BETWEEN THE HILLS AND THE SEA

LITERATURE OF AMERICAN LABOR
Cletus E. Daniel and Ileen A. DeVault, Series Editors

In the LITERATURE OF AMERICAN LABOR series we bring back into print some of the best literature that has emerged from the labor movement and related events in the United States and Canada. We are defining literature broadly; the series encompasses the full range of popular writing, including novels, biographies, autobiographies, and journalism. Each book includes an introduction written especially for this series and directing the reader's attention to the historical context for the work.

We believe that the titles in the series will be particularly useful to students of social and labor history and American studies. Our hope is that, both individually and collectively, the books in this series will contribute to a greater understanding of working-class experiences in our culture.

LITERATURE OF AMERICAN LABOR SERIES

BETWEEN THE HILLS AND THE SEA

K. B. Gilden

ILR PRESS

School of Industrial and Labor Relations

Cornell University

This new edition of *Between the Hills and the Sea* is designed by Kat
Dalton. The text, with the exception of the front matter, is reproduced
from the original version, published by Doubleday and Company,
Incorporated, in 1971. The cover photo is used with permission of
Wide World Photos.

Library of Congress Cataloging-in-Publication Data

Gilden, K. B. (Katya B.), 1914–
  Between the hills and the sea / K.B. Gilden.
    p. cm. — (Literature of American labor)
  Reprint, with new introd. Originally published: 1st ed. Garden City,
N.Y. : Doubleday, 1971.
    ISBN 0-87546-154-9 (alk. paper)
    I. Title. II. Series.
[PS3557.I3427B48 1989]
813'.54—dc20   89-15651
                                     CIP

Copies of this book may be ordered through bookstores or directly from
ILR Press
School of Industrial and Labor Relations
Cornell University
Ithaca, NY 14851–0952

Printed on acid-free paper in the United States of America
5   4   3   2   1

CONTENTS

INTRODUCTION

Between the Hills and the Sea centers on Mish Lunin and his wife, Priscilla, who were brought together in the aftermath of World War II by the hopes they shared that organized working men and women might transform industrial America into a more equitable and democratic society. Ten years later their dreams lie shattered. He now belonged, Mish Lunin thought, "to a damned generation, damned by its faith and its errors." The labor movement has lost its vision and daring; the tenants in their fetid housing project shy away from Priscilla's appeals for action; Mish has long since lost his union office and is politically isolated at his job in an electrical equipment factory; and their marriage is disintegrating. By depicting their lives in a New England industrial city during one eventful week in the spring of 1956, *Between the Hills and the Sea* reveals the cost for working people of the Cold War and its political repression. It discloses the human toll of what sociologist Daniel Bell called "the exhaustion of political ideas in the fifties."[1]

As the novel opens, Mish and Priscilla cherish memories of what they used to be and bite their tongues to avoid wounding each other verbally. Priscilla longs to rekindle in her husband the energy and talent for leadership that he displayed in the immediate postwar years as head of his large local union. These qualities had attracted her to him and persuaded her to leave college and the comforts of her pros-

1. Daniel Bell, *The End of Ideology: On the Exhaustion of Political Ideas in the Fifties* (New York: Free Press, 1961).

perous family. Although Mish remains ardently attracted to her, his
working-class upbringing has made him scornful of quixotic gestures,
keenly sensitive to the changed political environment of Cold War
America, and highly suspicious that his wife envisages working people,
including him, as her social mission.

The fate of the couple is not determined simply by their personalities, however. Their destinies are also shaped by the power of
corporate management and housing authorities, congressional investigating committees and legislation, their fellow workers' hunger for
income and security, fears and suspicions fanned by the Cold War,
and revelations by Nikita Khrushchev of Stalin's crimes. Neither Mish
nor Priscilla is a Communist. In fact, Mish was encouraged to run
for the presidency of his local union after the 1946 strike because he
was a capable organizer with a keen sensitivity to details, timing, and
power and a moderate. For a while, his politics made him acceptable
to both left- and right-wing factions in the local. He was driven from
office, however, because he refused to climb on the anticommunist
bandwagon or to renounce his friendship for Bob and Maria Ucchini,
two Communists who had helped found the local. Subsequently,
Mish's understanding of how much is involved in organizing effective
action leads him to shun, and even to ridicule, his wife's irrepressible
impulse to storm the barricades against injustice: "Priscilla, you're
living for something that's gone. Past. Over and done with. It WAS
and it IS NO MORE!"

The novel's authentic depiction of the efforts of two individuals to
reconstruct their own lives, after the visionary labor movement to
which they had once devoted themselves unreservedly collapsed under
the impact of the Cold War, provides rare insight into American
society in the 1950s. Although no local union underwent a political
evolution identical to that of the fictional EWIU-UV Local 317,
veterans of the postwar struggles in the Congress of Industrial Organizations (CIO) easily recognize every controversy recounted in *Between the Hills and the Sea*. Many activists of that era can also recall
all too vividly personal decisions and conflicts like those Mish and
Priscilla experienced. Their story seems to have been erased from the

pages of American history. It has been told, and told brilliantly, by K. B. Gilden.

K. B. Gilden

K. B. Gilden is the pen name of the husband and wife writing team of Katya and Bert Gilden. Both were very familiar with the industrial world of which they wrote. Katya had spent her childhood in the Irish and French-Canadian railroad district of Bangor, Maine, where she listened in on the conversations of neighborhood men and women and accompanied the children delivering home lunch buckets to their fathers' places of work in the gasworks, foundry, and roundhouse. Her distinctive writing style drew upon her varied experiences: studying English literature at Radcliffe College, composing advertising copy for women's fashions, writing for a special agency that sought jobs for boys out of reformatories, living in Harlem, editing a weekly newspaper, and then marrying Bert Gilden and moving to Georgia, where they were involved in interracial rural action programs.

Bert spent his childhood in Bridgeport, Connecticut, among mostly Hungarian and Swedish neighbors and worked on a city newspaper before going to Brown University to study literature. After college, he worked as a film press agent and served during World War II as a tank commander in the North African and European theaters of action, where he was twice wounded. On his return home, Bert was determined to become a novelist but took a job organizing farmers' training courses for veterans in Georgia.

In 1947 Bert met Katya, who was also fired by the ambition to write, and after a whirlwind courtship the two of them moved south and began working on the stories that ultimately developed into their first novel, *Hurry Sundown*. In the 1950s they returned to Bridgeport, where Bert worked in several factories while they completed the novel. Its publication in 1965, just as the civil rights struggle in the South was reaching a crescendo, helped the novel achieve immediate success. Paramount Pictures converted the book into a movie, which left the Gildens unhappy with its content but financially able to devote themselves unstintingly to writing their second novel. Bert died suddenly just before *Between the Hills and the Sea* was published in 1971. Katya still lives in Connecticut, where she teaches and writes.

Katya Gilden calls their writing technique *analytical realism*—a term deliberately evocative of organic chemistry. They explore the development of individual characters who are revealed and transformed by the conflicts and dilemmas of the situation in which they live. "My subject," she explains, "is the individual in the grip of history." Although the huge electrical plant, the Tidal Flats housing project, the mayor elected on a labor ticket, the influential conservative congresswoman, and various other personalities in *Between the Hills and the Sea* bring Bridgeport to mind, the events and personalities are all fictional.[2] This use of historical events as a backdrop against which to reveal the personal development of fictional characters is a distinguishing feature of the novel. This technique is also suggested in the title of a seminar Katya Gilden taught at Wesleyan University: "Inner Person/Outer World."[3]

The Gildens' own experiences had taught them that the lives of individuals cannot be divorced from the networks of social interaction and social hierarchies that shape personalities and through which individuals find expression. The vivid descriptions of factory work and the unrelenting rumbling of garbage trucks feeding the smoldering dump beside the housing project do more than provide a realistic setting for the action in the book: they also articulate the exploitation that is disguised by modern consumerism. The piecework gait of the women on assembly, their endemic resentment of the men around them (visiting dignitaries, foremen, set-up men, materials handlers), and their "constant interchange of anecdote and argument, friendship and feud, horseplay, festivity"—all "indiscernible at first"—reveal an

2. Jaspar McLevy was elected mayor of Bridgeport on the Socialist party ticket in 1933 and served until 1957. Clare Booth Luce served in Congress as a Republican from 1943 to 1947.

3. For biographical information on the Gildens and a discussion of their philosophy of literature, see Norman Rudich, "*Between the Hills and the Sea* (Un roman proletarian experimental des anées 1970)," *Europe. Revue Litteraire Mensuelle* 55 (Mars-Avril 1977), 79–90. Katya Gilden discusses analytical realism in two letters that she generously made available to me: Katya Gilden to Allan Lewis, October 21, 1971, and Gilden to Otto Brandstätter, August 8, 1973.

underlying design of human relations in production processes of far deeper significance than the objects with which and on which the women work. And all these human relationships are being shaped by and expressed in a specific moment in history.

Rise and Rupture of the CIO

The postwar history that generated and then shattered the dreams of Mish and Priscilla was marked by intense conflict over the future course of American social and political life and by the ominous escalation of global confrontation between the United States and the Soviet Union. The combined impact of strife at home and war clouds abroad transformed the daily lives and expectations of workers, as well as the character and role of the labor movement.

The industrial unions had been formed during the depression of the 1930s in an effort to organize all workers employed by the same companies, regardless of their occupations, race, sex, religion, or political beliefs. They pursued aggressive collective action to improve working conditions and the lives of workers and their families. Most of these unions had been expelled from the fifty-year-old American Federation of Labor (AFL) for violating its craft union principles and in 1938 had formed the Congress of Industrial Organizations (CIO). The industrial unions had contributed strongly to the reform impulses of Franklin D. Roosevelt's New Deal, and in turn had benefited from the government's encouragement of collective bargaining in industry.

Workers who had previously played marginal roles in craft unions and electoral politics, or been excluded from them, lent ardent support to the CIO where they worked and to the New Deal when they voted. Among them were women, Afro-Americans, Mexican-Americans, and especially the children of southern and eastern European immigrants who had come to the United States at the turn of the century. Their quest for security, status, and participation in national life was summed up in the 1937 battle cry of striking steelworkers: "You are not going to call us 'Hunky' no more."[4]

4. Ewa Morawska, *For Bread with Butter: The Life-Worlds of East Central Europeans in Johnstown, Pennsylvania, 1890–1940* (Cambridge and New York: Cambridge University Press, 1985), 273.

The uprising of the ethnics had unleashed new forces in American politics. Although most successful political aspirants from industrial neighborhoods sought a place for themselves within the American social order, rather than its overthrow, neither they nor their constituents had anything but contempt for the "rugged individualism" that former president Herbert Hoover and other conservatives identified with the American Way. Communist party members (like Mish's friends Bob and Maria Ucchini) earned prestige and influence among their neighbors by battling for the needs of the unemployed, creating new unions, and after 1935 forging a united front with Socialists, Farmer-Laborites, and other older radical groups, ethnic organizations, and liberal Democrats to further New Deal reforms. Because millions of Catholics were involved in the social and political movements of the 1930s, Catholic trade unionist groups were also formed by clergy and lay people to combat the Communists and uphold the teachings of the church within the CIO. [5]

Although the new industrial unions made slow headway during the last years of the depression, and conservative resistance frustrated attempts to extend New Deal reforms in Congress and in state legislatures after 1938, the economic boom generated by World War II produced an unprecedented increase in union membership and power. While CIO unions enrolled most workers in the auto, steel, electrical, and meat-packing industries, the AFL grew even faster. In addition to swelling the ranks of skilled workers in its traditional craft unions, AFL constituents such as the machinists, electricians, and teamsters directed successful organizing drives at mass-production industries in

5. The literature on these subjects is vast, but see Bert Cochran, *Labor and Communism: The Conflict That Shaped American Unions* (Princeton, N.J.: Princeton University Press, 1977); Nelson Lichtenstein, *Labor's War at Home: The CIO in World War II* (Cambridge and New York: Cambridge University Press, 1982); Maurice Isserman, *Which Side Were You On? The American Communist Party during the Second World War* (Middletown, Conn.: Wesleyan University Press, 1982); Nell Irvin Painter, *The Narrative of Hosea Hudson: His Life as a Negro Communist in the South* (Cambridge, Mass.: Harvard University Press, 1979); Ronald W. Schatz, *The Electrical Workers: A History of Labor at General Electric and Westinghouse, 1923–60* (Urbana: University of Illinois Press, 1983).

bitter competition with the CIO. The railroad brotherhoods and other unions independent of both the AFL and the CIO also grew rapidly. By the end of the war, more than 12 million Americans—32 percent of all nonfarm employees—belonged to unions. Although union representation remained rare in service and clerical occupations and in public employment, a record 83 percent of all mine workers, 67 percent of all transportation workers, and 87 percent of all construction workers were union members by 1947. Peak union membership in manufacturing—42.4 percent—was not reached until 1953, but during the postwar decade, for the first and to date last time in American history, the average production worker in a large manufacturing concern was covered by a union contract.[6]

Even more important than the expansion of union membership, and certainly more ominous to corporate managers, was the wartime expansion of the codified and informal authority of unions over work practices. Full employment during the war made workers bolder in challenging supervisors and regulations they found oppressive, while cost-plus government contracts and insatiable demand for their products had often sapped managers' resistance. Although the government had frozen wages and suppressed strikes, its War Labor Board encouraged industrywide bargaining, union security, recognized status for union officials within the plants, seniority rights in layoffs and promotions, and negotiation over fringe benefits and job classifications. These were matters business executives had long considered their exclusive domain. Long-established company and craft union policies of racial discrimination also came under attack, through the Fair Employment Practice Committee. At the war's end, therefore, the labor movement's sense of the changes it could effect in industrial life had expanded in many directions, while business leaders were issuing an alarmed cry for the restoration of management's "right to

---

6. Leo Troy, "The Rise and Fall of American Trade Unions: The Labor Movement from FDR to RR," in *Unions in Transition: Entering the Second Century*, ed. Seymour Martin Lipset (San Francisco: ICS Press, 1986), 75–109. The table "Union Density by Major Industrial Sector, 1930–1985" is on p. 87.

manage" and the defense of "free enterprise" against "foreign-inspired collectivism."[7]

A strike wave, informed by this conflict and which in turn defined its meaning for much of the American public, began in the fall of 1945 and continued through the following year. The most widespread demand among workers was for higher wages—a major increase in hourly pay to compensate for the rise in prices and the sharp reduction in weekly incomes that came with the end of war-induced overtime work. Employers countered with demands for dismantling of the contractual authority unions had secured under the auspices of the War Labor Board, tightening of production standards and workplace discipline, and unrestricted managerial discretion in setting prices, locating plants, selecting and introducing technology, and hiring and promoting employees.

During the early months of 1946 all of the major CIO unions were engaged in protracted strikes against the country's largest manufacturing corporations. The strikes by the United Electrical Workers (UE) against General Electric and Westinghouse were especially hard fought. The low wages paid women and union control over the setting of piece rates were among the prominent issues being contested. Massive picket lines shut down factories and offices each day, often in defiance of violent police attacks. But battles were waged not only with pickets; films and radio publicity, huge rallies addressed by well-known personalities, sympathetic strikes, and other tactics were used in an effort to win public opinion. The settlements resulting from the strikes gave workers wage increases based on the government formula of 18 1/2 cents per hour and raised but did not equalize women's pay rates. Equally important, most of the companies' demands were rejected. For General Electric, confronted by a strike in all its plants throughout the land for the first time since 1918, the workers' triumph

---

7. Howell John Harris, *Right to Manage: Industrial Relations Policies of American Business in the 1940s* (Madison: University of Wisconsin Press, 1982), 48–58; for a more negative assessment of the influence of the New Deal and the war on the labor movement, see Mike Davis, *Prisoners of the American Dream: Politics and Economy in the History of the U.S. Working Class* (London: Verso Books, 1986), 52–101.

was so galling that the corporation dramatically revised its labor and public relations strategies.[8]

At its convention in November 1946, the triumphant CIO resolved to spread the union gospel to America's many unorganized workers and to seek a "guaranteed annual wage" for every employed man and woman. It also adopted a political program that envisaged a significant expansion of the role of government in the country's economic life. The plan called for effective regulation of consumer prices, an excess-profits tax, and "an allocation and priority system" to direct materials toward the satisfaction of urgent social needs that unregulated markets had left unmet. Housing, infant and maternal health care, "day care of workers' children," national health insurance, a fair employment practices law, and secure income for the elderly held privileged places in the CIO's program. Public, civilian, and international control of atomic energy and a single development agency for the valley of the Missouri River were two of the most grandiose projects the convention endorsed. The importance of world peace was also stressed, to be secured by universal disarmament, self-determination for colonial peoples, and continued collaboration between the United States and the Soviet Union within the framework of the United Nations. This was not a socialist program, however. Rather, it represented points of agreement between the left wing and the moderates of the CIO, and in presenting it, President Philip Murray reaffirmed his own commitment to private enterprise.[9]

But despite the overwhelming support shown by workers for their unions in the 1946 strikes and the widespread popularity of the CIO's

8. Schatz, *Electrical Workers*, 167–87; James J. Matles and James Higgins, *Them and Us: Struggles of a Rank-and-File Union* (Englewood Cliffs, N.J.: Prentice-Hall, 1974), 130–49; Harris, *Right to Manage*, 139–54; Ruth Milkman, *Gender at Work: The Dynamics of Job Segregation by Sex during World War II* (Urbana: University of Illinois Press, 1987), 144–51.

9. CIO, *Final Report of the Eighth Constitutional Convention of the Congress of Industrial Organizations, November 18, 19, 20, 21, 22, 1946*, 38–115, 151–52, 156–58, 277–78. The famous declaration, that the CIO "resents and rejects efforts of the Communist Party or other political parties . . . to interfere in the affairs of the CIO," was adopted immediately after Murray's opening speech. Ibid., 113–14.

program, outside as well as inside of its ranks, the American labor movement was by no means a united force. The 4 million members of the CIO were then outnumbered by the 7 million workers in the AFL.[10] Although AFL unions had been involved in many strikes that year and had collaborated locally with CIO unions in the citywide general strikes in Stamford, Connecticut, Rochester, New York, Lancaster and Pittsburgh, Pennsylvania, and Oakland, California, the AFL's top officers remained hostile to the CIO and to its reliance on government power to achieve social reform. AFL unions regularly denounced CIO rivals as "Communists," and President William Green assured Congress early in 1947 that the AFL would not defend a Communist worker against dismissal. Moreover, factionalism was rampant within the leadership of the CIO, and both Walter Reuther's caucus in the United Auto Workers and the insurgent UE Members for Democratic Action had already raised the anticommunist banner against their rivals. The Gildens' novel quite appropriately depicts opposing groups selecting their slates for union office during parties celebrating the strike victory of 1946.[11]

"Back on the Same Side"

The lesson driven home to business executives by the strikes of 1946 was that they could not carry the day by reacting to labor's demands. Nor was it enough to win legislative restrictions on union strength and action, although the Taft-Hartley Act of 1947 provided business with a major success on that front. A new consensus in management circles had emerged out of the 1945 Congress of American Industry, numerous studies by industrial relations research groups, the admonitions of business representatives on wartime government agencies,

---

10. U.S. Department of Commerce, Bureau of the Census, *Historical Statistics of the United States, Colonial Times to 1970*, 2 vols. (Washington, D.C., 1975), 1:177. The CIO's claims to 6 million members in 1946 were based on a blend of mutually contradictory ways of counting.

11. George Lipsitz, *Class and Culture in Cold War America: "A Rainbow at Midnight"* (South Hadley, Mass.: J. F. Bergin Publishers, 1982), 56–86; Irving Richter, *Labor's Struggles, 1945–1950: A Participant's View of 1945–1947* (Cambridge and New York: Cambridge University Press, forthcoming).

and especially the experience of 1946. Business executives had to reformulate and battle continuously for their own policies of plant management and wage a systematic campaign to persuade not only their employees but the public in general of the dangers of "mob production" in the factories and of "socialism" in government.

Most major firms realized that they could not destroy their workers' unions as they had after World War I. At the same time, only a handful of relatively small companies went to the opposite extreme of welcoming active union participation in the creation of a new teamwork. Most managers tried to win their workers "back to their side" by enunciating comprehensive personnel policies, which they tirelessly sought to enforce, in the so-called second and third rounds of postwar strikes (1947 and 1949) and, more important, in the daily conduct of factory life. Managers avoided overt violations of labor law, went to great lengths to make their policies appear "fair and reasonable" and to apply them to nonunion clerical workers as well as unionized production workers, extended benefits from union contracts to all employees, devised union-free grievance procedures to defuse discontent, and encouraged the careers of local union officers whom they found cooperative. Corporations such as General Electric led the way in instituting job evaluation systems and formulas for piece rates and production standards based not on negotiation but on their own studies (as they had done in the 1920s, before they recognized unions). The crucial objective was to have management make the rules while reducing the unions' role to that of filing protests.

An ideological campaign accompanied management's daily effort to reassert its authority. The president of the National Association of Manufacturers contended that with proper instruction from their own employers the "millions" of industrial workers "with their families could be a mighty force, probably a determining factor, in the growing struggle between American individualism and foreign-bred collectivism."[12] Management's first objective was to persuade employees that their hopes for a better life could be fulfilled only through higher

12. Harris, *Right to Manage*, 137–52. The quotation from Wallace F. Bennett is on p. 190.

productivity: only under the guidance of skillful management could the economic growth needed by all members of society be achieved. This was not a matter of ideology, argued the business leaders. On the contrary, the quest for productivity made ideological controversies outdated. As executive Grover Coffin says to Mish in the novel: "The toughest job I have in this job is unfreezing people from outmoded frames of reference."

Although personnel managers in the 1950s still had to negotiate new contracts with unions every few years and cope with union protests against their decisions, their work focused now more on testing employees so that they might be assigned where their talents would be most useful to the firm and on sampling their opinions to determine how well management was doing and where troubles might arise. Universities played a large part in devising opinion research surveys and instruments such as the Minnesota Multiphasic Personality Inventory.

The mounting tension between the United States and the Soviet Union provided an ideal intellectual climate for the success of industry's campaigns. As international conflict escalated over Iran, Poland, Turkey, Greece, and Czechoslovakia and over issues such as the atomic bomb, the Marshall Plan, and the Berlin blockade, President Harry Truman declared the "containment of communism" the basic aim of American foreign policy and introduced loyalty screening of government employees and an attorney general's list of subversive organizations. Truman's Republican and Dixiecrat foes in turn hurled charges of "Communism, Controls, and Chaos" against the Democrats and against labor in the elections of 1946 and assigned the House Committee on Un-American Activities to investigate alleged subversive influences in unions, the movie industry, civil rights groups, churches, and ethnic fraternal organizations. Further, the Taft-Hartley Act, adopted in Congress over Truman's veto in 1947, had required all elected union officers to sign affidavits that they were not Communists or else have their unions excluded from the ballot at certification elections and otherwise denied all protection of the National Labor Relations Board.

Anticommunism not only legitimated business's goals; it also undermined labor's opposition. Although all unions denounced the Taft-Hartley Act and pledged to fight for its repeal, the AFL rejected the ardent pleas of the leader of the United Mine Workers, John L. Lewis, and decided at its 1947 convention that its officers should sign the non-Communist affidavits. The CIO authorized each of its constituent unions to choose whether or not to sign the affidavits, and many officers refused to sign. The new president of the United Auto Workers, Walter Reuther, however, used the affidavits as a loyalty test within his own union and launched raids against locals of the United Electrical Workers and the Farm Equipment Workers, whose leaders had not signed. In short, unionists were using the law they had all condemned to fight each other.

By 1947, though, the CIO had become so dependent on the government and the Democratic party for enactment of its goals (including any possible repeal of Taft-Hartley) that when the Democratic president declared anticommunism the guiding principle of his foreign and domestic policy, the CIO was obliged to follow his course. Many officers of its member unions were Communists, and many more remained committed to the original ideal of uniting industrial workers regardless of their political beliefs. Consequently, the imposition of the new policy on the CIO provoked ruthless battles within its ranks, and in 1949 led to the expulsion of eleven member unions, which were subsequently targeted for raids by other unions with which they had recently been allied.

By 1950 the CIO's bold dreams of only four years earlier had dissolved in a nightmare of congressional investigations, press exposures of "Communist ties," firings, and blacklistings. It was a time of mysterious figures shadowing activists, tapped telephones, deportations, imprisonments, mutual suspicions, and betrayals. Unionists who continued to adhere to the CIO's program of 1946 found themselves under relentless attack from the government, their employers, conservatives within their own ethnic communities, and fellow union members. Leaflets delivering charges and countercharges were distributed daily at factory gates, and lunchtime meetings where union stewards had once discussed members' grievances now featured celebrities denouncing communism and praising the American Way.

Leftist union officers were heckled by opponents, who distributed themselves in diamond formations around meeting halls. More and more members simply tired of the tumult and longed to go about their jobs in peace.[13]

The obvious outcome was a transfer of effective decision making in industrial unions to the full-time officials who conferred with management—professionalization of industrial relations on both sides of the table. Policy debate atrophied. But that was not all. Among those who resisted the Cold War drift of their unions and their country, the intensity of the battle encouraged a siege mentality, which crippled their own thinking. In the fall of 1947 the newly formed international Communist Information Bureau (Cominform) replied to the anticommunist Truman Doctrine by proclaiming that the world had been divided into two irreconcilable camps: a "Camp of War, Imperialism, and Reaction" led by the United States and a "Camp of Peace, National Independence, and Socialism" led by the Soviet Union. The pronouncement heralded a new rigidity in the world communist movement. It was soon followed by an open break between the Cominform and the Yugoslav regime of Marshall Josip Broz Tito and by a wave of trials, imprisonments, and executions of alleged "Titoists" in Eastern Europe. Among them were Rudolph Slansky, Laszlo Rajk, Josef Grosz, and Traicho Kostov, all of them Communists renowned for their parts in the wartime resistance to Nazi conquest. In the Soviet Union itself, between 1949 and 1952—the heyday of McCarthyite repression in the United States—thousands of people suffered imprisonment or execution on such charges as "rootless cosmopolitanism" and "worship of things foreign."[14] Persecuted and defamed by their own government and press, American Communists and their dwindling numbers of allies found it hard to resist the temptation to see only hope and progress in their own camp. They rejected all unflattering reports on the Soviet Union that emanated from the

13. See Ann Fagan Ginger and David Christiano, eds., *The Cold War against Labor*, 2 vols. (Berkeley, Calif.: Meiklejohn Civil Liberties Institute, 1987) for accounts of this epoch.

14. Roy A. Medvedev, *Let History Judge: The Origins and Consequences of Stalinism* (New York: Vintage Books, 1973), 474–85.

mouths of their enemies and believed the most fantastic charges leveled by Communist governments against their dissidents.[15]

The psychological blow to American leftists was therefore especially devastating when, in 1956, Nikita Khrushchev told the Soviet party congress that a legacy of rule by coercion and deception had undermined his own country's development. Supplementing his argument was a secret speech on the horrors of Stalin's crimes against his own people and party, a speech soon known around the world. Many American leftists concluded that their lives of struggle had been in vain.

Other leftists, however, remained determined to right the evils of American society that had radicalized them in the first place. Despite the swelling tide of consumer goods in American stores, the self-satisfaction of the country's opinion leaders, and the ubiquitous assurances that productivity—ever more productivity—would satisfy all their needs, most people who punched time clocks every day felt harnessed to a machine over which they had no control. And perhaps no one else did either. In fictional Shoreham, trucks kept feeding the burning dump at Tidal Flats. In the real world, the United States and the Soviet Union stockpiled atomic bombs.

Even corporate opinion researchers found most workers passive but cynical, believing their own future prospects meager and still favoring government measures that their employers had effectively opposed: planning for full employment, price controls, comprehensive social insurance, and legally secure unions. Only 14 percent of General Motors' employees in 1951 considered management "conscientious and principled."[16] Although union members continued to proffer their unions the needed support on picket lines, they no longer expected much from their organizations or their leaders. Above all, production workers felt harassed by the tempo and monotony of their jobs. Hence the seething discontent that stalks the factory floor in *Between the Hills and the Sea*. It breaks through to the surface in unexpected ways: a

15. See, for example, Derek Kartun, *Tito's Plot against Europe: The Story of the Rajk Conspiracy* (New York: International Publishers, 1950).

16. Harris, *Right to Manage*, 187–93.

mysterious leaflet, a lack of concern by workers for their machinery, their excitement when Mish walks through the plant on the way to executive offices, and, above all, the women's "zoo" demonstration.

The novel's conclusion evokes the question of how a labor movement might once again articulate workers' frustrated aspirations. At the story's end, Mish and Priscilla have been crushed, sentenced to upward mobility in the social hierarchies they had hoped to destroy. But both the factory and the housing project are astir with action, and working people are gathering to make their plans in the absence of their former leaders.

David Montgomery
Yale University
June 1989

BETWEEN THE HILLS AND THE SEA

ONE

The Sensitive Plant

I

1

He awoke to the clangor of concert music in a strange house with a strange woman, straining against a backside, long-curved and full-limbed, sheathed in night clothes and swathed in sheet. Plastered against Priscilla's back, he held her clasped in his crotch as if all that was unsolvable between them could be solved by fusion of the flesh, as if in a passion of possession he could by some epoxy magic, gelid, agglutinate, close the gap.

He held her as if he could by his fondlings and buttings, *come on turn around to me,* change everything over. Craving from her what she craved from him: the person she thought he was.

That he might be more or less than, or different from, or not at all. That might be no more than a figment of her imagination now at this late date fading fast.

Under the blankets she was wrapped so tightly in the sheet he couldn't tug it out from under her. Nothing doing there. Cold ass.

The radio grinned at him with all its teeth. The full philharmonic at four in the morning for crissake. He had fallen asleep on the news. He reached over to turn it off.

2

The alarm clock buzzed. He awoke in the dusk of morning, uncovered, chilled to the bone.

Out of bed he shut off the alarm, overwhelmed with the desire to crawl back in. The scatter rug trickled away under his groping foot. He tiptoed over the polished asphalt floor, treading thin ice.

Under a forest of dangling stockings, bras and blouses, kids' pajamas drying on the ceiling rack in the bathroom, he took a leak. Gurgle gurgle down the drain, out to the bay, up skyward, down from the clouds, greatest feedback of them all. Blinking he faced himself in the medicine-cabinet mirror. Cheeks gyved, gritty with a prickle of beard, sooty hair spilling over harrowed forehead, eyes hard as the nuggets of coal he used to cull from ash cans in ice-rutted backyards. As soon as he caught his expression it changed, became saturnine. Monkeyface. Michael Lunin, thirty-four years old, ten years married, father of two, Apt. 3C, Door J, Bldg. 2, Tidal Flats Park. Employed by United Vacuum Inc. (Electrical Products Around the Globe), Shoreham Works (Transformer & Generator, Cable-Cord-and-Code Wire, Radiosonics, Home Refrigerator, etc.), Bldg. 17 (Construction Facilities Div.), Dept. 11-E (Switch). Soc. Sec. No. 222–07–6303. Blood Type O.

His mouth was a graveyard of cigarette ash. He washed up, brushed teeth, sloshed stingy-sweet mouthwash around inside ballooned-out cheeks, spritzed. Swished his shaving brush in the wood bowl of soap the kids had bought for his birthday in January, under Priscilla's direction, from marked-down Christmas stock. Lavender-scented. Among sandalwoods and old leathers, spices and ferns she sought out, happily foregoing her personal taste, the Best Buy.

He stumbled back into the bedroom, still half-asleep. Fished clothing out of bureau drawers. Slowly the room reassembled itself, with all its familiar pieces in place in all their contradictions.

The bureau, good old Grand Rapids via Good Will, solid mahogany antiqued in celadon green. The sheet wispily dribbling from her side of the bed, the Big Sheet Bargain, three inches short, under the imported merino blankets her mother had given them. Her rummage-sale skirt—look at the label!—over the back of a chair piled as always with a couple of her father's briefs, a file of the academic journals in which her brother Ted published articles she never quite got through, newspapers from which she meant to clip articles. With her economizing Priscilla displayed the scorn for bourgeois comforts of one raised in bourgeois comfort. Thrift for her was more than a necessity, it was a form of self-indulgence. She reveled in it.

All on his account, all for love of him. Gratitude was due her. He begrudged it.

The curtains Priscilla had seamed together and hung over the tripartite windows, starchy-white when they moved into the project almost two years before, were almost as dark now, after regular washings, as the window shades behind them.

He started to clear the chair and gave up on it. He started to move her portable typewriter, open on the hassock with a sheet of paper still rolled in the carriage, TENANTS AWAKE!!! There was nowhere to put it down. Her canvas-enveloped guitar had to be taken from the closet corner before he could open the closet door. He dumped his clothes on the bed and began to dress for the day, Monday, the worst day in the week.

Priscilla's eyes, frozen blue, stared at him as he shivered into undershirt and shorts. Now she knows, he thought. Now she sees it. This is it, there isn't anything else.

"You feeling all right?" she ventured, cautiously.

"Fine and dandy. Wonderful."

"Mish, I can't stand it when you . . ."

She touched his arm as he sat on the edge of the bed pulling on his socks.

"Where were you before?" He tried to joke it off. "I was looking for you all night."

She watched him as he belted in his work pants, stamped into his battered work shoes, a thousand such mornings, her eyes stark with terror.

"Mish, please."

She reached for his hand and pulled him down for a kiss, as if she could rub out with a kiss what her eyes saw.

"Now you want to play."

Whitish eyelashes quivering over lean cheeks windburnt red, misted with the merest sheen of freckles and down.

Time was pressing. A fat chuck under the sheet, long and lithe and luscious. Sweet ass.

"Don't bother to get up. I'll grab some breakfast."

"Oh no, I'll get breakfast." Not to be outdone, love for love, she sprang out of bed. "Wow, this floor. You'd think they'd get the heat up. Where're my slippers?" She flung about the room, buttons out, unbosomed, pajama pants shrunk, pink-ankled. "Why are you dressing in the dark?" She snapped up the window shades over the fixed center glass and the two casements left slightly ajar, letting in a gust from the bay laden with the odor of ashes. "Look out there. Will you just look?"

He didn't look. He knew what was out there.

"Look, I'm pushed for time."

"Lucas has twenty women lined up for tonight, one from each building—"

"Fuck Lucas."

"Oh for godsake, Mish. Just because Lucas is trying . . ."

Lucas the lost soul, forever a stranger and alone, had knocked at her door one morning with his brainstorm, while her husband was conveniently away at work and her children at school. In two minutes Lucas was inside drinking coffee with her and telling her his whole life history, a tale of horrors so intriguing . . .

"Lucas has done all the spadework—"

Lucas was the kind who would confess impotence to a Priscilla so she'd take him into bed with her in order to prove otherwise.

"He feels the time is ripe now, we're ready to go. The women will have their husbands with them tonight. All you have to do, Mish, is provide a little leadership."

She had been out with Lucas till past midnight winding up plans. He had refused to talk about them with her when she arrived home and he refused now.

He escaped to the bathroom and combed his hair in the mirror. She followed him in, dropping her pants, and plopped down on the toilet. "Mish, it's been two years. You've got to—" She yanked at the toilet paper behind her drawing out a streamer, no economizing there, and, wiped, stayed on the pot, pants down, legs asprawl, earnestly beseeching him. "Mish, I know you've had a rough time of it. I know that better now than I did when it was happening. When Colangelo brought you down with his slogans . . . and then when he beat you again without the slogans . . . and when Mari and Bob and Ray and Marty, they all got after you to run once more, even though you were against it, and you all but won . . . The way you'd keep going with it, going and growing. . . ."

He wasn't listening. He didn't have to listen.

"When I think of what you were. . . . Why you sat up there with your negotiating team and took on Grover Coffin and his UV experts, his New York lawyers, all the might of one of the mightiest corporations . . . Why you could have become anything. You could govern this city . . ."

It was after his last defeat almost two years ago when he all but won the union election, all but made his comeback, that he recognized fully at last the precise nature of the bind he was in. And she in a panic over what she considered to be his poisonous pessimism had jumped at the chance to move out of their hole on Prince Street into the more up-to-date, and communal, quarters of a public housing project. He had spent his off-work hours since, building a hi-fi for their apartment, rigging up a camping trailer for their station wagon, fishing off the breakwater with his buddies for blues and blacks when they were running and reading through his father-in-law's library, law books excepted—these he was saving for his old age.

"Mish, I realize it takes time to get over these things—"

"I got to rush."

He escaped back into the bedroom and filled his cleaving pockets with wallet and keys, the daily debris of nuts and bolts, assorted papers, the leaflet. He paused over the leaflet he'd intended to show her Friday when he brought it home, tempted now again to show it to her. It had appeared out of nowhere all over the plant, but not in sufficient numbers to go quite around. Everyone was snatching for a copy, speculating on its source.

The mimeograph paper was soft, crumply in his hand from overhandling. Priscilla would latch onto it as she had latched onto Lucas, blow it up into a movement of major proportions with Mish Lunin at the head of it, at the bottom of it and in the thick of it.

She was right behind him at the bedside table, coaxing him as one coaxes an invalid to try a sip of broth.

"If you'd just reactivate yourself. Mish, you can't go on living like this. We've always had to be part of something bigger than just ourselves. We've always had to live with some purpose . . ."

"Jesus Christ, Priscilla, it's almost half past! Will you get a move on? Or let me shove off?"

"Break it up! Break it up!"

The children, up, rampaged through the dissension of their parents, creating diversions all over the lot.

"Break it up," they chanted, an intervention always good for a laugh.

He didn't laugh and neither did she. They regarded each other for a moment, numbly. Her mouth, chapped raw with little shreds of whitish tissue clinging to it, gathered in a knot.

The girl with the gay guitar who had come down from the university to join the United Vacuum picket line in the great postwar strike of 1946, and who quit college to marry the picket captain.

Striking up her guitar, a jangle of chords. Joyously lifting her voice, more tune than tone, in their song of the day:

If you've worked for UV all your days
Just ask the foreman for a raise
And he will give it to you
He will give it to you—

Put it on the ground
Dig it all around
It will make your flowers
Grow-ow-ow. . . .

Now it was ten years later. No more the picket captain she had introduced to her family as a mass leader, hero of the barricades. No more the chief steward sharpening himself up against Grover Coffin, UV-Shoreham's new director of industrial relations, architect of UV's new labor policy. No more president of an 8000-member union local, youngest local president in the country. Just a plain working stiff, likely to remain so for the remainder of his life.

The party's over, baby. The jig is up. History has played you a dirty trick.

The present lay like an unexploded bomb between them. Sidestepping it, she went off to the kitchen. He unfolded the leaflet in his hands. Nothing like it in language had been seen in or out of the plant in years. It was directed at Grover Coffin, now general manager of the Shoreham works and corporation vicepresident. DIG YOUR OWN GRAVE, GRAVEYARD. . . .

He tore the leaflet into bits, flushed the bits down in the bathroom and went searching through the laundry hamper for his identification button. He was not about to be pushed by Priscilla or Lucas or anyone else, not here with the tenants at the project, not out at the plant where the workers were at him again, *run!*, into one of those exercises in futility which now in Shoreham, in the year 1956, he was no longer willing to undertake. Futility, he thought, is the sharpest fear. The effort wasted. The child stillborn. The strikeout with all bases full.

And blood-won battles yet unwon.

He was not going off half-cocked and throw himself into something that would either never get off the ground or fall apart in the middle or peter out in a couple of weeks. Or blow up in his face. He was through with all that.

"Anybody seen my button? Goddamit, you put something down . . ."

Stephanie stood on the toilet lid, posturing between the medicine cabinet mirror and the door mirror arranged at parallel angles. A wriggly eight-year-old trying to catch the back of her head with the front. Losing herself in the reflections, reflection upon reflection, an infinity of reflections.

"If you hadn't married Mamma, who would I be?"

Greg wandered in and clambered up the pile of dirty wash.

"Where was I," Greg wanted to know, "when I wasn't here?"

Puffy with sleep, squinting up at him, demanding to know. Before he was born, before he got out of Mamma, before he got into her?

He pricked his finger on the button and pinned it, his photo in blue, on his shirt. His shirt, his uniform, Army surplus suntan, was bleached to ash and mottled with shadowy grease spots that no amount of bleach could wash out.

"Kids, it's too early in the morning."

They trailed him to the kitchen. Priscilla whammed pans on the stove. Crimson-splotched, flashing, the ragtag ends of a none too successful home permanent flopping about her face. "For crying out loud, kids, will you wait till I get through with your father?"

He crammed into his corner of the table and ignominiously drank his juice, shamed by her busyness. She loaded his plate, shame shame.

In a postclimactic vacuum, an estrangement in which words were superfluous, all said and done with, they made conversation.

"Scrambleds dry enough?"

"So much pressure in the shop," he mumbled half-apologizing. "Six machines to set up today and they want it last week." He'd already told her that six times. "And this wildcat walkout in

Hot Rubber last week." It slipped out of him inadvertently. "They all been on me."

"A walkout? You never mentioned—"

Turning from the toaster she was instantly on it, seizing on the walkout, back on common ground. Her eagerness aroused in him an old and obscure resentment. A walkout, three men suspended. Some picnic.

"And there's a retiming in the department this morning," he went on quickly, putting the walkout behind. "The turntable's all jittery. And as if that wasn't enough there's this visiting delegation coming through, NATO, BENELUX, some damn thing."

"I know. I remember a sosh field trip we took once to Fieldston Reformatory." Extending a sympathy he took amiss, Priscilla seated herself with her coffee. The sosh major and the con. "Our whole class parading down the corridor and this girl on her knees scrubbing the cement floor out of a bucket of lye. She looked up at me and my God—"

In the living room on the record player, blandly Mack the Knife—

"Oh no, kids! Not again!"

—committed multiple mayhem.

Priscilla handed over his paper bag of sandwiches. Held his jacket for him as he gulped down the last of his coffee.

Late. Riders to be picked up. On the split second.

"Come straight home, will you, Mish? The meeting's right after supper."

Dry-lipped he brushed her cheek, promising nothing. He slid his hand in under her bathrobe, smoothed it over the small of her back.

"Relax, hon."

"You too."

Truce.

Greg tagged after him to the door. "Daddy?"

"I got to run."

"Daddy?"

He slid the chain out of the slot, turned the bolt. "Yeah, yeah? What is it, son?"

"What happened to the dinosaurs, Daddy? Where did they go?"

3

"The mushroom cloud."

Eddie Kochis from next door settled into the sedan next to his station wagon on the parking strip. They glanced down the obliquely staggered brick buildings to the smoke funneling up from the city dump black as thunder, blotting out the shore front.

"I understand you're organizing folks tonight to do something about that," Eddie shouted out his window at him over his motor. "About time."

"Me? Why me?" he shouted back at Eddie. "I thought it was you."

Impatiently they back-smacked through a herd of boys who had dragged an abandoned car into the road behind them and were methodically stripping it down, removing from it everything that was movable.

He sped past block-long factories black with age, windows loftily eyebrowed—schoolhouse same vintage—desultory store fronts—houses reshingled with asbestos siding, at once upright and down-at-heel—to the corner where his riders stood clustered about the telephone pole. Without waiting for him to stop they swung inside.

"You're late. We got seven minutes."

The men, two of them from Hot Rubber, immediately started in on him. The wildcat walkout last week. The suspension of the union steward and the section chairman along with the crew leader. When the elected officials of your union are suspended for doing what they are supposed to do . . .

"In the old days we'd a-pulled the switch, everybody out! You run a good campaign against Colangelo this June, Mish, you'll be surprised . . . Mix it up with the company. Throw some weight around."

Up the slot and into the groove of the new expressway, channeled into the dog race, a hundred whippets whipping in and out under the whip on their backs: not to be late on the job.

Under the lee of a monstrous trailer truck zooming eighty an hour cross-country (that was a close one) and through a near smashup shooting out of lane (you take your life in your hands every time) and around the iron-railed curve into a morning already paling with haze, fetid with the fumes of chemicals.

"That leaflet on Friday, who put it out? Come on, Mish, spill it. You can tell us."

"Don't look at me. I know as much about it as you do."

Over the guardrail, against the horizon, the gray office tower with its illuminated emblem, UV, transfixed by a lightning bolt, and its lower flat-roofed buildings, spiked with water towers, stretching back and back for twelve city blocks.

"You mean you're not the one?" his riders pestered and plagued him. "Everybody's saying it's you."

"That's funny. I thought it was you."

Down the slot and under the Cedarbrook overpass, into the sluice of Raymond Street. Brick buildings banked with multiple-paned windows and interconnected with umbilical corridors, wire-fenced at the inlets. United Vacuum, founded fifty years before for the manufacture of electric light bulbs, had branched out into fuses and fuse boxes, circuit breakers, meters, power equipment, industrial installations, home appliances, radio and television, nuclear energy, computer technology, armaments; in plants from Shoreham on the east coast to dozens of others scattered across the nation and abroad.

UV MAKES THE WORLD GO ROUND.

ELECTRICAL PRODUCTS AROUND THE GLOBE.

IF IT'S UV IT'S THE BEST.

"It's a good leaflet," he conceded. "But with no name on it, nothing to indicate the individual or group behind it, what good is it?"

"If it's not by you, Mish, then it's for you. Something's brewing. Everywhere you turn."

His riders hit the gravel running for the gate before he stopped the wagon. One minute late they'd be docked fifteen. Savagely he nosed among the parking cars for the nearest spot.

"Hutcha like?" the drivers on either side of him yelled back and forth.

Number to play.

"Seven-o-six."

Number for the day.

With his lunch bag under his arm he sprinted for the gate, flashed his button at the guard in the sentry box, headed for his building. The March chill had magically lifted during his journey. A freshness in the air, a breath of warmth, a quality of light . . .

Over the concrete floor and up the iron-treaded staircase, through the swinging doors into 11-E. He caught up with the last of the stragglers at the time clock, nipped his card out of the slot and slipped it, face up, under the white face of the clock, stamp! The minute-ticking clock clicked the hour, seven, and yielded up his card.

Made it.

II

The interruptions that were to disrupt this day beyond recall began at seven-thirty.

He was tearing down the first machine, his eye on the blueprint he had taped on the wall beside him. A continent of lines specifying the dimensions and contour of the new contact screw by the ten-thousandth of an inch, the areas where it was to be slotted, threaded, chamfered, cut out of what grade and finish of stock. His mind occupied with the selection of parts required. His hands already in it, geared to dismounting and installing the sequence of precision tools that fed and formed, slid and revolved: each in turn to be loosened and then tightened with nuts, clamps, set screws, dowel pins, bolts; to be cushioned with bushings, held with chucks, adjusted for distance and angle, timed, tested. When Dirksen, the foreman, laid his hand on his shoulder.

"Say, Lunin, do me a favor?"

"Huh?"

"Show the job to the new material handler they sent up here to Switch?"

"Huh?"

"They send me this raw kid. Another hour the girls'll be screaming for the stuff."

He heard Dirksen only vaguely through the clatter of the adjoining machines and the presses in the next row. Stooped over his setup, delving through a chest-high maze, immersed in it, he didn't even look around. Collet out. Metal dust cleaned off. Next size collet in. Holding plate screwed fast—one jar, loosened by the vibration of the machine in operation, kerplunk.

"I got the turntable timing this morning. I got that VIP delegation coming through this noon. The window washers are behind schedule, the cartons have to be moved, I gotta find a porter, Tom's out sick. Hammill just called with a change in their specs and we already started the job, no idea what havoc . . ."

"Huh? Yuh?"

His shoulder hardened under the urging supervisory hand, with a resistance built into his bones. You don't knuckle under to a cop or a social worker, teacher or priest, merchant or landlord, any hand or voice of authority.

He had no personal objection to George Dirksen. He might have been standing in Dirksen's shoes right now if he had accepted the promotion to foreman when it was offered him. The offer had so excited Priscilla that she called her father at his office and her brother Ted at the university to inform them of it by way of negation. "Naturally he's not taking it, of course not. But . . ." It was shortly after that that she got busy with Lucas.

A foreman is a supervisor is a boss. To go over to the other side, become a company man was for him unthinkable. Join the rah rah boys? Take a cut in pay and make up for it in bonuses based on the amount of increased production he could wring out of the ranks? Every foreman is a son of a bitch, he has to be. The face of the faceless corporation, the buffer between top and bottom, the exposed punch of a five-ton press bearing down with all the pressure of the forces above upon the resistance of the forces below.

". . . they're running my ass off."

"Yuh?"

Just a month ago he'd been friendly enough with Dirksen, exchanging lunch sandwiches with him. Inside of a month Dirksen had developed devices he was already only too familiar with. Asking a favor, Dirksen issued an order. Pleading for sympathy, Dirksen implied mutual identity. Confiding his problems, Dirksen unloaded them. It was George Dirksen's job to get the job out. Extract the maximum from every individual under him.

"For Christ sake, Mish," Dirksen shouted at him through the din of machinery, "don't give me no trouble. I'm shorthanded. Come on."

"Are you nuts?" With difficulty he extricated himself from the entrails of iron and tempered steel. "Last week you want these machines set up week before last. Now you pulling me off?"

Dirksen's normally cherubic face was thinned down, harried, chamfered and milled to a fractional tolerance and it wasn't even eight o'clock yet of a fine spring morning.

"It's the new material handler for Switch," Dirksen explained to him, with a friendly squeeze of the shoulder that simultaneously propelled him into motion. "By nine the girls'll be out of materials, it'll be a madhouse out there. What the hell, you're on hourly rate. Knock off forty minutes, put the boy to work." With a gesture of largesse, doing *him* a favor,. Dirksen lifted socket wrench and gauge from him and restored them to their trays. "Take a break."

He stared at Dirksen in unfeigned disbelief. To leave the machine in disorder, the machine tool replacements only half assembled, the hand tools and the array of slide rules, squares, gauges arranged ready to his hand, the grease-blackened book of tables from which he made his calculations open to the page . . . Take an additional twenty minutes just to pour himself back into it. There had to be a catch.

Dimly, through the diffusion of oil from the double row of machines, he perceived the two operators down his aisle watching on the sly. Unable to hear but quick to scent a clash, Roscoe and Ewell nudged over from their attendance on feeding tube and spindle and concentrated instead on inspecting the finished pieces dropping into their baskets, letting the pieces trickle through their fingers, while they covertly grinned around and winked at him, cheering him on, made a victory signal of their habitual rubbing together of thumb and forefinger over the slipperiness of oil.

Room and men were bathed in a fine vapor of oil. Oil saturated the air. It clung to every surface, leaving a film on clothing, skin, the hair tucked back under their caps. It flowed through the intricately jointed anatomy of the machines, protecting them in their internal motion from overheating and the erosion of friction. It glistened on the bolts and pins heaping up in the baskets, glittered in the grooves of slottings and threadings, sparkled on the cutouts and chips and grit separated out in barrels, burnished to gold the pine-coned copper scrap. Roscoe and Ewell, spot-checking their pieces between side glances at him and Dirksen, continually reached for the oil-smeared rag dangling from their back pockets to wipe their hands off. Their tan coveralls were already beginning to darken with the day's permeation of oil.

Dirksen alone appeared untouched. Scrubbed pink, his taffy hair combed back in a tufted wave, white-shirted and black-trousered, immaculate and immune, above the hurly-burly in which he was so intimately involved, he bore himself with a manner as distinct as his change of attire since he was elevated from the ranks. He hovered at the door waiting, not staying an instant longer in the machine shop than he had to.

"Hurry up now, Lunin. Don't worry about the machines, you can make it. You'll catch up during the day."

So that was the catch. A month in his new role and Dirksen was completely predictable. You-can-make-it-Dirksen. On the double. Push it through.

"The hell I will. I don't catch up nothin'. This setup can take anywhere from three hours to three days depending on what I run into. I'll have Ledyard down on my neck, the whole works."

He picked up a wrench half as long as his arm, locked it on the feeding finger and standing back, gripping with both hands, prepared to remove the finger.

"Roscoe!" Dirksen beckoned down the aisle. "Say Roscoe, c'mere."

Jaw clenched and shoulders bulging, he strove with the snug feeding finger. He had the cams to change yet, the turret cam and the cams for each of the sliding tools—the pie-shaped cams with bites out of them that by their profile governed the programming of the machine. He had the turret stops to adjust after the turret tools were in, and the dogs on the turret wheel to be positioned at intervals that tripped the collet open and shut—governing the time and order in which the sliding tools would perform upon the subject: the brass rod. One error, one instant's lag, ram-jam, crack-up. Everything bust.

There were so many things that could go wrong with a setup. A slipping belt, a loosened bolt, a tool dulled, an inside or outside diameter off by a hairbreadth, and tolerances were thrown off, the whole process could be knocked out of kilter. And to discover the cause of a breakdown demanded infinite patience. Last time, his stock started scratching up during the trial run and it took hours to track down: the interior of the feed pipe was wearing out at a certain spot, abrading the twelve-foot brass rod as it passed through.

And holes. A million holes. Every hole had to be exactly right for what went into it.

"You can read this blueprint, can't you?" Beside him, by the blueprint taped up on the oily wall, Dirksen was conferring with Roscoe. "The tools are all laid out here," Dirksen said to Roscoe. "You fill in for Lunin till he gets back."

Roscoe squinted through his glasses at the blueprint. He was capable of handling minor repairs and setup and he was bucking for an operator-setup rating. Only he could never seem to hit it off with the oil. One day he forgot to check the spigot: the machine overheated, dulling all the tools; smoke filled the room, everybody ran. Another day he forgot to check the guards: the oil splashed over, splattering his glasses; drenched him head to foot; flew out into the aisle, everybody scat.

With his little ferret nose outthrust Roscoe skirted the machine, looking for what was in it for him. He was not about to be stuck with a job that required an ace mechanic. What's the catch?

"What about my quota?" Roscoe suddenly bethought himself and edged away. "I'm falling behind right now."

"You'll make it. You'll find time."

"Now wait a minute, I don't make my quota it comes out of my paycheck. Not anybody else's."

"Ewell!" Dirksen summoned the second operator from down the aisle.

Ewell who had been standing at ease before his four Brown & Sharpes, each of them working a different job, advanced slowly toward them, wiping off his hands.

"Watch Roscoe's machine for him," Dirksen instructed Ewell, "while he fills in for Lunin here. Just a few minutes. Half hour at most."

Ewell pulled himself out of his relaxed posture. His cap cocked back on his fair head, he moved down the aisle with the rigidity of a nobleman who, walking through crowds, listens only to his own thoughts, deaf to the outer world.

"Oh no," Ewell said to Dirksen with a touch of condescension, informing him of the obvious. "I run four machines."

Ewell was perfectly capable of attending five or even seven machines at once. And Dirksen knew it—that was the advantage of being a foreman promoted from the ranks, he was on to what went on. But Ewell had no intention of demonstrating his capabilities for Dirksen's, i.e. UV's, convenience. Suppose as a result he wound up with five machines regularly assigned him instead of four, at no extra compensation or very little more? The increase in feed, takeoff, odds for simultaneous snafus multiplied by the tensions generated— There was always some catch.

"Okay, you guys. Ewell take over for Roscoe. Roscoe for Lunin. Lunin, you come with me."

Dirksen wheeled on his heel, compliance expected. No use fighting it.

Accede or make a stand? It's always so much easier to give in.

He had the feeding finger out now and its replacement about to go in. For an instant he dallied in indecision: steel pad or nylon?

Roscoe and Ewell lingered with lurking grins, waiting for him to make an issue of Dirksen's order: as witnesses or covictims? Dirksen stationed himself at the door, adamantly awaiting him.

Briefly he processed the grievance—Lunin doing Dirksen's work on Lunin's time, Roscoe doing Lunin's work on Roscoe's pay, Ewell doing Roscoe's work along with his own . . . against the company's countercharges of insubordination. From a fuss on the floor here, calling in Fritz the steward . . . through Steps Two and Three up to the top brass, Colangelo handling it . . .

Go on give it to him, Roscoe and Ewell grinned at him. Let 'em have it, they urged him on with conjoined thumb and fore-finger circling over the slipperiness of oil. Operators in the next row were rubbernecking over and around their stamping presses and lathes.

He wiped his hands off on the rag hanging on the ledge of his machine and with a gesture at the two men, hands crossed and fanning out, back to your own machines, he followed after Dirksen. So the setup would wait. And be late. A lag in the gargantuan interdepartmental machinery of the plant, slam-jam . . .

Breathing heavily, Dirksen rushed him down the corridor toward the section manager's office, a glassed-in kiosk tucked in the corner of the Switch Department, where the new hand was sitting around on his ass on company time. Heaving and muttering, Dirksen shook out his starched white handkerchief and mopped over his maroon-mottled pink cheeks. He inserted the handkerchief in and around his collar, scrutinized it for streaks of grease, blew his nose into it and restored it, folded, into his pocket. Groping at his black bow tie, only slightly askew, as if it were strangling him, he twitched it straight. Gradually like a machine coming to rest, he subsided.

"Mish, I don't understand you, I swear I don't." Dirksen slowed his trot, smoothing the wattles and dewlaps of his shirt down inside his belt. "I make a request, a simple little request for you to pitch in in a pinch . . . You could get ahead. You could make good. If you'd just learn to cooperate."

The old company song and dance. A couple of men pushing hand trucks by recognized it on Dirksen's lips and formed their own song and dance in reply. *You can make it, yessiree, up to the UV presidency.* Just like George D. Hey, Georgie?

"I bet I can name fifty men in this plant just like you. All the ability in the world and no ambition. Good men. With a bad attitude. Pigheaded! You are your own worst enemy."

Approaching the section office, Dirksen touched over his lotion-stiffened tuft of hair. Fumbled at his black bow tie, askew again, clown eyes intersecting.

"Pigheaded. Pigheaded."

Dirksen's scolding, reaching a pitch of expostulation, was drowned under the shattering noise of the floor. At Dirksen's side he halted abruptly. A handsome young woman dressed in Easter parade best, fawn suit and black straw hat, gloves in hand, sailed past with a wave of her handbag at them and plunged into the thunderous maelstrom of the department.

"That Leora?" he said to Dirksen in consternation. "She coming back?"

"Sure is," Dirksen said, "thank God. Just dropping by today to say hello to the girls. Be on the line next week."

"Not in her old job?"

"What else?"

A new materials handler, the turntable timing, the delegation due this noon—and now Leora tripping through. Has anybody, he wondered as he tracked Dirksen across the floor to the kiosk, ever done an actuarial table on the life expectancy of company supervisors?

"Say what you may," Dirksen, his cherubic good nature recovered, offered a parting bit of paternal advice, "there's no better place to work in this city than UV and you know it. What's going to become of you, Mish? Where are you going?"

Dirksen bustled into the section office ahead of him. The unmistakable ring of concern in Dirksen's voice resounded through him with the alarm of a warning bell out at sea. The simple little request to break in a new man, was it as simple as it seemed? Or the symptom of some deeper disturbance? Dirksen who had accepted the foremanship he turned down forcing him into this role as a means of washing himself clean? The sort of self-defensive aggression in the guise of kindliness that can, if it isn't watched, boil up into a brawl . . . Or was Dirksen simply reacting to a disturbance that lay even deeper? The suspicion attached to a man who has declined promotion from the work force into the first rung of management. Sometimes weeks later the pressure will begin, the pressure from some potent source inside the company toward expulsion, the ejection of him who has rejected it.

In the last few weeks he had been shifted from one work station to another, had been started on setups and dispatched to maintenance, had lost out on an opening he'd sought in Generator. Meaningful or meaningless, the enigma of these dislocations had the power, at the merest note of concern in Dirksen's voice, to pierce him with fear.

What's going to become of you, Mish?

Where are you going?

"Where the hell you been?" Stan Ledyard, the section manager, yelled at Dirksen with his hand over his telephone. "Hiding on me?" Ledyard who had been a foreman himself knew the whole bag of tricks. When a man has too much coming at him from too many directions, try and find him. "Will you get after the window washers? And the sweepers, I want them through here just five minutes before that delegation."

"Mr. Dirksen," the clerk called over the cost accounts she was typing up, "the engineer and the inspector are waiting for you at the turntable."

"Sir?" The new materials handler uncoiled himself from the supply shelves on which he had been leaning while jiving the clerk.

Dirksen danced about the tiny office, flustered by Ledyard's accusation. Over Ledyard's phone he bawled out the boss window washer and over his own phone he hung up in the middle of a complaint from Quality Control and at the same time he hauled up the materials handler and presented him.

"Don Pinette, meet Mike Lunin."

Sucking at a particle caught in his back teeth, msp msp msp, Dirksen consulted the coded card from Personnel. He must have looked the boy over before he was hired, he must have approved him. But now he was having his doubts.

"I'm giving you the best man I got, son, to show you the job. Step by step. You'll catch on. Just one thing, though. Don't pay no attention to the girls. They're touchy. Flighty. Temperamental. They'll get you all excited. Well, that's the way they are. Just go your own way, do your job and you can make it. You'll make out."

Delighted with his briefing, the field covered in a nutshell, Dirksen snapped up his time book and trotted off, leaving the rest to Lunin.

2

"What did you say your name is?" he inquired on the way to the locker room.

"Don Pinette. Doc. They always call me Doc 'count of I worked in the drugstore."

"What'd you do in the drugstore?"

"Soda jerk. Short-order cook. Behind the counter. Servicing the waitresses—and, boy, did I give service!"

"Then you never worked in a plant before?"

"Don't tell anybody but I'm in it for the dough, strictly for the dough. Bought a car, you know, De Soto, used, but power—boy, has she got power! What a doll, two-tone, fire-truck red with cream on top. And a si-reen." He let out a siren blast, two-tone, curvaceously arching. "Course I gotta meet the payments."

The boy towered over him, youthfully glossy, tossing his tawny mane back. His gray sharkskin suit was pressed to a crease and his satin-striped tie was pinned down with a silver bar. He carried his work clothes still bundled in the package made up in the department store and his lunch in a black metal bucket unmarred by use. Altogether he was neat and clean, eager to make a good impression. Don would smile at the right people.

"Way I figure, if I work here for a year she's mine."

The locker room with the lavatory opening from it reeked of sweat, piss and grime, infused with the odor, pungent and acrid, of machine grease. Don stripped off suit and shirt, inserted his articles of clothing tenderly into the narrow aperture of the locker to hang slackly on the hook inside. Undressed he was a masterpiece. His collarbone branched out to an incredible width, a veritable yoke. His trunk descended in a tapered shaft to the twin columns of his legs. The whole bound together by his jockey briefs, white of a whiteness undimmed by launderings, in which his cheeky buttocks and more than ample privates were snugly pocketed.

"Don't you worry about me," Don assured him. "I'll get along."

Looking down on himself, appreciating what he saw, Don unwrapped his work clothes on the bench. He peeled the label off his jeans, opened them, stiff as a board with sizing, and thrust a leg in.

"Mostly chicks in this department, ain't they?"

"Up to the age of sixty. Then they're retired."

"Plenty a young ones. I spotted 'em." He zipped up his closure and tossed his tawny mane back. Nostalgic and anticipatory, relishing foretaste and aftertaste, he contemplated past and future. "Broads they're all alike. If you know how to handle 'em."

Don punched his navy blue T-shirt into his jeans, bracing his shoulders back with a castanet click of his joints. "They like you to touch their tits," he confided, "as you pass 'em by. Steal a little nooky. And them nigger gals, they're the best of all. Give off chocolate milk."

He handed Don his lunch bucket from the bench to put into the locker. Most of the men brought their lunches in paper bags. A green hand, previous experience confined to the passage between drugstore counter and back bar, rubbing past waitresses. And the racks of paperbacks decorated with undraped damsels. Forty minutes to run him through Dirksen's training course. *You can do it, sure you can, nothing to it.*

"The older they get, the harder they go for it," Don explained, stimulated by lack of response to enlarge and embellish. "You wouldn't believe it. With married daughters and grandchildren yet. Not tramps, what I mean lookers, wearing fur coats on. Why I had one, teller in the bank, used to stop in every day same time for coffee. 'You like tipped cigarettes?' she asks me. First time I ever laid eyes on her. 'Then let me'"—Don passed an imaginary cigarette over his chiseled lower lip—"'tip it for you.' How do you like that? Next thing I know she's dropping her key under her saucer. And then there's the stud dames."

"The what?" Leading Don out of the locker room he turned around and looked at him, hooked at last.

"Stud dames. You know, girls going with girls? You ever hear of that? But just before they get the rag on and right after, they gotta have a man."

"Boy," he shook his head at the boy, "have you got a lot to learn."

"What? What? What have I got to learn?"

Don pranced after him, bewildered.

"What have I got to learn?"

3

At the threshold of Switch he hesitated, seeing it as a youngster might see it coming in for the first time to work here, fresh from vanilla ice cream sundaes and his mother's apron strings and the greenery of a small town somewhere.

He felt the boy beside him flinch. Don might have noticed this interior before from the outside, flashing by at night on the expressway in his souped-up red De Soto: dingy windows blue-lit, bars of fluorescent lighting floating like barges through the gray murk above a concourse of machinery to which vague figures were attached, people working. He must have glimpsed it when he was sent up by Personnel to the foreman for approval. But to step inside it, commit himself physically to it . . .

He himself experienced a twinge of compunction. To cast this kid—green as grass with the sap rising in him, young Adonis in a jockstrap, Apollo in a T-shirt, the golden boy, rounded forehead smooth as stone, deep-set eyes clear as water, bulbous mouth raspberry-tender, throat arching like an oak—to cast all that into this . . .

Before them, activity swirled through the vast expanse of a chamber cobwebbed overhead with pipe and cable conductors. Every machine vibrated with its own peculiar hiss, stamp, rumble, clangor, crash, each sound localized in its own area merging into a din no voice could penetrate. Silent, unheard, subsidiary to the movement of machine and conveyor, a stationary prefix to it, frozen to the grindstone, keyed to it with a succession of motions so minute sometimes as to be barely perceptible, was the human form, the warmth of thinking, feeling, pulsating human flesh. The smell here, stronger than that of the locker room, was sharply chemical and metallic, thickly tarrish, aromatic with plastics, laced with traces of gas from the gas ovens.

Chaos. Yet even to the unpracticed eye, he thought, some pattern must be discernible. The machines were grouped in the order of their production sequence. Through a compartmentalization of processes, part of an ingenious scheme to elicit from the human units en route the utmost efficiency, the component elements were moved swiftly from work station to work station until they were united in the desired object: the electric wall switch, one-way, two-way, up to four-way.

To take charge of this boy was for him to assume a measure of responsibility for his success or failure—a weakness of which Dirksen was well aware and exploited to the hilt. He had to implant in the boy something of his own experience. He had to plumb out of him some workable essence. He didn't particularly want to adapt Don Pinette to the UV apparatus. He didn't especially like himself for it. Yet there it was.

You got to shape up, kid. Shape up.

"This is a vertical operation," he began, raising his voice against the noise, bent upon defining for the boy the general configuration of his task. He faced the boy, eyes fixed on him, as if by sheer intensity he could communicate the means of hearing that obtained in the plant: part lip-reading, part sound effect, part guess-work.

"In contrast to other departments, say, where they concentrate on a single aspect of the total product. Thermostatic controls, for instance. Paint touch-up. Here"—he gestured widely—"we take the whole switch from the arrival of raw materials on this end of the floor to the finished product all the way down there in final assembly."

As he spoke he felt something slide into his idle hand, a long stiff grubby substance. It was a stick of gum, with its wrappers thoughtfully removed.

Have some, Don gestured at him and stuck a stick of gum into his own mouth. Holding it jauntily between his teeth, Don surveyed the floor.

"I'm suppose to supply the girls," Don hollered into his ear.

Tossing back his mane, pawing the ground, champing at the bit, prick-happy, out to rape the works.

Where are they? Lemme at 'em.

He drew Don away to the side out of sight of the department, into a nook formed by cartons stacked high by the windows. He smoothed out a scrap of wrapping paper and, holding it up against a carton, sketched out a map of the floor for Don.

"Machine shop and ceramics here on the south side of the floor. Plastics shop on the north side over beyond final assembly. In between you have the main department."

He blocked out the main department, here the milling and drilling, there the brushing and polishing, subassemblies here and there, mercury injection in the center, final assembly and testing all the way back.

"A vertical operation? You don't say!"

With a leer and a wink Don dug it.

On top of a low carton he laid out the components of the switch for Don as he had once laid them out on the kitchen table for Gail, the wife of Priscilla's brother Ted, when she asked him what he did. Gail didn't take in a word he said. It was all sculpture to her. The ivory toggle— "Why it's a tower, a phallic symbol."

The zinc alloy support— "Why it's an African primitive, look at the symmetry of that figure, the hollowed oblong of a body and the heads top and bottom." The ceramic-belted button— "What a lovely navel." And so on through the plastic base and the two fillers shaped like flattened F's, the brass-angled contacts beveled with exact concentricity for the insertion of the screws. "Why it's perfect," Gail said. "I'm going to take it home and mount it and hang it on my wall." The woman was a mystery to him. He could never tell whether Gail was making fun of him or not.

"What are you smiling at?" Don asked him as he explained the function and site on his map of each part.

"Nothing."

"Tell me so I can smile too."

Don was jabbing the ivory toggle about, the tunneled tower, the phallic symbol. Bang bang for Rosie.

"And this is the button"—dimpled aluminum shells top and bottom with the glass-ringed ceramic sealed between—"which everything else is designed to hold in place. The women seal it at the turntable"—he located it on his map—"here at right center."

"Uh huh. The belly button. You like belly buttons?"

Another art collector.

With every procedure he defined, they went through the same fandango. To "make out" meant only one thing to Don: what a fella does with girls. To "put out," ditto: what a girl does with fellas. The distinction between the male contact, threaded on the outside, and the female contact, tapped on the inside, could be identified for him only one way. "The male is the one that fits into the female. Get it?"

How to clunk this lunk into a useful tool? How to convert this hunk of spunk into a smoothly functioning factor?

"Now I'll take you through your first run-through. After that you're on your own. Let's go."

"What you say they inject?"

As he hustled Don out onto the floor, back into the onslaught of noise, he gradually became aware of a strange scent, alien to this place. At first he thought it was the gum they were chewing, spearmint. Then he thought it must be some lotion Don had applied to his ducktail haircut with its cocky little lick in back. But the boy tossed his hair back freely, no lotion. Skin, sweat, a personal effluvium strong enough to penetrate this atmosphere yet too elusive to quite—? A scent of grass. The sweet rank grass in which lovers lie down together, a bed of meadow grass that, shining and lush, sways gently above, caressing the sky.

"Your first few weeks here you'll be completely occupied with learning the parts of the switch I just showed you. Where they're stored on the floor. How to handle them. Where they go to. When they're needed."

He led Don to the first stack of tote cans, containers about the size of a file drawer tiered one on top the other.

"You keep these filled at all times with materials for the nearest work station. When a production worker starts yelling for her materials you run for your tote can, deliver it where it's wanted and lift it into her bin."

Demonstrating, he lowered a tote can to the floor, hooked a drag roller into it and hauled it along at a run.

"Down. Hook. Run. Up into the bin. All you'll know of yourself for a while here is that run. And all you'll know of anybody else here is that yell."

Sure, sure, Don nodded, you bet. But his eyes were elsewhere. Traveling up and down Leora as she wended her way through the girls at their workbenches exchanging words of greeting.

"Now let's see you. What do you do?"

Don heard it or lip-read it or caught it from the expression on someone's face. Promptly, ignoring the drag roller, he bent over and picked the tote can up off the floor and carried it, loaded with screws, in his arms. He saluted Leora as he strutted past her.

"After you've done that a couple of hundred times," he said to Don, "and hoisted it into a bin as high as your head, you can forget about pussy because you won't be having any."

"Why? What's the matter? I'm strong enough."

"It's not how much strength you got. It's how you distribute it." Demonstrating, he lowered himself in a knee bend to the tote can on the floor. Elevating himself to his feet, he raised the can, spreading the weight of it from legs up through shoulder muscles, up to the height of a bin.

"From now on keep your pecker in."

But Don was resolved to carry the tote cans in his arms or precariously on his shoulder, displaying the body beautiful. He had the back of a bullock. He had brass balls.

Before taking Don on the rounds, he added a tentative schedule to the map he'd drawn up on the scrap of wrapping paper.

"You'll be scrambling all day long till you're onto this. The night material handler is supposed to leave all the bins full. You check that out as soon as you arrive. Keep tabs on how fast the stuff is used and keep refilling before the bins hit bottom. Never leave an area without filling up for the time you'll be gone. The trick is always to keep one step ahead of the game. Anticipate what the girls require before they have to yell for it."

"Anticipate. That's me."

Whoever in Personnel had placed Don Pinette in Materials Handling ought to be sent back to whatever School of Business Administration had graduated him. The job was one of the lowest in the plant, lowliest of the low, unskilled labor, no experience called for. Calling only for a Back. So the man had hired a Back.

Only to become an effective Materials Handler, the Back had to have a memory as long as an elephant's, the punctuality of a stop watch, alertness, initiative, judgment. He had to know his department as an Indian knows the forests, as a plowman knows the fields, as a mariner knows the waters. He had to figure out an itinerary adaptable to all possible contingencies if he wasn't to run himself ragged. He had to figure out the psychology of those he worked with if he wasn't to be pulled apart.

"You say you were a short-order cook?"

Don snapped his fingers in the air. Burgers with. Comin' up.
He wiped his cap back over his head. Well, it was something.
"All right then, let's cover the floor. First stop, the powder
room."

"The powder room?" Don, jogging along, shouted into his ear.
"You're kidding."

4

By a hundred signs it was clear to him as he steered Don Pinette
toward the powder room that this was destined to be one of those
days when squabbles broke out and machines broke down, when
everybody worked like hell and output dropped. It was Tom Riker,
Dirksen's assistant foreman, out sick today, who was in hiding.

He could hear it above the clatter like the hum of high-tension
wires. The visiting delegation of industrial, political and military
dignitaries arranged under the aegis of the U. S. Departments of
State and Commerce was not due in Switch until noon, their last
stop before the luncheon that was to be tendered them in the
executive dining room in the head office building. The appearance
of such a delegation was of no concern to him or to any of the
work force. Even the appearance of Grover Coffin, rare back here,
was of no particular concern. Old Graveyard, not so old, at the
peak of his prime, would breeze past him with a nod, "How's it
going, Mike?"—so much for auld lang syne over the bargaining
table, both of them on the rise together—and breeze on without
waiting for a reply, the manager always in touch with his men.
None of them, least of all he, gave a damn for Coffin or his delegation. Yet the atmosphere in Switch hummed with anticipation.

Anticipation sawed away at their sensibilities like an unaccustomed sound within the medley of sound, irritating, agitating.
Children reacting to the anxiety in the section office, Dirksen and
Ledyard all futzed up with housekeeping detail, company's coming, on your best behavior now? Not exactly. Prisoners about to be
viewed by a sociology class on a field trip? Not exactly that either.

It was an anticipation rife with insecurity. His own nerves jumped with the insecurity, the mistrust, the doubt in the air. All of them, anticipating, entertained a suspicion, a reasonable suspicion, that the descent of the dignitaries might prove prelude to the departure of the department from under them to elsewhere, anywhere from Birmingham to West Berlin to Bombay.

He could see the warning signals, as unmistakable as the flicker of lights on an overloaded circuit, in the activity around the turntable in the center of the floor. The turntable, a carrousel assembly, wheeled about the iron structure of gas ovens under the shield of a convex iron roof. Dirksen, an inspector and an engineer were gathered on the aisle side with time books and stop watches. The button assemblers, seated on their high stools in a circle around the turntable, were striving with madly dancing hands to keep up with the rotation. For the second time in a month the turntable was being accelerated. The women at their presses across the aisle kept glancing around at it. Last week Anna Lamianski was on the turntable for three days and she had nightmares every night. Anna had asked· Dirksen to transfer her to another job and Dirksen turned her down. So she talked it over with her husband and he told her it was crazy, quit. She quit. Now Bea was requesting a transfer.

He could smell the unrest. It came and went like the vagrant scent of grass that issued from Don Pinette, a scent out of the pores, the hair follicles, the sweat and seminal glands: the kind of scent that sends feelers out to the female, attaching her to the man who possesses it, to that man and no other: an emanation that wraps the pair around in each other's arms, envelops them.

Against the overwhelming presence of machinery, Don with his overriding need to make an impression pitted himself in all his muscular glory. Against the chatter of drills, the crash of presses, the rasp of abrasives, the resonance of metal upon metal, he strove to make his imprint, *I'm here*, to leave his trail behind, *he passed this way*. Against UV's equipment he posed his equipment, attempting to rouse the girls out of their enmeshment with inorganic matter into enmeshment with him, nature boy. He strode among them, an intrusive spirit, an escapee from the burgeoning spring day outside, demanding response.

Offering gifts of himself in which the women couldn't be less interested.

Don's path crisscrossed Leora's. Waving her handbag, *hiya* and *bye now*, stopping every once in a while to bend over a girl in affectionate conversation, Leora left in her wake a current of dissension, speculation, a ripple of rumor that traveled the grapevine. All eyes converged, not upon Don, but in the direction of final assembly. Surreptitiously they followed Leora as she wove in and out, vanished behind and emerged from, pursuing her in her progress to the ultimate assembly line. What would happen when she reached there?

He ushered Don first into the powder room. Aside from the machine and plastics shops the powder room was the only self-enclosed facility in Switch. The small room contained three molding machines supervised by a single operator, the darling of the department, Inga Kohlberg. Her job was not difficult; it was a privileged job, one always assigned to a person of some influence. In Inga's case, she attended the Lutheran church with Dirksen and had served on supper committees with his wife.

"Every morning first thing after you've checked your tote cans," he instructed Don, "you bring these sacks of clay powder in here from supply and fill that mixer."

Don waggled his fingers at Inga. At last his moment. The female contact. And in such close quarters too.

"Inga Kohlberg, Don Pinette your new material handler."

"Call me Doc."

Inga was too busy stowing trays of ceramic rings from her high-speed molder into her high-temp oven and too preoccupied with Leora who had looked in on her minutes before even to nod to Don.

"Is it true, Mish, that Leora's going back to being group leader on the line again?"

"That what she say?"

"She didn't say. But the way she's talking . . ."

Don swooped for one of the clay sacks on the floor and with swiveling hips swung it up to Inga's mixer.

Eschewing Don's leg which somehow in the process became entangled with hers, Inga hiked herself up on her stool. With a fetching little sweep under her bottom, she smoothed out her skirt. She was a bit of ceramic herself, pink-and-white glazed, her make-up still fresh on her this time of morning, her brown eyes bright and her brown hair, pin-curled for an evening date, plastered in waves under her becomingly turbaned kerchief.

"But if Leora goes back to group leader," Inga persisted, in fascinated horror at the thought of it, "after Amy's been replacing her all this time . . . Oh brother. They'll be hitting the roof out there. The night-shift handler"—she at last deigned to notice Don, with a peeve—"didn't take the last batch of rings out. They're piling up so, I can't move. Get 'em out of here."

"Every morning about nine," he instructed Don, "you move all these cans of finished rings here out to the turntable. And again at noon. And just before you leave."

Lightly Don lifted Inga, stool and all, out of his way. "Don't you move, sugar, I'll move you."

Blithely he hefted a tote can of rings from the floor and bore it out in his arms. Inga, stirred out of her indifference, stared after him.

"You'll drop a stitch in your back. You'll pop a gut. You'll be laid up . . ."

Puffed up with victory, Don high-tailed off to the turntable. He came back empty-armed and baffled.

"What goes on in this joint? Nobody talks. Nobody cracks a smile. They don't even raise their heads."

"You pick up your tote can like that again, I'll knock your block off. Now go back get the empty, put it where it belongs."

He might have told Don that within the cavernous gloom of this chamber, which not all the flotillas of fluorescent lighting could dispel, within its reverberant din, among the shadowy figures attached to the machines, bubbled a constant interchange of anecdote and argument, friendship and feud, horseplay, festivity. From this too, indiscernible at first, a design would emerge.

"In a couple of weeks, if you last that long, you'll be able to tell one person from another. In a couple of months you may become familiar with their personalities, their problems, their home life. Meanwhile you'll be doing well if you just catch their names."

"Why bother? With one date I'll be in on the inside."

Machine shop next. No chicks, no dames, no broads. His tool kit and his setup were lying in disorder just as he'd left them, untouched by Ewell or Roscoe. Don sprang back out of the spray of machine oil.

"All this machinery in here just to make them little doojiggers? All these things turning and screwing around just to put a little bitty hole through?"

It was a beginning. Beginning to make a dent.

From the machine shop, the basic operation, he and Don hauled the tote cans of oil-slick metal pieces to the secondary operation, the contingents of smaller machines on the floor that applied the finishing touches, drilling and milling, winging and swaging, notching and flanging, tapping, crimping, cross-milling.

At the head of the row of presses Maria Ucchini sat, singing. All day long Mariuch fed zinc alloy supports, the two-dimensional African primitive, eyed top and bottom, under the incessant plunge of her tapping head, her body absorbing in shudders downward the noise and the vibration. All day long, Mariuch sang her airs from *The Threepenny Opera*, starting in the morning with the shark's tooth, the jackknife, and progressing, with transpositions as suited the occasion, to happy endings at the end of the shift. Now she gloated, the tavern slavey, the pirates' sweetheart, over the fate of the gentlemen she served. Scrubbing the floor under their feet, she grinned to herself. Making their beds, she counted heads.

"Mish, it's murder."

With one hand Mari organized her supports on the side of her platform so as to entail a minimum of reaching and turning, with the other she continued to feed them under the descending tooth.

The up-and-down plunge jerked spasmodically through her, every moving part a threat, any momentary loss on her part of alertness or control an amputation.

"Old Coffin can take this job and stick it up his ass."

Mariuch was a thorn in the side of the company. At the time she was a shop steward she cost UV, easily, twenty thousand a year. Grover Coffin had tried every way he could to get rid of her. Suspended on her job, she walked half the women in the plant out with her. Fired from her job, she sued in the courts for re-instatement. Transferred from one job to another all over the plant, she took every company training course available and became one of the best all-around workers the company had.

Mari's husband, Bob Ucchini, had been a founder of the union and its moving spirit for many years. Bob's death, almost two years ago, had taken some of the jazz out of her. And a series of illnesses—every time she attempted nowadays to organize the women around a grievance, another illness struck her down. Illness hung poised above her like a guillotine. It had descended on her so often now she was frightened by it, inhibited from action. If it wasn't hepatitis it was gastritis. If it wasn't an operation it was a car colliding with hers putting her in a brace for months. Yet she had plenty of the old spark left. Mariuch was guide star of the women in the department; source of counsel; instigator of lunch-hour birthday parties, baby showers, pizza pools, sympathy cards and fund collections to be sent to the sick and the bereaved.

"Mari, this is Don Pinette. Your new material handler."

"Call me Doc," Don invited her, admiring her figure, trim in slacks outfit of polished cotton, her jogging bosom, her jiggling curls, her brown eyes boldly roaming.

Mari barely spared Don a second glance. One glance was enough. She knew all there was to know about him.

"Do you see what I see?"

Mari's eyes were on her work and all over the floor at once, on Luckner the time-study man stepping out from around the turn-table to consult with the Dirksen group, on Leora circling about mercury injection toward final assembly.

He left her whistling a booby-hatch army march. Pirate Jenny was now Tiger Brown.

"I know her." Don hitched after him, confiding into his ear. "I got her number. I been out with that kind. They feel you around. They put their hand inside, make a big deal of it. 'Oh m-m-m-y.'"

Pig-meat, young and tender.

He piloted Don around the turntable with its blue-flamed gas jets, its dizzying fumes, its three-inch posts at which women dextrously fitted together aluminum shells, ceramic ring, glass rim. The glass rim melting in the gas heat sealed the completed button.

"You can make it." Dirksen was encouraging white-haired Elsie and twenty-year-old Joan Hlavacek who had been brought in as a replacement for Anna who'd quit. "I can," Dirksen assured them.

So afraid were the women of being retarded they motioned him away with their heads as he passed them, pulled their backs in from Don.

"Shells from the stamping presses go here next to the ceramic rings. Glass rims. Pins. Every couple of hours." He inserted a note on the schedule he was making up for Don. "Then after the buttons go through the gas ovens you collect them. Every three hours. Otherwise they'll back up in the ovens and be ruined. Got that?"

"Mamma's little baby want shortenin' bread?"

Don had transferred his attention from the smoldering turntable to the sultry brown girl at the brush machine beside it. Inserting sealed buttons into slots on a small rotary table, she studied from under her glossy eyelashes sidelong the four men timing the nine women in the blue haze of gas flame.

Don tried again. "Then I deliver them buttons to you to be polished off, huh?" he asked her, logically enough.

"They say what goes up must come down," she pronounced with ominous certainty, her fingers inserting buttons into her brusher, her eyes fixed sidelong on the cluster of men, the ring of women, the posts revolving around the gas-lit hearth.

He handed Don a drag roller to haul over the filled cans of buttons.

"Thinking of switching jobs, Rita?"

"First Anna. Now Bea. Who next?"

"Don Pinette, your new material handler."

"Elsie has that child she's putting through college, she can't stop. At her age where would she find anything else? Not over there, boy. Here's my bin."

Casually from behind her Don placed his hand on the caramel smoothness of her arm. "Anything else I can bring you, babes?"

"If I had that job and I had a husband I'd have to get a divorce or give up the job. I'd be in such a state all the time he wouldn't be able to stand me."

"Call me Doc."

Absently Rita shook Don's hand off her arm. "Watching and waiting. Waiting and watching. What next? Who?"

At mercury injection, women dressed in hospital white sat before a glass shield and with a hypodermic needle, attached to a rubber tube from a bottle of mercury, injected, at the pump of a foot on the compressed-air pedal under the table, a drop of mercury into the button. With a continuous movement of the arm they shook each button for activation of the mercury injected and deposited it on a tray, the mounting trays to be removed by Don when full.

Women at punch presses brought down, with a plunge of the foot pedal, the plunge of the punch above their hands upon the injected button, plugging the puncture of the hypodermic needle.

Women at the electrical activation machine—a machine that loomed over the floor like a furnace, spectacular with running lights, green, blue, red—paced around the machine in tempo with its mobile, electrically charged track, sliding buttons between little knobs.

And finally, before final assembly, the women at the electronic tester. Automated, wired internally with relays that triggered impulses in programmed succession, the tester tested the arc of the mercury locked in the buttons, sorted the buttons into three different categories. Here at the tester one of the women nodded Don toward her, signifying a desire to speak to him.

"Yeah yeah yeah?"

"The best brain," she bellowed up at Don and nodded at the tester, "in UV."

The sum and substance of it all, a button. Less than an inch in diameter, a half inch in depth, aluminum shells dimpled top and bottom and pierced with a pin, ringed with glass-rimmed ceramic, weighted with mercury that shook like a jelly inside.

"You mean when I put my finger on the switch," Don said to him, incredulously, "all this goes on behind it?"

"The button's just one component. There's the crimped copper wire, the angle contacts, the blunt-tipped screws, the double-grooved . . . Just one goof, the wrong screw to the wrong place, you won't know what hit you."

"There's got to be somebody whose switch I can turn on."

A scent of grass, moistly swelling.

"Buttons! Buttons!"

"Bases!"

"Angel hair!"

The women in final assembly were yelling at the top of their lungs, projecting their desperation through the tumult by screech and semaphore.

"Come on"—he grabbed Don and ran him—"they're running out."

5

The women faced each other over a conveyor belt that extended across the back of Switch. The belt carried before them the evolutionary switch, to which one after another supplied and fixed into place a single component. Bins stationed between them provided the proper items at the proper point.

"Don Pinette, your new material handler. You got to give him a little time—"

"Call me Doc."

Out of the wreckage of their voices they lifted to Don faces ravaged with animosity. They needed an expert, not a neophyte. They were all on incentive pay and their ability to meet or exceed the standard depended to a considerable degree, in their estimation, on the alacrity and accuracy of the materials handler, on his devotion to the replenishment of their bins. Insofar as he might fail them, he was a menace to them. He was the enemy.

Their normal tension was exacerbated by the presence of Leora. Leora stood over Amy, svelte in her fawn suit, her black leather gloves and handbag stylishly clutched in hand, her handsome face demurely framed in a black straw bonnet with a brim peaked like a chapel and veiling under chin tied in a bow at the side. The imperfections of her skin were smoothed over with a tan cosmetic blended with a daub of coral over her cheekbones. Over Amy's shoulder Leora chatted with the girls across the conveyor, acknowledging their compliments on her appearance while, ostensibly above it all, she observed the rate at which the components traveled from their arrival through assembly to testing and packing at the far end. Amy, the incumbent group leader, housewifely in homemade apron over white-collared blue Hoover dress, gave no sign that she cared about or even understood the meaning of Leora's return. Center of the strain of dispute in the offing, Amy remained sedately focused on her work.

"Buttons! Where are my buttons?"

"Bases! Bas-zes!"

"What are you gawkin' at? Come on, kid, get the lead outa your pants!"

Driven not by the crack of the whip but by the count at the end of the day, the crackle of their weekly paychecks, they clamored from a half dozen quarters at once for instant service.

Now it was that Leora, who had been calculating to her own advantage the rate of production on the line, bestowed upon Don a tiny smile. During her regime no materials handler ever lagged. Don bowed in response. Some momentary convergence, perhaps a crossing of odors, of puissant grass and musky geranium, occurred between them. At the mere suggestion of Leora's smile

Don dove back to the buttons pouring out of the tester and without stopping to hook on a drag roller, without sinking at least to his haunches or even spreading his legs, he heaved up a tote can full of the mercury-loaded buttons and carried it to final assembly. His tight blue jeans wrinkled across his fly. His thighs bulged. His chest humped under his navy blue T-shirt. Up he reared the tote can, stretching with the weight, to the overhead bin, high as a drugstore coffee urn. Dumped the buttons in.

Openmouthed and round-eyed, moved as much by consternation as by awe, the women on the line craned upward from their stools. Don stepped back and dusted his hands off. His ears were tinged with red.

He grabbed Don, bonehead! and whirled him around, fatass! and with a whack across the back flung him into the aisles, sink or swim.

"Okay, bud. Zinc supports now. Springs over that way. Screws down there."

"Where? Where?"

"There, there and there!"

"Bas-zes!" "Tog-gles!" "Angel hair!"

"You get these goddam bins filled before they're out. This line'll be stopped—" An unimaginable catastrophe. "Faster. Faster."

He rushed Don from storage site to storage site, down one aisle for the zinc supports and down the next aisle for the crimped copper wire to be welded on them, in one direction for electrical screws and in another for pins. Everywhere the operators were screaming. Their production was accumulating, overdue to be dispatched. That one worker should hold another up, unthinkable.

"Before they get through with you, Doc, you gonna be such a woman-hater . . ."

"Bases! Bas-zes! What happened to my bases? I was calling first!"

"Filler!"

He rushed Don around the corner from final assembly into the plastics shop to gather the plastic components. Here two men working twenty machines converted a resinous powder—poured into forms, liquified, pressed—to hollow black bases, ivory toggles. Toggles and bases—cooled, weighed, tumbled—brimmed over the cans, monoliths of curvature and indentation, formed by injection mold into shapes no metal could with any facility achieve.

"Say, Mish."

Gene Bostic who belonged in Spray Paint, who had ten years seniority on his job, had been placed here in plastics when he was recalled from the winter layoff and he was strictly unhappy about it.

"Not now. Not now," he put off Bostic.

"I been gettin' such a kicking around."

"Not now. Later."

Always uneasy before Bostic, twinging with guilt, he hurried Don along who, slightly staggered by his exertions, was taking his time drag-rolling a light can of fillers.

Gene kept pace with him a few steps, a hardheaded Negro, hardness glinting out of his coveralled frame, his skin, his eyes.

"Mish, I wanna talk to you. It'll just take a minute."

"During coffee break, okay? If not then, lunch. I gotta get back."

Out of the resinous dust of the plastics shop back to final assembly. Leora was gone. Having displayed her charms and proved her powers, she had tactfully withdrawn before the onset of conflict.

He took one look at Amy, kindly and maternal in her apron among her bloused-and-skirted companions, but not incapable of a wasp's tongue when circumstance demanded. At Teresa sitting directly opposite, who had been having her differences with Amy. At the wavering of indignation, loyalties, self-interest down the double row of faces.

A hush extended down the entire length of the line. No one wanted to be the first to speak. Only the pairs of hands over the workbench were active, fitting buttons into plastic bases; jamming the angled brass contacts in; cushioning with paper-thin fillers; welding the crimped copper wire, called angel hair, to the zinc support; electrically screwing the supports, toggle-centered, down over the base assembly; placing the finished switch in contact position on the big testing panel under bulbs spelling ON and OFF; packing the switch in individual boxes, then into larger boxes of ten, then into cartons of fifty to one hundred; nudging the cartons on to a skid; building in a day a mountain of switches to be shipped to all corners of the world.

Over the hands, unwavering in their constellation of movements, a hubbub arose.

"Well, she looks good anyway."

"I thought it was a hospital she went to. Not a modeling school."

"She always did know how to dress. Every cent goes on her back."

"Went all the way to the head of Personnel, putting on the dog."

"She didn't say, she just implied."

"Howcome they give her the job back after six months out when they wouldn't let Anna . . ."

"Leora's a good worker, you can't take that away from her. When Leora was here, we made money."

The dispute was on. He beat a hasty retreat, drawing Don with him.

"What's eating them?" Don tugged at him. "What are they so excited about?"

It was a story no one could unravel in two minutes, if ever.

"Well that's it," he said to Don. "Think you can shift for yourself?"

The deep-set eyes glazed over. The smooth young jaw sagged. The T-shirt, black under the arms with perspiration, drooped out over the belt.

What else to tell the boy? He gazed back over the obstructed floor, every fulcrum, template, cam of its machinery, a moving part of him. Not all the lighting overhead nor all the window glass along the sides could brighten this room. A darkness clung to it, clouding the air, begriming every surface. A darkness clung to the person, to be scrubbed out later under the shower at home with a stiff-bristled brush, out of fingernails, out of ringing ears, out of the texture of the skin, and even then perhaps some vestige of it clung to the soul.

"Any questions now before I go?"

He lingered a moment longer in uncertainty. The confusion of impressions, the catechism of instructions—impossible for the boy to assimilate it all. Inga, Mari, Joan and Rene, Teresa, Villa, Jane, Earlene. Rita, Mabel, Amy, Lee . . . Don wouldn't have their names down pat for days. But they had his.

There was so much he should have said to Don. There was so much Don had to understand if he was to work with these women. That they all bore a grudge against the men on the job. Against Stan Ledyard the section manager, against Dirksen the foreman, against the inspectors. Against Lunin too. When a machine was down and he was called over to repair it—oh he was slow, he was stupid, he was making mistakes, he was dragging ass. For who was he to know more about a woman's machine than she did?

Once in Italy during the war, in the mountain country south of Naples, he had glimpsed from a distance a massive surface being borne aloft. It was surrounded by a swarm of people as it proceeded down the road. As he neared them he saw that it was an enormous circular table top supported underneath by a stout pedestal of a woman. She carried it square on her head, no hands. A dozen men buzzed around her, all set to set the table top straight if it should tip.

The tableau had made a profound impression on him. It colored his view of the women here on the floor. All of them on production while the men, high-placed and low, buzzed about, auxiliary to them.

Toward Don, the only male in the department in a position subordinate to theirs, the women would employ every means at their disposal to compensate for the discrimination, the petty tyrannies and the patronizing witticisms, the denial of advancement they endured at the hands of masculine authority. To complicate matters, Don, the lowest-classified male in the department, a beginner, unskilled, was receiving pay that exceeded theirs, even with incentive.

Still Don could, if he wanted to, hit it off with them.

If Don acted genuinely friendly toward them, they would in time accept him, take an interest in him, discuss his private affairs and theirs with him. They would debate in his presence, with his participation, ignoring his sex, such feminine issues as: Can men be trusted in love? Is it right for the husband to keep his wife from driving the car when she's helping to pay for it? Is it better for the mother to be at home with her children during the day or at night when she has to put them to bed? Are people in this country turning into beasts? No heart, no religion, everybody out for the buck?

If Don recognized that most of them, after their eight hours here, spent eight hours shopping for groceries, cooking, laundering, looking after their families, and before coming here were up making breakfast, tidying up, putting up lunches, arranging whatever had to be arranged during their absence . . .

If Don adopted the attitude from the beginning that there was always some valid basis for their complaints and accusations, their edginess and eruptions, and looked for the reason behind it . . .

He could have told Don which of them were divorced or separated, how caught in the web of a marriage from which love had fled they exerted a tremendous drive toward independence. And which of them, married, took pride in their work and their wage and the weight it lent them at home. And which of them had remained single rather than enter into marriage with a man they couldn't love. And which of them, the young, were still looking forward to marriage, to love and security and all that is supposed to be.

"Anything you don't know," he said to Don, "just ask. Never be ashamed to ask. Okay?"

"Leave it to me."

Don biffed him in the shoulder, snapped his fingers in the air, stuck his thumbs in his belt and hitched in his jeans. Strode down the aisle hips a-shuttle. Master of all he surveyed. King of the realm. Exuding his odor of grass.

A rough-and-tough cream puff. He wears his diaper low.

"Hey—stud hoss!"

"Oh, Doc-tah!"

"Pee-nut!"

Some of the older women who had been around were getting ready to give Pinette the business.

III

1

He was hardly back in the machine shop settling back into his setup when the mechanical breakdowns out on the floor began. Like youngsters sensing derangement, the machines broke out in a rash of temperamental crotchets. Dirksen bounced in, summoning him as he was adjusting the timing of his sliding and turret tools, and they had another scrap. He could be temperamental too.

"You want me in here on setup or you want me out there on repair? I told you last week you need another maintenance man here."

"Tom's out sick."

Tom, the assistant foreman, pressed into maintenance and everything else in emergencies, didn't count.

"I tried calling down to Maintenance for Willie. He's not available."

Willie refused to work in Switch. The women got on his nerves. He couldn't stand the women.

"Come on, Mish, stop stalling. I know you. You'll make it up."

"In here or out there? Make your mind up."

"Dear God. Holy jumping Jesus."

It was just one press. He let Dirksen overload him. But then it was another machine down and another. All morning long he was all over the floor debugging systems. And wherever he went he got an earful.

First, the storm raged over Leora.

"When they made Amy group leader, they didn't tell her it was temporary," the women in electrical activation declared.

"When somebody feels a little off," the white-uniformed women on mercury injection observed, "Amy never cracks down."

"Leora's bossy," Rita at her brusher proclaimed. "Talks to you like you're a child."

Mabel, an older colored woman in charge of salvage rejects, complained, "Leora always has to have her own way. Well she better not mess with me," she muttered enigmatically. "She better leave me alone, we'll get along."

To the trill of drills, Mari whistled a dirge for bygone bliss.

"When Leora was here, she had everything humming." Teresa, sitting across from Amy, stubbornly gave voice to the opposition. "We made out."

If it were only a matter of two personalities, Amy's and Leora's, or even a matter of who was to receive the six-cents-an-hour preferential paid the group leader, the emotion over them would not have been so widespread or intense. They were all affected by the dichotomy of Amy and Leora. A tug of war that entered into their bones, into the pattern by which they functioned here from second to second . . .

Final assembly was on group incentive: the pay increasing over the base rate in several steps according to the number of switches the group put out above the expected task. Theoretically each of the women on the line was stimulated by the challenge of team-work to ever-ascending flights of effort. Actually the team incentive tended to keep them all at loggerheads. Rene suspected that Earlene wasn't trying hard enough to keep up with the pace. Lily blamed Lee whenever they fell behind. In order to achieve top pay they had to arrive at seven thousand switches packed in the cartons by three-thirty. They never made it. No matter how hard or fast they worked. Even though three general wage raises had been negotiated by the union in the last three years, the average earnings of the women on the line were now, week after week, the lowest in the history of the department. And the main reason they were unable to succeed under Amy harked back to the backlog of problems accrued by the success of Leora.

The scuttlebutt had it that Leora had gained her promotion to group leader originally by permitting Stan Ledyard, the then foreman, to pour his filthiest jokes into her ear. Though this was one way of obtaining desirable posts, Leora did not need to resort to it. Under the influence of Stan's flatteries and promises to her, and his willingness to help out personally on the line whenever possible, Leora had whipped final assembly up to a new production record. As a consequence Stan was promoted to section manager. Leora went to the hospital. The task was upped and a higher incentive count set for the assembly line than it was capable of maintaining. The women were now producing as many switches as they had before Leora's advent, at a drop of fifteen cents an hour, a dollar twenty a day, six dollars per week.

Under Amy they had gradually become resigned to their inability to meet the revised schedule. But tensions gathered among them like a head of steam, with occasional outbursts against the tired, the unwell, the less nimble, the rebellious. Every once in a while Earlene would cry, "What are we, nuts? Killing each other for some lousy coupon-clipper? Another bonus for Graveyard?" Everybody would agree that something ought to be done about it. The outcry would eventually subside and once again they would be striving-striving, in the famous phrase, to make out.

With the reappearance of Leora, a mood of desperate hope ignited contention among the women in final assembly. The women were divided within themselves between their respect for Amy, sharp-tongued but sympathetic, competent on the job but with a firm sense of justice, never dictatorial, never overbearing, and their begrudging admiration for Leora, domineering, driving, with the power to attract others into her orbit.

"At least Amy's fair. You can always count on her to stand up for you."

"With Leora we were always ahead of the game. Leora's smart. She knows how to push."

"She's a rate-buster. She cut our price."

"Say, Mish!"

Earlene on the receiving end of the conveyor hailed him over from the stopped-up feedline he was dismembering.

"Can Leora walk in just like that and take over," Amy's partisans besieged him, "after so long out?"

"She broke down on the job here," Leora's partisans insisted. "Ledyard must have given her assurances when she left."

"What do you think?" They appealed to him. "What does the contract say?"

The union contract said that no foreman was to be permitted to perform a worker's work. When Leora let Stan Ledyard pitch in, in order to send up their production figure, they let her and him get away with it. Now they were in the hole, they were calling for the contract.

"You got a shop steward," he said to them. "Take it up with him."

They did nothing so sensible or so futile. Lacerated, lashing out, the women unconsciously accelerated their movements, those on Leora's side compensating for a missing factor, those on Amy's side showing their mettle. The components flowed ever more rapidly from hand to hand, the women hating the materials they handled, wrestling with them, incensed with them and yet intoxicated by a kind of exhilaration, the triumph of skill over substance. When the zinc supports turned out to be more difficult to handle than usual, the women took vengeance not on the insensate material but on the new materials handler, Don Pinette.

"What do you mean dumping this junk on me? It's so hard I can't make time on it!"

"Ain't been here two hours and already playing favorites! You give Rene the good ones."

"You asking to be Number One on my shit list?"

Don stood dazed under the unexpected barrage. Coming to Don's rescue, he took the objectionable zinc alloy support out of Don's hand and examined it. That piece of primitive sculpture, symmetrical, stylized with eyes and mouth at the head and foot of the hollow oblong of a body, offered a profusion of holes and corners, elevations, awkward to the hand in the process of swift manipulation. The metal was rough-finished, harsh of surface, edged with invisible burrs. The new stock coming in wasn't of the same grade as the old.

"It's these little tits," he said to Don. "It's tearing up their hands."

"Tits? Tits? What tits?"

"This metal when it's stamped out doesn't take a clean cut. C'mere."

He led Don back to the storage area, scooped up supports from half a dozen cans and accompanied him back to the line.

"Have them take their pick. Then fill the bin from the can it came from."

"*Wear gloves,*" Dirksen was forever admonishing the women when they objected to the materials. But gloves interposed a sheathe between them and the material, between the sensory fingertips and the article to be fingered, slowing them down. "*Then tape up,*" Dirksen would advise them. Some of them did, but the tape was always unraveling, getting in their way.

He pocketed a support for later contemplation. There was a time when no manufacturer would turn out a piece like that. Every tit would have been buffed down. But what difference did it make? The support would be completely enclosed in the switch. Between the squawks of the girls and savings per thousand, which came first?

The next time he intervened occurred when the friction over Leora reached its climax in a bitter clash between Amy and Teresa.

Up to then Amy had not entered into the fray that churned about her, adhering to her dignity as a stanch Catholic, as the daughter of a country postmaster and the mother of four children, all of whom she had breast-fed in infancy, every single one. (When she went to work on the night shift, Amy once revealed, she cut off a lock of her hair and left it on the pillow of her eight-year-old daughter so she could stroke it before falling asleep.) She held her tongue while Teresa, sitting opposite her, seized the opportunity afforded by her coming deposition to retaliate for past disagreements.

Doughy, dumpy, dull-eyed, Teresa shot her slings and arrows across the conveyor, failing to score until she flung out, "Of course you can't say it's because of her you're being downgraded. After all, you climbed up over Leora's back when she wasn't here. It's not her fault you took for granted it was permanent."

Taking this to be a slur both upon her intelligence and her reputation for fair dealing, Amy shrugged off her dignity, let loose her tongue.

"Why you stupid idiot, how many times have I covered for you when the work you spoiled wouldn't pass inspection? Leora comes back here, you think you're going to be on top of the world? Well let me tell you, you'll be out on the sidewalk. If you had the brains of a bird or the decency of a dog . . ."

Not only did Amy chide Teresa for every boner she'd ever pulled, every job she'd ever lost, but digging back into ancient history she threw up in Teresa's face the fact that sixteen years ago, back in Poland, Teresa had abandoned her husband and baby to Hitler and taking advantage of her American birth had escaped with a whole skin.

In her anger Amy went too far. She had only contempt for those women who had allied themselves so quickly with what appeared to be the winning party. For those who protested so vehemently on her behalf, a protest that cost them little since they had already apparently accepted the likelihood of Leora's restoration, she had only exasperation, thank you for nothing! But in taunting Teresa for the child she had deserted, whose grave, she claimed, Teresa had never even bothered to trace, she let bitterness carry her beyond the bounds.

"You know what they did with those babies? They banged their heads against the wall. They threw them in the furnace. And you never—"

"You dass—you dass take what I told you—all I been through— All right, all right you had your husband and your kids here, but I never done on the sly what you done—"

Separated from each other by the conveyor, obscured by the bases piling up on the bench before them, their voices raised in order to be heard, Amy and Teresa flailed out for all the griefs of their lives with accusations that destroyed every last vestige of mutual and self-respect. In an orgy of flagellation they reduced each other, themselves, to a bloody pulp on the table. Throbbing with horror, the women in their vicinity tried in vain to quiet them down. The tears rained down Teresa's cheeks mixing with mucus from her nose and trickled into her mouth. Still neither she nor Amy would stop.

"Moron! Any moron would have got around the consul—"

"You phony, you hypocrite, you put yourself up to be such a plaster saint . . ."

It was none of his business. An ex-wrestler, all his excess muscle runs to fat. An ex-union president, all his overgrown sense of concern runs to meddling. He abandoned the feed intake he was tying up and piloted Don, grinning in stupefaction, to the storage site. Hooking stacks of tote cans, they dragged them back to the line. Between them they began hefting up tote cans and emptying them into the bins. With the roar of tons of coal down the chute, the contents drowned out Amy's voice and Teresa's.

During the enforced pause the two women recaptured their breath and their control. Withdrawing themselves into themselves, they nursed their wounds in silence. Thenceforth they were not on speaking terms.

The women assemblers pulled themselves together, gathered together the pieces that had gone by without bolts or buttons and, anxious to make up for production lost, enticed Don Pinette into giving them a hand on the line.

"The material handler before you used to," they wheedled him. "Come on, be a good guy."

"Just for a coupla minutes. Till we catch up."

Eager to please, Don joined them. Rene and Pearl coaxed him in between their stools and, snuggling up to him as he stood there, conned him into jamming the angled brass contacts into the box-like plastic bases.

"See, it's easy. With your thumbs."

"You should have been here when Nancy was here," Pearl lured him on and on. "She was here during the war when we were making these wired outfits for the Arctic, you know? The insulation for them was piled up to the rafters."

Nancy was a legend, or maybe a myth, in the building. A slip of a girl, fresh as a daisy, and first thing you know she's up there on top of the pile of insulation and guys from every department are streaming in.

"Her daddy asked me to keep an eye on her and I said, 'Oh no, she's too fast for me.' In three months she was out, pregnant."

"You ought to work the night shift," Rene told Don. "I had it all during the war. We were next to the purchasing agent's office and all the suppliers were presenting him with bottles and every night this girl, Pamela, would cop some out of there. The boss is pleading with her, 'Please, you been here all night, do a little something. Touch the machine.' And he takes her martini away from her. Two minutes later he comes back and she has another martini in her hand. Where's the martini machine!"

"Tell him, tell him about the time you caught her on the floor of the john with the inspector. Man crazy. He's old as the hills, she's ugly as sin."

Don thought he could get a rise out of the fair sex? They'd show him who'd get a rise out of who.

Don was jamming in contacts by the hundreds while his work accumulated elsewhere. All the strength of his muscular body drained down through his thumbs into a minuscule pressure.

"You're doing them no good," he wanted to remonstrate with Don. And didn't. Let him learn.

Don winked around at him. "Doin' all right, huh?"

Just yesterday Earlene was raising the roof. "We got to make the company reduce the task!" They all agreed that this was the thing to do. Now they were conniving to dare, shame, inveigle Don by various ruses into finding time during the day to work with them. Scheming to beat the system, put one over on the company.

"Leave him alone," he wanted to remonstrate with the women. And didn't. Let 'em suffer.

If Don refused to work with them they'd make it so hard for him, they'd ride him out on a rail. But if Don continued to play along with them, at the end of three months, six, a year, their production quota would go up and their price come down. And they knew it. They knew better.

No one quarreled now. No one joked. Striving-striving-striving. Coffee break.

The men from the machine and plastics shops sauntered leisurely toward the table the women in the department had set up in one corner with coffee pot, crockery and buns, doing the ladies a favor. What was it today? Baby shower? Birthday cake? Farewell party? The table, ordinarily spread with sheets of wrapping paper, was decked out with birthday crepe and napkins, for the women's lunchtime celebration later on. Mariuch, in charge of arrangements, allowed the men a peek at the birthday cake, gorgeously iced, that Bea had made. It was Elsie's birthday. White-haired Elsie, groaning from her turn at the turntable, refused to divulge her age. Riding the cream waves, wreathed with green leaves, it was inscribed in yellow curlicues on top of the cake. Twenty-nine.

As soon as Elsie discreetly went off to the washroom, Mari allowed the rest of them a peek at the group present she had purchased, a potted plant. "*Mimosa pudica*," she read off the slip of paper attached. She was the plant expert in the department, the perker-upper of ailing plants the other women brought to her from home for diagnosis.

"It's called the sensitive plant," Mari said, lowering the tissue paper shrouded around it all the way down, performing a bridal strip tease. "Watch this."

They all stood about the plant in amazement, even Amy and Teresa, still pale and shaken; even the men to whom house plants were a thing of no interest, a woman's affair.

"Mish—"

Bostic nudged at him with his coffee cup, reminding him of his agreement to listen at coffee break. But even Bostic stopped himself, too diverted to go on, postponing whatever was on his mind for a more opportune moment.

They crowded about the plant, marveling at it.

Beginning at the crown, Mari moved her fingertips over the spread of foliage, caressing without touching, sensuously emitting from the palps of her fingers a siren song. The leaflets responded, folding up, erectile, a closure of liplets, under the movement of her fingertips, their movement centripetally engendering movement downward, a flutter of movement down the green sprays on both sides converging in the swollen base of the stalk.

Coffee putt-putted in the pot. The aura of coffee expanded to the walls of cartons surrounding them. Coffee, sipped down piping hot, refreshed, sharpened, kindled.

"Hey, let me try that."

"Let me."

"Now wait a minute. Wait—" Mari fended them off. "You do this too often, it won't react."

"Let me."

Don Pinette thrust himself forward. He placed himself before Mari like a Spanish dancer, his broad thigh positioned to tango off with her.

"You gonna let me do it, ain't you?"

Fresh from his session with the assemblers, his confidence revived, Don leaned intimately over her.

"I hear you a widow."

"Black widow. Come up into my chamber, you'll never come down."

Mari's eyes traveled over him, delineating his parts.

"Buster," Bostic grunted, "she gonna bust his britches."

"Let me see your hand."

Mari took Don's hand, sticky with cinnamon bun, and scrutinized it in all its hollows and mounds, its sprawling lines. Her tongue twinkled over her lips. Primed to touch over the plant, the chosen bridegroom, Don jocked himself up closer to her. Lightly Mari fluttered her fingertips up the length of his thumb.

"Sore thumb, huh?"

Paroxysms of laughter as Mari restored Don's hand to him. She reshrouded her plant. Coffee break over.

"Yoo hoo, Tom Thu-umb!"

"Pee Wee-eee!"

"I'm out of double-grooved screw-ews!"

The leaven of laughter spread outward over the floor.

"What's gotten into this place? Pixies?" Dirksen, called away from the turntable retiming by still another machine down, tore his hair out. "Over there by Mabel, Mish. A cracked chuck. And Rita—what's the matter with you, Rita?"

2

The window washers, due yesterday, arrived on their round of buildings in preparation for the party of distinguished visitors who were even now being greeted in the front office lobby by Mayor Kearnsey and Grover Coffin. Dirksen dashed about with a porter removing cartons from the path of the inside window-washing crew. Panes in the broad expanse of windows that girded the floor on two sides were closed, shutting out whatever breeze had strayed in.

"You're leaving streaks," Mabel kidded the inside washers from her salvage table as they plowed up the murky glass with their squeegee mops. "I wouldn't have you in my house. Would you, Mish? Your wife wouldn't let them in your house, would she?"

Home. Wife. As remote from him now, tightening a chuck adapter, as the moons of Jupiter.

The clatter, the dinginess, the odors were sealed inside the chamber, concentrated in volume. The sense of being immured in a cave intensified, with a claustrophobic oppressiveness. Suddenly surges and splurges of water thudded on the outer glass, geysering up from the hoses of the outside window-washing crew, flooding down the glass in riffling ripples, in diamond clusters of drops. The outside crew appeared, elevated on their scaffold, and began wiping clean.

"Just like monkeys in a cage," Mabel commented to him over her shoulder, obviously enough.

"But who's the monkeys," he answered her, just as obviously, "them or us?"

Obviously, yet out of a strain of zaniness on the loose, they grinned out the window at the window washers, who's the monkeys, and thumbed their noses at them. The window washers thumbed back. Wigwagged ears. Who's the monkeys?

And thus the chain reaction, the atomic pile building up all morning, was unwittingly unleashed.

Monkey, monkey in a zoo. Who's the monkey, me or you?

"Come on, come on, you fuckin' the dog," Dirksen, zipping by, rebuked them.

Suddenly, the windows clean, they were all exposed. Out of the cave, their cage. The plastering of muck that had prevented them from viewing outward and protected them from the outer view was eradicated. A raw glare of tans and grays, the supporting pillars of the expressway soared out of the shadowed street below into sunlight, bearing on its white span a coruscation of cars, a glitter of chrome and crystal shooting across a glimpse of blue sky. Every car contained a motorist, indifferent to them. They were under the highway. Underground. Beyond the windows on the opposite side of the department, behind windows like theirs, on floors like theirs, others, themselves a thousandfold, labored at linear assembly and rotary. In Switch, a subsection of a subdivision of Construction Facilities, they huddled over their work now, drawing inward from the outer view that so cruelly tugged at them, crashed in on them.

In the interlude Mariuch screamed.

He was stooping with Mari over her press, examining the tapping head which had stopped turning while the machine continued to turn, and Dirksen on his way back to the turntable, spotting conversation, time a-wasting, gave way to a small-boy impulse. Dirksen jabbed his finger into Mari's ear. Tempted by the sight of the curlicued silken-tender hollow tipped so opportunely upward, he thrust his horny forefinger forcefully into it, adding a screwdriver twist for good measure.

"What big ears you have."

Her scream ripped out.

The women jumped up from their presses down the row. A finger sliced off, at least.

"You dirty rotten bastard, keep your stinking hands . . ."

Dirksen, taken aback, backed off, reddening to his neatly tufted hair.

"What's going on here today? Has everybody gone crazy?" Dirksen sped off to the turntable, raving. "A bunch of lunatics! Get back to your work now. Back to work."

The women at the presses sank back in relief. Mari, Mari, they mouthed at her, don't make so much of it, he didn't mean anything by it, it was just a joke.

"Don't you ever EVER," she turned on them and harangued them, "let any of them get away with anything like that!"

The men timing the turntable, joined by Dirksen, glanced back at Mari, laughing. It was all over the floor. What is it, whassamatta? Georgie stuck his finger in Mari's ear.

Mari sat back on her stool trembling with outrage, invaded and degraded, besmirched. As if every small part of her weren't an invitation to violation, the elfin ears, her tendril of a mouth with its impudent underlip, her every curve and indentation.

"It's screwing itself out," he tried to resume his argument with her over what was wrong with the press. She claimed it was grease build-up.

Mari's eyes sparkled with pinpoints of pain. She had to retire to the rest room to compose herself.

He went back to Rita's brusher which he had been repairing when Mari interrupted him. In contrast to Mari's machine, which promised to be a lengthy affair, the brusher was no problem, a matter of replacing some worn-out stops. Rita, keeping an expectant eye on the developing situation at the turntable—"Any minute now it's bound to blow"—kept plaguing him with unwanted advice. "It's not shutting off when it should. The springs have got unsprung . . . Here it comes. Oh, Lord. Oh no. Here we go."

She should know. Rita had been watching the turntable from the time when, a month ago, a nice young engineer, recently hired, had come into the department and surveying the turntable area had seen his opportunity to clinch his contract by consolidating two operations in one. Four women at a separate workbench were fitting the ceramic ring between the aluminum shells of the button and sending the buttons on a conveyor to the nine women at the gas-lit turntable to be sealed. The engineer eliminated the workbench, the conveyor and the four women. By tripling their effort, the nine women at the turntable were able to amalgamate assembly of the button with their sealing operation.

"Of course we don't expect you to turn out as many completed units as before," the engineer had explained solicitously to the women when they were tried out on the new task. "It takes time to adjust to a new idea," he said to them, appealing to them to help him make good. That was why UV brought in bright young graduates, got rid of the old timber. New ideas.

Between the engineer and Dirksen, the task was then set at a reasonable rate of four hundred and eighty-five assembled-and-sealed buttons per hour. That was three weeks ago. Little by little the rotation of the turntable was stepped up and automatically the women stepped themselves up to keep pace with the demands of the machine.

The effect on the old-timers, accustomed to the rhythm of their former task, was devastating. Anna Lamianski was gone. Bea had thrown in the sponge this morning. Others were similarly being weeded out. Joan Hlavacek, a young hand, had been brought in as a replacement for Anna. The goal at today's retiming was six hundred buttons an hour. Eventually, as everyone guessed by this time, the company hoped to arrive with the nine women at the six hundred ninety output of the original thirteen women.

"Woo," Rita said, "that was a close one. I thought Elsie was about to fall out. But she's got that boy . . ."

Conscientiously the women were pushing themselves, trying like students to pass the test imposed on them, make the few cents extra an hour it would bring. Elsie, her white head hunched over the circling posts, was determined to hold out. With an agility acquired over the years, she matched herself against Joan Hlavacek, radiant with the energy of youth. Meanwhile Stevens the engineer, Luckner the time-study man, Shepasy the inspector on the lookout for any increase in spoilage, and Dirksen sought to identify among them the perfect combination: the milk of youth and the skill of experience, consolidated in a single person.

"Look, it's not that fast," Dirksen and Stevens interjected from time to time and took a turn at the turntable themselves to prove it. "Watch me." For three minutes they deftly dropped the sequence of pieces over the three-inch posts moving past them. The time was being tested in the pink of the morning for a few hours only. The job would continue, as the women were only too well aware, eight hours a day, five days a week, regardless of individual stamina or physical condition. "There." Dirksen and Stevens stepped back from their hand-over-hand stack-up of pieces —after all, women are supposed to be quicker at these jobs than men are. "You see? Nothing to it."

The gas-lit table wheeled about, heat and gas fumes climbing. The posts collected their toll of pellets, silvery, dazzling white, glassy. On and on.

With a crash, Elsie's stool toppled to the floor. She had jumped down so abruptly, jerking back from the merry-go-round spinning past her, her chair overturned in the aisle.

Her tannish face was lemon-tinged and her glasses were blurred. Still hunched over, her agile body concentrated to a point, she hugged herself.

"I can't do it," Elsie wailed, the admission wrung out of her. "It's too much. I can't."

"That's all right, Elsie," Dirksen assured her and upended her stool. "We thought you could make it. But if you can't . . . Aren't you feeling well?" he asked in concern. "You better go down to the nurse."

Elsie stood visibly riven by the choice before her, torn between the boy she was putting through college and her chances in the Dispensary where she might possibly be found wanting in sight, heart or some other faculty and sent home. Then try and get back in.

"Oh no," she said, hugging her elbows to suppress the quiver of her arms. "I'm perfectly fine. Just dandy. It's just I can't do that job."

"That's all right, Elsie," Dirksen said. "Only right now"—he scanned Rita at the brusher, the women at the electronic tester— "I don't have anything else for you. Get a slip from the section office and go down to Personnel."

Still she hesitated, torn between the turntable and her chances in Personnel. Sorry, we don't have anything today in your classification, we'll let you know. The old heave ho.

"Oh no." Dirksen barred her way back to the stool. "We don't want anyone collapsing on us, do we?" He helped her down the aisle. "They'll take care of you in Personnel."

"Stand on your seniority, Elsie," Mari hollered after her. "Stick to your guns— My God!"

The same thought struck all the women at once. They half rose from their stools in distress, gazing down the aisle after Elsie. Her birthday cake! Her party! Her present!

"Back, back, back to your work! She's all right. They'll fix her up—" Dirksen bustled about, getting things in hand again. But when he went searching for a substitute for Elsie, all at once everybody was much too busy.

"Not me," Rita said, sidling away. "My brusher's most ready now, isn't it, Mish? I got all these buttons waiting."

They were all riveted to their jobs like a house afire. It was Mariuch, whose machine was still down, that Dirksen collared and ordered up to Elsie's stool.

"I'm not feeling well," Mari announced loudly. "You can't put me on that job when I'm not up to par."

"If you're not feeling up to it, what are you here for then? Go down to the nurse."

Oh no, she wasn't going down to the nurse, lose half a day's pay. "I don't need any nurse."

"What's the matter then?"

"I'm indisposed."

"Indisposed how? What do you mean you're not disposed?"

In retaliation no doubt for her excessive reaction to his ear-jabbing prank, Dirksen was compelling her to spell out the nature of her indisposition in front of Stevens, Luckner, Shepasy. With shamefaced curiosity, a gleam of salaciousness, the men edged over, ears out, listening for Dirksen to goad it out of her. Did Mari still have her sex all there? Or had her last operation been a hysterectomy?

Mari was fair game. She could count on no backing from above. Although she was chary of tangling with management nowadays —and since her husband's death management was chary of tangling with her—it was known that any tactic that resulted in getting rid of her would not be frowned upon.

"Your machine is down," Dirksen reasoned with her patiently. "You won't be back at it till after lunch. You can't excuse yourself just because you're not inclined."

"I didn't say I was disinclined. I said—"

"Either you're well enough to put a day's work in or you're not."

"All right, goddamit, I'm menstruating!"

She threw it in their teeth. She gave them all they bargained for and more.

"UV killed my man. It killed my ability to have babies. What the hell more do you want from me? The whole works?"

She had no right to fling out such charges. It was intolerable. Bob's death was not attributable to the plant, he was fifty feet outside the gate when it happened. A cerebral hemorrhage can hit anyone anytime.

"Either you're well enough to work," Dirksen stolidly repeated, "or you're not. This is a lighter job than the press you're operating."

"All right."

Mari took a few steps toward Elsie's stool, then stopped in fake surprise.

"Where's the shop steward? Where's Fritz?"

"Fritz?" Dirksen spluttered, caught off guard. She had him hip and thigh. "What's Fritz got to do with it?"

No one had seen Fritz in the last hour, least of all Dirksen. Fritz was out running numbers. Dirksen, like the supervisors before him, shut his eyes to it. If Fritz was caught, he'd be fired. If Fritz wasn't caught, then it must be—Dirksen figured and Mariuch figured—because Fritz had protection. The numbers racket couldn't go on in the plant, they figured, without the company's complicity. "There has to be a payoff all along the line," Mari was always speechifying. "No one knows how high up it goes." Meanwhile Fritz took advantage of his relative freedom of movement as a union steward. Along the workbenches he was a welcome diversion. "Eight six three. Kiss it for me, Fritzie." Maybe today, maybe? "I hit! I hit! Touch me." The touch of magic.

"I want Fritz," Mari said to Dirksen. "I don't make a move without Fritzie here. In the disputed retiming of a job—"

"What dispute? This was all settled," Dirksen threw in, ambiguously, "weeks ago."

"I'm disputing. Mish, come on over here."

He finished putting Rita's brusher through a trial run, shit-shave-shampoo. It was in working order. Mari yanked at his shoulder.

"What's the contract say? Doesn't the shop steward have to be present during the retiming of a job?"

May or *must.*

"How did you get into this?" Dirksen yanked him from the other side. "Everywhere I turn this morning . . ."

He took the little grease-stained red book out of his pocket and went through the motions of searching the EWIU-UV agreement. Coffin's compromise. *May* be present.

"Fritz should be here," he said ambiguously and snapped his book shut.

Mari dug her heels in. "Go get Fritz."

Dirksen was going frantic. Half the posts on the turntable were whirling by with a shell or a ring or a glass rim missing. He'd have done much better to do without Mari. But now of course, he couldn't back down.

"Go on, Mish," Mari demanded. "Go bring Fritz here."

"Don't you do it," Dirksen roared at him. "Don't you leave this floor!"

For an instant he thought Mari was about to call the women at the turntable down from their stools. Rally the whole department around her. Everybody out! Down to the union hall!

But her hand crept over her stomach and his own stomach cramped with hers. The old glow faded from her face. Instead, allowing Dirksen to nudge her toward the turntable, she raised her voice even higher.

"Oh no," she cried, allowing herself to be dragged by the heels, eased past the embarrassed young engineer to Elsie's stool, "you're not putting me on the Torture Wheel! You're not shoving me into the Gas Oven!"

And up onto the stool.

Her hands danced over the posts in concert with the other hands. Virtually the whole department had suspended animation insofar as possible, taking in the scene.

"What is she saying? What did she say?" It was relayed from one to the other.

"What are we doing here?" she addressed her fellow assemblers as she fitted and sealed. "Working ourselves out of a job! The more we put out, the fewer there'll be of us. Another minute off! Another penny more! And next thing you know, we'll be out the penny too. We used to be friends in this shop. All for one and one for all. Coffin's turned us into cannibals. For what? For the minutes. The minutes and the pennies. The pennies and the minutes. UV's getting richer by the minute on the minutes and the pennies old Graveyard squeezes out of us."

"Mari Ucchini," Dirksen warned her, "you got a big mouth. Shut it."

"Ah, you'd like us all to be like the Torture Wheel here. Automatic. That would suit you just fine, wouldn't it? Only we're not automatons. We have eyes to see with. Ears to hear with. And mouths to talk."

"You're not paid to talk. Do your work."

Mari shut her mouth, but out of the corner of it trickled a murmur that passed from woman to woman.

"Stretch it out."

Every third post whirred by with no part of the button on it.

"Now look, girls."

The men at the turntable consulted among themselves, glanced at their watches. The rotation of the table was slowed down to a less taxing number of revolutions per minute.

"How's this now? Okay?"

Victory. All smiles.

After a while, unnoticeably, the cycle was revved up. Faster, faster, Mari's hands wove over the posts, moved by her psychic compulsion: an irresistible need to outshine everyone else.

3

He was delayed a few minutes beyond the general exodus for lunch, checking over the stubs of Mari's press. The row of presses had previously been operated by men, paid at the male rate. To the men displaced, the women operators were intruders, usurpers, thieves in the night . . . The gear was slipping and the machine repeated and he pulled his hand out from under the head just in the nick of time.

"You notice Dirksen wouldn't let Inga take a press job. Said it himself. 'It's not fit for human beings.' "

Bostic lurked over him, lingering till he was through. He had never felt quite comfortable with Gene Bostic since the time years ago when he somehow or other let Nick Colangelo muscle Bostic out of the stewardship in Spray Paint. He sometimes wondered if Gene ever thought that if he had been able to stay steward, other factors being equal, he might be where Colangelo was now.

"So I got my pink slip just before Christmas." Bostic stood over him, spilling his troubles. "This fellow I'd never seen before, Reiner, come in from some other department and bumped me. Claimed he had eleven years seniority to my ten. Thank God for those blizzards end of January. I was out shoveling snow for the city for godsake at three in the morning. You ever been on a snow crew? Christ— And even for that I had to go begging my barber, the politician."

He avoided looking up at Bostic. He had a crick in his neck at the mere idea of looking around at Bostic.

"All winter long I was picking up and delivering curtains for Mae to do up after she was home from work. And you know Mae, she don't even like to mend the boys' socks."

The Indian princess. The African queen. Keeper of the civic auditorium.

"Up every night doing up curtains. Now I find out, today, just this A.M., this Reiner had no seniority over me. He's two months under. And he's still over there in Spray Paint holding my job."

"What do you come to me for? Get Fritz to go take it up with your steward over there."

"But that's just it. Fritz was in on it. He was the one arranged it with my steward. Reiner's his buddy. Fritz walks in on me in plastics now like big daddy, I owe him a favor. He got me called back to work."

He left the press and walked down the corridor with Bostic to lunch in the locker room. He still couldn't look around at Bostic. It put a crimp in his shoulder just to have Bostic in his powder-dusted coveralls beside him.

"What good does it do you to come to me? I got no influence. Almost anybody you'd go to in the union would be better than me."

It was impossible for the union to tamper with the seniority list. If the company had made a mistake it was up to the company to rectify it.

"Why don't you go to the section office? Have them take it up with Personnel."

"I already been there."

Inadvertently he looked around at Bostic. Yellow-splotched eyes glinting with scorn. Scorn of him—if I hadn't tried there first, why would I be here talking to you! Scorn of himself, for having to plead with him for the so-called sympathy of his ear.

"What they say?"

As if he couldn't guess. The busy office, the jangling telephones, window washers, porters, the change in the Hammill order, and Bostic there with his beef requiring a request to Personnel for a search through two sets of employment records.

"I made them let me through to Ledyard himself. And Ledyard said, 'What do you come to me for? It's up to the union to handle it. Go to Colangelo.'

"So now," Bostic said, "I want you to go with me to Colangelo."

Bostic had a plan. Bostic held him at the door of the locker room describing it. The crux of Bostic's plan was provided by the Tenant Committee that Mish Lunin was supposed to be launching at Tidal Flats tonight. The Bostics had been living in the project since it was opened.

"Now I been through this tenant deal before, Mish. I told your wife and I told that fella with her, Lucas, it's no go. What I mean, we can't stand up by ourself. We got to tie in with something bigger. What I mean, politics."

"Yeah?"

"You know this Judge Rinaldi who's running against Kearnsey for mayor next fall? Well my barber tells me that Rinaldi's depending on Colangelo to deliver the labor vote. So we give Nick this housing issue to take to Rinaldi. Make it look like he can deliver the tenant vote too."

"Yeah. I don't follow . . ."

"Then while we're there with Nick, him and us, I slip it to him what a raw deal I got here in the plant. Gimme my job back!"

Passionate with his plan, Bostic had him up against the door. A hardheaded, two-fisted, straightforward character twisting himself into such knots . . .

"Nick's very hot on this election. Rinaldi's promised to make him his labor adviser."

It was truly a remarkable plan. The labor vote. The tenant vote. The colored vote in the person of Bostic. The progressive vote in the person of Lunin. Why not?

"This afternoon, Mish, right after work. We'll catch Nick at the union hall."

"Well, I promised my wife I'd come straight home today. Let me think about it, huh?"

Another Ledyard, Bostic's eyes accused him. Another run-around.

With Bostic on his tail he pushed open the locker-room door to the badgering awaiting him inside, that was becoming a lunch-time habit.

On the backless benches drawn up before the olive-drab lockers, the men were unpacking their lunches. Few of them ever went to the company cafeteria for lunch. Sometimes they sent down for a hot dish. They ate here, consuming with their food the exhalation of toilets and disinfectant, the sweat of feet placed up on the bench when changing in and out of work shoes.

The locker room was Capitol Hill at lunchtime. In the past few weeks Capitol Hill had abandoned its free-wheeling debates to zero in on a single target: a drive to draft Mish Lunin, the unwilling and unready, into candidacy once again for the presidency of the local against Nick Colangelo, the certain victor at the polls. Or to put it another way: HAS LUNIN TURNED CHICKEN?

"Peanut butter!" Roscoe thrust his sandwich accusingly up at him as he passed through to the washroom. "With jelly. Eighty bucks a week and I'm no better off than I was in nineteen-forty."

In the next room with Bostic, mute now, he unzipped over the yellow-stained trough of the urinal. Through the open arch the men's voices plashed at him in broken waves of agitation.

"Two cat fights in one morning. What more . . ."

"So he tries to shove my machines onto Ewell. Next thing I'll be on short-work week . . ."

"I says to the boss, I says, 'That . . . ain't . . . my job!' "

He rubbed the gritty gray sliver of soap into his hands, dripping black into the black-splattered basin.

Even the voice of Cusak, the lathe operator, reminiscing, was a rebuke to him.

"First time I went into the mine I had my shell hat on and my belt and my hard-toe shoes, I was a man! I go down the pit elevator and man, I'm telling you, my legs are sheared off. I get out, I'm walking on stumps. I start breathing the dust, with all the t.b. we had in our family. But I went back next day. And the next. And the next."

He wiped dry on the gritty gray paper toweling and tossed it, unsuccessfully after Bostic's, at the overflowing wastebasket.

When he came out they were all concentrated on baiting Don Pinette, who was sitting with his lunch, somewhat subdued, on the end of a bench by himself.

"It's not how big a dick you got, Doc, it's how you use it."

"You thought you could make time with them? With that bunch of cock-teasers out there?"

He plowed through to his locker to take out his lunch bag. Over the grating they had taped up the leaflet he hadn't written, the mysterious leaflet that everybody in the plant was pinning on him.

DIG YOUR OWN GRAVE, GRAVEYARD
NOT OURS!!!

While the talk died behind him he scanned it for the fifth time since last Friday, looking for clues. Tan paper, flecked, pretty good grade of stock. Mimeo not so good, blurred and blotched in spots, a home job. And the style, it was the style that was the giveaway. Colangelo's strike leaflets criticizing United Vacuum with catchy slogans, said to be devised by his niece, a budding journalist, were models of courtesy by comparison.

It was directed at Grover Coffin and charged him with the invention of techniques for turning workers into the willing prey of profit-hungry investors. Wolf versus the lambs, the kind of thing that used to drive Coffin crazy. Creating division between employer and employees when plainly they were an interdependent unit.

HEAT'S ON IN HOT RUBBER

Three days ago the crew on the missile job in WIRE & CABLE was cut from five men to four and the time from fifteen minutes to eight for handling fifteen hundred pounds of hot rubber.

The men refused to work it. Their lead man was suspended.

When the steward tried to negotiate it with the foreman and the section chairman tried to negotiate it with the section manager, what happened?

The steward and the section chairman got a week's layoff apiece and three warning notices for non-cooperation. One more notice, they'll be out of a job.

When the men we've elected to represent us can be punished by the company, what's left of our union? Who's going to stick his neck out for us after this?

Everywhere it's the same story. Six assemblers cut to three. Improved methods. Efficiency.

Coffinism!!!

Graveyard is getting away with murder! Bypassing seniority. Rate chiseling. Classification pirating. Upgrading based on favoritism. Pitting young against old, women against men, race against race . . .

In the form of a newssheet, in two columns, featuring subheads reminiscent of those they used back in 1946. Replete with names and incidents. Boss Powell Pulls Foul in 22-BB! Mutiny in Mangler! The Snake Pit. The Slave Galley. The Rat Race.

He peeled it off with the tape attached, careful not to tear it.

For years, nothing. Now this. It burned their fingers. It offended. Caused discomfort. Yet, gloating, they read and passed on. It rode around in pockets, transferred with the daily debris from pants to pants.

The men were watching him. Their eyes bit into his back. The shark's tooth. The jackknife.

"If you didn't put it out, Mish, who did?"

Mari, the natural suspect, was out of the running. If it were Mari, the news of it would have been all over UV by now. No one ascribed it to Mari.

"Why don't you ask the steward in Hot Rubber?" he suggested, still scanning the blotched paper. "That section chairman over there? They're the ones suspended. They're the ones had the time."

Both Colangelo men. Probably seeking to enlist some protest action in the plant against the penalty imposed on them, citing common ground. But the style. The style was larger than that. It threw out larger loops.

He took his lunch bag out of his locker and brought the leaflet with him back to the bench.

"Everything's moving, Mish. The whole plant's boiling. Flare-ups all over the lot. Everywhere you look, another flare-up."

"What's moving? Show me what!" He waved the leaflet under their noses. "Show me one word in this, just one, that tells where it comes from, who's pushing it, what it's leading up to. Then you can say it's moving!"

About to tear it up as he had torn it up this morning, fling the bits in their faces. Ewell with his head in the air and Roscoe with his nose out, Cusak the ex-miner with his legs tucked under the bench, Palermo who was always for whoever he happened to be with and Jackson who never said anything, Bostic with his problems and Pinette sorting out the contents of the manila envelope he'd been given in Personnel this morning. All so smart. *Go ahead,* the colonel said, *I'm right behind you.*

Only this time he couldn't bring himself to tear the crumpled sheet across. He dropped it on the floor and sat down, disgruntled; dug sandwiches and thermos out of his paper bag. With his foot he straightened out the sheet on the floor and toed at the tape.

Moving, my ass! Flare-ups, just that.

The men who had pulled the illegal walkout in Hot Rubber last week were working the job today, while their group leader, their steward and their section chairman paid the penalty. Amy's friends in final assembly, championing her all over the lot, had already dumped her. The Torture Wheel turned.

His election campaign was being mapped out for him.

"Between now and June, Mish, if you get right on it, you're in. Call the old bunch together, Ray and Marty, line up some new elements. You have supporters in every section, Mish. You'll have spokesmen in every department. Put out the publicity, the funds'll roll in. This whole place is a powder keg . . ."

Nobody took out paper and pencil to start listing names. Nobody volunteered to speak to the spokesmen. Nobody reached for the five-spot to start it rolling.

"Hit the beefs, Mish," Cusak, spooning last night's leftover stew out of his thermos jug, advised him. "Hit 'em with the beefs. You can't miss."

Up from the mines, his legs tucked under the bench as if cramped for space, his father a miner before him, a lifetime in the mines and the struggles of the miner's union and Cusak still thought a Colangelo would let himself be booted out of office on the basis of beefs?

"You got to put the principle back into it," Ewell informed him. "That's the missing factor today. Whatever else you can say about Bob Ucchini, and you can say plenty, he had principle. He never ran this local as a pocket operation. He built a system into it. He spread the responsibilities. We had unity in those days. We had strength. We had organization."

Now Ewell said it. Now. After they had chased Bob out of the union hall and down the street one night, out to lynch him. Who killed Bob Ucchini? UV or us?

Ewell was a talker. Ewell was a thinker. Ewell had a long memory. The old days. The old bunch. The old leadership. Bring it back! Dig it up out of the ground! Ewell was a romantic, lost in a past that was never that simple.

"You may not remember this, Mish, but I remember, that day in Spray Paint you took on Coffin," Bostic reminded him, getting his digs in. "Remember how you stood up to him over that No. 3 spray gun? How you fought him to a standstill over a fraction of a second?

"There was a time, Mish, when you let nothing get by. Not a goddam thing. You think you can ignore it now? Turn your head the other way? Forget it all?"

His sandwich was dry as sandpaper. He liked plenty of mustard and mayonnaise in his ham sandwich. Priscilla didn't. "It'll make your bread soggy." An eternal argument.

He swallowed muddy coffee out of his thermos cap. He liked plenty of milk and sugar in his coffee. Priscilla liked hers black and sugarless. His coffee was always a bastard.

"What's holding you back, Mish?" Roscoe plucked at him. "What are you afraid of? You all but won the last election. You did win it. It was stolen from you. Right in the election booth."

Roscoe sprang up from the bench and tippytoed toward the lockers with his sharp little nose outthrust.

"You want to know how they did it? I'll tell you how they did it."

Sideways, stealthily, relishing the rascality of it, Roscoe peered down into the lower grating of a locker.

"Colangelo had his watchers watch the legs under the curtain of the booth. And when somebody left the booth they could tell by the way he stepped out he was just pushing the curtain aside. He hadn't swung over the lever for the curtain. So his vote wasn't registered. Then Colangelo's watcher would slip in right after and reset the jiggers on the machine. How about that?"

"Sure it was stolen," Palermo seconded Roscoe. "But not like that. The watchers just waited to the end of the shift and voted everybody in who hadn't showed up."

"No, that's not how."

They all had their own version. A million ways to steal an election. Hilarious with it. Everybody loves a rascal.

"Mish, you should have had more watchers."

"I was counting on you guys."

For two weeks now off and on they had been having their fun, putting the screws on Lunin. They didn't push the company. They didn't push the union. They pushed him. And he had played the prima donna being wooed.

His second sandwich was gummy with processed cheddar. Chewing, swigging his coffee, listening, all the while he was studying the smudged leaflet planted on the concrete floor between his feet, as if the key to its identity must be hidden in it somewhere. It lay there like a blueprint, like a Sunday-paper puzzle tumbling with numbers from which, if you followed the numbers with your pencil, the picture would emerge.

"I'm not the leader Ucchini was," he was forced to say in self-defense and hesitated even to say as much. One toe in the water and you're in over your head, you're drowning. "I'm a follower. When the pieces are all there I come along and put them together. Where are the pieces? I don't see the pieces!"

But even as he said it, the pieces swarmed up at him out of the paper on the floor. Clustering, cohering, almost, it seemed, in prearranged order.

"All right, you asked for it. I'll give it to you straight. No matter what kind of campaign we mount, no matter what kind of rank-and-file slate we assemble, no matter if we mobilize this whole plant against him, we don't stand a chance. Nick'll beat us out."

"You mean you won't take him on?"

Colangelo had grown in his mind to monstrous proportions. Soft as a pussycat. Tenacious as a rat.

"All right, I'll state the obvious. Colangelo has every resource on his side and you know it. He has control of the union office, the office equipment, the secretary, the paper and the stamps, the funds—all those essentials that even with honesty and auditing he can charge off to petty cash. He's in control of the election committee, everyone on it is his appointee. And the election committee appoints the checkers and the watchers who control the election.

"He has his lieutenants everywhere inside the plant. Maybe all the way up to Coffin. Maybe right here in this room right now. He has his lines out to the city and state labor councils, the international. And the press, the politicians, the diocese.

"For Nick it's not just the presidency of this local that's at stake. It's not just the hours off the job he can spend on union business. It's the position it's put him in. It's the connections he'd normally never have access to. The exec meetings in the New York headquarters up there on the twentieth floor. The banquets he rubs shoulders at. The communion breakfasts. The jobs he can snag for his friends and the favors he can dole out. It's what he can do for Judge Rinaldi when Rinaldi runs against Kearnsey—right, Bostic? And what Rinaldi can do for him. It's the deals."

In the world of Nick Colangelo every human relationship was founded on a deal. Beefs, principles, the true interest of the workers, their class consciousness—all that men like Bob Ucchini lived for and died of? What's right? What's wrong? Nick never occupied himself with any such drivel.

"You saw the spread on the Jackson Day Dinner in the *Tribune* last week. Nick in that crowd around the governor. You punks and your gripes are no threat to him."

They sat hunched on the benches, chewing at their sandwiches, wincing at his insinuations. Who was the stoolie among them?

"Jesus, Mish, you're already campaigning."

"Now wait a minute. I'm not through yet—"

"Do I have to join the union?"

It piped up plaintively from the end of the bench where Don Pinette had laid out the materials from his Personnel envelope. Brochures, pamphlets and papers in a panoply of colors, arranged according to category. Group Insurance Plan, UV Employees Savings and Bonus Plan, Unemployment Compensation and Social Security Information . . . Payroll Deduction Authorization and other forms to be filled out . . . UV Education Series #5 How To Identify Communists, Subversives and Traitors in Unions . . . UV-EWIU (AFL-CIO) Agreement . . . Maybe Don would make a good materials handler after all.

"Not till after your thirty-day trial period," Palermo answered Don. "If you last that long."

"Everybody keeps saying that," Don complained. "If I last that long."

"If your job lasts that long," Bostic jived him. "They gonna turn you in for a conveyor belt."

"But do I have to join? I'm only going to be here a year. Just long enough to pay for my buggy."

"It's like insurance," Cusak said brusquely, impatient at the interruption. "You got to have it."

"It establishes the ground rules between us and management," Ewell took the time to explain. "Under what conditions you can be transferred from one job to another, your eligibility for upgrading, length of service increments." He picked out the little red paper-bound booklet and tossed it to Don. "Read it."

"I already have," Don said. "I'm covered. It says that non-members get all that anyway. Why should I let them check off my three bucks a month? I don't have to, do I, Mish?"

Good God, back to that one again. After all these years. The new element coming in. Do I have to join?

"You're going downtown," he said to Don, "you take the bus. The bus is going downtown anyway. Still you have to pay. Okay?"

"If everybody took the same attitude you do, Mish," Jackson who never said anything said from behind, "that you can't buck the power of the opposition, we never would have had a union here in the first place."

"What are we suppose to do, Mish? According to you, just lay down and take it?"

"Ask yourself that. Ask yourself why Colangelo has been president of this local for six years. Longer than anyone else before him."

What they needed here was a candidate with the enthusiasm and drive, the blind passion of youth. Untainted by doubt, uninhibited by the past. What they needed was a wily old hand who had the confidence of his supporters, who knew the ropes well enough to tie Colangelo up in knots. That perfect combination: the strength of youth and the skill of experience.

"I've been in this too long, far too long to pick up the ball and run with it just because somebody calls the signals."

Without restraint all that was most painful to him, all that was most bitter, all that had been storing up in him for the past six years, all that he wished least to give voice to, rushed out of him.

"All right, I run again. With one blow, one little pinprick, Nick takes care of it. A vote for Lunin is a vote against Uncle Sam. You're unpatriotic. You're a security risk. You're jeopardizing UV's contracts. You're destroying your jobs."

"Oh, that old stuff . . ."

"Everybody knows it's just smear tactics . . ."

Frightened by the mere mention of it, they vied in their haste to deny fear.

He should never have said it. He should never have revived it. A fool to have exposed himself. A waste of breath.

"It's no accident we have Nick in the leadership. It's not just happenstance."

He spat it up to the last bitter drop, the bitterest.

"Nick knows this membership. He knows instinctively how far his members will go at any given moment, how much militancy they're capable of, how much they'll let the shoe pinch before they howl. He knows what stance to adopt before the union, before the bosses, before the public. He knows the moment in history he's at, the circumstance of time and place, the mood. And he meets the needs of that moment.

"He never ignores the will of his followers sufficiently to isolate and thereby sever himself from them. He always pays sufficient attention to the common will as he interprets it to carry enough of us with him. He fills the bill."

He unwrapped his coffee cake with a crackle of wax paper. Cusak's spoon fell to the floor and he retrieved it for Cusak, one of those nickel-plated spoons from the old country, worn down to the brass and weighing a ton. It was sticky with grit-peppered stew. Cusak used his paper napkin to wipe it off, his small eyes screwed up, squinting at him in consternation.

Ewell pulled his billed cap from the back of his head down over his nose.

"You're not—you're not—" Roscoe sprang up. "You're not saying—"

That Lunin is coming out for Colangelo this election.

"Why not?" He swept Roscoe aside and pointed at the leaflet on the floor, all the pieces down there, coalesced. "Do you see one word in this, one single word against Colangelo?"

Not a word.

"Whoever is behind this is fighting Coffin, not Colangelo. And you want me to fight Colangelo?"

"To fight one you got to fight the other."

"We fight the union, the company gets lost in the shuffle. Is that what you're saying, Mish? It's a godsend to Graveyard?"

"I'm saying—" He was saying too much. One toe in the water, he was in up to his neck. "I'm saying it's not here! Where is the action? Where are the troops? What's happening? For two weeks we've been beating our gums and nobody's even suggested the first elementary step."

He said no more. They scrambled for the leaflet, re-examining it.

UNLESS AND UNTIL EACH AND EVERY DEPART-MENT DECLARES WAR ON COFFINISM . . .

They had to start where they were. In Switch. They had to start with what they had. Fritz.

How long was it since they'd had a departmental meeting? They had to persuade Fritz to call a department meeting in the next day or two. At the department meeting they had to present Fritz with one or two grievances they were sure he could win. Then with Fritz at the helm the whole department had to appear in a body at next Sunday's union meeting, with a proposal for action on behalf of the men in Hot Rubber and a program for strengthening the union. Not in opposition to Nick, no. As encouragement to him, helping him in the exercise of his office.

They had to build up to the Sunday meeting. There had to be a turnout. One little spark may set off another . . .

They no longer pressured him. They were pushing themselves.

"Where's Fritz?"

Fritz had not arrived in the locker room yet. He was down at the gate on his usual noontime foray, picking up a pizza from the Pizza Parlor delivery truck and incidentally turning his numbers slips in to the driver. The truck was late today.

They waited for Fritz with their plan, a plan with as many bends in it as human ingenuity can contrive.

"Boy oh boy, Mish." Bostic sidled up beside him. "You sure are a master at getting yourself off the hook."

4

Fritz appeared like the dawn, loaded with packaged pizzas, bringing a breath of the outside world into the stale locker room. His face shone brick-red over the white boxes, under a shock of frizzy red hair square-cut across the top. Fritz was a favorite with the women in the department. They were forever ruffling up his hair, cooing baby talk at him. Fuzzy wuzzy wuzzn't fuzzy, wuzzee? Rita threatened to send him to her beautician to have his hair straightened and Mabel opted for her neighborhood barber to have it conked. Fritz was popular with the men too. He was always good for a decision on whether it was in the 1940 or 1941 Series that Mickey Owen muffed the ball. Fritz could become quite prickly however when contradicted. His opinion was paramount.

"Say what are you guys doing in here?" Fritz lowered his pizzas to the bench and began jerking at the strings. "It's gone up forty degrees outside. We could be eating on the mall."

Immediately the chill imprisonment of the room was dispelled. They jumped up out of their cramped self-involvement and fell over their feet getting to the window. Open up. Let the air in.

"I phoned the Pizza Parlor for these an hour ago and they just showed up. Half apiece." Fritz began opening covers. "No—no chipping in. I did all right with the pups last night."

In a suffusion of tomato pungency, Fritz transported them to his phone booth call to his bookie downtown, to a southern track under the lights, to the realms of ease and expertise.

"I had ten bucks on the daily double. Paid six-fifty." With a stroke of his knife Fritz sliced through the pie and began distributing the wedges.

Brown-curled around the rim, studded with sausage, mushrooms, anchovies, bacon, specked with oregano and anise seed. Lips slavering over the napkins. Tongues drowning in a welter of juices.

"We better make time," Fritz warned. "I just passed those VIPs downstairs coming into the building. Dirksen's down there with Ledyard receiving them. Just as soon as the brooms go through, he wants us out on the floor."

Before the Bronx cheers could erupt, Fritz was on to the next thing, solicitously querying Bostic as he supplied him, "How's m' boy? They treatin' you all right?" And before Bostic could reply was off and away to the next one. "Louie makes the best. Never get 'em from Punchy. He shorts on the anchovies. Mish . . ."

He wasn't hungry. The food he had eaten without savor or satisfaction balled up like a lead dumpling in his stomach. But to refuse Fritz was to be a bad guy. Not to cram down gratefully what Fritz so generously offered was to kick him in the face. The brick-red face smiled over him with golden eyelashes and golden pricks of beard and strong square teeth.

"Come on, Mish." Fritz thrust his pizza at him. "Take it while it's hot."

To hesitate was to inject a moral issue. Make everybody else look bad. The touch of corruption, they all took it for granted. The guy who lives by the book, who really believes in him or likes him if he believes?

He accepted his pizza like everybody else and dipped it in his mouth.

He ate stolidly, ignoring glances and nudges. None of them was willing to open up on Fritz. How can you pressure a guy when you're eating his pie? With his sauce on your chin. Bostic cleared his throat once or twice and thought better of it, why should he be the one to rouse Fritz's antagonism?

Ewell pulled himself up out of his loose-jointed slump and fixedly stared at him. Don't fight the union leadership, get the leadership to fight the company, wasn't that your idea?

Cusak poked him from behind, prompting him. Start where we are, begin with Fritz, here's your chance.

He nodded at them. They gave him the nod.

Fritz said, "What's the matter with everybody? You look like your nag just lost in a photo finish. Something eating you, Mish?"

He had proved his point. He was vindicated. Nothing was stirring here. Nothing was moving. You can't plant seed in frozen ground.

Yet he couldn't answer Fritz, force his natural answer up through the juices of mushroom and sausage. Oh no, nothing, nothing at all.

"The guys here were talking," he began, tentatively. Amazing how hard it was. He was running full tilt into a brick wall. "We'd like a department meeting tomorrow night."

For once Fritz didn't bridle. He didn't blow his stack at the mere hint of aspersion. He retorted with fact.

"You know how many people showed up last time I called a department meeting? Two."

"It was storming." To talk to Fritz was like walking through tar.

"Yeah. And I was out in it. Two people. I swore off then. I got other things to do, I got responsibilities. My wife works the swing shift."

Tomorrow afternoon Fritz was helping a neighbor move. Thursday he had to take his daughter to her dancing class. Friday was Friday-night shopping night, who would stay for a meeting?

"Maybe next week. What's the big crisis? What you so steamed up about?"

They told Fritz. They climbed all over him. Calmly, his strong white teeth plowing through piece after piece of the whole pizza he had reserved for himself, Fritz disposed of their attack with his facts.

Dirksen shoving Roscoe's machines onto Ewell? Switching people from job to job as he saw fit today and every day?

"The company's got a right to transfer to comparable work. Of course what's comparable sometimes . . ."

Bostic on injection mold when he should be in his paint booth?

"That had nothing to do with me. All I did was take care of you. You know Nick's niece, the one who helps get the union paper out? Up with it till after three in the morning sometimes. Well, Reiner's her boy friend's father and if she goes to Nick about who's where on the seniority list, what can he do? The company'll show Reiner has a day over you. What have we got out of it? One sore chick."

Mariuch, the turntable, speed-up?

"Don't talk to me about Mari. First she takes a man's job on a woman's pay. Then she comes hollering to us for equal pay, which if there was she wouldn't have gotten the job. A royal pain in the ass. Mari takes care of Mari."

Final assembly? About to blow up out there?

"Open the door, Jackson," Fritz ordered. "Open it wide."

Jackson reached for the door and opened it. The light of the corridor invaded the locker room.

"You hear what I heard when I came up the stairs? All the way down the hall? Stick your head out," Fritz ordered Jackson. "A regular circus. Laughing like a bunch of hyenas down there."

Fritz was not unsympathetic toward them. He didn't deny the problems.

"Sure, I know conditions are lousy. I know it stinks. But it's easy enough to sit around here, Capitol Hill, and kick it around. All a union official has to do is bang on the boss's desk, shoot his mouth off, call a stoppage. That's all there is to it. You remember the strike two years ago?"

They shuddered, remembering. Whoever heard—whoever in the world heard of a union coming out of a strike with a cent less an hour than the company offered to begin with? No other gains.

"There was a recession on. Now there's another recession brewing. You don't know. You don't know what we're up against these days."

Last fall when there was a cutback in UV's defense orders, Nick spent a week in Washington pleading against it. Now there was another cutback hanging fire.

Last month UV installed a machine a block long in 9-C, with three men working where twelve had worked before. The local and the international yelled to high heaven, and how far did they get? Saved the third man's job. Now there was another monster machine due in 11-D.

Last week the steward and section chairman in Hot Rubber were penalized for the action of the men. Yesterday the union exec was out seven hours with management over it and no settlement in sight. Now Mari tries to stop the turntable . . .

"And what happens to the union? What happens every time? Just when we need all the solidarity we can get. Our members quit. Get disgusted, a little sorehead, it's all over. We've lost a third of our membership in the last two years. And as if that isn't enough, where's Nick today? Where is he?"

Nick was up at the State Legislature testifying in committee against a proposed right-to-work law.

"And if they put that gimmick over, we lose another third of our membership. Where'll we be then?"

Fritz stuffed down the last of his pizza and, glancing at the clock, leaped up. "Come on, come on. Any more of this yakking, you know where Switch'll be?"

Way down south in Dixie. With a brand-new facility built with the help of government money. And all the improved methods they wouldn't put up with here put through on a greenhorn crew.

Fight? Who you going to fight? What's to fight?

"Gonna rename this room. Frustration Junction."

They followed Fritz on the run. The sweepers zoomed down the corridor with their brushes.

"Right behind us," the sweepers whispered.

Cusak minced after the sweepers with a fairy wiggle of his fanny. "Our system," he intoned, "is a collaboration between capital and labor. Capital creates the jobs and labor does them."

"Productivitee-ee," Palermo sang out behind him, "is the key-ee."

"Meet the UV family."

At the entrance of Switch, Cusak stopped short. He fell back against Palermo. Palermo stepped back on Bostic's foot. Behind Ewell, Roscoe and Jackson stretched up on their toes. Fritz rammed his hand rearward through his shock of red hair. Pinette stumbled over Lunin. Across every face flitted a wild and soaring glee.

Through the double doors at the end of the corridor behind them, the delegation of dignitaries was pouring in.

And through the doors before them . . .

"Holy Mother of God."

The monkeys had taken over the works.

5

When the delegation marched four abreast into Switch, their last stop before the official luncheon in the executive building, they were greeted by a sizable placard removed from the packing area and printed in lipstick.

NO DOGS ALLOWED

Resourceful, dynamic, eagle-eyed, the captains of industry, tailored in grays and charcoals, correct in soft-collared shirts and slim ties, escorted by the brass of three countries in epaulets and braid, and guided by Dirksen, dove into aisles and defiles vibrating with the chatter of machinery, everyone industriously working, and vibrant with signs in lipstick, eyebrow pencil, mascara, machine oil, solder, grease pencil.

Posted outside Inga Kohlberg's powder room:

DO NOT FEED THE ANIMALS
ZOO FOOD 10¢

And over the turntable:

SQUIRREL CAGE

At Mari's press:

WATCH OUT FOR SNAPPING ALLIGATOR

By Rita's brusher:

THIS TIGER WAS RAISED BY A LION

In front of the women pacing in a circle around the spectacularly flashing electrical activator:

SEAL POOL
(PERFORMING SEALS)

Even at mercury injection where the women garbed in white, wearing white stockings and shoes, regarded themselves as equivalent to hospital staff in status, probably because of their clinical apparatus and the association of mercury with poison, a sign had been erected, painted with crimson crosses, dominating the center of the room.

FIRST-AID STATION
Emergencies Treated Here

And so it went. HIPPOPOTAMUS AFRICANUS (African Hippo). CAMEL RIDE 10¢. GOAT FARM. COILED COBRAS. THIS IS WHAT WE PLAN TO DO IN FIVE YEARS.

Eyes darted sidewise seeking Grover Coffin, the central figure of the delegation, the host. Coffin was most visible by his absence. Nowhere among the group. Nowhere in sight, ahead or behind.

In the wake of passage, everyone leapt to the same conclusion. Coffin was off at one of those high-level conferences presaging upheaval that always seemed to take place at United Vacuum in the month of March.

A banner of wrapping paper spanned Final Assembly:

KEEP OFF THE GRASS KEEP OUT OF THE MOAT KEEP HANDS BEHIND RAIL

KEEP MOVING

And across the cartons of switches:

REST ROOMS THIS WAY $\longrightarrow$

$\longleftarrow$ PARKING

ENTRANCE—EXIT

$\longleftarrow\!\!\!\longrightarrow$

TWO

Some Careless Rhyme Still Floats . . .

I

1

The quarrel between them, so long latent, skirted and averted, postponed, began creeping up on them even before they left the house. He had come straight home from work. After showering, stretched out in bed in his shorts for a quick nap, he entertained her with the trials of Pinette.

"*He's* chasing them, *they're* chasing the buck."

The clean sheets on the bed were roughdried, starchy with air and sunshine. Priscilla, sitting cross-legged on the spread beside him, was mending through a lapful of children's jeans. Patches over patches, sew-ons over peeling iron-ons, scraps hacked out of outworns to fit over the holes of worn-outs.

"Come on in here with me." He fussed at her skirt placket, mussed up her blouse. "For an old lady you're still a pretty good lay."

"Cut it out. The kids are out there."

Nevertheless she nudged over. With fanatic gleam and spitted thread she speared the needle's eye. Simultaneously hemming and attaching, she drove the needle like a Mack truck through quadruple layers.

"There's always someone out there," he complained. "Ever since we been married."

In a lighter humor than she had seen him for some time he went on recounting the day's events. They laughed over the zoo show.

"How did Coffin take it?" she asked, sharing the full savor of it with him. "I bet he's wild."

"He wasn't there. They say he's flying back tonight."

She pricked her finger, she licked it and, balked by a snarled thread, she abandoned her patching to trace over his eyebrows, tattoo down his nose, tweak at his chest hair. He was falling asleep.

"But if a thing like that happens, just out of the blue," she wondered, "it must mean something. What do you think it means?"

"Nothing." He was at once on his guard, alert against her prodding, her readiness to read some deep meaning into a passing incident.

"But what specifically brought it on?"

"How the hell should I know? Don Pinette. Spontaneous combustion."

"Mish, don't do this to me!"

She jumped up, spilling spools and shears, pants. Zipped and buttoned herself back together.

"It's getting so the only place it works any more is bed. And that's not enough, Doc. It's not enough for me! You've grown so hard and cynical. You've changed so."

"I'm not cynical." Surprised by the charge, he suppressed a spurt of anger—*he* was doing to *her*? "I haven't changed. I saw things before the way they were. And I see things now the way they are. It's circumstance that's changed. Not me."

He didn't bother to tell her about the locker room debate. He told her no more. What was there to tell?

He dozed and after dinner conciliatory, not wanting to fight her, wanting to please her, he went along with her to the meeting.

According to Priscilla, representatives from the twenty buildings in Tidal Flats Park were to meet in the apartment of a Mrs. Leggett on the dump side. Lucas had discovered the woman, wasn't that lucky? and had persuaded her to let them use her apartment, wasn't that proof positive? when everyone over in that section was supposed to be so scared. Tonight they would form a Tenants Organizing Committee, with the aim of mobilizing the entire project around a single initial issue. Of the multitude of miseries the tenants railed against, she and Lucas had fixed on the city dump that bounded the project eastward as the prime mover.

Priscilla heard his grunt of reluctance as he locked the door and chose to ignore it. She was bringing him along. She had won him over.

"Will you stop worrying about the kids, Mish?" She tried the door, firmly locked. "They don't light matches. They won't drink the iodine. Steph," she called through the door, "slide the chain."

"If she slides the chain," he commented dryly, "how do we get in later?"

They were leaving the children alone for the first time. Sitting on the living room floor in their pajamas, listening to their parents' latest LP.

It lilted, muted, in the dimly lit hall.

2

"Mrs. Kochis!" Priscilla pounded on the apartment door next to theirs. "Mrs. Kochis! Eddie's coming with us," she explained to him over her shoulder.

He'd believe it when he saw it.

After inordinate delay the door opened a chink to darkness within, all the lights out. Mrs. Kochis peeped out at them from behind the jamb, half a face, obliquely sliced.

"Shshsh," Mrs. Kochis hissed at them.

"Is Mr. Kochis ready?"

"Sh. The TV."

Mrs. Kochis ducked back to a babble somewhere behind her. Pneumatic drill of laughter. Applause.

"I missed that one." She returned reproachfully to the door. "You want Ed now? Tonight? What's tonight?"

"Our Tenants Committee, Mrs. Kochis, don't you remember? You said you thought Ed . . ."

"Oh, tonight. Is it tonight? Milton Berle's on tonight. The Lord Jesus himself couldn't drag Ed out of here."

"What about you?" Priscilla urged Mrs. Kochis, bent on demonstrating the mood she claimed to be so widespread among the tenants, all up in arms, about to shoot the works. Mrs. Kochis, as Priscilla well knew, never went anywhere. Eddie wouldn't allow her to go running around nights. Her place was at home with her family where she belonged.

"Mrs. Kochis, we're leaving Steph and Greg alone. I told them if anything comes up to call on you."

The door was closing. "Sure. Sure. Anytime."

Priscilla, undampened, bounded downstairs half a flight ahead of him. Her ragtag yellow hair bounced about her neck. Her unlined red jacket jounced over her hips. Her skirt, unevenly lengthened, flounced over her bare calves. The red-white-and-blue girl, who belonged on her father's boat in the harbor, up jib! up mains'l! . . .

Lean and purposeful, flushed, buoyant, she strode through the clutter of ten-year-olds in the lower hall.

"Hi, Peg. Hey, Cookie. Say, Joe, hutcha know?"

"Eddie Kochis!" she burst out wrathfully as soon as he caught up with her outside. "Just give him his bag of popcorn and his can of beer and his comic book. He's got it made."

Eddie Kochis. Sprawled out on his easy chair with his white-socked pups propped up on a hassock, his chest heaving with the yacks of the gags.

On behalf of Eddie Kochis he bridled with an old, obscure resentment, the resentment that had been with him from the very first words Priscilla ever spoke to him.

"They got a problem with their oldest boy," Priscilla went on, assuming the Kochis problem, any problem, as her own. "Here it is March and he still won't go to school. Won't leave his mother and whenever she tries to take it up with Ed he just treats it as a joke. 'Go to it, boy, give 'em hell.' When I finally got her to call Child Guidance, they couldn't give her an appointment till June. Then she backed out. Eddie wouldn't approve."

Exasperated with Kochis, with all the obduracy of inertia in this world, Priscilla plunged ahead undeterred. They proceeded toward Building 19 through a haze of ash. The day had been unexpectedly warm after a prolonged winter lasting late into the month. It was the kind of day when the earth softens, crumbles, opens up, yields forth the first shoots of crocus under the sunny lee of a house, along the basement wall. Not along these houses. Precipitated by the warmth of the day, a suspension of soot ascended over the flat rooftops into the evening sky.

The four-story brick buildings stood like children's blocks, rectangular slabs hedged with cars radially parked on the concrete apron; separated from one another by narrow courts paved in asphalt and gravel. Rectangular windows, the large fixed glass in the center flanked by casements, jeweled the dark façades with the blue-whites and ambers of lamplight. Priscilla never stopped to wonder, he thought, which window is mine? She never asked, which one am I? She knew. She was never lost among the stars. She cut expertly between the buildings and through the overflow of cars parked wherever they could nose in. Building 19 was located in the corner of the project diametrically opposite their own, adjoining the salt marsh that was being filled in.

"This way, it's shorter." Priscilla beckoned him on.

The dump rolled in on them. The air thickened. Litter underfoot crept upward. From between the buildings it breathed upon them its odor of stale vomit. On the asphalt path through the gravel court a little girl raced out of the outer darkness toward them, hugging roller skate, slat, wagon handle, the makings of a scooter. A tot panted past them, droopy-drawered, dragging after him a baby buggy three times his size, cleaned out of some attic, the torn wicker of its hood springing up like unkempt hair.

Beyond the last line of buildings, an ocean of rubble spread outward to the lawn-bordered boulevard on Shoreham Beach; hills and valleys of rubbish, acres of smashed glass, broken bedsteads, arms of timber, tons of plaster from demolished buildings, paint and oil cans, chemical wastes from factories, grease and sludge, scrap, the discarded daily news and packagings of two hundred thousand households.

The soggy earth smoldered, smoke filtering upward through layers of rotting refuse. Here and there slivers of flame flickered. Showers of sparks drifted on the wind. Even as they walked the dump-side road, dozens of small fires burst out. A fiery fragment soared like a skyrocket in the sulphurous air. Smoke, white as steam, blacker than night, orange with the fumes of some volcanic material below, swelled over an igneous field, an infernal plain, a last scene of man perishing in the noxious vapors he himself has produced.

"It'll be all ablaze by tomorrow," Priscilla predicted grimly. "It'll burn all week."

Tidal Flats Park had been located here on a prediction. In five years, Shoreham's mayor, Roderick Kearnsey, had predicted when he sank the cornerstone of the project, the marsh fill—started a decade before—would be completed and planted with trees and grass, provided with picnic tables, slides and swings, tennis courts, skating rink in the winter. From the buildings to the beach it would be all one park. The five years had passed and another five years and Rod Kearnsey was still mayor and the marsh was still being filled.

The dump was always burning. Sometimes the fires, temporarily quelled, burned underground for days and then all of a sudden out of nowhere they were all over the place. Sometimes the fires, taking contagion from each other, joined in a general conflagration. Fires were a natural phenomenon on the dump. They were so commonplace that several weeks ago Rod Kearnsey had ordered his fire department to pay no further attention to dump-fire calls from Tidal Flats. It was costing the taxpayers too much money to tie up engines and personnel there. A little smoke never harmed anyone. It just killed the rats.

Who started the fires? Eternal riddle of Tidal Flats. The kids, according to the city. Your kids. The kids start the fires. The city, according to the kids. The men in charge of the dump for the city, they started the fires to eliminate the paper, the old mattresses and bureaus, everything that was inflammable and so extract most easily what was non-flammable: the metal. The superintendent of the dump, the commissioner of public works and the scrap-metal dealers, they were all in it together. It was a three-cornered plot, according to the kids, between the truck drivers on the spot and Mr. Whoosie in city hall and one Huffsy, king of the junk yards. So long as someone had a stake in it, the dump would never be closed down, it would go on forever. The dump was a gold mine.

Now after supper the kids clambered through the debris, their playground. Strange lands to be explored, perils to be dared, treasures to be gleaned. Atop a pyramid two boys bent over a stovepipe fitting it together, wielding and banging, forcing and forming, wrestling with it.

He paused to watch them, the two heads so intently bent, black-shaven, tawny-tousled. A Trojan horse? Eventually they would sell the stovepipe for a few pennies to the scrap dealers, their friendly enemy. Industriously they rammed a spike into the stovepipe head, gouging out holes. Eyes? One wiped his streaming eyes and nose with hand and sleeve; the other sniffed back his phlegm, choked on it, swallowed, spat. Summers they ate the berries from shrubs that managed to grow through the smothering deposits. Intestinal infections, respiratory ailments, skin rashes ran rampant through Tidal Flats.

"Come on. What are you standing there for?" Priscilla called him. "Nineteen's down on the end."

Priscilla had taken him along this route compelling him, and he didn't like being compelled, to view close up, bare his eyes to what he lived with, habituated himself to and fulminated against at those times when it became unlivable. She rubbed his nose in it. She immersed him in it.

All his wife wanted was for him to get rid of the dump.

"Are you coming? I promised Lucas we'd be on the button."

No one but Priscilla, who despised television and therefore thought she could safely dismiss it, and Lucas Ford, the fey faun, the suffering saint, would plan a Tenants Committee meeting on a Milton Berle night.

She fell back, waiting for him. "Honey, you that tired?"

"Bushed."

"We'll make it short and sweet. Just the one point, okay?"

She was ahead of him again, laughing back at him, bright lips, flash of teeth. Her cheeks windburnt, the skin around her eyes whitish from the sunglasses she wore—taking the children on long beach walks in the winter, pointing out birds to them, fifty kinds of gulls, ducks. "What did we see today? A glaucous gull!" Her identifications were not necessarily accurate. It was her mother who was the true bird watcher. But Priscilla named the birds with such confidence, such enthusiasm, it hardly mattered whether she was accurate or not.

"Everybody's agreed on what has to be done. It's just a matter of working out the next step."

With a flourish of her hands she drew him onward, fetched, lured, seduced him into it. The girl with the gay guitar who had set herself at the head of the UV picket line, adopting their cause and contest as her own. Turning with her hands out: Come on, everybody now, the chorus, sing!

She slipped her arm through his, hastening him past the last few buildings. The girl who quit college to marry the picket captain and went to live among the workers, adopting the life of a worker's wife. "What's the matter with her?" his father, the old worker, had asked him. "Is she crazy?"

"That Mrs. Kochis!"

She was still fuming over the Kochises, trying to explain away their delinquency.

"If she'd just get up off her butt and make an effort to improve the situation instead of complaining all the time. All she ever thinks of is how they can get out of here."

Mrs. Kochis daydreaming over her ironing board, furnishing a pink split-level with bleached mahogany, matching appliances.

"She can't wait to get out of here!"

And neither can anyone else, my girl. Neither can anyone else.

On behalf of Mrs. Kochis, he prickled with the annoyance at Priscilla that never quite left him. A minor annoyance, a grain of sand, a tiny pimple in the tender fold of a membrane radiating discomfort.

"All we need now is someone with the experience to pull it together."

"Why not leave it to Lucas?"

His question, an attack, didn't warrant a reply. Lucas was living here illegally with an older sister, paying her room rent. At the first whiff of publicity he'd be out and his sister and her children with him. Aside from that, Lucas's attraction for women didn't extend to men.

Under the low-wattage light of a vestibule, Priscilla searched through the rust-flecked mailboxes with their missing and obliterated names for a Mrs. Olive Leggett.

"This is Door A, isn't it? I thought this was Door A."

It would result, as every other attempt of the tenants at Tidal Flats to organize themselves had resulted, in a flock of eviction notices, rent raises, and petty harassments designed to eventuate in the malcontent moving out under his own steam.

Door A, it turned out, was not on this side of the building facing the dump as she had expected it to be, but on the opposite side facing away from it. They were directed by a seedy little Negro who insisted on guiding them part of the way. After an influx of Negroes and Puerto Ricans into the city, Lowell Stanton, the director of public housing, was forced at last to admit them in numbers. Some of the buildings in this section, where the welfare cases were generally placed, were now going almost completely colored.

On Door A someone had incised with a sharp instrument in letters a foot high: SUSIE IS A SNAKE.

II

1

From the minute he sat down in Mrs. Leggett's apartment, he sat back. He had nothing to say here of any value to anyone.

The meeting went just about the way he anticipated it would. It was neither short nor sweet nor to the point. All talking all over the map. Whenever Priscilla tried to guide the discussion into the proper channel she was overrun. Lucas being Lucas let spontaneity rule the roost, awaiting his opening.

Mrs. Leggett herself said very little. She moved through her living room in plump white placidity, her glossy hazel eyes fixed on the room beyond. Her mouth pursed, under a pug nose, gave her face a snouty appearance. She was solid rather than softly plump; her round head thrust slightly forward from her stumpy body on the solid smooth whiteness of her short neck. In person she was immaculate. A soapy-scented moisture emanated from her. Her buff hair, indifferently cut and combed, looked as if it were still wet from the shower, stringily plastered down over her forehead. Her starched pin-check cotton dress bristled with cleanliness. Her whole apartment was immaculate. The brown asphalt-tile floor gleamed as if just polished around a green shag rug upfluffed as if just laundered. Not a mote of dust on the end tables, not a streak on the glass top of the coffee table.

The apartment was well furnished.

Print draperies hung at her tripartite windows from traverse rods under a cornice, in violation of regulations. (*Use only win-*

dow shades and fixtures supplied: in other words, no hardware in the woodwork!) Framed rustic scenes of the kind sold in dime stores for a dollar or two decorated her walls. (*Hooks, nails, screws, etc. strictly prohibited:* no holes in the plaster!) Her walls were painted pale green. (*Painting to be done only by our maintenance men:* in a uniform tan, before you move in or after you move out or when you can catch them once in eight years!) A washing machine bulged from her kitchen entry. (*No major appliances, use the coin washing machines in the basement, put up and take down your own lines in the drying areas as needed:* and politely wait your turn!) She had a nice set of bouclé furniture, no humps and no hollows, no scuffs in the fabric.

Mrs. Leggett moved from time to time to the bedroom beyond the living room to check on her little boy who had been sick all day. "Pore little thing," she announced once in her flat down-East accent, "he's had the diarrhea so bad. He's all wore out but the buttons."

Once she brought her little girls out in their frilly white nightgowns, threaded with yellow ribbon, to say good night to the company before going to bed.

Otherwise Mrs. Leggett did not participate in the meeting. She stood by the sofa with folded arms listening, head cocked, mouth pursed, an impenetrability about her like the impermeable thick whiteness of her skin. At least she had been concerned enough to let them use her apartment, a commitment from which the most vocal sometimes backed off.

2

He was not at all surprised that so few of the building representatives Lucas laid claim to were present. Priscilla kept turning at every creak in the hall. Where were the Dolans? Where was Mary Lucharski? When she spoke to them this afternoon . . . Only five materialized, all of them from the immediate vicinity, all colored and all women. Priscilla fell upon Gene Bostic's wife, Mae, when she arrived, like a long-lost friend.

"Mae! Am I glad to see you! How you been? How're the boys?" Mae Bostic proved to be the main bottleneck of the evening. A woman of superb bearing employed at the civic auditorium, Mae always managed to convey with a glance that she functioned in her job less as caretaker than as hostess for the director and his visiting performers. The vacuum cleaner she plied was an optical illusion. Rather, it was personal relationships she manipulated to suit her taste. Mae kidded her bosses and she kidded herself and she enjoyed the effect she created. What their actual attitude was toward her she was much too proud to investigate or give a thought to. She accepted their compliments at face value and returned them in kind.

"Where's Gene?" Priscilla asked her. "Why didn't you bring him? We need the husbands."

It was not a very subtle put down. Mine's here, where's yours?

"He wouldn't come," Mae answered her promptly. "Why should he? First Tenants Council we ever had here he went overboard. They built this place up with no play space in it anywhere. Turn a coupla thousand kids loose, running up and down the hallways, chasing between the cars, vandalizing . . . Well sir, the fathers got together and they demanded a spot for a basketball court, a baseball diamond, a yard with seesaws and a sandbox, all that stuff. Throw some empty apartments together, clear some part of the basement for bad weather, you know? And you know what they told us?"

Mae smiled with a provocative dimple at Priscilla, giving her put down for put down, reminding Priscilla that she was a Johnny-come-lately here. The Bostics were among the half-dozen colored families admitted to the project at its inception, thanks to Mae's knack for string-pulling.

"Patience, they told us. That's the price of progress. Just a little patience and we'll have a park here."

"And where is it?" Priscilla helped her out. "The dump—"

But that was not the point Mae was building up to. "And you

know what they did? First thing we knew, Marty Rakosczi—you know Marty, Mish—he got his notice. Then all of a sudden overnight our vice-chairman disappeared, left us holding the bag. If I hadn't put a word in for Gene here and there . . . And two years ago, just before you arrived on the scene, Priscilla, some fellows got talking to Gene and they drew up a list of grievances a mile long. Covered the waterfront. They circulated it and everybody signed it and we were all running to meetings every other night of the week shouting the roof down. Then the un-American Committee came to town, you remember, and they called one of our committeemen as a witness and next morning his best friend had painted a hammer and sickle on his door. He took his wife and babies and flew the coop. Left town. The housing office called in the ringleaders. And if I hadn't dragged Gene out of it in the nick of time . . ."

Mae glanced about her, conveying it all. Maybe you white folks can find yourselves another place to live. But us! She was not about to allow a Priscilla and Mish Lunin, a Lucas Ford, a Mrs. Leggett to lead any of these poor black lambs on the sofa to their slaughter.

"You want to organize this place," Mae advised Priscilla, "it's not going to be easy. Anybody that's been here any length of time, they know what the score is."

Priscilla, put on the defensive, was unable to restrain her protests of explanation. They had moved here two years ago, June, from a cold-water flat on Prince Street (surely no paradise for white or colored) after the house they were living in was condemned for the new expressway. They had moved here to her parents' distress (not unmixed with admiration) and against her husband's misgivings.

"My father wanted to give us some land to build on but I refused. This was so superior to what we'd had, four rooms all modern, heat and hot water, decent bathroom, at a price we could afford, who needed anything more? And with the park due facing the bay, why this could be, I thought, the beauty spot of the city. Isn't that right, Mish?"

Cringing, he slouched low in his chair and crossed his knees up high before him. Priscilla was committing what he considered a basic blunder. She let it slip out that she was here more by choice than by necessity. If there was virtue in her choice, there was also folly. The more fool she.

Unaware of her blunder if it was a blunder, unaware even that she was confirming Mae Bostic's cautions, Priscilla gazed past Mae to the three women sitting with Lucas on Mrs. Leggett's sofa, and in a fervor of self-explanation, with irresistible sincerity, made clear her position. She was willing to share the conditions of their existence. She had thrown her lot in with them. So what's the holdup? Let's go!

"How long are we to let this dump continue? If we who are the victims of it don't act . . ."

"The dump?" Scornfully Mae waved it off from before her face. "You can forget that. Gene has some notion about getting Rinaldi to beat the mayor over the head with it. I told him who'd get beat. Beat and buried."

"Rinaldi? Why that's brilliant. When Lucas and I polled the tenants, they all agreed the dump . . ."

"You asked, so they answered you," Mae said. "So what? If you're going to do something, why don't you all do something you can do something about?"

"But, Mae! How can you—"

"Ladies. Ladies," Lucas called them to order.

Lucas perched on the arm of the sofa like a mythological figure gracefully disposed, half-god, half-boy. His black hair sprang up in glistening tendrils, thinning back in twin bays over his temples. A youth of uncertain age out of the slums of Detroit, a generation out of the Kentucky mountains, in the course of wandering the continent from city to city he had stopped here. For how long was anybody's guess. He had confessed once to Priscilla in some quivering moment of rapport that he had had a nervous breakdown a few years ago and spent several months in a state hospital.

When Priscilla in turn revealed Lucas's hospital episode to him, swearing him to secrecy while seeking his sympathy for Lucas, it merely reinforced his initial mistrust of the man. Unashamedly he took advantage of Lucas's candor to vindicate his attitude toward him. At the same time, illogically, he suspected that Lucas had never been in a mental hospital at all. It was just possible that it was just a good story, the right story to reach the heart of the right woman at the right moment.

Beyond that, he wasn't even sure that Lucas was primarily interested in women. He had met him a few weeks ago walking through the project with his arm around the shoulders of a nine–ten-year-old boy. "This is my son." Lucas had introduced the boy, looking down fondly at him and squeezing his shoulder. "I'm taking him to a show." It was fine and generous of Lucas to take such an interest in a neighbor's boy. But it had struck him strangely all the same.

Lucas perched like a bantam rooster in a henyard over the women he had collected here tonight. He commanded them in his bass voice, dominating the proceedings. They all rustled up when he spoke, fluttered to attention at his word. Priscilla too.

"Better start taking notes," Lucas ordered Priscilla and she meekly accepted the pencil he passed her. "Let them have their say," he reprimanded her and she mutely bent her head over her notebook.

Lucas threw the floor open. But even while they were all freely having their say, Lucas seemed to dominate them. It was at his command and pleasure that they gave vent to their frustrations. He had them on wires, playing them until the moment matured when he should break in.

Hard with suspicion of Lucas, he stretched back in his chair till his joints creaked, saying nothing. What's the guy up to? Where's he taking all this? Some crackbrained scheme? Some insane mission?

Every woman, it soon developed, had come here tonight with a purpose of her own. And for every purpose Mae Bostic waited —her elaborately coiffed head thrown back and her face, the copper-brown face of an Indian princess, splendidly attentive— with her little hatchet on the ready to chop it down.

Mrs. Knowlton, leader of the contingent on the sofa, was on the warpath over the terms governing her rent payments. She delivered herself with the nonchalance of the tall and rangy, the briskness, crisp as celery, of coherent argument and the crackle of irrepressible rage.

Where was a copy of her lease? Nobody had ever received one. Where was a copy of the rent-income schedule? Nobody had ever seen one. She was a dayworker and her earnings varied from week to week. Her husband was in construction and his earnings varied with the season. Her oldest boy had a dish-washing job last summer but then he went back to school for the year. She had had three rent raises based on family income, including the boy's, when they were all working.

And when she went to pay rent at the office, taking time off from work and rushing to get there before five, what did she find? A waiting line clear out to the hall and the clerks behind the window giggling and gossiping, going off for coffee and cigarettes, and at five sharp, bang goes the window right in her face. Then she was charged a penalty for late payment of rent. How about that?

"This is no low-cost project, it's high-cost. You open your mouth, they bite your head off. You put up a squawk, they put you out for overincome. The more you try to get ahead, the more you fall behind."

Priscilla in a whirlwind of taking notes hopelessly shook her head. You could never unite the tenants around this one. Too many on Aid to Dependent Children, Old Age Assistance and Social Security paying the minimum.

"We been through all that before." With a flicker of her peaked brows and a flick of her shapely shoulders, Mae demolished the argument and went into attack. Nobody had ever been rude to *her* in the rental office. They always greeted and treated *her* with the utmost respect. It was all a matter of manners.

"You handle yourself right, you can handle them," Mae sermonized. "Some people don't know how to keep things to themselves. That office don't have to know anything more than what you want them to know."

"Anybody steps on me," Mrs. Knowlton retorted, "I don't kiss their foot."

"Ladies. Ladies," Lucas interposed. But did not intervene despite Priscilla's imploring glance: Get them back on the track!

The three women who had come with Frances Knowlton flew to her support. You don't have to *tell* that office a thing. They *know* who's working in your family and where and for how much. They know everything around here. There isn't anything goes on they're not on to. And if they can't find out any other way they barge into your apartment looking for unauthorized persons on the premises, disturbances, leakages, vermin, any excuse.

"There's no privacy!"

That social worker, some social worker, not even a trained social worker, nosing into your personal business and spreading it around all over. A social worker is just another kind of a cop. A spy. She has a regular espionage system operating here.

"Get rid of her!"

The women drew in apprehensively, contracting, even in the fever of their complaint. What's said here tonight will be in the housing administrator's book by tomorrow morning.

Priscilla scribbling up a storm shook her head in despair. You could never unify the tenants in a campaign against the social worker appointed to the project. Mrs. Condon ruled by fear and favor.

"If everybody was law-abiding," Mae stated with emphasis, staring straight ahead at no one in particular, "you wouldn't have no interference. If everybody conducted themselves like they should and followed the rules and kept a clean house . . ."

So it went. Mrs. Leggett roused herself sufficiently out of her glazed hazel-eyed daze to stomp off to the kitchen and bring back a cereal bowl into which she emptied the ashtrays.

Maintenance! Here the government had spent all these funds to construct this project so slum dwellers could move into it out of

the slums and failed to provide the funds for adequate maintenance. In another five years this too would be just another slum.
"It's not buildings that makes slums," Mae lectured them. "It's
people."

She always scrubbed the floor in her hall when it came her turn,
but there was always the woman next door and the one downstairs who didn't and spoiled it for all the rest. *She* never left her
clothes in the washing machine all day and up on her lines and
got into scraps with the neighbors over it. *She* never let her young
ones run wild all over the lot when they were little, she locked
them in if she had to go out, day or night. It wasn't *her* child playing outdoors who, when he had to crap and couldn't make it to
his third-floor apartment, let it go in the first convenient corner
inside. And that trash out in the pathways, those broken bottles
you had to wade through sometimes, all the cussing and carous-
ing and cuttings, the police here every other Saturday night, it
was none of *her* doing.

All these people coming up from the South and these Spanish
don't know the meaning of responsibility, they're the ones. No
respect for the rights of others. No religion. No law. No sanitation.

"Why I went into this girl's place one day to borrow some rice
and there was this big fat roach on the floor right by her foot.
'Why don't you sweep it up?' I asked her. 'He ain't doin' no harm,'
she says to me. 'He's dead.'

"Oh they carry it up here, they bring it in here with them"—
Mae flung her hand out a disdainful distance—"bag and baggage."

Mm hm. Ain't it the truth! In another instant Mae would have
them persuaded that it wasn't the Housing Authority that was to
blame for the lack of janitorial services, clotheslines, toilets accessible to youngsters outside. Not Lowell Stanton, the city's dictatorial administrator of public housing, or Mayor Kearnsey his patron
and protector, but People—the family across the hall.

Priscilla regarded Mae with shocked astonishment, her red
cheeks flaming redder, her blue eyes blazing bluer. Mae Bostic was
a friend from years back, from the time when Gene was a shop
steward at United Vacuum, the first Negro steward in the plant.

Only Priscilla was never as close to Mae as she assumed, assuming that because Mae was by definition a victim of society it automatically made them the closest of friends. To Mae the assumption was presumptuous. It was Mae's supreme boast that no one ever put anything over on her.

Mae had first put the colored women on guard against the white folks. Then she had disposed of the colored one by one and all together. Now she was leading them into assault against their own.

For Mae too, it shortly became clear, had come here with a purpose very much in mind, for which she sought support. Having lopped off the diversionary issues, she was now ready to spring the issue that inspired her. A red-hot one. Not only at Tidal Flats but at the four other housing projects in the city. Television.

She had just bought an almost-new RCA from Gene's cousin, new picture tube in it, rabbit ears on top, good reception, no more snow than anybody else gets. But Mr. Stanton, after years of forbidding TV, had recently decreed that every tenant's set must be tied in with the master antenna he had arranged for in each project. First there was the installation fee for the hookup, then the fixed annual fee for servicing the master antenna and in addition a flat monthly fee for electricity to be paid with the rent in perpetuity. Anybody missing a single payment was cut off and had to start all over again with the thirty-five-dollar installation fee. Not only that. Gene could have his cousin take care of the hookup and repairs as they arose. Mr. Stanton however had contracted with a company to cover all repairs and adjustments, with a surcharge for every call whether the man fixed anything or not.

"Now *there's* something everybody's burnt up about," Mae declared, hoarse with indignation, shaking with it. "They'll sign a petition against *that* in a minute!"

Priscilla, letting her notes slide, was twisting and turning, in the grip of contrary drives: her impulse to jump in and push through the issue they had decided upon beforehand, the dump! the dump! the one issue she believed had a chance of success; and her conviction that any decision that had to be pushed through, even if

previously consented to by all of them, was in principle undemo-
cratic and therefore bound to fail for lack of accord.

Her cheeks thinned down, carved to the bone. Her throat
arched, constricted to the sinew, throbbing with the desire to
formulate. Out of this confusion, this blind groping . . . In the
first place it was doubtful that 50 per cent of the tenants had
television yet. In the second place Mae herself was not as militant
on this score as she would like to think she was. Mae had
not mentioned the arbitrary Mr. Stanton by name but had referred to him as "certain parties." Once a petition was drawn up
to be circulated, would Mae be one of those to circulate it?

Out of this chaos, this groping, this frenzy of outrage upon
outrage . . .

"Milton Berle!" Priscilla burst out, unable to constrain herself.
"There was a time when you could talk to people. You could knock
on anybody's door and they'd talk with you. But nowadays nobody wants to talk. It's all shush-shush. That goddam TV . . ."

Mae started as if she'd been slapped. Insult my TV, insult me!

"Ladies."

3

In the course of the past half hour he had received from Lucas
out of the breast pocket of Lucas's black jersey a piece of paper
reduced to such minuscule folds it could have been safely swallowed. The writing, when he unfolded it, was hardly decipherable,
in light lead pencil crisscrossed with creases and smudged with
erasures. Evidently Lucas's draft for a leaflet to be handed out,
his call to arms. Why was this project, the largest housing project
in Shoreham, situated in this location to begin with? Could it be
that the Bayside Businessmen's Association plotted this in cahoots
with our so-called honorable mayor as a means of converting waste-
land into a rental and commercial area? (He grimaced at the style,
a style of insinuation he was not unacquainted with. Oh God, a

Red!) Can it be that the merchants up and down these streets are reaping profits galore? . . . We live in an atmosphere of terror. We got Russia right here, the iron hand of Joe Stalin. (Oh God, an anti-Red!) Talk about Big Brother . . .

It was a hodgepodge, poorly conceived, misspelled hither and yon, but Lucas would fight to the death for it. This was his proposal.

He passed the paper on to Priscilla for her perusal. Stalin is dead.

Passively draped over the arm of the sofa, his pallor sheathed in black jersey black-belted into black pants, his forehead crowned with springy curls and his wrists veiled in listless wisps, Lucas let the women whip themselves up to a pitch of ire. Lucas was the sort who seeks out a stage and an audience on which to exercise his gifts, who must see himself reflected in others' eyes, behold the man.

Then Lucas began to speak.

"You are all wrong," he told the women and they blanched as if accused of mortal sin. "You've all missed the point. Why—are we—here?"

The pale green walls of the room melted before his gaze. His *here* spread outward from this apartment, this building, this cluster of dwellings ensconced upon this barren heath at the edge of the sea, to the crescent of smoke-stacked factories, the power plant, the sewage-disposal plant, outward to the encompassing city.

"Shoreham, asshole of America. City of Big and Small Industry. Spilling its contamination into the waters and the air. A working-man's town. Producing the things everybody uses and nobody thinks about.

"The stink of plastics, the gases of acids are in our lungs and our gut and the blood and bone of our children. Our crowded hospitals—our rotten schools—our forgotten recreation—anything's good enough for the workingman. Nobody cares. Nobody thinks about it. Not even ourselves.

"We are what is left behind by the lords of creation when they go off to their estates in Hillcrest and their head offices in New York and their trips to Bermuda.

"We are the refuse swept under the rug of civilization."

Lucas leapt up from his perch and small, not five and a half feet tall, bestrode the room like a colossus. Even Mae the proud one, the untouchable, quailed under his gestures.

"That's Shoreham. Now Tidal Flats. What are we doing here? Why have we been condemned to this spot? Who are we?

"We are the asshole of the asshole."

Starkly Lucas stabbed his forefinger into the center of his black-jerseyed chest.

"They built these houses on top of a cesspool, a burning dung heap. And they sent us into them. The trucks that haul in the sludge, the slag and the spoilage out of the plants and the buses and the cars that carry us home from there, what's the difference?

"Which is which?"

Lucas laid it on. It released the outpouring Priscilla had hoped for. The rats that invaded your kitchen big as squirrels. The bugs in your cupboards big as your thumb. The flies on your supper table, the soot on your window sills and wash line, the sicknesses and the days lost from work and school.

"A virus, the doctor says. What kinda virus? Virus from the dump."

"Festered and festered. Ten dollars for salve, didn't help none."

"Swung a rat by the tail in her face."

"They don't care nothin' bout us and our kids. They think we don't care. Well, they got another think . . ."

Priscilla was satisfied now. With her zest and her gusto she was off like one of her paternal ancestors, salvation bound.

"Everywhere we turn we're in violation. If we keep a pet we're in violation. If the kids play in the halls they're in violation. The chain and bolt on my door, it's in violation. But the joke, the cream of the joke is, this whole shebang is in violation. In violation of Federal regulations, state health laws, the city fire and sanitation codes.

"Oh yes, I know, Mae, I know it seems like a lost cause. You can call and write and yell to high heaven and nothing happens. Every once in a while some bright new secretary of the Chamber of Commerce or some bright young lawyer trying to break into politics raises enough hell to bring the inspectors down and they investigate and they castigate and they issue statements to the press and that's the end of it. Still it's a backlog. We have a case. We're in a strong position.

"The right, the right is with us."

She unfolded her perspective. They were not alone in their plight. Odor and smoke drifted over the Bayside section of the city; were carried on summer evenings out to the fine residences on Bay Point; and on certain days, under certain conditions, yellowed the sky as far as Sherwood Heights where her father and mother lived, two miles away. There were all these people outside who were directly affected. There were forces of some standing in the community who would respond if appealed to. Any number of resources that could be counted on.

"How to reach them, that's our problem. That's our job. And once we've focused public attention on this, all the other issues you've raised this evening can come into play. First things first. The rest will follow."

Among her notes Priscilla had jotted down a list of potential allies. The PTA of the South Bayside School of which she was secretary. Any action proposed here tonight she would be sure to present at the board meeting tomorrow night. The local chapter of the NAACP. "Gene is on one of the committees, isn't he, Mae? Anyhow one or both of you can take it up, if you will, with the president." And the union, EWIU-UV Local 317.

"Mish, you have a meeting next Sunday. Introduce it from the floor. Ask for a resolution."

Her blue eyes transfixed him, compelling response.

Only two disruptions occurred in the flow of the meeting from then on, both of them caused by him. The first one now over the union.

"Introduce what?" he asked her.

She had been doing her damnedest to impress upon them in their small ranks how much influence they possessed. The strain showed in the tendons of her neck, in the whitish crinkles around her eyes.

"Why what we've been talking about!" she cried with a rasp in her throat. "What we've been tackling here tonight!"

"What's the union got to do with it?"

"The same thing everybody else in Shoreham has! There are union members all over Tidal Flats. Must be fifty of them."

More like thirty. Who rarely attended union meetings.

"You can get them together on this. You were their president once."

"I'm not president now."

"Oh, Mish." She slackened back out of her tension, full of concern for him, smoothing over the breach. "Of course. Colangelo is a prize pill. But you still have plenty of followers. The phone rings at all hours. There's always somebody dropping in for advice . . ."

She let it go.

"Mish is right. Before proposing action for others we'd better draw up a plan of action for ourselves. Though there's no reason why we can't work simultaneously inside and outside the project. Anybody?"

Recovered, Priscilla smiled expectantly around, fingers upcurved beckoning, urging it out of them.

Lucas slumped on the floor resting his spine against the foot of the sofa, his draft leaflet forgotten in the shuffle. He had discharged, in the intensity of attaining his climax surpassing himself. Fulfilled, sweated, spent, he required at least for the moment no further proof of his being.

Plans for action were not wanting. Hold a mass meeting, publicize, get it into the papers. Besiege the Housing Authority office with telephone complaints, tie up the switchboard. Delegation to the Health Department. March on City Hall. Rent strike. Frances Knowlton and her contingent spitting-mad enough to try anything. Mae Bostic with her peaked brows raised, tolerant as a

toddler's mother; Olive Leggett with her pouted mouth, mum as
a monument: neither one of them ready for anything drastic.

A letter then to every tenant announcing the formation of the
committee, calling for its expansion into a permanent council and
setting forth its goal: DUMP THE DUMP! House meetings in
every house to lay the basis for a public meeting, speakers, maybe
the minister of Fran's church, maybe a doctor, maybe a resident
of Bay Point, a trade union spokesman, a city councilman. And
out of the meeting the forms of pressure to be adopted.

The letter then, the absolute minimum, required not too much
from anyone but the initiators. Lucas already had a draft leaflet
to base it on. Frances, Priscilla and Mish would get together with
him tomorrow night to knock it off. By day after tomorrow it
could be mimeographed, who would let them use a mimeo for
free? Paper, stamps, stuffing the envelopes, and if not by mail
then how? It should be out by the end of the week at the latest,
with a target date included in it for house meetings next week
and the public meeting next month.

"What's the best night, Mish?"

"Just a minute. Not so fast." Compelled again into response, he
threw up another roadblock. "Who's signing your letter?"

"Nobody." Lucas shot up from the floor, a stiletto of righteousness.

"It's a letter, isn't it?" he said to Lucas. "A letter has to be
signed. Who are your officers?"

"What officers?" Lucas, standing over his chair, roared down at
him. "Who the hell needs officers?"

"If this is to be a public affair, everything has to be open and
aboveboard," he said. "You should have some provisional officers."

In the ensuing imbroglio it became apparent, to him anyhow,
that Lucas, far from looking forward to open letters and meetings,
harbored a taste for the secret, the conspiratorial: the agitational
figure skulking around corners in the dark, scattering the seed of
his message; who appears at anonymous gatherings like this one
to proclaim his cause and then, folding his cloak about him, disappears into the mists of time. Lucas had not brought his sister

here tonight any more than Mae had brought her husband, but Priscilla had not remarked on her absence.

It was also possible that since Lucas could not very well be an officer himself, and most especially not top officer, he wanted no part of officerships. To most of the women here however, unaware of Lucas's dubious status, it could only appear that Lucas was afraid to sign. And if he was afraid, why shouldn't they be?

"Why can't we just put Tidal Flats Committee at the bottom?" one of the women inquired. "Wouldn't that do it, Mr. Lunin?"

"We can," he told her, "but in this day and age, unless people are convinced there is something sound and solid at the core they stay away in droves. First thing they want to know is: Who's Behind It?"

"What is this, Big Brother?" Lucas thundered. "Stah-leen?"

"Stalin is dead."

But no one paid attention to such trifles in the uproar. The women themselves craved the sense of something sound and solid at the core, something that wouldn't crumble at a touch.

The letter should be signed by four officers, but who were to be the officers?

"Mae, you're an old-timer. You're elected."

Raising her hands, Mae shunted the mere thought of it away in horror.

"I'm no good to you. They say Tidal Flats is one-fifth colored now. That still leaves four-fifths white. Where are the white folks? You need somebody who'll bring them in."

Lucas could not be chairman. And Priscilla? She was twisting and turning again, riven by contrary drives. She too was vulnerable to exposure. When the reporters started scratching and digging and found out Who She Was . . .

"Not right now," she begged. "I'll work for it with everything I've got but . . . When it gets going, when there's a much larger group involved, then if you want me . . . Mish?"

"Same here," he said to them, averting his head from her. When the reporters announced Who He Was . . .

"Mish, I honestly think you should."

Her blue eyes rested on him, brilliant, close to tears. Rise up to the stature of what's needed! Where's your guts?

"Mrs. Leggett?" Adamantly he passed it on.

Mrs. Leggett barely stirring out of her torpor shook her cocked head. She wasn't one to take hold.

"I'll sign it," Frances Knowlton volunteered. "Somebody has to be the goat."

She would sign as chairman pro tem and one of the women with her as secretary pro tem. Priscilla glowed. Both women, both colored and no men. But that would do it. The committee was in business now. A going concern.

Before they left, Lucas emptied Mrs. Leggett's cereal bowl of its ashes and holding it between his hands, his stern visage concentrating downward upon it, he went about with it from person to person. The women as if prompted beforehand each dropped fifty cents into the bowl. Priscilla, surprised, scuffed about her pockets and finding nothing there extended her hand husbandward. Fifty cents.

"Good idea," she said with the clang of her half dollar into the bowl. For the letter of course. It was launched.

Lucas halted before him. The grave lines of Lucas's face slashed down, converging, toward the bowl in his hands. Another fifty cents.

Lucas bore the bowl of jingling coins across the room to Mrs. Leggett who without wonder accepted it.

"For your hospitality."

"Sure," she muttered. Her shorn buff locks, escaping from a bobby pin, fell unevenly over one eye. She shook her hair decently back into place. "Thanks a lot."

Smoothing her cotton dress, the admirable housewife, she accompanied them to the door and held it open while they filed out.

They departed with the illusion that a great deal had been accomplished in the space of a few hours. When actually . . . He swallowed the sourness in his mouth. Gene Bostic was about as likely to take up Tidal Flats with the august Dr. Vaughan, president of the NAACP, as he was with Grover Coffin, general manager of the Shoreham works of UV.

III

1

Priscilla was delighted. "Wasn't that simply marvelous?" she rejoiced as soon as they were alone with Lucas. "The way those women took over. What got into Mae? I could have bopped her. But that Knowlton, she's a firecracker. And those others with her, every one of them sharp as nails. Lucas, you were tremendous. If only we'd had more people there to hear you! You'd think that after all the time we spent contacting . . . That collection you took up at the end, Lucas, I thought it was for the kitty. What was that all about?"

In brooding silence Lucas walked with them toward his building. He kicked at the slivers of glass from a shattered arc light.

"You weren't *renting* the place from Mrs. Leggett, were you?" Priscilla's voice sharpened, anathema! "I mean she's just as much a part of all this as we are. With as much to gain or lose."

"It was an act of love," Lucas said.

"Love? What's love got to do with it?"

"Mrs. Leggett is a whore."

It was the way Lucas announced-pronounced it that jolted. The word coarsely croaked out of that delicately curled mouth, spat out with relish and revulsion.

"You mean," Priscilla asked dangerously, "that we were holding our Tenants Committee meeting in the apartment of a known prostitute?"

It was the way she said it that jarred—her annihilation of anyone who stood in the way of action. It incited his immediate empathy with Lucas, with Olive Leggett.

"Those women went there tonight," Lucas stated, "as a testimony of love for Mrs. Leggett. To let her know she's not alone. To let her see that she's not so low they wouldn't go there. To demonstrate their regard and respect. They were all her sisters tonight."

"Love! A white prostitute in a mixed section? They're supposed to love her? When she's hustling their men? Taking a bite out of their paychecks? Why everyone around must be onto it. No wonder nobody showed up!"

"That four dollars," Lucas went on, musing on it with a reverberant tenderness, "was a gift of love. To help cover the time she might have spent otherwise. For once in her life after she's closed her door behind her, she can lift her head up. She can feel the difference."

"For godsake, Lucas, is this a housing problem or is it the Salvation Army? And that apartment of hers . . ."

"What do we care what she does?" he interrupted them, the peacemaker. "As you said, Priscilla, she's in this with us. It's the same smoke." They were following another route home, but the ashy haze was heavier now, shrouding the lights in a brownish halo. Smoke pricked the eyes, penetrated nose and throat, invaded lungs and bronchial tubes, flowed through the air sacs, branch and twig, into the bloodstream. Without let or leave, some soluble part of it into some insoluble part of them. He struggled with a cough. "She chokes on it too."

He got the deserts of the peacemaker. They both fell on him.

"Oh, please, Mish! She's parasiting on her neighbors, peddling it in the plain sight of kids. Did you get a good look at her apartment? I can tell you right now she's taking from the state and the city and all the guys she can lay. And she's either putting out for Stanton's stooges or paying them off."

"A woman left like that," he found himself excusing her. What the hell, she must be in the stable of some pimping politico. "With a family to raise. She can't make ends meet on ADC."

"Let her get together with the other welfare mothers then and fight for more dough."

"That'll be the day. Tomorrow or next week?"

Priscilla's breath hissed in and out her nostrils. More than sarcasm was involved. He was taunting her. Casting doubt on, detaching himself from, placing himself in opposition to the bulwark of her belief. You get together, hire buses, storm the legislative chambers, lay down the law.

"All right then! Let her do what everybody else does. Look at Frances Knowlton and she has her husband. With five youngsters, going out to housework."

"Mrs. Leggett would tell you that what she does for a living is no more degrading than scrubbing somebody else's floors."

Through the medium of Mrs. Leggett they exchanged blow for blow.

"You know everything, don't you, Mish?"

With inexplicable venom, Lucas assaulted him from the other side.

"You know all the answers, don't you?"

Lucas's face was ravaged with torment.

"You even know what's real and what isn't!"

Rapidly Lucas walked away from them.

He stared after Lucas in bewilderment, disconcerted by the intensity of his onslaught. In some unfathomable fashion he had marred Lucas's concept of what he was doing, and the flaw was in him. Come back, he wanted to shout after Lucas. Let's explore this a bit. Explain yourself.

"A hooker's pad," Priscilla groaned. "Jesus Christ. Where do we stand now? I could kill Lucas."

"Maybe Lucas knows something we don't know."

"Of all the half-assed sentimental . . . . Crazy as a bedbug. She must be slipping him some. Now where do we go from here? I thought you didn't like Lucas."

"He got those women to play along with it, didn't he? And Mae Bostic of all people."

"*That's* what was bugging her. Now how do we save the situa-

tion? There must be some way to salvage . . . All right, all right, I
get it. When I was for Lucas, you were against him. Now I'm
against him . . ."

"Whatever you have there now, whatever it is, Lucas drummed
it up. Eliminate Lucas, what have you got?"

Lucas, it was his guess now, had been in all the warring factions
of the Left at various times, or all at the same time the better to
test them out; and had been expelled from every single one of
them. He was unstable, unreliable and impossible to deal with. Of
a temperament given to constructs based on his own theories but
incapable of sticking to any preconceived plan of action. In the
middle of their public meeting, if it ever came to pass, Lucas would
rise up from the audience and blast the living daylights out of
every sponsor on the platform.

Alongside him, *sss sss sss*, Priscilla was striving mightily to bottle up her rage and, *tk tk tk*, was busily revising, projecting. When
the whole thing was so shot full of holes . . . She was a woman
of vision and determination, prone to exaggeration. In those periods and situations when external circumstance was ripe, exaggeration served to power her determination, provide the steam for
transforming vision into actuality. But when external circumstance
was otherwise, no matter how she huffed and she puffed . . .

She had dragged him out of the house tonight and put him on
the spot before those people for a piece of stupidity. He was seething over it.

"Priscilla, there's nothing there. It's not in the cards. You're
beating a dead horse."

"How do you know? Till you try it. You have to try."

"Dead, Priscilla. Dead dead dead."

"Then you try anyway. It's worth the try. Mish, it's not the
horse . . ."

Go ahead say it. *It's not the horse that's dead. It's* . . .

They walked on in silence hugging their arms close to their
sides, jerking back when by accident they touched. Out of the
sleeping shadows of parked cars, here and there a car growled
into wakefulness and with a grinding of gears and glitter of lights

backed into their path, swerved and swooped off. The eleven-to-seven shift, not many plants on late shift now. Jobs were tight.

"When I think of the ability you have going to waste . . ." She moved close to him, twined her arm through his, pressed through the sleeve of his jacket. "Mish, it breaks my heart."

With all her vision and determination she had snatched at this means to rescue her husband from his quiescence, seeing him restored through it to his proper role: spokesman of the delegation, chairman of the organization.

Her motives were no more calculated than Lucas Ford's. Call it opportunism. Call it ambition. Call it devotion. Desperation. A blind and baffled effort to make things right.

2

Now they walked with their arms around each other. Above them the buildings loomed, murmurous, pulsating, jampacked with lives that in their assertive vigor refused to be boxed and tagged. A figure hurtled out from between parked cars, chasing someone or being chased. "Mother-fucking cock sucker . . ." A rush of drunken breath. Whhhht.

They hastened toward home as they neared it, toward their children summoned suddenly out of oblivion. Hurried, with a throat-gripping spasm of anxiety, as if behind their own door doom awaited them. Climbing the stairs after Priscilla, he reached along the grubby wall. Like the dump smoke, like the residues of the plant, the grubbiness, absorbed, coursed through him. Her heels flailed above, disappeared around the corner of the landing.

"Damn, the light's out up there."

They fumbled about in the dark with the keys—my God, I hope they haven't shot the chain! and burst through the door as if exploded out of a cannon. All the lights in the living room were on, the overhead globe, the lamps on the end tables, the floor lamp by the bookcase. The LP was still playing, the same LP replaying itself over and over.

Their children hadn't drunk the iodine or been carved up in cold blood. They had been left sitting quietly enough on the floor listening to a record and they had taken out of storage boxes and closets every construction set they had ever been given. Blocks and Lincoln logs, plastic panels and jointed rods, villages, farmyards. A highway layout complete with toll stations and service stations, bridges and overpasses, signs and signals. A primeval landscape of papier-mâché, furnished with rubber dinosaurs and ferns. Mister Potato Head. The floor was covered with what must have ended up in a squabble, a glorious smasharoo. And scattered over all in pastel snowflakes, the box of jigsaw puzzles Ted's wife, Gail, had brought them last Christmas, a marvel of art and fantasy and totally impossible for any child to put together. Robinson Crusoe's adventures on land and sea, fragmented forever.

He giant-stepped through the jumble and tiptoed into the narrow bedroom. The children had dutifully turned off the light here. They lay in the same cot curled together for mutual protection, bundled in sheet and blanket. He extricated Greg to deposit him in his cot. The child embraced him tightly with arms and legs. "Daddy?" "Yeah." "What happened to the dinosaurs, Daddy?" "Yeah." "Where did they go?"

He tucked the boy in, fast asleep, his hand lingering over head, shoulders, limbs, sturdy and tender, all the parts joined. The kids were getting too big for one bedroom.

He waded gingerly back through the living room, lifting his feet at the least crackle underfoot, to close the outer door to the hall. The Kochis television was going stronger than ever. Priscilla was in the kitchen alcove fixing his lunch sandwiches for tomorrow. A pot of coffee was bubbling on the gas range and she had a boxed coffeecake open on the table.

He turned down the volume of the record player and began picking up, separating out, making order of the chaos on the floor.

"We'll just go ahead with it, Mish." Priscilla, taking half a ham out of the refrigerator, spoke over her shoulder. "We'll have to watch Lucas like a hawk of course. And drop his girl friend, she has to be a stoolie."

She smeared mustard over bread, laid cheese on. "Of course
we still have Knowlton, she's a find. And we still have the building
representatives who weren't there tonight. As soon as we have
the letter ready we'll visit them with it. Try to catch them when
their husbands are home, brief them on what's up, consult with
them. Set up the house meetings. It may take a little longer
than we thought. But the important thing, it's in motion now. We
have to keep it moving. Keep up the momentum."

With knife sharpened till it whistled, she began slicing up ham,
mindless of her fingers. "Coffee's ready now. Come on in. Leave
that till later."

"Priscilla." He went into the kitchen and took cups and saucers
down from the shelf. She was longing for a little praise from him,
a little encouragement. He had no praise, no encouragement to
give her.

He forced himself to say it at last, out loud, in the open. "I
understand what you're up to and I appreciate it. But if you're
doing this for me . . ."

"For you?" She whirled about with her knife. In the close con-
fines of the kitchen he stood with the steaming coffeepot in his
hand and her knife pointed at him. "You think I'm in this for you?
This was all dreamed up for your benefit?"

Ferociously, cheeks scarlet, she denied it. How dared he place
such an interpretation on her actions? It was all pure and holy.
No gain, no advantage to be reaped.

"If I was looking for advantage . . ."

Go ahead say it. *Why would I have married you?*

She didn't say it. Heaving, flashing, biting her lip, she didn't
say it.

"Okay then," he said. "You're doing all right without me. Just
leave me out of it. Count me out."

"The hell I will! We need every man we can lay hands on. If
the women start doing this by themselves, the men'll find a million ways to sabotage it. You, you slumping there in your chair
all evening, everything we came up with, you torpedoed it with a
look. You could sit there through all the things that were said

there tonight and not *feel*. . . . All I'm asking is for you to go through the motions, take a hand. . . ."

He poured the coffee into their cups, passed hers to her end of the table black, added sugar and milk for himself. He was back in the locker room all over again. Only now he was spilling coffee over the rim of his cup, sprinkling sugar over the lip of the spoon onto the table, shaking evaporated milk out of the encrusted hole in the can in flying drops.

"It's licked before you start. You don't have the support behind you. You don't have the forces to swing it. No matter how much effort you pour in at this point, no matter how you take and run with it, no matter how close you come to making it, it'll be defeated. And defeat, don't let anybody ever tell you different, is defeat. It's not victory in disguise.

"That's my judgment of the situation."

He was talking to the wall. Priscilla lifted the coffeecake out of the box on its circle of cardboard and thumped it down on the brown enamel-top table, slashed through the raisined crust with her butcher knife. It was not a matter of the situation or his judgment. It was his attitude that was at issue. A lack of confidence, a failure of nerve, a compulsive retreat into negativism. The disabled veteran. Traumatized.

Your guts are cut out, you scoop them up and stuff them back in. The hill is higher, you climb it.

"Priscilla, you're living for something that's gone. Past. Over and done with. It WAS and it IS NO MORE!"

They drank their coffee and they munched their cake. The brown, ivy-bordered enamel table top rang tinnily with the bump of tableware. If what had brought them together to begin with— her ardor for a life beyond the personal and private, his involvement with the commonweal—was gone, what did they have left between them? Love? What's love? And if not love, then what?

"What are we supposed to do then, sit it out like everybody else? Sit back like the Kochises, all the rest of them, not lifting a finger to help themselves? Waiting for the day they can get out of here. The day that never comes."

Instantly he was everybody else, he was all the rest of them. At her note of condemnation—more the victim than the victims!—the tiny grain of resentment it never failed to evoke in him swelled like an abscess.

"After all, I'm not somebody who just wandered in here looking for a cause to play with," she said with the self-justification he always found so insufferable. "I'm not just someone who's here and gone. I am one of the inhabitants of this place. I've *identified*."

Identification!

Almost, almost he said it. *Who needs your identification! They need what you could have!*

Was that what he, her supreme identification, needed out of his marriage with her? If that was so . . .

He couldn't say to her that her identification with him, with them, with this way of life was a farce. Go back to your family, to your orderly house on Sherwood Heights, to your living room with the books and the bird prints, the chintzy bedroom. . . . Any more than she could say to him that he'd failed her. To say it was to make it so, to alter irreversibly what they were to each other.

They didn't need to say it. It was boiling over in them.

Identification, shit! A lot of good your identification . . .

Conk-out! Flop! I gave everything I had, I worked hand in glove with you, you were my work—and now you're nothing? Nothing!

The truth. The truth laid bare between them. There is only one hitch to a showdown with the truth. It may not be the truth. For the truth, the minute it's grasped . . .

"All right, you're so goddam objective," she said, growing leaner and keener, objective herself, pinpointing a grain of sugar on the table with her knife and propelling it in a straight line. "Let me ask you one thing. Just one little thing?"

All evening long she had been pushing at granite. Pushing him. Pushing Lucas. Pushing the women. Pushing the absentees. With an invincible resilience pushing and pushing. Pushing herself.

"Tell me this. Tell me just this one little thing." She brandished her knife at the window innocuously curtained in cotton trimmed with rickrack.

"Is there a dump out there? Or isn't there?"

He nodded. Beyond and above emotion, motives, attitudes, conflicts, the dump was there.

"Is it a problem or isn't it?"

He nodded. The problem was there. The problem was always there. A million problems.

"Then it is a good idea to try and find a solution to it? That's all I'm interested in. Tell me that. It is a good idea, isn't it?"

She swept her finger over the window sill, wiped by habit with the dishcloth when she did the dishes after dinner. Her finger came up blurred with soot.

"A good and necessary and inevitable idea?" Her tone softened, entreating him.

"Sure it's a good idea." He took the coffeepot from the stove again and refilled their cups. "A great idea. A stroke of genius. Anybody can have a good idea. The trick is to execute it."

He thought she was going to throw the cup of scalding coffee at him. She looked at him wildly with her hair askew like Mrs. Leggett's over her eye, her fair face flooded with red, open-mouthed.

"Priscilla, this is cuckoo. Right now I couldn't move ten people in this project. We're on ice—"

"Where are you going, Mish?"

Carefully she emptied her coffee into the sink. With an expression of violence unappeased, savagery seeking satisfaction, a gloating glimmer of a grin she hurled the cup at him. It smashed against the wall.

"What's going to become of you!"

Appalled as if she'd shot a gun at him, she backed away from him, backed out of the kitchen. She fled through the living room over crunching plastic, slammed shut their bedroom door.

Under the dull gray light of the dull gray globe overhead he sat in a stupor over his coffee. Under his hand the table was coated with invisible motes of soot.

The record spun out its thread of light irony, nasal, insinuating, winding about him. Weekend before last they had driven down to

New York with Mariuch to see *The Threepenny Opera*—Mari had seen it four times—and gone on to the Village Vanguard afterward. Stayed over with his sister Irene in Brooklyn. They were happy then.

Who gets the children? Who keeps the furniture?

After a while he pulled himself up and moved with his cold coffee into the living room and bent over his task. Picking up. Sorting out. Picking up. Sorting out.

THREE

A Matter of Family and Friends

I

No, he said to her. No, he was not going to take on the housing authority, the city fathers, or Rod Kearnsey—her bugbear—the ten-term mayor of Shoreham.

No, he said to Ewell, Roscoe, Bostic. No, he was not going to take on Nick Colangelo and the EWIU, AFL-CIO. Nick, his nemesis, the little gray man who had been a nobody, a nothing, slipping and sliding into any crevice, until all of a sudden he wasn't so little and he wasn't so gray. A gladhander with a barrelhouse voice that bounced off the walls of the big barn of a union hall.

No, he was not going to take on Grover Coffin of United Vacuum, whose star had ascended with his and had extinguished his. Coffin, UV's labor brain, his antagonist and partner. "Now you and I, Lunin, we understand. . . ."

Go through the motions? Go from take-a-hand to take-in-hand? No. Nothing doing. Not again. No.

His no, she thought, they thought, was weakness. His no, he thought, was his strength.

Because it wasn't there. The movement wasn't there. When it's there you see it in the faces around you. You feel the thud of it in your fingertips. When the movement starts, personalities, backgrounds, relationships, purposes, none of it matters: people are seized up and swept into an amalgam that rolls like a tidal wave over the landscape, transforming its contours. Personal hangups, connivings, it all flows together. The whole is greater than the sum of its parts. Even though in the end the movement may stand or fall by the character of the amalgam: the personalities, relationships, backgrounds, purposes that made it up.

The movement wasn't there. Dissatisfaction. A few stirrings. That was all. There is a tide in the affairs of men, and an ebb tide.

When it's there, like love, you know it.

Methodically, concentrating with a rigor that excluded misery, he distributed the pieces of various sets on the floor in piles according to affiliation. Reaching out from his seat on the sofa in widening arcs until he had to go down on his knees to pry under the bookcases, scrape out from under the record cabinet, nudge over the easy chair, lift up corners of the rug. Searching out, extracting, shuffling together. Jigsaw scraps of Robinson Crusoe's bearded puss that might or might not fit into any one of six different puzzle frames. Where the hell did the frog come from? The red cam wheel? Was the farmyard ever complete or was it one of Priscilla's school-fair prizes? Turning everything over for a barn roof that wasn't anywhere.

Tenderly—to music saccharine, satiric—Mack the Knife and Polly parted.

He looked for logic, pattern, function in what was apparently disparate. He sought out guidelines, focal points around which to cohere the scattered. If he had to believe that this was a hopeless tangle, that these fragments were all random, a collection of broken connections, that it didn't matter a damn whether he allocated them in the right piles or not, whether he deposited them in the boxes and string bags where they belonged or not, it would have been enough to send him climbing up the walls. There had to be a basic design. There had to be main and subsidiary junctures. There had to be highlights, accents, clues to missing parts. He looked for the shape. The shape.

Suavely—to music nostalgic, derisive—Mack the Knife and Jenny danced.

A tenant meeting in a hooker's pad. It was a laugh; why didn't they have the sense to laugh it off? Instead they were caught in a flare-up (like the dump sometimes, can after can inexplicably exploding) of hostilities contained over the years. The strike was their courtship. The union was the substance of their marriage. She was married to a situation that no longer existed, a perspective that was no longer possible and a man that he, perhaps, no longer was. Mish and Pris. Pris and Mish. Where the coffee was always hot, the beer was always cold and the spaghetti would always stretch. She thought it would go on forever.

He raked the blues and greens and tawny browns of the Robinson Crusoe puzzles into one central heap and arranged the cardboard frames in a semicircle around him. Reinforced with a shot of rye, he applied himself. Leave it to the kids? Helter-skelter into box and bag, never to be unscrambled. Leave it to Priscilla? Let her walk in on this tomorrow? Give her that much edge on him? Slam-bang into box and bag. . . . It had to be straightened out. Now or never. Do or die. Does it fit? Will it function? This was his talent and his limitation.

With obsessive urgency he sifted through.

Shipwreck.

Shelter.

Goatyard and cornfield.

Footstep in the sand.

Battle.

Rescue.

How long? How many years?

He did not however go back into the kitchen to sweep up the cup Priscilla had thrown at him. She smashed it. Let it lay.

2

He knew right away, right from the beginning, that she was a girl he had to land in bed with or a fight to the finish. "Are you the picket captain?"

In windbreaker and jeans, her hair afly, so sure of herself, hip to it all at no personal cost.

It was early January 1946, eight months after he'd come back from the war. On a Saturday afternoon, the shag end of the week, just a few hours to go, the mass picket line down to stragglers strung out for blocks before the massive battlefront of brick buildings. A raw wind blew from the bay through the vacant lots across the street spitting grit and every now and then a spatter of sleet. He had his mackinaw collar up over his ears and his lumberman's cap down over his eyes and to counteract the monotony he was trying to read a book held between his gloved hands as he marched.

Priscilla buttonholed him, demanding picket signs for the student friends she had brought with her, handbills for them to pass out, locations to be assigned in the line. He snapped his book shut and shoved it into his pocket, irritated with her, the kind of irritation that plucks at ego and genitals, win her or wipe her out. She adjusted her guitar strap over her shoulder and from the instrument, slung like a dead bird across her bosom, plucked a few chords. She eyed him with bright expectation.

"Wouldn't you like to sing?"

As if they never sang. Song sheets were stacked up in cartons at strike headquarters before the mimeograph ink was dry on them. Song leaders dished it out like hot soup on the line. But nobody was singing this afternoon. The pickets were interested in one thing only. Getting home.

Then Priscilla spotted the young chicks, who had been on picket duty all week, making a beeline from the picket line to the bus line, and she blew a gasket.

"Well I like that." She had come here to pitch in, not to pinch-hit. "Where are they off to?"

He blew too.

"When do you think they do their duds?"

With disarming humility, a deference toward him that both flattered and offended him, she stuck her hand out.

"Give us a chance, huh?"

Her apologies rendered, good cheer restored, she fell into step beside him and, strumming, looked about for the excitement from which to take fire. The strike, a nationwide strike against United Vacuum, was one of a series of postwar strikes that had broken out in the major industries of the country, steel, auto, electrical, the largest strikes ever held by workingmen anywhere at any time in history.

Multiple-paned windows loomed over them, blackly blank, plastered with huge X's of tape. Police cars clustered at the gates: scuffles every other week or so over how many pickets, how far apart, how many feet from the plant. Picket signs jogged along, tall above their bearers. FORCED Strike means FORCED Slump . . . OUR Blood UV Profits . . . UV CAN PAY A DEUCE MORE A DAY . . . UP 25¢ an HOUR for WOMAN POWER . . . Living COSTS . . . LOCAL 317 . . . LOCAL 3 . . . LOCA . . . LOC . . .

Up and down they plodded, back and forth over a sidewalk humped and fissured, crumbling under their feet.

Priscilla let out a deep breath, turned a dazzling smile on him. "Isn't this great? God, what an experience!"

She struck up her jangle of chords and lifting her toneless tune, her voiceless voice, with an exuberance so genuine who could resist her, she put it on the ground, spread it all around, made your flowers grow-ow-ow.

She lighted up a dismal afternoon.

3

They stashed her guitar in her car and adjourned from the picket line to a steamy little coffeepot down the street to warm up. The red-topped counter in front was crowded and the red-topped tables in back were all taken except one right under the red jukebox. They jammed themselves in. Bebop blared.

Over the smeared-off red square of table top they leaned toward each other in order to hear and be heard. Under the table, planted on its iron pedestal in the floor, their legs met knee to knee. Amid the bustle, the noise, the reek of unwashed pop bottles piling up in damp wooden cases stacked in the rear and the acid vapor of coffee boiled all day in the urns, their table was an island. It was Eden. The bread they broke together was stale cheese Danish.

The vibration of disturbance between them became palpable as a charged field. Polarized, magnetized, in every particle of themselves compelled to fusion, they leaned toward each other and talked.

He was badly in need of a girl. He had lived through the war on the hope of marrying Elisabeth Kallen, a girl who used to live with her family downstairs from his family, in the second-floor back on Liscomb Street. He would go back to high school to pick up the credits he needed for college, then go to the university upstate on the GI Bill, catch up in his education with Elisabeth and somehow or other in the process of it marry her. A fantasy if ever there was one. He picked up the pay phone in the PX at Devens the day after disembarkation, shortly after V-E Day, and called Elisabeth at the *Atlantic Monthly* in Boston. With a weekend pass in his pocket. "Mish, how lucky!" she said. "Come right away. If you'd called tomorrow, I wouldn't be here." He helped her pack and rode down with her to Washington in the crowded troop train, both of them standing all the way, and yielded her up in the station to her husband, a lieutenant commander in the Navy.

He arrived home in Shoreham to find his mother in the last stages of an illness that taxed human endurance and his family at each other's throats. His older brother, Petey, had moved in with his teen-aged wife, Peg, and their baby. His beautiful sister, Irene, how beautiful she was he had never noticed before, was killing herself between her job and Mom and feuding with Peg over the pots Peg never washed clean enough to suit her. His baby sister, Jennie, was growing into a holy terror, sassing teachers, pulling the tablecloth off the table with the dishes on it in unaccountable fits of temper. And Pop—they all laughed in despair over Pop and wept with hilarity. Sunk in hypochondriac gloom, Pop read all Mom's symptoms into himself, followed her diet and would have injected her insulin into himself at the same time if he hadn't been afraid that it was really morphine. As for his mother, the flirt, the scold, that poor lump of a woman in the bedroom, when he went in and kissed her on the cheek, he who had been spared and she the disabled one, she whispered to him with a breath that smelled faintly of nail polish remover, "Mish, I been waiting for you." Then commanded him, "Mish, look at me. Don't turn your face away. I lost one leg. They gonna take the other. It's no use. The doctor he only wants his money. Mish, do me a favor. Find out where they keep my sleeping pills and give them to me?"

All this in four small rooms. Elisabeth Kallen didn't last five minutes after he reached home.

He should never have stayed over the first night. Before he understood what was happening, they had his old cot made up for him in the kitchen and he was forced to assure them that of course they had room for him here, of course they weren't squeezing him out. Jeanette got him aside and wept on his shoulder. She wanted her shepherd dog Gary back, she couldn't live without Gary who'd been shipped off to Aunt Luba's chicken farm in the country the minute Mom fell sick. Irene got him aside and pleaded with him, "Get Pete and that bitch of his out of here. They're taking Pop for every cent he has." Peg, flinging her youth at Irene the incipient spinster, snaked him off into a corner. "Petey will never grow up," she confided to him, "till he leaves this family. If somebody has to be the prop to him, at least let it be me. You know what he does? Kicks me out of bed every morning. 'Go take care of my mother.' Well I didn't get married and have a gorgeous baby just for that." Pop took him out into the hall and spilled his troubles. "You got to get Irene away from here. You see, she fixed up the parlor last year to make it nice for her friends to come to, and now when Peg diapers the baby on the couch . . . Peg does things for Mom I could never ask Irene, she doesn't have the stomach for it." Pop preferred Peg the lightweight to

Irene whose thwarted yearnings were a shame and a humiliation to him.

Lying in his old cot in the kitchen between the copper cylinder of the boiler and the white cube of the gas range, blinking up at the blue glimmers cast by the pilot light, he could hardly breathe. The air was poisoned. Gangrene swelled through his veins. A serpent had slithered up out of the sea and was coiling itself tighter and tighter about them all.

He should never have stayed the summer. Irene spent her vacation in Brooklyn renewing acquaintance with an old boy friend who worked in the post office. Petey decided to transfer with Helioglund Aircraft to Texas. Jennie went to live with Aunt Luba in the country. When the last of the family had cleared out with their tears and their tensions, when Petey had disappeared down Liscomb Street, wife, baby and baggage, in the secondhand Studebaker bought on Pop's credit, when the house was quiet at last, he sat with Pop in the kitchen over a glass of tea.

"You have a companion?" Pop shyly-slyly asked him.

He was outraged. At the implication that the family exodus had been engineered by him so he could remain in possession, bring sweetheart or wife here to share the place with him.

"They sucked you in," Pop slyly-shyly suggested two minutes later, taking the opposite tack.

He was enraged. At the implication that he'd been conned into taking over, that he could be conned.

Left with his father to see his mother through to the end, he returned for the interim to his old job at United Vacuum. A widow from down the street looked after her during the day and he spelled Pop nights. The end came and went and he was still at United Vacuum.

"Nobody is ever trapped by anybody else," he said to Priscilla over the little red square of table top. "You're trapped in your own debris. You start spitting out thread like an insect and before you know it you've woven yourself into such a cocoon . . . All I did was go back to my old job for the summer. And I was caught."

"Caught? How?"

"Obligations multiplying from one day to the next. Commitments . . . The warworkers were being laid off, some of them shop stewards. The GIs were being rehired in their place, sometimes at lower pay. The company was claiming superseniority for veterans and naturally the veterans sided with the company. Patriotism first. It blew up a storm in the union."

"What did you do? How did you handle it?"

The union, the job and the union, it was what she craved to know, the hard fact and the inside track, with an eagerness that puzzled him. Other girls listened to such stuff with a tin ear, their eyes glazed over, they changed the subject.

"Well, I was the man in the middle."

He drew up the salt shaker on one side of their cups and the pepper shaker on the other side.

"Here we were all fighting each other to no one's benefit but the company's. So I suggested at a meeting that we form a committee to thrash it out. Never make a suggestion. All of a sudden I was chairman of a six-man committee with the whole dispute dumped in our laps."

"And?"

"On the one hand I had to agree with the idealists." He twirled the salt shaker toward her. "The issue wasn't one of superseniority for veterans versus layoffs for warworkers. It was enough jobs for everybody. If UV couldn't provide it, then let Uncle Sam step in.

"On the other hand"—he twirled the pepper shaker toward her —"I had to agree with the realists. That that wasn't the way it was going to pan out."

"How did you resolve it? Two irreconcilables. Or was it four? Or more?"

"Couldn't. We had to come up with a formulation that would unite as many people as possible without fully satisfying any of them. On the one hand I was running to the GIs"—he retrieved the salt shaker—"trying to persuade them to reject superseniority as a company plot to split the union. On the other hand I was running to the warworkers"—he retrieved the pepper shaker—

"trying to persuade them to support accumulated seniority for GIs, time worked with the company to include time spent in the service. And once that was unenthusiastically accepted . . ."

He restored salt and pepper to their place by the napkin holder and trotted forth the sugar shaker.

". . . we tried to steer the conflicting parties into areas of common concern. In general, we launched a drive for increased severance pay and unemployment compensation. In particular, we opened fire on day-to-day issues. Hitting speed-up incidents. 'Hyatt (Hotshot) Lovett guns down Purple Heart vet Bill Orr with gunned-up Grid Wire schedule'—that sort of thing. Instead of UV using GIs against the union, the GIs started piling grievances on UV."

"Yuh? Yuh?"

"That's it."

"That's all?"

"Well, not quite," he admitted. "The Ad Hoc Committee on GI Status gave birth to a permanent Veterans Affairs Committee. Then Bob Ucchini seeing that I was single and unencumbered and therefore presumably crazy enough to run my ass off promoted me to the Legislative Committee. Jesus, Joseph and Mary! Another bind."

Pepper and salt back into service.

"V-J Day. The fruits of victory. Pink slips flying all over the lot. Rumors flying, the work force is about to be cut in half. This in spite of an almost limitless backlog of consumer orders. In the middle of a boom we're having a bust. According to the company, reconversion to peacetime production is being slowed down by a shortage of machine tools. According to the union, the company is deliberately curtailing production in order to bring about repeal of Federal price controls. From there we all start fighting among ourselves. Half our membership accuses the union leadership of causing unemployment by their stand on price controls. And the other half . . ."

"You sure you want to hear all this?"

"Yes, yes. Go on."

Flutter of whitish eyelashes. Cheeks resting intently between knuckled hands.

"You writing a paper or something?"

"God forbid. Go on. What happened?"

"It's still happening."

In her eyes, the humdrum glowed. The ordinary was exalted.

"Half our Legislative Committee was agreeing with the editorials in UV Highlights, the company paper. Prices should be determined by a law older than Congress, as old as commerce among men. The Law of Supply and Demand."

She accepted the pepper from him (those shady realists).

"And the other half"—the salt (those pure idealists)—"was agreeing with the editorials in Lights On!, our union paper. Price controls must be retained, reduce the profit margin!

"The yelling and screaming that went on. Stalin got into the act. State power. The whole deal. The anti-price controllers were ready to kick Ucchini out of the presidency. 'Get rid of the Red gang!' And Ucchini was giving it right back to them. 'UV, those sons of bitches, they've made billions out of the war with their cost-plus from the government. While we were stuck with the wage freeze and the no-strike pledge. The head office is plastered with V-plaques from the Army, the Navy and the Air Force that you earned and you want to promote their prices and their profits?'

"Charges. Countercharges. Chairs were flying."

"And you? Where do you stand?"

"In the middle."

Salt and pepper. Moves and countermoves. A life-and-death clash.

On the one hand he was with the union leadership. Keep price controls, cut profits. On the other hand he was with the opposition. They knew and he knew that that was not the way it was going to pan out.

"We asked an expert from the international to come in and conduct classes on wages and prices. Everybody's educated now on the wage-price spiral. Take the lid off prices, wages never catch up. If we let go now, when will it end?"

Salt and pepper were retired to the wings.

"Still you meet a member on the street and he buttonholes you. 'What do I care if I have to pay two bucks more for a radio? If I can just lay hands on one! Better legally over the table than black market. Right?' "

Sugar commanded stage center.

"Right now," he said gloomily to the girl who, so fresh and fair, so frank and free, regarded him with a kind of enraptured amazement, "in the middle of a strike, in the middle of the winter, I have to round up six busloads to Washington next week, with 'Save Price Controls!' plastered on one side of the bus and 'End the Wage Freeze!' plastered on the other. And if you can reconcile those two, you're a hell of a lot smarter than most other people."

"But UV can well afford—"

In her earnestness she sprang hotly to the cause. Catching herself, raking nervous fingers through rumpled forelocks, she peeped at him from under her hand.

"I like your mouth," she said. "Those kooky little quirks." Delicately she touched the corners of his mouth.

He ordered more coffee. His words blurred, dragged.

"I—I was planning to go back to school last fall, pick up the credits I need to apply for the university. Maybe after this strike . . ."

"What for?" She was horrified. "What can they teach you that you don't already know? You—you're what it's all about!"

Music throbbed, horns and drums. Their slightest gestures became weighted. His fingers thickened on the glass sugar shaker. Hairs stirred up his arms. Her fair, almost shaggy eyebrows crinkled. Her short, straight, whitish eyelashes lowered. Her cheeks, overheated, reddened under the faint sheen of freckles and down.

For any of the men sitting up at the front counter the next move would have been obvious. Excuse me a minute. Into the phone booth to arrange with a friend. Then to ease her toward it.

Let's get outa here. The male plug into the female socket, the connection is made, the current is on.

"What's your last name?" he asked her. Rising from bed after a night of love you ask that. "I didn't quite catch it."

"I am Joe Barth's daughter," Priscilla said.

She said it with a lift of pride, sure of recognition. With male brusqueness as if to tone down pride, she stuck a cigarette into the corner of her mouth. With male bravado, I know the score, she waved her match out, and with a male compression of her mouth took a long drag. Above, her blue eyes glistening begged understanding.

Joe Barth's daughter! It made her at once more and less accessible to him. She was no raw kid out on a jaunt in rebellion against her family background. She was living up to her background.

Joe Barth was a legend in Shoreham. Idol of his father's generation, the immigrant poor, to whom he represented a radicalism older than theirs, as old, they believed, as America itself.

"Joe and Flo. Flo and Joe. They were always there," she said with a masculine tap of her cigarette as if to tamp down her overweening pride and pleasure·in them. "In it," she added and threw her head back taking the long view of them, critical of them as if to forestall an unspoken criticism of his, "but not of it."

In it but not of it.

"They went everywhere there for a while and everywhere they went they took my brother Ted." Flashing with pleasure and pride in him. "But me, I was so much younger, a nuisance." Abysmally abject, mourning some long-ago lack in her herself. "They had to leave me with this aunt that I loathed. Kicking and screaming at the door."

Kicking and screaming at the door.

Awkwardly Priscilla pulled herself up out of her cramped seat, tucked shirt, over flickers of taut flesh, into jeans.

"Where's the john?"

He thought she was the straightest person he had ever met.

She disappeared through the curtain between the cases of empties in back. He shut himself into the telephone booth up front and called Betty Kimmel to cancel their date for the evening. Betty was always assuring him that she and her husband were about to break up. Only they could never bring themselves, because of the housing shortage, to give up the apartment they shared. Betty was not the girl he so badly needed.

"How about later?" Betty said.

"No," he said recklessly and, hanging up, experienced for a moment there in the booth the most intense regret for the loss of those hours with Betty peacefully floating in a vacuum.

When he stepped out of the booth, Priscilla was back at their table gaily gabbing away with one of the men from the counter.

He was furious. She couldn't tell one from the other. Giving everybody the come-on. Afternoon of a slummer.

He contemplated slamming out the front door into the street and charged back down the aisle furious enough to haul the man up and hurl him to the floor.

"I hope I'm not intruding," the man said and with a flourish of his coffee cup yielded up his seat to him. Then he reached for one of the wooden cases, upended it under him and sat down between them at their table. "Mind if I join you?"

Get lost!

An inoffensive little guy he had trouble placing, vaguely recalling him from occasional Veterans Committee meetings. Nick Colangelo, a spray painter in 5-G, usually in spattered coveralls or, as now outside the plant, in some grayish-brown outfit under his Eisenhower jacket, all tones of grayish-brown or brownish-gray. An oldish young man or a youngish older man—it was years before he recognized that Nick's hair, combed up in a crest over his brow, was not gray at all but rich brown and that his complexion was not pale as putty but rugged tan. He saw Nick as slight of build, a meagerness about him that might have been due to the hang of clothes become cheesy after the sizing had been washed out of them or to childhood malnutrition. He didn't see Nick or think of him as husky. Maybe Nick developed muscle during the time of their acquaintance. Maybe he was muscular all along.

"You're sure I'm not butting in?" Nick said to both of them, addressing Priscilla, his burring bass voice reduced to a purr. "As I was saying to the young lady here, what's all this fusses with buses?"

The other counter sitters spotting the pretty girl Lunin had cornered and sizing up the situation drifted down with their hamburgers and coffee.

"What's all this fusses with buses?" Nick repeated without raising his voice.

They gathered in close to hear Nick. It was a pleasing voice resonant of depths in reserve, intimating warmth, understanding, very *simpatico*.

"Riding to Washington and back in one day. Knocking ourselves out. Wasting the money out of our treasury. For what? Hold the price line! My grocer ain't got salt on his shelves. Salt! Let them hike up the price and we'll be flooded with salt. I give it a year. A surplus of goods, the prices'll fall back to where they are now. Lower."

Tipping back on his box, addressing Priscilla, Nick regaled them all with the ABCs of economics. Very impressive.

"With our industrial capacity expanded by the war, in no time at all our inventories will start accumulating faster than the customer can buy. Everybody'll be competing for your buck. Just leave it up to the operation of the free market. It all evens out in the end."

Very sharp. Well put. Nick took every lesson learned in the union hall and turned it into its opposite.

"Yeah." He scrutinized Nick over his coffee cup: a married man with three kids horning in on another man's girl? the pundit preening his ego? what?

"We already been through that one," he said to Nick. "It was called The Great Depression."

At the height of the ensuing polemics, Bob Ucchini the union president blew into the coffeepot on a gust of wind, with Gavin the international rep trailing him.

"Say, Lunin."

With his seaman's beanie on the back of his prematurely white head and his navy pea jacket swinging like a cape from his shoulders, Bob descended on his table, the crowd parting for him. Bob came on like a pirate, a gypsy, with the face of a sagacious gnome and the élan of a bandit, a diamond-chip sparkle in his anthracite eyes.

"We got to push the buses. The hearing's been moved up."

Priscilla rose to her feet in awe as he introduced Bob to her.

"Bob Ucchini. My God. All this in one afternoon."

And to Gavin, the scarred veteran of organizing drives in the South, "Not *the* Frank Gavin?"

She rushed off with him in their wake, Nick left behind, forgotten. That was where the mistake with Nick Colangelo was made. He was ignored. Why all the fusses with buses? It rang down the years. Why all the frenzy of effort over matters that in no time at all vanished without a trace.

"Wait till my brother Ted hears about this," Priscilla crowed. "He's dying for contact."

He had to leave Priscilla in the vestibule of the union hall while he went inside to an emergency meeting, everybody looking daggers at her: no one admitted without a union card, no camp followers! When he came out she was setting up a system for screening volunteers.

They had supper with the Ucchinis. Mari, called Mariuch, to distinguish her from all the other Marias in the plant, had been his sister Irene's closest friend when they worked in blouses together and she was Mari Salvaggio, called Marisal to distinguish her from all the other Marias around.

"Sing for her," Mari urged him. "Sing your father's song for her."

"Sing it," Bob ordered him and began singing it himself in Russian.

A song Pop half-hummed, half-crooned while he tinkered with the engine of his Chevy, a song as melancholy and tender and deep as night on the steppes.

Bob tried it on his piano, a full Tchaikowsky symphony.

Priscilla tried it on her guitar, chords.

"Go on. Sing it."

He sang it to her in translation, uncertain of the words, leaning toward her over the ledge of the piano, a song as lost as the wind in the grass of the steppes.

> I love a girl
> In a little town
> Where is the girl I love
> Where is the town?
>
> Where is the street?
> Where is the house?
> Where is the girl
> That I love?

They went to the Bus Benefit Dance afterward in a barren upstairs hall downtown. He twirled her to jive. Skipped her through polkas. Holding her from behind, left hand clasped over her hand on her hip, right arm extended with hers, he glided her through a slow czardas. They joined a conga line or was it the kola? Doseydoed.

By midnight he was so high, in the middle of the dance floor in the middle of a circling ring he was flinging out from his haunches a quite creditable kzatske, whirling, leaping, as good as his brother Petey, almost as good as Pop sometimes at a wedding celebration.

Higher. Higher. Higher.

Hai!

4

It was all there, right there in that first encounter between them. He with his hard-nosed matter-of-factness, mistrustful of her good intentions. She with her spontaneity, her sincerity, ready to plunge into any crusade she could believe in. She romanticized the humdrum and that antagonized him. She glorified the ordinary and that attracted him. He was irritated, antagonized, attracted, drawn to her by his very resistance.

They walked the picket line with a vibration of disturbance between them. He was there because he had to be there, it was his function to be there. She was there, like an adoptive parent, because she wanted to be there. Out of curiosity? A sense of adventure? Generosity of spirit? He should have been grateful. He was suspicious.

That difference between them was to run through their marriage like a fault underseas in the earth's crust likely to produce at unexpected moments shiftings of rock, fractures and cleavages, earthquakes, volcanic upheavals.

> Gdye eta ulitsa?
> Gdye eta dom?
> Gdye eta barishnya
> Shto ya lyublyon?
>
> Zdyes eta ulitsa
> Zdyes eta dom
> Zdyes eta barishnya
> Shto ya lyublyon.

II

1

"The epitome of convention," Priscilla said, slowing her prewar roadster to a stop in front of her family house, apologizing for it. A pleasant Dutch colonial on a street of similar small colonials, stucco villas, of a kind built in Sherwood Heights during the twenties. The kind of a house that he and Irene and the Kallen kids would eye as they passed by on one of their exploring expeditions up from the harbor through the rising ridges of the city. "I choosey this one." "I'll havesy that one."

Gray-shingled and green-shuttered, lawned and hedged, cedars at the windows clipped to a point, a few brown leaves from the sprawling oak in the side yard scattered over snow-tinged grass. No neon-tubed storefronts, no zigzag stairways up through tiers of back porches, no scummy dishcloth in the sink. In the round-arched door, framed in a peaked-roof doorway, three slots of glass marched upward like ascending notes. He had known such doors before. Come in and stay out.

On the flagstone step Priscilla inserted her key in the lock over the tongued door handle. They scraped their feet off on the rubber mat and hung their coats behind the sliding panels of the closet inside, a place for everything. It was two days after the price-control cavalcade to Washington. He resented her bringing him here and putting him on the spot, though he would have resented it even more if she hadn't.

Priscilla dove ahead of him into the hall.

"Joe! Flo!"

She ran up the carpeted stairs toward whatever goes on in the upper story of such houses, disappeared around the angle of the landing. He was left alone in the lower hall. All the wood polished, dustless, the pride of some colored girl who had been coming in three days a week for years. On his right, a glimpse of mahogany dining table, bowl of flowers between candlesticks. He walked into the living room on his left. It extended from front to rear. Cross-beamed ceiling, a vista of cream-and-green prints, chairs comfortably arranged before the fireplace.

He inspected the bookshelves in the niche beyond the fireplace. Jacob Riis. Florence Kelley. Proceedings of the Hague Peace Conference vol. II (1907). On the shelf below a row of old friends. *The Jungle, The Pit, The Call of the Wild, The Harbor.* Steffens' *The Shame of the Cities, The Autobiography of.* . . . "You're going to the library," Boris Kallen, his father's friend who lived downstairs, would say, "I'll tell you what to bring back." Everybody should have a Boris in his life.

He began leafing through the Steffens looking for that old passage, the prostitute they watched through the window across the courtyard who accommodated ninety-seven clients, as he remembered it, in one night. The figure intrigued him. If you figure ten hours, allowing time for change-over and setup, that makes how many per hour?

Joe Barth surprised him with the book. He came in from chopping wood outside carrying an armload. Frosty air clung to the rough bark, to the wool flannel of his shirt, the gray-specked hair that fringed his bald dome.

"What're you reading?"

Crouching before the fireplace, bundling newspapers into a tapered roll, the lawyer at his manual task eyed the mechanic with book in hand.

Hastily he slid the book back into its slot in the shelf, a whole phase of his life with its illuminations and confusions.

"A little problem in piecework. Here let me . . ."

"No, no." Joe fended him off, not to be robbed of his prerogatives. "This chimney's a bitch." Poking his head into the dusky cavern of the fireplace, he waved his lighted taper up the chimney to warm it up. Withdrawing, he fed paper and wood chips into his up-whooshing fire.

"Instead of studying for her midyears in history, gov and ec, she went to Washington with you. Is that it?"

Accusation or statement?

"Try and stop her."

"I know," Joe said. "That's it."

Priscilla presented her mother and father to him with an air almost of anxiety for them, that they commit no bloopers. She presented him to them with an air almost of triumph, a real live specimen, straight from the horse's mouth. Elevation of the laboring classes. Liberation of the masses. Isn't that what it's all about?

She retired to a corner of the sofa and curled up against the cushions, bright eyes on the alert, to watch the show. They were testing him. She was testing them through him. Like a child bringing home to Mama and Daddy her accomplishment, deserving their approval, testing them with it: Are they going to keep their word? You said! You promised! Now here it is.

When they spoke she glanced at him: Aren't they wonderful? When he spoke she glanced at them: Isn't he great? In that language of enthusiasm he was becoming accustomed to.

They had the look, weathered yet unworn, of innocents enjoying their own innocence, of people who have been fighting windmills all their lives and have thrived on it.

Joe's chairside table was heaped with publications and briefs. Not so much union stuff as he once had handled. Civil liberties was his province, not negotiations. A habeas corpus for a CO who had allowed himself to be subjected to typhus experiments and then, after having been bitten by infected lice, had decided that that too was a contribution to war and had gone to jail where now, after the war, he was still incarcerated.

"What do you think of the prospects for maintenance of peace, Mr. Lunin? Is the labor movement at all concerned about it? Or will it join with industry and government in a drive against Communism?"

(What are your politics, young man?)

Flo busied herself about the cocktail table with glasses, very thin, and silver, thick, and embroidered napkins that shook out like handkerchiefs. As self-effacing as it is possible for a large-boned woman to be, she brushed by in her plain green dress, of a wool as soft as velvet, and deftly circumvented legs in her bulky cross-tied space shoes, and bestowed her smile, the beaming smile, under tightly combed-back wheaten hair, of a Chinese peasant. COs. Peace. Communism. Scattering explanatory murmurs, she supplemented Joe. A schoolteacher out of Minnesota, she had traveled east during the First World War to attend an anti-war conference and when she approached the young law-school graduate who addressed the socialist section he invited her up on the platform with him. She stood at Joe's elbow.

"Will you have sherry, Mr. Lunin? Or would you prefer, let's see, bourbon? scotch? rye?"

(Young man, what are your drinking habits?)

They plied him with their sherry and their little hot cheese things that melted in his mouth and their questions. How much influence did Bob Ucchini actually have in the EWIU? Were the Catholic trade unionists organizing an opposition faction? What was the reaction to UV's latest wage offer? How long would the strike last? He was the authority. The oracle. As if he could deliver the answer to them on their silver platter. Every once in a while they glanced at Priscilla with concern as if at a false move from them she would shatter like one of their goblets.

He returned the honors.

Fire snapped in the grate. Reflections glimmered in the framed bird prints hanging on the walls between the draped windows. A light snow was falling outside.

"On a Saturday afternoon in January 1919," he began, eying them for the effect, "a few years before I was born, a young man stood out on that step there—no, not that step, it must have been on Bancroft Avenue then—" Formidable houses with granite steps, wide porches, bay windows, turrets. "—and rang the bell. It was snowing hard. The trolleys weren't running. His sheepskin coat was covered with snow. When the young lawyer came to the door he didn't want to let him in at first. The lawyer's wife had just had a baby and she'd caught the flu and the doctor was upstairs with her and they didn't know whether they were going to be able to pull her through."

He told the story well. He'd heard it often enough.

How Joe Barth invited Pop in to have a cup of coffee with him and while the coffee was heating Pop told him what the crisis was. As the result of a series of paralyzing strikes, race riots, bombings, bank holdups the year before, Federal agents had swooped down in a single night on nests of suspected Bolsheviks across the nation and cleaned them out. The prisoners picked up at the Russian Workers Hall in the Bayside section of Shoreham were locked up in a storeroom in the post office basement. When Pop's friend Boris Kallen went down to the police station to inquire about them, he was arrested too. A postman leaked the word out to Pop. A mandolinist who had been rehearsing for the Russian Christmas Ball was manacled to the storeroom wall. There was a boy in there suffocating with asthma. And a woman, half-crazy, with six little children just landed in this country after a train journey across Siberia and six months in the Chinese refugee camps.

"Here are my keys to the Shoreham Bank Building," Joe Barth had instructed Pop. "Go into my office on the second floor and get my typewriter and bring it here."

The fire hissed, reflected in the birds on the wall and the snowy windows.

"And you are that man's son?" Joe stared at him for a long, crackling moment. "He covered my typewriter with his coat."

"And the forums," he said to Joe. "You remember your forums in the Unitarian church downtown about ten years ago?"

They all piled into Kallen's sedan and rode downtown to the forum where Joe Barth and his wife brought together emissaries of every persuasion from the outside world to debate the burning issues of the hour. From all over the city, from all the nationality enclaves and social strata the aspiring of mind converged on the forum, challenged the speakers from the floor and engaged afterward in hot debate, settling Hitler and the League of Nations, the CIO and the NAM, over paper cups of pale fruit punch. The forum was also a date mart. Marisal who was a fervent follower of Father Coughlin—social justice! he tells the truth!—met Bob Ucchini who was a passionate pro-Communist, historical materialism! the music of the spheres! Irene met . . .

"Remember the time you brought together William Z. Foster, Norman Thomas and the chairman of the Shoreham Chamber of Commerce?"

"And you were there?" Flo said to him, wonder-struck. "You were one of those people out there?"

Husband and wife gazed at each other in bafflement, caught between sentiment and irony.

"Well."

They gazed at each other, at him, at Priscilla curled up like a pixie in the corner of the sofa.

"Well."

All their chickens had come home to roost. He was in some degree their creation.

The subsurface tensions were cracking, slightly.

He had another one for them.

"I was coming home one evening with Petey from stealing coal on the railroad tracks."

Stealing?

"The dicks had been chasing us and we'd split, I had the coal. Three months in the reformatory."

Reformatory?

On Liscomb Street when a girl got into trouble, she was pregnant. When a boy got into trouble, he was having a run-in with the law.

"Petey ran up the bank. I ran through the yards. Over and under freight couplings. Right in the path of a locomotive. With this burlap potato sack. Into the gasworks. And the gas guards joined in."

"You weren't . . ."

"They didn't . . ."

Flo plucked her skirt over her knees, long strong legs smoothly clad in service hose. Joe brushed at the wood splinters still clinging to his well-cut corduroys. Priscilla's raw bare legs came out from under her skirt down firmly to the floor. Her hand flew to her cheek. She was with it. The burlap bag lumpy with stolen coal. The tingling fiber of burlap. The tang of its smell.

"Did they—nab you?"

He was tempted to say yes. To be the victim, the hero. Arrested. Tried. Jailed. To draw on her pity with his pain. Which came first with her, pain or pity? Did her pity require another's pain? Or did pain, wherever it occurred, require her pity?

An appetite for horror in disguise? The need to create a sensation?

That was an aspect of it.

"We wound up at the corner of Liscomb and Stone," he said. "Front of Mroz's Cash & Carry, just across the street from home. In a crowd surrounded by police. You were up on the back of a pickup truck," he said to Joe and Flo, "and you had your boy with you, not much older than we were, passing out handbills. We stood there like fools with our coal and listened to you tell off the police. Denounce the Democrats for stealing the city blind and the Republicans for bankrupting it."

Rod Kearnsey, perpetual Independent Labor candidate—this time for mayor, was their man.

"You said Kearnsey would open up the coal depots. Take ownership of the gas and electricity. Reopen the factories."

There was a prolonged silence. He had touched a nerve.

Flo went about the room turning on lamps. Joe prodded at a log in the fire. It tumbled off the grate with a shower of sparks. He pried it up, giving it leverage.

"You know what Fred Eckstrom used to say," Flo said at last. "Fred and I wrote all Rod's campaign material for him in Joe's office. 'I wonder,' Fred used to say, 'if Roderick will ever understand what this is all about?' "

"Looks like he never found out," Priscilla said with asperity.

She sprang up from the sofa, spilling napkin and crumbs, and began knocking things together on the tray.

"At last they had it, the great labor candidate! Champion of the forgotten man—"

"Now, Priscilla."

"Now Rod Kearnsey is mayor of Shoreham and Joe Barth—"

"Priscilla!"

He had an inkling then, an inkling that never hardened into certainty, that under Priscilla's spontaneity, her impulsiveness, her flaming altruism, lurked a spark of fierce ambition. An ambition she would have denied, aghast, oh no, never! Joe Barth might have acquired wealth if he had chosen to devote his energies to that end. He might have acquired, more important than wealth, importance. Instead he had dedicated himself to certain principles and to the candidate, out of the carpenter's union, who apparently personified those principles.

Was it possible, he speculated for the merest instant, that Priscilla was looking for another Roderick Kearnsey? The man of the people who would lead the people into some splendid tomorrow?

Hoping to succeed where her parents failed?

That was another aspect of it.

This sweet and simple girl. This glittering dangerous creature.

"Eckstrom?" he said to them. "Not the Eckstrom who used to work with my old man in Forge & Foundry? Both canned for signing up union members in the—can."

"That's Fred. Blacklisted out of every plant."

In a moment they were all laughing like old cronies, friends from the same hometown united by chance after years apart.

The tensions had melted away, not quite.

Joe recovering himself squared off, got his licks in.

"I promised you, did I, that Rod Kearnsey would take over the utilities? Reopen the factories?"

"You did."

"We went pretty far in those days. A lot farther than you'd go today?"

"Right."

"I didn't urge the crowd of you on the corner to go take it over yourselves?"

"No, sir, you did not."

"Well, I didn't go far enough."

Having rapped his knuckles with that one, Joe hauled up from his chair. "Come on upstairs, young fellow. I have something I want to show you."

They all trooped upstairs. Paused on the landing. Oval of a gentleman in winged collar, wispy hair parted in the middle, drooping handlebar mustache, eyes fixed on white and distant vistas.

"My father. A rootin'-tootin' revolutionary. Went barnstorming over the country with Debs. Every whistle stop was decked out in red to greet them."

Flo and Priscilla burst into laughter, sharing a family joke.

"We've been going rapidly downhill ever since."

Joe climbed ahead of him. "They were all so pure in those days. All so honest and trusting. Everything was so clear to them. My father was always off to Zurich, Brussels, The Hague, some international convocation that would unite humanity in peace and brotherhood, do away with the machinations of kings and capitalists. The great blow for him of course was the First World War. That workingmen would take up arms against workingmen."

The innocent eyes, not so innocent, glanced back, rested sidewise on him, the workingman. The betrayer. Rod Kearnsey, the carpenter who defaulted on his promise.

"In the end he was defrocked. For lying down, with more courage I must admit than I have, on a siding with three war resisters in front of Shoreham Firearms."

Priscilla and Flo burst into laughter, sharing the family joke.

"Beside them, you and I, Mish," Priscilla explained, "are just a couple of pikers."

"In here. My study. And my mother—"

"Oh, come on," Priscilla protested. "You've made your point."

"Not yet."

More bewhiskered gents, bone-collared ladies. More book-shelves, volumes of leather-backed cardboard files, white-stenciled on the orange backs. Over the massive oak desk, relic of another era, a copperplate engraving of the Shoreham waterfront: sailing ships and other vessels floating on little wavy lines against a motley collection of buildings in the background. An odor—when Mom entered a house she could always sniff it out, Yankees! An odor of women, she claimed, who didn't wash their corset covers often enough or clean out their cupboards. The odor of attics, old papers crumbling away in barrels, sun-warmth, dust.

When Joe removed the engraving from the wall, it left no light spot behind: everything kept in order here, regularly repainted and repaired.

"We came as coopers and wheelwrights," Joe said and traced a path back from the docks in the engraving, relishing the artisan role, a step up the social scale apparently rather than down in his estimation. "Located about here. Dropped the wheel hoops and spokes after a while and stayed with their barrel hoops and staves. The family never attained to any particular prominence but they were all outspoken."

He rehung the engraving and began scanning his bookshelves, stretching, stooping.

"Stuck their necks out. Skipping a generation here and there. Transcendentalists, abolitionists, anti-trusters, suffragettes. Couple of manic depressives, those too. Had an uncle used to plan utopian communities in his manic period and during his fits of depression we had to put him away. True believers. Disillusionment might give them pause, doubt never. Man might fail but ideas didn't. Good was good, evil was evil and where the two shaded into each other, steer clear, don't get fouled up. Naïve? Yes. Foolish? Often. And futile? Could be."

Joe found his volume, tightly wedged in, and inched it out. It did have a fur of dust on top and he whisked it off with his finger. Flo quick with a dustcloth out of a desk drawer, upset. "Doesn't

Ruby . . ." Always a Kathleen, a Helga, a Ruby. Joe unclasped the brass fastening of the marbleized cardboard file.

"Do-gooders they say nowadays do no good. Well, we've done what we wanted. We followed our lights as we saw them. Selflessness has been our self-indulgence. It's been our luxury and our vice."

Whether Joe was placing him at a remove, the object of the Barths' do-goodism, or taking him in, fellow toilers in their plaid shirts, he was not quite sure. The innocence at any rate had not been easily earned.

"There we are."

A splotchy newspaper clipping. Row of men in caps down over their eyes, coats down to their ankles. Strikers Part of Red Terrorist Gang.

"Recognize any of them?"

They were unrecognizable.

"Barucik, the mandolinist in the post office cell. Kallen . . . And here." Joe turned the tan pages, neatly dated on top. A lady in a flowerpot hat, fur choker. "The biggest Red in Shoreham. My wife. A charter member of the League of Women Voters." He searched again through his bookshelves. "Now where is it, what year? This is really a prize. It was all about to be carted off to the dump when we moved from the old house. And Flo—she spent months—"

Another newspaper clipping, the print too fine and too faded in spots to be readable. Flo supplied a magnifying glass from the desk drawer.

"Priscilla, don't sit off in the corner. Come here. See what you can make of this."

Priscilla peered through the glass. "It's an editorial, I guess. 'Communists have captured and turned to their purposes the powerful trade unions in the nation . . . in preparation for a great general strike . . . during which they will seize control of the country. . . .' My God. 'Property owners such as the Reverend Theodore C. Barth would do well to reflect . . .' Oh no. '. . . when encouraging agitators . . .' "

"The date," Joe said. "Look at the date."

"Shoreham *Clarion & Messenger*. I can't find . . ."

"Up there in the corner. Flo wrote it down."

"June 15, 1878? Look at this, Mish."

He read it over her shoulder.

He was cut down to size. Deflated. Robbed of his romance and originality. No rebel. No wild-eyed revolutionary. A moderate young fellow. The Barths had been through all this before.

At the head of the stairs Flo stopped them and brought a shoe box of loose snapshots out of Ted's room.

"I found these the other day. From before the war. Tucked away in that trunk they sent over from England."

Mother, father and daughter put their heads together. Ted on a boat trip up the Volga, faceless between Flo and Joe.

"We were devoured by bedbugs. Our camera was confiscated. But the Russians! Ted picked up the language overnight. Have you ever been to Russia"—Flo beamed about at him—"Michael?"

Ted on skis whipping down a white slope, his face lost behind sun goggles.

"Could have made the Olympic team. Only it was 1940 . . ."

Ted lean and easy in a dark suit, hand in pocket, before some sort of building, his face sun-struck, blurred by a light leak.

"He was at the London School of Economics for his postgraduate year when the war broke out. He stayed all through, a statistician for the Labour Party by day, hospital orderly nights. He's back now taking his Ph.D."

Ted was the hope of the family. It shone in them, quietly contained in Joe, confident in Flo, blazing in Priscilla.

"We think he's going to be the American Harold Laski."

There it might have ended. With a cordial invitation from Flo as they trooped back downstairs: "Why don't you bring the Ucchinis over some weekend night when Ted's home? He'll have someone down from faculty, I'm sure, and we'll have friends in."

If it hadn't been for the telephone. The telephone had been ringing for him off and on all afternoon. Bob was out of town at a district strike meeting. Ray Pelletier, Bob's second in command, hadn't shown up at headquarters. Mari was frantic, calling on Lunin at the Barths' for advice.

Taylor and Baylor, the self-constituted goon squad (otherwise known as the Education Committee, if you can't educate 'em one way, educate 'em another), had been overheard planning to overturn some cars tonight. The lab maintenance men were being sneaked in daily to service the sensitive equipment and they had to be stopped. Baylor and Taylor, supermilitants, rough stuff, that's what it takes? Or provocateurs, company stooges?

He got hold of Marty Rakocszi. "Track 'em down. Try all the taverns. Put Ed and Connie on it too."

With Priscilla hanging over his shoulder. "What is it? What's happening?"

Then Mari again. "It's Ray's wife, Yvonne. She's gone off her rocker. Her mother sent her eight hundred dollars four years ago to bank for her and they had to live on it. She blames Ray, when he was president he was spending out of his pocket. So she's been trying to deposit little by little ever since to make it up and now her mother's wired her for the money."

"Where's Ray?"

"Down with bursitis."

"Put them on emergency relief. That'll quiet her down a little."

And Priscilla: "What's the matter with Ray? Why isn't he . . ."

When they came downstairs, the telephone for him again.

"I got to get back there." He hustled into his mackinaw.

"We thought you might have dinner with us," Flo suggested. "Priscilla . . ."

"Priscilla." Joe took her in hand. "You have a paper to finish. Exams next week."

A bus trip to Washington singing all the way, bundling up through a freezing breakdown on the way back under buttoned-together coats—or midyear exams? Live it or read it. Be it or talk it.

She kissed her father and grabbed her windbreaker.

"Oh, history," she said. "History's a drag. Let's go."

In her pride and pleasure in them, in tacit obedience to them, in defiance of them, out of her own perverse necessity, Priscilla laid a trap for them with him. They side-stepped it. Rather than risk her rejection, the destruction of their integrity in her eyes, his eyes, their own, they went along with her. She tuned up her five-string guitar, listen to this! The free and equal blues.

Joe and Flo watched them from the peaked-roof doorway down the snow-thickened gravel path, through the snow-tufted hedges.

Priscilla fled with him down the path from the house, from those dry-as-dust clippings and letters preserved between the pages of files. They shut themselves up in her car and he drove around the corner to the next street and braked up in the snow-hazy blackness between streetlights. They put their arms around each other inside each other's jackets and kissed and clung, seeking themselves in each other.

Minutes later they strode into the union hall, a former church emptied of pews and filled now with a mad scramble of tables and folding chairs.

"Mish, we got to get wires out. That son of a bitch Taft just made a speech in the Senate against union monopoly. They're gonna slap a law on . . ."

More fusses with buses?

"Mish, we got to send a delegation down to the *Tribune*. You seen the job they done on us tonight . . ."

Red Cell Directs Strike Strategy.

A city hall demonstration next week. A new company drive to drive a wedge between production and maintenance workers, everyone in Maintenance would have to be visited. A night club celebrity would be on the picket line Monday, line up the sound trucks, radio stations . . .

They swarmed on him, and Priscilla with him. She loved it. She was in love with it. A visitor from outer space, ignited by the excitement around her, igniting it.

Aspects upon aspects. Countless aspects.

2

"Oh, to be in Zurich and not to climb the mountain!" Pop would reminisce. "Wasn't that a shame? I worked." It would be his epitaph.

Lev Lunin ran away from home when he was nine years old, after a row with his father over kissing the hand of a drunken priest. In Tula he worked in a samovar factory. In Zurich he worked in a foundry, stumbling each evening from the fiery forge into the fire of sunset on the snowy peaks. In Le Havre and Liverpool, he worked on the docks. On the S. S. Victoria he worked in the hold. In Pittsburgh, he worked. In Hibbing, Minnesota, he worked in the open-pit mines during the summer and all winter he worked in the woods and, when he stumbled out of the woods in the spring, he was so eaten up by crabs in his crotch if it wasn't for the blue ointment . . . In Idaho he worked in copper and in San Francisco on the hook. He gypsied across the continent with the boomers and wobblies and drifted back east to Shoreham to visit with Boris Kallen, his friend from the old country who had escaped with him over the border, and while he was staying with Boris he came down with pneumonia and was nursed by a girl from down the hall. So at the age of nineteen he settled in Shoreham. In Shoreham he worked in the foundry.

Wherever he went it was all the same thing. Hard work. Hard and bitter to make a living. Honest to live, hard to live. Who does the hard work, that's what it's all about no matter where you are.

Old country, new country it was the same thing. He trusted no government, no religion, no industrial or financial organization, no institution however benevolent. The world is run by piecards.

"All on my back!"

Priscilla and Pop never arrived at a common understanding. The two of them got off on the wrong foot to start with and they remained out of step, neither one of them ever willing to acknowledge it.

He had been reluctant to bring Priscilla up to the third-floor back on Liscomb Street. Not because he thought Priscilla and his father wouldn't get along. In fact, he thought they would. Pop, a confirmed pessimist in private, waxed genial in company; he bloomed with sociability: he liked a good time. As a matter of fact, he hoped that Pop would be impressed. Joe Barth's daughter. Underneath, he must have harbored a childish longing, the gnawing of a hunger never fulfilled, for the old man's approval.

His reluctance stemmed from the time, months before, when his father had shyly-slyly asked him over a glass of tea, "Do you have a companion?" Implying, as he interpreted it, that he had turned his brother and sisters out for the sake of a vacant bed. If he brought Priscilla home now and that should prove to be the outcome, then in Pop's logic, for all practical purposes it must have been his intention to begin with.

Nevertheless, on a Sunday afternoon when he had an errand in the neighborhood, no chance to hit the sack, he stopped at the house and took Priscilla up the zigzag of stairways through the back porches to his door.

The radio was playing a concert of light classics and Pop was stretched out on the couch replete with a dinner served him by the widow who had taken care of Mom. Pop was very popular with widows and ladies with husbands on their last legs who needed someone to drive them to and from lodge meetings, weddings and funerals. He never wanted for a good Sunday dinner. Even during the week after an exhausting day's labor, he was off like a grasshopper visiting around.

At the sight of Priscilla, Pop hastily pulled on his natty gray gabardine jacket with the black-bordered silk handkerchief overflowing from the pocket, and reknotted his not-so-somber tie. So this was the girl! Kindling up, all primed to play the gallant.

Priscilla leaned her canvas-enveloped guitar by the couch and said with surprise, "Oh, what a nice place you have here!"

Pop was immediately disconcerted. On the one hand: what did she expect, a garret? On the other hand: was she making fun of him, such a palace?

Knowing Pop, wincing with it, he tried calling Priscilla's attention to the framed Chinese tapestry over the buffet as justification for her amazement. People always noticed the tapestry and inquired about it: a length of green silk so finely embroidered it looked beaded; its figures, white-faced and white-stockinged, splendidly robed, enacting in three panels a story everyone invented for himself.

Priscilla gave the tapestry no more notice than if it had been the usual three-paneled mirror, ornately framed, extending over the heavy walnut, squat-legged buffet. Instead she tossed her gloves onto the buffet and without a second glance at the tapestry said to Pop, "Mr. Lunin, your son is a genius."

He caught Pop's umbrage at her indifference to the tapestry. What did she think it was, a Coney Island souvenir? Or did she think that such a work of art was too fancy for the likes of them?

Cheerfully, with eager interest, Priscilla pumped Pop's hand. "You're Russian, aren't you?"

Stiffly Pop allowed her to pump. He had arrived on these shores some forty years before. When his children brought a nationality questionnaire home from school to be filled out, he tore it up. Nobody has the right to ask you your nationality or your religion or your politics!

"*Govoryte po-russky?*" Priscilla said to Pop.

Impassively Pop removed her coat. He spoke English fluently, though with an accent of which he was unaware. (Also a smattering of Yiddish, Polish, German, French and Croat.) He read English, at least the newspapers. He even, he often boasted, thought and *dreamed* in English.

"*Ochen plocho,*" Pop answered her with a feeble attempt at a joke. "*Y vi?*"

"*Ochen chorosho,*" Priscilla said and burst into laughter with her own joke.

He had to intervene. "That's all she knows," he explained to his father. "She doesn't know any more."

"It won't stick," Priscilla confessed in a meek small voice. "I can't learn it."

Pop, unable to decide whether he had been more insulted by being asked whether he could speak his native tongue or by being told that she couldn't learn it, refused to crack a smile. But in an effort to smooth things over, he hurried into the kitchen and returned with a clutch of bananas and a bowl of walnuts. Pop the food spender could never buy just a half dozen bananas and Mom the food scrimper was always screaming the roof down over him because of it. "They'll be black before we eat them, you fool. The cupboard in this house will never be empty so long as there's a grocer anywhere to put one over on you." Now that she was gone there was no restraining Pop. A double claw of bananas. Pop twisted one off, the yellowest, and peeled it down halfway.

"Have a banana."

Pop thrust the fruit, amid its petals, at Priscilla: his first law of hospitality, the offer of food. Making amends.

"Oh, no, thank you. I couldn't." Priscilla drew back. Her hand splayed appealingly over her stomach. "I'm not hungry."

In high dudgeon Pop withdrew the banana and foisted it off on his son. Did he look like he was starving!

"You go on about your business, Mish," Priscilla smiled up at him. "Your father and I will make out just fine."

He had promised Anna Pogany on the strike-fund committee that he would pick up the contributions Mroz of the Cash & Carry had collected on the block. When he left, Priscilla was cozying up to Pop on the couch and Pop was cracking walnuts. The wrinkled walnut shells snapping between the jaws of the nutcracker and dropping with a clack into the glass bowl.

A simple little thing. Walk diagonally across the street to Mroz on the corner and pick up the kitty from him. As active as he was in the union he should have known better. Mroz was just opening up for his late Sunday afternoon trade and he had to take his Sunday papers outside first and attend his waiting customers; the beggar always comes last. Mroz was also having a little trouble with his oil heater—just a little adjustment, Mish, if you will—and a load of troubles with his son at school to get off his chest. Naturally it turned out that it was Pekar, the shoemaker in the next block, who now had the kitty. Pekar had put it together with the contributions he'd raised from the Hungarian People's Fraternal Order. At Pekar's, in the flat back of his shoemaking establishment, a family dinner was in progress. Pekar's son Kalman, now Carl, a high school classmate, was visiting with his bride and she had to be introduced with toasts in Tokay wine all around and a taste of the chicken paprikash with dumplings. Also, Julie had some potato salad she'd just made that she wanted to send over to Pop and a suitable container had to be found.

"You know what is the secret of good Hungarian potato salad?"

"No, what is the secret of good Hungarian potato salad?"

"Good potatoes. Ha ha."

When he climbed back up his stairs and opened his door, Priscilla, lounging up against the console radio, was playing her guitar for Pop on the couch and singing to him.

> When you go to Sevastopol
> On the way to Simferopol
> Just you stop a little farther down.

A bouncing lyric of collective farm life that was going the rounds. Aunt Natasha drives the tractor. Grandma runs the cream extractor.

> There's a little railroad depot
> Known quite well by all the people
> Called Zhankoye, Dzhan Dzhan Dzhan.

"Come on," Priscilla coaxed Pop. "Sing the chorus with me. It's an old Russian folk song."

Grmph grmph. Pop slid low on the couch in embarrassment.

> Hey Zhan
> Hey Zhankoye
> Hey Zhanvili
> Hey Zhankoye
> Zhan Zhan Zhan.

A joyous jangle of chords.

Hrsk hrsk. Strangulated throat scrapings.

He rushed Priscilla out of there as fast as he could.

"Awfully shy, isn't he?" Priscilla whispered to him as they galloped down the stairs.

He could never explain Pop to Priscilla any more than he could explain Priscilla to Pop. He tried.

"But I thought you said that he likes music. That he likes to sing."

He tried to explain to her that her song was neither old nor Russian nor folk. A paradise of husky Jewish farmers. Not permitted to farm in the old days, now look at 'em. Emancipated. Glorious.

"Of course. How stupid of me. Is he prejudiced against Jews?"

He tried to explain it to her. "Pop's oldest friend, they hid in a cellar together for two weeks in the first strike ever called in the city of Tula, they hid in a cemetery all one winter night waiting for the guard to pass on the border, they roomed together here, they went out with their girls . . ."

"What's the matter then? He's not ashamed of being foreign-born, is he? He shouldn't be ashamed," she said compassionately. "The Russians have as old a culture as we have. I'll bring him a book."

"No, he's not ashamed."

He tried to explain to her that with Pop one nation was as good or bad as another, no culture was superior or inferior. The only thing Pop ever gave Winston Churchill credit for was his proposal for a universal language. But why English? Why not Esperanto? Goulash? Alphabet soup?

"I think he's sweet," Priscilla pronounced her judgment on Pop and stuck to it.

Pop was a craggy old crab, a sour dour old misanthrope so convinced of the folly of all human emotion that he had never, he often proclaimed, kissed any of his children even in infancy. When he appeared at the widow's for dinner carrying cake, bread and two kinds of rolls, when he went miles out of his way to drive a couple home from a name-day feast, it was never in his view an act of solicitude. It was obligation. He would allow nothing, no airy-fairy sweetness, no gesture of tenderness or gratitude to dissipate his tragic sense, his acceptance of the way people are, an acceptance that festered in him like a narcotized wound.

After parting with Priscilla he returned home ostensibly to change his shirt for the evening, actually to have it out with Pop. Here I bring home a person so lovely, so openhearted and you, you slap her in the face.

Pop had taken off his suit in order to spare it, no more company was likely to appear, and wrapped his worn maroon bathrobe over union suit and socks, not undressing completely in case he might after all want to go out again. He was reading the Sunday paper and the loose sections fell in heaps about him: impossible ever to reassemble a newspaper after Pop was through with it. Only his snow-swirled dark head showed over the top and his hands gripping the pages, scarred with innumerable burns.

"I thought you liked pretty girls," he said to Pop.

"Who said she isn't pretty?"

A page turned, loose pages slipping out from under. Ads, showers of ads. Eloquently Pop shunted them aside with his foot. All the trouble he'd had with Irene over clothes, stocking money. And here this one was running around bare-ass.

"She's all right," Pop conceded. "If she'd fix herself up a bit. A peacock," he added, reversing the proverb, "in crow's feathers."

"She's helping us out with the strike. Doing a tremendous job on the food drive."

Wordlessly Pop passed him the sports section and with glasses elevated regarded him for a moment. The pink bare legs, it was a crying shame. Chasing all over town with his son in every hole and back alley, it was a scandal. When she could be up in New Hampshire skiing from the mountaintops. Must be—tap, tap—a screw loose somewhere.

"I suppose Joe Barth," Pop commented from behind his newspaper with maddening irrelevance, "has enough socked away."

He ripped off his shirt and flung it away in disgust, marched off into the closet of a bathroom and scrubbed himself with icy water out of the faucet down to the waist, shouting through his father's shouts—"Wait, I'll heat you up a little water!"—"I thought you respected Joe Barth! I thought you thought the world of him! I thought you appreciated—"

"Who says I don't respect Joe Barth? Who says I don't appreciate? If he has money, let him have and enjoy it. Better him than somebody else."

"What money!"

He exploded with it, the into-the-guts insinuation that his feeling for Priscilla was inspired by calculation.

"They have a nice house, they keep it up," Pop reasoned. He brought in a kettle of tepid water, quicker than the boiler, and poured it into the sink where it began seeping out at once under the blackened metal stopper. "I bet they have three cars in that family."

They did.

He had returned home to have it out with Pop. He was no match for him. Having driven it into his gut, the old man drove a little further.

"He's not making it out of the law. It has to come from somewhere."

"What do you mean!"

He knew damn well what his father meant.

In his father's folklore, in the folklore of Liscomb Street, in the forklore of the *We* down here as distinguished from the *They* up there, any family that had lived in this country for several generations, staying in the same city and growing with it, was bound to have accumulated some backlog. Savings, stocks, property handed down increasing in value over the years, accruing interest. A step-great-grandmother here, a bachelor uncle there, always something for the heirs. Maybe a block of Liscomb Street tenements? A chunk of United Vacuum?

In his father's folklore, in the folklore of his street and his kind, there was always something these lawyers latched onto. Trusts that fell into their hands, some of it sticks to their fingers. Transactions with the government they got wind of, buy up a tract under cover, sell sky-high. Tax accounts of clients looking for loopholes, loans at 12 per cent, bankruptcies. They didn't make it on their cases and their contracts, even the most high-minded of them. Especially the most high-minded. They have something in the background.

Joe Barth did.

There Pop sat in his shabby maroon robe, swathed in the virtue of his folk morality; lolling against the cushions of the couch Irene had bought and Petey's baby had sprayed and spat up on: shoving his store-bought glasses up over his forehead (he'd tried every pair in the dime store till he hit the one that suited him best, isn't that what the eye doctor does?) and glinting up at him, eyes alight, with all the satisfaction of having struck home. Asserting his primacy over his son, you're no different from anyone else. Over Joe Barth, he's no different. Over Rockefeller, Du Pont, all the rulers of this earth.

For every dollar a man gets that he didn't earn, another man earned it and didn't get it!

That other man being of course himself, Lev Lunin. He never had a penny he didn't earn by his own hand. He never made a penny off the sweat of another's brow. He never owned anything but his personal effects. He, the cheated, the robbed, had this much over them all.

"For godsake, Pop, will you go to a specialist and get yourself a decent pair of specs?"

"I ain't buying no new specs. I'm still in hock to the docs for Mom. Why? You need a loan?"

The corkscrew process by which his father converted an expression of concern for his eyesight into a request for a loan sent him flying out of the house.

"Hey you want to take your girl out?" Pop hollered at him over the bannisters down three flights of stairs. "Here, here's a coupla bucks." Cutting him down to the ground. "Don't let her spend her money on you. Hey, Mish!"

Whang! The car keys. Did he want to use his father's car tonight? He did.

Pop had no objection to Priscilla. Who wouldn't take out a Priscilla Barth, marry her if she'd have him? It wasn't Priscilla he twisted the corkscrew into. It wasn't Priscilla he was putting the sign on, with eyes as mild as a child's:

Don't worry, my son, Joe Barth will fix you up.

A jeer deadly in its inaccuracy.

In his father's folklore and his own the world was divided not into continents but into *We* and *They*. *They* constituted authority: self-centered, corporate, committed to the defense of its own power and possessions, ever hungry for more. *We* constituted their prey: those who were taken advantage of, who hung together in their toil and their abilities, their needs and longings, their rebelliousness, who lacked the will and the ruthlessness to exploit their fellow human beings. *They* issue the orders. *We* carry them out. *They* are out to squeeze the last drop of blood out of us. *We* don't let them. The *We* who were The Doers had no truck with the *They* who were The Takers. More than oceans lay between.

But to escape from The Doers to The Takers if you can, why not?

It was the damnation of his father's blessing that he most violently rejected.

Out on Willow Street, a lane of tumbledown shacks in the original factory district of Shoreham, the Barth Barrel Works, founded almost two centuries ago, still stood. He had passed it once or twice taking a short cut to somewhere else. A rusty-red structure, built like a stable, that had grown mainly in length, abutting on the backyards of houses in the next street. The works had gone out of wooden barrels years ago, he gathered from stray bits of conversation in the Sherwood Heights living room, and gone into steel drums. A salvage operation, conditioning used fifty-five-gallon drums for re-use, under the supervision of Joe Barth's—and Pop's—old side-kick, Fred Eckstrom. The man who had written the campaign handbills for Rod Kearnsey's first election to office.

The Barths rarely referred to the barrel works. Having a decent respect for their privacy, he never referred to it either. A little pisspot outfit, probably lousy working conditions, must have made plenty during the war. Their skeleton in the closet. He never once stopped there. He never set foot inside. There was no such place. It didn't exist. He was not after Priscilla Barth's money, what money!

Was he?

3

Ted was crucial. Ted could have stopped it when no one else had that much influence on her. He sometimes wondered afterward if she would have surrendered so completely all normal reservations toward him without Ted's sanction. Or if he would have abandoned so completely his native caution without a Ted Barth somewhere in the picture.

Whenever she spoke of Ted, those first few weeks, it was clear that she hoped to bowl Ted over with him. Ted, according to Priscilla, was madly in love with Gail, a fantastic actress married to a fabulous director, an absolute bastard, who was starring her in a way-out play running in New York in a loft off Sheridan Square, the smash of the season. This she related to him with bated breath, hinting at passions of awesome dimension. Ted, the idolized brother, was glory-bound and therefore Ted's girl, anything that pertained to Ted, belonged on the heights with him. Gail had something Ted didn't have, a kind of living that wasn't his, and Ted was in love with her. Priscilla was in love with Mish, countering her brother's drama of extremes with a drama of her own. And Mish was in love with Priscilla, a kind of living . . .

Ted was the measure of her aspirations. He had to make it with Ted.

His first night out with Ted, Ted was supposed to pick Priscilla up at school en route from Cambridge and meet him in Shoreham on the corner of Liscomb and Stone. It was the evening before the city-wide rally that was to be held downtown in support of the United Vacuum strike and he had a full schedule of last-minute rounding up ahead of him. The bars from Liscomb to Cedarbrook were his precinct.

He was waiting under a streetlight with a bundle of *Calls* at his foot, frozen to an icicle, when a sleek little convertible slid up and the door swung open. "Hop in." He ducked inside. The car shot out into the street. No Priscilla. A young man who controlled the wheel with a finger if he touched it at all. "Where to?"

"How did you know me?"

" 'If you see a stubborn, stiff-necked, snub-nose guy with a cleft in his chin and a spot of mischief in his eye, that's him.' "

"That what she said?"

"She's tied up tonight with her transportation committee. Swears she'll have the entire student body here at your rally tomorrow. Half of it anyway. I understand we're covering the pubs?"

He was intensely disappointed that she wouldn't be with them, and enormously relieved. He had no taste for touring her through the taverns. In an excess of zeal on the part of some brain, probably lying around at home with a can of beer on his chest, he was out beating the bushes for sympathizers not reached by the central labor council, radio spots, leaflets at plant gates. He had his team on the east side of town, Marty Rakocszi had his on the west side. Ray Pelletier was checking out the churches and lodges. Bob Ucchini, president of the local, and Herb Cranston, leader of Bob's opposition, were addressing meetings in two different public halls. They would all join together afterward at the Blue Bird on Cedarbrook Avenue, just up the hill from United Vacuum, for a final prerally briefing.

Ted skimmed a *Calls* off the top of his bundle at a stoplight and scanned it.

"You're expecting a one-day walkout by every plant in the city?"

"Well, steel's on strike and auto's on strike. They'll be at the rally anyway. We think. ACW and ILG are in their slack season right now. They'll be there. They say. And all the union shops that are working will march from their jobs at ten to Liberty

Square. The arrangements have been made. The banners have been printed. The pledge cards are in. Who knows? If this cold snap holds up . . ."

"You don't take much for granted, do you?"

"If we have one thousand, it'll be meaningless. Five thousand, a miracle. Ten thousand, we've won the strike."

"What's your estimate then?"

"I don't know."

"Take a guess."

"After we get together with Ucchini and Cranston tonight. All right?"

From the hunkville hangouts on Liscomb to the rooming-house resorts on Bancroft. From the neighborhood of Forge & Foundry, Shoreham Firearms, the large unorganized plants, to the back streets meandering off into shoals of little grinding and polishing, finishing and fabricating shops, no one knew quite how many.

"You gonna be out tomorrow?"

"You gonna be out tomorrow?"

"Here, here, give 'em to your friends."

"When you get to work, talk it up. Call 'em out."

"UV sets the pace. What we gain will help you."

Ten o'clock. Liberty Square. Speakers. Entertainment.

"We want ten thousand of you there."

In this weather? Brrrr.

He went about his business, knowing that he was under Ted's scrutiny and too occupied to take it into account. Ted too, while observing him, put his time to good use in pursuit of his own interests. Ted's doctoral dissertation had to do with a comparative study of working-class goals in England and the United States. He had his political, economic and historic factors lined up. And he knew the British firsthand. He was just a few months home from the Labour Party victory in the summer. He had worked on the Labour research staff during the war, he had stumped for Labour candidates in the Parliamentary elections and the Labour program was as much his at this point as if he had personally invented it. What he lacked was familiarity with the current American scene. He was no closet scholar and he didn't intend to rely solely on books for his source material. It was an ambitious project and he hoped to produce a work of immediate pragmatic as well as academic value.

Ted filled him in as they drove around. In the dead hour between the last of the after-supper crowd and the arrival of the swing shift, they warmed up with a hot toddy at the Paradise Rest. They sat in a booth opposite the bar where he could catch the customers as they appeared.

"You know you fascinate me," he said to Ted. "Here we been talking all evening long and I don't understand a word you've said."

At twenty-seven Ted was already professorial, but lightly so. The faceless boy of the snapshots grown tall. His long body shifted about with an awkwardness that was oddly supple. Bangs slewed over his brow. Through the lens of his glasses his eyes were magnified into large dark pools. His accent, clipped and drawled, British or Harvard or both, put a distance between himself and others, a distance overcome by an eagerness for communication which caused him to stammer at times. He was brown in midwinter from skiing weekends and a week down at Daytona Beach where he had been dabbling with the nascent sport of stock-car racing. The ambitious scholar tested his reflexes against wind, sun, snow, track, Gail's bastard of a husband, in order to be able to live with himself as scholar.

Ted removed his glasses, steamed up in an atmosphere so steeped in beer the wood back of the booth sweated with it and the plastic seat clung dankly to their pants. He breathed on his glasses, wiped them with a soggy paper napkin.

"N-n-none of it?"

Laski and Marx? Keynes and Means? The causes of cyclical crises? The problem of economic surplus? Class struggle or class collaboration?

"Well, some," he admitted.

With the elongated squirm that was somehow graceful, Ted shifted shoulders and hips, began all over again.

"Where are you going, Mish?"

"My team'll be reporting here pretty soon. Then the Three Crowns on Spenser."

"W-where are you going?" Ted repeated, digging in.

He nursed his sweetened rum and hot water and jumped up with his *Calls* to greet a bevy of newcomers.

"Running around all over the lot," Ted said to him when he sat down again. "You win your strike, you lose your strike, where do you go from there? Where's UV going? Where's the U.S. going? Where's it all going in the next few years? The next ten years?"

The newcomers drifted over with their beers. From the Paradise Rest on, he settled back and let Ted carry it, accumulating a floating talkathon of gas hounds in their wake.

Ted knew where they were going. He scrunched his spine down in his seat and poised, tensile, as if it were physically embedded in him, soared off with it.

The British revolution. Voted into power by the industrial and white-collar workers, intellectuals, soldiers in the field. Banks, coal mines, public utilities, transport and communications to be nationalized. A comprehensive system of social insurance and health services to be administered by the government. Education for all, agricultural reforms, freedom for India and in the course of time all the colonies. The continent would follow suit, France and Belgium, Italy, Greece. Indeed, the transfer of ownership from private to public would be quite simple for them. Native fascists and Nazi expropriators who controlled the industries had only to be ousted by the prodemocratic forces now in a position to assume leadership.

And if Western Europe went socialist, how long could America hold out?

Ted's perspective was met with general skepticism.

"That easy? Not a drop of blood spilled?"

"It's already been spilled. We had the war."

"Voted in?"

"Voted in. Democratically. If socialism doesn't bring with it an expansion of democracy, the game's not worth the candle. We're at a point in history where the possibility is present . . ."

"It'll never be."

"It's been. I saw it. I was there."

"Washington won't let it. They're too smart for that. They'll find some way. Europe's on the rocks, it needs all the help it can get. And we'll come in with our money . . ."

"Ah, now we have it. Now we're getting somewhere." Ted was exhilarated. He had his communication, a two-way process, going and coming, an experience not always easily achievable for him. With fingers conjoined, rolling at a mote scraped up from the clammy table, he put his question. "Who's we?"

Who's we? Who's Washington?

"United Vacuum or you? Who is we?"

The gas hounds had their own idea of where it was all going. It would end up with a bomb on Moscow, the sooner the better. It would end up with the United States the last bastion of reaction, capitalism would make common cause with Catholicism and the Pope would move to Chicago, direct his crusade against Communism from there. Stalin would march over Europe and England and the next thing he'd be right here in Shoreham if he wasn't here already.

Where are we going?

Everybody pitching his two cents in, shooting his mouth off.

"You gonna be out tomorrow? You gonna be out tomorrow? Take some of these with you. How many you need to cover your plant?"

Where was the country going, peace or war? Where were the companies going, prosperity or depression? Where were the workers going, bargaining with the company for raises and improvements or going beyond that demanding a piece of the pie, a seat on the board of directors, participation in the decisions by which their destinies were shaped. Or going beyond that, the whole hog . . .

"We're standing in the door right now, hat in hand, begging—

no, *coercing* crumbs out of them. And you talk about the whole board table?"

"All right. Suppose they can't provide sufficient and continuous employment." Ted goaded them. "Suppose there are no jobs. Your compensation's run out, all the palliatives. Then what?"

The Achilles' heel of the money machine. Breakdown.

Gloom descended. It was past midnight. They were in the Blue Bird on Cedarbrook Avenue around the corner from United Vacuum, waiting for Ucchini and Cranston to appear with final instructions for tomorrow morning. They weren't receiving unemployment compensation. There would be no paycheck at the end of the week. Strike benefits couldn't last long. Fuel oil at home was running low; stoves were turned off all night. The years of the Depression gnawed in their bones. A steady job, security, unsolved in the past, uncertain in the future.

They sipped their beer slowly, sipping the froth, not blowing it off, squawking at the barmaid, too much head on it. All taverns are alike. Skunk holes. Soaked in skunk juice.

Pleasurably Ted offered them alternatives. Back relaxed against the smoky-tan wall, leg cocked up on the seat of the booth. The barmaid had brought her little Scottie in with her when she came to work and she had her locked up in the back room, in heat. The Scottie whined and whimpered, scratched and butted at the door.

"Suppose," Ted offered, "the level of employment can be maintained in peacetime as it is in war by massive expenditure of Federal funds. Building schools, hospitals, financing all kinds of social projects—"

"That'll be the day!"

"Back to WPA!"

"—extending credit at low interest rates to industry to stimulate new production of capital goods—"

"Wasn't that Herbert Hoover's idea?"

"All the cream goes to the top and what's left goes to us?"

"—and regulating profits and taxes in such a way as to induce the corporations to spread their surplus earnings. Return enough to the investors to attract further investment. Pay you enough to meet your needs. While at all times retaining ownership in their own hands. Would you be content with that?"

The money machine in perpetual motion? Primed by the public till?

"Suppose . . . ?"

The little dog yelped.

"Why don't you let her out, Hazel? It ain't natural."

"What I'm searching for," Ted confessed, "is some indication of the American worker's level of development."

Ha! Marty Rakocszi and Ray Pelletier, in now with their reports, gave the professor a lesson.

"The American worker." Marty, the surveyor of public opinion, collector of clippings, waltzed up and down the aisle between the double row of booths, solid in his bulky wool jacket. "The most backward worker in the world. In Europe they *hate* the rich." With a chop of his hand. "I know. I was shipping out back in '37, and we had this German deck hand . . ." Finger across his throat. "But here on Saturday night we put on our chesterfield coat." Buttoning down his front. "And our Homburg hat." Flipped on. "And we're cock of the walk. Right?"

Right! Applause. Whistles. Cheers.

Ray Pelletier, the analytical one, neat as a pin, precise as a cutting tool, sliced through to the core.

"There always has to be a Columbus," Ray said. ("My father, the dreamer," his children called him. "Dreams," his wife, Yvonne, said, "that no one ever yet saw come true.") "But look what happened to Columbus."

Right! That's it. On the button.

"You've been very quiet, Mish." Ted leaned with an elongated lunge of his body over the table. He was sitting back at his ease, enjoying it all. "What do you say? You think the fight for change will stay within the system? Or do you think you'll have to change the system?"

"I don't know."

"Come on. You must have an idea."

The research sleuth on the trail. Scholarly, glasses glinting. Pullover, a soft heather knit, over loose-collared white shirt. "I honestly don't know. I wish to hell I did."

"Come on, Lunin, give. Spill it."

"Okay then. You mean over in England they're getting ready to get rid of capitalism? While here . . . How about the king and queen?"

"The king and queen?" Ted was puzzled by the obvious.

"They gonna get rid of them?"

It was a mean trick. A Pop trick. The corkscrew jab in the gut.

"The king and queen." Ted shrugged it off. "They're just figureheads. Symbols."

"And the lords and the ladies? They gonna get rid of them?"

"Well, the peerage. It's an anachronism of course. Eventually it will disappear. Except perhaps as a means of bestowing honors."

"And the big stockholders and the landholders? Are they out?"

"Not exactly. The nationalized properties will be paid off in time out of earnings. Other than that, the tax levies will be practically confiscatory. And the death dues . . ."

"You mean those who have it will still have it. And those who are trying to make it—"

"Will still make it," Ted ruefully acknowledged. "Only that much harder."

Some revolution.

"Buh-but you see, the g-general increase if the state can m-manage—"

"What do we want here?"

A resonant voice rose from the back booth, Nick Colangelo, the little gray man who wasn't there.

"What are we crying for? We got UV on our necks, that's enough. You want the whole goddam government? I was in the army I had it. That was it."

Another revolution.

Ted reached over to his jacket hanging on the outer side of the booth and took a notebook from his pocket. He began jotting down.

"So in your opinion, Mish, there's no likelihood—"

"I didn't say that. I said I don't know. One thing you better add to that thesis of yours."

"Yes?"

"The subjective factor."

All in good fun. All in good fun.

The bitch in the backroom was barking her head off. Marty stuck his head outdoors to see if either Bob or Cranston was in sight and pulled back in quickly. There was a pack of dogs outside growling and howling, snapping.

"They'll bite somebody," Marty chided the barmaid. "In a situation like this the gentlest male in the world will turn vicious."

The men drifted over to the bar and piled onto the barmaid.

"Every time the dogcatcher catches my shep out like this, it's five bucks. Rounds up ten hounds in the pound on a call."

"It's the bitch's fault. She's the one excites them. They smell her from half a mile away."

"She ought to be kenneled. There ought to be a law. Why don't you kennel her?"

"I will not." The barmaid, wiping the bar with a wet rag, was huffy. She had her dog inside. She had her locked up. She was the affronted party.

Bob, and then Cranston a few minutes later, pelted in on a blast of frigid air, barely slamming the door against the snarling, raging torrent that surged after them. The dog in back and the dogs out front hurled themselves with irresistible clamor against the walls that separated them. It was torment not to succumb to them.

"Open up for godsake. Let what will be, be!"

"They'll tear the joint apart."

A soprano moan. Agony.

Bob and Cranston brought in with them the effulgence of their meetings, the fragrance of success.

"How does it look?"

"What's the score?"

"Ten thousand?"

"More," Bob said positively.

"You're outa your mind."

Cranston's men gathered about him at the bar. Bob's men gathered about him at Ted's table. Cranston, crimson from outdoor cold in his peaked white parka, unfolded his map of the Liberty Square area on the bar. Bob, with his knit seaman's beanie folded down over his ears, stooped over the map he spread out on Ted's table, issuing instructions.

Bob Ucchini and Herb Cranston were on the outs. All during the fall and even during the strike, Cranston was organizing Catholics in the union with the avowed purpose: Kick the Commies out of office! Bob from his incumbent position was assailing Cranston as a disrupter, a splitter, a company tool. "Stalinist stooge!" "Fascist flunky!" The epithets flew. And the threats. "Now that the war is over, we'll get you, you Commie bastards!" "You're what we fought the war against, Hitler!" Wait till this strike is settled . . . Wait . . .

Easy to make light of. But in its density and weight the opposition between them was unresolvable. Cranston was saving them all from totalitarian slavery. Bob was saving them from imperialist adventurism, the atomic holocaust. Both of them honest men, impugning each other's honesty. Ferocious over what they considered outside interference in the affairs of the union even while they consulted their outside sources. Capable of cunning only in the interest of the creeds they served.

Yet for the duration of the strike they maintained a working relationship of sorts. Each had his own sphere of influence, Bob's predominant, Cranston's still merely a minor threat. The forces polarized around them were both hard-core and fluid, with a certain amount of go-between.

He could never feel toward Cranston the indignation Bob thought he ought to feel. Cranston was perhaps a little too much in love with himself, but then so was Bob and who isn't.

Bob marked his map for them, a hectographed blue web of

streets leading into the square. Picket-sign depots. Sound-truck locations. First aid. Canteens. Who was manning this station. Who was responsible for that section.

Cranston up at the bar marked his map. "The UAW contingent will assemble on the south side. Rizzio, you coordinate with Perry. Wear your identification button. Everybody got your buttons?" Union buttons. Work buttons.

It mounted up. The certainty of it. The sweep.

From time to time Bob glanced nervously toward Cranston's back. Finally he passed his lists over to Ted. "Will you read these off? Marty, check him out. Mish—" A gesture of his head, follow me. Bob trekked down the aisle to the can. A few minutes later, he strolled after Bob and was drawn into a nook hung with aprons and mops where they could confer without undue interruption.

Bob was still buoyant with his meetings and committee reports. Almost every plant in the city would be shut down tomorrow. The downtown merchants were planning to serve coffee out of their stores to demonstrators. With such backing, under such pressures from the public, how long could UV hold out?

"Christ, it's cold out there tonight. We had fifty people call in they're out of fuel oil. If only the weather . . ."

Shivering in his peacoat, Bob drew him deeper into the nook. Soiled aprons hanging on hooks brushed their cheeks. The faceted face was suddenly pinched with cold, harrowed, ashen.

"Mish, I don't know how to tell you this."

Security, he thought grimly. Bob and Cranston had crossed wires on security and where there should have been a surplus of volunteers they were short.

"Mish—"

Shuddering, Bob rubbed his hands up inside the sleeves of his peacoat.

"Mish— Scottsy's a fag."

It didn't penetrate. He was unable to grasp it. Scottsy, the field organizer sent in by the international to guide the strike . . . who by sheer force of personality stood astride the factions . . . jumped them over the hurdles. Scottsy had been killing himself day and night for a week with tomorrow's program, staging it, and he had been assigned tonight to bed. A good night's sleep.

"Where'd you get that? There's so much shit on the loose—"

It was a main function of their information committee to combat rumor-mongering.

"Mish, he made a pass at Bertha Donahue's boy. She came straight to me. She wouldn't lie."

Bertha's boy, a sixteen-year-old kid who still thought sex was something invented by idiots.

"He could have imagined—"

"It's no imagination."

"Jesus Christ."

The personal and organizational ramifications . . .

Scottsy was too likable, too popular with everyone, to be dismissed out of hand. There would be an outcry of foul play.

To report it to the international? It would ruin the guy. It was too late to bring someone else in.

If it leaked out as it was bound to, at any moment, if Cranston who was something of a moralist caught wind of it . . . if the company . . . if the police . . .

They needed Scottsy too much. They couldn't keep him. Who would speak to him about it? That alone presented insurmountable difficulties.

"Mish, somebody's got to hold things together." Bob was passing the buck to him. "You get along with Cranston. If this isn't contained . . ."

Scottsy. Scottsy feeling over a kid. Not Jimmy Scott.

"What was that all about?" Ted asked him when he returned to their booth.

"I couldn't explain it to you," he said, still dazed, "in a hundred years."

"Hey!"

Cranston and his men up front, Bob and his men from the rear made a dive for the street door. An oldster walking his Saint Bernard in the late hours had taken it into his head to stop at the Blue Bird for a nightcap.

"Don't bring that mutt in here!"

The Saint Bernard bolted through the door dragging his master on the leash, heading for the backroom where the Scottie must have scratched every inch of paint off the bottom panel of the door. Amid laughter they succeeded in shoving the oldster and his massive pup outside.

"You're a man-hater, Hazel. You're taking revenge."

Amid laughter they trooped out, scuffled through the lovesick pack, kicking at ribs, swinging belts. The pavement rang with their footsteps down the incline of Cedarbrook Avenue, veering toward United Vacuum at the foot of the hill. Below them the plant lay like a cathedral, a fortress, its light-studded office steeple spearing the stars. Under the plant floodlights police cars huddled, keeping watch over the few pickets who, beating their arms for warmth, heads tucked in, stamped back and forth between the gates.

Beery and boisterous, the vapors of beer joints cleaving to them, they dashed for their parked cars through beery breath issuing from them in drifts in the arctic air.

"Anybody want a lift?"

"Anybody need a push?"

Car doors clanged. Engines gurgled, wheezed. Grit rolled like iron shot under the tires.

"All right now, how many?" Ted asked, reminding him of his promise.

He considered. He was new at this. He had listened to Bob Ucchini and Herb Cranston, Ray and Marty, the team reports, the disputes. He suffered the doubts and the pitfalls. He counted it on his fingers: so many from United Vacuum and the electrical locals, so many from Royal Steel, Auto Body, the IAM, Mine-Mill, UMW, clothing, jewelry, Allied Pharmaceutical, Apex Valve, Shoreham Battery . . .

"Full house," he guessed, recklessly. It was in the throb of his fingertips. It was in the tingle of his ears. "We'll fill the Square."

"Just one more question," Ted said to him as they turned from Bancroft down Stone to Liscomb Street.

He knew what it was. He had been preparing for it all evening.
I don't know! God knows I don't!

"Where is this going?"

"It's up to her," he said. "She has everything to lose. I don't."

4

In the morning Ted accompanied him on the security round of
Liberty Square, chatting with the knots of men gathered at
strategic points to watch for rows, internally or externally caused,
which they would move in on and move out. No one was worried
about security. The cold had cracked. The air was gray, soft with a
hint of snow, and gay with the contagious spirit of a large crowd.

He and Ted hoisted themselves up on the iron fountain in the
center of the Square and what they saw was hardly to be believed.
Thousands and thousands flowing in from the radial streets as
far as the eye could reach, bright with union banners and placards
just as Scottsy had plotted it.

The PA system worked perfectly for once, amplifiers bringing
the platform close. Speeches were short, as promised. Entertainment was good, most of it out of the plant. Mary Farrell, wasn't
she a beautiful girl? didn't she have a lovely voice? Ralski, what
an artist he was, his cartoons projected upon a screen. Petersen
with a line of patter that skewered UV and broiled it on a spit. A
Hollywood star gave her blessing. Priscilla and her guitar at the
mike riding the crest, borne aloft on the waves of mass singing.
Which side are you on? Which side are you on?

"Just one more question," he shouted at Ted over the topmost
rim of the three-tiered fountain. "Who the hell is Harold Laski?"

Ted shook his forelock back in the wind, laughing. The notion
that he would be the American Harold Laski, doing for America
what Laski had done for Britain, mentor of the labor movement,
ideologue of a labor party, theoretician of a socialism adapted to
the conditions of his own country? He could never measure up
to Laski, a man of such immense erudition.

"I am going to be," Ted said and touched his shoulder over the embossed summit of the fountain, "the American Ted Barth."

He arranged for Ted to teach a weekly class in labor history at the union hall. Ted arrived with cards and graphs, equipped to interview his students. Bob, carrying on ferocious arguments with Ted over the nature of social democracy, was nevertheless impressed with him. They had something Herb Cranston didn't have. Cranston could have the clerics. They had the academics.

In turn, Ted invited him, the political novice—not Bob, the expert—up to Harvard to lead a graduate seminar on the hottest issue of the hour. Is Labor a monopoly? The seminar wound up in the master's suite at Dunster House at four in the morning.

"You see? You see?" Priscilla was jubilant. "Didn't I tell you, you two would hit it off?"

Ted and Priscilla took him to New York with them to see Gail in her husband's latest play. "What do you think of it?" The interplay after the show between Gail the actress, her husband the bastard, and Ted who was trying to take her away from him was much more dramatic, and disturbing, than the play.

Did he love Priscilla more for herself or for what she brought him? The living room in Sherwood Heights. The idyllic walk along the Charles. The backstage of the Village loft and the rambling cold-water flat occupied by a half dozen couples, all in a rage of creativity, all from families of some means and even note, all here today and gone tomorrow, off on an impulse to Rome, Coral Gables, Tokyo.

An aura. An era.

He had to absorb Priscilla and Ted Barth, enlarge himself through his absorption of them, make what they had part of himself. Without becoming part of it. He had no desire to attach himself to the middle class. For ultimately he had, like his father, too much contempt for it.

And that was still another aspect of a love that asked no whats or whys, but simply was. His aspect.

III

1

There never was a strike like it.

Two weeks before Christmas, 1945, United Vacuum had reverted to its prewar practice, the annual Christmas gift: a wholesale distribution of layoff slips. Whole departments were eliminated. Workers with more seniority bumped workers with less seniority, displaced persons jousting and jostling for jobs equivalent to those they were accustomed to. But this was mere routine. A few days before Christmas the blockbuster fell. United Vacuum announced to its plants throughout the country the cancellation of its current contract with the union and its terms for the new contract soon to be negotiated, take it or leave it.

The grievances accumulated during the war? The long-postponed wage adjustments?

"The union," a United Vacuum spokesman declared, "has changed its policy from one of cooperation with management to one of intransigence following the postwar switch in the Moscow line. The terms we propose are more than fair in the light of expenditures related to peacetime conversion."

"This is no walkout," Bob Ucchini thundered from the platform of the Local 317 union hall, "it's a lockout! The company is out to break the spirit of independence we acquired during the war."

Each side had waited for four years to get even.

To Priscilla it was all great. The bleak street and the biting wind. The clashes with police and the crack of night sticks, the immense protest afterward in front of city hall. The hilarious paddy wagon tales. The *sub rosa* tales of this foreman and that engineer tipping off the strategy committee to the company's next move. But if this were all, it would be like almost every other strike before and after.

From all over the state, workers in non-struck industries maintained a steady flow into Shoreham of financial support: voting a portion of their union treasuries, pledging a percentage of their paychecks, digging into their pockets to fill the hat passed around every membership meeting.

Churches in Shoreham collected boxes of children's clothing. Supermarkets stationed cartons at their door for food donations. Affluent liberals opened up their homes for parties. Stars flew in from Broadway and Hollywood to march in the picket line. Local 317 saw its own faces in *Life, Look, Collier's,* Fox Movietone News. The Shoreham *Tribune* was forced to couch its criticism in stories so subtly slanted the unsubtle reader construed it as encouragement.

The local mobilized every resource within its reach and within its ranks. Talent scouts, who had talent for what. Putting on skits, square dance calling, writing, art. Picket signs that were masterpieces of satire. Ida Pucci and her accordion, Kallen and his balalaika band, Shorty Spofford's blues combo, always something going at strike headquarters. The pots in the mobile soup kitchens bubbled.

They had that kind of spirit. They had that degree of unity. They had organization.

Priscilla drove the sixty miles down from the university every other afternoon, whizzed back late evenings or stayed over, cutting early classes. She was a whirlwind of energy, errand girl for ten different committees. Soliciting the churches and stores. Dispatching press releases and speakers. Swooping down with Mariuch on the welfare office where a half dozen tenants who had received dispossess notices were staging a sit-down. Rounding up youngsters to address envelopes—she could make a mailing sound like a feat of international diplomacy. Stacking up chairs with the sweep-up crew.

Nights they cast themselves into each other's arms on borrowed beds as if flung together by the day's events, ravaged with the hunger and anticipation of every minute apart. Stroking, caressing —involvements they should have been able to shed like their clothes, like the sheet they tossed off, enveloped them, throbbed through them, interfused. She sat up, a long lithe girl, and searched his pockets for matches, talking through the cigarette she stuck in the corner of her mouth. "So you think there'll be a break in negotiations?" "Come on back down here." "Mish, what's the trouble? Something's troubling you." "Scottsy." "What about Scottsy?" He had to tell her about Scottsy. "So I talked to him. All I said was, 'Everybody's got a right to his own personal life but—!' And, Jesus Christ, he up and cleared out."

Time to leave. Into the shower together. She wore someone's crimson rubber cap, chin strap dangling over her collarbone. Shimmering with wetness. Ooo. Do we have to leave now? Do we have to? That clockwork slash of the shears. We have to.

The UV strike ended in a smashing victory for the union. An eighteen-cent-an-hour increase for the twenty-five cents demanded, very good. Establishment of industry-wide bargaining procedures, essential. Improvements in working conditions and fringe benefits, real progress.

Priscilla, not a member, no card, was winked through the door of the Shoreham Armory with him. Inside, they stood with the crowd listening to the new contract, roaring, pounding the floor, swept up on the tides of elation, the culmination of the past weeks —you're on a roller coaster you can't get off, you have your finger in the dike you can't pull out. While the situation that had brought the two of them together dissolved in thin air. Going-going-gone with the hammering of the gavel, with the scrap of paper Ucchini and Gavin held up between them.

"By our united strength standing solidly together . . ."

Back to work Monday. Back to the grubbing and the grit.

"When do we get married?" Priscilla formed the words at him through the voice vote ratifying the contract.

The ayes had it without hesitation, doubt or objection from any quarter.

He scarcely paid attention to Gavin's speech. Gavin the international rep, veteran of the Harlan mine fields and the southern organizing drives, throwing a sop to Cranston's clique—or the company in defeat.

"All through this strike United Vacuum found only one chink in our armor. Stah-leen. A victory for the union would be a victory for Stah-leen. I promise you now if there be any among us . . ."

A shimmer of chapped lips, lipstick in shreds. Red cheeks hazed with the merest sheen of freckles and down. Eyes too direct, too honest, too trusting.

He listened to Gavin like almost everyone else in the hall. With a tin ear. Eyewash. Hot air. Politics. Whether it was the U.S.A. or the U.S.S.R., UV or the EWIU, Ucchini or Cranston, it all amounted to the same thing. Who's going to be top banana?

He wanted to take Priscilla by the hand and disappear from the armory with her but he was due up on the platform to deliver his report. And Bob had invited them afterward, a special mark of his favor, to his grandmother's birthday party. Bob's grandmother was one hundred years old this week, the oldest person in Shoreham and still going strong.

"I'll tell Bob we have to skip the party," he muttered to Priscilla when he left his chair.

"Oh, no," she protested, "we can't do that. It'd be taken as a—a personal repudiation."

He took his seat next to Bob on the platform, assembling excuses. He never had the chance to begin. Bob seized him by the sleeve and thrust a newspaper clipping at him. "You see this?" Everybody had seen it and was laughing over it. At a luncheon ceremony opening the annual Italian Festival, the mayor of Shoreham had introduced the famous and beautiful and very conservative lady who represented the district in Congress to Bob's grandmother. In the newspaper photo, to vast local amusement,

Bob Ucchini, anathema to the congresslady, was standing behind his seated grandmother. The grandmother receiving the hand of the *grande dame* was dressed in a Sunday version of her daily costume, in peasant black over high-topped shoes, with a bit of white underblouse showing above her open collar, and a black kerchief, from which the ends fell loose, covering her head. She was a personage in Shoreham, admired and quoted. In the middle of a blizzard, it was said, Nonna would appear at the door of friend or relative in her black kerchief and her black dress open at the neck, with a pot of ricotta under one arm and a bottle of wine under the other, and march in announcing, "Today we make ravioli."

"You know what she said?" Bob whispered to him while he waited for Gavin to finish his speech. "There she is, this gracious lady bending over her in her flower hat and her make-up and her perfume and takes her hand. And my grandmother turns around to me and says in Italian—you know what she said?"

The grandmother had asked Bob in Italian, "Who is this whore?"

Laughing over Bob's grandmother, he took the rostrum from Gavin and delivered his report. It was Bob's night. It was Bob's triumph. He departed from his mundane warning of retaliatory anti-labor bills in the offing to pay tribute to Bob. Whatever else you could say about Bob Ucchini, he never hogged the leadership. He spread it. When responsibilities were allocated, Bob never asked beforehand: Are you for me or against me? If you could do the job, do it.

"Let's give Bob a hand."

A five-minute standing ovation.

2

At the party, in the basement of the house inhabited by various generations and branches of the Ucchini family, he eased Priscilla into a corner and with his back to the eddying company tried to shelter for a moment what was uniquely theirs, unique only to themselves, tried to hold the moment, fragile as a bubble, expansive as air. When? How? Where? Before it should scatter to all comers. Hey, they're gonna tie the knot! There was too much going on. There was always someone pursuing them. They weren't left alone for a single moment.

They were dragged into the circle around Bob's father, Mast' Anton', the master carpenter, the storyteller. Holding forth on his throne, the rustic chair his sons had made for him brought in from the grape arbor back of the house. How he came to America, how he pounded the pavements looking for a job, how he rode the subways unable to read the signs when suddenly—rising up out of his rheumatism with the ribaldry of it—the call of nature . . . How he bought a piano for Bob when he was just four years old and how the piano had to be hoisted up through the third-floor window and all the neighbors who were buying parlor suites, Model Ts, gathered in the street below to watch . . . How Bob, Shoreham's child prodigy, gave a concert in the Civic Auditorium when he was eleven years old and how just when he was supposed to go over to Italy for training under a celebrated maestro suddenly—rising up out of his rheumatism with the awfulness of it— The Crash . . .

Bob's first teacher, his mother's cousin, arrived, The Blind Musician led by one of his daughters. The Blind Musician roamed the streets always led by one of his daughters, and anywhere he heard the sound of a piano in a house, any house, he would walk right in and listen, render criticism. He could stand in the kitchen giving a lesson to a pupil in the parlor and call out his corrections, "Third finger on the B-flat!"

"Priscilla! Mish! Come here."

They greeted The Blind Musician, a gray-maned upstanding man with the eyes, damaged at birth, of a movie monster.

And Mariuch's mother, The Poetess, had to recite to Priscilla, while she heaped her plate, a letter she'd written to the Pope about peace. On her breast Mari's mother wore a large pin printed with the photograph of her youngest son, killed on the beach at

Salerno. She fondled the pin out of habit as she recited, chanting her elegy.

"You think that's a good letter? The letters I write are nothing. The writer you should have known, the real writer, was my father Esopo. Mari, tell them about Esopo!"

Esopo, the folk poet of a mountain village outside Naples, was such a poet, if there had only been someone in those days to write down the poetry he composed, he would have been one of the great nineteenth-century poets of Italy.

"He was fifty-two years old before he knew there had been another Esop in this world."

And the grandmother escorted by the son she lived with.

"Nonna!" "Granny!"

She apologized for being late. She had already celebrated her birthday at four parties this week before coming to the important one, the family party, and she was a little tired.

They settled her about with cushions and translated her comments, screaming with laughter.

"Come here, over here, everybody. You've got to hear this."

The son had worried about her whereabouts all afternoon. He had let her off after the luncheon to visit with Angelina and three o'clock, four o'clock, five o'clock went by and not a word from her. The weather wasn't so good, the streets were slippery.

She had found Angelina down with heart trouble and she fixed up some tea for her and they spent some time together. Then since she was in the vicinity she went to see Margarita, laid up with her kidneys, the kidneys are gone. And two doors down, Stella in so much pain . . .

"I hope," the grandmother said of her friends, all in their seventies, "that when I get old I won't be like that."

She beckoned Priscilla forward and looked her over with eyes like polished marble.

They all held their breath, as if some final judgment hung in the balance. What will she come out with next?

A woman hewn of stone. None of the shrinkage of age. Rather,

her bones jutted under her skin as the rocks jut under the mountainside. She had the large craggy hands of a workman.

"What is she saying?" Priscilla asked Bob, faint with apprehension.

"She is saying," Bob translated, " 'You are a doll.' "

Priscilla kissed her.

Now they could go, but no. The birthday cake. They couldn't leave without partaking of the birthday cake.

The long table, set up on trestles along the wall, was partially cleared. The scampi tinged with lemon and garlic, the scaloppini dark with Marsala, the sausage hot and sweet seeded with the licorice tang of fennel, the cheese-stuffed pasta blanketed in tomato sauce, the green salads and the oregano-sprinkled breads were set aside for latecomers. Wine splotches on the tablecloth were covered with napkins. The basement lights were turned off.

The birthday cake was borne in, festooned with icing, candles flickering like flags in a mist of molten wax. Flame flickered over the low plasterboard ceiling, the white-washed walls. The guests on tiptoe clustered about the table, closing in out of the darkness that lurked in the corners.

The grandmother's face, yellowed in the candlelight, ridged and gullied, descended over the cake. Mouth sucked in—toothless, she chewed steak with gums as hard as nails—and chest heaving, she gathered the breath to blow out a century of candles. Her husband had died years ago, crushed under a landslide of gravel when a section of US 1 was being laid north of Shoreham. She had come from Italy, sent for by her brother, with her nine children and the pots and pans she still used. Her breath expired. Puffing out their rosy-tan cheeks, her great-great-grandchildren blew out the remaining candles.

"Mish, wait. Wait a minute. I have to talk to you. Don't go yet."

All evening long, along the laden table and the benches against the opposite walls, a murmur had been creeping, rasps of anxiety hastily muted. Gavin, who was spending the night in Bob and Mari's third-floor apartment, stayed downstairs with the festivities. Although the union victory party was scheduled for Saturday night, members kept filtering in uninvited, spilling over with mutual congratulation, kibitzing, reviewing and reminiscing. Actually hankering for information from either Bob or Gavin or both, scenting trouble. There was a bunch over at Herb Cranston's tonight, they reported, lining up a slate that would cream Bob in the June election. Some of them had come from there. Some of them were going there. Nick Colangelo dropped in. Just to wish The Signora many happy returns. He lingered on, talking with Gavin.

Confabs behind doors. Consultations on the stairway.

"Son of a bitch," Mari grunted under her breath. "After what we've built up . . ."

Bob shushed her down and trundled her off with a tray of glasses to be washed. It was a wonder she didn't throw the tray at his head. Mari was a favorite with reporters, the torchbearer, galvanizer, "UV's Red Flame." There is no room in a marriage for two dynamos. If one is the star, the other must provide the setting. But with Bob and Mari, if they didn't function together they destroyed each other. They were fighting all during the strike over failures of preparation, mistakes in tactic, missed meals, Scottsy. They would have split up any number of times, it's all over, washed up, only the strike—they were shackled by the strike, the strike held them together.

Philosophizing over Bob and Mari, he uneasily tracked down Priscilla. Priscilla tracked him down. Everybody in their path nudging: look at them. As soon as they found themselves alone they went seeking each other.

3

The union contingent ended up in Bob and Mari's apartment on the third floor, dancing to old phonograph records, drinking and arguing, making time with each other's mates. Ray Pelletier brought along his wife for once. Yvonne clung to him with frail gay prettiness, almost happy. Ray was getting a seven-dollar-a-week raise under the new contract. Marty Rakocszi's wife, Helen, barged in upstairs a half hour after Marty's arrival downstairs, trailed by Yusskevitch, her admirer. The victory celebration slated for Saturday night was being pre-empted. Noise poured through the apartment, a babble of voices over the music.

Twice he was beckoned away from Priscilla into Bob and Mari's bedroom, first by Bob and later, separately, by Gavin. Both of them approached him with the same proposal. Would he run for chief steward in the June election?

His future over the next several years was being determined in the bedroom and all he wanted was to get the hell out, get off by himself somewhere with his girl.

"But why bother with this now?" he demurred. "Can't it wait?"

No, it couldn't wait.

"But why me? Why not Ray? He's the one with the know-how."

"Yvonne'd kill him. She can't forget when Ray was president he spent money out of pocket. She never knew where he was. Ray'll help you out."

"Marty then. I'll keep on with the legislative committee. There are all these anti-union bills coming up in Congress now to break the so-called labor monopoly—that lousy Senator Taft—"

"That's all being taken care of. That's one thing labor's united on. Even if they manage, between the Republicans and the southern Democrats, to pass something, we'll put such a campaign on, Truman will never sign it. It's because of the job you did on legislative everybody's pushing for you. Marty'll be right at your elbow. You can count on Marty."

For one reason or another neither Ray nor Marty was available for the office.

Both Bob and Gavin, separately, brushed aside his pleas of insufficient experience. The organization was there, firmly entrenched, of stewards and section chairmen throughout the plant. All he had to do was implement it. Strengthen the grievance machinery. Master the system of job classification and ratings. Acquire skill at negotiation. The old heads would guide him. He'd learn.

All he had to do.

It didn't occur to him that for Bob Ucchini and Frank Gavin he fitted into a context that far transcended the limits of UV-Shoreham. That Gavin's speech at the armory earlier was more than eyewash: it was a straw in the wind. That the standing ovation for Bob might possibly be the overture to Bob's swan song. That the first salvos had been fired in a power struggle that would split the local, the international, the labor movement wide open in the next five years. A struggle in which he would stand stubbornly between. Courted by both sides. Tugged and torn. Caught in the crossfire.

He had only the vaguest notion that conflicts of global dimension were at stake. Ted Barth's: *Where are you going?*

Reform or revolution. Patch the system up or scrap it, start all over again. Uncle Sam. Or Uncle Joe. Or—the halfway measure, divided and negated by the countervailing influences—the Clement Attlees of England and Europe. Rival world trade union associations blockading each other with accusations and denials of Soviet forced labor. American trade union expeditions into foreign trade unions to rescue them from the Communists who had originated them, pitting leftists of various stripe against each other, liquidating not only the enemy but sometimes the organization as well. Freedom of Enterprise vs. The Iron Curtain. For the Marshall Plan or against it. For the Baruch Plan or against. The fate of the Greek guerrillas. Iran. Indo-China. Guatemala.

He foresaw none of it. If the General Executive Board of the EWIU-CIO in New York was about to engage in a civil war to the death, as first Bob and then Gavin indicated, then it was not, he suspected and the suspicion wouldn't go away, over pure principle and policy, program. It was over that old bone of contention: who gets what. Who gets control of the hierarchy of offices, funds, political connections, distribution of staff jobs down to the last little pissy-assed messenger boy, the determination of where the group insurance and the staplers are to be bought. Ideals and convictions notwithstanding.

In Bob and Mari's bedroom he swung his leg over the arm of the comfortably upholstered chair and considered. It was a restful room, the walls painted a soothing coffee-tan, the furniture off-white. The twin white lamps on the dresser cast pools of shaded light and the white string rug covering the uneven floor was thick, muffling footsteps. Outside the closed door a constant hubbub streamed through the hall, twined with the tinkle of music. *I wonder who's kissing her now.*

Bob paced up and down the room, keyed-up, kinetic, persuasive.

"Mish, I can see what's coming! UV isn't going to take defeat lying down. Just as important as what they're trying in Congress is what they'll try in the plants. The organization we achieved, they'll split it every way they can from inside as well as outside. The contract we won, they'll nullify it on the floor if they can every day of the week.

"We can't sit back now. We have to consolidate our gains. In the only way we can. An alert membership. A membership that's on it. And there's just one key to that: every worker in every department has to feel that every legitimate beef he has on the job it'll be acted on. That's the spot I'm asking you to fill.

"Chief steward, Mish. You can swing it."

Bob had been in and out of the presidency of the local; it made no difference to Bob which office he occupied so long as his influence remained paramount. So long as he could, like The Blind Musician, feel free to step in anytime, anywhere and render his opinion.

To Bob he said: "Now you know, Bob, I don't always go along with you."

Bob smoothed out a ripple in the bedspread, straightened the rug with his foot, always putting to rights, never still.

"That's all right. All right." Bob lifted his right arm, swearing to it. "I'm free to put the screws on. You're free to resist. Okay?"

"I ain't agreed to nothin' yet."

The door to the bedroom burst open and Nick Colangelo stopped stock-still in the doorway as if he had surprised them in a tableau, in the midst of a bed-bouncing scene.

"I beg your pardon." Nick retreated, embarrassed. "I didn't mean to interrupt you. I was just looking for my hat."

"You must have left it downstairs."

"Well. I'll say good night."

"Good night."

"See y' round."

"See y'."

The sort of man you see around out of the tail of your eye. After further discussion with Bob he departed from the bedroom. He had till tomorrow, when the nominating committee would meet, to think about it.

Out in the hall the party was heating up. Somebody had ordered up a case of beer. A half dozen fifths stood on Mari's prized pine chest. Marty Rakocszi was popping corks in the kitchen, the perennial bartender. A dusky-rose girl, twice-divorced, was leaning on her arms over the table to Marty, her long black hair and her breasts drooping toward him. Marty's wife, Helen, was loudly stomping in the living room with Yusskevitch, a lumbering steamfitter in Maintenance.

He located Priscilla in the nook behind the parlor grand Mast' Anton' had bought his son in the days when everybody else was buying buggy rides. She was dancing with Colangelo.

A pussycat tiptoed up his spine, sunk its claws into his skull. In a flush of enjoyment, a one-drink girl who'd put away more, with her hand on Nick's shoulder and his hand on her behind. Nothing under her dress but her slip, no girdle, no pants either, what the hell did she think goes on? With her head reared back, her bright lips on a level with Nick's, talking away on a knotty point. From behind he seized Nick by the shoulder.

"I thought you'd gone."

Nick surrendered her at once. "We got caught in a conversation," he explained, resonant with understanding, and withdrew.

"What have you got against that guy?" Priscilla, still flushed with her conversation, upbraided him. "He's not so dumb. He has plenty to say."

He had no more than slipped his arm around Priscilla, trying to recapture their moment—never time for a moment of mood, emotion; no time to sustain the moment, to prolong, to deepen —when Gavin, the old war horse, grabbed hold of him.

"Can I see you a minute?"

He didn't want to see Gavin.

"Go. Go on," Priscilla urged. To her a summons from Gavin was tantamount to a summons from the Messiah. "I'm not about to evaporate."

In Bob and Mari's bedroom Gavin loosened his collar and his belt and stretched out on the bed, without removing shoes or bedspread, to rest. He pulled the pillows, rolled into the semblance of a bolster, down under his grizzled head, flattening them out. His hand strayed down his shirt unbuttoning and crept inside over his athletic undershirt massaging. Gavin suffered from a malady no doctor could diagnose to his satisfaction: cramps. Ulcers? No. Angina? Prove it. Psychosomatic, are you nuts? Wise old eyes that had seen too much of fact and fancy peeped out from between pouched lids. If Gavin noticed anyone watching his by-now unconscious rubbing of his belly he'd rebutton quickly, like a cripple denying his disability.

The third finger of Gavin's left hand was short by half. He had come up out of the rough-and-tumble of the thirties, had ridden the rails into towns where it was worth his life to seek out a contact in an outlying house, to be passed from contact to contact with literature secreted under his shirt. Outside one town he was flogged and left for dead in a ditch and when he came to in jail he was chained to his bunk, left without medical attention for three days. Lucky to lose no more than part of one finger. An orphan, a vagrant, a laborer, he had educated himself, chipped out of the shell of his ignorance into discovery of the world. Not an organizer like the organizers around nowadays whose work was always organizing, no matter what. Frank Gavin knew the shops from the inside, working from unskilled to skilled. There was no one in the UV management who could beat Gavin at slotting a job. Rumor had it that he regularly turned down UV offers that would have placed him immediately in the middle executive bracket.

"Shut the door," Gavin said from the bed.

He closed the door on a hubbub that poured like an avalanche through the hall, twined with a thread of music. *Painted lips, painted eyes, Wearing a bird of paradise.*

"You're not about"—Gavin's slitted eye peeped open—"to be seduced by Bob, are you?"

He settled on the foot of the bed by Gavin's crossed legs. His attitude toward Bob, he thought, was perfectly plain. Whether Bob was a card-carrying Communist, a fellow traveler or an unwitting pawn he didn't know and didn't want to know. He reserved the right to agree with Bob when he thought Bob was right. And to disagree with him, as he frequently did, when he thought him dead wrong.

"You'll only kill your usefulness," Gavin warned and punched back his pillows. Head propped up, jowls sagging, Gavin contemplated him.

"Take a tip from me, Mish. I know. I been burned by the Reds."

He thought his attitude toward Communism was perfectly clear. He had argued it out enough, God knows, with self-proclaimed party members. With Communism in the abstract he agreed as almost anyone else he knew would: "If that's Communism, I been a Communist all my life." But with Communism in the concrete he parted the ways. How could he, a workingman, not believe in the only country in the world governed by the working people? Very easily. He didn't believe it. He had too much of his father in him to believe it. The world is run by piecards! There are always those who reap the benefit. He didn't believe that the time of the classless society had come or ever would come. Or if the time did come that it would be a paradise, all problems solved, all conflicts resolved, man's inhumanity to man forever at an end.

He was all for it. But not with it.

Gavin peeled back his withered undershirt and tenderly rubbed over his wincing, whiskered belly.

"I can see so well what's coming," Gavin said. "The leadership of this local is too far out on a limb. The company's going to chop it off so fast, and what they don't chop the membership will. We've got to develop the independent element here. To protect and advance what we've won."

He had for Gavin a respect that was close, almost, to Priscilla's awe. But he was not about to be drawn by Gavin into an assault on Bob. He was tied to Bob by ties of friendship, loyalty, gratitude— the grandmother downstairs. He was incensed that Gavin should think he could lure him into it. While he was sitting on the foot of Bob's bed in Bob's bedroom . . .

"If you're looking for someone to knock Bob off," he said to Gavin, "what are you doing here? Go over to Herb Cranston's! I've known Mari since I was a kid. She got Bob to get me into UV when I dropped out of school. Everything I know about trade unionism they taught me—"

"Whoa. Slow down. Cool off." The dark eyes laughed at him from between the puffed lids. "I'm not dumping Bob. For one thing, I couldn't. What I'm saying is, it's only common sense we have to broaden out."

Bob was too far over in left field. Cranston was too far over on the right. Cranston himself would never run for top office. In another year Bob would eliminate himself. Each of them would back a slate of candidates they thought they could count on to attract the broadest support.

"What we have to avoid, above all, is a civil war in the local between Bob's clique and Cranston's. They'll drag the whole damn membership into it. We have to advance someone who can unite all the elements. And there's only one way to accomplish that, Mish. By concentration on the trade union issues, the day-to-day issues that affect the men on the job.

"This year, chief steward. Next year, the presidency."

"But Bob—"

"Bob'll accept it. So will Cranston."

"All I'm interested in is the principle of it. And already you got

me so messed up in the politics—I'm not ready for it. It's not up
to me. I got other plans . . ."

The door burst open. Colangelo again. Backtracking out in
shocked surprise, wagging his finger at him.

"What's this, an orgy? You keep disappearing into the bedroom."

"Are you still here?"

"I'm going."

Go and good-by.

"I just wanted you to know I wasn't trying to cut in on your
date."

"Okay. It's okay. All right now?"

After some further discussion with Gavin he left the bedroom
even less decided than before, thinking that much more about it.

Out in the hall the party was getting out of hand. Bob intercepted Mari as she scooted past. "We better send these people
home. They'll wreck the joint."

"Don't be such a stick!" Mari shook him off. "They got to loosen
up sometime." And with a bawdy chuckle she scooted on, pausing
only to groan over her pine chest. "They come in here with their
goddam butts and they don't care where . . ."

He bushwhacked through to the living room, looking for Priscilla, for that lost moment of theirs outside time and space, that
moment together that was not to be diverted or despoiled. Ray
pushed by him propelling Yvonne, hysterical with laughter, protesting in torrents of French, to the outer door. In the center of
a raucous audience in the living room stood a lady, cloaked in
a magnificent black Persian lamb coat with stand-up collar, her
blued hair swathed in a toque of satiny black plumage glistening
with purple and green lights. She was expatiating on the prowess
of her young man. The young man came barely up to her
diamond-pierced ear. Charlie Meadows, an ex-UVer who had gone
into the Merchant Marine, hearing that there was a party on had
brought her here. With the turbulent hair of an Irish poet and the
face of an obstreperous small boy, he stood now beside his lady
in the sober cloth of a petty officer. Meek as an acolyte he ac-

cepted her accolades. How many times a night. Timing each time. Dimensions. Thrust.

Six-by-eight glossies out of the lady's capacious handbag were being passed around, snatched from hand to hand. Photographs of a twenty-room Tudor mansion, in which Charlie was apparently ensconced for the nonce. Front view, rear view, gardens. Her husband, God rest him, had left her very well taken care of.

"Aaah, you're just babes in the woods."

The lady downed her double scotch and in a booming bass challenged all the males present, or the witness of their wives, to outmatch Charlie. Verbally.

"You're a bust. Technique, variations, forget it. Give me a good old pile driver anytime."

"I got it! I got it!"

Mari scooted into the center of the crowd.

Silence! Silence! Mari wants to speak.

Piano keys crashed. A dishpan was banged with a ladle.

Mari was hoisted up on the piano bench but not before she had laid down on it a layer of newspaper.

"I got it!"

Eyes round. Curls dancing. Impudent underlip outcurled.

> There was a rich widow in Kent
> Who invited upstairs a young gent
> She didn't ask him his name
> So widespread was his fame
> He came and he came till he went.

Priscilla was in the bathroom throwing up.

"Are you all right?" He rattled at the locked door. "Are you all right in there? Let me in."

"Don't be silly. Of course I'm . . . agh . . . agh . . ."

Helen Rakocszi was in the kitchen with her head down on the table, bawling. Mari fussed about the stove throwing coffee into her coffee-maker.

"Is Priscilla all right, Mish? You want some coffee for her? All that wine and then the mixed drinks—Helen, Helen, you hear me?" She pried up the bloated face. It thumped back down on the table. "Oh God. Go find Marty, Mish. Helen, Marty's still here."

Marty was in the bedroom with Gavin.

The subsurface palaverings of the evening. Scurryings in the walls. The enigmatic ridges and gullies of the grandmother's face hovering over the birthday candles.

Who struck the first blow wasn't certain.

A dispute in progress down the hall erupted into a clamor and the two principals, Bob Ucchini and Nick Colangelo, came to blows. Bob shoved Nick toward the door, out! Nick grasped Bob's collar at the throat. One of them threw a punch. A large part of the party rushed down the hall to the melee. The two men were wrenched apart.

Bob with his arms pinned back shouted, "Any fool knows Trieste was a Slovenian city to begin with!"

Nick struggling against his subduers bellowed, "He's giving Trieste away to Tito!"

In the confusion there was a movement of Italians toward one another. Yusskevitch shouldered through from the rear—"Hey, you! Hey, you!"—with his nephew right behind him. An anomalous pool milled about of those who were for whatever Tito was for and those who were for whatever Truman was for, regardless of national origin. Mari dove between arms and legs and managed to pull the outer door open wide enough to expel the antagonists into the outer hall.

"Down with Tito!" Nick bellowed.

"Yeah. Up with Mussolini!" Yusskevitch jeered.

The whole party might have plowed in and gone tumbling down the flights of stairs if two of them, Marty and himself, hadn't bludgeoned past Yusskevitch and taking Nick by the arms bundled him out between them. The remnants of the birthday party in the basement surged upward. What is this riot? A shame. A disgrace.

"He's giving Trieste away to Tito!" Nick bellowed down to them, sure of sympathy from below.

Someone from upstairs flung Nick's jacket down. Someone from downstairs tossed Nick's hat up.

"Viva Trieste!" Nick bellowed as they hustled him down the stairs.

"Viva Trieste!" as they forced him out of the murk of heat and smoke into the cold night air.

They trotted him into the flood-lit yard. "Which is his car? Where are his keys? Better drive him." They packed him inside.

"Viva Trieste!"

The widow squired by Charlie was getting into her car, a car as slick as black ice, a black bullet of a car, the kind of a car that glides through cities late nights, bulletproof, on missions suitable to diplomats and gangsters. She held the door open on her side. Lapped in opulence, her coat unfastened falling in folds about her ankles, she leaned out toward them.

"Need any help?"

He arranged with her to be driven back from Nick's house. On the return journey, seated between the widow and Charlie at the wheel, the velour sumptuously smooth behind his back and the dashboard before him streaked with the lights of a thousand night cities, he was overcome with depression, the loneliness that shrivels the soul. Beyond the car, patches of dirty snow lined the narrow streets. Brittle frame houses closed in. Lost, loveless, abandoned in a city of black icicles.

"Tell me something, sonny," the widow said to him. "What were they brawling about up there? What the fuck got into them?"

Up in the Ucchini apartment the company had left. Frank Gavin leaned over the piano. Bob played. And Mari, embracing the two men, threw her eyes and her ass around. Swaying together they sang with a sweetness breaking out of their throats that would break your heart. *Oh Danny boy-y-y* . . .

Where was Priscilla?

In the bedroom on the bed. Out like a light.

4

And so the first months of their marriage were consumed in a highly charged election campaign.

It was a good marriage, a sound marriage in which the cracks showed only occasionally.

"Come see the purple finches," Flo Barth called them to her side at her living room window on the day of their wedding, "how they perch."

They watched the birds with her a moment. Flying from perch to perch in search of food or a nesting spot or whatever. The male, rosy-feathered, landed on the side-yard fence and the female, white-flecked brown, right behind him. He pointing one direction, she pointing diametrically opposite, commanding between them a full-circle perspective on food, security, the next move. The male took off from the fence, the female right behind him.

To be. To do. There was never enough time to be. There was always too much to do. They were always in a crowd, always in a crisis. Excitement. Challenge. Growth. An endless hassle.

To be was to do. They were what they did.

He was elected at a time of high tide, at the turning of the tide. Cranston's candidates won several stewardships, a seat on the executive committee. Nothing to worry about. Anyhow they didn't worry him. They were Bob's worry.

He didn't understand what was happening to him while it happened. He didn't see the process of attrition setting in that would eventually undermine him. He didn't count the casualties until it was too late.

FOUR

Of Victors and Victims

I

The time a year and a quarter later, a fine blue-and-gold day in mid-September 1947.

The place the Labor Conference Room on the third floor of the Industrial Relations Building, United Vacuum, Shoreham Works.

On one side of the table the union team. Michael Lunin, recently elected president of EWIU-UV Local 317. Maria Ucchini and other members of the negotiating committee. Gene Bostic, new steward in Spray Paint. Frank Gavin, the international representative. Except for Gavin, the one professional, they are on company-union time, in their work clothes, off their jobs and due back in an hour or two.

On the opposite side of the table the company team. Grover Coffin, director of Industrial Relations. Members of his staff, his supervisor from Spray Paint, his time-study man and methods engineer. All dressed in suits appropriate to their status and income. Undivided among themselves, strictly under Coffin's thumb.

Speedwriter taking notes, non-verbatim. Experts and lawyers for both sides on tap.

Atmosphere friendly. Ashtrays all around.

The issue: a fraction of a second in Spray Paint.

According to the scuttlebutt around the plant, Grover Coffin was the architect of UV's new labor policy. Following the 1946 strike Coffin had been invited, so the scuttlebutt had it, to a secret conclave of UV's top directorate in Philadelphia (why Philadelphia? unless it was to lend authenticity to speculation?) to participate in an analysis of the company's position. His analysis left a lasting impression.

"Something happened in this strike," Coffin was supposed to have stated at the Philadelphia conclave, "that must never happen again. Somewhere, somehow, the employees got the idea that they were in the driver's seat. That they had control in their hands. This is the attitude, gentlemen, that must be reversed. This is the fantasy that must be eradicated."

As a result, a few months afterward, Coffin was promoted from Personnel on the first floor to the executive suite of Labor Relations on the third floor and was given a free hand to develop his theories. Coffin eschewed the hard line, take it or leave it, that had precipitated the strike to begin with. He made no attempt to weed out militants, leaving it to the Taft-Hartley Act and the Cold War to mitigate their effect. He did not stride up and down and shake his arms and hurl accusations during the altercations that broke out now and again over work stoppages. He left the heroics to the lawyers.

He named Building 3 the Industrial Relations Building and housed under its roof all functions affecting employees, health office and classrooms, house organ and discount store as well as payroll accounting, hiring and firing. He substituted the door sign "Employee Relations" for "Labor Relations" in the departments that dealt directly with the union. In the company paper he replaced the incendiary words "workers" and "labor" with "employees." All foremen were now consistently referred to as "supervisors." Only the Labor Conference Room where the actual meeting of labor and management occurred remained, obdurately, unamenable to semantics.

Coffin, from the beginning, refused to admit any distinction between labor and management. Serving their common interest and the public interest, union and company representatives met to iron out the snags that are bound to develop in any mechanism. Just keep the issue specific. Keep it technical. Eye on the ball.

At the moment Coffin was not so much annoyed at Maria Ucchini as amused by her. Long and narrow of head, thin-lipped, his ruddy complexion taking on a bluish cast from the slate tone of his shaped hair and his suit, he appeared to be as solemn as his nickname. Graveyard was not however lacking in humor. Without the crack of a smile or a pause for recognition, it mumbled out from under the mustache he didn't have as if by inadvertence. Minutes, sometimes hours later it evoked a taste on the tongue of vinegar pickle.

"Now, Mrs. Ucchini, that is an irresponsible, irrelevant and uncalled-for insinuation." A formidable rustling of the diagrams his secretary had deposited before him. With a boardinghouse reach across the table, on the diagonal, Coffin courteously presented the first set to Mrs. Ucchini. "Now if you will take the trouble to look through this, Maria, you will see that the number of motions . . ."

Sets of diagrams were distributed on both sides of the table.

The trouble in Spray Paint had started a few months ago with the introduction of a spray gun of a slightly different model from the one in use. A sprayer had a row with his supervisor over the No. 3, claiming that it took him a fraction of a second longer to cover so many square feet with it than the No. 1. Not only should he not be penalized in his pay, the sprayer claimed, for the lag in his production quota, but he should be compensated for the extra skill required in its use. The other sprayers with the No. 3 backed the complainant up. It so happened that the employees in Spray Paint were about 30 per cent Negro and the rest mainly Italian. The Italians, being older on the job and wary of any tool that might entail a change of routine, had by and large avoided being stuck with the No. 3.

Now to the general embarrassment, not only Coffin's, Mariuch was implying that more than a fraction of a second was involved in the dispute. In cadences throaty, purling, hardly raised above a whisper, the voice of sweet reason, she charged the company with gross race discrimination, from apprentice training up through administration and all stops between.

The embarrassment was the more acute because of the presence of Bostic. It was well known that Gene Bostic had been maneuvered by the Ucchinis into the stewardship of Spray Paint through a by-election to fill a vacancy. He was the first Negro steward in the plant. Mari was now demonstrating to Bostic, and therefore to all the colored workers, her willingness to stick her neck out on the race question on every occasion that offered, even on the highest level. No one doubted that her concern was sincere. But it was also political, and no one on the negotiating committee, especially not the anti-Ucchini members, wanted to be caught out in the open espousing her politics. No one wanted to step on Bostic's toes either. The dilemma would have been easy enough to dispose of in Bostic's absence. In his first participation in top-level negotiation, Bostic sat at the table with attention fixed not on the company men across from him but on his union confreres, watchful, mistrustful, hard-eyed, glinting.

"Now as you can see from these diagrams, the number of motions and the amount of pressure and the coverage are exactly the same for the No. 1 gun and the No. 3."

Coffin with the assistance of his aides flipped through the diagrams pointing out the breakdown of figure and tool in motion.

"Given the same proficiency on the part of the operator . . ."

Gavin was immediately on them. When was this time-motion study made? With or without the consent of the worker involved? Did they take any film? No filming, in the open or on the sly!

"This is the manufacturer's study," Coffin insisted. "They tested out the No. 3 under every conceivable condition. Given the same degree of proficiency on the part of the operator . . ."

"Manufacturer!" Gavin pounced on it. "No wonder—"

"Proficiency!" Mari interrupted them. "That's it, that's just what I mean. You've given the colored equipment," she said to Coffin in her night-club contralto, not to be contradicted, "that puts a premium on proficiency and they're making five cents an hour less with it than they did with the No. 1, handling the same workload."

"Mrs. Ucchini."

Coffin raised his hands in despair to his ears, as if to shut out a note of shrillness, of stridency, of hysterical denunciation directed against him for no discernible reason.

"We can do without these, if you'll pardon the expression, red herrings injected into the proceedings. If it's your purpose to create confusion, we can accomplish nothing here but waste of time. Now those of us who seriously want to unravel this, let's get on."

"Are you baiting me?"

Mari's small bouncy figure, trim in tan blouse and slacks, rose up out of the chair. She was furious with Coffin. Not for his red-baiting—that was standard for the course. Not for his race-baiting as she conceived it—good, he was exposing himself. For his woman-baiting. Coffin was demeaning and isolating her in the company of men.

"Gavin," she commanded. "You heard him."

Mari was always all sex. The chip she carried on her shoulder was an invitation. Her walk, the hell with you all, was a provocation. She conducted intercourse with her eyes. If she never moved another muscle, her eyes did it.

Never more so than now. Her eyes practically plucked Gavin up out of his chair. Go save my honor from this dastardly traducer! There was a rumor around the plant that Frank Gavin had once been her boy friend. There was also a rumor that Coffin would have liked to date her if he could without compromising his position and that was why he gave her such a hard time.

With visible effort Gavin nailed himself to his chair. Under cover of riffling through the diagrams once again to find the flaw, he ignored her. Gavin was not inclined these days to extricate the Ucchinis from the consequence of their follies. If Mari wanted to bring up charges of race discrimination against the company, this was not the time or the place. The international maintained an anti-discrimination committee under a full-time

Negro director, where such charges were to be lodged, weighed and processed for handling on the proper level.

Mish.

With her eyes she spoke, stepped on his foot, compelled him.

On the other side, with a scrape and shift of his chair, Gavin pressed him.

He was thoroughly exasperated with Mari. When she had approached him beforehand about using the grievance to open up the guns on race, he had turned her down. Now she was trying to entangle him in her tactic by fiat where persuasion had failed. He was still smarting from the last time he primed the gun for the Ucchinis on race.

Besides, he had his own red herring that he was itching to toss into the proceedings. A number of recently upgraded sprayers, Italian and Negro alike, were being paid at the bottom of the wage range in their new classification, receiving a dime below the top pay in their previous classification. This zigzag in the wage structure occurred throughout the plant, cutting across race, sex, politics. A bit of figure finagling that saved the company, he was convinced, a pretty penny. Merely to raise the subject of overlapping pay grades was to set off a bomb under Coffin. And unite the union negotiating committee around a common cause.

He turned his eyes away from Mari. It was no good. She was still standing, expecting defense by her union against the boss. Men on both sides of the table were cringing and coughing. The speedwriter gaped at Mari, pencil suspended from pad, reveling in her temerity.

Bostic.

Audibly Mari looked toward Bostic for vindication. Gene Bostic, the focal point of it all, spray painter, steward, Negro, had not opened his mouth up to now. He was an articulate enough fellow, vocal with his gripes at meetings of the Stewards Council, unhesitant in lambasting union officials for their deficiencies. But when the spray-gun grievance was processed on the lower levels, Bostic had not been so quick to lambast the department foreman —or was it "supervisor" to him? He let the section chairman first and later the Grievance Board take up the cudgels while he stood by, watchful, on the alert for the first sign of betrayal.

Bostic sat at the conference table in his spattered coveralls and thumbed through the stapled diagrams, unresponsive to Mari's impelling eyes.

Inexperienced? Intimidated? Feeling, out of the habit of subjection, that his job depended more on Coffin's good will toward him than on Mari's good offices? Even though the superseniority conferred by contract on the stewardship, which she had wangled for him, saved him from being laid off?

Bostic's silence was painful. Mari had brought him this far. Now perform!

In a sweat of sympathy and irritation with Bostic, with Mari, damning himself for identifying with them, he cleared his throat of a skein of strains and launched prematurely into his own explosive irrelevance.

"If it's a matter of proficiency rating, Mr. Coffin—" he said and disdainfully flicked the diagrams back toward Coffin. "If the No. 3 requires special proficiency as Mrs. Ucchini just suggested and as the operator states in his grievance and as you yourself, Mr. Coffin . . ."

The company claimed it could analyze a job with scientific precision. The union denied it. What happens in the book and what happens on the job can be entirely different things.

"Then perhaps, Mr. Coffin, we'd better review the rating structure in that department—"

"Bostic?"

Before he could open it up, Coffin cut him off, addressing himself to the steward.

"Now I'm not prone to be diverted by red herrings," Coffin said to Bostic, "but since this unfortunate innuendo has been thrown into the hopper, I don't think I can let it go by unchallenged. Do you think, Bostic, that United Vacuum makes a practice of racial discrimination?"

Bostic fingered the squashed bridge of his nose.

"Well?"

Mari who had settled back in her chair with a little wriggle of dissatisfaction, just a modicum appeased, intervened.

"You're talking to him," she rebuked Coffin, "like a plantation master."

"Why don't you—let him speak—for himself, Mrs. Ucchini?"

As silken as she was velvet, Coffin folded his arms on the table and pivoted about toward Bostic, man to man, excluding her.

"Go ahead, Bostic. You can be frank with me. There's nothing to be afraid of."

"Well . . ."

Mari's eyes on Bostic commanded-demanded: Give it to him! Lay it on the line!

Gavin inserted his hand inside his jacket with the surreptitiousness of one suffering a heart ailment.

"Well . . ."

The speedwriter dropped her pencil and everybody jumped. The methods engineer, stooping to retrieve the pencil as it rolled away, bumped his head against the girl's and came up red-faced.

"Well . . . sir . . ."

Men on both sides of the table, even Mari's partisans, writhed in their discomfort with a malicious-delicious glee in her discomfiture.

So this is your boy!

The brow creased vertically over the squashed nose. The mouth fumbled. Bostic was wild. Plantation, what plantation! From Red Bank, New Jersey. Afraid? Forced against his will and advantage to decide which way to jump.

"You see . . ."

The air was suffused with the man's inner tumult. The cream walls of the shoe-box room shimmered with it. Marty Rakocszi, the business agent, heaved and struggled with a rising sneeze that expelled itself with a squeal and a splatter he barely caught in his handkerchief.

It had gone on long enough. Too long.

"You don't really expect him to answer that, do you, Mr. Coffin?"

Coffin snapped to, passed his diagrams back to his secretary and sent her around to collect the rest.

"All right, Lunin. Now that we've settled this spray thing, what's the next item?"

The union's negotiating committee was tired of it, disgusted with it, ready to give up on it and Coffin guessed it. Gavin was just about to signal Bostic that he could return to his department. Frank had no intention of saving a case Mariuch had spoiled for the sake of a victory she would assume and broadcast as hers. He'd trade off the spray-gun grievance for another item on the list.

"Now wait a minute."

"What's the matter, Lunin?" Almost Coffin smiled at him. "You have a reservation?"

Coffin had had his fun with Mariuch, had pulled her leg, pinned her ears back. Now Coffin was prepared to deal with him. Not with the same technique however. The partnership gambit. Partners in nothing else, they were partners in peacemaking, no?

Knowing that he was contentious, Coffin invited objection from him. Went out of his way to invite it. As if by the mere act of spilling it he solved it, on Coffin's terms. Come let us reason together, Coffin invited him. Between the two of us we can straighten this out, can't we?

Through over a year of hard bargaining Coffin had persisted in this attitude toward him, a suggestion of complicity, of mutual accord lurking in the background, the expectation of reconciling what was not necessarily reconcilable. It was hard for him to believe that Coffin was serious in his attitude. The director of industrial relations was appointed by the corporation to fight for it. He was elected by the men in the plant to fight for them. Now let us not muddy up the waters.

Coffin's almost smile toward him, the rosy gleam of almost intimacy through his slate-blue haze, had its history in a strange interlude they'd shared. In the spring when he was first married he had taken his wife, Priscilla, and her brother, Ted, out to dinner in The Bottoms, the Italian section, at a little hole-in-the-wall restaurant owned by Bob Ucchini's cousin. As they entered, Ted recognized a customer at the bar that he had interviewed the week before for his thesis, UV's personnel director. "How are things going?" Ted asked Coffin. "Terrible," Coffin said. "Oh, you know each other?" Bob's cousin inquired over the bar and fixed them up with a table in the corner. "He's a great pasta-fagiol' man," Bob's cousin said of Coffin.

The great pasta-fagiol' man brought his plate over to their table and entertained them through dinner with an account of the current state of affairs at United Vacuum.

"Every year when March rolls around something happens. Every male on the staff starts up like a buck rabbit. Everything's in upheaval. Firings. Hirings. Promotions and demotions. Transfers. People you've tolerated all along, headaches you've put up with, all of a sudden it's unbearable. Out the window! We call it the March syndrome.

"The man who outlasts it all, who weathers every storm, is the one with the sad, weary, resigned air, who sticks to his desk doing the jobs everyone else shuffles off on him. All those little pesky snarls nobody else will tackle. Cultivating his anonymity. A threat to no one's ambitions."

Spooning up his thick soup, sopping up with chunks of garlic bread. A non-stop monologue.

Three months later, shortly after the union election, he met Coffin in the Labor Conference Room. He walked in for the first time as chief steward and Coffin walked in for the first time as chief of employee relations and they both stepped back over their heels. You!

Coffin never mentioned their dinner in the restaurant to him. He made no mention of it to Coffin either, the great pasta-fagiol' man's manner forbade it. But the intimation that shared experience could lead to shared interest hovered between them. They shared the human burdens, didn't they, of Shoreham's largest industry, a plant with a fluctuating work force of eight thousand to five thousand, whose function was the production of goods for profit.

He did not smile back over the conference table at Coffin. Those quirks in the corners of his mouth spontaneously twitching, encouragement to Coffin's eagerness, he restrained with an iron bit.

"Yeah," he said, "I have a reservation. Just when did we settle this?"

The fight had started in Spray Paint with an argument between a sprayer and his foreman over a fraction of a second. It ended up in Spray Paint.

Rather than pass the grievance on to a higher level, the New York headquarters of union and company where the officials would tear their hair out over it—how did this ever land here? something that should have been settled on the floor in the first step!—the two teams betook themselves from the conference room to the department in a last-ditch attempt to reach determination.

Coffin brought his full team into Spray Paint: engineers, personnel director, lawyer, top expert in washer and refrigerator finishes. Lunin and Gavin brought in their full team: their negotiating committee, Bostic, their lawyer and their expert.

Outside a paint booth, watching a sprayer cover washer sides with his No. 3 gun, Coffin trotted out his stack of diagrams all over again. So many motions, so much time per motion.

Gavin and the union expert put the sprayer through the motions again, demonstrating. "You're not counting where he picks up. You're overlooking where he has to turn."

Inquisitively Mari skirted about the adjoining spray booths, with a mutter that would penetrate armor plate. If it was all the same, why was it most of the colored had the No. 3 and the whites the No. 1? Why was it the two whites with the No. 3 (obviously a couple of shleps the foreman had it in for) weren't making out any better with it than the colored?

Bostic spoke up. Treading a quagmire, testing it out every step of the way, Bostic at last found himself on firm ground. He aligned himself with the union group and explained the job to Coffin.

"The coverage is just as good with the new gun, Mr. Coffin, but it's harder to apply. Maybe it's the air mix. Maybe it's the paint we're on now. Maybe it's in the color, the viscosity's different."

Coffin walked away from him. A whisper against the new paint coming in and they'd all be squawking, No. 1 as well as No. 3. Nothing would pass inspection.

The Negro sprayer in the booth knowing he was under observation was of course holding back. The supervisor went for Vittorini, his fastest operator, to show what he could do with the No. 3.

The union lawyer started screaming contract violation and the company lawyer started screaming no such thing.

When the supervisor arrived with Vittorini, Mari muscled in. "You're pitting race against race!"

She snatched at Vittorini's mask and shook her finger in his gentle, inoffensive face. "Don't you do it! Don't you touch that piece of crap! Always remember you're just another wop to them!"

Mari was muscled out, a thorn in the side of law and order. The supervisor brought in three other sprayers. Nick Colangelo. Ange Baldessari. Liscio. None of them would touch the No. 3 without the nod of the union.

"Realistically, Lunin, it's so close," Coffin confided in an aside, "what's to be gained from going on with this?"

He stepped back from the embroilment between the two lawyers, Coffin and Gavin, Bostic and the experts, and surveyed the scene. Amid the fumes and heat the sprayers, goggled and masked with respirators, swooshed their guns over washer sides shuttling to the ovens.

He forgot race. He forgot the two-dollar cut in pay per week on the No. 3. He forgot his endeavors to steer the bargaining in a direction that would bridge the divisions within his negotiating committee: the need for eliminating overlapping pay grades, for establishing a single-rate pay structure. He forgot the possibilities: somebody in Purchasing must have goofed with the gun; somebody in Paint Chemistry must have slipped up; somebody was trying frantically to compensate down below for a flaw up above. All he could see was the man in the booth with his thumb on the spray gun and the man outside with his thumb on the stop watch. All he could think of was the fraction of a second.

He rejoined the group and like Mari burst out of the bounds of the specific and the technical.

"What are we, crazy?" he said to Coffin. "What have we come to? To be fighting like this over a tenth of a second. What are the goals of your civilization when this much effort is poured into computing the last fraction of this man's time? What kind of society is this? What are we trying to progress to?"

Coffin and his contingent continued with their specifics a few minutes more. But it was all over. They knew it themselves. The company would have to let this one pass.

Only the look on Coffin's face, the look Coffin turned on him, the look of pained surprise, of disappointment deepening to disgust, that look remained in his mind. No more intimations of intimacy. No more hand-in-glove, we fellow employees. He'd shut the door in Coffin's face. No macaroni and bean soup here, mister.

He emerged from the Labor Conference Room later with his cohorts, leaving Gavin to clean up the details. They tramped down to the main floor together and returned through the buildings to their departments. Talkative, exhilarated with the joy of combat, the ceaseless contest with management over minute differentials that made all the difference in a day's work. The last two items had gone fast, everyone pitching in with his own angle, exchanging the high sign, conceding here, winning a point there.

"Didn't I tell him! Didn't I give it to him!" Mari exulted all during the rehash. "He won't forget that one in a hurry."

But as soon as the others had scattered, she changed her tune.

"Why didn't you back me up, Mish?" she upbraided him as they neared her job in Rheostat.

She was still furious with Coffin. "Son of a bitch, I had him dead to rights. I had him on the run. And just as I have him up against the wall, that bastard Gavin puts the kibosh on me.

"And you. You're just as bad as he is. Why didn't you let Bostic answer Coffin? Why'd you shut him up? The chance of a life-time. He could have landed him one right on the kisser."

He had some difficulty recalling when it was he had shut Bostic up.

"Mari, Coffin had Bostic on the griddle— Never mind. The whole grievance was about to fall apart. It's getting to the point in this local where nothing's being fought through on the merits but on who sponsors it."

"All right, okay, you fought it. But why didn't you fight it on principle?"

"What principle?"

"The women and the colored get the worst deal in this plant. And today was a prime example of it!"

He was exhausted by his own vehemence.

"Wake up, Mari. Half our own crew were dragging their feet. We were losing Gavin. I had to find common ground, the scrap of common ground . . ."

Mari grew morose. Her throaty voice thickened, throbbed with mourning. It was awful. Dreadful. Everything was going down the drain. With one hand the union tried to cope with the company and with the other it was repressing and negating, destroying its own resources. Whatever was accomplished here in Shoreham, New York pulled the rug right out from under it.

"You think you can carry Gavin? You're playing right into his hands. He was playing you against me back there. He's playing you against Bob. He'll play you till he has every progressive out of the leadership. Including you. Go ahead, line up with Gavin. Find out for yourself."

With the dignity of tragedy, majestic in her carriage, a sliver of a figure enticingly bosomed and hipped, she mounted the iron-treaded stairway to her department.

The worst of it was, he sometimes thought that Mariuch was the smartest one of them all.

In the afternoon after work he got it on the other side from Gavin.

2

"Haven't they landed you in enough hot water? Haven't you learned your lesson yet?"

He was driving Gavin from the union hall to the railroad station before going home to dinner. Gavin was white and tired, his pouched eyes sparked with pain. His left hand with its foreshortened middle finger picked at his tie unknotting and strayed downward unbuttoning, unbuckling, half undressing in the car.

"You had the perfect out. All you had to do was back away from it. 'You blew it, baby.' Let her bear the onus. Instead you plow in . . . They trapped you before with Bostic. And you're still paying for it."

It was true. He had been elected in June on a coalition slate arranged by Gavin in order to avoid the vicious contest impending between Bob's faction and Herb Cranston's faction, which now called itself the Freedom Caucus. The two factions had more or less agreed on a list of candidates, so many yours, so many ours, so many neutrals, with the scales still tipped in Bob's favor. Shortly after the election Bob had come to him with a resolution that was to be introduced, he said, by Gene Bostic, a spray painter, at the next membership meeting. Bob wanted his assurance that he would advocate support of the resolution by officers and members and transmission of it to the District Council and the General Executive Board.

"I'll take care of my people," Bob said to him. From his position as section chairman of Radiosonics, Bob could mobilize on occasion at least one third of the active membership. "You take care of the rest."

He was none too happy with the resolution. He had opposed superseniority for veterans a few years before and so had Bob. Now he was being asked by Bob to support superseniority for Negroes. "SINCE Negroes were not employed by UV in numbers until the war . . . And SINCE they are consequently last to be upgraded and first to be laid off . . . THEREFORE special measures are necessary to overcome the handicap imposed by previous discrimination . . ."

Suspension of seniority, the most precious of the protections gained by organized labor . . . It was out of the question. He knew it would be voted down. The minute workers feel they may be bumped out of turn, there's bound to be friction.

"Have nothing to do with it," Gavin had advised him when he showed him the resolution. "It's a grandstand play. All right, all right, Bob means well by it. He means well enough, God help him. But when it's defeated, what have you got? The colored will be disgruntled with the whites. The whites'll go on the defensive, and offensive, with the colored. It'll only exacerbate the existing situation. Get you off to a bad start. The whole thing's cuckoo. Don't let them bring it to the floor."

But Bob and Mari had descended on him in his apartment, bringing Bostic and three other colored with them. Bostic went to work on him with a cold chisel. "What about the DPs? Seniority or no seniority, the company found a place for them and you didn't let out a peep! If there's anybody in this country got seniority, it's us." A gingery young woman took a long look at Priscilla. "You're carrying. Why don't you sit down and enjoy it?" "I am?" "Mm hm. Never missed one yet." It turned out to be one of those evenings, ferocious and funny. To reject them for whatever reason was to lose them. How could he reject such people? They would obtain sufficient signatures on the resolution in the plant, they promised, to guarantee a substantial vote. He would issue a statement covering its pros and cons.

The rest was history, not exactly as Gavin anticipated it but near enough.

Cranston's Freedom Caucus went into a frenzy over his statement. Lunin was fronting for Ucchini. Ucchini was fronting for the Commies. The Commies were fronting for Moscow. The whole scheme was hatched in the Kremlin, not to eradicate inequities but to foment turmoil.

The CIO national office sent its FEPC chairman to the District Council to explain the fallacies of the resolution being circulated in United Vacuum by EWIU-UV Local 317 with the apparent encouragement of our good friend and brother, Mish Lunin. The NAACP national office communicated its displeasure through a letter to the chairman of the Shoreham chapter, released to the press, condemning Mr. Lunin's praiseworthy but misguided efforts to secure special treatment for Negroes. All the Negro wanted and needed was to be treated the same as everyone else.

The resolution was presented at the membership meeting bearing the names of over four hundred signers, white and black, Catholic, Protestant, Jewish. Bostic, who introduced it, received hearty applause. The secretary-treasurer read the official messages sent in against it, offsetting Bostic's appeal.

Lunin stepped down from the chair amid a rising storm of speeches to express his own views. Applause and boos. The boos had it.

Cranston took the rostrum, not a strong speaker but sincere, persuasive. "It's perfectly clear that no one wants this thing but a little gang of conspirators who've pushed the colored into it and browbeat the whites into supporting them under threat of being labeled hatemongers."

Bob Ucchini took the rostrum to address the body he had so often before presided over, and with all his old ire and fire, his ringing eloquence, he flayed them and swayed them.

Cranston's men rushed the rostrum. Bob's men rushed Cranston's. In the uproar Bob was escorted out of the hall under bodyguard. Mari too, she commandeered her own bodyguard. Blasting right and left as she was marched out by her protectors. "I know you, Chickie, who fixed you up when you were thrown out of your flat? I know you, Randolph, where would you be— And you, my fine Mafia cousin . . ."

Having failed to achieve superseniority for Negroes, Bob and Mari achieved it for Bostic by ramming through his election to the stewardship in Spray Paint when the regularly elected steward resigned. It was said that Bostic had thanked them with tears in his eyes, though Bostic was scarcely the type for tears, for saving his job for him when he was about to be laid off.

Cranston had not raised any objection to Bostic's election up to now. Herb was too shaken up, almost as shaken up as Bob was, by the charge of his light brigade. A petty racketeer known as Tookalook had penetrated the Freedom Caucus with the aim of taking it over. It was Tookalook and his clique, sporting American Legion caps, who had led the assault on Bob, yelling, "Go back to Rush-sha!" Cranston was having his troubles.

The whole thing was a hornets' nest.

"You knew what the situation was there today," Gavin said to him, and with clothing loosened sagged back, legs under the dashboard, loosening his joints.

He knew.

Bostic sitting in on the negotiation of a grievance, Mariuch egging him on, Lunin bailing them out.

And in the background, off-scene. Cranston hostile to every act of Lunin's that smacked of commitment to the Ucchinis. Tookalook out to torpedo Cranston with Lunin's lunacies. Bob with his still considerable forces and resources, among which he counted Lunin, blowing the horns of virtue (civil rights!), beating the drums of logic (peace and trade!), waving the banner of the international working class (*avanti popolo! a basso fascismo!*). And the DPs. Forty Poles and Hungarians brought over from the German camps by relatives in the city, under the aegis of churches and relief agencies; most of them bitterly anti-Soviet; all of them desperate to make a place for themselves, one tiny place, contributing by their presence to the grumblings and rumblings, the ferment.

"You're the youngest local president we have now, Mish," Gavin said to him. "How old are you? Twenty-five? Twenty-six? You have a long way to go. I know how you feel about Bob and Mari. They're family."

Abruptly Gavin sat up, tight-strung, and searched about as if trying to locate himself in a strange city, looking for a particular street, a route that mustn't be missed.

"Take the next block. Go back to UV. The mall side. Believe me, Mish, I know what it is to be torn between personal and organizational loyalties."

Gavin had never acquired the burly, bustling manner of some professional trade unionists. He had not made his way upward. He was always a little apart. He ate himself up.

"I know what it is to be torn between what's right and what's real. If you can ever begin to determine what's right, what's real."

"If you're building up to something," he said to Gavin, "I wish you'd say it outright. And if it's what I think it is, the answer is no."

"You're going to have to detach yourself from the Ucchinis."

"No."

"That's not all there is to it, Mish. That's just the beginning. Follow the mall to the rotunda. Stop there."

The mall, a street divided by a grassy strip, ran along the east side of United Vacuum. Before the office tower was built, it had been a main thoroughfare providing a pleasant prospect for the public entrance and the balconies that decoratively embraced at intervals the second-floor windows. In mild weather, workers spread out over the grassy strip of the mall with their lunches.

Gavin opened the car door at the small stone rotunda where the lawn widened out. The rotunda was ringed with barberry bushes and the iron stanchions of park benches long ago removed.

"Right here," Gavin said. "This is it. X marks the spot. Andy Lucas, you remember Andy? No, he was before your time. Killed in Spain. Popped his head over the trench to see what was going on and bam. Just about your age.

"There was a time back then when half the Communist Party in Shoreham was Hungarian. Refugees from the Horthy terror after the First World War. Andy used to bring a box down here every Thursday noon and address the workers who were lunching around. One day Bob Ucchini went up to Andy and asked him if he could use his permit to speak. Bob and Ray Pelletier and Marty Rakocszi and a few others were trying to organize the plant. Andy put Bob in touch with me. I put Bob in touch with the organizing drive in UV plants elsewhere. I moved into Shoreham to help him out. I educated him in Marxism. Over a period of about two years. It opened up the sky for Bob. It gave meaning to who he was, and where and why. It saved his soul."

With his shirttails hanging, Gavin stepped out of the car over the curb and tramped about the patchy grass. The barberry bushes were turning color, olive tinged with maroon, dotted with crimson berries. Like a child, Gavin folded his fingers at the base of an unkempt branch and pulled upward over the brambles, stripping it. He edged back into the car with the leaves nested, a maroon-stained green blossom, between his two fingers. He regarded the blossom so neatly gathered in puzzlement and scattered it outside, slammed the door.

"We better get going if we're going to make my train," Gavin said impatiently, as if he hadn't requested the detour in the first place.

The streets flew by. They caught up with the late afternoon traffic on Bancroft Avenue, bumper to bumper in a line of blaring horns. He was caged in the car with this painful man who unburdened upon him those things which he ought better to have kept to himself.

"You see, Mish, in those days I thought I could substitute politics for religion. Politics was my religion. But the minute you enter politics, you enter into action. And the minute you enter into action, the erosion of your ultimate purpose begins. There has to be something out there for you that's larger than action, larger than politics, larger than knowledge. A point of reference. Something that lays down the ethic. Something you can turn to for light in your time of need. Do you understand that?"

No, he didn't. He squirmed at the least hint of religiosity. He was not about to be drawn into Gavin's private search for grace. The ethic has to be in you. The light has to be in you. There is no help anywhere out there.

"Someday you'll know. Someday you'll find out."

He had some idea of the road that had brought Gavin to religion. The party promoted Gavin and the party broke him. Suddenly Gavin had found himself enmeshed in a welter of hair-splitting polemics, errors of policy and corrections of error that compounded the original error. Heresy trials. Slanders. He was the class enemy, a left sectarian, a right opportunist, an imperialist wrecker. Gavin went back to work in the plants just to be able to lay his hand on a machine again, place his living flesh on tempered steel, reality. But reality, the humdrum, unless it was infused with vision, could never for very long satisfy Gavin. One night somewhere on the road between Lynn, Massachusetts, and New Britain, Connecticut, Gavin experienced conversion. He went to Mass in the morning for the first time since he was a boy, confessed himself to the priest and was given fifty Stations of the Cross as penance. Gavin never became a good pious churchgoer but he never quite gave it up again.

The Ucchinis had their own version of Gavin's conversion.

"For some people," Bob would say with one of his grand generalizations, referring to himself perhaps, "it's the substratum of theory that counts. The stupidities men make of it are just a passing phenomenon. The music is always there. But for Gavin the stupidities were it. He fell into the hands of some nut who turned rat later on. And he had what amounted to a nervous breakdown."

According to Mari, Gavin had gone through a crisis all right but it wasn't because of politics. "You ever meet his wife? She was a nothing. A slut. I picked her up out of the ditch. I put the clothes on her back. And Gavin married her. He ran around on the side till after they'd had a couple of kids. Then he started going steady with this girl in the New York office, a really fine girl, the best. And he knocked her up. I'll never forget one night, she was boiling herself in the bathtub, so full of ergot, quinine, laxatives— That's when Frank got religion."

They snaked through the traffic-choked street toward the railroad station, a tan structure not unlike an Italian church with its belfried clock steeple. Its round-arched windows glinted darkly with the light of the setting sun through black tiers of track. Gavin nudged his spine about, seeking a spot that would yield him some ease.

"The hell of it is I brought Bob into it. Well, that's what I have to live with. I've tried to talk with him. I've pleaded with him. Slow down. Back off. Play it safe. No. He still thinks he's in the thick of battle, mid-field. When all the time he's fighting with his back to the brink of a precipice.

"I don't want to see you go down with him, Mish. There's no reason for it. You can't save him. And even if you could, what good would it do?"

True enough, Bob still thought he was running the show. When all the time his fellow workers were falling back under the daily onslaught of headlines and radio. Bomb Moscow. Canadian Red Spy Ring Revealed. A UV defense contract with the Atomic Energy Commission jeopardized by certain suspect elements in the union . . .

"If we went to war with Russia tomorrow," Gavin said, "do you doubt for a minute that Bob would have a group in there ready to go out on strike? Commit sabotage?"

True enough, Bob had been in Radar during the war, a technician on some sensitive electronic measuring device. There was no telling . . .

"How long can you tie yourself to Bob's kite? How long can the union allow itself to be fractured by controversies that, believe me, Mish, have no foundation anywhere on earth but in the wishful delusions of the Bob Ucchinis?"

He circled the railroad station seeking a niche to insert himself in. They still had seven minutes if the train was on schedule, which it usually wasn't. He was halted behind trucks by the red light under the viaduct.

"All right," he said, resting on the wheel, "we do the big scene in one of those anti-Nazi movies around. Throw the Red to the dogs. Is that your point?"

"My point is the Taft-Hartley non-Communist affidavit," Gavin said. "The AFL unions are signing it. When the CIO convention meets in November, half the unions will vote compliance. And when the EWIU convenes in February, what are we going to do, Mish? What are you going to do?

"It means Bob's through. How about you?"

"Now wait a minute, you're jumping the gun—"

"I don't like it. Personally I'm against it. But it's going to carry, Mish."

The green light blurred. He almost ran into the rear of the truck ahead of him. The car stalled. He was so stunned he couldn't, under the rain of horns and the fogs of monoxide, get it started again. He flooded the engine.

"I thought we were all going to stick together on this affidavit thing. I thought if we all refused to sign—"

"We have to remove the party-liners from positions of leadership if we're to fight the rest of the Act. Now take it easy, stop gassing it."

"It won't pass the convention. It can't. Not without one hell of a row."

"Stay out of it, Mish. Have nothing to do with it. Disappear if you have to when the vote is taken. Don't say a word. Not one word."

He parked the car behind the station under the high span of the platform, facing the posters mounted on the grille under the stairway. Green-peaked pixie peeking around green-arrowed pack of Wrigley Spearmint. Loudspeakers boomed with a voice as hollow as a robot's. The New York train was late again.

"Whatever happened to Scottsy?" Gavin asked, conversationally, marking time. "Lit out right after your big downtown demonstration, in the middle of a strike, nobody knows why or where. The best kept secret in UV. Who put the skids under him? Who was the hatchet man?"

No. He shrank under it. One of those acids in the plant, one touch and you break out all over, inflamed. Not that again. This wasn't the same thing. Not the same thing at all.

"You have to make your mind up. You have to see it in the framework of the larger picture—"

His mind was already made up. Years ago. "Nobody has the right to ask you," his father said and tore up the school questionnaire, "your nationality or your religion or your politics."

"We don't have a choice, Mish. The NLRB won't certify us as a bargaining unit if we don't comply. It won't deal with your local if you don't sign."

A roar on the tracks above of an approaching train, still a few minutes away. The concrete underpass of the station was splotched with the muck of footsteps, eternally wet.

Gavin heaved out of the car and, bent almost double, pulled himself together, shoved the shambles of his shirt into his pants, fumbled with flickering mid-finger up his buttons.

"Piano lessons," Gavin said through the car window. The grimace of a cramp splayed down his pitted cheeks. "If it wasn't for piano lessons . . ."

He hopped out of the car in concern. "Maybe you better come home with me. Rest up a while."

Irascibly Gavin waved him off.

"He had this scholarship to Juilliard. And his folks on relief."

The grimace twisted into a thin grin.

"Bob's never forgiven this country for not making a concert artist out of him."

Up the long iron staircase to the platform, from landing to landing, up to the roofed shed and the open sky above, Gavin climbed like a crab. Man cannot live without God. Man cannot live without prayer. Man cannot live without guilt, inborn and inherent in his every act. Man cannot live without hope of salvation.

He drove home to Prince Street on the bumpy road by the freight sidings along the waterfront. Refracted in the spars of barges, in a mote of dust on the windshield: the face of Bob Ucchini. Ucchini's dead. Drop him.

Bob in his black-knit seaman's beanie and roll-collared black jersey. The premature white hair, the anthracite eyes, the face of a sagacious gnome.

The wiry upright figure at the piano, blunt fingers gymnastic, separate entities under supreme control prancing over the yellowed keys, the little finger on a rotation all its own. The wiry figure and the fingers on wires, maestro.

The ringing eloquence, Italians and their voices, what an instrument the voice is.

He turned the corner into the cross street without even knowing it, stopped blindly at the bakery for buns and a cake.

"Should I sprinkle some powdered sugar on, mister? Mister?"

How long can you be the dupe of Bob who is the dupe of comrades who are being duped. A chain of dupedom.

He passed the market and had to drive around the block again to pick up milk and beer, potatoes, the heavy groceries.

Home. The gray ramshackle house crammed between the assorted storefronts of Prince Street.

If you can't have peace at home, Mariuch would say, where else is it? She and Bob were building a house for themselves on the outskirts of town. Every weekend on the house, Mari's bottom up the ladder, Bob's head down the hatch. A little Cape Cod to be painted yellow, with frilled curtains to be hung crisscrossed in the windows. Already Mari was giving away zucchini they'd grown, basil leaves. Next year they'd put up a garage. Year after, the patio.

Loaded with grocery bags, he stumbled up the decrepit stairs of his house to the second floor. The first floor was rented for storage by a secondhand furniture dealer and the smell and the sound of disuse penetrated the walls, an echoing emptiness of worn chairs and dressers jumbled one on top of the other. Through the battered door at the head of the stairs, painted a cheerful red over cracks imperfectly sealed, Priscilla's typewriter jingled. The telephone jangled. He jiggled his key into the lock, with arms around his groceries, and almost dropped it.

Oh God, he prayed, turning his key in the lock. Oh God.

3

The day before he was married to Priscilla he had rented a room from one of the women assemblers in the plant that would have to do until they could locate an apartment. The best bedroom in the house. Dark mahogany furniture kept polished with lemon oil. Draperies and bedspread in ashes-of-roses taffeta.

"All hand-shirred," Amy said to Priscilla when she showed them the room, lifting the flounced skirt of the spread to display its fullness.

"Horrors," Priscilla said as soon as Amy was out of the room.

He couldn't understand what she had expected. The room was clean, quiet, away from the street, facing the backyard. They were lucky that Amy was willing to let them have it. Hardwood floor. Stomp stomp. Good mattress. Thump thump. He was determined not to move Priscilla into his father's place. It would sour the marriage.

Three weeks later Amy gave him notice. "I need the room," she said to him coldly as she counted out his rent.

"But why?" Priscilla demanded, mortified, when he told her. "Because we're having so many meetings here? She should be the first to understand."

No, it wasn't the meetings. Though the meetings every other night or so over his election campaign must have had something to do with it. It was the pickle juice Priscilla had spilled one afternoon on the shirred bedspread while eating pickles out of the jar. He tried to explain to Priscilla that her carelessness, never bothering to turn the bed down when she sat or flopped on it or gave it over to their guests to sit and flop on, expressed a contempt for Amy's property that extended to Amy.

Priscilla couldn't understand. What was this confusion of persons between themselves and their property? A person is a person. Property is nothing. Why was he attacking her over Amy's property? She had the utmost respect for Amy.

"But ashes of roses, ye gods! It's a wonder I'm not permanently frigid."

In a fever of mutual misapprehension, they chased down every last clue to an apartment until they arrived at the hole on Prince Street. What did she want, to wallow in romantic misery? Not his idea at all. A single chamber running from front to rear of the house, with a bathroom and a few kitchen fixtures tucked into an el—the landlord's excuse for blowing the rent ceiling.

Priscilla liked it. Now this was something like. Convenient to UV and the union hall. On a through street, easy to give directions to. Space enough for twenty people. "Come here, Mish, look!" She peered out the dusty front windows. "Do you see what I see?" A glimpse beyond leaden roofs of the harbor, masts of freighters penciled on the smudged sky.

They mixed colors, rubbed down furniture, pleated the heads of yellow sheets on drapery pins, put up room dividers and put in studio couches for the convenience of out-of-towners passing through. Pasting down square after square of linoleum on his knees, sweating out miscalculations, he regretted Amy's golden floor, the grain flowing through the gloss like honey. Over the linoleum they unrolled their prize buy, a cream-colored drugget rug bordered in green and strewn with stylized blue and yellow flowers, primitive yet sophisticated, perfect. Priscilla slung her guitar on a peg over the library table they used for meals. Open the doors, everybody, and come on in.

They came, they saw, they approved. Joe and Flo, Ted and Gail, Bob and Mari, Ray and Marty. An endless stream.

"Quite a place you have here."

All but Pop.

"Why don't you," Pop suggested, "look for a nice three-family house to buy, in a nice neighborhood? The tenants will pay it out."

Priscilla was shocked. Millions, billions of people lived under conditions much worse than this, what was the matter with it? Because it was in the slums? That was just the attraction of it for her, it was in the slums.

He was outraged. He knew very well what Pop meant. That he should go ask Joe Barth for a down payment, if Joe didn't have the sense to offer it . . . take out a GI mortgage . . . and join the ranks of landlords, handle with rent collection, evictions, leaky pipes . . . So the old man could sit back on his couch glorying in his own incorruptibility.

Priscilla suffered only one major disappointment living on Prince Street. She had not anticipated that she would stay home during the day while her husband was away at work. She had planned to walk with him every morning to United Vacuum, lunch bag under her arm, one of the army of working wives. She attempted it for a few months. She took a job in the Snake Pit. "One of the worst departments in the plant," she announced proudly. In it and of it at last.

She went at it with all her slapdash slap and dash, the union maid who never was afraid. Her fingers went numb, her mind was benumbed with the tedium of it. She did manage after a while to gear herself to a task so pinpointed it required the merest twist of her wrist. Only she had to throw the whole of her being into it. She couldn't subordinate it to herself. It swallowed her up. And the chitchat, the companionship she had looked forward to, the opportunity to exchange opinion? The women were all on an electric-blanket binge just then and all day long it went on, the virtues of one kind of blanket versus another. They were working for what they could buy with their pay. What had she imagined?

"If I had your education," they said to her, "you wouldn't catch me here."

The first prerequisite for a worker who hopes to gain influence is competence on the job. One day Priscilla was slow; the next day she had too much scrap; at the end of the week group earnings fell off. "You've got to stop driving yourselves so hard," she protested. "Sure, sure," the women agreed and went right on driving. They finally figured out among themselves that Priscilla was working in order to promote her husband in the union. Having discovered a rationale for her behavior, they relaxed with it. Not

Priscilla. She was terribly hurt. How could they imagine such a thing?

One afternoon when she returned from work more than usually discouraged, he persuaded her to quit. There were some people who could never adapt to mass-production industry and she was one of them. She wasn't making any contribution this way. Why kill herself?

Priscilla cried over it, terribly. His father, arriving uninvited for dinner with a bag of groceries, was alarmed. Priscilla flung out on the couch in torment, moaning as if something she held fast in her heart, the world, had cracked to pieces.

"What's the matter with her?" Pop whispered to him in reproach. "Something happen between you?"

"She's not making out on the job."

"So what? She'll get a job in the office."

"It's not the same thing," he said and stroked her heaving back, trying vainly to soothe her.

"Of course it's not the same. It's better."

"It doesn't pay as well," he said to his father.

This Pop understood. He unpacked his groceries muttering one of his gloomy incantations, trotted out whenever the occasion suited.

"Too light for heavy work. Too heavy for light work."

From then on Priscilla had divided her time largely between the union hall and the house, making her contribution.

He unlocked the glossy red door of his hole on Prince Street and, staggered by his clash with Gavin over Bob, with Mari over Gavin, with Coffin over the fraction of a second, he lurched inside spilling potatoes. The two studio couches, the library table they used for dining, the bridge table they never used for bridge and the drugget rug on the floor were covered with mimeographed sheets of paper. Priscilla was neck-deep, as she had been ever since Congress overrode Truman's veto a few months before, in the union's campaign to repeal the Taft-Hartley Act.

"Careful where you walk," Priscilla warned him over her phone call and continued into the phone, "Oh, no, Mrs. Wilson, you're not bothering me one bit. That's what I'm here for. Fire away."

He skirted the rug. Last year: CITIZENS COMMITTEE TO DEFEAT TAFT-HARTLEY. Then: VETO TAFT-HARTLEY. Now: REPEAL TAFT-HARTLEY. Next as it went up through the courts: APPEAL TAFT-HARTLEY. Burning issues that all too soon burnt themselves out, receding into a past as remote as the ice age. Delegations to the mayor, the governor. Eighty thousand demonstrators parading through downtown New York. Cavalcades to Washington. All the fusses with buses.

Strewn in pink, blue, green, yellow, white sheets over the naïve flowers of his rug.

"We're putting together a Fact Folder on it, Mrs. Wilson. It's not just that it compels unions to get rid of Communists in office, that's just one minor aspect of it. You see, anyone can be tagged a Communist. My husband. Me."

Oh, Priscilla.

"You. Then it devolves on you to prove otherwise. You see? But that's the least of it."

She'd been out sailing her father's skiff in the bay and she was tanned and tumbled. Her washed-out rose polo shirt slopped over shrunken yellow shorts. Her long legs were drawn up on the couch, deck-fashion, ankles spliced, knees askew, inviting rape.

"It hamstrings labor at every turn. Bans the closed shop. Forbids sympathy strikes. Requires the union to open up its books, not the employer. Makes the union liable to damage suits . . ."

With cigarette in hand reaching for pink and blue sheets, she rattled it off.

"It virtually reverses the Wagner Act. We're back in the age of the injunction. The Wagner Act? The Wagner Act, Mrs. Wilson, was labor's bill of rights. Uh huh. Uh huh. I know it's hard, that's the trouble with it. It takes a Philadelphia lawyer . . ."

He disengaged himself from the cakebox dangling precariously from his finger, the potatoes and the cans of beer. Bent over and licked her cheek. Salt. Sun.

"And this two–three-month cooling-off period before a strike can be called . . . Which organization did you say? How many copies? Would you like a speaker too? When?" She groped in the air. He supplied pencil and calendar. Ran his finger down the silvery sheen of her tanned leg. "You don't see what's wrong with it. Well, Mrs. Wilson . . ." She held the babbling telephone away from her ear. "That's the third one today. They call for information and what they want is a full-scale debate." He placed his hand over the mouthpiece. And a hand over her belly. It didn't show yet. No fullness of the waist. It showed in her face, in the bloom that diffused from her in a warm mist. It showed in her bosom, straining against the bra under her shirt. "Let's grab a bite—" She caught his straying hand and held it. "—and get outa here. Go to a movie." "Oh, it's a panel discussion. All right, Mrs. Wilson. Fifty copies. I'll mail them out tonight." She had no more than finished with her telephone— "A movie? What movie? I have all these folders—" —and the telephone was ringing again. "Oh my God, I forgot. Springfield's been trying to get you for an hour. Mike Garceau. Operator 3. The company's sneaked the machine out." He was on the line with Springfield trying to get through to Garceau when there was a knock at the door and Priscilla opened up. Soft as a pussycat Nick Colangelo slipped in. Greeting her with low-toned intimacy. "Say, champ." Looking around, a whoop of a whistle. "Nice place you have here." Nodding toward him at the telephone. "You're lucky with your wife. With my wife it's all—" A clamping motion of his fingers. Gimme gimme gimme. Mike Garceau came on, excited. Collins & Ware in Springfield, on strike for the past four months, had built a horizontal boring mill for United Vacuum, ready to be delivered when the plant was struck. Two hours ago, during the picket line changeover, the machine was sped out of C&W on a freight truck. It was due at UV-Shoreham tonight during the late shift.

As soon as Garceau hung up, he twirled the dial calling around to prevent the delivery truck from entering UV. Nick gestured at him with his hat—sorry to bust in on you at a time like this—and tossed it on the couch, from which Priscilla was hastily clearing mimeographed sheets. She began to clear the floor as well, plunging to her knees and picking up pinks, blues, greens and yellows in sequence. Her swollen breasts drooped, her bra, unhooked, hanging askew under her polo shirt. Nick dropped down on his knees beside her to help her out. Tied up on the telephone, he watched Priscilla and Nick crawling over the floor, Nick contesting every headline on the sheets in order to provoke her passionate, proselytizing response. Her faded shirt, parting from her shorts, crept up her spine.

"But you're talking against yourself, don't you see! The NLRB which was formed to guarantee the unions a fair shake has been moved over into a quasi-judicial position. With powers of review vested in one man, the counsel, who can easily become a tool of the bosses—"

Nick, his mouth an inch away from hers: "Is that right? Only somebody has to regulate—"

"Do you have to be protected from your own organization? It's up to you to control it, democratically. You're giving away your prerogatives! It'll castrate the labor movement."

"That's what you say. In principle we're democratic. But in practice, what are we? Somebody has to watch over . . ."

Priscilla thought she was making time with Nick on her level. Nick thought he was making time with her on his level. In Nick's book, girls were raised to withhold themselves from men—that was the whole fun of it, that was the game. She lures. He pursues. There was no equal give-and-take. If she gives, he takes. Nick helped Priscilla to her feet at the card table, retaining her hand an instant, enjoying the come-on. Wriggling her clothing into place all unawares, Priscilla reached up under her shirt to yank her bra down from around her neck and refasten it behind.

OF VICTORS AND VICTIMS 255

"You're lucky with your wife," Nick spoke over his shoulder to him while he arranged for a picket line to be thrown around all possible delivery gates. "She's right in there with you." Priscilla sifted a post card mailing for her mother's International League for Peace and Freedom out of the material on the card table. Nick pocketed a post card. He'd think about sending it.

"One thing I don't understand about you guys," Nick spurred her on, "you want to disarm the country, leave it defenseless. The Russians'll mow us down."

"But don't you see if we have the Bomb they'll have it too? We'll be over our heads in an arms race that can only lead to total extermination. We have to learn to live with the Reds—"

Oh, Priscilla.

He finished with his pickets, put a call through to the Teamsters. "But is that legal?" Priscilla interrupted her tête-à-tête with Nick to ask him.

"Is what legal?"

"What you're doing now. Is it legal?"

"How the hell should I know?"

"You see? You see?" She waved her rainbow of papers under Nick's nose. "He may be engaging in a secondary boycott—or restraint of trade— You'll be so fouled up—"

His calls completed, he faced Nick. It's sticking up his jock! Treating himself to a hard-on on my wife! I'll kick shit . . .

"Have some dinner with us," Priscilla invited Nick and floated off to the el. With one hand she mixed yesterday's casserole on the stove and with the other she continued her discourse over the counter.

He followed her into the el without waiting for Nick to explain his purpose and went into the windowless cell of a bathroom to wash up, leaving the door ajar. They had scrubbed and patched and painted, installed cabinets and linoleum, wrought a revolution piecemeal. The hole on Prince Street remained a hole. Impossible to keep clean. Impossible to heat in winter, the oil range a fire hazard. The apertures around the pipes under the sink were stuffed with steel wool against the incursion of water rats from the docks three blocks away. On a June morning, their first summer, they awoke to a peculiar smell. What's that? They searched the apartment high and low. It was their cream-colored drugget rug with the pastel flowers scattered through it and the green border around. The rug stank like a camel. Everytime hot weather hit, it stank to high heaven. Our camel.

"You see," Priscilla whispered through the bathroom door, "he's not so bad, listen to him. He's only saying what a lot of others are thinking. He can be reasoned with."

Nick sat down with them at the library table. The table was set with straw mats and pottery plates, which he duly admired: "Taste." He refused dinner, he'd already had his, but accepted a beer and lifted it in salute to them: "Team."

What Nick wanted here soon became apparent. He wanted Gene Bostic's stewardship in Spray Paint. The paint crew (how many? five?) had met this afternoon (where? the Blue Bird?) and they had decided that Bostic was not their man, they'd never elected him.

"Now I got nothing against Bostic, you know that. I don't hold his race against him. But when a man who's had less years in the plant than a lot of us have is kept on the job while we're laid off—"

"Just as long as some of you too."

"However that may be, it don't go down so good. When a man with as little negotiating experience as Bostic has is supposed to represent us—"

"He's learning."

"And there's 30 per cent colored in the department and most of the rest Italian and when the vote was counted it was all Bostic, you know something was put over on us. They sneaked in a by-election—"

"In the union hall!"

"And nobody shows up but a handful—"

"Whose fault was that?"

"And Liscio gives the word out. When Bob blows the whistle, Liscio jumps, you know that. The vote comes out according to order. Now I'm not going to make a big political mishmash out of this, which I could. All I'm concerned with is democracy in my department." Nick lifted his beer to Priscilla. "Right, champ? There wasn't a quorum present when the vote was taken."

Priscilla was distressed. "Are you insinuating that Bob . . . Bob would never . . ."

"Oh, I got nothing against Bob. Bob has a right to his own viewpoint. Only one thing I can't stand about him. He's always knocking Uncle Sam. Other than that . . .

"After all," Nick disclosed to them confidentially across the table, "my grandfather marched with Garibaldi."

If Nick was here, it was because he had Herb Cranston behind him. If Cranston was toughening up, it was because Tookalook was pressuring him. Cranston was counting on his fingers the number of Local 317 delegates he could count on to the national convention.

"We want you, Mish, to call a new election for steward in Spray Paint."

"Jerk off."

"Mish!"

"Pick up that telephone right now, Mish, and tell Bob you're calling a new election, let him keep his hands off. What have you got to lose? You hold a fair election, Bostic wins again, fair and square, that's it. The atmosphere's cleared. Now you call Bob while I'm sitting here—"

"Up yours."

"Mish!"

"You got a beef against Bob," he said to Nick, "you go to him yourself. Tell him yourself."

Nick had not forgotten that he was once thrown out of Bob's house. Viva Trieste! He would not go talk with Bob. Calmly Nick jabbed the beer-can opener into a second can of beer. The metal gave with a gasp of escaping air. Nick would drink with them. But not eat with them, share their bread and salt.

"You're acting kind of foolish, aren't you, Mish? We're petitioning tomorrow for a new election in Spray Paint. If you try to sidetrack it in any way, there's a bunch of us will raise it at the

membership meeting this Sunday. And not only from Spray Paint.
You with us or against us?"

They had him cornered. A bunch of them—distributing themselves about the hall, several in second row center behind Bob's
contingent, some in the middle row left, some in the middle row
right, more back center, the diamond formation—had become
very adept in the art of disrupting meetings. Charges, countercharges, insults hurled. He'd have the whole Cold War right in
his lap.

"You check out that election, Mish. You'll find Liscio voted in
colored who weren't even there."

It was not inconceivable.

Nick was not skimpy-gray at all. He was robust-brown; his hair
richly brown combed back in a crest; rich laughter lurking in the
brown of his eyes; husky brown arms resting on the table, richly
turfed.

Priscilla showed Nick to the door shoving copies of her Fact
Folder at him. "Read the quotations from Section 8(b) (4)," she
instructed him. "It's an octopus. It'll strangle us."

She followed Nick halfway down the stairs with it. "It strength-
ens Coffin's hand. It's a weapon in the hands of UV."

A nice girl. A proper girl. But one of the roving kind.

"You didn't have to be so rough on him." She reappeared in
the doorway. "You only antagonized him that much more. You
could have tried at least to win him over."

Kiss her. Kill her.

She had such enthusiasm, as if enthusiasm could make it so.
But not much sense of organization. Taft-Hartley was all over the
room again, a windfall of leaves feathered with the snow of some
Call to Action left over from a month ago. Probably the two qualities, enthusiasm and organization, could not be mated in the
same person to a high degree. She depended on him for the
slow, hard, patient process, the overall pulling together. As he depended on her for the flash and splash, the instant magic without
which there's no go. The gas has to be in the engine. The yeast
has to be in the dough.

Priscilla knelt on the floor clicking sheets together and stapling them. She punched with her stapler. *Bite* and *bite* and *bite*. Jump her. Let the phone ring, let the door bang.

"Look, Pris, let's get outa here before somebody else—I gotta get somewhere I can think! The convention's just six weeks away. Gavin says that in order to beat Taft-Hartley there's a move on to dump the Left—we'll have a fight in the local over delegates-at-large— Where's a good movie?"

"Dump the Left? But they can't! Once they give in to one thing . . ."

To her it was all for love. All for love. She was the amateur, outside and above the erosion of routine, the hard decisions, the compromises. Integrity. Principle. The shining vision of the self. And while she devoted herself, the opportunists were in there every minute scrambling over the back of her accomplishment for position, for favors, for crumbs of so trifling a nature sometimes she'd never believe it.

He called Bostic. The youngest boy answered. Laughter in the background, kitchen pots. A continuation of family banter as Bostic neared the phone.

Bite and *bite* and *bite*.

"Hey." With pleased surprise. Bostic was still brimming with his performance today at the paint booth. " 'If it's not the gun, Mr. Coffin, then it must be the paint.' Man, did he fade!"

"Anything happen in the department afterwards?"

"Well, no. They all waiting to hear, did we win it or lose it."

"Anything after work?"

"Well, no. Everybody scatted. Why?" Growing edgy, guarded. "What's up?"

"Colangelo was just here. He wants to be steward."

"But he's nobody! He's noth-thing."

The squeaking jaws of the stapler. *Bite.*

"I just thought I'd let you know."

"Yeah. Sure." The voice flattened, receded. "Sure. Thanks."

"He's petitioning for a new election. We'll back you up of course."

Bostic was Bob's headache. Let Bob handle him.

"Yeah. Sure. I understand." Dwindling away.

"Ask him to dinner next Saturday," Priscilla, signaling from the rug, tried to get her word in. "Ask him to bring his wife."

He called Bob. He had to call Bob.

"I understand you drove Gavin to the station," Bob said to him before he could begin.

"The news sure gets around."

"I understand he's had his orders to line you up on the Taft-Hartley vote at the convention. Or did he ask you here and now to sign the non-Communist affidavit?"

He was annoyed, more testy with Bob than he should have been. No time to speak to his own wife. Not world enough nor time nor privacy even to catch a little nooky on the run.

"If there's anything you can be sure of in this world, Bob, I'll never sign that thing. Okay?"

"Not okay. A non-Communist oath as a qualification for office, it's a purge! These goddam phonies, they're yielding on it before it happens. Then they have to make it happen. We've got to make sure our delegation sticks together—"

"Colangelo was just here. Hollering irregularities in the Bostic election."

Bob brushed it off. "Now? Two months later? Forget it."

"He's petitioning tomorrow for a new election."

A prolonged pause. Bob regrouping.

"If Nick was there," Bob said, "Cranston must have sent him. And if Cranston sent him, that means Tookalook . . ."

"Yeah."

Bob had maneuvered the election and now he was being maneuvered. Forced to reinforce Cranston against the threat of Tookalook. The rackets, Bob had once estimated, between the numbers and the pools and the sweepstakes, collected a quarter of a million dollars out of the workers in the plant every year. If Tookalook enlarged his base in the local by taking over Cranston's caucus, if he started swinging his baseball bat . . . Cranston at least was honest.

And there was Bostic. The opposition would run to Bostic to convince him that he was being used by Bob to front for him. They'd run to the colored sprayers and try to convince them likewise. Then they'd run to the whites, convince them that all the colored . . .

"What are you going to do, Mish?"

"I told Bostic we'd back him to the hilt."

"Mish, you can't afford— All right. All right, I'll talk to Bostic. You stall off the petition, I'll talk to Bostic. Okay?"

Aaaah. Aaaagh.

"Ask Bob and Mari up for Saturday dinner too, huh? There wasn't anything wrong with that election, was there? If there wasn't anything wrong . . ."

He dragged Priscilla up from her papers. "Change your duds."

"But I've got five hundred of these— Fifty to get out to that Mrs. Wilson—"

Heaving, glistening, a quiver of dismay in her eyelashes. It all rested on her.

The first law of organization. If you have to do it by yourself . . .

They left the corpse of Taft-Hartley on the floor. Defeat Taft-Hartley. Veto Taft-Hartley. Repeal Taft-Hartley. Appeal Taft-Hartley. What's Taft-Hartley?

Down the warped stairs.

Where's a good movie? When were we last at a movie?

But hold on. Halt. Ray and Marty galloping up from the sidewalk.

"Caught you just in time."

The pickets at the UV gates on the lookout for the Springfield truck, they wanted something to hand out to the workers when they came off their shift. Explaining why.

"Collins & Ware has been on strike for four months! Isn't that enough why?"

"Well, you know how people are these days, they don't take nothin' by word of mouth. Got to know the who and the what."

Who was going to get out such a leaflet at this time of night? Who was going to do the work? Not Ray's wife. Yvonne was still sore at Ray for stepping out on a weekend night to a conference around the corner that ended up two days later in Boston. Not Marty's wife. When Helen wasn't running around to the priests with her marital problems, she was running around the taverns just to pay Marty off. They wanted the old man home nights. Union activity, who needs it? Unless you're getting something out of it for yourself. Neither Ray nor Marty would put their wives to work on the leaflet. They wanted the old lady back home tending the home fires.

Back up the stairs. The three of them over Priscilla's shoulder, pounding it out on the stencil. Unless we stick together. Unless there's solidarity. All for one, one for all.

Down to the union hall. Inking the mimeograph cylinder. Roll. Enough for tomorrow too, they'd have to throw a mass line in case the truck showed up again. Till it was settled.

4

At the crack of dawn, six-thirty, he walked Priscilla to the Raymond Street gate and stood opposite her distributing, catching glimpses of her through the throng. She loved the morning at the gate, the fresh blue air, the freshness of paper sticking to her fingers as she tried to nip it off fast enough to meet the press of on-comers, their hands reaching out to meet her halfway. She loved it when an occasional shopmate from the Snake Pit greeted her. "Hey, Pris! Where you been keeping yourself?" "Hey, Jean! Esther!"

She abandoned her stance and burrowed into the crowd so that for a moment he lost her.

"Amy! Amy, guess what?" A whisper into Amy's ear.

"No! When? Turn around. It don't show."

Laughter. Kisses. "Hey, Bertha. Mary. Guess what. She's . . ." Bosom pals.

As the clock approached seven Priscilla ran toward stragglers, thrusting into their hands. A man stepped back to ask for extras for friends. With a tremor of eagerness she tore off a handful. In the afternoon when he came home from work she would be waiting. "Well? How'd it go? Did it hit the nail?" No throwaways littering the aisles. Success.

II

1

The time a year and eight months later, spring of 1949. A beautiful May morning.

The place a suite in a New York hotel on the mezzanine, equipped with business facilities. Easels displaying charts are stationed along the walls. Tripod and slide projector are set up on one end with the inevitable rubber cable running underfoot, tripping up the unwary. A screen suspended from the ceiling. Polished board table, telephones attached at each place, buttoned for switching, sharing and amplifying calls. Cool drinks all around.

The UV-EWIU national contract is close to agreement. Specific provisions relating to individual plants are being wrapped up. The big holdup, the last holdout is Shoreham.

Sequestered in the hotel suite to iron out their differences, Grover Coffin and Michael Lunin, with their respective associates, are contending, as they have been for weeks, over what they consider the main issue of the negotiations. Not the fringe benefits, these have been settled. Not the wage offer, acceptance of which the union has left to the end for bargaining purposes. Over Coffin's bug and Lunin's bug. The job itself.

The present contract is due to expire day after tomorrow.

No contract no work.

Coffin's stature had perceptibly increased in the course of the bargaining sessions. The current general manager of the Shoreham works had taken a cruise to the Bahamas in March during the annual executive upheaval and had not returned since to his office. It was reported that he was on the road to retirement, and speculation was rife concerning his successor. No one had much doubt any longer who it would be.

"These things go in cycles," the dopesters in both union and management prognosticated. "One year the companies are after a banker to head up the plant, a budgetary brain. Economizing. Another year it's the ace promoter, the marketing whiz. Gimmicks. Then the engineer's the wonder boy. Technological development. New products. Now . . ."

They all cocked an eye at Coffin and kidded him about it. Who's going to be The Man in the Top Tower Office?

The industrial relations director. The man who can handle the men.

Coffin had succeeded in confining the collective bargaining this year largely to Benefits. This was not the year, he let it be known, when the union could hope to obtain substantial wage increases or changes in company practice. This was the year for Benefits. After exhausting its arsenal of statistics and surprise stratagems, the union found itself boxed in with a four-cent wage offer from the company in place of the ten cents asked. A few concessions in piece prices, service credits, no more. Knowing itself to be internally divided and therefore unprepared for any protracted action, the union then opened up on the front most likely to yield. Improvements in paid holidays and vacations, sickness and accident coverage, hospitalization, pension plan. Benefits. The Benefits Coffin had in mind, it turned out, were next to nil. A diversionary front.

Lunin had also acquired stature in the course of the negotiations. What promised to be a lousy contract, it was generally acknowledged, owed whatever real gains were incorporated in it chiefly to him.

He was perplexed and tickled by his present position. On the one hand, he was in bad odor with certain top union officials for his opposition to the vote on the Taft-Hartley non-Communist affidavit at the last national convention and his continued refusal to sign. On the other hand, he had never been stronger than he was now with the rank-and-file officialdom. He was one of the few local presidents who had been able to hold right and left factions in the membership together. And he was a bit the hero of the hour for the persistence with which he had countered Coffin in what was to both of them the key issue: to be avoided at all costs by Coffin; to be pursued at every opportunity by Lunin. Their mutual bugaboo. Who determines what the job consists of?

For him it had begun over a year and a half ago with the new spray gun in Spray Paint. From the set-to over the No. 3 gun, he had advanced to a struggle for the elimination of overlapping pay grades and the establishment of a single-rate grade structure with automatic progression based on job classification. On the broader categories of job classification he arrived at agreement with Coffin without too much difficulty. But on the fine points, and it was all fine points, they constantly clashed.

Coffin would produce his books as evidence. When a new tool, a new machine, a new method, a new material, any change at all was introduced on the job, the job was analyzed, graded and point-rated by the book. So much training, so much skill, so much initiative, physical demand, hazard: fourteen different elements measuring the degree of effort involved, the factors correlated by formula with the rate of pay. It was all scientifically defined, according to Coffin. In the realm of higher mathematics.

"Baloney," he would say to Coffin. "Why should we go by the company book?"

It couldn't be done by yardstick, he had insisted. And he persuaded the local to develop its own system of job evaluation. "We'll be glad to accept the company's point-rating charts, your time-motion studies, all the material you're willing to give us," he told Coffin, "and take it under consideration." Then under the guidance of Gavin, the old expert at slotting the job, and with the aid of Priscilla's brother, Ted, now an economics instructor at the state university, and the participation of the workers on the floor, he launched a job-evaluation procedure that could only be described as quite unscientific, rule-of-thumb.

When a change of tool or machine or method occurred, one of the men on the new job, selected by his peers, met at the union hall with men on related jobs, on their own time after work. A thorough discussion was held concerning the job and where it stood. "How much is it worth? Why?" The man on the new job attempted to prove through a step-by-step breakdown of his machine and his performance that he merited the highest rating and classification possible under the given conditions. The men on related jobs, unwilling to let anyone get ahead of them, would raise their objections. "Oh, no, I'm doing the same thing on such-and-such and it's only rated . . ." The discussion could go on for minutes, for hours, for days. Until a conclusion was reached out of the pooled experience of those who did the work.

Sometimes the man on the new job was upheld. Sometimes he was knocked down. Sometimes there was unanimity. Sometimes not. Sometimes it ended up in individual or common disgruntlement. But this was the way it was shaken down. Not by charts, although the company's material was included in the total estimate. It was based on the doing of the job eight-plus hours a day five days a week at a pace that was tolerable, with allowance for the obstacles and interruptions that crop up in any normal operation.

In the past six weeks he had worked day and night with his committee, reviewing every ambiguous job in the plant. After endless meetings on the subject, columns in *Lights On!*, leaflet distributions, the members were united on their goal. The Shoreham local sent its president and its business agent, Nick Colangelo, to the contract negotiations in New York with a definite mandate.

"Don't fall for any petty-cash offers from Coffin that he'll just take back later with his reclassifications and his reratings and his retimings. This year, this contract: job protection first!"

Several of the Shoreham demands were now embodied in the proposed national contract. The remaining demands were bogged down in a deadlock with Coffin. For three days now the Shoreham negotiators on both sides had been closeted in the mezzanine suite. Hours of debate over a figure here, a phrase there, passed back and forth over the table. Only minimal accords were reached.

This morning, with the expiration of the old contract no more than forty-eight hours away, Coffin's strategy was plain to the union team. Coffin would dilly-dally over details till the last possible minute, sometime today, and then spring a slight increase in the wage offer, maybe half a cent, as bait for finishing up on his terms. It was only a question of when.

Coffin had never looked more fit. He positively glowed through his glacial haze. His slate-colored hair, snow-edged, brightly framed his face, and he tossed his head back, on his mettle, with an alert and sparkling challenge. When he shed his jacket in the heat of the morning, his long-sleeved shirt was miraculously fresh, glazed-white.

"Now, Lunin, we all want to do what's right and reasonable. Why do you assume otherwise? With the new go-no-go gauge, which you must admit is a safety factor, those jobs no longer require a Class-A operator. Retiming has nothing to do with it."

"Yeah, but when you install the go-no-go, you not only downgrade the operator, you change his motion pattern—"

"Simplify it."

"That's what you say. And you retime the job. We're insisting that a steward must be present during every time study—"

"Time study! Steward! Gavin—Colangelo—you can see that this is patently dragged in— When a time study's completed you file your exceptions, if any. The mere presence of the steward would make a fair study impossible. Is that what you want?"

Coffin no longer looked at him as he once had with a suggestion of intimacy, an intimation of partnership. He gave him the Mariuch treatment, trying to isolate him from his fellows.

Under Coffin's hand lay UV's job-evaluation manual, a fat volume in red leatherette binding, to which Coffin referred now and again for verification of degree differentials in various types of work.

Under his own hand rested Local 317's job-evaluation report, the final draft typed up by Priscilla at home on what was left of Ted's thesis paper, with its red margin line, and clipped into a shiny black thesis folder. From it he cited example after example of arbitrary job classification and the train of consequences thereof. The two books, Coffin's and his, each a guarded document, pranced about like dogs on the leash, barking out their hostilities. UV's book he called *From the Top Down.* And his, *From the Bottom Up.*

The talks recessed without progress at noon. No sign yet of the half-cent hike in the wage offer, raising it from four to four and a half cents, which the union representatives hoped to stall off. No falling for that bait! Sandwiches were served at the table to some grumbling by the lawyers. "Might as well be locked in." Coffin, the great pasta-fagiol' man, held his bun off before biting into it.

As a clock bonged twelve outside, Coffin's telephone buzzed. Long distance. Here it is! Gavin was poised to jump, cut Coffin off. No business transacted during lunch! With a roguish non-grin over the canary he was swallowing, Coffin pressed his amplifier button.

A tenor wail, ululating with the nostalgia of lost love, flooded the room.

Two hundred miles away in Shoreham, on the mall outside the plant, during the lunch break, United Vacuum was entertaining its employees with its new radio and recording artist in person, star of a major motion picture recently released, sweetheart of every girl, buddy of every boy, son of every parent, Wally Rayne. Employees packed the mall and the sidewalks, the bays of the buildings, hung over the balconies and window sills. Each of them had been presented on punching in at work with an autographed record.

Outside the gray window ledge of the hotel room, within the gray court of windowed walls, sunlight plummeted downward in blue-misted shafts.

Above the rotunda on the grass strip of the mall, downy clouds floated in a mild blue sky. The boyish voice yearned and wept. A sea-roar of applause. Squeals, shrieks, ear-splitting whistles.

The concert, arranged some time ago, fell quite by chance on a day when contract negotiations were going into their final phase.

Tilting back in his chair with his cheeseburger, he was mesmerized by the voice. Bad enough to have Wally Rayne up there in Shoreham this noon. He had not expected to have him right here in the room with him. He was boiling—how he could have let Coffin pull such a stunt, how he could have let such a thing get away from him . . . And he was frozen to his seat by the sound. It poured through his veins, releasing sensibilities rusty with disuse. Somewhere out there the sky is blue. Water ripples. A bird soars. Somewhere, somewhere I'll find you . . .

In the chair next to his, Nick Colangelo, munching his food, hummed along with Wally. Nick, who had proved to be as good a shop steward as Bostic, neither better nor worse, he had to be taught, was thrust upon him in the last election as part of his coalition slate, the result of a deal between Gavin and Cranston. Nick was neither the best nor the worst business agent the local had ever had. In any contest that depended on who could holler loudest, "Bust the bosses!", Nick would win by a landslide. He could always be counted on to champion the spectacular grievance. But the routine cases, the chores and the bores that piled up on him daily, he let all too many of them slide. An uneven performer. Temperamental, unpredictable, a law unto himself. Nick sang under his breath as he chewed, relishing the familiarity of words and rhythm, shoulders jogging.

Gavin barely touched his roast beef interleaved with lettuce. From his corner of the table he offered his pickle in its paper boat to any taker.

From the rotunda, guarded all around by motorcycle cops, over the microphone the piping of a sweet young chick broke through. "Any more at home like you, Wally?"

A feminine chant, bouquets from the balconies, boomed through.

Wally, Wally, come on up here
Wally, Wally, come on up here

A mighty chorus swelling from the mall, male as well as female.

Wally, Wally, come on up here
Wally, Wally . . .

Somewhere Frank Gavin plucked leaves up from the barberry bush at the base of the rotunda. The leaves bunched between his fingers in a rosette, maroon-stained green. Scattered.

Somewhere Nick danced with Priscilla, his hand fanned over her fanny.

Coffin dropped his telephone back and began chit-chatting with the lawyers about the expanding television market. Three million sets manufactured in the country this year, expected to more than double in 1950. Picture tubes alone . . .

Just a pleasant interlude, that's all. Back from show biz to biz.

It was hot for May, very hot. The three windows back of the board table, partially open, let in so much heat and grit, steam from the kitchens below, traffic noises from the street outside the court, they had to be lowered to the sill. Schneider the union lawyer jived with Whiting the company lawyer. "Where's your air conditioning, UV?" "Suppose you tell us." Dissolving in amiability, lawyer to lawyer.

All afternoon long whenever Coffin appeared about to spring his announcement on the wage offer, "Gentlemen, I have been authorized . . ." he managed to stall Coffin off. "There are lags and snags on every job, Mr. Coffin. That's what Paragraph 9 . . ." "Schneider, Gavin, we can solve this in a minute . . ." Colangelo whirred through slides on the screen he had already shown twice, illustrating. Coffin couldn't find a chink among them to slip through. "Lunin, you're deliberately obstructing . . ." The two books, the red and the black, snapped, snarled, growled, yelped.

He was hot. His shoulders, hunched too long over his precious pages, braced for the blow, had hardened into concrete. His shirt was plastered to his back from pattings of water on the back of his neck at the water bottle. He itched with anxiety, apprehension. His head thrummed with Wally Rayne's sign-off song. *NOW is— the OW-ah—when WE must* . . .

Shortly after four o'clock his telephone rang. Long distance. Ray Pelletier calling from Shoreham.

"The company," Ray informed him over the telephone, "just passed out a flyer all over the plant announcing its offer of a five-cent increase in the hourly rate."

Cool as the ice cubes in his glass, Coffin sipped at the transparent straw of his long cool drink, mouth puckered. All the fanfare around Coffin's telephone calls, all the flurries around the door . . . Coffin hadn't even been trying to announce anything here at negotiations. He'd gone directly to the employees at this last minute, having softened them up first with the concert. The maximum anyone had expected from the company now was four and a half cents.

"Where are you now?" he asked Ray over the phone.

"In the union hall. We're holding a meeting."

Through Ray's voice, fresh, keen, ebullient, he could hear the response. He pressed his amplifier button and, holding his telephone up over his head, facing the board table, switched his speaker up to full volume.

NO! NO!

BOO-OO! BOO BOO BOO!

He still had his mandate. Job protection first. Dough later.

The bargaining session broke up at seven-thirty in an impasse over a word. *May* or *must.* After hours of adamant resistance, Coffin in a conciliatory mood proposed a compromise: a shop steward *may* be present during the disputed retiming of a job. Lunin stuck to his guns: a shop steward *must* be present.

In the corridor Coffin smoothly disengaged himself from press and radio interviewers.

"Will there be a strike?"

"We're narrowed down to a few minor clauses."

"What about the five cents?"

"More than generous. It'll be accepted."

Equally confident, Lunin let Colangelo grab the mike.

"What about the five cents?"

"No dice. We're as far apart as ever."

"Will there be a strike?"

"Absolutely. If UV thinks they can buy us off with a penny . . ."

Company and union descended together in the gilt-barred elevator to the lobby. Expelled by revolving doors into the street they dispersed. Whiting uptown, Schneider downtown. Company representatives took a cab to their hotel three blocks over on the east side. Union representatives sauntered toward the corner just a block away from their hotel on the west side. At the corner Nick gazed wistfully after the green-topped yellow cab disappearing into the strident pack, imagining an evening of executive high jinks. In the purple dusk darting with lights, out of the grime of pavements and masonry, excitement stirred. Quickening, beckoning, pulsating, the ache and allure of spring.

But as they turned the corner into the narrow cross-town street, all Nick said was, with a snort of wonder at himself, at them, "The time we put in. Nobody could pay us for the kinda time we put in."

It evens itself out. Why all the fusses . . .

2

They stopped to pick up papers at a newsstand adjoining the rail of a subway stairway. On the spur of the moment Nick decided to take the subway downtown. His wife, can you beat it, expected him to pick out a credenza for the dining room while he was here and time was getting short.

In the hotel Gavin went straight up to his room to call the union officials and go over the latest developments with them. "No need for any more huddles. Leave it to me. I'll do better than you can, Mish." He left it to Gavin. He had neither the mind nor the heart to cope with intramural hostilities. Gavin would do better than he could.

He tried to call home from the hotel grill. The baby had been running a temperature when he called in the morning, wouldn't eat her cereal. The line was busy of course. He stepped out of the booth into the amber dusk of the grill.

"Lunin! Over here."

The Springfield crowd.

He threaded through the shoals of glossy black-topped tables to their semicircular orange banquette in the corner.

"Hey, I hear we got five cents! Siddown siddown." A chair shuffled up for him. A parchment menu was shoved into his hands. "Not another cent, they said. This is the year for Benefits, they said."

"Not so easy. Not so fast. We're turning it down."

"You mean you're holding out for more?"

He was quite the man of the hour, giving them a rundown on what happened today. Not a bad feeling at all, considering that not so long ago he'd been strictly poison. Against Gavin's advice, thrust forward by leftists who needed a broad spokesman, he had led the floor fight at the convention opposing compliance with the Taft-Hartley affidavit. The liberals and moderates had deserted him, sick to death of the whole Red issue, in a frenzy to have it off their backs so they could go ahead with things that had to be done, so they could talk and act freely without fear of unfounded accusations, unsuspected manipulation. He lost on the resolution, but managed to amend it with a time extension for compliance. Then a change in the bylaws was introduced by a leading liberal, which out-Taft-Hartleyed Taft-Hartley, excluding Communists from membership in the union. Again he led the floor fight, supported mainly by known Communists, the kiss of death. And by the somewhat conservative small-town, small-plant delegates who didn't give a damn about anybody's politics—they weren't dumping good people, some of them the best they had, from their rolls. The new bylaw had squeaked through, paired with another that everyone wanted, the extension of the one-year term of office to two years. When he returned home from the convention, Bob Ucchini landed on him. "Why the hell did you let them stick you out front? For Christ sake, Mish, we got to see you're kept inside."

He was still inside. Enhanced now apparently by the very qualities that had made him objectionable. Against the dictates of authority and common sense, against the obvious course of events, he posed his obdurate self. Comply! He defied. And had not only defied but, it would seem, survived.

He had some trouble convincing the Springfield crowd that his obduracy at the bargaining table over his musts wasn't just a dodge to jack the company up another half cent.

"You've seen this Coffin in operation," he said to them. "You watch him. He's here to prove to all the hot-shots he can top their raise and still reduce labor costs. He'll skin us alive. It's his stock-in-trade. We've had it. Nothing doing. No more."

"They all do that."

"He outdoes them. They're learning from him. *May* for *must*. Some compromise. He's the philanthropist. We're the ingrates. That's Coffin."

"You sure you won't change your mind overnight? Take what you can get, forget the rest?"

He was jarred. Ash dropping off the butt of his cigarette burned his fingers.

"After all these months we spent preparing? All these weeks we been bucking the company? That's just window dressing? Our whole local's sold on this. Nobody's wavering. Not a crack."

He wasn't hungry. He was too tired even to scan the bill of fare. The parchment faded before his eyes. The faces around the table —admiring and skeptical, with the admiring skepticism of those who have made their peace with the nature of existence, subordinated their personalities to its limitations—frightened him.

"I can't swallow a thing, do you mind? I haven't showered yet, I stink—I got to call my wife."

"Hey, here's your drink . . ."

He had the middle of three connecting rooms on the ninth floor, Colangelo on one side of him and Gavin on the other. Usually they barged through the rooms exchanging incidental intelligence. He put the membership job-evaluation report away in the shirt pocket of his Gladstone and locked it in. Priscilla had typed it up in final form in a day-and-night tear and delivered it to him at the airport as he was leaving. "Guard it with your life. I didn't have time to correct my carbons!" He didn't let it out of his hands, standing over it while excerpts were multilithed at headquarters. The early drafts had created quite a stir, furnishing the basis for the union's surprise moves.

He didn't bother now to knock at Gavin's door to find out how Gavin was doing with headquarters. Gavin would handle it. It was Gavin who had guided them through the intricacies: standardization of wage structure, codification of job practices, the achievement of a means by which workers on the same job or in comparable jobs would not be placed in competition against themselves. It was coming. The union knew it. The company knew it. It had to come.

Lounging on the bed he kicked off his shoes, phe-ew, and reached for the telephone on his night table and asked for an outside line. The switchboard was busy. He waited interminably for the operator to put his call through to Priscilla. He peeled his shirt off, waiting, and threw it on the floor. Rotated his head to get the crick out of the back of his neck.

"We have your call now, sir. Go ahead, sir."

"You left a call in for me?"

The telephone pressed against the rim of his ear burned, swelled, amplified.

He had Graveyard Coffin on the line, an impossibility.

"Yes, sir. About that offer you made this afternoon—"

He stared at the recessed black door at the foot of his room.

It was no more than a fleeting impression. The call was cut short at once. The Shoreham operator: "The line is still bus—"

Shirtless and shoeless he rushed into Gavin's room and grabbed Gavin from his telephone and rushed with him to Nick's door.

Nick—he should have guessed—Nick vanishing down the black maw of the subway, removing himself from the scene of plaudits. Nick at the mike, no dice, absolutely not, with that glimmer in his eye, at the helm. If five cents, why not five and a half? Going to the General Executive Board with it. Waving it over the rostrum at the union hall, we won! we won!

They rushed through the back-to-back separating doors into Nick's room. "Yeah, I get the picture." Calmly Nick continued with his telephone call. "Just a minute, fellas—" He waved his cigar at them from the edge of his bed. "Will do. See you."

He wrenched the telephone out of Nick's hand. The line was dead. He tapped the bar.

"My brother-in-law, the druggist, he must think I own a drugstore," Nick said and circled his finger around his ear. "His uncle just died, left a Chrysler New Yorker they want to sell me. The gas alone for godsake . . ."

"I thought you were on your way to Houston Street to buy a credenza."

"So I changed my mind. I'm pooped. Chryslers. Credenza. My wife and her family. You're lucky—"

"You contacted Grover Coffin. Operator—operator—" He clicked the bar. "I want a call traced." His chest was flushed with splotches of color under the matted hair. He smelled with sweat. Throbbed with a vicious gratification. At last, at last, his dislike of the man justified. Gratification outweighed for him at the moment the grossness of the betrayal.

"What is this?" Nick appealed to Gavin who stood leaning back against the dresser, quizzically studying them both. "What's got into him?"

The operator couldn't or wouldn't furnish the requested information.

"If it was an incoming call, I have no record of the caller. If it was an outgoing call, it'll be charged on your bill. Who is this again?"

"Mr. Lunin."

"Oh, Mr. Lunin. In 912. We have your party now calling back."

He looked at the molded black shape, slippery in his hand, the perforated orifices, ear and mouth bracketed. A comedy of crossed wires. He declined the call.

"I know you never liked me," Nick reproved him. "I know how hard you been working. I know the kind of pressure you're under." Nick offered his hand. All is forgiven.

He brushed by the extended hand and walked out of the room. Gavin followed, closing the doors behind him.

"Well?"

Leaning back against the dresser, always leaning against something nowadays as if he needed the prop, Gavin pulled at his elongated chin. He was emaciated, a delicately boned specter, his eyes reduced to pinpoints behind his black-rimmed glasses. Several locals had detached themselves from Gavin during the past year.

"What's your pleasure?"

Archly Gavin peered at him through his glasses. A council of war? Twenty-four-hour surveillance?

"I don't suppose he can do any harm now." He twitched the socks off his feet and shot them at his shirt on the floor. He was still shaken by the voracity for vindication that had taken possession of him. For that twinge of gratification he would have sacrificed all his accomplishment. He would happily have seen the ship go down. "He knows we're onto him," he said to Gavin. "All we have to do is open our mouths, he's through."

Gavin cracked his knuckles. Thin humor creased his chops.

"Aren't there enough people around, Mish, who want to put your neck down without you adding to them?"

3

By ten o'clock he was in bed sitting up with a paperback whodunit, comfortably putting the pieces of a murder together, mating this clue with that. The bed was firm, the pillow was plump, the linen was smooth, his flesh was fresh. Relaxed, he drifted sleepward. He had talked with Priscilla earlier. Stephanie's temperature was back to normal. "Every time she goes up a degree, it doesn't mean it's polio," Priscilla remonstrated. "Anyhow it's not the season for it. All right now? Fill me in." She was dying to hear. He was dying to tell her. He omitted the incident with Nick. "What else?" she demanded. "Nothing else." "Something's wrong." "Nothing's wrong." "Then why are you breathing like that?" "I'm not breathing. Do you have to breathe with me too?" He had hung up laughing. The duo.

So in his good firm bed in the good medium-priced midtown hotel he scrambled and unscrambled Raymond Chandler, chased shamus and tart through the palmy hillside villas of southern California. At a tap on his hall door he reluctantly swung out from under his light blanket. Springfield with a bottle wanting to bull all night.

In his pajamas, finger in book, he opened his door. A beautiful blonde straight out of the pages of Raymond Chandler walked in, statuesque, high-heeled, with a determined little short-gaited step that was not to be interrupted, ever, by obstacles in her path. She sailed past him into his room and set her handbag down on his glass-topped dresser.

"I'm afraid you've made a mistake," he said to her. "You're in the wrong room."

"Oh no," she said. A nice girl in blue dress and blue pumps, as nicely modulated as a new-model car. "I never make a mistake. We have a date."

She took a blue comb from her handbag and began combing her curls up in little short strokes, in his mirror.

"Isn't this 912? Aren't you Mike Lunin?"

He placed his hand on the small of her back and steered her back down the lane between closet and bathroom.

"You don't want me?"

"There's been a mistake."

Handing back her handbag. Inhaling the powdery bloom of her skin. Propelling her with a pat at her bottom.

"I ought to charge you for that."

Pout. Out.

Toodleloo, Baby Blue.

He unlocked the door to Nick's room on his side and slid back into bed, wide-awake.

The knock arrived on the button, a few minutes later. But not from Nick's door. From Gavin's. Gavin burst in with Nick behind him and advanced to the foot of the bed. Nick's eyes wandered about, from bathroom to closet, over ceiling and floor, drapery and drawers. The sense of a just departed presence was acute.

"Looking for something, gentlemen?"

"Not unless you wear Evening in Paris perfume," Nick said amiably.

Tit for tat. Coffin for cutie.

An intonation over the telephone wire evaporated like a scent in the air.

His good humor—how far will this clod go?—faded at once. As deftly as he had backed him up into a corner that time over Bostic, Nick now had him trussed hand and foot, stilettoed. You smear me with Coffin. I smear you with her. Mutual blackmail. Equally unprovable.

A blonde in blue. The more she's denied, the more she multiplies.

With the glimmer of his eyes Nick spelled it out for him. Think of Priscilla and her family. Think of Ray's wife, Yvonne, and Marty's wife, Helen, sure as shooting that every excursion for the union is just an excuse for boozing and bumming around. Think of the women in the plant, scandalized because so surprised. Lunin? Not Lunin! The good family man.

For every slight in the past, every gesture of scorn and impatience, every cross-eyed look, Nick scored him off.

Playing around during contract negotiations. Tsk tsk.

Smash the smirk off his face.

"What's the matter with you, Lunin, can't you take a joke?"

Nail him with it. "You sent a floozie up here to frame me."

"Who, me? Why me? If you had somebody here . . ."

Slug him. Gavin interposing, "Mish, are you out of your mind? This place is crawling with dicks. The company . . ."

Expose him, publish it, shout it out. "Well, you see, his wife was always giving me the eye and he was always—"

Dump him. Out the window like a sack of potatoes. Wham. His paperback fell from the bed with a soft thud. With soft solicitude Nick retrieved it.

"Any good?"

He began to laugh. There was only one way to foil that genial face hovering so close to his, that geniality so brazen nobody would believe it, you couldn't make it up. Say nothing. Bite your tongue off.

"Will you two kindly cut out the charades?" Gavin ordered them. "I brought Nick in here to make peace between you. We have some chance for a settlement tomorrow."

"Sure," Nick said. "I'm ready anytime. Forgive and forget, that's my motto. Okay?"

"That creep, that crud," he said to Gavin as soon as Nick was out of the room. "You bring him in here again, so help me . . ."

"You're all charged up," Gavin said to him. "Simmer down. Get hold of yourself, Mish. We're settling tomorrow."

"Settling?"

Beside this, the immensity of Nick's trick with the girl diminished to child's play. Nick's treasonous call to Coffin, hinting that the *musts* were for sale, dwindled to a mote.

"Settling? On what terms? The Board promised to go along with us. They committed themselves. My people are ready to walk."

Gavin strolled about the room picking things up, a lamp, a blotter, anything, looking underneath, examining the article, replacing.

"You're no kid, Mish. Don't you know by now," Gavin said to him wearily over his shoulder, "that what goes on at the bargaining table, that's just for the record? The real deals are made upstairs."

He gaped up at Gavin like a fool. The rim of the ear he had

pressed against the telephone, overhearing Coffin and Colangelo, tingled as if scalded, frost-bitten. Two small moles over Nick's mouth danced like bloodspots before his eyes. Graveyard's cat's-eye cufflinks. The refraction of Gavin's glasses.

The guarantees they had slaved over under Gavin's guidance, the phrases and figures they had battled for inch by inch against the company's iron resistance under Gavin's generalship. Window dressing? A stage set? While all the time behind the scenes, behind closed doors the real action . . .

Sucker bait!

The word had been passed down. Shut Shoreham up. Knock it off. The agreements are being concluded.

He dove for the Gladstone he kept by his bed and unlocked it with the key he kept under his pillow and pulled the job-evaluation report out of the shirt pocket.

"And what about this? What's this?" He thrust it at Gavin. Gavin's genius.

Gavin picked up the paperback whodunit and leafed through it with flickering mid-finger, scanning the contents. Gavin who had gone into the coal fields with Harry Sims who never came back, who still bore the scars of Gastonia, who had fought on the overpass at River Rouge, who had testified before the La Follette Committee and challenged the Dies Committee, veteran of a civil war whose martyrs and place names few remembered now or cared about if they did remember.

"It's not that bad a contract, Mish. This just isn't the year."

"It's never the year! Every year we let these things go by. Next year. It's always next year."

"Taking all the factors into consideration, from the overall view, it's the best we can get."

That was what Gavin had said when the non-Communist affidavit won at the convention, with the time extension tacked on. "Not so bad." And when the purge bylaw followed it, cushioned with safeguards. "The best we can get." Yet when the expulsions started, Bob Ucchini was one of the first to go, then a dozen other past and present officials. Then members began dropping out of their locals, stopped attending meetings, paying dues, either in fear of attack or in sheer disgust.

Not so bad. The best we can get.

"You immersed yourself in it too deep." Gavin barely glanced at the black thesis folder. "Now you have to pull out. You oversold yourself on one perspective, Mish. Now you have to adjust your sights. It's not defeat, it's only your pride you have to swallow."

Absently Gavin wiped his glasses with his shirttail. "When you've lived as long as I have you'll know Rome wasn't built in a day. We made our point. On to the next phase." His eyes were brown-pouched, the eyes of a phantom. "You made an impression. You won a lot of recognition. There's a vacancy on the General Executive Board. You could do more good on it than off it."

"Is that what they sent you here with? 'Line your boy up. Straighten him out.'"

"I was making an observation," Gavin said, "not a promise. Got a shot of something in your bag? Take it. Get a good night's sleep. Negotiations tomorrow at ten. Should wind up by noon."

Shirttails hanging, Gavin took his departure through the black door in the upper corner of the room.

He lay back on his pillow. A fly walked upside down in the circle of lamplight on the ceiling. Soon it was buzzing around his lamp bulb, imprisoned in the white inner circle of the lampshade. Flies breed on refuse. He must have smacked three of them in the room tonight. Where from? The wire-braiders—the air was so thick with lint in Wire Braiding it would burst into flame sometimes from a machine spark, a lighted cigarette. The machines were so snowed over they had to be stopped every few hours to be cleaned off. The maintenance men who serviced the machines would never wear a mask, so hot and choking in there. The girl operators pushed back their bandannas and goggles, tore off their masks. Six braids per machine, three on one side of the operator and three on the other: the jenny wrapper revolved and the cotton spiraled about the rising wire from two directions and every time a thread broke the operator ran from one side of her machine to the other to repair and restart her braid. All day long the revolving, spiraling, twisting, breaking in the lint-thick air. No ventilation ducts till the union came in.

The wire-braiders were waiting for him to return with a new formulation on production quotas written into the contract, which they had written up themselves.

Cat's-eye. Cat's-paw. A rage for self-justification.

The decision was made from the top down, not from the bottom up, and this was what he couldn't swallow.

4

He switched off his lamp and dressed quietly in the dark. Gavin's door was suspect. Colangelo's door was suspect. The telephone was not to be trusted. In a phantasmagoria of mistrust he buttoned his job-evaluation report inside his shirt.

Like a private eye, target of cop and killer alike, he eased out into the hall. Eschewing the elevator, he skipped down rippling flights of exit stairs. Cream figures in the crimson oriental rug tracked him through the lobby. Gilt-framed mirrors menaced him at every turn. From high-backed chairs, concealing, loungers sprang out at him. The orange-illuminated entrance of the grill room, the white-illuminated length of the desk lurked in wait for him, traps. Hallucinatory as if he'd drunk himself cockeyed, he escaped into the street.

Crossed Broadway against the light, through labyrinths of charging monsters. Dashed down the tomb of a subway and up an escalator, out. Ducked past glaring displays, dress-suited dummies. Amusement parlors crackling with the shot of pinball machines.

It's over, Gavin said, the campaign that consumed your energies, the love that lighted your dreams. The door is shut and bolted. Accept accept accept.

Someone was following him. In a defile of brownstones he opened a creaking wrought-iron gate, trod down into the areaway past peeping venetian-slatted basement windows, secreted himself behind a trash can under the arch beneath the stoop. Footfalls in the deserted street, approaching. A dog yapped inside, a pesky little terrier that wouldn't let up. Footfalls receded. Hiding in tunnel darkness behind an ash can, dog yaps pelting about his ears.

Briskly he swung into the nearest drugstore. A fluorescent wilderness. Telephone booths were a long hike back through acres of cosmetics and syringes, camera goods. In the middle booth a bulky fellow with back hunched against the glass panel, unidentifiable. He waited in his booth until the man was through before he punched his change into the coin slot.

He was not the colorful dynamic leader Bob Ucchini had been. He'd been the detail man to Bob the dynamo, anchor man to Bob's charisma, backstop to the star. Components that together make up a good partnership as they often do a good marriage so long as each understands his own role and values the other's. Then Bob under pressure, from the left perhaps for its own good reasons as well as from the right, stepped down from the leadership and he stepped into Bob's shoes. He had attracted his own components. Not colorful, not dynamic. Dogged.

His dimes clinked through. His quarter chimed. Oh God, he prayed—(should have made it person-to-person, goddamit)— don't let it be Yvonne. It was Yvonne.

"Ye-eh."

The languid plaint. A woman who spoke always with face averted, sighs escaping her out of wordless depths of suffering, begging the query: What's the matter, Yvonne? What's wrong? For someone to take her hand and draw it out of her. Not Priscilla's pep talks about what a great man Ray was, how brilliant. Not Mari's efforts to organize her, activate her around some outside interest. Someone to tip that still pretty face about, look deep into those diffident eyes, touch that passive skin, gently press that limp hand. What's the matter, Yvonne?

Alerted by the jingle of coins, recognizing his voice, Yvonne instantly warded him off. "What do you want? Are you cuckoo? Calling this time of night."

"Yvonne, I got to speak to Ray. Is he there?"

"What do you want with him? When he's awake. When he's asleep. Why don't you leave him alone?"

With her liquid l's, her sagging cadence.

Yvonne fought him over the telephone, defending her sleeping mate and her young from depredation.

"What do you care for him? He has to go to work in the morning. He's tired, he gets sick, he gets hurt, who will take care of him?" Ray had had a siege of bursitis during the strike three years before just when everyone was so busy. Yvonne couldn't forget it. "Who came to see him? Mari for a minute. You call him here, you call him there, but when something happens I'm the one, it's me, me . . ."

A woman who worried all night over what the future might bring, eventualities she could only too vividly imagine.

"In the end I'll be the one to save him. Because I—LOVE—him."

His three minutes were running out.

"Yvonne, we're about to settle the contract. I got to talk to him about the contract."

"Yeh?" She was instantly intrigued. "What we get?"

"Five cents."

"Five cents. Phooey," Yvonne said.

But she did call out to Ray or Ray called to her from his bed.

A tiff with the operator for more time. Gesturing frantically to the drugstore clerk for more change. Ray on the line insisting, "Give me your number, I'll call you back." A dispute erupting in French in the background.

He gave his number to Ray and went to the cash register to break a five-dollar bill. A customer at the counter up front squealed about on his stool. Twenty-four-hour surveillance. This one's too big, Lunin. It's bigger than you are, bigger than Shoreham, bigger than the EWIU. Who rules on what the job is. Who sits in the driver's seat?

Back in the booth he tried again. Busy signal. The Pelletiers wrestling it out. Who has the upper hand? Who's boss?

The trouble with Ray, everyone said, is his wife. Ray was president of the local in the early war years. He was elected for a term to the Shoreham city council. He could have gone far. But Yvonne . . .

They were working on the first draft of the job-evaluation study one night in the hole on Prince Street, and it must have been almost twelve when Ray left for home. Ten minutes later, Yvonne came panting up the stairs, disdain in every breath she drew for every step upward she took on the rotting stairs. She walked into their chamber of horrors, where rags and tatters of laughter still lingered amid the debris, and demanded to know:

"Where is he? What have you done with him?"

"You should have been here," Priscilla sought to allay her wrath. "You should have heard him. That Ray, when he gets going . . . He's really living!"

Yvonne refused the glass of water he brought her. She refused the brandy he offered. She refused to sit down on his couch. She stood in the center of his room in her droopy black coat, a skinful of bones, without sinew, without pith, and gathering structure, height, towering with passion she pointed at him:

"You are—my—devil! You are Satan to me!"

She was engaged in a mortal struggle with him for the soul of her husband.

"And you," she said to Priscilla, "you're worse than Mari. You're the worst one of all!"

She slammed down the stairs, a creature of stings and nettles, full of ginger, a woman to be reckoned with. He followed her through the midnight streets with his car to give her a lift home. She wouldn't set foot inside.

Ray rang. His voice came over the wire fresh, keen, the cutting edge of a fine analytical mind. Before he'd half begun explaining the situation, Ray was all the way through it.

"You mean the international is wielding the whip for the company?"

Over Yvonne's bitter complaints. Didn't she tell him he was wasting his time?

"You mean we fought for industry-wide bargaining all these years and now they're tying us up with it? Don't let them palm it off on you, Mish. If you present it to the membership, they'll take it for a double-cross. You heard us this afternoon. We won't go for it. Without our job guarantees that contract's out."

"That's what I want to know. Where do we go from here?"

"Pull the switch!"

Between them they divided up the exec and the stewards in the key departments. Mari for her division. Amy for the wire jobs. He'd check back with Ray in twenty minutes.

He finished with Ray and called Marty Rakocszi. Ray was the analyst. Without hesitation Ray cut through to the core of the apple. Marty was the researcher. The collector of grass-roots opinion, the keeper of files on UV in his basement that went back for years. Thoughtfully, shuffling from foot to foot, Marty would give him the all-around view, complete with ifs-ands-and-buts plus quotes from clippings he seemed to pluck out of the air.

Of course it was Helen who answered, fluttery, hoarsely gasping, wound up as usual for disaster.

"Ooo, I thought it was my sister in Albany."

Why did the husbands let their wives jump out of bed to the phone? Or was it that women were always on the jump?

After he had smoothed Helen's feathers down she was amenable enough. "Marty?" she sang out. "Hey, Mar-tee-ee." Coyly mock-coyly. "For you, sweetie-pie."

Must have been making a night of it.

"Yah?" Marty in shocked astonishment.

"Ya-ah?" Marty amused.

"Yah." Marty solidly reassuring.

For once Marty didn't hedge. He'd covered the taverns earlier in the evening and had gathered the mood. "You can't do a back flip now, Mish. They won't buy it." And the data. "Coffin knows

he's got a strike deadline. You heard those stories all over, how
they been pushing hell on production the last three months, piling
up inventory? Well, there's no backlog in Warehouse. In 11-G
they're behind on orders. Same in Wire & Cable, all the stuff's being
stamped in Spanish, some deal in Venezuela. The new dryer's hit
a bug and they're back for readjustments. Construction just expanded their sales staff.

"The company ain't ready for a strike. Stick it out."

Marty would call the section chairmen. Check. Call back in
twenty minutes. Check.

While the white-aproned porter mopped the terrazzo floor outside the booth, he panicked inside it lest the store close before
he was through and, quaking, made a few more calls. Soiled apron,
muddy waters swishing outward, a shimmer to be traversed. . . .

He went back to his hotel room sure of his ground, reports from
a network of sources backing him up. He went to bed shaking
with a chill sweat of nervousness, fire in the pit of his stomach.
From the corners of the ceiling, Gavin's voice crashed down on
him. *Do you have to take on everybody?*

All night long Gavin's face shone down on him like the face of
one newly dead, in all its expressions and angles. An enigma.

Gavin the teacher who had nurtured a favorite pupil up to the
point when the pupil would turn and destroy him.

Gavin the arch-conspirator, under orders from the Kremlin,
dropping Bob with Bob's compliance and replacing him with
Lunin until Lunin too lost his usefulness.

Gavin the secret agent, under instructions from Rome or Washington, displacing Bob the leftist with Lunin the progressive and
ultimately displacing Lunin with . . .

Gavin the honest realist, trying to save what he could of the
old trade unionism while he built the new.

Demon. Guardian angel.

All night long he disassembled and reassembled the pieces of
Gavin. Gavin glancing through the glass door of the hotel dining
room at a bevy of officials seated around a damasked table, a

waiter in monkey suit hovering over them. "How long is it since they walked a picket line?"

"How do you choose," Gavin once said to him, "between corruption and elimination?"

Corruption. Or elimination.

Was it Gavin who had sent up the blonde in blue?

All night long he pleaded with Gavin: Stay with us! But underneath he knew. When your own international rep won't go along with you . . .

In the morning Gavin wasn't in his room. He went down to the coffee shop alone. In the waiting line he kept an eye out for Gavin and when his turn came left word with the hostess to direct Gavin to his table. But it was Nick who dropped down in the chair opposite his at his table and ordered.

"Where were you last night?" Nick asked him, with the glimmer of a jest. "Calling Bob for advice?"

"I thought I ought to give you a chance to go through my wastebasket."

Still no sign of Gavin.

"If you're looking for Frank," Nick said, in command of information, "he's not here. Had a family emergency. Trouble with his older boy. Chased the young one up on the roof and threatened to throw him off. The cops called him home. We kept knocking at your door."

Bennett, a vice-president of the international, took Gavin's place at the bargaining table. "Now let's see if we can't clean this up today." Cheerfully Bennett rolled up his sleeves and with admirable ease sifted out the essentials. Bennett and Coffin and the lawyers exchanged views. Every time Lunin opened his mouth, they stared around at him from a long way off, then plunged ahead. Company and union shared problems that could only be solved through joint effort, give a little, get a little.

Finally he stood up and headed for the hall door.

"Where are you going?" Bennett thought to inquire as he reached for the knob.

"Back to Shoreham. What do you need me for?"

It turned out they did need him. They needed his assent. He withheld it.

That night at the armory in Shoreham in the last hours of the old contract, the new contract was presented to Local 317 for approval. Bennett delivered his speech of recommendation with the persuasiveness of an energetic and enlightened personality. In the midst of his speech shouts broke out.

"Go home!"

"Sellout!"

In a body the membership rejected the contract, Cranston and his caucus leading the pack, more militant even than the militants. Nick threw up his arms. Lunin gaveled for order through tumult, everyone making his own speech. The chief steward called for a strike vote. Next morning they hit the pavements.

The strike lasted one day. He knew. The membership knew. They couldn't take on everybody. They couldn't buck the company and the union both. The decisions had already been made, behind their backs, over their heads. The heart had gone out of it.

He heard two weeks later that Gavin had moved to Wyoming for his health. He never saw Frank Gavin again and he never stopped wondering about him. He missed Gavin and missed him the more because of his mystification. He turned it over and over in his mind sometimes like an odd drill bit, speculating over the many facets of Gavin.

III

He first learned that Colangelo was planning to run against him in the June election, at the end of his two-year term, from Bob Ucchini. Bob was still working in the plant though he was out of the Radiosonics lab and out of the union, shorn of his skills and his power. He had not seen Bob in several months. Either he stayed away from Bob, more or less unconsciously, or Bob quite consciously stayed away from him. By a circuitous route he received a message from Bob that he was to meet him at nine o'clock Saturday evening in the parking lot of the A&P on Bancroft Avenue, in the left rear away from the building. Bob would not be driving his own car. A black Ford two-door, license number RD-871. If the radio aerial was up, he was to leave his own car and join Bob in a third car that Bob would indicate. If the radio antenna was down, he was to go on to Beach Road opposite Lighthouse Point and park among the neckers, Bob would find him there.

He telephoned Bob at home after he received the message, though he knew he had no business telephoning him, and said, "Look, what is this shit? You want to talk with me? You come here or I'll come there."

If Bob's telephone was tapped, let it be tapped. If Bob's house was bugged, let it be bugged. If Bob's car was being tailed by the FBI, let it be tailed. It had nothing to do with him. He wasn't going to go slinking around parking lots, making himself an object of suspicion by playing cloak-and-dagger. Anything they had to say to each other, let it be out in the open.

"All right," Bob said. "Why don't you bring the wife and kid over Saturday afternoon? It's nice out here now."

He was not so noble and above-it-all as he thought he was. As soon as he hung up he realized how rash a visit to Bob's house would be, particularly at this time when his feud with the international had reached critical proportions. Still out of sheer bullheadedness he couldn't bring himself to call Bob back with excuses, backing out. Instead he jittered all week over it.

The local was under severe pressure from several directions, riding out a storm that was solely of his making. The end of it was not yet in sight. His deadline for signing the Taft-Hartley non-Communist affidavit had long since expired. Along with a number of other union leaders in the country he continued to delay. If they all held out long enough . . . Truman had won the labor vote in the 1948 presidential election with his pledge, as a principal plank in his platform, to repeal Taft-Hartley. Why should he jump the gun on Truman? Several cases challenging what amounted to a test oath as a qualification for union office were pending in the courts. Why should he beat the courts to the punch? He didn't like the affidavit. He didn't believe in it. Nobody has the right to ask you your nationality or your politics or your religion.

"The Constitution specifically forbids both Congress and states to pass a bill of attainder," his father-in-law, Joe Barth, advised him. "Traditionally the Supreme Court interprets a test oath as a bill of attainder, an imposition of pains and penalties in restriction of the civil rights of the individual. But historically," Joe warned him, "the court has been very reluctant to render an opinion on the constitutionality of an act of Congress, which may be construed as infringement on the powers of the legislative branch. Much depends on the climate of the day. Just four years ago, in 1946, in the case of U.S. versus Lovett, a rider to an appropriations bill that would have denied salaries to government

employees accused of being subversives was struck down. Now we
have an entirely different kettle of fish. The climate, to put it
mildly, is not conducive . . ."

Resistance to the affidavit might encourage its demise, he decided, whereas surrender to it would only serve to confirm it.
When the legality of it was determined, then it would be time
enough for him to consider. He didn't sign.

It led to a lot of stupid arguments.

"If you were in Russia you'd have to sign."

"But I'm not in Russia. I'm here. In Russia I wouldn't sign it
either."

"If you don't sign that means you're a Communist, don't it?"

"If I was a Communist and I did sign, I'd be in the pokey. If
I'm not a Communist and I sign, what have I proved?"

"If Bob was our president now, what would he do?"

"If Bob was our president and we elected him to it fair and
square . . ."

Every meeting of the local turned into a raging historical debate. To sign was to protect America from subversion. To sign
was to desecrate the American heritage. The fair body of this
land lay upon the rostrum, inviolate, violated, the virgin ravished,
the human sacrifice.

It was simply something he couldn't do to himself.

In January the National Labor Relations Board had served
notice that it was denying certification to EWIU-UV Local 317
as a bargaining unit until such time as its presiding officer com-
plied with the requirements of Title I, Section 9 of the law. He
went right on bargaining with the company. They didn't need the
services of the NLRB in order to bargain, at least for the
moment.

In February the international sent John Bennett to Shoreham
with orders to him to comply. It wasn't a matter of personal
choice. Like or dislike, it was union policy. Bennett left the local
with an ultimatum. Unless it removed its non-complying officer,
the international would impose a caretaker administration over
its affairs and its treasury. Forgetting the affidavit and the appeals

to their patriotism, the members, in outrage at the threat of a
trusteeship, voted two to one against Lunin's removal. Rather than
give up their non-complying officer they would withhold per
capita payments to the international if necessary.

In March the climate changed.

Observing the embroilment of EWIU-UV Local 317 with its
international, two outside unions moved in to raid the local and
in the process of wooing favor with various leaders on various
grounds split factions into fractions.

Grover Coffin, general manager of UV's Shoreham works, announced that certain defense contracts slated for the plant were
being canceled or reallocated due to security problems and general
uncertainties stemming from conditions in the local.

One Russell Luchin, president of an AFL local of electroplaters
in another plant on the other side of Shoreham, absconded on
his birthday to parts unknown with nineteen thousand dollars
in credit union funds and his treasurer's wife. The treasurer, left
in the lurch, was indicted under the same section of the Taft-
Hartley Act as the affidavit for filing a rigged fiscal statement with
the government. All over the city union members began clamoring for enforcement of the Act. The Act was their defense against
malfeasance by their leaders.

Overnight he was besieged with pleas to sign. "You can say that
that part of the law is no good. But the other part— We can't
have everything." "Look at all the mess this has gotten us into.
Half of Radar was laid off last week and there's more coming."
"Sooner or later you gonna have to sign anyway. Spare us the
agony."

"But we already have laws covering embezzlement. The credit
union funds and the union funds are two separate . . ."

His rejoinders were futile. Principle crumbled, degenerating
into quibbles. The only principle at stake was his personality.

"Did it ever occur to you, Mish, that you may not be so right as
you think you are?"

"Trouble with you, Mish, you never learned to roll with the
punches."

It was in this context—amid rumors of impending mass layoffs; daily warnings from the international by registered mail; solicitation and badgering of workers at the plant gates by field organizers of the two outside unions—that he was to go pay a friendly call on Bob Ucchini.

2

The yellow Cape Cod on the outskirts of town was set back from the road on its plot of lawn, screened from the medley of neighboring Cape Cods by a row of firs on one side and rose bushes on the driveway side. Tender shoots of new grass tapestried the grayish winter lawn. Jonquils and spears of blue hyacinth, blossoming early in the April warmth, bordered the sunny front of the house under picture windows crisscrossed with frilled organdy curtains. The garage on the side had been finished last year. Bob was trundling a wheelbarrow of gravel out back, laying the foundation for the patio. Mari was pruning her rose bushes along the driveway. Everything in progress. Hence the saying around UV, behind her back: Mari takes care of Mari.

Priscilla lifted Stephanie out of the car. "My," she said with surprise, "it's nice out here."

Bob came around the side of the house and eyed his grass. "Looks like I got the lawn licked. I put in a dormant seed last November."

Mari scootched down before Steph and nuzzled with her. "Talk to me, aren't you going to talk to me? You ready for your nap? Sleepy-teepy, beddy-bye? Why don't you," she suggested to Priscilla, rising and starting in with her snipping again, "stay out here with me? Let them take care of the baby."

Once inside, Stephanie snapped wide-awake. She scampered about in her overalls, a wiry little black-eyed girl, too restless and curious to nap. Bob kept a supply of balloons on hand for visiting tots. While he spoke to their elders he blew up balloons and tossed them around the room. If they tired of the balloons, he produced a clay pipe and blew bubbles for them. When they were old enough, he showed them how to blow bubbles themselves.

They mixed drinks in Mari's beige-and-white electric kitchen and in the living room, Steph chasing about underfoot after her pink and blue balloons, they examined Bob's latest acquisition. His old piano was too big for this house. Through a cousin, a jazz guitarist turned lutanist, "student of Hindemith," Bob had hooked up with a young string group, "all mad for this antique music." Under the white ruffled curtains in the window stood what appeared to be a miniature piano on a stand. "Look at the casing. Beautiful, isn't it?" Bob said, with fingers sentient in the air for the grain that swirled through the tawny wood. They pored over the brass blades and strings in back, Bob explaining the sound process. He depressed a key. A chiming timbre.

"It's all in the touch," Bob explained. "The touch controls the pitch."

Bob wasn't altogether satisfied with the instrument. "Made in Europe about fifty years ago. Supposed to be a replica of the clavichord Bach played. But I suppose I could never find one . . . outside a museum . . ."

Blunt fingers, expert in the testing of electronic pulsations, struck up a romp. Raindrop runs of notes, vines and tendrils, startling shifts of rhythm. The complexities of a forgotten age. Fresh to the ear as the clink-clank of Mari's pruning shears in the rose bushes outside the half-open end window.

"You've got to come down out of the clouds, Mish," Bob said to him, playing. "Where the hell do you think you're headed, riding your white horse?"

"Now you sound like Frank Gavin."

"You should know. We were both schooled by the same man."

Bob was not like Gavin. He had none of Gavin's weariness. Sitting erect on his bench, fingers plummeting over the keys, commanding their tone with his touch. The anthracite eyes sparked, no sagging pouches swallowing them up, no haggard lines fanning out beneath. Though he was outside the union now, Bob found plenty to keep him busy. Conducting campaigns to get back in, which got nowhere. Giving help from behind the scenes to Gene Bostic and the Fair Employment Practices Committee he had encouraged Bostic to form in the plant, with no appreciable results so far. Hearing out people who came to him seeking guidance, some of them openly in his department, some of them secretly at odd meeting places, and drawing up blueprints with them for actions which they seldom carried through. Running for mayor on the Progressive Party's peace-and-plenty platform, garnering mainly exhaustion for himself and his backers. Practicing and rehearsing with his music group, a lutanist, a violist, a madrigal singer with whom he was more than half in love, for recitals in each other's homes attended by maybe three buffs. He still had his job at UV, though transferred and downgraded from the Radiosonics lab to the Washer-Dryer line. He still had his wife though Mari—pained and relieved to find that he was not after all infallible, irked with him for his failures and wrung with compassion for him—could not be especially easy for him to live with at this time.

"I deal with what is," Frank Gavin once said. "Not with anybody's pipe dreams."

Bob still danced to his pipe dream, the grand vision. Disillusionment had taken no toll of him. Under his emphatic black brows his black eyes still gleamed; undimmed by doubt or regret. He still moved with an irrepressible *élan*. The Blind Musician correcting the false note in the parlor from the kitchen. The rock-hewn grandmother appearing at the door in the middle of a blizzard with a pot of ricotta under one arm and a bottle of wine under the other, marching in. Today we make ravioli.

"What are you waiting for, Mish?" Bob asked him. "For the international to do to your whole membership what they did to me? They'll expel the local."

"Expulsion? Maybe. It's a possibility. But when there are two other unions out to take us over. . . . What's that? Play it again."

"Okay, you're not expelled, you're raided. The Teamsters are collecting their cards, the Machinists are collecting their cards, and first thing you know they'll be petitioning the NLRB for new

bargaining representation—then where'll you be? We'll wind up
with four different unions in the plant. Just what Coffin would
love. Right in his lap. A present from Lunin to Coffin."

Stephanie hitched herself up from the floor by Bob's pants and
added her doodlings to his intricate plaint.

"It's all right, let her, she can't hurt— And there's a third possibility. What about your election this June, Mish? How's it shap-
ing up? Is Ray running with you?"

"Well—Ray. He's having trouble with Yvonne. All this spy stuff
in the papers nowadays has her so wrought up—and these attacks
on me—and their oldest is in the Army. She won't let him."

"And Marty?"

"Well—you know Marty. He's with Ray. Without Ray . . ."

"Colangelo?"

"Oh no. Not him again. You can't sell me . . ."

"I've got news for you. All the time you've been so wrapped up
in bread-and-butter issues and day-to-day developments, Colangelo has been after Pulaski . . . Horvath . . . Walton . . . Your
coalition is kaput. The Cranston caucus has lined up its own slate
with Colangelo heading it."

"What! Oh no. Not Nick. He's incapable . . ."

"They have John Bennett behind them and the tacit support
of the international. Maybe outside money. They'll mount such a
drive against you . . ."

"Oh no. No. Nick hasn't even serviced his office adequately.
He doesn't stand a chance. Everybody knows . . . I saw Pulaski
yesterday, he's perfectly friendly. Except he's so hot on the
Poles . . . And Horvath . . ."

Bob suspended his playing to retune, and peeped cautiously
under the crisscrossed curtains at a car parked across the street in
front of a house perched like a marshmallow on its knoll.

"It's getting so every time I spot a gray Plymouth sedan, oh-
oh. They stop me on the road. 'Hey Bob, we want to talk to you.'
Where am I going? Where've I been? 'None of your goddam
business,' I tell them. I don't crawl." He dropped the curtain with
a flash of his old denunciatory fire. "They can kiss my ass!"

Edgar Hoover shooting pictures? Eavesdropping? Noting down the license plate in the yard?

Bob banged chords on his instrument, an instrument keyed so low it couldn't be used for anything but chamber concerts.

"Sign it," Bob hissed at him under cover of his chords. "You got to sign that affidavit."

"But you—" Over Bob's frantic signals to tone down. "You're the one—"

It was Bob who always said, "Hold out!" It was Bob he was protecting in a sense: so long as I stick to my rights, he still has some defense. It was Bob's respect he had to preserve, or what was he? A weak sister. Crap-out. Just another phony.

It was to Bob he had once said: "If there's anything you can be sure of on this earth, I'll never sign that thing."

With Stephanie in his lap Bob blew up a green balloon, puffing with comic heaves, twisted its neck into a knot, twanged its skin with his fingers, rubbed it on his pants and in his hair, clowning. Planted it on the wall. Blew up a yellow one for her, longer and longer and LONGER. Released it, untied. It rocketed off in the air.

"Sign it," Bob muttered through his teeth. "You might as well sign."

From the brass wastebasket by his bookshelves Bob uprooted newspapers until he found a discarded envelope. He turned the envelope over to the blank side and scribbled across it with stubby pencil. Outside, Mari and Priscilla chatted, treble notes, melodious contralto and clear soprano, interweaving. Bob held the envelope up for him to read, the thick pencil lines skipping at the lines of the flaps:

"There are CPers who are resigning from the party and signing."

Bob tore the envelope across and across again, the rasps skipping at the flap lines. He deposited the bits in the brass bowl of an ashtray and lit them with paper matches, tearing match after match out of his matchbook. The holdout who hadn't given in soon enough.

SIGN IT!

The rest of the afternoon was a confusion of shimmering, translucent balloons popping. Wormy shreds. Stephanie bawling on the potty, balloony pink plastic pants. Rainbow bubbles wafting.

"Nick'll never make it. It's impossible. I just won that vote against removal from office, two to one."

Several times he was tempted to spill the whole story to Bob. How Nick tried to play footsy with Coffin during contract negotiations last year. Each time he saw the spreading grin. So he fixed you, huh? You caught him with a telephone call. He caught you with a call girl in your room.

Sign.

They stood in the driveway defiantly lingering over their good-bys. Bob with the strain in his face and in his pride: the untouchable legitimatized by his callers. And they, the callers, asserting their legitimacy: who didn't have the right to stop by this house for a friendly afternoon visit?

"Anything I can do about your job, Bob? You should at least be in testing."

"Nononono. Not a thing." Bob was afraid to fool with it. "I was acquiring an elitist attitude. Now on the line I'm more in tune . . ." Saving his pride with little stories, who said what to him yesterday, who he met on the street. In tune with the masses.

Mari ran back and forth with coffeecake left over from their coffee together; a pot of African violets, giving precise instructions on their care; a magazine article she thought they should read. No one ever left Mari's house empty-handed.

"I suppose Bob could sue the international for political discrimination against him. Under another section of Taft-Hartley," Joe Barth suggested whimsically at family dinner next day in Sherwood Heights. "Compel them to readmit him to membership."

"Are you saying that he has some recourse?" Stunned, he dropped the knife and fork with which he was mincing meat for Stephanie.

"It would have to be explored. Bob won't do it."

"For Christ sake, why not? Here I am knocking myself out over him, worrying myself to death . . . It's not only him, there are a dozen others."

"I suppose it's a matter of principle. He won't sue the union, any union, in the first place. In the second place, he won't validate the Act by bringing suit under it."

"Principle?" Ted said. "Or command decisions? From East Twelfth Street—or by some Machiavellian twist, Pennsylvania Avenue? Wherever these things originate."

Ted had helped initiate an academic-freedom committee at the university and he was having problems.

Over the dinner table the Barths pondered the Lunin dilemma. To sign or not to sign.

"Bob or no Bob," he told them, "the more I think of it the less I'm inclined."

The Barths advised him dispassionately, in abstractions.

"I suppose you could enjoin the international from interfering in the affairs of the local." Joe paused to dab butter on his roll. "Under another section of Taft-Hartley. It has everything else in it."

"N-n-no." He couldn't bring court action against the union either. He had a member's horror of wasting dues money on internal litigation.

"In today's atmosphere," Joe conceded, "I suppose it would take years." Ruefully he relinquished his legal whimsey.

Flo quoted Thoreau at him, her plain face shining over china and silver and embroidered linen cloth.

"What do men do when confronted with an unjust law? They refuse to pay taxes. Fill the jails. Resign from office."

"Quit? And leave the field to Colangelo? I don't see what good that would do."

"You'd have a clear conscience. You would not have contributed toward expansion of the injustice by acquiescing to it."

"But that's not the way slavery was ended," Ted reminded her.

"Thoreau notwithstanding. It's a matter of what your options are. You don't seem to have much latitude, Mish. Stand pat, you're demolished. Move, you compromise. Is it better to survive at some sacrifice of liberty? Or to maintain liberty no matter what the risks? Given the flux of historic conditions, does one strive for a constant or a balance?"

"How did slavery get into this?" Priscilla inquired.

They all burst into laughter. Their family joke.

Priscilla in one of her tough masculine moods, talking through the cigarette stuck in the corner of her mouth, had no patience with options or risks. "Bennett doesn't give a damn about the T-H affidavit at this point. He just wants it out of the way. Millions of people, government workers, scientists, teachers, everybody in defense, God-all knows how many have signed loyalty oaths by now. It's already past history. What Bennett is really concerned about is the T-H ban on the checkoff. Getting around it by getting the companies to agree in the contract to a voluntary checkoff of union dues from wages. Without regular collection of membership dues, how long can the unions last?"

She had always insisted and she insisted again: "The affidavit is the least of it."

She was also quite angry at Bob. "If we'd even breathed of giving in before, he'd have axed us so fast. Friendship, what we've been to one another, what we've been through together, none of it would have counted. Off with our heads! Mari knows it too. Mish knows it. Don't you, Mish? You know it."

He knew that she was upset with the Ucchinis over their house. She had fussed half the night over it, writhing between criticism and sympathy. Bourgeois heaven! All that energy expended . . . They built it as a haven from all the hullaballoo. A pleasant place for people to come to. Now where are the people?

Suddenly, punching her cigarette out on her soiled dinner plate, she smashed up, a face seen through a goblet of water, all brightness and wetness, fractured.

"*No pasaran! No pasaran!*"

With a clatter she gathered her mother's gold-rimmed china plates together and headed for the swinging door to the kitchen.

Gail, not a Barth yet, midway between divorcing her bastard of a husband and marrying Ted, in fact living in the state with Ted in order to establish residence for her divorce, was baffled. She arched about in amazement.

"Now let me get this straight, Mish," she said to him across the table. Her slender neck tilted as if she carried a vase of inestimable worth on her head. With her dusky eyes she plucked him up and tucked him away somewhere under her piled-high coils of dark hair. "Let's begin all over again. Slowly, please. You won't sign to something you're not—I mean you are—I mean—? I tell you what. Let's all assume the lotus position."

An official notice of suspension of Local 317 by the EWIU-CIO was delivered to the local's office by registered mail Monday afternoon, to take effect in five days if the local did not in the meantime conform with policy.

In the afternoon edition of the Shoreham *Tribune,* Grover Coffin announced the transfer of the Radar Division to the new United Vacuum plant in Charlton, Tennessee. Every effort would be made, he promised, to place the employees with other departments in the plant or with other companies in the city.

Ray and Marty stamped up the stairs on Prince Street with the news about Colangelo's candidacy. Pulaski was talking up the Teamsters. Something had to be done right away about uniting the people in Radar against the company's move.

On Saturday in the forenoon, his last hour of grace, he signed the Taft-Hartley non-Communist affidavit in the office of the CIO lawyer, with the lawyer's two partners, impatient to be off for the day, as witnesses. The office secretary stamped her notary's seal upon his signature. Now that wasn't so hard, was it?

Immediately afterward, with a hundred details claiming his attention, he went up to his father's place on Liscomb Street and sat around brooding. Pop made tea in the kitchen and brought it to him in a glass on a saucer, too hot to drink. "Put your spoon in. The spoon draws the heat." The old man looked at him in his

misery as the old-time housewives of Liscomb Street would look
at a daughter seduced and abandoned.

Now you know. Now your eyes are open.

In the weeks that followed his signature didn't save him. He
had waited too long.

3

He was defeated by a cloud of witnesses. During his years of
office they swarmed over the air waves, paraded through the headlines, subjected the nation to a barrage of alarms that left no man
unaffected. John Rankin, J. Parnell Thomas, Richard M. Nixon,
a host of interrogators. Louis Budenz, Elizabeth Bentley, Whit-
taker Chambers, Ginger Rogers' mother, G. Racey Jordan, FBI
undercover informants, a host of accusers. Gerhart Eisler, Bertolt
Brecht, Judith Coplon, William Remington, Alger Hiss, Scien-
tist X, Hollywood writers, government officials, college professors,
labor leaders, ministers, actors and artists, a host of criminals before the bar. Hopkins and Roosevelt, Condon and Henry Wallace,
White and Morgenthau, Oppenheimer and Lilienthal, the nature
of two decades, Depression and War, the direction of the postwar world, a host of issues in the balance. Agents of the international Soviet threat, from within and without. Espionage rings,
conspirators to advocate the overthrow of, infiltrators into, leakers
of information, transmitters of the atomic secret, recalcitrants refusing to turn over organizational records and mailing lists, to
name names and even open their mouths at all. Hearings, investigations, contempt citations, perjury charges, searches and seizures
and arrests in the night, trials, jailings, deportations. Security
checks, security ratings, security clearances and denials of clearance, reversals of clearance. Resignations. Firings. Blacklistings.
Heart attacks. Suicides.

It was still mounting when Colangelo ran against him for the
presidency of the local in the spring of 1950. In Russia they now
had The Bomb. In England Klaus Fuchs had confessed to having

provided the Russians with reports of his activities while he was a member of the British wartime scientific team at Los Alamos. In the United States Harry Gold who claimed to have been Fuchs's American contact with the Russians was arrested in late May. In Shoreham a smudged photostat of a post card, alleged to have originated in the Lunin apartment, circulated around UV like a dirty picture. NO MORE A-BOMBS!

He was defeated by Nick Colangelo and his slanders and slogans.

"Worse than the Communists are those who do the work of the Communists."

"A vote for Lunin is a vote for Ucchini. A vote for Ucchini is a vote for Stalin. A vote for Joe Stalin is a vote against Jesus Christ."

Slogans and slanders. To deny them was to spread them.

Nick professed to be just as distressed by the slogans as he was when he confronted him with them. Times like these who knows where the hell it starts?

"Aaah, it's all politics," Nick said to him, comfortingly. "And you know how politics is. Don't lose any sleep over it."

He went to Herb Cranston with it. Cranston, clean-cut and starchy in his open-collared white shirt, listened to him attentively with inclined head.

"I have waited for four years, Mish, for you to break with Bob. You haven't done it. That's why we're running our own slate. Where do you stand on Alger Hiss? With Bob or your own government? Guilty or not guilty?"

Alger Hiss was not an issue in the election. Colangelo's performance as business agent was.

He was defeated by his members, by a kind of frenzy that swept through United Vacuum that June. To expel The Enemy Within. Tear the traitor out of their bosom. Oust the foreign agent. Out! Out! They were sick to death of the incessant cries of treason, the peril of self-exposure in every unguarded word. They wanted peace in the local, peace in the plant, peace in the land. They wanted the soothing, smoothing touch of Nick Colangelo.

Even if he had disclosed at this late date that he had caught Colangelo red-handed on the telephone with Coffin during contract negotiations, it wouldn't have helped. Nobody cared. Company stooge, so what? Colangelo was working well with the company, wasn't he, on reallocating the people in Radar. With a change of union leadership, it was hinted in the company weekly, *UV Highlights*, there was a possibility that Radar might not, after all, be transferred out. The Lunin forces immediately filed a complaint of unfair labor practice against the company with the NLRB. The complaint only further publicized the company hint. UV's employees longed for the assurance provided by union alliance with the company. Out of the abrasive day-to-day hostilities into harmony. To crawl into the bosom of, be rocked in the arms of, sink into the warm bath of. They were in league with the company against The Enemy Out There.

Sometimes, thinking of it, he thought how stanch they must have been to stand up for so long against the siege from Without to Within. They were clobbered into submission before they crumbled.

He ran against Nick Colangelo for the presidency two years later. In 1952 there was the wage freeze, there was the production squeeze, there was discontent. Cranston's Freedom Caucus had disappeared for want of an object. The slogans and slanders were no longer bruited about. They weren't needed.

He was defeated by the Korean war. He was defeated by Julius and Ethel Rosenberg. He was defeated by United States Senator Joseph McCarthy who sat at every breakfast table like a guest in the house.

He was defeated by Boris Kallen.

As he was going into the last two weeks of his election campaign, an obscure diemaker in his late fifties, close to retirement, was summoned to a hearing in Washington by a Congressional committee investigating the activity of "Red Cells in Defense Industries." Bruce (Boris) Kallen had been politically inactive for many years. He had not even been active in the union in recent years. He devoted himself chiefly to a committee for aid to

Birobijan, a province in far eastern Siberia where Soviet Jews, who
so desired, it was said, were building a national homeland for
themselves. The aid consisted of collection of funds and clothing,
celebrations in song and dance, the circulation of publications
profusely illustrated with photographs of pioneer life. The committee had been listed by the Attorney General as a subversive
organization.

Why Boris? Why not Bob or Mari, Jensen, Lukacs, Chadwick,
Donovan, Revels—any one of whom would have provided a
more satisfactory target? Boris had a memory of radicals and
radicalism in Shoreham that extended back over thirty years. He
was one of those young men who had been rescued from the post
office storage room by Joe Barth after Lev Lunin came knocking
at his door on a snowy afternoon in January 1919.

Boris Kallen had hidden in a cellar with Pop during the first
strike ever held in the city of Tula. They had escaped from Russia
together, roomed together in Shoreham, courted girls together.
The Kallens had lived below the Lunins on Liscomb Street for
five years and from the time he was twelve, Mish Lunin mooned
after Boris's daughter, Elisabeth.

"What color's your hair, Elisabeth?"

Slim-jim girl in sloppy Joe sweater, tomboy pants, treading the
ridge of the schoolhouse fence. She picked a strand of hair out of
her elastic-banded braid and held it up to the sun, rainbows.

"Mud color."

He'd hung around with her brother, Carl, making fun of the
oldsters: their fathers and the fathers of the neighborhood
gathered in Pekar the shoemaker's little slot of a shop, exploding
with political argument. "AKs," Carl tagged them. *Alte Kuckers.*
Old Craps.

Boris's children were grown now, the son an engineer in California, the daughter married to an embassy official abroad; the two,
especially the girl, a source of pride to him. Thus Boris was both
harmless and vulnerable.

Joe Barth consulted with his son and son-in-law before consent-
ing to accompany Boris to Washington.

"I've tried to find another attorney for him. Jack Grodinsky would take it but he's a cardiac—and I suppose he's afraid of his name. Todd Bailey might take it on, only he wants a pledge from Boris that he won't resort to the Fifth Amendment, plus assurance from him that he is not now and never was. If the American Civil Liberties Union here would assign me to it, that would settle it. Only they want Boris to admit publicly that he was and is. And Boris won't even tell me!

"Nobody will touch it. Seems to be open season on lawyers in Washington this year. Smears. Ejections. Disbarment. Contempt charges. Some of them in prison now.

"You two have more at stake in this than I have. Shall I turn him down?"

In his upstairs study, surrounded by his family archives, Joe swung about from son to son-in-law. Nobility glistened on his tanned bald pate. Innocence peeped out from under his tangled brows. Large-knuckled hands tightly folded. He was itching to have a go at it. Joe enjoyed a snobbish certainty that he was above reprisal.

Ted had come down from upstate where he had just won a stock-car race for the first time. "Pure fluke." The dust of it still clung, a trace of his fiendish, black-goggled, victory grin. His first lead had blown a radiator tube on the three hundred and nineteenth lap of the half-mile oval. His second lead started belching smoke just ten laps from the finish.

More important (the racing like the skiing being a refuge from what was most important to him), Ted was also in the final stages of the too long delayed book that had developed out of his thesis on the class consciousness of the American worker. And he was sweating out his too often postponed appointment to an assistant professorship. He was quite tense on both scores. His academic-freedom committee had cost him too much in lost time and opportunities.

With a shifting of his elongated body in his too small chair, neither too prompt nor too hesitant, Ted made up Joe's mind for him.

"Are you asking us?" Ted accused his father. "Or testing? Kallen is obviously just their opening gun. How much do they have on him? Where is it leading? To that whole old crowd at UV? All the 1905ers in Shoreham? If you're going to be a patsy for the Commies . . ."

Better and better.

"I don't see what else you can do but go with him," Ted said. "It's up to Mish. He's the one . . ."

"What do you say, Mish?"

He could say no less than Ted. He had to face his father too. All the AKs.

"It's Bob they're after. It must be Bob."

There were plenty of sleepless people in the city the night Boris Kallen took the train to Washington with his attorney.

"What is your occupation?" Kallen was asked by committee counsel Charles Stoltz.

"Frustrated millionaire."

"Have you ever been under the discipline of any organization?"

"Yes, sir. United Vacuum. Every day from seven to four. Make your quota or out you go."

"Will you please describe for the committee the nature of your employment?"

"Gladly. First you apprentice to be a toolmaker and then a die-maker and after that, if you're smart enough to keep it up, a tool designer. You've been through an eight-year college education. Now in my job . . ."

"I have before me a copy of the Communist *Daily Worker*, September 24, 1936. In it is listed the names of contributors to Spanish relief. B. Kallen, one dollar. Is that your name?"

On advice of his attorney Kallen declined to answer. Even though, regretfully, it was another Kallen.

"Now you're $999,999.00 short," Stoltz quipped.

"Mr. Barth, I must say that is a very engaging witness," Stoltz confided chummily in the corridor outside the hearing room during a recess.

"I should pay *him*," Joe Barth said.

Nevertheless:

"Were you a member of the Communist Party when you were naturalized as a citizen in 1938? It is a fact, is it not, that since 1920 you have been dedicated to the overthrow of the United States Government? Were you present in the company of Bob and Maria Ucchini, Inez Revels, Vince Donovan . . . ?"

"I hope you don't mind if I ask you to speak a little softer? I have a ringing in my ears. Perforated eardrums caused by . . ."

Kallen was shown a crowd photograph purported to have been taken at a meeting on Second Avenue in New York City, with a white head in the foreground circled in black ink. Would he identify the circled head, please, as that of Bob Ucchini?

"Did you say blob?"

KALLEN INVOKES 5TH 14 TIMES

It was a misprint. Boris had resorted to the Fifth Amendment only four times, no mean feat under his hours of grilling. His Constitutional privilege of remaining silent in areas that might lead to self-incrimination—or, to his mind, the incrimination of others—provided him however with no more than a legal fig leaf. He was as damned by his silence as he would have been if he had spoken.

On his return to Shoreham, Boris was fired from his job. He was summoned to a hearing by the state insurance commission investigating "links" between the Birobijan committee and a fraternal lodge of which he had once been vice-president and which was in the process of being disbanded as a Communist front. Then he was hauled up before the immigration authorities, charged with falsifying his application for citizenship in 1938. For two weeks his name was never out of the headlines.

Boris's children were not mentioned. But United Vacuum was. Over and over again.

In the plant the atmosphere was such that when workers asked one another, "Do you know this Boris Kallen?" the answer invariably was, "I hope not." An old-timer attempting to raise money to help Boris was sternly admonished by a fellow old-timer, equally under the protection of Boris's silence, "Forget him. He's dead."

"Are you a Jew, Mish?" Yusskevitch, dropping by his machine, inquired of him, seriously. "I mean your name, Lunin, and his name, Kallen, ain't it related?"

"Well, no," he confessed. "But you know Grover Coffin? He's my first cousin."

Thirty per cent of the union membership failed to cast a vote in the mid-June election. Those who would not vote for Colangelo abstained from voting for Lunin. Even so, he carried 33 per cent of the vote.

When he was approached again in 1954 to run again against Colangelo for the presidency, he resisted it.

"But conditions have changed," Ray Pelletier argued. "Everything's going to hell. I'll run with you. Marty will run with you. We'll draw up a sure-fire slate. You can't lose."

"I couldn't win steward in my own department. Colangelo has it sewed up so tight."

He should never have argued back. Once you argue back, you're already one foot in it.

"Sure he has it sewed up tight," Ray said. "All you have to do is cut the thread."

The Korean war was over. The Rosenbergs were dead. The atomic secret was a thing of the past. A recession loomed. The local had just been through a disastrous strike during the winter: lost, according to the membership, for lack of leadership from above; lost, according to Colangelo, for lack of support from below.

On his way home from Marty's one night he stopped at a service station for gasoline. He honked twice, thrice, by the pumps, hopped out of his car and went inside the dimly lit station to investigate. Between tires untidily stacked and shelves neatly packed with cans of oil loomed the twin peaks of a rusty felt hat. A big fat slob of a guy in dark khakis sat tipped back in his chair, immobilized before his twelve-inch television screen. The Army-

McCarthy hearings. Slowly the man tilted forward, brought himself massively to his feet, rose upward, goggling at the screen.

"Son of a bitch, he wants to be dictator!"

He drove home from the service station to Prince Street, transfixed, and woke Priscilla up out of bed.

"All right," he said to her, "I'll run."

He was defeated by Grover Coffin.

Grover Coffin's powers reached far beyond his management of the Shoreham works. He was widely recognized as the architect of United Vacuum's labor policy, a policy familiarly dubbed in industry "Coffinism." He had been rewarded with a vice-presidency in the corporation and as such, from his office in Shoreham, he drafted United Vacuum's new security program.

Coffin knew very well that UV-Shoreham had been an object of Communist concentration in the city since the late thirties. He was well aware of who the Communists in the plant were, their dwindling numbers, their losses due to defections and the attrition of the times. For years Coffin let them alone. He sat back while the union weeded them out of its ranks, reduced them to impotence. Then when there were less than ten dues-paying members in the entire plant, all of them in middle age, capable only of stirring up a little dust now and then, lighting a few sparks soon quashed, then unwillingly, as if forced to it, he moved.

It began, without objection from any quarter but the far left, with the prompt discharge of Boris Kallen after his first hearing. A company that spent millions of dollars yearly in the promotion of its good name, and the name of its goods, and that was engaged moreover in the production of goods for the national defense, was not obliged to retain an employee who exposed that name to public obloquy. As Congressional investigating committees continued to net UV witnesses across the country and as the Kallen deportation case, Shoreham's own little sideshow, dragged on through postponements and appeals and repeated announcements in the press that UV's Red Cell was about to be called to the stand, it became evident that sporadic firings, sometimes on shaky grounds that opened the company to possible suit, were not enough to meet the problem. Public relations, personnel and legal departments could not be left to flounder with it any longer by themselves in each locale. A clear-cut directive was needed, definitively stating the company's position.

In the late spring of 1954 the Kallen case was being retried in Federal court. Over Joe Barth's strenuous objection, an FBI informant employed at UV was introduced and, as he named members of the one-time party club, subpoenas were served at their homes and at work. The old names known to everyone. Vince Donovan, Steve Lukacs, Inez Revels, Tom Chadwick, Ron Jensen.

"But Bob? What about Bob? Isn't he? . . . They must be building up to Bob. Holding him for the last. And Mari . . ."

It was an old drama by now, a bit of a game.

Bob went to his job every day braced for the touch on his shoulder of a U.S. marshal. Mari, excluded from union membership, continued to handle negotiations for the girls on the floor and to speak out at meetings of the local. No one could shut Mari up. No one tried.

In the midst of the mildly titillating diversion of news headlines hinting every day at mysterious key figures yet to be summoned, sensational exposés yet to come, Grover Coffin issued United Vacuum's "Statement of Company Policy Toward Security Risks."

Henceforth employees who failed to cooperate with an authorized government agency would be suspended with pay for a three-month period, at the end of which period if they failed to clear themselves by cooperating they would be permanently discharged. The policy statement did not stop here however. Henceforth employees whose habits, tendencies to loose talk, nationality background and other attributes rendered them subject to external pressures were to be observed and reported upon to the company by their co-workers and supervisors. To this end, lest irresponsible charges take the place of knowledge, the company was to undertake an educational program for its employees. Classes were to be conducted on "How to Identify Communists,

Subversives and Traitors," "Twenty-one Grounds for Denial of Security Clearance," and "American History."

With the appearance of UV Policy 451-2B, witnesses who had been shuttling from the Kallen case to government investigating committees, taking refuge in the Fifth Amendment wherever and whenever, were suspended from their jobs.

Mish Lunin on the eve of the Local 317 election was badgered by radio and press interviewers seeking his opinion of the new policy.

"This policy circumvents our whole union contract," he declared. "It enables the company to fire anybody anytime for any reason."

Nick Colangelo, similarly besieged, pointed out, "Our union back in 1948 took its stand on this issue. Now the company is taking a stand."

To say that the UV workers were terrorized by "451-2B" would be at once an exaggeration and an understatement. There were those who went to work every day wondering, like Bob Ucchini, when the ax would fall. There were those who packed up their children and belongings and disappeared overnight to some part of the country where they were unknown. There were those who painted hammer and sickle on the apartment door of the latest witness, their erstwhile friend and neighbor, dumped red paint in his mailbox. There were those, the vast majority of them, who, having nothing to fear, feared nothing, they said.

He lost the election to Colangelo by 187 votes. Considering the circumstance, he might have interpreted the defeat as a victory. He didn't. The thin line between being in and out is it.

He was defeated by himself, by who and what he was, by the irreversible facts of his own life, by his own intrinsic nature. He was defeated by every move he ever made and every word he ever spoke, spontaneous, accidental and inevitable.

He belonged, he sometimes thought, to a damned generation, damned by its faith and its errors. Everything he had ever touched and would ever touch was tainted. He was a walking plague. Typhoid Mary.

The Kallen case was stalled for a few weeks while Joe Barth moved for a mistrial, with the contention that UV's policy statement constituted an attempt in effect to prejudice the verdict.

On a torrid July day he left his building with the herd stampeding out at the end of the shift. As he neared the gate he glimpsed Bob Ucchini's white head through the crowd just ahead of him, the buoyant lift of Bob's hand waving to the guard as he passed through. Outside the gate the Cedarbrook overpass of the new expressway being built stood like a ruined temple in a desolate landscape of dirt heaps, rocks, acres of demolition. The tumult of road machinery, incessant for weeks, had moved on elsewhere for the time being and in the white-hot afternoon the quiet dinned.

At the curb Bob paused, probably waiting for him as he sometimes did. Bob stood aside while the crowd trampled past and seemed to pivot on the curb toward the parking lot where he would meet Mari. Then with arms outflung like a suicide jumping off a bridge he pitched forward into the road.

The anthracite spark, the élan of the gypsy, pirate, outlaw chief, the imperious voice of The Blind Musician, the step of the rock-hewn grandmother, the face of a sagacious gnome.

In the greasy muck of the roadside a shrunken little gray worker in baggy chinos.

The women tried to stop Mariuch. They tried to draw her away.

"Come here, Mari," they called to her coaxingly. "Come into my car. I want to talk to you a minute." "Mari, come."

She flew through the restraining women and men in her path with a shriek that tore the hair off their heads.

He tried to hold her back. "Mari, the doctor will be . . ."

She tore out of his arms and threw herself down upon the wizened form in the gutter like a mother shielding her child from the rain of bombs.

"Bob! Oh my God, Bobby! Roberto!"

Roberto.

Roberto.

Roberto.

4

The world is mean . . .

The floor of the living room in the apartment at Tidal Flats was clear now. Robinson Crusoe was bedded down in his puzzle frames. The bits and pieces of the children's rampage were sorted away in their boxes and bags. A few leftovers, the red cam wheel, a green rubber frog, plastic odds and ends that didn't fit anywhere. Shove them out of sight, out of mind. Years later they swarm up at you out of limbo, disrupt all your so-tidy devices. It's the miscellany of items, those little inconsistencies you're unable to account for, that torpedo the system.

He fiddled with a model car, a touring car of the twenties, broken in two. Could it be fixed?

Everything in the room had its association and attachment, whole and indissoluble. Priscilla's guitar, steel-stringed, leaned in the corner, what did she play today, here we go loopty-loo? The drugget rug on the floor, our camel, the smell gone out of it now, the yellow and blue flowers merging with the grayed ground. The record spinning on the spindle, the hi-fi components Bob Ucchini had selected for him the week before he died . . .

He took the touring car into the kitchen and, with the enormous concentration of the slightly drunk, mixed the epoxy out of two tubes together—"one drop holds two tons"—and applied it to the break. Singly out of the tube the glue is ineffective; together it works. Clamped the car in a vise to set overnight.

Stepping over, around and through the fragments of the cup Priscilla had thrown at him, he brushed coffeecake crumbs off the table and deposited them in the sink, swept a cockroach off the sink side, scabby brown, and flushed it down the drain, sprinkled roach powder, poison green, around the sink edge on the wall. Butcher knife, shreds of ham clinging to the blade, hickory hilt nested firmly in his grasp, he stabbed through the gush of water from the faucet, wielded with swordsmanship and wiped off, mirror-bright, razor-edged.

The yellow cup painted with plumaged birds: on a camping trip years ago they had stopped at a pottery kiln in New Jersey and sorted through the rejects until they had collected triumphantly almost a full set of dishes, with Greg in arms and Steph at their heels crabbing away.

He switched off the phonograph, lifted the record from the spindle. Still putting off the moment when he would have to go into the bedroom, he blew a suspicion of dust off the record and slid it into the jacket on which Mack and Pirate Jenny, slickster and strumpet, tangoed. Skirting the rump-sprung couch, he went back to the kitchen. As an afterthought, against the unlikely possibility that one of the kids might come wandering in here in the dark, he swept up the shattered cup on the floor, even contemplated for one mad moment piecing it together with the epoxy, and poured it, rattling, from dustpan into wastebasket. Off to the dump.

He turned out the lights and at the door of his bedroom turned the knob. So beautiful a girl. Why did she have to challenge the parents she cherished? They defended the cause, they didn't live it. So she had to take it a step further, live it out for them?

The room was thick with smoke.

He rushed through the dark to the window, wrestled through the mesh curtains and snapped at the shade. The shade halted limply halfway. Leaning out over the sill he reached for the handle of the outswung casement. Fogs of smoke issuing out of archeological layers of rubbish smoldering in the sodden earth, borne on the salt chill of wind from the bay, embraced him. Mistily the neighboring buildings unfolded in staggered angles to the outer darkness, each of them split down the middle by hall lights and irregularly checkered with the lights of tenants still up; a galactic ship drifting through space, freighted with the demand, *Do something!* In the obscurity beyond, rising from ground level like the light of dawn, ruddiness glowed. *Put out the fires!* He pulled the casement haltingly inward on its rusty rod and latched it.

No, he said to all the windows of all the buildings, *no.*

Behind him Priscilla was coughing with the smoke in her sleep.

No, he said to her, *no.*

We were all so pure in those days, we were all so honest and trusting. We dug into our own pockets. We put out. We stepped blindly forth.

Coughing, she would rasp herself awake.

The second casement window, flanking the fixed center glass, was jammed. In the dark he took his toolbox out of the closet. He tapped with his pliers at the fixture in the sill, twisted with his wrench, pried with his screwdriver. The track needed sanding, the latch wouldn't catch, one snag led to another ramifying.

No, he said to his tools. *No,* he said to Marty and Mari, Ray Pelletier, Bostic, the rest of them. *No.*

Even after Colangelo won he'd kept going. Conducted training classes for stewards. Coordinated grievances in departments where he still had contact. Got out the local statistics on inflation and profits for the anti-wage freeze drive. Covered *Lights On!* when the editor was out sick. There's always the problem: who's going to do the work? So long as he was content to do it unofficially, Nick was content to let him. But after he almost took the election in '54, Nick froze him out.

He crouched at the window, twisting at the flat-headed screws weather-hardened into the fixture. Strain spread through his shoulders and loins. His eyes watered over and blurred with the smoke.

"I meant to smash you with that cup," Priscilla said from the bed, wide-awake. "I really did. I didn't mean to miss."

"Next time try a little arsenic."

"You're tearing the curtain."

"These lousy cheap curtains." He clawed at the wispy folds whipping about his head.

Stung beyond bearing she pounded on her pillow, her lumpy little pillow. In her self-abnegation, in her renunciation of the creature comforts she was born to, in her penance for the possibilities that were hers and were denied to others. Not saying it, not even yet saying it. What have I done to myself? What's it all been for!

"This is impossible. Impossible."

Who gets the children when? How do you divide the books and the records? Or do you go on with it, making a fresh start, she with a part-time job, a university extension course, or he back to school nights—always making fresh starts, in an extended postmortem?

"Look, Pris, this doesn't have to be— This just isn't the time! The times are against it! You're asking me to lead people—"

"Lead or follow, head or foot—you should know me well enough by now to know I don't give a damn which you are! So long as you're in there, fighting what's wrong. Win or lose, you fight it! Fight!"

"—into certain defeat. Defeat! Leaving them decimated and demoralized. Back of where they were before they ever began."

"And what are they if they don't fight? What are they? What are you?"

"I'm not risking my home, my job—or anyone else's— You've never taken account of the cost. The living cost. Never!"

"Shut up, shut up, I'll go insane. . . ."

He secured the latch temporarily with wire and undressed. Jangle of belt. Plop of shoes. Slipped between the sheets. All juiced up, the potent male paralyzed.

He switched on the bedside radio out of habit, waiting for the news on the hour. She pressed against her side of the bed, her breath sharp in her nostrils, in and out.

"Today . . . what transpired last month at the Twentieth Congress of the Communist Party of the Soviet Union. . . . Nikita Khrushchev . . . revelations . . . the Stalin terror . . ."

Here it comes.

Like a death knell. What he had always known, with a knowledge lodged in his gut. And never believed. True or false, false and true, so true so false. The dream of a workers' paradise.

". . . slave labor . . . death camps . . . millions . . ."

"Pris, are you listening to this?"

Sharply in and out. Not listening.

"Listen!"

She whipped the blanket off the bed and, wrapping it around herself, stalked off to the couch he wouldn't sleep on in the living room.

". . . the trials . . . the so-called doctors' plot. . . ."

Freedom from oppression! Emancipation of the masses! Down with the bosses! No more dumps!

"A ruthless dictatorship . . ."

The betrayal of Bostic. The disappearance of Frank Gavin. Bob toppling into the ditch.

A man and woman who had functioned so well together for all their flaws, destroying each other. What's right, what's wrong, what's real?

In the living room in the dark, Priscilla was quietly strumming. *I dreamed I saw Joe Hill last night, Alive as you and me* . . .

The independent who had done the best he could for the best as he saw it, the tool—the fool of forces outside his control, he turned over on his face and pulled his pillow down over his ears.

No he said no he said no he said no he said no.

FIVE

The March Syndrome

I

It wasn't until Tuesday afternoon after lunch that he completed the setup he had begun on Monday. Before trying the machine out with stock he operated it manually. Spindle revolving. Okay. Sliding and turret tools coming in, in the proper sequence. Okay. Collet opening and closing. Okay.

Now for the trial run. Still operating manually, he raised the end of the feed tube and lifted the stock, a twelve-foot brass bar, and rammed it in. Then lowered the feed tube until it was even with the spindle. Rammed the stock on into spindle and collet. The stock balked at the collet. Holding the stock with his pliers, he hammered it against the feed finger and forced it through. The stock projected beyond the collet. Okay. That done, he tried the cutting tool. Clean cut? No scratches? Okay. Forming tool . . .

Surgically prodding with his hand tools through the internal mesh of machine tools, he was dimly aware of a whinny, a whine, the siren of a distant ambulance. Surfacing, he saw Ewell down the aisle drunkenly swaying and stomping his feet in an agonized dance. A moan squawled out of Ewell.

Through the interstices of machinery, faces spluttered and splintered. Gusts of laughter spilled through the iron blare.

"Your machine is leaking oil," he alerted Roscoe.

"If it was my car," Roscoe replied, "I'd worry about it."

The investigation of yesterday's lunchtime follies had been proceeding all day. With the questioning of each employee by staff men from Personnel, the comedy instead of receding with the passing hours renewed itself. Now old Graveyard's back! Now he knows!

Watch out for snapping alligator. This tiger was raised by a lion. Monkey monkey in a zoo . . .

Laughter circulated, illicit, disruptive. Through the medium of Don Pinette the messenger, his tawny hair curly with sweat, his dusky raspberry mouth curved with mischief, the latest cracks were passed from one area to the next. As soon as the laughter subsided a little, someone would recall Dirksen pelting about yesterday ordering the signs down, a nuthouse, Commies! And Ledyard shooting in and out of his office with coveys of executives in a miasma of commands countermanded, who's responsible? who started it? And the girl clerk dashing from desk to file all morning, madly doing nothing, where's the guilty party? somebody has to pay!

Anarchy reigned. Irreverence romped. An employer's nightmare. Everybody busy, looking as if they were working, and nothing happening. Scrap!

The women, aghast at the magnitude of what they had wrought, bent over their tasks, unable to suppress the gurgles that welled up in them. Not only had they succeeded in giving United Vacuum a black eye, that was bad enough. They had embarrassed the government of the United States.

And the men laughed at the women. Whatever gaiety and warmth existed in this place, the women were the source of it. The ability of women to turn any cave into a bearable habitation. With their coffeepots and their plots. To reduce any scene to a village stream where, gossiping, they scrubbed their wash on the rocks.

Mabel simplified her sorting at the salvage table with a back flip of her hand. Into the waste carton. Jackson, laughing at Pinette's description of Mabel, let a roll of brass worth maybe two hundred dollars run through his stamper before he noticed the hole was off.

"Say, Lunin, listen to this!"

He had neither the mind nor the heart to listen and laugh. Glumly he tested out his first run-through.

"WILL MICHAEL LUNIN PLEASE REPORT TO THE SECTION OFFICE. WILL MICHAEL LUNIN . . ."

The clerk's voice over the public address system, generally used for plantwide announcements, cut through the noise of the machine shop, startlingly shrill.

". . . PLEASE REPORT AT ONCE."

"But I'm not through here," he argued back at the loudspeaker disk over the door. "Gimme time to finish, goddamit."

"Mish, it's for you, Mish." In concern Ewell and Roscoe and Palermo, popping around from his lathe, started toward him.

His heart banged up through the top of his head. Something had happened at home. Priscilla killing herself and the kids with the butcher knife. Moving off with them to Flo and Joe. A car in the street . . .

In the section office Dirksen and the clerk, grave with a message too important to be conveyed by lesser functionaries, passed him on to Ledyard. Ledyard, pale and puffy under his sleeked-down black hair, half rose from his desk.

"You're wanted in the front office, Lunin. Mr. Coffin wants to see you."

"Is this a put-on? I'm not finished with my run-through. Jackson's machine is down—"

All of a sudden there was plenty of help on hand. Tom, the assistant foreman, Willie from Maintenance, a couple of utility men to fill in wherever relief was required.

"What's he want?" Phlegm thickened his throat. His heart trip-hammered. "In relation to what?"

Outside Coffin's cursory "How's it going, Mike?" on rare occasion, without pause for an answer, they hadn't met in years. Shortly after the contract negotiation in the New York hotel suite, *may* or *must*, Coffin had been promoted from industrial relations director to works manager. And shortly after Lunin's deposition from union leadership, Coffin had been appointed to a vice-presidency in the corporation. The intimacy of interchange that had once been theirs, such as it was, was canceled out. The possibility of his being summoned by Coffin, up there in his top tower office, was so remote as to seem to him bizarre.

"He doesn't think I staged that show, does he?" he ventured a wild guess. It was too silly to warrant an answer. The one thing that the women had all admitted to was that the show was solely their doing; they were all in it together. "What is it then?" he demanded of Ledyard. "What's he up to now?"

With bureaucratic mystification, Ledyard—if he knew he wasn't telling, if he didn't know he wasn't letting on—handed him his pass, already filled out.

In his confusion he forgot to stop at the washroom for a wash-up. He met Don Pinette in the corridor pushing a pallet back from Supply. "It's all over Supply now," Don grinned at him. "And getting out to Warehouse. What a laugh. They're rolling in the aisles."

2

Downstairs on the first floor he was halted by a guard in the gray uniform of the industrial security system. He submitted his pass and flashed the photograph button on his breast pocket. Instead of waving him on into Fuse Block, the first of the departments to be traversed on his passage through the buildings, the guard reached for a wall telephone and checked him out. He had to sign in as he entered Fuse Block and wait for the time to be stamped opposite his signature, and sign out when he left, waiting again for the time to be stamped.

Through embankments of solenoid magnets and coils, under networks of heat exchangers and water conduits, past assemblies and iron-treaded staircases and on into the umbilical corridors that connected the buildings, he was halted and checked by the guards. He could not recall ever having seen so many guards before, even during the Korean war, inside at their posts and outside at intervals in guard towers. The guards were mainly equipped, having the local police at their beck and call, to handle pilferage, deal with drunks, spot firebugs and cranks, quell minor disturbances. The guards stood like bulkheads between the gray concrete compartments. It was a long time since he had taken such a journey.

"What is this, a concentration camp?"

The guard was not amused. They were here to prevent unauthorized persons from entering the premises without permission and to prevent authorized persons from leaving without permission. . . . Defense secrets, industrial secrets, microfilm secreted in the heel of his shoe, in the tip of his ballpoint pen? Oh no. Being who and what he was, he couldn't swallow that. The guards were part and parcel of the grand strategy known as "Coffinism." They were stationed here in order to create an atmosphere of intimidation. To hamper the mobility of workers and keep them from free congress with one another.

Old friends greeted him all along the way. "Say, Mish. Where you goin'?"

"To see Graveyard."

"You're kidding."

"No kidding."

"What for?"

"Search me."

He was fatigued from a poor night's sleep, shook-up over his collapsing marriage, crabby with the day's work, jumpy. Relaxing, he slowed down.

"What's your hurry?"

"No hurry."

"Say, Mish, wait a sec."

Ray Pelletier was up on the platform of his two-story-high cabler, pouring bags of diced plastic rubber into the hopper. He scrambled down the laddered steps through clouds of steam, his small-boned frame agile under his soggy overalls.

"You know that idea I been working on?" Ray's thin face was flushed with enthusiasm. "I got it. Hey, hold on—what you doing here? Where you going?"

Hastily Ray checked over the array of gauges and levers on his control panel. The temperature stood at three hundred and fifty degrees, his plastic rubber heating to liquefaction. Ray was churning with an idea he had been nursing along for improving the flow of compound through his tube nipple. And plagued with doubt, should he do anything about it.

Surveying an operation that filled half the room, from the water trough that provided the cooling process to the huge capstan that handled the cable, Ray was carried away with it.

"I just now licked it. That tube nipple is the Achilles' heel. On soft-core wire every time it loses uniformity, I have to stop— And on solid-core—"

Straightaway Ray launched into the workings of his cabler, a machine that was an enigma to the plant engineers and even to the engineers in the plant that built it. Every few months the plant engineers would bring around a party of visiting experts to hear Ray explain how he ran and repaired the cabler. Ray himself stood in awe of it. He was amazed at what it could produce. How do you make a piece of cable that thick, two hundred feet in length? How? A problem even to ship it.

"Ray, I haven't got time. Just one thing." He bethought himself and dug the crumpled leaflet out from under the hardware riding around in his pocket. It was here in this section that the Hot Rubber crew had pulled the stoppage last week when their number was reduced, leading to the suspension of their group leader, their steward and section chairman. Ray had been bending his ear about it over the telephone all weekend.

"You guys trace this down yet?" he asked Ray now. "Did your steward or section chairman have anything to do with it?"

When Ray talked labor, he was the cool, precise analyst, his chestnut eyes appraising. But when he talked his cabler he was all impatience, hot on it, chestnut eyes aglow. Caught between the two, he was swamped.

"They swear up and down it musta been you. Get a bunch of us together, Mish, we'll match up the circumstance and the persons that could have— Can you write this up for me today? Meet me by the gate—"

"Say what is this?" The foreman barged between them, catching them with the leaflet.

"I'll give you the dope and you or Priscilla can write it up—"

"Come on, come on." The foreman hustled him along.

"Not today," he shouted back, resisting. "I got to get home—"

"By the gate. It'll just take a minute—"

The conversation consummated constituting somehow a victory over the foreman, over the works.

He straightened up out of his crotchets. Advancing through departments, sections, divisions, he grew tall and taller.

"Hey, Mish," Marty Rakocszi called down from a casting inside which he was working. "Come on up here a sec."

He crawled up into the casting. "I just now ran into Ray," he said to Marty.

"Yah? Did he mention that leaflet last Friday?"

"Couldn't tell me a thing about it, it's the damnedest thing— You hear anything from those gas hounds around the Blue Bird?"

Marty scrutinized him quizzically, past his beeping apparatus. "I hear they been giving you the business in the locker room. Is it true you're running again?"

"You listen to those cats on Capitol Hill—"

"Aw come off it, Mish. Knock it off. I know you better than you know yourself. Guys like you, you never give up. Till the day you die. It's so much part of you— You can't help yourself."

They crouched up in the casting like trolls in their hole. Below them, gray-garbed guards were dashing about. Walkie-talkies exchanged shouts, robot voices, unintelligible. Lights were flashing. Bells were ringing. A peal of alarm.

"Hey, you, what the hell you doing up there?"

He was grabbed and hauled down, protesting.

"For Christ sake, I don't know what goes on in that casting. If you talked for a year, I wouldn't understand it. The worker, he don't know except for the one particular thing he's on . . ."

The kid who couldn't travel from his home room to the principal's office without becoming embroiled en route.

As he was signing out with the guard, one of Marty's buddies left his job and delivered a message to him.

"You want to walk through this department, Lunin, and talk with somebody in it, you go right back and start all over again. If any one tries to stop you . . ."

He grew.

From fuses to plugs. From cable as thick as his arm to wire as fine as a hair. From tool and die to industrial diamond. "Say, Mish, you remember Saul Pelotti? Got a good job out of this with a firm dealing in diamond dust." From electric furnace to vacuum tube. From radio to refrigerator. From small motor to steam iron.

A landscape trembling with the sonic boom of punch presses.

"Say, Mish . . ."

The afternoon sun slanted dustily through the windows. Rows of figures poured themselves into their meat grinders. In all their pride and contempt doing the work of the world, holding the whole world up on their backs.

"You're going to see *Graveyard?* Himself? Well, you tell him something for me."

"Okay."

"He can suck my left tit."

He entered the first of the office buildings, the precincts of management. The corridor changed color, tired tan. The floor changed texture, worn tile. The UV trademark, linked letters transfixed by a bolt of lightning, was present everywhere on door and floor, in blurred black and white. Through the open doors regiments of typewriters and calculators filed back, nicely groomed girls tapping away, crisp young men scanning over. Personnel (a surplus of applicants lounging in the doorway), Insurance and Employee Benefits, Payroll. Dispensary One

Flight Up. Training Classes, Third Floor. A supply cart rolled out of the freight elevator, stacked high with the weekly *UV Highlights!* fresh from the printer. He lifted one off the top. "UV Brainiac Aids Scholarly Research . . ."

He was smaller by a head.

He was alone, unaccompanied by the negotiating committee with which he used to parade through Industrial Relations. He hadn't washed the machine oil out of his ears. His grease rag was still hanging out of his back pocket. For the first time he harbored a sneaking sympathy for John Bennett, president of the EWIU, who had to live in a fifty-thousand-dollar house on Long Island, wear hundred-and-fifty-dollar suits from Hickey-Freeman, drive around in a new Pontiac every year in order even halfway to equalize himself with the company chiefs.

Corridor clean cream. Floor polished brown. He took a couple of wrong turns in search of the outlet to Building 1, the executive tower, and was lost in a maze of windowed doors, firmly closed. Quality Control, Materials Control, Production Control, Traffic Control. Plant Layout. Product Research, Product Improvement and Engineering, Product Design. Purchasing . . . He tried the door of the men's room, a chance to wash up. Locked.

A door swung open. A man coming out looked at him inquiringly. Inside the door, earnest able men pored over papers in paneled cubicles, doing a job within the closed circuit of their jobs, masters of technique, the slide-rule, the draftsman's sketch.

"You're in the wrong slot, Mac," the man said to him before he could ask. "The shops are back thataway."

He was a unit of the machinery allocated on paper to its proper grouping. Less than the machinery because he was cheaper and more easily replaceable. A hand.

Zero.

Corridor white. Floor slate-blue. Outside the windows the pillars of the expressway swerved north over the disheveled storefronts of Cedarbrook Avenue. Out from behind the scenes into the carpeted, glass-fronted lobby. Into the daylight.

He skirted along the curve of the diorama that partially circumscribed the lobby (UV in Home—Industry—Defense) toward the receptionist's desk in front of the elevators. Sales and public relations men were milling around after lunch, making their farewells. Regional directors apparently, called in for a briefing on the new model something-or-other being developed here. They stepped away from him as he passed them, shrinking from contact. Waiting for the receptionist to call the top-floor office, out of the corner of his eye he caught a portly middle-aged gentleman examining the plantings that bordered the curved sweep of window, a replica of the plantings on the outside, so exactly grown and trimmed that indoor and outdoor merged. The gentleman stooping rubbed a leaf, was it real?—and feeling himself watched, surprised in the act, stiffened and with soldierly bearing joined the nearest group.

Monkey monkey in a zoo, who's the monkey . . .

He pressed the elevator button, his nails grime-rimmed. A micrometer nested weightily in the tail of his pocket, resting against his groin.

Over the elevator the UV insignia was emblazoned in gilt. Inside the elevator it was inscribed in white on the carpet, etched on the ceiling light. Pressed to the rear by the crowd who had entered with him, he began his ascent. Doors slid open and closed, admitting and discharging. Field offices out of New York: Marketing, Promotion & Advertising, Community Relations, Accounting, Systems Analysis.

"When you go to work for United Vacuum it's constantly hammered into you," Grover Coffin had said that long-ago night of the March syndrome, in the little spaghetti joint in the Bottoms owned by Bob Ucchini's cousin, " 'This is the world.' The external world becomes more and more remote to you," Coffin said, lapping up his soup with chunks of garlic bread, "even threatening. Even the best minds, the most creative, the most determined to remain independent, sooner or later they all give in. You ask no basic questions. You seek no ultimate meanings. You eat, drink, sleep, socialize with, live UV."

They had sat at their corner table, Ted and Priscilla and himself, soaking up Coffin. They understood of course that he was going through the wringer of a managerial reshuffling. At the same time they thought he must be pretty democratic, eating here, and liberal too, letting them in on his company view. Not unlike those engineers who had slipped them funds and information during the recent strike.

"On the rubber mat before the executive dining room," Coffin said, "on the silver, the glasses, the dishes, the damask, UV." His spoon described it over the checkered tomato-stained tablecloth. "On the drapery swags over the windows, UV. On the towels in the lavatory, on the toilet-paper fixtures . . .

"After your first interview you go through your battery of tests. Your performance studies. Your psychological. Finally the physical. You enter the last door at the end of the last corridor and you drop your pants and they stamp you on the backside. UV."

Thus the great pasta-fagiol' man.

On the fourth floor an easy-breezy Ivy Leaguer shouldered into the elevator. Offered a startled smile, half appealing, half appeasing, and slouched back in a corner. One of the new breed, no rigidities. Closeted, they rose together.

Up the remaining flights so fast it was like Cusak going down the mine shaft for the first time, legs sheared off under him. You can make it, yessiree, up to the UV presidency.

3

In the foyer of the executive suite, he presented himself at a convent window behind which a girl, nunlike, her white collar flaring out over the shoulders of her black dress, murmured into a telephone. No clatter of machinery here. No bustle of sales engineers. No pressure. Typing muted. Courtesy the order of the day. Even stepping out of the elevator with the Ivy Leaguer, after you, my dear Gaston, my dear Alphonse. Then, after stepping out after him, the Ivy Leaguer breezed off, bemused with his clipboard, down the hall.

The girl's black hair swept back without a part over her forehead, which crinkled slightly as she spoke, and fell smoothly with barely a ripple to the starched white collar of her dress. He took the chair she indicated and sat lightly at first, minimizing contact between his oily clothing and the vinyl back and seat. Gradually he sank back.

The slate-blue walls glimmered with framed glossies, mementos of Coffin's ascent to the summit. UV employees receiving their fifteen-year service pin, a Coffin notion. UV's interplant bowling championship match, a Coffin promotion. UV's three annual scholarship awards to deserving sons of UV employees, a Coffin inspiration. UV's television star, Wally Rayne, bathed in holy light, singing on Thanksgiving eve, *Praise God, from whom all blessings flow* . . .

No doubt now of who sat in the driver's seat. The company was the light and the life. The company was the source of bread and bounty. The company was the great earth mother, as kindly as nature itself and as ruthless.

He unfolded the UV weekly he had lifted off the supply cart in Industrial Relations. UV cryogenics team assists medical research with miracle device. Fascinating.

He took a magazine from the table beside him, *Corporation Management Monthly*. Profile of the man behind the scenes who more than any other in the past ten years has helped shape the course of . . . belief in the free enterprise system . . . equity among all segments . . . ability to place the right person in the right place and build through cooperation. . . . Yes, indeed.

He swiped United Vacuum's *Annual Report to the Stockholders* off the top of the stack on the table and before rolling it up to stuff into his pocket glanced through it. New defense contracts. The all-electric home. Nineteen fifty-five a peak year, profits and dividends up. Increased wage and fringe benefit costs offset by cost-reduction program. Federal Trade Commission investigating price practices, told profit levels essential to finance expansion and attract continued investment flow.

"Miss, do you have a match?"

"I don't think so. Mr. Coffin doesn't approve of smoking during working hours."

He rested on his butt at two-forty an hour in the cool clean quiet of Coffin's paradise. He sat in his waiting chair, chained to it by every contractual gain he had ever extracted from Coffin: his seniority, including his war years; his yearly wage increment; the ratio of his payments, shared with the employer, for his health-and-accident and life-insurance policies, his family-hospitalization plan, his pension fund; his month vacation due him now at last this summer. The old saw, you have nothing to lose but your chains? It was a new song now, you have nothing to lose but your job! He was chained by his gains. He was chained as fast to this plant by links he himself had forged as his great grandfather the serf had been chained in his vassalage to the manorial estate.

Coffinized.

The Ivy Leaguer fled by with his clipboard and standing by the elevator spared him a placating smile.

"Michael Lunin?"

From the hall a secretary tripped forth, tall and willowy in pale wool. She approached him with an angelic dimple. Her gray eyes were luminous with humor and understanding.

"So sorry to keep you. This way, please."

Her dimple floated back over her shoulder like a trailing scarf.

He uprooted himself from his chair and in a dazzle of glossies, glossy pictures, glossy pages, plunged after her. In a daze of blurred images. Coffin with the mumble of dry wit escaping from under what would have been his mustache if he'd had a mustache, "Mrs. Ucchini, please!" . . . Coffin never avoiding, always urging objection out of him, "Lunin, you usually have something to say . . ." The long hot afternoon of stalling off Coffin's nickel offer when all the time Coffin was stalling him . . .

Down the narrow path of the hall soundlessly screaming as in a nightmare. Help! Save me!

At the final flush door she half-turned, a slenderness of curves tautly poised, in high-heeled pumps, on her toes. She held open the door for him to pass through.

Bladder twitching. Bowels pressing. Limbs dissolving.

Over indigo turf, spongy underfoot, past sofas cantilevered on steel legs and tufted leather chairs, toward the bulky oak desk that had been through the wars, to the extended hand.

"Well, Lunin."

"Long time no see."

4

Immediately, as if no time at all had elapsed since their last confrontation, they assumed the same posture toward each other as they had when they left off.

Blinded by the expanse of glass behind Coffin's desk, the smoky vistas of the city blazing with the hyperclarity of technicolor, he almost walked into Coffin's hand, his own hand raised, before he noticed that Coffin, on the telephone, was merely motioning him to draw up a chair. Disconcerted, he pulled up the nearest chair and, surreptitiously wiping his hands on his pants, dropped down into it. The leather chair was too low, tilted at an angle that brought his knees up higher than his hips. Rearing himself erect, he placed his elbow on Coffin's desk and propped his jaw in his hand. Coffin swiveled away from him and continued into his telephone without lowering his voice in the least.

The snow had crept up Coffin's temples until it wreathed his cap of slate-colored hair; but his skin was still ruddy, with a ruddiness in his cheeks as rich as stage make-up. The snowier his hair, the younger he looked. Alert, vigorous, trim, on it every second. Swinging about from stark-white wall to smoke-smudged sky and back again, he toyed with a glass swan from his desk, small enough to fit into his hand and heavy enough, if hurled, to kill someone. Coffin was either prying for information over the telephone or confirming it.

". . . the worst possible time. One of these March reorganizations. Every man I call has been plastered to his phone since Wednesday, what's going to happen to him? I suppose some of them when they find out will be jumping out of the windows."

The glass swan rolled in his hand, head jutting out, bluely crystal-curved.

"Richards—you don't mean Richards . . . Are you sure? When someone's been at the top so long, no one can topple him . . ."

The swan came to rest on an open folder. Flow-chart diagrams. Over his desk Coffin craned toward a blackboard standing across the room on casters. Four panels were chalked up on it, filled in with yellow and blue shadings at various levels.

"But just one minor slip-up. He must have had some sign, there must have been rumblings from below . . . I suppose it became impossible for him to admit the initial misjudgment. Once the unshatterable image is cracked . . ."

For a moment after he hung up Coffin contemplated the blackboard across the room, blank-faced.

"If you'll excuse me, Lunin, for another minute?"

With an escaping mumble, "Hanged on an ironing cord," Coffin jabbed at his intercom. Rapidly, firmly, objectively he moved in on the crisis, whatever it was, to terminate it. "Rosemary, get Anderson in Chicago right away, tell him the S–140 is through, unload. Have Mason, Glenn and Hirsch here for a meeting at four, they better clear their desks for the night. No more calls now."

In spite of his injunction Coffin accepted two calls Rosemary had pending.

On one line:

"Richards resigning? Don't you believe it. He'll be board chairman yet . . . Executive infighting—where you guys pick up this garbage . . . Listen, Ken, there are two things that count above everything else in this company. Group loyalty. And performance. The fastest way for a man to disappear around here is to start a personal contest. One or both contestants will disappear. Every individual on my staff knows he has the security of the rung up. Not by vying for the upper hand, that only undermines the group. Loyalty. And performance. We're in the business of producing goods to meet the market, in as great quantity as we can, of as high quality as we can, at the lowest cost we can. And that takes all of us solving the problems together. That's where the drama is. There's your story.

"Of course, between you and me, Ken, when a two-billion-dollar-a-year enterprise jumps to four billion, there's bound to be some reshuffling. You'll be the first to know . . . Oh, the tour yesterday? About as usual . . ."

And on the other line:

"Richards! How's it going? We're up to our necks. Revising the procedural manual. You know how it is. With it, everybody follows a pattern. If it's not in the manual, don't do it. No leeway for originality. And without it, complications ensue—communications failure—duplications—the void. Panic. Write it up! Lee was just going over the final draft when he was picked to head up St. Louis. Leaving me high and dry . . . S–140. Now, Rick, with all the promotion behind it . . . Who's putting the skids . . . ?"

Coffin could anticipate, but he was not going to be the one to deliver the bad news. His swan was taking a beating.

"Listen, Rick. Listen to me, this is important. Sometime before midnight tomorrow night I'm hoping to get home. You know what I'll do when I get there? I have a little Hammond organ. If it's a nice night I'll open my window and my neighbor across the lawn—he's a surgeon, under strain all the time—will open his window. He'll play his organ and I'll play mine. Neither one of us trained. Improvising. All by ear. Started with the accordion . . . All right, your boat. In a couple of weeks . . ."

Coffin disconnected his telephones. Everything has to happen today. Today of all days. That's every day. He shut off his intercom. For the next quarter hour he was out of the building. He couldn't be reached.

"Now, Lunin."

Carefully Coffin polished over his swan with his handkerchief. Expert at deflecting opposition with delay, dispersing it with irrelevancies. He held the swan up, balanced on his fingertips, solidly transparent, shimmering with glimmers of light from the scattered vistas of the city.

His arm on Coffin's desk hardened, muscles bunching, braced for the Indian wrestle. Only the thin line of leather inlay in the desk top lay between.

(They're no smarter than we are. Just about the same proportion of brains and stupidity.)

"Something came up here in my office today, Lunin, that I think will interest you."

Coffin restored the swan to its marble pedestal on his desk and wryly glanced him over. The grease-streaked arm with its branching veins, bared to the elbow under the rolled-up sleeve, did not remove itself. "Ordinarily I'd leave this to my Industrial Relations director, it's his territory."

(If this has anything to do with the bargaining unit, I'm mum! I want Fritz here. I want the chief steward.)

"But as you may recall, I came up through Personnel and Industrial Relations. I've never lost my concern with that facet of the business. That experience has proved invaluable in keeping me attuned to the organizational pulse."

(Not a word to him. Not one word.)

Coffin flipped through the folders on his desk, annoyed at finding them out of sequence. At the peak of the structure— responsibilities delegated downward to hosts of subordinates; decisions cleared upward through a series of superiors; schedule programmed according to priorities—Coffin wrestled with the setup of a day disrupted by unaccountable breakdowns.

"My finger's always on the organizational pulse. There are far too many people in management who haven't the slightest idea of what goes on back there in the shops. I do. In fact, I feel that the relative harmony we've achieved at UV owes no small part to the insights I gained from direct contact with you, Lunin, and others like you. It was my credo from the start that cooperation is preferable to conflict and you helped familiarize me realistically with the obstacles I had to cope with. I think I can take pride now in the job I did so long ago in bringing company and union together."

Once upon a time, eons ago, UV and EWIU were locked in mortal combat. Then Grover Coffin appeared on the scene. To UV he said: "Fools that you are, stop fighting your own workers! Work with them." To EWIU he said: "I can do more for you in my position by boring from within than you can by battering from without."

In place of hostilities, turmoil, chaos in the land, costly to both sides, under the benign influence of Coffin the two sides, between them, regulated and codified the relationship of employer and employee, established guidelines for dealing with every occupational contingency, hammered out a *modus operandi* for resolving conflicts cooperatively. Of course they still engaged in an occasional skirmish. Over the usual paradoxes. Raise pay, and absenteeism on Mondays becomes a major headache. Reduce hours, and everybody's out moonlighting to the detriment of his major job. But such differences were of no great significance. The main thing was, UV and EWIU had learned to live with each other. They recognized their mutual dependency, the stake they shared in the well-being of the company.

"I suppose that nowadays you must feel a little out of it," Coffin said, an eye cocked at him, sun-bright, seeing through to his backbone, not missing a thing, not one damn thing.

"In some ways you're a relic of the thirties, Lunin, the period of explosive social change. When you came back from World War II it was already over. That '46 strike was the last gasp. We absorbed the changes. We went into a period of consolidation. And you never quite adjusted to it. You'd won what you were after and you didn't know what to do with it. You had to keep on fighting. You had to go on being the supermilitant. While the labor movement, like every other cause once the battle for acceptance is past, settled into its place in the sun.

"The action central to the times, the adventure, the excitement have moved elsewhere. The focus today is on a different arena. Growth. The phenomenal growth of American industry. That's the dynamic of the fifties, Lunin. With all the challenge and satisfaction and reward it offers for personal growth.

"Not to move with the times is to die on the vine. To move is to give full rein to your abilities, to possibilities you may never have suspected you had in yourself. United Vacuum is moving in a direction, in the future, that I'm sure will especially appeal to a man of your background. That is, if you're seriously interested in improving the common lot, not just making a noise. Change doesn't have to come about with a bloody bang."

He eased back in his ass-back chair. The upholstery was comfortable, the view through the window wall was pleasant, he was on company time. The conversation had nothing to do with the bargaining unit. It was strictly between the two of them. He was being propositioned.

"According to our records you were offered a promotion to supervisor some weeks ago. The most critical problem we have in Personnel, finding competent supervisors. Men able to give leadership. You turned it down. Why?"

"Can't you guess?"

"All right. You thought you'd have to tear yourself apart? I wouldn't want anyone to tear himself apart. To serve a constituency, it takes everything you've got."

Rosemary, murmuring apologies, had supplied Coffin with what he was looking for, a red leather portfolio, and cleared the desk. Coffin reordered the contents of the portfolio while he spoke; several stapled reports interspersed with graphic figures, like those on the blackboard across the room, encased in glassine. Then leaning back he folded his hands behind his head, much looser than he used to be in negotiations, unbuttoned.

Free. The fifteen minutes expanded as he expatiated on a new facet of the business, a new dimension, that for him wedded certain inner tendencies—his sympathies and his pragmatism.

"We like to look ahead. We try to anticipate trends. More and more in the future the corporations will have to assume a larger share of social responsibility. We're increasing our staff in Community Relations to explore lines of action on the outside. Perhaps more participation in philanthropies. Perhaps a foundation that will fill a certain public need. And there's my own pet project. What we can do on the inside to benefit our work force, to make their daily work more challenging and rewarding, open-ended. A chance for growth."

For his purposes Coffin had brought in a consulting firm. Shoreham was to be the pilot plant.

"A consultant always brings in a fresh breeze, the context of a broader view. And our staff, mired in the detail of where we're at, always reacts in the same way. Show me! We've had quite a hassle here over these proposals. To me they're very intriguing. Take a look."

Coffin slid the portfolio toward him. Explaining to him, Coffin riffled through pages of progress reports, black type blacker than black on white paper whiter than white, tables and charts with shaded legends in the corner, graphics glistening through glassine.

"You once said something to me, Lunin, I never forgot. It's stayed with me. It stuck in my mind. And my craw, I might add. 'There's so much more to the man on the job,' you said, 'than just a set of motions.'" Coffin tapped the portfolio. "Well, here it is. An attempt to learn something of his reaction to the mechanics of his environment. His interaction with others. Who he is. His total life structure."

The portfolio was tentatively titled *Studies in Human Performance*. It staked out the groundwork for a four-year research project to be undertaken in conjunction with one of the universities, probably Pennsylvania or Columbia or the School of

Management at MIT, and in collaboration with the U. S. Department of Labor where, fortunately, some spadework was being done in the field.

"First phase,"—Coffin tapped through pages stapled in pink paper flap—"psychological. An analysis of the factors that contribute to the work performance of the employee. His emotional make-up, his family pattern going back to early childhood, his formative habits relating to presence or absence of parental authority. His adaptability to one skill or another as determined by his personal endowment, his previous training and his predilections. And the means by which his performance, and his perspective for himself, can be raised either in the specific skill in which he is now employed or by retraining in a skill more suitable to him.

"Second phase,"—in blue flap—"methodology. We'd move as quickly as possible from concepts into techniques. Selection of tests for pinpointing personality and skill affinities. Development of educational procedures that will be most effective with our range of age and intelligence.

"Third phase,"—buttercup yellow—"application. Matching the man to the job. Enabling him to advance in it. Renaming jobs, if necessary, from apprenticeship to subprofessional level, to encourage the achievement of maximum potential through maximum upward mobility.

"In other words, an end to dead-end jobs. An end to square pegs in round holes. Release of hidden talents. Self-fulfillment. Growth.

"You can play a key part in this, Lunin."

He fumbled in his pocket for a cigarette and fished up his pack, crushed under the weight of his micrometer. He knocked out a limp cigarette and stuck it in his mouth. No matches. Nowhere.

Coffin, glowing with the zest of ideas that sounded better and better as he sounded them out, leaned toward him with his lighter, not the least abashed in his eagerness, a father humoring a favorite child, the recalcitrant come home.

"Let me outline it for you. We'll start out with a small team. A psychologist, a sociologist who's worked in group mental health, an occupational specialist, someone in charge of data, a finance officer. Plus, on my insistence, a control—the man they always leave out. The one that it's all about. Who sees the problem from the inside looking out. Who can act as a backboard to all the theories and statistics the others throw at him. Who will bring to bear his plant experience, his criticism, his objections. With absolute honesty. No holds barred. Anything less than honesty would impair the validity of our results.

"You have some hesitation? Your attachments. There's nothing in this that can possibly compromise your loyalty to your attachments. It affirms your loyalty to them. We want you to stand up for your own. We want you to give us a hard time. Without that we're dead.

"You'll be making a permanent contribution to the science of manpower utilization, on which any type of organization can draw. Our findings can be of value to any industrial society. In the process of it, you yourself, Lunin, become a prototype of what we hope to accomplish.

"How does it sound to you?"

It sounded good. It sounded wonderful. Idyllic.

It sounded as if he was being bullshitted and brought to heel by a past master.

"I don't mind admitting to you there's opposition to this. From below, Personnel resists it. It means an eventual upheaval in routines for them, staff changes. And from above—not a single vice-president on the board with me hasn't expressed reservations. Those out of engineering are willing enough to devote resources to technological research. The fiscal advisers will go for experimentation in systems. The sales promoter will drum up the dough to restyle an ironing cord. But investment in people? Oh no. Where's the payoff!"

It sounded selfless. Visionary.

It sounded as if Coffin, consolidated on this pinnacle, was shooting for some further height. The operational vice-president on his way to a directorship, out of Shoreham into the conclaves of intercorporate royalty.

"I've had to fight for this. I've gone way out on a limb— Persuading them that either we continue to make progress in our employee relations or we revert to a period of unrest. Arguing that automation being upon us, the more we automate the more we need to know of what makes the human being tick if we're to prepare our employees adequately for the transition. Convincing them that whatever we do for the good of the employee we do for the good of the company and the nation as a whole. The feedback is the payoff!"

It sounded unimpeachably genuine. There was no doubting Coffin's sincerity. He was in dead earnest.

It sounded like a gimmick. One of those hot-shot panaceas that loom up sometimes, very big for a while, serving the proponent of it well, and then it fades, leaving his pawns entangled in it.

"Just a few hours ago I received word that I'd won the day. Human Performance is being budgeted under Long-Term Planning. But now that I have it, do I really want to risk it?"

Practical. Candid. In motion.

"It's tooling up for the sixties, Lunin. Maybe even the seventies. You don't have to give me your answer now. But since I've gone to the length of giving you a total picture, I'd like you to give me your impression of it. Your honest impression."

"My honest impression?"

"Completely honest. If you'll just keep in mind one point. In your present job—setup, isn't it?—you have certain prescribed actions to perform, dictated by the nature of the machine. You also have certain discretionary actions, dictated by your own choice and decision—your way of tackling a task that makes you better or worse at it than the next fellow, your own distinctive style. In management we are faced with a similar dichotomy. Targets of necessity. And targets of opportunity. What we are discussing now falls in the realm of choice, decision, the target of opportunity."

He envied Coffin. He envied him his flow, his sparkle, the scope of his command. Envying him so much that he wouldn't for anything, not even for Coffin's place behind his desk, not even for the fulfillment of every demand UV workers had ever dreamed of, give up the privilege of rejecting him?

"Now, Lunin, you always have something to say. Say it. Spit it out."

He didn't know where or how to begin.

5

He was vividly aware, during Coffin's discourse, of comings and goings around him. Rosemary tiptoed in, in her high-heeled pumps, and with a sweet pea of a whisper, "Nice write-up," placed an out-of-town newspaper on Coffin's desk. (According to Mari, Coffin's first act in office was his order for fifteen *Daily Workers* to be delivered every morning to his top executives.) Coffin barely glanced at the crayoned column. "Did Larry get the film?" he snapped after the retreating Rosemary. "It's in his desk drawer." "In my drawer, please. Not anyone else's." Minutes later Rosemary drifted in with the film. Coffin unrolled it, examined the exposed strip against the outdoor light. "You're sure this is it?"—and catching Rosemary's budding smile through the back of his head—"I'd laugh too if it had happened to someone else." Behind Rosemary someone slipped into the office unannounced and seated himself beside the blackboard. (Coffin's latest act in office, Mari claimed, was his selection of an ex-CIA agent to head up Plant Security.) The gentleman amiably disposed by the blackboard might have been Coffin's organ-playing neighbor or the professor who was to direct the Human Performance project or President Eisenhower. From his chair beside Coffin's desk he scowled around at the visitor, absolutely sure for certain that he was UV-Shoreham's new security chief.

And, sucking at his broken-backed cigarette, he leafed

through the pink-, the blue- and the yellow-flapped reports while Coffin attended to other business. *Conceptual-verbal,* the so-intriguing correlations of personality and skill components . . .

He was looking for the catch. Where's the catch?

There was the swan on Coffin's desk, removed and handled and wiped clean and restored to its pedestal, brilliantly polished.

There was the micrometer in his pocket resting against his inner thigh, calipered and calibrated to turn at his twist of the screw to the ten-thousandth of an inch.

There was the actuality back there in the shop, the irrepressible turbulence of it. And there was the fantasy of his being up here with Coffin amid white, chrome and indigo, encased in glass. The panorama of city roofs extended below like a sea of shingle to an orange smudge on the blue horizon, the dump burning, an image on the screen, vitrified.

He saw everything with double, triple, quadruple vision. So many angles to it, so many aspects.

Aspects upon aspects.

He was to be the backstop, the devil's advocate, the workers' spokesman on a high-powered team, what's wrong with that? He was to be the experimental prototype into which every effort is poured, no expense spared.

A glorified guinea pig. A sounding board. They talk it up, he thought, they fill you full of promises, they promise you the world and then . . . He'd end up at a dead-end desk with his nose in a pencil sharpener. He'd wind up like the poor stooge stoolpigeon at the Kallen hearings. In the boiler room.

At one moment he was sure that he was the object of Coffin's long-term reflection, the flaw in the system that Coffin had never quite overcome, the tube nipple that was forever gumming up the compound. And now Coffin, to the satisfaction of his emotional make-up, had figured out the role in which Lunin could smoothly function.

At the next moment he was just as certain that Coffin had no intention of placing him in any such role at all. Caught in an organizational squeeze with his way-out project, having to make a fast decision on it, stop or go, Coffin had on inspiration called in Lunin for an opinion. Lunin was being brain-picked for whatever it was worth in passing.

He believed every word that Coffin had said to him and he didn't believe a word of it.

UV assuming social responsibility?

All on my back!

No more square pegs in round holes? Ability tests? Transfers? Of all the labor-busting dodges! A mandate for overriding union agreements on upgrading, merit ratings . . . for shifting jobs on any pretext . . . screening out the unwanted, firing at will . . .

Total life structure?

Prying into and appropriating that part of the worker's life that belongs to himself and himself alone!

No compromise, Lunin, between your loyalties and your potential?

Pasta i fagiola!

And the Human Performance Studies through which he was thumbing on Coffin's desk. Superbly outlined and defined, the work of a genius surely.

He saw it as a front. Some R&D outfit, out for UV dough, had sold Coffin on it and now Coffin had to steer it through. An excuse for a tax write-off. Or Coffin had sold the R&D on it for the purpose of obtaining a government grant to UV, cost-plus, Uncle Sam footing the bill. The company would make money on it for godsake!

Simultaneously he saw it as a hoax. Coffin, sensing unrest, fearful of having the boat rocked under him at this particular juncture, had seized on it as a convenient cover for the purposes of this interview. Under the guise of inquiry, he was seeking information: "Say, Mike, what's going on down there?"

They were right back at the same old stand in the same old stance. Facing each other over Coffin's Job-Evaluation Manual. After all these years Coffin was still trying to get him to swallow the company book.

He was being swallowed up by UV. In the draperies hanging in fluted columns at the corners of the window wall, he discerned the repeated indigo figure camouflaged by the folds—UV shot through with a lightning bolt. In the indigo carpeting on the floor he spotted, or imagined he did, a pattern, UV infinitesimally interwoven. Rosemary wheeled a cart in with electric coffeepot and shaker—"Would any of you like a Bloody Mary?" —and sure enough . . . At the bottom of his cup, UV. Coffin's tie clasp, his foulard necktie, his herringbone sleeve, if you looked at it a certain way . . .

Coffin was on the telephone again with Richards, burying the ironing cord.

"You stupid bastard"—all cordiality—"let it lay! You were never the type to tear up cereal boxes. . . . I have to be able to foresee events before they occur. If I stick my head in the sand for a single minute"—all patience—"somebody'll walk right up over my back. . . . Oh, you heard. You know that word they keep flinging around nowadays, *alienation?* I call it counter-alienation. Counterinsurgency? That's a hell of a note—don't tell me you're tying up with a think tank. . . ."

The silent man by the blackboard, CIA or CID or whatever, a watchdog, hummed to himself. *Way down upon the Swanee river, far far away* . . .

"And to top it all off," Coffin, hanging up, addressed the watchdog, "he's breaking up with his wife. After twenty years of marriage she comes pissing in his ear, 'I don't like or love you any more.'"

Everything at sixes and sevens today. Even the weather. In the third week of March, on the first day of spring, Rosemary had to turn the air-conditioning on in the office.

"Now, Lunin, back to you. Let's debug for once before we start. What have you got against it?"

He hitched himself up out of his slope-bottomed chair, the steel frame so comfortably padded in tufted leather. He crossed the room to the blackboard. "Pardon me," borrowed a stenographer's stool from against the wall and toted it back to the desk. Scrunching his butt into position, he took one last lingering look through the red portfolio. His last chance to make a lasting contribution to the species, all other chances being, it would seem, foreclosed to him.

"There's nothing wrong with it. I got nothing against it. It's a beautiful project. An emancipation proclamation."

He began drawing junk out of his pockets. Piece by piece he laid it out beside the portfolio, under the swan poised on its pedestal. "But you don't need no four years and no research to find out will it work."

From his right pants pocket an assortment of bolts, the micrometer, the zinc alloy support, eared and eyed and rimmed with invisible burrs that tore at the fingers. From his bulging back pocket the UV *Annual Report to the Stockholders* and the grease rag stuffed underneath. From his breast pocket, folded, the tattered leaflet he'd been saving since yesterday's Capitol Hill debate. He opened it up over his hardware. It was stamped across with a ribbed shoe sole.

Coffinism . . . Coffinism . . . Coffinism.

"There's that." He slapped the portfolio. "And there's this." His arsenal. "Insofar as the worker on the job is concerned it's Human Performance. But insofar as you're concerned, from where you sit, it's still the Human Push Button.

"If the time ever comes, Mr. Coffin, when your study goes through, I'd want to be sitting across the bargaining table from you. Not on the same side."

Coffin whisked the leaflet back at him, unruffled. "This is your answer? This bunch of hoary clichés? A few minor incidents blown up into such hysteria— We know where it comes from."

"Where?"

"The same source as that circus in your department. Now don't jump, I'm not probing."

The swan, bluely gleaming, came back into play, Coffin ruddily through a blue haze rubbing it over.

"You won't believe this, Lunin, but the toughest job I have in this job is unfreezing people from outmoded frames of ref-

erence. Come now, the perspective I've presented deserves
more than a snap reaction. Free yourself. Exclude everything
but the guts of the matter. Strip down."

He was mesmerized by the swan, transparent glints upon
glints.

("If you didn't marry Mamma, Daddy, who would I be?")

For an instant he had the illusion, mirrors upon mirrors reflecting, that he was in negotiation flanked by his associates,
sustained by his supporters, thousands upon thousands of them
back in the shops.

The mystery man at the blackboard was humming again.

"All I can say to you then, Mr. Coffin, is what they'd say in
my department. It's not how big a dick you got, Doc. It's who
gets screwed."

He remembered to retrieve his micrometer, he'd need it, and
left the rest on the desk. The mischief with which Don Pinette
had infected Switch was in him. Borne on waves of an ancient
and dizzying elation, all discipline thrown to the winds, restraint out the window, he strode forth with cheeky buttocks.
He'd told the boss off.

As he waited for the elevator to rise and re-embrace him, take
him down again, fantasizing, Coffin's real intention at long last
revealed itself to him in the full splendor of Todd A-O Pan-
Vision. He was to be the star of a publicity build-up spread
through the pages of *Life, Time, Fortune* and the *Saturday
Evening Post.*

Hero of a true-life fairy tale.

II

1

He returned through the buildings and the umbilical corridors
that joined them, alive. Liberated as if he had survived a long
and debilitating illness and recovered from it by magic. Gal-
vanized. He'd shot his mouth off. He had been at the top, he'd
caught a glimpse of the sky and been offered a piece of the pie.
And what had he said? Shove it.

"You see him, Mish? What'd he want, Mish?"

He knew who he was. He had his identity. Workers were leaving their stations and running down the aisles to him as he
passed. He was holding meetings all over the lot.

"Some research deal he wanted to ring me in on."

"What'd you tell him?"

"What do you think?"

Coffin's proposal was summarily chopped down to size. Research? Everyone had his own interpretation of it and no one
had any doubt of what it meant.

Marty Rakocszi crawled down out of his casting and crowded
him into a niche, out of sight, behind two idle Burgmasters.

"Research? He could at least have offered you something like
they did Miklowski. UV fixed him up with some old jig-borers in
the garage back of his house, on a long-term note from the bank.
Showed him how he could pay some bohunk a buck and a quarter
an hour, take seven for himself. Now they're subcontracting

jobs to him hand over foot. Subcontracting, that's the latest wrinkle. The new runaway shop. I dropped in on Mick the other day. Jesus, you should see the place. When he was here, Mick was always hollering to the union, 'Room, room! We got no room to turn around in.' Now he's so packed with equipment, coupla moonlighters operating way under scale, no union, no nothing."

In Marty's opinion, if Coffin was trying to buy Lunin out he should have been a little less subtle with the price.

Ray Pelletier stopped him in front of his cabler in plain sight of the foreman and when the foreman intervened, he included him in on it.

"Research? Retraining? Listen, John, listen to this one."

The foreman, sagging in the last hour of the shift, listened and laughed.

"Training you up to do better? Aaaah. We get that all the time in the supervisors' classes. UV has an enlightened policy toward its employees. Don't fuss, don't cuss, don't crack the whip. When you give an order always explain why. Reason with them. Remember every man has his own quirks. Use psychology. But when it comes right down to it on the job, there's only one kinda training that counts. Get the job out! Come on now, Ray, haul ass before I kick the livin' shit . . ."

In Ray's opinion, if Coffin was trying to rope Lunin in he should have been a little less crude in his device.

"To think you'd fall for that— Man, he must be hurtin'."

What did it all mean? The consensus was, it meant of course that there was much more trouble in the plant now and to come than any of them had guessed. It meant that Coffin anticipating that Lunin would run again for the presidency of the local, that his campaign would polarize the lurking rebellions, that he might even win election, was willing to go to the wildest extremes to remove him from the scene.

Through the murky glare of department after department he saw with heightened vision what Coffin must see here: an obdurate unwieldy mass that had to be whipped into shape, driven in a direction. Each of them milling around in his own indifference, conscious only of his own area, oblivious of the composite picture. Gearing up for quitting time, wherever it was possible they goofed off.

A tall thin droopy chap caught his eye. The face under the billed cap was abraded with the grit of experience. He was sweeping up around his machine, scraping his broom over the same spot, must be five times over, slouchily slouching it out. Somewhere under a bench the sweeper had secreted the surplus he had managed to achieve over the production target, saving it for a slow day. Sooner or later the UV pros would catch him at it. The short cuts he had devised between himself and his machine would be incorporated into the routine. Quotas up, without compensatory allowance for production kinks. Higher and higher. Faster faster. Screws skipped. Finish skimped. Turning out garbage.

The broom scraped back and forth, skirting the aisle as he walked by. A pale eye shot up at him, a glint of humor, kind to kind.

With quickened ears he singled out through the din the notes of an exacerbated argument.

"It ain't passing inspection!"

"You got what the job calls for!"

Under the quiescent surface incessant internecine warfare. The same old war. The company out to extract as much as it could from the work force. The work force out to give no more than it had to to the company.

2

Switch was still going full blast when he signed back in. He stepped unnoticed into the machine shop. Ewell, standing before his four machines, was busy completing his daily time sheet. Master of the art of pencil-pushing, Ewell adjusted his figures for the day to his own advantage, but not too much so. At the same time, he scanned Roscoe's time sheet, with his usual gesture of disgust. Its peculiar mathematics was too much for Roscoe. "You're cheating yourself."

From his private cache Roscoe brought out a batch of contacts and added them to his count for the day. One of his machines must have been down during the past hour or his materials had been held up and he didn't want to fall below his average earnings. By a sleight of hand no one could unscramble, Roscoe succeeded in adding the selfsame batch of contacts into his day's tally at least one day every month.

"Mish! Hey."

They converged on him. His relief man yielded up his place at the setup he'd just started. "What happened?"

"Nothing much."

"Oh, come on. You look like you been to the moon and back."

He was a changed person. He was himself again, all charged up, tingling at every touch with shocks of static electricity. Instead of continuing with his new setup for the remainder of the hour, he made a great show of tidying up his toolbox.

"Three things I learned these last few days. Number one, yesterday in the locker room. The grievances are piling up and the union is losing membership. Number two, this afternoon in Coffin's office. We've chained ourselves lock, stock and barrel to the company juggernaut and where it takes us we go. Number three, on my way back through the plant. Everybody's out to beat the system his own way."

"Now you're talking. Now what?"

"We sit down with the contract and we list every contract violation we know of. And we figure out the action that'll mobilize the works."

"Colangelo—"

"Never mind Colangelo. With him if we can. Without him if we have to."

"When?"

"Sooner the better."

"Tonight." Ewell pinned him down. "If we're going to make

time before the Sunday meeting— Couple of us from here. Some of the girls out there—Amy's still sizzling over Leora. Mari can always pull her friends in the key departments. And Bostic, he's got a following among the colored. I'll talk to a couple of guys after work—I bet we have twenty people without half trying."

"Tonight," he agreed. "Seven o'clock. Where?"

Where, that was the touchstone. Whose house? Who would bear the onus?

"Well . . ." Ewell paused in what was a flight of fancy for him, entailing a degree of energy foreign to his contemplative nature. Thoughtfully he lifted his cap back. "It can't be my place. Six kids in four rooms."

Roscoe had no telephone. Cusak was too far out of town. Palermo and Jackson were equally unsuitable or unavailable. They looked expectantly at him.

"Not my house," he said with relish, refusing them the easy solution. "My wife has these tenants organizing . . ."

He took a stroll out on the floor to consult with Mari.

"My house," Mari said promptly. "All right, all right, it may be a mistake but you won't get anything else. If they're not ready to come to my house for something that concerns them just as much as it does me . . ."

"You two billing and cooing again?" Dirksen swooped down on them. "What are you cooking up now?"

Bostic was absent from the plastics shop. "Didn't you see him?" his partner inquired. "He was looking for you a while back. His old lady called him home."

Restlessly, unable to stay in the machine shop till the whistle blew, he sneaked out to the can for a leak and a smoke. There he encountered Don Pinette.

"What nice legs you got," Don said, standing behind him as he washed up.

"I thought it was girls' legs you were interested in."

"What I mean," Don said, "look at mine." He twitched his jeans up over his shaggy shanks. "So big and thick," he said unhappily, "like a hog. Clumsy."

Don dogged him to the window and struck a match for his cigarette. "You married, huh?"

"Ten years."

"Any kids?"

"Two. Girl and boy."

"Hey, that's great. Nice to have a family. First the son. Then a daughter."

He craned around at Don and scrutinized him closely.

"The girl is older. Say, who you dating?"

"I'm trying. Inga Kohlberg."

Sweetheart of Switch. China doll of Lutheran church suppers.

"You think she would go out with me?"

"She give you the brushoff?"

Hesitantly, with an air of apology, Don begged him, "Will you put in a word for me?"

All this in the space of just a few hours.

3

Through the gate with the velocity of a buffalo herd the first shift stampeded and over the curb toward the parking lot.

Lost in the mass, he already half regretted his impulsiveness. He was no more sanguine about the results to be obtained by a union campaign than he had been this morning or yesterday or any time in the past two years. He had been precipitated into action by Coffin, where Priscilla and everybody else had failed, out of the nature of his own emotional make-up—if Lunin was Coffin's hangup, then Coffin must be Lunin's. It was his own subjective mood that had altered, not objective conditions. A swell from below perhaps, an upsurge, but not of the magnitude required to effect one iota of difference.

Yet there was something there, more than he had originally estimated. He was willing to let himself be carried by the pressures the others placed on him.

Ray Pelletier plucked him aside with his idea for the tube nipple. They walked along the broken sidewalk together. Ray was still brimming with his cabler and its idiosyncrasies and the invention he had arrived at today after all his months of tinkering around. He thrust a crude sketch and the stub of a pencil at him.

"Just take notes on this as we go."

"Ray, I have to get home. I had a fight with my wife and the way we left it—" Ray should understand that. "We're getting together at Mari's tonight to see what we can do about the situation in the shop. Seven o'clock. I'll see you there."

But Ray couldn't wait for tonight. He wanted it down on paper, now, concretized outside himself.

"Just rough it out, you can fix it up later. Won't take any longer than it takes to get to your car. The problem is, we're having constant trouble obtaining and maintaining a uniform center on soft-core wire. And making solid wire out of round."

He began jotting down under the sketch, trying to keep up with Ray through the jostling of the crowd.

"Now if we increase the two wrench grooves on the tube nipple to eight, evenly spaced around, it'll even out the flow and pressure of the compound. Got that? This will result in a 10 per cent saving on compound every hundred feet of wire. Also, save the operator's time every time he has to stop and center after uniformity is lost. Got that? Under these new conditions the operator can then use a larger size nipple on the control wire, thus eliminating tape wrinkles, roving centers, variations of diameter—"

Midstream in the crowd, Ray stopped dead. From his thin cheeks, honed to the bone, the flush of enthusiasm ebbed. Now that he had his idea verbalized, out of his system, he was seized with doubts. Once he had received two hundred dollars for a similar suggestion and the company, he was convinced, had made thousands on it. On the one hand, any innovation of his while he was employed at UV belonged to UV, not to him. On the other hand, if he kept it to himself it would be of no service to him: it applied only to the machine he was working and to that specific production. On the third hand, if he submitted the idea and it turned out to be a stroke of genius, funny how likely it was to have been thought of first by someone higher up. On the fourth hand, how did he know that after he'd received a few bucks for his brain child it wouldn't be used later on to retime and reclassify him? Maybe John, his foreman, who now saw him as a resource, who came around to encourage him and draw on him, would take it into his head to regard him as a threat, would start looking for ways to get rid of him . . .

Shadows of dilemma flitted across Ray's thin chestnut-tinged face.

"Have Priscilla type it up anyway," Ray said, too hot on his idea to kill it off even if it should kill him. "Make it look good. I'll keep it on tap."

While he dawdled with Ray, Marty spotting the two of them together shouldered through.

"I just now seen Ewell. Is it true we're meeting at Mari's tonight? Boy, have we got a beef . . ."

"Ewell? Is he in on this?" Ray took back his sketch with the notes on it and put it away. "Jesus Christ, we're on the move."

"You notice those two new Burgmasters in my department, Mish? That job was always Labor Grade 9 and now the company claims . . ."

"Save it, save it for tonight."

". . . it requires less skill when it requires more skill. Now nobody'll touch . . ."

Suddenly they were inundated. Spotting Lunin and Marty and Ray together, the old team, the crowd coalesced around them.

Everybody spouting beefs. Everybody making speeches. A floating crap game.

"Everything's gotten too big. The union's too big. The company's too big. The government's too big. You got a complaint, who you gonna complain to? Ain't nobody anymore can do anything for you. Pass the buck!"

"You been in Small Motor lately? One floor all machines. Where are the people?"

"It's easy enough for them to tell you this automation is a snap. With the old rig I'd set up my speed and feed, my horizontal and vertical, see what was what every minute. But with this new thing, the size of it, the output, the responsibility of it, the danger. One tool a little off, one scratch in the material —it can throw a drill a hundred feet. I don't sleep nights."

"Putting out ten times as much. Am I getting ten times more pay? Where's the extra going? Who's making it? Even discounting the cost of the equipment—"

"They skim the cream off the top. Organized robbery."

It was so hot outside they were shedding their jackets. The temperature had freakishly mounted in the last few days until now the air was sultry, Fourth of July in the third week of March. The rows of cars in the parking lot shimmered with heat.

"Write it up, write it up! You got a case write it up, bring it to me. We'll set up a committee to collate . . ."

He was in it, committed.

Mari was waiting for him by his station wagon, loaded with Elsie's tissue-swathed plant and Elsie's birthday cake left over from yesterday. She was surrounded by women.

"The Snake Pit, twelve inches to a person. Stools, we're fighting each other for a stool. I go home with my arms numb, my hands slashed—look at my hands. And my nerves—"

"Write it up." He maneuvered through to his door.

"I'm riding with you." Sending his morning riders off to find themselves another ride, Mari climbed into his front seat. "My car's in for a checkup and I have to stop by Elsie's."

"Mari, I got to rush. Pris'll have my head. She has these tenants—and, my God, her PTA tonight—"

"So it'll be like the old days. A three-meeting night. Just fifteen minutes."

"Yeah, fifteen going. And fifteen coming."

"Mish, Mish! Mariuch!"

A woman dashed up to his wagon as he was backing out.

"You wanna see something?"

Concupiscently, with a salacious smile, her downcast eyes moistly anticipating, the woman snapped open her handbag, parted the pouch, lifted back the folded pink silk scarf inside, laid bare the contents nestled beneath. The Blue Bird contingent knotted about Marty shifted over to her and peeped down in curiosity.

"How do you like that?"

In the bottom of the handbag the woman had stowed, compactly dovetailed, the inner parts of a small radio. Looking back toward the plant, she raised her thumb.

Drivers were spilling out of their cars in the bumper-to-bumper line to take a look. He couldn't back out. Another mass debate. Mari holding forth.

"Sure, sure, I want what's coming to me," she lectured the woman who stood smugly, queen for a day, clutching her fat black handbag under the long black coat over her arm. "But I want my right to it recognized! You fight back, fight in the open. Not on the sly!"

The men to a man upheld the woman. "Look at these purchasing agents, look at these execs with their expense accounts, look at the prices they're charging. . . ."

Larceny was the leaven of society. Larceny was the glue that bound it together.

"Remember—remember that business in Washing Machine back in '52? That was fabulous. The guy who started removing the motor part by part? Pretty soon all his buddies were helping him? Working the night shift. One night they'd lower the lid over the back fence. Next night it was a side. Till he had the whole thing at home and assembled it."

They were all looking back over their shoulders at the back fence, the high chain-wire fencing barbed on top, over which on moonless nights, men had passed from one to the other the agitator, the tub . . .

"That's the trouble with us," Mari declaimed. "That's why we don't get anywhere. Everybody in his own little shitty-ass way—"

He backed out of his parking space through them, jerking Mari back in her seat, shot past the lined-up cars with a rattle of gravel, and jounced out into the street under the highway.

III

1

Mari set Elsie's potted plant down on the floor of the car and clamped it between her trousered legs. She placed the hatbox containing Elsie's cake upright in her lap and clasped it to her bosom.

"Our zoo show yesterday, it's all over UV now. Dopes, if they hadn't tried to question us— You're hitting every pothole. What did old Graveyard have to say about me?"

"Nothing." Mari always had to be the one the spotlight was trained on.

Desperate to reach Priscilla and irked with Mari for the delay she was causing him, he passed the expressway entrance and took the underpass to Cedarbrook. The long dusty uphill street glittered with traffic climbing at a snail's pace, interrupted by the outpourings of intersections. He idled through green signals blocked by cars ahead of him, only to arrive at corners as the red flashed on.

"That's what he called you up there for, isn't it? To finger me."

"Not exactly."

"Everything that happens in the plant, according to him I'm the one behind it."

"Then why didn't he call you?"

"Because he didn't have proof! They burnt their fingers on

me too often. He thought he could sneak it out of you without you even knowing."

She set her box aside momentarily and took a moist astringent pad from a compact in her handbag. Chin up high, she scrubbed over her already washed face, her neck, removing every last vestige of grime and cosmetic. Her freckled nose tilted ceilingward. Her pert underlip curled out. Her bosom thrust at the buttons of her polished cotton blouse, smudged over as if cupped by fondling hands. Dulled and drained by her day's work, she shone. Aggressively the culprit.

"Well, Coffin did link up the performance in Switch yesterday with that leaflet on Friday," he acknowledged reluctantly, unwilling to give her the satisfaction.

"What'd I tell you! Every time the spirit of opposition raises its head, it's an outside plot again. The long arm of the Kremlin. Through me. Always me. The last of the party liners. I did it."

"Well, did you?"

Mari saddened. She slumped.

"If only it were so! If I'd written that leaflet and had the means to smuggle it in and spread it, do you know where I'd be right now?" Delicately she touched her shoulder, bursitis, her stomach, gastritis, her knee, a touch of arthritis. "Laid up for a week. If I was the instigator yesterday, is there anybody in the whole works who wouldn't be onto it?"

He intended merely to pat her knee in comfort, if he had any intention at all. It was an automatic gesture springing as much out of old association as any immediate concern for her.

He had known Mari since he was a kid. Mari with her air of something mysterious lurking in the background, something marvelous about to happen, her husky voice breathless with things she could tell you if she only would. Mari faking her way and his sister Irene's way, under age, no experience, into a job with the Nu-Vogue Blouse Company, a sweatshop in a loft. The two girls running home to their families Saturday afternoon, throwing their pay envelopes on the kitchen table, taking a dollar for themselves and running off to whatever excitement it is teen-age girls run off to. Mari sleeping over with Irene, Irene sleeping over with Mari, whispering their confidences till the break of dawn. It was Mari who grabbed the ballot box up after a union election in the blouse loft and raced down the stairs with it to the street screaming, "They stuffed it, they stuffed it," chased by the business agent of the union. It was Mari who administered her father's enemas when he was dying of cancer. Mari who . . .

Well, Mari.

He touched her knee and he clutched it. Through the thin cloth of her slacks, a bubble, a beat. Mari was all there, as much as ever, too much so.

With a wriggle she jiggled the box back into her lap. When she spoke she kissed the syllables.

"You think Coffin was out to buy you out, you got another think coming. He's out to smoke you out. Turning down supervisor and now this—oh, boy, has he ever got it in for you! You've no choice now, Mish, but to keep doing what you're doing and push it through. It's your only protection."

It was her only protection.

"Son of a bitch, he's getting ready to pull a fast one and he doesn't want you around when he does it. Reduce the work force," she speculated, eyes rolled heavenward, "move a division . . . ? Remember last fall when they moved Washer-Dryer to Mobile? Fifteen hundred people out. And there was Coffin up there in his tower showing off his razzle-dazzle charts to the press, how he was going to bring Steam Iron in from Aliquippa. Colangelo swallowed it. Stopped us from striking. And what did we wind up with? Fifty, count 'em, fifty jobs in Ironing Cord. Oh no, he doesn't want you around making waves."

She dropped the hypothesizing and began making plans for tonight. "Now about this meeting, are we aiming for specific goals? Or do we leave it up to spontaneity?"

She brooded over past errors. "We aim, we're rigging it. Let it develop spontaneously, it may build up out of the needs expressed there. Or blow up in hot air. Or go off half-cocked."

"We have to aim," he said, "we have to nail it to something. The mood is on now, but moods fluctuate. Everybody's insecure. Nobody knows what's coming next. All hanging onto what they got."

Between traffic lights uphill they began identifying the pieces. He always came back to that. What do we have to work with? What are the pieces?

First of course, the leaflet. They had to find out where the leaflet came from, make contact.

"There are only three people in UV who could have written it. Me and it wasn't me," he said. "You and it wasn't you."

"Who else? Who?"

"Bob Ucchini. The style is Bob's, the method of attack—"

"Oh, Mish. Mish— It wasn't just UV we were fighting in those days. It was the whole rotten system. We had class consciousness. We had morale. We had a vision. We thought of ourselves as makers of history. We were changing the world."

She turned her face toward him, starkly porcelain without make-up, and he didn't doubt her, didn't doubt that given the slightest leverage she could have moved worlds and might yet.

"Any little activity we undertook, it was part of the greatest thing going. The best. We gave ourselves to it day and night. Everything else was subordinate."

Again he was moved to touch her. He had always regarded her as a sexually desirable woman and had never felt any desire for her. That old-time whisper around the plant, "You know Mish and Mari, they're just like that," was so baseless that neither Bob nor Priscilla had ever bothered even to tease them with it. She was the older sister. He was the kid brother. She was Bob's wife and that put her out of bounds, though he suspected now that she was more faithful to Bob dead than she had been to him alive. He was inextricably involved with them both, with a mixture of affection and annoyance. He respected them for their politics and resented them for the trouble they brought on him. He refused to submit himself to them and he returned to them time and again, no matter what their blunders. "If only you'd stayed away from the Ucchinis," workers in the plant would say to him, "you'd be all right now. You'd be way up there." He couldn't stay away. He was drawn to them by a fate outside himself. He was thrown together with them.

He should not be driving Mari home now. He should not have agreed to have the meeting at her house tonight. He touched her arm and clasped it and with a little shudder, a strangulated gasp, she settled into his clasp.

"Mish, slow down. Stop the car!"

"Oh, for Christ sake, Mari—"

"Ta-ree-sa! You can't pass her by, she sees us." Mari poked her head out the window and shouted back toward the disconsolate figure plodding up the crest of Cedarbrook Avenue. "Where are you going, Teresa? You need a lift, Teresa?"

He was forced to pull over. He didn't know what Mari had in mind. That she would transform Teresa by example into a stalwart for tonight?

"Poor thing, she's all alone now," Mari filled him in. "She did have this friend staying with her. Only her friend was always short on her end with the rent and bills, though every once in a while she'd bring in extra food. I told Teresa, 'It never works out. Make her pay you a flat sum. Then if she brings in extra, you can make it up.'"

Deftly she had rearranged Teresa's life for her.

"Only she didn't follow through. She stood it and stood it till natch one day . . . Going home, Teresa? It's right on our way."

Teresa climbed into the back seat with a tale of woe. She had almost reached the UV parking lot when she remembered that her ride home on Tuesdays was with Amy. She'd hustled all the way back to Cedarbrook to catch the bus, having palpitations with every step. The first two buses were just pulling out and the third one shut the door on her.

Teresa thrust her face between them from the back, seeking to enlist them in her feud with Amy who was by derivation to blame for her near heart failure, the bus driver who wouldn't respond to her pounding on the door, the unseasonable heat.

Mari rapidly lost interest in Teresa. Teresa would be of no use at the meeting and in any case Amy had already promised to be there.

"Okay, the leaflet." She resumed preparations for the meeting. "That's one item. There's bound to be someone there who can track it down."

"Trying to show off what a great mother she is," Teresa wailed between them, reliving the bitter injustice of it. "What's she got to brag about? I lighted a candle every day for my baby. I paid a lawyer downtown . . ."

"And those three guys suspended in Hot Rubber," he said to Mari. "We have to come up with a demonstration of support for them if we're to restore confidence. You open your mouth, you're out on the street, nobody lifts a finger."

The leaflet. The suspensions. Mari had pencil and envelope out of her handbag, scrawling down an agenda, back in harness.

"She thought she could make me cry. But I didn't cry." Teresa, her wounds opened afresh, was howling again. Tears splattered out of her red-rimmed eyes over cheeks as flaccid as overkneaded dough.

"And the grievances. A Court of Complaints," Mari chortled, getting creative with it.

Location? Hours? How to man it?

"I been without a husband for sixteen years. Still I never went with another man. But Amy, she has her husband and family. . . ."

"This Sunday union meeting. We have to present ourselves in numbers if we're to have any impact on Nick."

A turnout on Sunday. With the time so short.

"What we expect to get out of it—what are we shooting for?"

Warmed up to their working partnership they batted ideas back and forth, with Teresa providing the background music. Absently Mari passed her a tissue.

"I could have told the whole of final assembly who she was

stepping out with. I could have named names. But I wouldn't do that on her."

"He has to take up the contract violations. Initiate an all-out membership drive. Broaden his slate to include representation from all elements."

"If we cover a tenth of this—"

"Everybody'll have their own ideas. There's all this automation creeping in—"

"I'm no prude. If a woman has a boy friend on the side, that's her business. But when she starts carrying herself so high and mighty—"

"You mean Amy's having an affair?" Mari at last woke up to the import of Teresa's diatribe. "With who? I don't believe it."

"I caught her in the Three Crowns with this fellow." Their attention captured, Teresa nodded her head between them, suddenly round-faced and pink-cheeked, blooming.

"When?" Mari asked her.

"Oh, I got the goods on her all right. Christmas week. Monday night."

"And what were you doing in the Three Crowns on a Monday night?"

Teresa retired to the middle of the back seat in high dudgeon. "I had enough! Everybody thinks she's such a saint. When I know better! Making a nothing outa me!"

Mari, twisting around, tried to mollify her. "Yesterday noon we did something together, no feuds, no fights. If we can just stick together like that, maybe we can even do something about reducing the standard in final assembly. We'll talk about it tonight."

"You talk, you talk," Teresa said wrathfully. "I know how you all talk. You should be ashamed of yourselves talking like that. When the company gives you a living."

"Who gives WHO a living?"

Mari all but climbed over the back of her seat. Teresa holding herself aloof, sniffling and simmering over her injuries, would have nothing further to do with them. They rode on in silence.

Elsie was not at home, a half hour of Mari's gossipy persuasions eliminated. She left the cake and the plant with an upstairs neighbor and came panting back down the front porch stairs.

"You think they didn't get her in the dispensary?" she addressed herself to Teresa, making amends. "Told her she had high blood pressure. After that turntable, whose pressure wouldn't be up?"

Teresa, not to be appeased with Elsie's problems, remained unapproachable. Wrapped in her winter coat, she steamed and steamed. Two blocks before her house she insisted on being let out at a grocery store.

"Lovey-dovey," she jeered at them over the seat as she hauled herself out. "You think I didn't see? I seen. All lovey-dovey! Now wait a minute, don't go yet. Just you wait a minute."

Teresa rushed over to the plank, supported by two crates, on which newspapers were laid and snatched one from under the awning winch that served as a weight. She thrust the paper into the car window at them, black headlines outspread.

REDS DENOUNCE STALIN TERROR

"There, there, that's who killed my baby! Look what your Stalin did. You think you're so goddam smart, what do you think of him now?"

She threw the paper in Mari's face and blubbery, swollen with righteousness vindicated, shook her fist at her.

"Killer! Murderer! You murdered millions of them. You not gonna murder me too!"

She tramped back across the sidewalk and into the grocery. Slam!

"Stupid bitch," Mari muttered after her. "Some people have a mentality—born flunkys."

Shaken, she smoothed out the newspaper and folded it lengthwise, reading to herself as he drove. An inquisitive and critical intelligence, a challenger of constituted authority who never in her life, she swore, had taken any crap off anyone.

3

In the once semirural section where Mari lived, a shopping center complex, against which she had rallied the residents, was being carved out of farmland. Under the wooded rock ledge, clusters of development houses cascaded. Service stations squatted in clumps on the roadside. Competing landscapers confronted each other. A drive-in eatery blared with teen-agers. A front yard sprouted with cemetery monuments on display.

Halfway up the lane from the main road he stopped before the yellow Cape Cod with the ruffled curtains crisscrossed in the windows. Mari rustled through the paper to the run-over page, grunting protests.

"Heard it on the radio . . . thought it was just more of the same old jive. . . ."

She closed the newspaper, unnaturally quiet. Her brown eyes strained in her porcelain-pale face, fixed on the blurred windshield.

"I don't believe it," she said. "I can't. The Soviet Union. The workers' state. That it wasn't perfect the way the *Daily Worker* said—of course. How could it be? But this."

Stiffly she heaved out of the car and stood in the open door rubbing at her joints.

"If I had to think for a minute that what Bob went through was mistaken . . . That Herb Cranston was right all along . . ." Wearily she gathered her coat and handbag off the seat, and her scribbled envelope. "That the Colangelos . . . the Teresas . . . That it can't be any better. That no matter how we try, we can't rise above . . . No, I don't believe it. It's not true. It's a lie."

"Mari—" He reached toward her. She walked blindly away from him to the house between the tall line of firs on the north side and the rose bushes along the driveway. All she had, what she'd built up for herself.

He left the car and followed her in an agony of compassion and impatience. He had to get home, if he still had a home. The minutes were flying away under his feet. She veered to the driveway and, stopping at her hose faucet, soaked scrunched-up newspaper under it.

"Here, go clean your windshield. There's bird shit all over it."

"Mari . . ."

She brushed water over her eyes and cheeks and down her neck, drenching her collar.

"It wasn't just for Russia, Russia was the least of it. It was for peace, for brotherhood, a decent life. It was for this country. For ourselves. Ourselves."

"I know—"

Helplessly he held her, wiping her wet face with his hand.

"We didn't bleed for nothing! We didn't bleed for nothing!"

Together, they stumbled up the concrete side steps and entered the house. Across the driveway a child stood at the window watching them, eating ice cream custard from a paper cup, licking the wooden spoon. Mari's sister-in-law who lived with her was due from work soon. He closed and bolted the door.

In the tidy beige-and-white kitchen with its plants in the window and decorative plates on the wall, he fixed himself a drink and tried calling Priscilla while Mari showered. The line was busy as usual. He tried calling Lucas Ford. Busy too. The two of them busy with each other. Two minutes later he dialed Priscilla again. All the circuits in that area of the city were busy. He finished his drink and called the operator. "I'm sorry, that number is temporarily out of order."

Mari, tightly belted in a voluminous white terry-cloth robe, her head turbaned in a white towel, interrupted him. She had turned on a record in the living room and she came jigging in, snapping her fingers to the music. Her mouth was freshly lipsticked. Her eyes danced over him leaving no part unstroked.

"Family trouble, huh?"

He didn't want to discuss his family trouble with her, to articulate what to him was too fragile for expression, let alone exposure.

Mari danced around him, swaying out of his grasp.

"She's been holding out on you, huh?"

He was not about to commit to her remedial attention what to him was too private to be shared.

"Tell me something, Mish." He pulled her down into his lap and she kissed him on the mouth, running her tongue between his lips. "In all the years you been married to Priscilla, how many other women have you wrapped your ass around?"

He wouldn't admit it to her.

"None, huh? And yet you're sore at her all the time. You're always chewing her out."

"Not always." He kissed down into the moist softness of her neck, into the soapy-sweet softness in the opening of her robe.

"You've never given her credit—"

"She'll never really know what it's all about. There are things she'll never—"

She took his head between her hands and tenderly kissed his forehead, the tip of his ear.

"Ever try explaining to her?"

"How can you explain? There are things you can't explain."

"If I was your wife," Mari said, "I'd fart in your face."

She paraded into the living room, her robe fanning out behind her.

"Now all they have to do tonight is show. Look—" She ran past Bob's clavichord to the window. "My andromeda's out! It's out since this morning."

Before he could get away from her she had him cutting sprays of andromeda, white-belled blossoms dripping like raindrops among the glossy leaves, and wrapping them in wet-down newspaper to take home to Priscilla.

SIX

A Chinese Tapestry

I

A flare-up or a fire? A mood or a movement? A tidal wave that rolls over the shore sweeping up everything in its path—or a fizzle?

Tonight would make the difference. This week up through the Sunday meeting would tell. Against his better judgment he had undertaken it. As a probing operation, a test run, no more. Yet if it proved futile after all, as he had claimed from the beginning that it must, he didn't dare think where it would leave him afterward.

He drove home to Priscilla with it, bringing it to her like a gift, Mari's admonitions ringing in his ears. "All she wants of you is for you to be a man again. What's so terrible about that? When they take your manhood from you, that's the worst. It can kill your life together. I know." And groaning over the past five years at UV. "Oh, how they cut our balls. . . . You came out of Coffin's office today full of jizzum. Now go home and tell her you adore her."

He couldn't tell Priscilla that he adored her. Like his father who boasted that he had never kissed any of his children, not even when they were babies, he was wary of sentiment. To define what he felt for Priscilla at any one time was to falsify it.

"Go tell her," Mari urged him in some feminine fantasy of

romance, out of this world, "that you worship the ground she walks on."

It wasn't love women craved, it was admiration, whether of their bodies or their minds or their behavior. He did admire Priscilla, so much sometimes it would have tried him beyond endurance to say it. He admired her and anathematized her for what he didn't admire in her.

"You may think you love me now," Mari said to him at her kitchen sink, flowing around him with her robe and her garden shears.

He didn't think any such thing.

"Proximity and opportunity, that's all it is. What would we do with it if we did it?"

He had to face a few unpleasant facts about himself. If he could have thrown her on the floor and had her just for the hell of it, it would have been all right. If they could engage in an affair with no responsibilities attached, emotional or otherwise, meeting in motel rooms and returning refreshed . . . But in order to do that he had to be that kind of person. Mari had nailed his weakness. He couldn't remain detached. It would lead to such devastation . . . or such a desert of meaninglessness . . .

"Of course she's not altogether without fault either," Mari mused. "Activity isn't enough. She has to dress a little better, set her hair once in a while. Put on the glamour. I'll talk to her."

"Oh no you don't!"

He drove home to Priscilla bringing her his gift of himself, his hard appraisal of what he was up to, and his feeling for her, his boundless and indefinable feeling.

On the expressway he sniffed smoke among the normal fumes, the smoke of burnt chicken feathers. Even with a diesel chimney blowing black in his face from the truck ahead of him, the odor was unmistakable. A yellow haze, drifting inland over the city from the dump at the seaside, penetrated the late afternoon air with the odor of a freshly plucked chicken being singed over the flame of an open wood stove.

He was not alarmed at first. Fire bloomed sunset orange on the east horizon. Then torrents of black smoke spurted up through the enveloping blaze. Bad as the dump fire last summer, midsummer.

He descended into a pall that banished all other preoccupations from his mind. He sped past pedestrians dimly hurrying along the sidewalks, heads hunched in their collars. The squawl of sirens forced him to the curb. Fire trucks roared past him, clanging into the access routes to the dump.

2

At Tidal Flats, policemen directed him around yellow barriers to a parking area six buildings away from his. He stepped out into a blast of furnace heat. Crowds milled about the foggy courtyards, shuttled hither and yon by firemen hauling hose through to the cordoned-off road that bordered the dump. The hose slithered past his feet, asbestos-gray, endless. Fiery tatters twirled in the air and fluttered in cinders to the ground. A fireman being helped from the fire stooped over a car fender, wracked with retching.

In a numbness of reality too unreal to be believed, he pushed toward his building. "Stand back, stand back," the loudspeaker blared above him. "All you people, go back inside!"

"Just as bad in there as it is out here." The people eddied about him wiping eyes and coughing.

"Go back into your apartments! Keep your windows closed!"

"Closed! That's a hot one."

"Asphyxiated"—he gathered—"suffocating." A baby in Building 20 nearly died this morning. From closed windows.

He was pressed back with the crowd out of the path of an arriving engine company. A little girl at his knee gazed trustfully up at him, stroking a kitten in her arms. He was elbowed aside by a shrieking mother. She whacked the child across the arm and the child, too stunned to break into tears, clutched her kitten to her. The mother whacked harder, hard enough to send the animal hurtling. He was almost capsized in a whirlpool of shrinking women, darting small boys, as it scampered between their legs, one of the fat and furry rats that flourished on the dump.

Past the fire engines he caught sight of Lucas Ford. Lucas sprang from group to group, inserting himself. "I hired a hall," Lucas trumpeted back at him. "Pulaski Hall. Seven o'clock."

"Priscilla? Where's Priscilla? My kids?"

"Who? What? Oh, Priscilla."

Lucas disappeared, upraised arm pointing, Priscilla was at home, a safe distance from the center of the conflagration. The hubbub increased as he neared his own driveway. Tenants from the dumpside sections swarmed in, seeking respite. His entrance was clogged. His stairway was packed, an escalator of passengers up and down. The door to his apartment stood wide open. He had to batter into his own foyer. Command post.

A stranger holding a clipboard of untidy papers jostled him aside and addressed the buzzing living room. "Can you beat it? There are still some people afraid to sign. You know what I tell 'em? If there's anybody going to be evicted, first one'll be me."

He took firm hold of the stranger's shoulder. Offended, the stranger turned on him.

"Who are you?"

"I live here."

"Oh. Willenski's the name." They shook hands. "You looking for your wife?"

"That's right."

"Somewhere in there." Willenski gestured vaguely at the living room and followed him, voluble with explanation. "I'm on afternoon shift and when I woke up this A.M. and heard what was going on . . . Mrs. Lunin typed up these petitions for me, I stayed home from work . . . Ask her to do a dozen more for Pulaski Hall tonight, okay?"

Waving his sheets of signatures at him, the man backed off and out through diversionary conversations into the outer hall, on his rounds again. Priscilla was not in the living room, which seemed to be overrun with experts swapping theories. It had been a long cold winter and dry, no snow at all or rain since the January storms. When the temperature changed and the hot sun hit two days running all the scattered fires smoldering underneath joined forces . . .

He was coming in on the tail end of a series of events that, as nearly as he could piece it together, had begun shortly after he left for work in the morning. At eight o'clock, flames were shooting higher than the rooftops. Tenants started calling the fire department. No fire trucks appeared. A couple of boys on their way to school smashed the pane of the firebox on the street corner and turned in an alarm. Fire trucks at last. A brief search of apartments ensued. Where was the fire? No fire. Where were the juveniles responsible for turning in a false alarm? Who were their parents? As the firemen left, a rock was thrown at them. The fire trucks took off. A night worker, roused out of sleep by his wife, managed to get through on the telephone to the fire chief. The fire chief responded as he had been responding to every call to a dump fire for the past few months. He couldn't tie up his department on the dump. "I have strict orders from Mayor Kearnsey not to bother with fires out there. It'll burn itself out."

Another tenant, a disabled veteran, called the Board of Health. The nurse on duty informed him that she couldn't do a thing for him. "Why don't you call Public Works?" Public Works suggested that he call Mr. Stanley, director of Public Housing. Mr. Stanley wasn't in yet at nine o'clock. By some ruse the tenant wormed Stanley's unlisted home phone out of the clerk. "You knew what that place was like when you moved in," Mr. Stanley answered the complainant. "Why did you move there?"

Sparks blew in over the window sills of houses on the dumpside and were slapped out before they could ignite the curtains. Windows were closed tight. The windowed brick cells heated up like bake ovens.

Around ten in the morning a woman ran screaming out of Building 20 with her baby in her arms. She had left him napping in his crib while she went out to rescue her wash on the lines from the soot. When she returned she found her baby gagging and choking, struggling for breath. A neighbor took the baby from the screaming woman and applied mouth-to-mouth resuscitation. A second neighbor called emergency hospital for an ambulance. The baby was treated at the hospital and sent home. By this time Building 20 was thoroughly up in arms. That beautiful little boy. An only child. Polish refugee couple. Lived through the war and the Nazi slave labor camps and the DP camps and now they were here just a few years, this baby. Wayne Strunski.

Building 20 adjoined Building 19 and in due course Olive Leggett, the pariah, was summoned downstairs to a parley in the courtyard. Mrs. Leggett denied any knowledge of a tenant-organizing meeting in her apartment last night, referring her inquirers to Lucas Ford, Building 11, 3D. Lucas Ford's sister in Building 11, 3D, denied any knowledge of Lucas, she had no one rooming here with her, and referred her inquirers to a Priscilla Lunin who was rumored to have been talking up a Tenants Council. Mrs. Lunin telephoned Mayor Kearnsey. Mayor Kearnsey agreed to order the fire department out but turned down flat her request for an appointment to discuss with a delegation from Tidal Flats the immediate cessation of the dumping operation.

"Find me another dump," Rod Kearnsey had said to Priscilla as he had been saying to every such request for the past seven years, ending the matter.

Wayne Strunski was home no more than an hour when he went into convulsions. The baby's father, who had been summoned from his job by the hospital, called in the family doctor. The doctor advised the parents to remove the baby from the project at once and for good. The Strunskis bundled up their baby and fled, leaving panic in their wake.

From then on the door to the Lunin apartment was never closed.

"Say, Mish. Over here."

In his living room, in the middle of one studio couch, Gene Bostic was holding forth. His three sons, Bostic said, were asthmatic. He couldn't believe it at first when the doctor told him.

"All three of them?" "All three." He had overcome their asthma with his own home cure. Musical instruments, each of them on a different instrument, clarinet, trombone and tenor sax. They were to play this Friday night at the Elks in a jazz combo contest. His wife had called him from work this afternoon to go round up the boys and ride them over to her sister's for tonight, or no jazz contest.

"Can't sleep in their own house. If we're gonna live here, we gotta figure something out."

"Heya, Mish. C'mere."

On the studio couch opposite Bostic, Eddie Kochis from next door was holding forth. He always told his kids, Kochis said, to watch the quiz shows on TV. If they had the brains or the talent, they could go anywhere in this country. But if they turned out to be schlemiels like him, they'd be just where he was.

"What the hell, in the next few years they gonna throw this whole project open to the jigs and the spics and insofar as I'm concerned they can have it. First chance I get, I'm gettin' outa here."

Between the two couches on the faded flowers of his drugget rug, a hatful of money, collected for the rental of Pulaski Hall, was being counted out.

A high-strung blonde squirmed past him, nudging her daughter before her. "Pull up your sleeve, Ruthie. Show them. Bare your arm."

The girl, about ten, sullenly tugged up her sleeve.

"Show it to them. Don't itch it! Show the lady. Teacher won't let her sit next to no one."

She paraded her daughter around, displaying the round tan arm, white-powdered over a freckle of festering blisters. "Pull up your blouse, honey. Show them your back." She fingered back the girl's blouse collar. "Spreading. From the dump, the doctor says. Don't know what it is, he says. Expose it to the air, he says. What are they waiting for here? An epidemic? Somebody has to die?"

She marched her daughter back out.

In the kitchen Frances Knowlton, the crackerjack of last night's meeting in Mrs. Leggett's apartment, was seated at the table with the telephone pulled in from the living room for privacy. A pencil was stilettoed jauntily through her smooth black pug. Nonchalantly, in the gray uniform of the house-cleaning job she had evidently skipped today, she leaned over the telephone soliciting speakers for Pulaski Hall tonight from a list of city officials on the table. Laconically she polished off refusals. "If you can't speak, then come and listen . . . If you can't come, then send a representative . . . If none of you all can make it, I'm just lettin' you know."

In Steph and Greg's room Mrs. Knowlton's five children were occupying themselves, over Steph and Greg's strenuous objections, with showers of jigsaw puzzles, logs and blocks, highway set, dinosaurs, crayons, model cars, Candyland.

Priscilla had retired to her bedroom from the interruptions of the living room, and amid women and tots and coffee cups she perched on a hassock with her typewriter set on a chair before her and frantically, with flying fingers, was copying notes for her PTA report tonight. Pink-elbowed and pink-fingered she attacked the budget cuts of the Board of Apportionment, so much wrong, everywhere you look, everything you touch. Harried, answering questions over her shoulder, x-ing out, thriving on crisis, glorying in it. Sat back and, with a sigh released, blew her bangs upward.

Nothing had stood still today. Priscilla's hair was shorn up to her ears. At some point, she had razored off the ragtag ends of her home permanent, zzzst zzzst zzzst without hesitation, with barely a glance in the mirror. Her hair hung now from the crown of her head in an uneven circle. Her bright eyes were narrower, her pink cheeks leaner, her harum-scarum movements pared down.

She saw him.

"Oh, there you are. Where you been? Isn't this—"

He thought for a moment she was going to say "marvelous."

"—amazing? You should have been here an hour ago. What's the matter? You mad?"

"No, I'm glad. Jumping with joy."

The women scooped up their children and whisked out of the

room, leaving husband and wife to themselves. The breadwinner was home.

"You're not still mad, are you? Last night you said . . . What's that you got in your hand?"

Priscilla swam up from her typewriter, shaking back her now non-existent curls, radiant, glistening, beautiful.

He was carrying his thermos bottle tucked under his arm and in his hand the andromeda bursting in sprays from its newspaper wrapping. He didn't remember taking it from the car. Ivory bells spilled out of glossy leaves in grapelike clusters, uncrushed, waxen in their perfection.

"A present from Mari," he said shortly, all his fine feelings, his praises gone by the board. "She said to put them in water. They'll last for a month."

He dropped the andromeda on the dresser and gathered clean clothing from drawers and closet. Priscilla pursued him with the missing mate to a sock, ticking off details he already knew.

"Last night you said there was nothing. Now there's so much— We have a minister and a doctor lined up for Pulaski Hall tonight —only I got this damn PTA at school, the budget hearing's next week and the ceilings are falling down on the kids. I have to be there."

Not to be there, it was the supreme defection. Not to be there for whatever reason, withholding the commitment of one's presence.

"So if you'll hold down Pulaski tonight, Mish. We can't rely on Lucas, he's sure to fly off on a tangent. Frances will chair but she's depending on us. Somebody has to see it through."

What did he want of her? What kind of person did he want her to be? Tootsie-wootsie bringing him his beans and his slippers? Pussy on tap? There is no room in a couple for two activists. If one is the dynamo, the other has to be the rock. If one projects, the other protects. Hard enough for Bob and Mari, never resolved. With children in the family it was impossible.

House or plant? Or school? Which was it to be? Even if he

could have put it to her and she would listen, which she wouldn't, it was too late. Everything was in motion.

With his change of clothing folded over his arm he headed for the bathroom. Bostic intercepted him at the door.

"We can weep and we can holler, you know damn well they ain't go'n do nothin'. We're gonna have to beat 'em to it. Figure out for them step by step a plan they can follow. Work out a workable plan for them. Know what I mean?"

He had no idea whether Bostic was referring to the meeting at Pulaski tonight or the meeting at Mari's, to his transfer from Plastics where he didn't belong to Paint where he did or to the protection of his sons' sensitive air passages. Bostic had no faith in any prescriptions but those he himself thought up.

"What's this? What's this?" Priscilla was right on them. "What plan?"

He slid out from between them and locked himself in the bathroom. Standing in the bathtub he soaped down, hair slopping over his eyes, curtains whipping about him, the water hot as he could stand it hitting the back of his neck. The grime washing away, washing down the drain, all of it washing away, washing washing washing.

The door was pounding. "Let me in!" He reached through the curtain and unlocked it. Mistily through the steam, Priscilla with a clean towel and the andromeda in a pickle jar. She turned the key behind her.

"Bostic says Ewell called him about going to Mari's tonight," she shouted above the rush of water. "Why didn't you mention—Turn off the water so I can talk to you! We're not supposed to use the water." She was filling the jar at the sink faucet. "Turn it off!"

He poked his head out through the curtains. Amid the disorder, his discarded clothes on the floor, the jar of flowers on the laundry hamper, Priscilla stood in a flush of perspiration and steam, Joan of Arc with her haircut, consternation and inspiration mixed.

She'd take care of Pulaski. He'd take care of Mari's. Someone else would deliver her PTA report.

His head was cracking open. Stop, stop! Too much too fast. Stop!

"Did Coffin really have you up in his office? Did you really—"

He stopped her with a kiss, stepped out of the bathtub dripping wet and covering her with his naked wetness kissed and kissed; splotching wet hands over her, backing her up against the towel rack, kissed, every marriage is a misalliance; kissed till she kissed back, kissing water-slick shoulders, water-tangled chest hair.

"Ah, Mish, you're you again."

The door was pounding. "Hey in there."

Kissing. Flooded with warmth on warmth.

Doorknob rattled. "Mrs. Lunin, you're wanted . . ."

Kissing.

A croak through the door. "Mrs. Lunin, I'm sorry but that social worker's up here. Snooping."

"Mish, I've got to . . ."

Kissss.

"Mish, you nut, look at me. How can I go out there?" White blouse blobbed with wetness over her breasts, blue skirt darkly splattered. "What'll I tell them? Look at you. Wow."

With an underhanded twist at him and a backhanded twist at the key, she was out the door.

"Tell them you were giving the baby a bath."

3

Tingling, restored, his clean clothes clinging damply to him, he bore the jar of flowering branches into the living room and set it down on the coffee table over a mass of papers. The room was thick with heat and smoke, generated as much from inside as out. The door to the hall stairways was closed now.

Bostic shared a couch with Kochis now, peddling his pet plan. "If we could get Nick Colangelo to get Judge Rinaldi to attack the mayor with this, THEN we'd have something."

"Rinaldi, he'll just use this for a political football," Kochis objected from his pet stance, reality. "You think if we had Rinaldi in office it would be any different?"

"We have to get to the mayor ourselves," Priscilla hammered it out, in pursuit of her obsession. "Get an appointment out of him tomorrow. Thursday at the latest. March on City Hall. That's what has to come out of Pulaski tonight. A showdown with Kearnsey."

At the tripartite windows the massive bonfire beyond the last buildings leaped upward into its own roseate field of cloud, inciting the experts to excited speculation. How long would it take to bring it under control, a day, a week? Wartime fire-bombings, the oxygen could be sucked out of the air creating a vacuum. Evacuation, you'd think they'd evacuate the families down that end. From their distance, not so distant, the fire watchers watched fascinated, spectators before a view, apart from it and one with it, of universal incineration.

It was awful. Dreadful. Intolerable.

"Do you see what I see? See. Down there."

At once they were all at the windows.

"Down, down there. Just below."

Directly below them the city dump trucks, rerouted, were passing down the driveway, an interminable column of green beetles, on their way to discharge their daily load into the dump.

"It's getting late." Unobtrusively he took hold, clearing the premises.

The crowd dispersed for dinner, declining Priscilla's urgent invitations. (She had only a heel of ham in the refrigerator.) Between himself and Bostic and Eddie Kochis padding around shoeless in his white socks, they parceled out the buildings for final coverage to a corps of responsibles, a chain of their kids—let no tenant claim afterward he didn't know about the meeting.

"Now, Bostic," he said.

Bostic elected to go with him to Mari's after dinner. After all, the job comes first.

"Now, Kochis. You going to drive these ladies to the hall later? Or are you going to stay home and watch wrestling?"

The assignment of lining up cars for those lacking a ride was thrust upon Eddie.

"Now, ladies."

Frances and Priscilla were shaking down the program. Keep it simple. Keep it brief. Invocation. Speakers. Open the floor for discussion. Resolutions for action. Proposed organization. Election of temporary officers. Collection. Singing?

"I got ironing this high."

Collecting her children, Frances sailed forth like a pioneer woman out to bring the crop in against hail and locusts.

The living room was empty, a desert of ashtrays.

"She's petrified," Priscilla said as soon as the door was closed. "On the telephone she's great. But the platform . . ."

"That woman's not afraid of anything."

"She exhausted herself here. Her husband's serving a party tonight after work and she has to do up his boiled shirt and his jacket. What do you bet she doesn't show up? He's so jealous of her . . ."

Priscilla's confidence had departed with the company. Frightened at the proportions of what she herself had bodied forth, she stormed about, slapping food together.

"It'll be a fiasco. Everybody has an excuse. Brother's getting married. Sister's getting divorced. This one's on welfare. That one's in the post office. Defense, credit rating . . . The personal always takes precedence over the public. So wrapped up in their own problems they never solve the common problem. Self self self first and foremost."

"You've done all you can, now forget it. There'll be at least a dozen of them there who've had enough experience."

She was at the telephone. She was at the door. Greg and Steph were clamoring.

"What's for dinner?"

"Ham."

Ham for lunch, ham last night, ham the night before. No more ham!

"Why do you say he's jealous? Maybe he's proud of her."

Priscilla paused in the act of tearing open a loaf of bread. She quieted down. A sidelong spark from under the white eyelashes.

"Ah, Mish, can we get together only when . . ."

Her hand flew to her head.

"My hair! Is it awful? I was so exasperated with you when you left, I just hacked. You went out of here like a walking corpse."

This morning the marriage was in ashes. And now?

"Tell me, tell me what happened today!"

He was too busy on the telephone to tell her. She had to gather the gist of it in crumbs.

They were just settling down at the table when the doorbell rang again. No more! Don't answer it! Go away! He opened the door on his father. Groaning for every step he'd had to climb and heaving for every breath he drew, the old man lurched in toting a sack of groceries that towered over his head.

"Whassamatta? What's going on here? How can you stand the stink? Phew phew phew."

Pop plunked his bag of groceries, his reproach and his revenge, down on the kitchen table, scattering bread and plates. He regarded the children with surprise. What were they doing here? Didn't their parents have the sense to get them out of here as fast as they could? He'd have kept them at his place.

Wordlessly martyred, Priscilla began unpacking the bag. She had told Pop a thousand times he could drop in anytime, but this she didn't need tonight. She'd told him he was always welcome to dinner but please not to bring anything. Borscht! That commercial junk, all the vinegar and sugar they put in, that's what was eating out his stomach. Marinated herring! The old man slung his rakish fedora hat on a knob of his chair and Priscilla removed his hat to the hall.

Pop was here, using the dump fire as his pretext, to pressure them yet once more, without ever mentioning it, to quit Tidal

Flats. What was the matter with Joe Barth? Couldn't he take better care of his daughter? And his grandchildren?

Priscilla tossed potatoes into the pressure cooker, intent on serving her father-in-law a regular dinner. Pop protested. What was she cooking? She didn't have to cook. Who needed her cooking? Just open up the can of salmon he'd brought and turn it out on a plate, slice an onion over it. "Potatoes? You know I can't eat potatoes." A new food bug. "Too much starch. Gravy, you're not making gravy, are you? Is there any fat in it?"

"You can't make gravy without fat."

"I can see you're all tied up here. You're in a hurry. I'm going."

"No no no. Sit down, will you? Just sit."

"My God, what have you done to your hair? Priscilla, do me a favor, go to a beauty parlor. I'll give you ten dollars."

"You don't like it? I love it. Why do you buy this kind of cottage cheese? Tastes as if it has flour in it."

And so through dinner Pop and Priscilla each tried to undermine the other's generosity, each of them embarrassed by the obligation to gratitude imposed, Pop attacking through his bounty their insufficiencies and Priscilla defending their sufficiency here and her father's policy of non-interference.

The telephone rang throughout the meal, punctuating their explanations to Pop of what had occurred.

"Shshsh." Priscilla chopped down savagely. "The Shoreham *Tribune*."

"Why do they call here?" Pop grumbled.

"Is it true that Tidal Flats is organizing a Tenants Council? Who the officers are?"

"Why do they ask her?"

"You're the reporter, come down here and find out for yourself. Live here a couple of days."

THIS IS NO WAY TO LIVE!

Mariuch called with her latest report. Ray would have to be picked up. Yvonne was meeting her godmother from Maine at the bus station.

"Now, what? A meeting? Another meeting? The union? The company? Another election?"

HAVEN'T YOU LEARNED YOUR LESSON!

Pop elevated himself from his chair and pointed with his fork across the table. "Who's that?"

Between Steph and Greg stood a little girl calmly stuffing herself with ham and potatoes.

"What's your name, sweetie?"

The little girl hid her face in her hands. Someone had misplaced a child.

The telephone rang. Pop took the telephone out into the hall and thumped it down on the hall table. It rang and rang. No one dared stir. The old man sat back in his chair, fierce as an eagle, his silvery hair, so carefully groomed beforehand, standing up on end.

"Maybe it's her mother." Priscilla jumped up. "I have to . . ."

Priscilla joyous from the hall. "Flo! I tried to reach Joe this morning at the office for some advice and he was out . . ."

Not her husband, not his father, but this her true fount of approval.

"And I tried to reach you. You've no idea . . . No. No, not now —what *is* it? *Tell me what it is* . . ."

It was the telephone call that ended all thought of meetings for the evening. Pulaski Hall, Mari, fires and fury, it was all wiped out. The personal took precedence over the public. They dropped everything. They left the children with Pop and they ran.

II

1

Flo had said that there was nothing to be alarmed about. Joe was having a little trouble lately with his eyesight, headaches, that was all, and Dr. Palmer was sending him up to Sprague Memorial for a checkup. Personally she thought it was fatigue, suppressed too long, asserting itself. A few days' bed rest would do him no harm. She was driving him to Sprague early tomorrow, and he wanted to talk with them before he left. He insisted on it. Joe had spent the afternoon with Eckstrom at Barth Barrel, going over his business affairs—Barth Barrel where he rarely if ever set foot! And he was seeing Boris Kallen now in his study, going over the appeals brief he was preparing for a Supreme Court review of the case. Ted and Gail were due to arrive any minute.

"Nothing seriously wrong, of course not. But I think you should come. He wants you here."

Nothing seriously wrong, but the mind always leaps to the worst, as if by anticipating the worst you can both fortify yourself against it and forestall it.

Nothing to be alarmed about, but the sight of the dingy white laundry truck Boris drove nowadays parked in the driveway at this odd hour, and Ted's little MGA at the curb, sent shocks of alarm coursing through them. He could feel Priscilla's tremor as he slid in behind the MGA. Her face under the jagged bangs was raw with fright.

"She was trying to get through to me for hours and I had the phone so tied up . . . What for? What for?"

"We don't know anything yet. There's no sense . . ."

Priscilla was out of the car ahead of him, racing up the gravel path to the round-arched door with the three slits in it like ascending notes. Up a path that was changing irreversibly under her feet toward her one certainty, a condition of her life, already receding. Joe was always there to catch her if she fell.

She ripped out of her jacket even before she reached the door. His resentment of her—that having her alternatives she chose to live not for herself but for those who had no such alternatives, no such security in the background; and railed against them, self self self, how dared they not live beyond the self as she did for their sake!—faded away. He hurried up the path after her, separated from her by an unbridgeable distance. That long agony which no outsider could ease for her had begun.

The door was unlocked. The tawny paneling of the hall glowed discreetly, dusted by Ruby, the three-days-a-week maid who had been coming in for years, with a wax-dampened cloth. From upstairs, Joe's voice and Boris's resounded, lustily singing in Yiddish to a rhythm thumped out on Joe's desk.

> Lo mir lo mir lo mir trinken
> Ain glezele wine
> Tsuzammen!
> Tsuzammen!

A drinking song that swelled with the vibrant baritone of young men making a night of it.

From somewhere far back in his memory: Boris and Pop in high spirits after a wedding, pounding late night on the kitchen table.

> Lo mir lo mir lo mir trinken . . .

Priscilla stared upward, thunderstruck. The song faltered abruptly on the second *tsuzammen.*

"Poor fellow." Flo beckoned them into the living room. She was speaking of Boris. "Joe's trying to cheer him up. He came here with some idea that Joe was calling him in to beg off from his case. Because of this Stalin thing. Boris has been brooding about it ever since the first reports of it leaked out a month ago. And today when it was confirmed— He's all broken up over it."

"But Joe?" Priscilla demanded. "What about Joe?"

"Joe . . ." Flo was arranging plates and napkins on the low round table before the fireplace. "Ted and Gail are washing up. Have you eaten yet? Are you hungry? There's no sense, ever, in proceeding on anything but the optimum premise, is there? It's quite a while since he's had a thorough physical, which he keeps postponing. He should take some time off away from everything, which he won't allow himself. Maybe better eyeglasses . . . Pris, will you put on coffee?"

"What's the not-so-optimum?"

"We'll meet that when it comes, if it comes," Flo said. "At every stage, as the facts come in, we'll assume the optimum within the range of possibilities and take it from there. Use the drip, Priscilla. Gail prefers it."

"What's this about options?" Ted emerged from the lavatory— off the short passages between living room and kitchen—stripped to the jeans, wiping down.

"Oh, games theory," Gail groaned from behind him. She came out pulling a jumper down over her dance tights. "You set up a model of all your prob-ba-ba-bilistic courses and play them out. Then you never have to live it. Life is the anti-climax."

The Barth living room was normal. White translucent china, gold-banded, and folded, ecru linen napkins on the table before the fireplace, too warm tonight for a fire; legal publications and wild-life and peace appeals piled up on the end tables; framed bird prints on the walls; the ricochet of conversation. And Flo moving firmly among them in her bulky molded shoes, the green pair, and her Liberty print, small green figures swaying over her large-boned hips. In another minute they'd be consuming drinks and salted nuts with Ted and Gail's tidbits of faculty farce.

"You can all go up to Joe together when he's through with Boris."

"Mish, will you make some calls?"

Priscilla, only a little less distraught than she'd been when they arrived, dispatched him to the telephone while she measured out coffee from can to pot. They had left the house too hastily to inform anyone but Kochis next door.

He tried the tenant meeting first. Pulaski Hall, a million light years away, dinned like a grotto with the surf of voices, the scrape of chairs. Lucas, caught on the run, boomed over the wire. Lucas didn't mind their absence one bit. The hall was filling up. Frances Knowlton was there and so was her husband. A self-help brigade was being organized on the spot, listing families willing to take in emergencies overnight. There was talk of stopping the city dump trucks from dumping. . . . Lucas was soaring, no secret cells now. The revolution was on.

Then Mari's house.

Mari exploded. "Where the hell are you? My place is jammed. You CAN'T?!" Then crestfallen. "Oh Jesus. Oh Jesus. Is it bad?" Quickly she recouped, started restructuring. "He'll be just fine up at Sprague. They'll take good care of him. These local yokels— wanted to give me a hysterectomy for a cervical polyp. At Sprague they snagged it out with a scraping. . . . Guess who's here, you'll never guess. Mabley from Hot Rubber," she said, tempting him, whetting his appetite. Mabley was the suspended group leader, an old-timer, knowledgeable, responsible, the kind that every company considers the backbone of its work force and every union considers the backbone of its membership.

"Did you ask him who put that leaflet out?" He was hooked, his numbed interest leaping. "If anybody knows, it's Mabley."

"If he knows, he's not telling. Anyhow it wasn't the steward or the section chairman. They think you did it. Whoever it was, they're not coming out of the bushes."

"Then we've got to keep beating the bushes. Get Mabley to chair tonight if you can. Go as far as you can with what we laid out. Anything you decide tonight," he promised recklessly, "I'll go along with."

"We're voting to form a rank-and-file caucus with you at the head of it," Mari told him and hung up.

With the click of her telephone he knew who had authored the leaflet. It was unlikely, it was unthinkable, it would be denied up and down, and yet . . . It was the only answer that fitted the conditions. It threw the accepted scene into chaos. It opened up such possibilities, fluidities to be coalesced, factors to be aligned, approaches to be broached, resources to be pooled, new combinations . . .

Throbbing with it, a crazy daydream, he traveled the million light years back into the living room.

"It was pretty cloudy up there. Ceiling five thousand feet according to my radio. So I decided to climb above the clouds. Only the cloud didn't stop. It just went on, endlessly."

Ted, stationed before the fireplace was giving an account of his flight lesson this afternoon in his instructor's little blue-and-white Cessna, a test flight, solo. The three women gazed up at him fascinated, as if the flight of the Cessna had the power to hold at bay, at least temporarily, the upstairs room.

"I was flying blind. Visibility zero. And I completely lost my bearings. You can't imagine what it was like. Lost in cloud, utterly disoriented. I didn't know whether I was flying up, down or sideways."

It was not just another anecdote out of Ted's fund of sporting feats, the fiendish grin of dust and glory. Hair slewed over his forehead, collar loose, tie dangling, shirt cuffs falling from his wrists, he had not yet put himself together again. Through the shimmer of his glasses, his eyes were glazed. He held the saucer of his coffee cup with both hands, gripping it with all his nerve, sinew, intelligence.

"Stripped of myself, everything I am, everything I'd ever learned. Useless. Where was the sky, where was the earth?"

The terror and emptiness of that moment clung to him.

"Finally I dropped out of the clouds in a tailspin. Or rather, I discovered I was in descent. I leveled off. I landed."

"But you might have been killed!" Priscilla cried up at him.

"You didn't say a word! You swooped into my dance class and collared me," Gail cried up at him, "and out to the car. Not one word about it all the way down here!"

Right now Ted was lying in a swamp somewhere, a sodden body to be extracted from a tangle of burnt-out fusilage. Search parties out for him, police helicopters, the telephone here in the hall jangling.

"I was all shook up when I got out. Jensen, my instructor, walked up and took one look at me, and he said, *'You have been there.'*"

Jensen piled him at once into another Cessna. An instruction plane, fully automatic, all the controls, gauges and so forth, practically tells you what you're doing.

" *'Fly strictly according to the instruments.'* "

The plane was equipped with special windows. A grain, Ted supposed, in the glass. He was supplied with special goggles. He went up again, shaking. Jensen radioed him from the tower to put on his goggles. Through them, the window glass looked just like a mirror.

"I flew for a while strictly by instrument. Then I knew there was something wrong. I knew it wasn't going right. I was absolutely certain. So I began to straighten out. And Jensen radioed me from the tower.

" *'Take off your goggles.'* "

He had the plane upside down, in another tailspin, heading for the ground.

"When I fell into the shack I was walking on my knees. There was your call in from Shoreham for me to call back."

Flo plucked at a fold in her cheek where no fold existed, her flat-planed face ageless in its plainness.

"You mean," she said to Ted slowly, absorbing it, "that you couldn't exercise your judgment? You couldn't rely on the evidence of your senses?"

" 'You fly strictly according to the instruments,' Jensen said to me."

"But if the instruments are wrong?"

" 'If those instruments are wrong,' Jensen said to me, 'you're gone.' "

"Are you saying that you surrender yourself completely?" Gail uncoiled herself from the sofa and arched upward to her feet. "You're nil? The controls are everything?"

"You are controlled by the controls," Ted said. With a brittle gesture he straightened his glasses. "You are governed by the objective realities. Not your subjective reactions."

"Why that's the worst thing I ever heard of in all my life!"

Buttoning his cuffs, Ted wandered off to the corner of the bookshelves where the reference works were stored. At the table they silently gathered up the dishes, disturbed by eddies of meaning that eluded them. Up, down or sideways? Everything? Nothing?

"And after a while," Gail called after Ted in an access of private intensity, between the two of them, "you begin to feel like the instruments? Instrument of the instruments? Is that it?"

Shuddering in her sweaty black leotard, Gail picked up and handled, fondled, each piece before placing it in the tray to go out to the kitchen. She stroked over the pewter beaker Flo had used as a cream pitcher, lip and belly. Snapped open the lid and sniffed inside. Held it up to the light, grayly luminous, her mouth outpouted and her hand belly-curved.

"As long as I'm alive, *I* am the center of the universe. *My* perceptions. *My* emotions. *My* responses."

"Sure." Ted crouched over the circle of encyclopedias he had opened on the floor. "The old saw. If a tree struck by lightning falls in a jungle at midnight, did it fall?"

"What are you doing? Just what in God's name are you doing?" In one continuous movement from table to Ted, Gail was bending over him, appalled. "What are you looking up there? Facts? Formulas? Anything, anything to keep from feeling! This is your *father*, Ted. This is *Joe*."

"Gail, we're all under tension—"

"All of you, at it at it at it. Is it Joe you're concerned about or is it that case up there in his study? Can't you be *still* for a minute? Let yourselves *feel*? Mish, give me a penny."

Mystified, he gave her a penny. The woman baffled him. He could never tell whether she was seeking his sympathy, allying herself with him or making fun of him. She never even looked the same to him twice in succession. Now pallid, her dusky hair drooping down her back, tied with a limp black ribbon, colorless, hands palely reaching out of her tight black sleeves.

She flipped the coin over on her wrist. "Heads or tails? What's your bias, Mish? Which is it for you ninety times out of a hundred? Sixty? We'll feed you into a variable equation. What outcome follows what choice?"

"Ted, will you help Gail with the tray?" Flo said. "Just unload into the dishwasher. Pris, bring me a whisk broom." Priscilla, frozen between her idolized brother and his ideal wife, had to be nudged out of the room. "There are crumbs all over this sofa. Mish, the books."

Pages and paragraph headings starkly exposed.

Cerebral cortex, physiology of.

Eye, neuropathology of.

Tumors, clinical diagnosis of.

Swiftly closed. Back to the shelves in alphabetical order.

Flo, joining him in the corner to help with the books, had a rational explanation for everything. Gail was upset, she'd had another miscarriage last month. Ted too was upset. It looked as if he might be passed over again this year for a full professorship. The Laski of his generation adrift among Keynesians.

"They keep moving him away from political economy into courses in business economics, industrial planning . . ."

"But Joe?" he asked her, now that she was alone with him. Flo had a tendency to confide things to him sometimes that she kept from the rest of the family, as if with him she could be free or as if with him it didn't matter. "Is there more to this—"

"We don't know. A slight blurring in his right field of vision. Headaches. Maybe just a passing phase, something easily correctable. Sometimes," she acknowledged, reflecting on it aloud, "he remembers things that happened long ago as if it were yesterday. And things that happened yesterday . . ."

Boris tramped downstairs. Immediately they all rushed into the hall. Boris, rugged as a brick, burnt-orange, eyes snapping, two-fisted, always throwing this and that together, always a step ahead of you, groped along the bannister taking the bottom turn in the stairs, ashen, stooped, the pinpoint glint in his eye of a man who suffers a consuming disease which he conceals from the knowledge of others. He rekindled at the sight of them.

"The whole family together."

For Boris that said all that there was to be said.

Flo walked Boris to the door, troubled. "Did Joe tell you . . ."

Joe had told Boris that he was taking a week off with Flo, and Boris wished Flo a good time.

In the reverberation of Boris's departure the four of them pulled themselves upstairs. Flo remained below. The green stair carpeting was worn white over the treads. Flo had talked about replacing it last fall. It wasn't like her to let the carpeting go.

2

"There is no Birobijan."

Flesh crept. Scalp crawled. The heart lurched, ruptured.

"A wilderness. A burning plain. A frozen waste. A swamp. In the basin of the middle Amur. On the other side of nowhere. The edge of hell."

Joe pivoted about from his desk, glass in hand, greeting them. The face was the face of Joe but the voice was the voice of Boris.

"In the city of Borisov in White Russia he worked in a match factory with a bog behind it. At night they met in the woods. They knew that one of them might be an informer. They knew they might be caught. They knew what the penalty was. And still they went. He was ten years old."

It wasn't a glezele wine Joe was pouring for himself. It was the family brandy, produced on festive occasions. They distributed themselves around the study, on the couch, the floor.

"Of the people he had left in Europe only one survived the Holocaust. A cousin, a partisan, a hero who had stood up under the Pilsudski dictatorship in Poland and then the Germans. A few years ago the cousin wrote to him from Lodz. 'Get me out of here!' Boris couldn't understand it. With all that behind him, all the political persecution and imprisonment, now he wants to quit? Had he perhaps come into conflict with the party leadership? Did he perhaps after all harbor bourgeois aspirations? Was it perhaps that the new Polish regime being in need, understandably, of educating Catholic Poland to socialism was giving preference, understandably, to Polish Catholics for the very purpose of overcoming the anti-Semitic lag? He never heard from his cousin again.

"Mish, you know Boris. You see what I'm getting at?"

Yes, he knew Boris.

His own mother and father had quarreled all their married life. One could scarcely utter a word without being contradicted by the other. A window shade couldn't be raised without provoking a clash, should it be up or down. Boris and Mary Kallen quarreled over politics. Boris subscribed to the *Freiheit*. Mary subscribed to the *Forward*. Boris sent their daughter Elisabeth to the schule, where she learned Yiddish. Mary sent their son Carl to cheder, where he learned Hebrew. Mary hung a pushke on her kitchen doorpost, a blue can with a gold Star of David on it, into which she pushed her spare pennies for the founding of a Jewish homeland in Palestine. Boris collected funds for miners in West Virginia and miners in the Asturias and finally for Birobijan, a homeland in far eastern Siberia for those Soviet Jews who might wish to settle there, rich in iron and tin to be mined, limestone and marble to be quarried, grasslands to be cultivated, forests to be cut. One night at the height of one of their quarrels, Boris tore the pushke down from the kitchen doorpost. Pawns of British imperialism! Opponents of their Arab brothers! Petty bourgeois nationalists! Not in his house! Mary ripped open a set of posters he had sent for to advertise a choral concert and tore the posters to shreds. Over their differences they turned into wolves. Their two children ran upstairs to the Lunins swollen with weeping. . . . Yet the two children grew up bright and ambitious, the pride of their parents.

Overthrow the government of the United States? Boris never fought the government. He fought his wife. With Boris it was all words. Marvelous words. Rainbows.

Nothing could break Boris. His wife reviled him with her last breath. His son, Carl, moved away from him to California and changed his name to Collins and every cent he made over subsistence went to the psychoanalyst. His daughter, Elisabeth, to whom he had been so close, was married to an embassy official in Ankara and didn't dare write to him, even through relatives. He had been ousted from his occupation. The organizations he had devoted himself to were liquidated. He was ordered out of the country and he would have gone but for the mandate imposed on him by the deportation order. He had to defend the political freedom for which he had come to America from the forces that would curtail and destroy it.

No matter what happened to Boris, he could endure it all. Because it wasn't for himself, it was for others. It was for that land where already, demonstrably, class and national animosities had been eliminated, where all cultures, fully developed in their distinctions, dwelt in equality. It was for such a land everywhere, for the world of his children's children and their children, a legacy larger than wealth.

It was for the Truth and for the Truth they schmeiss you, that's to be expected. But when the Truth turns out not to be true?

Rainbows.

Hogwash.

"Yes," he said to Joe, "I know Boris. I understand what you mean; I talked to Mariuch today and she still can't take it in, she won't. But what you're driving at—?"

"He believed," Joe said. "He really believed. What's that song you used to sing, Priscilla? Auntie drives the tractor. Grandma runs the cream extractor. He fell for it, goddamit. The whole bit.

Zhan zhan. And you know what hurts him the most? That he was a fool. That he was proved the fool. All the lies and the murders, all the horrors and the loss, it was all his fault. He was a sentimental sap, a crackpot. . . ."

Ted hunched forward from the couch, intent on his father's every word. Any sign? Any symptom? Gail lounged on the floor, all black arms and legs, hitching about in confusion. What's this Boris business! Priscilla sank back against the couch cushions all but fainting with relief. Joe was all right.

"I advised Boris that he could take the opportunity now to cop a plea, on grounds of disillusionment. Make a deal with the prosecution in exchange for the withdrawal of his deportation order. Agree to furnish a little info which they indubitably already have. Cooperate.

"Boris wouldn't hear of it. He's lost his pride and his virtue. He can never again speak with any authority. But he still believes. In every single thing he believed in before, except that it doesn't yet exist."

Joe unlatched the corner cupboard and brought out four shot glasses, unstoppered the decanter and poured, spilling just a trifle.

"If he'd been more sophisticated, if he'd recognized that here were two power blocs engaged in conflict for global hegemony, if he'd simply chosen one over the other and cast his lot with it no matter what perversion of purpose might occur in the course of realpolitik and human proclivities, would he be any better off than he is now? I wonder.

"The truth is, in the bottom of his heart Boris never believed at all. He knew what every Jew knows and rebels against. That there is no spot on the face of the earth he can call his own. All Boris has is his own stubbornness."

Joe passed the shot glasses around to them, just a trifle unsteady.

"Now he's stuck with his deportation and I'm stuck with his appeal for review. He's still denying he falsified his application for citizenship. And I'm still arguing that ancient issue: Constitutional rights are not to be abridged for the non-citizen in any proceeding, including the application for citizenship. From the very beginning I knew that this was my case.

"At any point it may be thrown back into the lower courts and smeared all over the front pages again. Next time, Mish, you may be subpoenaed. And you, Ted, you're not that immune from the aftereffects even at this late date. And I can assure you it's just as fatal to be shot by the last bullet in a battle as the first."

Joe was having his fun with them, teasing, testing, putting them through their paces.

They held their glasses, disconcerted, waiting for his toast, swishing the brandy about, a fruity vapor that went to their heads. Joe, pursuing his flights of paradox, wasn't ready yet for his drink.

"Without belief the Communists might never have accomplished as much as they did. With belief they were fools. Their chief contribution in this country has been their ability to project major social issues and mobilize support around them. We'll miss that. And the chief contribution of the anti-Communists has been —their anti-Communism.

"Holy Innocents. True Believers. And you want to know something? I believed a little bit too. We all did. Even the most rabid antis.

"Now you see what I'm driving at? Now do you understand? Mish, you know."

Yes, he knew now. All too well. He sat on the floor at Priscilla's feet, his back against her legs, afraid to look around at her. What she had refused to accept from him, over and over to the verge of breakup, her father was telling them now. It's gone, it's past, it's done with.

"What happens when the dream becomes a nightmare? When the heavenly city turns into the city of dreadful night? Don't underestimate the impact of all this. On the political direction, internationally. Here at home. The Left in disarray. The Right riding high. The corporations in control. Militarization on the march.

"It'll take another ten years to absorb it, if not more."

"Belief!" Ted snorted, unable to restrain himself another minute. "What's belief got to do with it? When faced with the task of feeding a population, organizing a viable means of production and distribution, the revolutionaries in the classic manner began cannibalizing themselves.

"Now the truth is out. Now the air is cleared. Good! No more heretical hairsplitting. No belief, no faith, no stars in our eyes. No utopian delusions. We take a good hard look at the status quo, where it needs changing, how to change it. Within the context of a proliferating technology, complexities so vast . . ."

Joe lifted his glass, the small liquid quivering.

"Next year in Jerusalem!"

They drank, tossing off the family brandy, the Barth family joke.

"Is that what you brought us here for? To catch us up on Boris? It's sad of course, it's tragic but— All that will count in the end is that Russia made the first attempt at complete socialization, however imperfect. And so long as there is imperfection, the revolutionary cycle continues: institutionalization above, ferment below, upheaval, chaos, consolidation, institutionalization. Boris is just an incidental casualty."

"Boris? Who was talking about Boris?" Joe said in the voice of Boris. "What Boris? When Boris? Mish, tell them."

"He wasn't talking about Boris," he said from his place on the floor, the bottom of the well, laying his head against Priscilla's knees, afraid to look up at her. "He never mentioned Boris. He's talking about us."

"Art is long and so is history," Joe said to them. "Life is short. You have to live."

3

Joe had called them together to broach a plan to them, his plan for them, which he had been harboring for months. Prompted by his visit to Dr. Palmer in the morning or by the prospects of the Kallen case or by Stalin unveiled, he felt he had to present it to them at once. And he wished them to accept it at once, tonight, on his say-so. He had gone into all the aspects of it thoroughly during the time at his disposal, and he was satisfied that no alternative was possible for them. Yet with circumlocutions, soliloquies, reminiscences, he put off explaining it to them.

Joe was animated. He was eloquent. He was puckish. He appeared vigorous, tanned from the weekend afternoons he spent at the Bay Point marina calking his skiff. He scratched his back hair up over his bald dome. He pulled at his ear. He twiddled his nose. He diddled with the girls.

"At my age every minor malady brings with it intimations of mortality." He took the girls into his lap. "Next time you cut your hair," he said to Priscilla, "save a little for me? And that union suit of yours," he said to Gail, "pee-oo. Go on." He threw them back at their husbands. "You got me all hot and bothered."

Joe joked about the brandy. The brandy was Joe's quintessential joke.

Joe's mother had been among other things an advocate of Total Abstinence. She had barnstormed about the country at one time denouncing Demon Rum. If only the millworkers would stop spending their all on drink, beating their wives, starving their little children, and turn their minds instead to improving their lot! And what was Barth Barrel manufacturing then? Brandy casks, the finest California white-oak cooperage. Whisky barrels, beer butts, tuns for Barbados rum.

Prohibition almost ruined them. When Fred Eckstrom took charge of the plant in the early thirties, he asked Joe if he should go on with the manufacture of barrels for the liquor trade. Joe said no, no more barrels. Eckstrom was a metal man. He bought used steel drums from service stations and adapted the Barth installations and the Barth work crew to renovating them for resale. Barth Barrel had done quite well with the renovated steel drums, especially during the Second World War. But if they had stayed with the barrels for the liquor trade!

Joe was breaking out the last of his father's brandy, a domestic distillation aged in the wood for over forty years. Fruity in the nostrils, wry on the tongue, it slid down their throats with a golden glow.

"You better watch that stuff," Ted said to Joe as he refreshed his glezele.

"When a rich man gets drunk," Joe replied in the voice of Boris, savoring it on his tongue, "he's having a good time. When a poor man gets drunk, he's a bum. Remember that."

Amid laughter Flo tiptoed to the door and beckoned.

"Mish. I'm not interrupting anything important, am I? Your father called. I told him you'd call back."

Firmly she piloted him past her bedroom telephone down to the hall below. She hovered over him while he dialed. "Has Joe told you yet," she whispered, "what he wanted you here for?"

"Well—no." He pondered, searching back for hints, clues, in Joe's habitual leaping from tangent to tangent that sometimes turned out not to be tangential at all, every brick in place. "I don't think so."

"He's talking a great deal."

"Well—yes. He's always a great talker."

Pop was in a dither. "How is he?"

"He's all right. He's fine."

"I don't feel so hot myself."

Give Pop a set of symptoms, he'd assume them all.

What Pop wanted was to take the children from Tidal Flats and put them to bed at his house.

"This smoke. I can't open a window. I can't breathe."

Over the wire, a wheeze dredged up out of the depths of the bronchial tubes, such a wheeze as penetrates the walls of apartments in the stillness of the night, a cough racking and rattling, raking up out of spongy tissues a slug of phlegm to be expelled.

"I got emphysema."

"Then why are you going to a heart specialist for it? Okay, okay, take them."

With mingled exasperation and guilt, guiltily resenting the exasperation inspired in him, he cut his father off. Flo was still hovering by.

"If you try to stop him from talking so much," she whispered, following him to the foot of the stairs, "you can't. He'll just quote Boris at you. *Don't tell a pauper to economize.*"

He paused at the stairs and embarrassed by a flood of affection tentatively touched her freckled arm.

"Flo, what is it? There's something more to this— What are you holding back from us?"

"Nothing. Not a thing, really. He's a bit of an actor, you know." She beamed at him and gave his hand a little pat of reassurance. "He can put on quite a performance."

Upstairs he paused at the door of the study, the familiar study all cozy and golden in the parchment-shaded lamplight. Nothing had changed during his absence. The orange-backed files, labeled and dated in white ink, going back more than a hundred years, lined the shelves. The etching of Shoreham harbor, hand-colored by the bone-collared maiden in the oval frame, hung over the glass-paneled bookcase containing old-time publications that would eventually be consigned to a library. The desk with its ledge of pigeonholes in back, was strewn with papers over and under the glass top that covered the writing surface. The desk jutted out to the doorway, leaving barely enough space for passage past Joe's chair into the room.

Joe was surrounded by mementos of a family who, he liked to claim, relishing his putdown of Johnny-come-latelies, had beaten Karl Marx by a century or two, the true sons of Jamestown and Plymouth. He could quote by the yard from his files. "The promise of democracy can be realized only through an equitable division of wealth." "In our classless society"—sic!—"there are two classes: the propertied and the propertyless." "The whole system of labour for wages is wrong, an accursèd system." "Anything short of the abolition of capitalism is useless."

Beside the window, above his desk: a plaster death mask of Josiah Barth the peripatetic cooper, eyelids drooping in a repose that could never have been his in life. On the opposite side of the window: a bronze medallion, green-tinged black, commemorating a world peace congress convened in Brussels in 1848 by Josiah's closest friend and associate, Elihu Burritt, the learned blacksmith. On the back ledge of the desk: the white marble bust, slightly yellowed about the earlocks, of Annie Barth Lowe of the Hillcrest Farm Phalanx, communitarian and crusader for universal rights.

Under the glass desk top, Joe's favorite among the items Flo salvaged from the barrels in the attic of the old Barth residence: a browned handbill of the mid-1830s, calling the masses to rally against a judge—"those drones who fatten on our blood"—for his verdict—"conspiracy to riot"—pronounced upon twenty-some journeymen seeking higher pay. Behind the glass panels of the bookcase, under lock and key, redolent of mildew and the mildew preventive Flo regularly inserted: a collection of periodicals published by girl cotton spinners, crying out their enslavement and rebellion.

Inside the orange-backed files on the bottom row of the open shelves opposite the desk: a miscellany of correspondence and news clippings, records of forgotten organizations, fund appeals, circulars. Account books of a Shoreham Trades Assembly. Minutes of the first convention of a Federated Coopers Union. An attack by the Locofocos on the Banks and the Money Power. A declaration of independence by mechanics and farmers "from both old parties." Workingmen's associations, leagues for factory reform, lyceums. A land cooperative in Pennsylvania, a producers' cooperative in Ohio, a consumer cooperative in Illinois.

"Where is it all now? How did it disappear?" he once asked Joe in amazement. Countless ventures founded on brotherly love, the communal vision, self and society united, one for all and all for one! Foundering on ungrateful soil, ungentle climate. Lack of training, lack of markets, cut-price competition. Internal dissension, external pressures. The ascendancy of commerce and industry, private accumulation, every man for himself!

It was all still here, according to Joe. Seedlings stamped out time and again whose roots time and again sent up new shoots.

On the upper shelves, in orderly progression: the relics of the Reverend Theodore Barth, mainly speeches and sermons delivered during the time of labor unrest in the 1870s, the anarchist agitation in the 1880s, the anti-imperialist campaign in the 1890s against annexation of Hawaii and the Philippines. And the public and private papers of Joe's father, starting in 1902 with a proposal for uniting the trade union struggle for economic gain with the socialistic struggle for overthrow of the wage system. "Between his advocacy of revolutionary aims," Joe would comment, "and his espousal of the electoral process in order to achieve them, he never quite pulled it together. And neither have I."

In the tall steel file by the couch, in the top drawer: Joe Barth's memorabilia of the socialist-oriented Independent Labor Party which he helped found in Shoreham some thirty years ago and which on his insistence repeatedly ran Roderick Kearnsey for mayor, a socialist-minded member of the carpenters' union, rather than the middle-class attorney who was after all merely a sympathizer. "We put Rod out front," Joe would point out when Priscilla grew contentious over what might have been. "He took the hidings. I just stumped for him."

Somewhere along the line, probably when the cooperage became a thriving business, the Barths had made the transition from brotherhood to philanthropy. But the question in this family—Joe would say, allowing time for a tale or two out of school on uplifters of the downtrodden—always remained the same. How did they choose to live? For themselves alone or with concern for the good of all? Self-supremacy personal, racial, national? Or human fellowship?

In this cramped study the dry husks of a once green and limitless continent.

Nothing had changed in this room since he went downstairs to the telephone. Joe sweeping along and the others lost in perplexity, Priscilla's face as blank as a baby's. Lingering in the doorway and scanning the room, seeing it as pleasant as ever with its predominant browns and touches of color, the volumes tightly stowed in their shelves, the sailcloth-covered couch under the sailcloth-curtained back window snugly inset between bookcase and steel file, he had a glimmer of why Joe was taking so long to speak his mind. Looking around him, looking down the road he had traveled for decades, centuries, Joe, for the first time in his life, was unsure of his bearings. Joe never made the smallest practical decision without wrapping it up in the appropriate abstraction. It was no small decision he had come to now.

"... adrift without purpose. What were those slogans we used to shout? *One big union!* Well, now we have it. What were those songs we used to sing? *The international working class shall be the human race.* Will it? Here the labor movement invests its funds in the very bonds that guarantee perpetuation of the system. Abroad it comes up with no shining alternatives. Socialism itself may be untenable. The operation of industry by the state too cumbersome. The exercise of power too coercive when concentrated on top, too ineffectual when dispersed below.

"UV may be as good as we can get. Right, Mish?"

Startled, he detached himself from the doorway and squeezed past Joe's chair to his place on the floor among the legs. The workers had botched it again. The common man had failed the faith. Whatever he had brought into this family—a medium for Priscilla, a resource for Ted, a living proof to Joe and Flo of their innate decency—was now no help but a drag.

"Come on, Mish, don't look so surprised." Gail lying back against the bookcase poked him with her black-sheathed toe. "You've just been deposed from your pedestal, that's all."

Ted and Gail, Mish and Pris, a foursome once, an aura about them, the cosmos can be yours! Then the shrinkage set in, no more cosmos. They didn't see each other much or go out together ever any more.

"No, no, let me finish. Let me get this out."

Imperviously Joe plowed through Priscilla's protestations, "I don't understand, you can't mean . . ." and Ted's impatience to pinpoint the fallacy, "Songs! Slogans! If you apply the proper measurements to input-output, then centralized planning . . ."

"... smack up against a failure that raises all kinds of doubts. Did we start off on the wrong foot to begin with, on the wrong road, in the wrong direction, and persist in it, bigger fools than Boris? Our trust in scientific progress, reason, the nature of man—?

Men are too diverse to submit themselves for very long to any cooperative effort, with the possible exception of war.

"A dead end. Everything we ever gave our energies to at a dead halt. I have seen the future and it doesn't work! That's where you are now. That's what you're stuck with. Humanity, what's that? A sick gag. Individualism rampant—me first and devil take the hindmost! The individual depersonalized, fragmented, alienated—there's your vocabulary. We've been through these periods before.

"How do you survive it? How do you function between a day that's gone and another that hasn't yet dawned? What's your recourse?

"You retire like Henry Wallace to your farm," Joe said to them, "to raise a better chicken. Or you die like Einstein wishing you'd been a plumber."

Joe had finished. He put on his glasses and, stooping, tugged at the lower left drawer of his desk.

"Joe, what are you talking about!"

Priscilla came to life with a rapid-fire rendition of all the excitement they'd been through in the past few days, the scene at Tidal Flats, the circus in Switch, Coffin's summons to his office. A popular uprising on the brink.

"Tell him, Mish!"

Joe paid her no attention. Straining at the drawer, he pulled it out full length. "Mish, you're the closest, will you help me get at this?"

"You can't keep making adjustments in an illogical structure." Ted too came to life. "When I came back here in '46, labor was going full steam ahead. That rally for the UV strikers in Liberty Square—we climbed up on the fountain, Mish— If only it had kept moving ahead! You had your union recognition. You had your collective bargaining. You won your big strike. And there you stopped in your tracks!" Ted cried out at him with sudden bitter accusation. "Everything changed. You tangled yourselves up in your job ratings—your contractual gains—your 5 per cent increase this year and 2 per cent next—how many paid holidays—"

In back of the manila folders in the drawer, one of those deep drawers that take the place of two, a gray, grained metal box had been jammed in, about the size of a cashbox, but much heavier he discovered when he started lifting it out, fireproofed. He heaved it up on Joe's desk, Joe brushing papers out of the way.

"Now look, you guys—"

He was suddenly shouting. The whole lot of them so righteous and comfortable, ensconced on their rosy-posy little pile of archives, with no conception, none whatsoever, not even Priscilla with her modicum of experience and the expansive glow in which she enshrined it, of what went into the job, his job, any good machine job. He clutched his head, going crazy with it—a morass of shop mathematics, charts, tables, formulas, blueprints and Rube Goldberg drawings, machining methods, the cutting qualities of copper, brass, steel, alloys galore. He dug his knuckles into his eyes—the concentration on close tolerances, a parade of forgings and castings, irregularly shaped parts. He held his hands out before him, clawed out—the tons of stock handled, the ingenuity required in complicated setups and layouts, the selection of feed and speed, the devising of tooling. Precautions against jam-ups that would damage equipment and product. The unavoidable hazards, flying chips, dropped clamps, eye injuries, burns and cuts, crushed hands, toes. Under working conditions described on the company point-rating sheet as: "Good. Slightly dirty. Usual machine shop noise."

Joe was having trouble inserting his key into the lock of his box. He squinted at the keyhole sidewise, sighted on it, removed his glasses and vigorously wiped them. He took the key from Joe and rammed it in.

"Everything's changed? Nothing's changed!" Bursting out, he was right back in his quarrel with Priscilla over the past weeks, only now in reverse. "Nothing! Not a goddam thing. Myself, the other fellow—Ewell, Bostic, Mari, Rita— All I know is, we go to work every day, we put the work out. And no matter how much we earn, no matter what benefits we win, we're still in the same spot. We make what UV makes its money out of. And we own nothing, neither the machines we work nor the materials we work on nor the stuff we turn out. Not even the labor of our bodies—we've sold that away. Nothing's changed. It's all the same—"

"You stopped at the bargaining table! You never advanced to the next stage. You never asked for a piece of the action. You never demanded your just share in the government—"

"Mish, Mish, what's the matter with you? Ted!" The girls tore at them and they shook them off.

"There is no union contract," he answered Ted evenly, "that isn't based on the premise, the works belongs to the company. If it's ever to be any different, it'll take another type of organization to lead the fight. You show us something better—"

Bob Ucchini had tried it. Joe Barth had tried it. How many others?

The spasm passed. They were both saying the same thing.

"So UV owns you hand and foot, is that it?" Joe said. "And yet when Coffin offered you something better today you wouldn't take it. May I ask why not?"

He was flabbergasted. After all they knew of him, after what he'd been all these years . . .

"Splendid," Joe said. "Just what I wanted to hear. You had to be your own man. You had to have your independence."

And Joe opened his gray, grained metal box.

4

In the next half hour Joe disclosed the plan he had been nursing along, unable to bring himself before to mention it to them. Even now, cushioning about the pressure he exerted with a persuasive rationale, he was reluctant to deliver what amounted to a body blow: his tacit recognition of their impotence.

Joe took out of his box the deeds to a tract of land he owned on Hilltop Road in Hillcrest, made out last December to his son and his daughter. Roughly five acres, more than enough under the two-acre zoning out there for two homesites. With land in

Hillcrest valued at about five thousand an acre and going up, they'd have sufficient base for financing construction, Mish on the GI Bill and Ted on FHA, at costs of, say, twenty thousand. The accumulated income from Aunt Harriet's trust, which hadn't been touched, should cover furnishings. Miss Keane at the office would give them a list of small retailers from whom they could obtain credit and discounts.

"You know lawyers. A lawyer always has someone on the string owing him something. J&G can have a crew there for you this spring. George Raleigh at Mechanics Savings, if you need any cash before your loans come through—"

They regarded one another with consternation. Hillcrest, a village about eight miles north of Shoreham, was a bulwark of conservatism, of old Shoreham wealth tucked away on back-road estates and new wealth taking refuge from the income tax levies of neighboring states. In the Hillcrest country store, no chain markets yet, the tang of vinegar and spices, of vanished kegs and bins, permeated shelves, bags, even packaged foods. The country club had only recently admitted its first Roman Catholic, an Italian physician active in Shoreham politics.

"N-n-now Joe," Ted, reduced to stuttering, interrupted him, "th-the university is sixty miles away."

"That's right. Too far to drive. Too close to fly."

"But, Joe, I told you before," Priscilla reminded him, "when we had to move from Prince Street, there's nothing for us in Hillcrest. It's a regular management compound."

"Good. You'll have a good school system then."

Hillcrest was the least of it.

"Barth Barrel."

The one thing in his life Joe never wanted to think about, that he had tried to ignore and forget and thrust out of his consciousness, that he alluded to only on rare occasion, humorously, the family skeleton in the closet.

"A good sound enterprise. Has kept us afloat for over six generations. Except for that time back in '30 when I had to pull Eckstrom in. Now in the last few years it's begun to slide again. The plant needs modernization. The equipment should be automated. Up-to-date costing—Fred carries the books in his head—and some effort to find new customers, perhaps a judicious infusion of outside funds— It can be made to pay for itself, for the employees and for you.

"Mish, you'd go in as the inside man handling production. Ted can go in as the outside man handling the business. The perfect symbiotic relationship. I've already spoken with Eckstrom about it. He'll break you in."

Instantly, regarding one another with alarm, they rejected it.

Gail elevated her spine from the floor, on her elbows. "Barrels? You want Ted to give up what he's doing to run a barrel factory?"

"Steel drums," Ted corrected her. "Reconditioned steel drums."

"Oh, steel drums." Gail was slightly mollified. "You mean like in Haiti. In Port-au-Prince I used to sleep on the veranda and all night long through the blinds—" Her father or mother, one of the triplex parental marriages. "From out there in the country somewhere—" She rose to her knees, clapping to the beat. "The steel drum bands. *Dam*boula, *dam*boula, *dam*boula—"

"No, not like Haiti," Ted corrected her. "Like here. Trash cans."

Ted was profoundly humiliated. How large his eyes were behind the glasses, how long his eyelashes . . . The doctoral dissertation designed ambitiously to affect the political thinking of the decade —that sank from view without a ripple after the initial accolades. The painstaking trend studies, published in professional journals, on the three Marxian theses: "the declining rate of profit"—when obviously to the professionals profits were on the climb; "the impoverishment of the working class"—when wages were never higher; "the proletarianization of the bourgeoisie"—when it was the proletariat that was becoming bourgeois. The book manuscript that stayed two years on an editor's desk, always encouraged, until it was returned. The call to a Canadian university offering a full professorship and succession to chairmanship of the department, the contract following his interview to be mailed within the next few days . . . that never came.

Still Ted might have made it. If he had been content to confine his theorizings, controversial though they were, to his lectures and writings. If he hadn't descended from the ivied tower to the committee room and involved himself in controversial activities, none of which he regretted. The Progressive Party, now defunct, an Academic Freedom Committee, now disbanded, a conference on East-West trade.

Ted was disappointed but not defeated. He had like his forebears his beehive of correspondents, exchanging observations and critiques. He kept abreast of innovation, the opportunities for more exact prognostication opened up by computer processing. He was teaching a course this year in statistical inferences. A colleague, in psychology, was taking him along on industrial consultation trips, one to Texas at the end of this week. He was being considered for a visiting lectureship at Upsala next fall, and he was already scheduling flying side trips for himself to East and West Germany, Yugoslavia, Italy, to gather data on a single type of production, yet to be selected, under different forms of economy. He had applied to the State Department for a research grant for the purpose, why not? Gail didn't think that he was going to Upsala or anywhere else and he knew that this was what she thought. He went right on with his preparations.

Above all, Ted remained to his family the great man who was to be, his trials and tribulations being the sure evidence of one on the road to glory. Not that he was so sure of it himself. It was the fact of their expectation that sustained him.

Joe punctured the illusion. By his awareness, he confirmed those painful wounds Ted would not let himself feel before. After eight years at the university he was an assistant professor without tenure and with no immediate prospect of advancement.

"Not just trash cans," Joe corrected Ted. "Fifty-five gallon containers for bulk shipment of paint, grease, iron filings, copper scrap, powders, solvents, liquids, gels, all kinds of chemicals. You take a small and necessary job and perform it with competence, without pretension, at a fair return for your efforts, what's wrong with it? Ted, you were never satisfied to be the pure intellectual. You were always caught between two poles, thought and action, and instead of supplementing each other, the two canceled each other out. That's where you got your lumps. Mentally you always needed the physical and particular. Now here it is. Pick it up and see what you can do with it."

"I suppose it was the most egregious arrogance—" Ted removed his glasses and rubbed at a redness in the corner of his eye, a prickle of dust or an incipient stye. "What one might have become under other circumstances. . . . To put it in its kindest light, let's just say I stopped at a lower level. A case of arrested development."

"You can continue with your writing. This may serve as a catalyst—"

Rubbing his eye, Ted left the room, a boy of thirty-seven, and went into the bathroom and turned on a loud gush of water. Gail sprang up from the floor.

"You don't know what he's been through! You don't know what it means to see someone dry up year after year. Even his babies—" She pounded at her sides. "You don't know what it does to the husband to see his wife go through—"

She ran out after Ted.

Priscilla stirred up from the couch to follow them and Joe motioned her back.

"Mish will talk to them," Joe said to her. "Mish will talk them around. You'll have something that's yours," Joe said to him. "With what you've learned at UV—"

He shook his head. He wanted it no more than Ted did. Apprehensively he glanced back up over his shoulder at Priscilla. She sat with her legs tucked under her, her lean form limp, her pink face puffy, a blob. Traumatized like Boris, floundering in a quagmire, disintegrating.

"With a little success under you, you'll be surprised how attitudes toward you will change. You'll be so much more effective than you are now. Any social contribution you want to make, don't worry, there's always plenty of opportunity—"

He kept shaking his head at Joe. "Joe, please. Joe, no. It's not I don't appreciate, I do—"

"At the last ditch there's only one thing that counts. To have the means. To be able to *afford*. Ten years from now—"

"Crap."

It was Priscilla who stopped Joe.

"Of all the goddam crap. Pardon me, Joe, but you sure can build a case. You see Palmer in the morning and he gives you a hard time about a checkup. You see Fred Eckstrom this afternoon and he gives you a bad report. And you push the panic button. We got things to do!"

In the end they all thanked Joe and refused him. Ted was going to Upsala. Gail, if they didn't go, had some idea of choreographing *Anna Christie* for the university's ballet festival next spring. Mish had his rank-and-file caucus, he was committed, it was already in motion. And Priscilla—

"We're not copping out! We're not dropouts. Don't you realize how it would affect everyone else if we just up and vamoosed? We're in it to the finish."

They left the deeds in the box. Ted had no present use for the property. Priscilla was afraid that it might be used by the city housing authority to evict them from Tidal Flats. "Save it for the kids."

"All right, all right." Joe sank back. "Give yourselves a couple of weeks. Fight it out. I was hoping you'd take my word for it."

"Forget about us. We'll take care of us. Joe, it's you we're concerned about!"

"Go on now, go," Joe said crossly, pushing them back with their contrite kisses and tears and pats on the shoulder. "I'm all right. You've worn me out."

They trooped downstairs too perturbed to formulate their thoughts. "It's what he wanted us to say," Priscilla muttered over and over, clinging to it. "We gave him the answer he wanted. No sale. It's what he wanted from us." Yes, Priscilla, yes yes yes.

"Mish, would you mind taking these glasses down?"

He returned up the stairs and Joe closed the door behind him.

"It's a mess, Mish. But a comparatively simple operation. You'll see how to straighten it out. Just be careful of Eckstrom, don't hurt him, he's set in his ways."

"Joe, I'm sorry—"

He precariously stacked the shot glasses, unable to lift his eyes to Joe.

"She's not going to stop the dump. You're not going to overturn UV. The whole thing's nonsense. You see what I'm trying to do, don't you? You and Ted—"

He put the glasses down in order to restore the heavy box to its place in back of the bottom drawer.

"Joe, I—"

Joe helped him clumsily back up to his feet, supporting his arm, holding onto it for support. "Always remember, Mish, you are the same as my son to me. In my eyes you are the same to me as my son."

The gray-blue eyes rested on him, innocent, benign, serene with more than confidence, a lasting pledge.

Flo took the glasses from him in the kitchen. Ted and Gail were getting ready to leave. "You sure you don't want us to stay over?" No, no, she didn't, they'd just be in her way in the morning.

"He's as alert as he's ever been," Ted said cautiously.

"More."

She stepped away from their embraces, their attempts to warm and comfort.

The night air outside was fresh with the first stirrings of spring, tinged with a wisp of smoke, the faintest hint, burnt chicken feathers. The gravel crackled under their feet.

"You notice Flo didn't go upstairs with us," Priscilla said as soon as they were out of earshot of the house. "She wanted nothing to do with it."

While Priscilla read Gail a sisterly lecture on the fallacy of counting delayed periods as pregnancies, Ted drew him away from the sidewalk to his car, into the lee of the car door.

"You don't think, do you," Ted said and glanced up at the house to the dimly lit window of the hall that led to Joe's study in back, "that that plant is on the rocks? That that's what's behind all this?"

That suddenly the money was running out? That there wasn't enough money, the money wasn't there?

In the shelter of the racy little car they stood very close, with hand on each other's shoulder. The inside-outside man pulled inside out.

III

1

"There's nothing wrong with Joe but overidentification with Boris," Priscilla reiterated all the way down from Sherwood Heights, as obstinate in her rejection of change in her father as she was of any suggestion of change in the times. "Gail is right. Joe is a poet at heart. He resists the necessity for professional detachment. There's no psychic numbing there."

He drove with one hand on the wheel. With his right hand he held her hand in his lap, tightly interlocked. They had gone along so long in their fixed routine and now the walls were blown out. In this new emptiness, everything changed, they gripped hands till it hurt, united in their need to find each other again and so to find themselves. Or nothing changed. Flo had parried every attempt to pin her down to a specific ailment. "Just as soon as I know, you'll know. Right now I don't know anything." She didn't want them worrying themselves to death for nothing. Still, strangely, they felt surrounded by an emptiness in which all their familiar landmarks stood at a remove.

He would have preferred bluntness from Flo. To acknowledge the worst that can happen, he had learned long ago, in the war, is not so much to lend yourself to needless worry as to prepare yourself for anything. Not being told, they worried too, flitting from one fear to another in their minds, disoriented, in limbo.

"We did the right thing. He gave us every out and we didn't

take him up on it," Priscilla reiterated. "Every rationalization. Just the way he did with Boris."

"Priscilla, he pleaded with me! I acted like an absolute heel."

It was still all too much with him. Joe striving to reintegrate him into the family on another plane. Joe's expression, so oddly inflected, of final full acceptance of him. *The same as my son to me.*

"He was tempting you. Not that he didn't mean it, he meant every bit of it. Advocate and adversary, arguing both sides to the hilt."

She slipped under his arm and with both arms around him burrowed her head into his chest, making herself small. "Let me crawl inside you." He held her faster to him.

"It can't be anything much—" It came up muffled from under his arm. Priscilla straightened up, her mind made up, solidified on her original conclusion. "A man can't look and talk the way he does . . . Remember the time we thought sure with Steph, polio?"

He remembered the volumes Ted had left open on the living room floor, Ted's rough guess, and his mind shied away from it. So long as you don't know, it's not so.

"A tempest in a teapot. Where are you going?"

Inadvertently, traversing the Bottoms to Bancroft Avenue, he took the narrow side street up past the Ucchini house where they had celebrated their engagement, the grandmother's hundredth birthday, the strike victory. A sanctuary light burned in the window under the peak of the roof, a candle flame feeding itself in a neon-red tumbler of melting wax.

"He's given his life for these people!"

With a heave of her body, in a paroxysm that passed through her like an electric shock, she flung it out at the shadowy, shambling frame houses.

Abruptly he loosened his hand, withdrew it to the cold circle of the wheel. How she hates us—hates and blames . . .

"Pop took the kids home with him."

"Oh God, now we'll have to pick them up. I thought we'd stop by Pulaski."

He swerved abruptly around the nearest corner, disregarding the stop sign. "All right, Pulaski then. Pop'll keep them overnight."

"What's the matter with you now? What are you mad at? You get these mads on—attacking Ted out of the blue— He'll have the fights on TV turned up so loud. They have to be in school tomorrow. Turn around, we have to go get them."

"You don't have to go anywhere. I'll drop you off."

He bent over the wheel, back with a bang. They were right back where they started from, back before tonight, before their reconciliation this afternoon, before their quarrel, before their good years. Right back on the picket line that blustery January afternoon. Showing off, he thought then, a princess among the peasants bestowing her goodies. She hates us, he thought now, an angel of mercy among the lepers, kidding herself into kissing the sores.

Pulaski Hall was dark. The night clouds, pink-tinged with the reflection of city light, descended in a steamy orange glow over the rooftops on the bayside. Smoke was blowing out over the water toward Bay Point a half mile away, the yacht club and the dwellings adjacent to it, with acres of greenery slanting down to the shorefront.

"I hope their windows are open out there." Priscilla rolled the car window down and inhaled the stink with satisfaction. "We'll see some action then."

He circumvented the lantern-lit road barriers to deliver her inside the project. The tenant self-help brigade was on the job, transporting an aged man out of a building on a litter or mattress or some kind of cot. Ghostly in his winding sheet of bedclothes under the beam of flashlights, attended by solicitous women, he was lowered, tilting like a picture of the descent from the cross, over the shallow stoop.

"Lucas!" Priscilla shot out of the car and raced after the bearers. "Is that you, Lucas? What goes?"

Still her irrepressible outcry, her cry of anguished antagonism, rang through him. She despises us.

2

Liscomb Street was always for him a journey back.

Jefferson School squatting dark in its barren yard, with the iron-bar fence around it, the chain wire beneath kicked out. Over the bar, painted with an undercoating of yellow (always a puzzle, why yellow if it was going to be black?) and then with a coat of black, the blackest black, glossy, soon blistering, Maudie Dukas skinned the cat. To the cheers of the boys and the jeers of the girls.

> I see Boston, I see France
> I see a hole in Maudie's pants.

He had tagged after Elisabeth Kallen walking the iron ridge of the schoolhouse fence, not Maudie Dukas.

> Michael and Elisabeth up a tree
> K-I-S-S-I-N-G
> First comes love, then comes marriage
> Then comes Michael an' a baby carriage.

Out of the tendencies in himself fanned by that attachment he was now married to Priscilla Barth.

The mystery of it.

A little park at the corner of Liscomb and Coombs, more a collection of untended shrubbery than a park. It was only after his mother's death that he learned from his father that theirs had been a romance right out of the books. Pop was courting a Jewish girl, Mary Rolnick, whose family forbade her to marry him. Mary had a shopmate felling seams with her in men's suits, Sophie Muratov, a girl brought over from the old country by a suitor who paid her ship's passage. Sophie's suitor handled in cattle and when he came calling on her Saturday nights, he had crumbs of manure nesting, offensively, in the wrinkles of his sheepskin jacket. After Mary introduced Sophie to Pop, the plot began to thicken. There ensued among the four of them avowals of undying passion, threats of suicide, even an attempted shooting of Pop by Sophie's suitor from behind a lamppost in the Liscomb-Coombs Park. ("Nitwit, *he* should have hidden in the bushes and waited till *I* was under the lamppost.") At the same time they were all opposed to the institution of marriage. Emancipated spirits, apostles of Freedom, strangers to Church and State. The plot began to unwind when Pop introduced Mary to his friend, Boris Kallen. Boris broke off with another girl in order to marry Mary. Pop married Sophie. And the ex-suitor made his first million in meat during the war.

Through such twistings and turnings . . .

Puerto Ricans were moving into Hunkville. Pausing at the stoplight, he was startled to observe the tall-lettered sign in the window of Mroz's Cash & Carry: BODEGA. Mroz of the battered felt hat and the soiled whites who used to reward good report cards with ice cream cones. Kids who would have starved during the Depression if it wasn't for Mroz slipping them Fig Newtons and bananas. Gone now. Buried a month ago.

A snatch of music, staccato. An eruption of voices, lilting. "*Hasta luego, Alfredo.*"

At Number 97 he locked the doors of his station wagon and the tailgate, ashamed of the clicks. Instead of going through the dark alley to the back he took the front entrance. On these porch steps in the summer evenings, the women, Hungarian and Slav, would sit confiding their female secrets in broken English, the common tongue. Boasting of their husbands. "When he passed through a town, they used to lock up the nuns." Yelling at their children in the street, complaining of daughters who got into trouble, babies, and sons who got into trouble, the cops. "The trouble with kids is, *they won't listen!*"

On the fretwork rail that divided the porch, boy and girl perched, tussling. In the bay windows that bulged like chunky cheeks on either side of the porch, light glared through the cracked, unevenly drawn shades. Nothing was ever soft or quiet in this house. No sickness was ever announced with decorum. They ran shrieking through this door to greet the visiting relatives, with wringing of hands, tearing of hair. Surrounded by whispers of awe and pity, a breath of scandal. Sugar in the blood, water on the brain, blood in the urine. "The best thing is to go fast. Apoplexy. That's the best way."

The hall was as decayed as ever, the wall paint scarred. When he was a boy the walls were covered with layers of peeling paper. He had never known love in this house. Never the love of parents for each other and their young. If only I'd died before I was born! If only I'd been struck blind before I ever laid eyes on you. Here little children, eat my flesh.

He stumbled over tricycles and baby carriages at the staircase. Pop had once built a bicycle for him out of wheels and a chain and a saddle that didn't fit. Up! On! Ride!

He'd wake up nights when Pop was on the late shift, hearing his footfalls up the stairs. In the kitchen the teakettle hissed on the stove. A stirring about, a tinkle of teaspoons in glasses of hot tea sweetened with cherry preserves, splutters of laughter.

Down these stairs, one evening of their last summer together, he helped his father carry his mother to the car outside in the street, that poor stump of a woman bundled up in a blanket, galled with sores. Pop drove her in his car to the shore, to the grassy headland, above the beach, where their friends were accustomed to gather bringing a picnic supper and setting up their games of cards under the trees. Later Pop drove her, as he always used to do, down to the deserted end of the beach and sat with her for a long time inside the car watching the tide break over the rocks. Foam-crested waves, blackness dappled with moonlight. Over and over and over again the same thing, never the same.

The steam of fish being cooked with hot spices seeped out of the door of the second floor back. In the spring as soon as the

Bing cherries were on the market, Mom and Mary Kallen would buy up baskets of them and set the children to stemming and stoning them. They'd stone the cherries till their fingers were black with the juice, snitching one every once in a while, sucking the cherry off the stone, until their mouths too were black with juice. The steam of cooking cherries filled the house.

The house was alive with voices. Cherries? You call these cherries? In the old country *those* were cherries. Walnuts, what walnuts they were, with meat that tasted of honey. Mushrooms, you could go into the woods in the morning and fill your shirt with mushrooms, not a poison one in the lot. Nothing in America was as good. Everything in America was fake. "So why did you come here," the children would ask, feeling themselves personally criticized, "if it was all so good in the old country?" "For you little bastards. To give you a better life."

People, what people they were. . . .

He galloped up the last flight of stairs, come here in flight from confusion, in longing for some sort of wisdom. Affirmation maybe. Something. On the third floor front he squeezed past the wringer washer blocking the hall, connected by hose to kitchen faucet inside, knocked against a diaper pail, tipped over a standing mop.

With a stitch in his side, panting, he arrived at the third floor back. Pop and his labored breathing, inhaling fumes of molten metal all his years as a molder. Emphysema? Or, as he sometimes hinted, scars of arrested tuberculosis? Or, as he more recently insisted, going to that old fart of a doctor of his, hardening of the arteries?

His father's door vibrated with the din of TV. Pop, who never lifted a finger to anyone, was a wrestling fan. Leaning against the doorframe he pounded, over the noise.

"Ssssht!"

With a ferocious shush, Pop let him in. The fights were over. The news was on. The news was sacred to Pop, not to be interrupted, ever. No one was permitted to speak, even during commercials.

"The kids—I just want to—"

"SSSHT!"

He couldn't rouse the children now, asleep in Pop's bed in the bedroom. It would create too much of a disturbance. Worlds hung in the balance.

Pop stood before his television set like a conductor, attuned and absorbed. The couch was made up with a folded sheet and a blanket, a pillow slip dog-eared over a couch pillow, and his pajamas were laid out. Pop was half-undressed, in his boxer shorts, a splendid physical specimen with the muscled shoulders and back, the bronze skin of a youth. He was still capable of doing knee bends with Greg and Steph to amuse them.

In spite of childhood malnutrition, in spite of the ignorance and superstition in which he was born, in spite of the homeless wanderings and blunderings, the burn scars and the scarred lungs —truly a remarkable man. A miracle.

The white head nodded in concert with the comments of the announcer. Stalin unmasked. An attempt to obtain statements from Togliatti, Thorez . . .

He left his father in peace till the news would be over. The green glass bowl on the buffet was filled with fruit Pop must have bought on the way home with the children. Pop the food spender, always afraid of being caught without food in the house, starving to death. Mom the food scrimper, always trying to save enough in the pot to go around. Irene, leave some for Mish! Mish, leave something for Petey! Petey, what about Jennie?

He broke off clusters of grapes, plucked the dusky grapes from the stem and popped them into his mouth, spat the seeds out in his hand. Over the buffet, in a narrow strip extending from the corner of the room to the door on the right side, hung the Chinese tapestry his mother had bought from a drunken sailor on the eve of her wedding. The sailor had come into the tailor shop where his mother was working in the slack of the factory season before Christmas, mending pants, and had rolled the tapestry out on the counter before her, the heirloom of an oriental dynasty, and offered it to her for a hundred dollars. She refused him of course.

Four hours later the sailor staggered into the shop again. The shop was open late, Christmas week. She bought the tapestry from him for twenty-five dollars, every cent she and her affianced had saved for setting up housekeeping after their wedding.

The tapestry was too beautiful. She couldn't resist it. Or maybe Sophie the flirt, the tease with her impudent eyes and her up-tilted nose and her mouth pursed in appreciation of her own daring and deviltry (in her photograph on the buffet she leaned upon a high-backed, elaborately carved chair with arm sleeved in lace up to the elbow and bosom fruitily corseted), had been unable to resist the sailor. Had succumbed in the course of her banter with him to his temptation, the silken scarf unrolled on the counter top. What did her bridegroom think of her purchase? What was there to think? He married her womanly foolishness along with the woman. A tapestry embroidered in silks so fine it could be drawn through her wedding ring.

The children later would take the tapestry out of the buffet drawer and unroll it on the bed, lose themselves in its exotic landscape.

"How much is it worth, Mom?"

"A million dollars." Mom would wrinkle her nose, pucker her mouth in foretaste of her own quip. "But what's a million dollars worth if it don't mean nothing to you? Not a cent."

They had a million dollars rolled up in a linen dish towel in their buffet drawer.

When Lev Lunin was out of work he pawned his watch, Sophie pawned the diamond engagement ring she'd bought herself. But not the Chinese tapestry. When the house caught fire, almost everything they had was ruined by water and smoke. Not the Chinese tapestry. They grabbed the tapestry along with the children and flew down the back piazza stairs. Once, urged by neighbors to have it appraised, they invited the Chinese laundryman from down the street to come look it over. The laundryman could tell them nothing but he returned with a friend from the Chinese restaurant downtown, an expert. The expert couldn't read the gold-threaded characters embroidered into the border, they were in a dialect he was unfamiliar with. But he did say that the tapestry was made for the home of a very wealthy man. If you placed a value on such things, the expert said, no value could be placed on it. It was priceless. No price anyone could pay you would be enough. But if such things were of no interest to you, if you didn't care for them, then a nickel would be too much. He told them what they already knew.

They never attempted to sell the tapestry. If it was worth as much as the man implied, they'd never get it. Somebody else would make the profit on it. They'd be the suckers. But if the man was just being polite, trying to save their feelings, if it was only a piece of junk after all, a Coney Island souvenir, they didn't want to find it out.

Before Lev and Sophie's twenty-fifth wedding anniversary, their children removed the tapestry from the buffet drawer and had it framed as a gift to them. It was hand-cleaned at the French Cleaners and mounted under glass at the Art Gallery Shoppe, with a burnished molding around it, very plain, in the best of taste.

"Look at it," Sophie and Lev bragged to their visitors after the anniversary party at the lodge hall. "What a good frame the children put on it. Cost them a fortune."

One by one he plucked the grapes from the stalk, half-listening to the TV and contemplating the tapestry. He switched on the bridge lamp across the room and tilted the arm up, adjusted it to focus on the framed length of silk over the buffet.

It was supposed to be very old, centuries old, but the colors were brilliant in their freshness. Scenes of a story embroidered on the green silk ground of the tapestry in three contiguous orange panels, from right to left. In the right-hand panel the prince arrived on his white charger bearing a plumed fan and was received by the father of the bride. In the center panel a banquet was being prepared in a pavilion by the women of the house and their servants. In the left-hand panel, under a tree sinuous in trunk and foliage, a girl waited, sinuous of posture, modest yet coquettish, her body turned away, averse, and her head posed over her shoulder, receptive, toward the messenger who deferentially, hands tucked into his sleeves, addressed her.

The white-faced, white-stockinged figures, robed in blue, purple, saffron, rose, were arranged in formal attitudes, stylized yet spontaneous, appropriate to the situation. The whole sequence moved like a dance to slow music. The border of the tapestry was embroidered in stitches so small and even, repeating the color of the robes, they glowed like fine beading. The gold thread intertwined was untarnished.

He dragged the lamp over the floor and focused its circle of light directly on the girl in the left panel. So coyly turned away from the messenger, from the banquet in the center scene, from her prince on horseback, yet turning toward: an asymmetrical interflow, disjointed yet harmonized, of lines, every line of every leaf of the tree down through every fold of her garments. Desirous and resisting. Avoiding and inviting. Curious and fearful. Pro and con. Yes and no, no and yes.

"Pop, it's late—"

"Sssht!"

John Foster Dulles, glasses ashine, mouth drooping like the beak of a discontented bird. Clarifying some pronunciamento of Ike's. Onward to the brink.

Foaming beer steins, clarity bubbling up from the stem, up and over.

"Pop, I just want to—"

"Sssht!"

Today on Bikini atoll an H-bomb test . . .

Girl in brassiere stroking her armpit, sumptuously smoothing, hairless, odorless.

"Pop—"

"Shuh!"

Weather girl. Sports.

His nightly ritual fulfilled, Pop snapped off the TV and, still reflectively tuned in, rendered his invariable judgment.

"Whichever way they turn, their behinds are still behind them."

3

Grumbling, his father marched into the kitchen and filled the teakettle at the sink. Why couldn't they leave the kids here for tonight? He had the couch fixed for himself. He had food in the icebox. He'd give them breakfast.

"In such a hurry to yank them back into the fire and filth."

"You have to get to work. There's school— Why were you listening to Channel 7? I thought you liked Howard K. Smith."

"What difference does it make? They all take it from the same script. Well, how is he?"

"I told you he's all right. Just going to Sprague for a checkup. Pop, I can't stay. It's too late. I'm beat."

Pop banged the kettle down on the burner. "We'll have a glass of tea together."

He'd have given anything to sit down with his father now over a glass of hot tea. To inquire after his health, urge him to consult a more competent doctor, insist he stop dosing himself with laxatives and vitamin pills. To ask about Petey, whether he'd heard from him lately. To recall the outings Mom would take them on— all week in men's suits and Saturdays in the tailor shop, up every night till midnight with her housework and dressmaking on the side, and on Sunday she'd pack her four little ones into a trolley car with picnic basket, paraphernalia, off to Waterville forty miles away to visit her sister, Luba, on the chicken farm. To catch up with him on neighbors: the girls who used to dance the czardas in folk costume at the Hungarian hall; the fellows who'd gather at the Sokol hall, on shots and beer all day and night—anybody else would reel out wrapped around a lamppost, not them.

To chat.

"It's just I had a bum night last night. One hell of a day—"

A Hungarian seven-layer cake was out of the bakery carton, stacked with chocolate cream between the layers and coated with chocolate icing. Such a big cake, it had to be eaten.

"He's all right, is he? They call you to Sherwood Heights with such alarms just to tell you he's all right? Mish, don't talk to me like I'm a child! He's got cancer? A blockage?" Pop's hand rested over his esophagus. "They're going to operate?"

"Pop, for Christ sake— Something with his side vision."

"Cataracts. You young people, you hear but you don't listen—"

"Joe's not that worried about it. Nobody's worried—"

In an effort to divert his father, to avert the rash of ruffled sensitivities that always, inevitably, sprang up between them, he added what he had no intention of adding. He blurted it out.

"He's had this land out in Hillcrest he's deeding over to Priscilla and Ted. He'd like us to build there."

"Hillcrest. Hm." Pop calmed down. He let the tea steep a few minutes. He had changed into his pajamas, but too hastily. He rebuttoned, straightened out the rumpled stripes. He combed through his tousled hair with his fingers, making himself presentable.

"What you going to build with? How you supposed to keep it up?"

He had never intended to say it, but once started he had to go on with it. He dropped a lump of sugar in his cup as Pop poured the tea. No cherry preserves.

"Oh, some wild idea he has for Ted and me to take over the barrel works. Me as the inside man. Ted as the outside man. Modernize the plant. Put it on wheels."

Maybe he had intended to say it. Had carried it here, or it had carried him, for this express purpose. To hit the old man over the head with it: Joe Barth has come through at last!

"He wants to make you partners with his son?"

"Something like that." He tried a tip of the cake with his spoon. "Fifty-fifty?"

"Of course Ted hasn't the slightest desire and neither have I—"

"You got it in writing?"

"What writing? What kinda tutti frutti . . . All these years they been so nice to me—"

"Signed and sealed. On the dotted line. It's always the brother-in-law that gets railroaded out of the business."

They were screaming at each other.

"Listen to me, Mish! For once in your life listen to me. Joe may have the best intentions in the world. Ted may have the best intentions. You go downtown tomorrow to the best legal firm in Shoreham, draw up a partnership contract."

"I don't want the goddam business! I didn't make any decision—"

"You made your decision when you married that girl."

The near empty kettle, restored to the burner, sang, whistled, throbbed, jumped.

"They mean right. Of course they mean right. But as soon as a man's in business he's out for himself. That's the nature of the animal. Don't you take no promises from them. Don't you depend on no understandings."

He shut off the burner; how many times had Pop burned the kettle? He drank his tinny tea and tried in vain to shut out the advice that poured on and on, vulgarizing, undermining, poisoning.

"In black and white. Ironclad. Look at Boris. Look at Mroz. Look at . . ."

A hundred stories. The folklore of Liscomb Street.

You know who started Wheel Cogs? A factory complex covering three square blocks. Boris Kallen! Boris went in with Pevsner. Boris was the toolmaker and Pevsner was the bookkeeper—what did Pevsner know about wheels and cogs? Today the Pevsners were showered with gold. And Boris . . .

You know what killed Mroz? From shoelaces door-to-door to peddling with horse and wagon to renting a store to putting a down payment on the building the store was in. Living over the store and installing the brother he brought over from Hungary on the top floor. Two brothers married to two sisters bringing up their children in the same house, could anything be closer? Yet when the sons, cousins, teamed up to buy a wholesale warehouse together on Mroz's credit, what happened? As soon as the warehouse was on its feet, don't you think the cousin found a way to frame Albie and kick him out on his ear? Over a matter of seventy-five dollars, Albie lost a seventy-five-thousand-dollar business. That's what killed Mroz.

And Jennie, right in their own family. Jennie drove the egg truck for Aunt Luba and she bred the chickens and she built up her chicken coops till she was running a regular chicken concentration camp; every time the lights were turned on the chickens would start to lay. Then a real estate speculator came along and Luba sold the farm out from under Jennie. . . .

"You'll do the dirty work and Ted will make it. You know what will be? You'll be left with nothing. Zero. Five years older. Don't wait to find out what's in Joe's will. Nail it now."

"Once and for all," he finally managed to stem the flood, "I am not going into that business. I've never even set foot in the place! I told Joe no."

"What are you going to do then? Be a slave for UV all your life? Make them rich?"

It was Pop who had the final say as he always did, with the corkscrew twist in the gut.

"For me to run that barrel factory," he said to his father, "that's what you'd like, isn't it? That would make you happy. So you can ride me with it. Look down your nose at me. A boss no less. A bloated plutocrat."

"Who's riding? Who's looking down? I'll have a son a manufacturer, I can go to Florida in the winter. In Florida, they say, is paradise."

"Pop, what do you want? Just what the hell do you want for me?"

"The best. Always the best, what else? Only the best."

The old gent who shared the apartment with Pop came pattering out of the tiny bedroom behind the kitchen, awakened out of sleep, bright with curiosity. Father and son fighting, shame, shame. A shame for the neighbors.

The children lay asleep in their underwear under the quilt of Pop's double bed. Father and son, not speaking, tugged socks onto rubber feet, pulled polo shirts over obdurate heads, scrambled under the bed searching for a missing sneaker. They hoisted the children up piggyback and passed through the living room, past the Chinese tapestry and the photograph of the young woman leaning with elbow and bosom on the carved chair. A million dollars! What's a million dollars worth if it don't mean nothing to you? Not a cent.

Gripping the gritty bannister with Stephanie on his back, he followed his father down the flights of stairs.

They're dead. They're dead. The house was full of voices. *They killed them.* Who's dead? Who was killed? *Sacco and Vanzetti.*

They unloaded the children into the back of the station wagon.

"You want the quilt for them? I'll bring the quilt."

"For Christ sake, Pop, leave it! Will you leave it? Just leave it!"

When he slid in behind the wheel, his father knocked on the window opposite for him to open up. The Hungarian cake tied up in its bakery carton was placed gently down on the seat beside him.

SEVEN

Flight of the Cessna

I

1

At coffee break, Wednesday, Mari nudged up to him, shared secrets dancing in her eyes. As if they had indeed gone down on the floor together yesterday. And would again today. And tomorrow. And every day. All in her eyes.

She showed him the letter that had been drafted last night by the self-constituted rank-and-file committee, a call to the membership to attend the Sunday meeting. Money had been volunteered freely to finance the mailing. The signers—the old trio: Lunin, Pelletier, Rakocszi. Mabley had agreed to the letter but wouldn't agree to sign.

It was a good letter. Unity. Expand the membership. Broaden the leadership. Revitalize the grievance machinery. Build the union. UNITED ACTION IS THE ONLY LANGUAGE THE COMPANY UNDERSTANDS!!!

"I couldn't find out who was behind that leaflet, though. Everybody's deaf, dumb and blind."

"I know who was behind it," he said to Mari and drank his coffee, grown cold while he read. "Take an educated guess."

"Oh no." All at once it struck her too. The foolery faded. She sank down on a convenient carton. "You're crazy. It's impossible." But already she was as sure of it as he was, denying it. "No. No, it's not. It can't be." She didn't want it to be. "Never."

She had every reason not to want it to be, everything in her doubled up against it. But who else could it be? It had to be.

"If he's the one . . . Herb *Cranston?* After he fought Bob so, now he's fighting Coffin?"

Cranston organizing the Catholics in the union: Kick the Commies out! Bob assailing Cranston and his cohorts: Splitters, disrupters! Cranston's Freedom Caucus driving Bob out of the union hall, out of union office, out of the union.

"Herb was always a strong union man, Mari, you can't take that away from him."

"You can defend him? You're still standing up for him? He's the one put Nick where he is. He swung the membership—"

Cranston clean-cut and starchy in his open-collared white shirt: "I have waited four years, Mish, for you to break with Bob. Where do you stand now on Alger Hiss? With Bob or your own government? Guilty or not guilty?"

"What he did, Mish, what he did to us . . . There's too much blood under the bridge."

Mari was white with shock, her cheeks mottled, her arms goosefleshed. She went back to her press muttering and shaking her head. Not Herb Cranston. No. Never never never.

Yet she saw it. He could swear she saw it. If Cranston could swing the membership one way, why not . . .

Cranston's faction in the union had disappeared with the disappearance of its object. But Herb had been in Hot Rubber at one time and he still had friends there, and he still had lines to almost every department. Under Colangelo he had not held any prominent office. But then he had never been ambitious for high office. Cranston viewed himself not as a power but as The Brain behind The Power. Whether at this point, a minor steward in Maintenance, Herb remained The Brain behind Colangelo was problematic. And in any case, to think of him simply as a brain, a Machiavellian manipulator, was a mistake. Cranston also conceived of himself as the moral arbiter of the union, the Keeper of its Conscience.

He had no sign that Cranston was on the outs with Colangelo. He had no proof that he was the author of the leaflet. He couldn't approach Cranston directly. Since the 1950 election they had avoided each other like the plague. It wasn't a matter where he could just walk up to him, "Say, Herb, what about this?" It was a matter that had to be conducted through second parties, through preliminary conversations delicately leading up to . . .

He couldn't even get to Cranston. If the leaflet had originated with Cranston, if he had the apparatus to distribute it, if it wasn't just a one-shot affair—then all concerned had had the discretion to cover up their tracks, the discipline to hold their tongues.

All morning he wrestled with it. Yet everything—bolts in and out with a twist of his wrench—that had been going so hard with him lately tripped a light fantastic. Even when he called Priscilla at noon, heavy with foreboding.

"Did they arrive at Sprague all right?"

"Yes, Joe's being admitted now. Flo's very upset."

"Oh my God. What is it?"

"That H-bomb blast on Bikini yesterday. Another one! After all our protests. She wants me to give powdered milk to the children. And to get Ellen Hamer on her anti-bomb committee to send off wires to Eisenhower. When I'm so damn tied up right now—"

He hung up, buoyed up. What can you do with such characters?

It was warm enough again today to eat outside. The mall was lined with lunchers. Arms scissored up as he appeared, reaching for a handshake. The word was out. The contest was on. He strolled down the strip of gray winter grass with Ewell, Cusak, Ray and Marty at his shoulders, others queuing up behind. The promenade was tantamount to an announcement. The challenger was in the ring.

"So you're running against Nick again?"

"No, I tried that. Let's just say we're helping him along the way he wants to go. Okay?"

"What if Nick don't go for it?"

"Then we'll see."

"You think we got a chance?"

"Not if you're not there this Sunday."

Sunday was a hangup, Palm Sunday. But there was no time to be lost. Before Nick's nominating committee trotted out his slate of trusted lieutenants, the clamor had to be raised for inclusion of representatives from every faction in the local. If Nick ignored the clamor, there was still less time to be lost. They would be forced to nominate their own slate of candidates, mount a campaign.

"Our first job is to get the turnout Sunday."

He surveyed the groups of lunchers who offered him their encouragement.

Langston and his buddies—dissenters who had quit the union in disgust. So loud to vote out Nick when they had neither a voice nor a vote.

Sig and his buddies—inactives, too busy with their own personal lives, too fatigued from overwork or too indifferent or too lazy to participate.

Buzz Burney—the uncommitted, standing pat on fact: somewhere along the line the initiative had passed from the dues payers to the piecards and there was nothing anyone, Nick or Mish or Whosis, could do now to reverse the process. The fatcats were in control and the guy in the dungarees was lost.

The Starvik bunch—with laughter, a twinkle of tongue, a malicious gleam. Urging him on, they took a positive pleasure in the laxness of the present regime. They preferred the warm human touch of corruption. Honesty, integrity, virtue, who can live with it?

Mari rallying up the women—no one took the women too seriously. All of them temporaries. Marginals. Even the lifers.

It wasn't simply Nick he had to contend with. It was the atmosphere.

He was besieged with beefs as he walked. A request a year ago for male classification in reflector packing. Tool payment for various girls who had been deducted. Restoration of service for . . .
They had gone to their steward. They had taken it up with the

Grievance Board. They had pushed it and pushed it until they were exhausted with it.

"A nickel an hour. Over a hundred bucks I lost this year. More, when you figure my average earnings are computed . . ."

He was greeted everywhere with the recurrent rumor of impending moves. Remember when they brought in Ironing Cord last year, replacing fifteen hundred workers with fifty, how they shut us up with it, and now Ironing Cord, they say, is about to be moved to Lewiston, which is being shut down . . .

The atmosphere was with him. The atmospheric pressure. He was wafted along on a friendly breeze.

In the distance, through the crowd dispersing back to work, he thought he glimpsed Cranston by the rotunda, the tall head rigidly upraised, the billed cap uptipped from his upstanding lick of light hair, stiff-necked as ever, the righteous bastard. But by the time he arrived at the rotunda, waylaid a half dozen times on his way, there was no one there. Bayberry bushes with a few of last fall's yellowed leaves clinging to the brambles, a few shriveled scarlet berries.

When he re-entered the building, a heavy-set fellow, lingering in the doorway, stepped out of the shadow and accosted him. His face under the slanting hat brim was vaguely familiar.

"Oh, you," the fellow said. "I thought Marty was with you."

"Marty's already inside."

The fellow followed him up the iron-treaded stairs, keeping himself two steps below, dissociating himself, but continuing to address him.

"So you're way up there again. Hero of Coffin's Creek. I hear it was a rout."

"That remains to be seen."

He smiled to himself, mounting the stairs. Coffin's proposal was becoming more and more incredible to him. All the steps upward in UV opened to an old-time militant, old friend of Bob Ucchini, old neighbor of Boris Kallen, son-in-law of Joe Barth?

It didn't occur to him then who the fellow was or what he imagined he was conveying by speaking to him. He returned to Switch on a wave of ebullience. It's moving.

He was almost immediately drawn into a renewal of turmoil, an eruption that would bring him face to face with Nick Colangelo before the end of the afternoon in a premeeting test of strength.

Shortly after lunch, notice of a week's suspension apiece was delivered by the section office clerk to three women in Switch. Management, unable apparently to single out the actual instigators of the zoo show had resorted to arbitrary selection and left it to Dirksen, the officer at the bottom of the heap, to pick the victims.

Maria Ucchini was naturally a top choice, on general principles. Rita Davis, the colored girl on the brusher, had an annoying habit of mumbling whenever she felt overburdened and broadcasting it wholesale when the burden continued. And Teresa Siemens, surprisingly, in final assembly: Teresa was a slow worker and a *kvetch* and Dirksen had been itching for a long time to get rid of her.

Teresa was the first to receive her notice. Instead of accepting it meekly, guilt being her lot in life, she spilled her batch of angel hair all over the conveyor belt and rushed across the floor to Dirksen.

"It's a mistake! It's that Amy, she's out to get me—I didn't have nothing to do with it. I didn't even have one of them signs in front of me."

Dirksen hit the ceiling. The notices were not to be handed out until five minutes before quitting time and the green girl clerk had bollixed up his orders.

"You rode home with Mariuch, didn't you?" Dirksen accused Teresa in self-defense. "You're in it up to your ears." Furnishing a basis for counteraccusations later that the company had spies out tailing the Lunin wagon. "You had your fun," he said to Teresa, "now take your medicine like a lady."

Rita upon receiving her notice darted across the aisle at once to Mari who was just receiving hers. They stopped Teresa on her return trip to final assembly. The three women descended on Dirksen before he had a chance to make himself scarce. Meanwhile, Don Pinette blithely drag-rolled his tote cans through the center of action and regaled all and sundry on his itinerary with a blow-by-blow account.

"And what's the reason for this?" Mari demanded of Dirksen.

"It says there. 'Participating in an unauthorized demonstration.'"

"What demonstration?"

"Get back to your work! You got two hours yet. Any other company you wouldn't be suspended. You'd be out."

"There was no demonstration," Mari declared. "We were all in our places. Weren't we, girls?"

"That's right," Rita seconded her. "I was right there at my brusher."

"I never got up, I didn't even look," Teresa swore.

"Work stoppage then," Dirksen conceded. "Whatever you want to call it."

"There was no stoppage," Mari said. "What stoppage? When did we stop?"

"You slowed down production—"

"No slowdown. We didn't slow down for a second. Look up our work sheets."

"Well, you're stopped now. You're making a scene. Get back to work."

"No scene. We're processing a grievance."

In the old days Mari would have processed the grievance herself, at least through the first step on the floor with the foreman. Now thinking it over, she beckoned to Don who had been hanging around grinning and sending reports circulating down the aisles.

"Get Lunin."

"Don't you dare!" Dirksen grabbed Don by the shirttails.

"Mish!" Mari bellowed. "Mish!" all three women trumpeted. They stamped their feet. "Mish!"

Dirksen dashed down the aisle to the milling machine Lunin was setting up in order to forestall him, the three women at his heels.

"You intervene in this, Lunin," Dirksen warned and pulled the switch on the miller to make sure he was heard, "and I will personally see to it that you get suspended right along with them."

Mari craned up over Dirksen's shoulder. "We won't go back to work till this suspension order is rescinded. Handle it for us, Mish."

"I already talked to your union steward," Dirksen objected. "Fritz went along with it. There's nothing to handle."

Mari's head popped up again. "He's bulling us. Go ahead, Mish."

The same to-do as the other morning over her, but this time he sent the run-through he was spot-checking clattering into the bin and wiped his hands off on his grease rag. Moved by a curious sense of lightness—he was larger than this narrow aisle between machine rows. Larger than Teresa who was backing off a safe distance positioning herself to reap advantage here if there was advantage to be reaped and to flee if flight was indicated. He was larger than Switch, larger than UV. The inner tightness of the past several years that could only be defined as fear, the anxiety of fear, had evaporated. Dirksen's threats held no terrors for him.

"Okay, let's take the time," he said to Dirksen, giving him formal notification that he was stopping work to institute the first step of the grievance procedure.

"Okay, it's your funeral."

Grimly Dirksen matched watches with him and entered the time in his form book.

"These girls are being suspended, Lunin, as you well know, for good and sufficient cause."

"Was there any disruption of production?"

"They caused a disturbance—"

"Did anyone leave her bench?"

"They violated company discipline and they embarrassed the company and caused it a loss of prestige."

"Was there any time lost?"

Dirksen's face, all pink ears and pale brows and pinched jowls, quivered over his twitchy bow tie. He was trying hard to contain the situation. He was afraid of bungling it.

"There was no interruption of production," he said to Dirksen. "Nobody left the bench. Nobody walked out. There was no unauthorized anything. You haven't got a case. Tear up the notices."

"Tear it up, tear it up!" the women crowed from behind Dirksen.

Dirksen refused to rescind the notices. Willynilly they were into the second step of the grievance, heading for the section office, the three women trailing them.

"Write it up, Mish, write it up!"

"Will you tell them to get the hell back to work," Dirksen growled at him, "till we settle this?"

"I don't tell them nothin'. I'm not their boss."

"GET BACK TO YOUR WORK!"

In the office, one eye on the clock—if the time spent in palaver amounted to less than twelve minutes, the company paid for it; if over twelve minutes, the union paid—he wrote up the pertinent information, spelling out in no uncertain terms the relief desired: withdrawal of the suspensions. He was just about to sign it, inside the twelve minutes, when Dirksen snatched the form out from under his hand.

"It has to be signed by the designated union representative."

Dirksen had sent for Fritz. Mari, backed up by Rita and Teresa, who was exhaling little moans under the tension, stood firm at the office entrance. The three women clamored at Fritz as he passed them, his rectilinear frame unswerving. Fritz paid scant attention to explanations of the grievance, either Lunin's or Dirksen's. Not only had his position been usurped but his paid time off the job, and not just twelve minutes. This could go on for days.

Dirksen handed the Statement of Grievance form over to Fritz. "You have to sign this."

"I have to read it first," Fritz said. Elaborately he removed his work cap and ran his comb through his curlicued orange hair, took his black-framed glasses from his coverall pocket and set them astride his longitudinal nose.

Either Fritz had trouble reading the handwriting, numbers were more his style, or he had trouble understanding what he read. Halfway through, he paused to nod past the clerk to Stan Ledyard. Stan was shuffling papers around his desk, meticulously keeping himself aloof from Dirksen's problem.

"I have to think it over," Fritz said at last and, pocketing the grievance, strode out.

The women flew after him. "Fritzie! Fritzie!"

Every woman on the floor switched around on her stool.

"He won't sign the grievance," Mari yelled. "He's stalling us off."

"He's sold us out," Rita broadcast it.

"Sellout! Sellout!"

"PULL THE SWITCH!"

With a wide gesture Mari slammed down the on-off lever of her press. Down her row of presses the din of drills and taps subsided. Row after row pins between gear and wheel were pulled, plugs were pulled. The flashing lights of the electrical activator out, the mercury injection needles down, the conveyor at a standstill.

Suddenly silence.

"If they're going to suspend any of us, they gotta suspend all of us!"

Every movable bin was lowered from workbench to floor. Up on the benches went the girls. They hiked their skirts up over their knees and crossed their legs. Stomachs in, bosoms out, they let loose.

"GO CALL COFFIN! WE WANT GRAVEYARD!"

"Sh! Shshsh!" Dirksen ducked up and down the aisles trying to quiet them. He had his slowdown now, his work stoppage, his unauthorized demonstration.

Joan Hlavacek, the beauty of the turntable, swung her superb gams under Dirksen's nose.

"WE WANT GRAVEYARD!"

Dirksen caught hold of Fritz. "For crissake, sign the goddam thing!"

Stan Ledyard issued from the section office. "For crissake, Mish,"—Stan caught hold of him as he stood lolling with a group of male operators who had joined him outside the office kiosk, enjoying the scenery—"stop 'em!"

"You stop them," he said to Stan. "Get on the mike. Phone for the guard."

Stan was not about to sound off over the amplifier or call in aid from the outside if he could help it.

"Tear up the suspensions."

Stan Ledyard retrieved the Statement of Grievance from Fritz. "All right, Lunin. Sign it."

He signed in the office. "Where's the duplicates?" Duplicates signed. "Now, Fritz, let him sign too." Fritz's signature was affixed.

2

At the end of the shift the women marched in a body to the union hall. He accompanied them less as a spokesman, they needed none, than as a symbol of masculine support. The Grievance Board met every Wednesday from eight A.M. to eight P.M., and they intended to present their case to be acted upon forthwith.

In the union hall—lofty with groined arches lighted at the peak with globed fixtures, distant and dim; and vast in its emptiness, its folding chairs stacked against the walls—there was no sign of the Grievance Board, due at four for its third three-man sitting of the day. The long table before the dais was unoccupied. The women swarmed through the sacristy door into Colangelo's office behind the dais. They took possession of the desk telephones to call home and other obligatory points. Noisily they dragged in folding chairs and dropped them open around Nick's desk.

Fritz had preceded them here and stood beside Nick with folded arms. Nick, the little gray man not so little and not so gray, waved them forward, welcoming them.

"That's right, make yourselves homely. Well, what can I do you for? Ah, Lunin."

Nick rose and came out from behind his desk to put his arm around his shoulders. The eyes that seemed as if they must be leaden gray, impenetrable, flashed over him, translucent brown, twinkling with lights of laughter.

"Still the ladies' man, I see." Playfully Nick squeezed his shoulder and gazed around. "Only now it seems to be a harem."

"Where's the Grievance Board? Don't they sit at four any more?"

"Keep your shirt on, Lunin. Fritzie, cool off. Ladies, will you simmer down please?"

Volubly, with the logic of the mundane, Nick sought to take the steam out of them. O'Boyle—poor fellow had a bad fall when he was cleaning a nest out of his father-in-law's chimney—was on sick leave. Mary Rosario was held up by her baby sitter who hadn't shown up, she'd be here as soon as she located another one. Carbone was probably caught in a conversation somewhere. The business agent had left for New York an hour ago to go over the suspensions in Hot Rubber.

"We were out with management seven hours yesterday," Nick said, "and couldn't get them to lift those suspensions. All day Monday I was up at the State Legislature testifying against this new right-to-work law they're trying to put over on us. I put in a full day today in Spray Paint. I'm dead on my feet. But I'll pinch-hit. Let no one ever say we don't service our membership. What's the beef?"

Amy presented the situation. Stable and matronly in her well-kept blue herringbone coat, a woman unknown to Nick and therefore presumably much more of a threat to him than Mari, she described the events leading up to Monday noon's—no, not demonstration—blowup. Not forgetting to include, over Teresa's interruptions in the background, the effect of Leora's intrusion and the company's suspected plan to restore her to the group leadership of final assembly.

"The company brought it on. They lit the spark. If there's going to be any suspensions, let them suspend themselves."

Nick perused the Statement of Grievance. He commended Fritz for his hesitation in signing it.

"While the steward and section chairman in Hot Rubber remain penalized, every union official in the plant feels personally on the spot. Fritz had to exercise restraint."

He commended Lunin for his willingness to stick his neck out. "Most anybody would have stayed out of it. Especially when the company has some ground. This—on top of what we're already into. *Gesu, Giusepp' e Maria!*"

"What ground?"

"Now let's be reasonable, Mari. Let's apply a little common sense. If you think UV doesn't have copies in its files of those artistic signs you ladies cooked up— How does it look? I'd hate to see anyone make a political football out of something that has such a poor chance—"

"Are you rejecting us?"

Down on Nick's desk went the ladies' handbags. Off came their coats.

"Now wait a minute." The women were about to stage a sitdown in the union office over what was manifestly a kooky stunt. "I didn't say I was rejecting you. I'm just giving it to you straight. You're letting yourselves be whipped up to serve ulterior purposes— All right, I tell you what. I'll take it up with the Grievance Board. We'll try submitting it to management. Good enough?"

Before their eyes the grievance disappeared into Nick's desk drawer as it had disappeared previously into Fritz's pocket. All their not inconsiderable determination went down the drain. The women didn't stir. As Nick chipped away at their confidence with his potshots at Lunin, their attention had shifted from the merits of their cause to the two men. It was Lunin's turn now. They waited expectantly.

"I didn't have nothin' to do with it," Teresa proclaimed from the background. "I was just there."

"Shuddup, Teresa." Furious whispers in the foreground.

"I was just walking along and they stopped me in the street and pulled me into the car . . ."

"Quiet!"

"When?" he said to Nick.

"You know as well as I do, Mish, these things take time. We're so piled up here. We got such a backlog—"

"When?"

"I told you I'd speed it through. As soon as the girl has it typed up tomorrow, it'll be sent over to Industrial Relations. What more can I say? How long it will take from then on . . ."

"How long, Nick?"

"Time, damn it, time. Time to go through the established channels."

Time was the enemy. Time was the saboteur. Mari, Rita and Teresa would go home for the week, catch up with their chores, relax a little, and by next Thursday they'd be back at work. And as time went by, the matter of their lost pay would recede into the past, dwindle away. . . . The case would be submitted in writing to Industrial Relations this week. Industrial Relations had a week to reply in writing. If the reply was in the negative and if the union exec after discussion decided to go back to management with it, the contractual time allowed would amount to another three weeks. And if still unsettled and still pursued, then on to the headquarters level: six weeks. If no agreement was reached within six months, it would pass up to the final step, arbitration. With mutually agreed-upon time extensions at every stage. Months. Years. Ending up with some college professor arbitrating over the UV copies of the signs.

"Monday morning," he said to Nick. "If the suspensions aren't canceled and the three women aren't back at work by Monday, with full restitution of pay for tomorrow and Friday, we're taking a vote in Switch on a walkout."

"We can't back you up. We're in no position—"

He started for the door. The women picked up their handbags and their coats. Nick escorted them out through the hall to the vestibule, amiable all the way.

3

It didn't occur to him till later as he neared home, generally pleased with himself, that Teresa had not left the union hall with the other women. She had stayed behind in the office with Fritz, waving the crying towel.

The dump was still burning itself out. In the streets surrounding Tidal Flats, trucks lined the curbs: city sanitation trucks, industrial trucks, private refuse trucks from the outlying suburbs. At Tidal Flats all the access routes to the dump were blocked by tenants standing arm in arm.

Men, women and adolescents stood with locked arms, facing police cars and refusing to budge. Lucas Ford, pale in his black jersey and pants, flew from post to post, weakest link in the chain, the outside agitator.

He hailed Lucas. "What happens when the paddy wagons arrive?"

Lucas spread his arms wide. All lie down, let themselves be run over.

Upstairs in the apartment, Priscilla was winding up a steering committee meeting. Bostic had encountered a couple of old buddies in the street, sanitation men taking the air outside until the impasse was resolved or quitting time arrived—whichever came first—and had brought them upstairs to the meeting with him. The committee was split up and down in a squabble between those who advocated immediate cessation of the dump operation and those who were interested in advancing a practical means, Bostic and the sanitation men among them, for easing the nuisance.

"What you have to do is lay down a six-inch layer of dirt every night like they done out on Long Island where I worked."

"All you're doing is providing them with an out. No more dumping! We'll get a cease-and-desist order. . . ."

"Now you know damn well, baby, they ain't gonna stop. Only hope you got is to make 'em do it right."

"Do it right, they'll go on with it forever!"

"What do you think, Mish?"

Fix it up. Or throw it out. Eliminate or ameliorate.

He'd been thinking about it all his life and he hadn't found the answer to that one yet.

It was no idle debate. The mayor's office had called an hour ago. Rod Kearnsey was granting the tenants their request for an appointment. He would receive a delegation of three tomorrow afternoon at four o'clock.

"By that time he figures the fires'll be out and the fuss'll be over."

"Delegation, my eye!" Priscilla said.

A night watch was being established, lest the trucks left locked in the streets overnight be reactivated and smuggled through with their loads to the dump. Priscilla signed up for the ten-o'clock patrol. She'd be there with her guitar. He signed up with Bostic for predawn. The human chain would be maintained until the dump was ended, Priscilla claimed, or, Bostic amended, improved.

They dined on Pop's despised jar of commercial borscht, too sweet, too vinegary, doused with sour cream, and the extra can of salmon he had stowed in the refrigerator. After dinner they took refuge for an hour, from telephone and doorbell, in Pop's remedy for all harassments: a drive in the country.

Numbed to insensibility by the succession of stresses, they argued as they drove. About Lucas Ford who had abandoned his job in order to attend full-time to the organizing. "If you're going to depend on everyone being a Lucas, Priscilla, this thing can't last." About his disposition of the suspensions with Colangelo. "But why did you give him till Monday? Why not tomorrow?" You should have. You shouldn't have.

Shouting at the children in the back seat: "Will you be quiet? Can't you stop fighting for just one minute?"

It was not like their clash of the smashed cup night before last. It had none of the misery of her sudden outcry in the street last night. It was an almost cheerful sort of argument. They were on the move again.

Blacktop wound through Hillcrest. Half-fieldstone houses stood half-screened by trees behind curving driveways. Sunset glimmers of glass climbed the wooded hillsides. Gray branch and evergreen shone, sunset-tinged.

"This road," Priscilla directed.

Past a rash of raw-boned ranches going up, desultory farmhouses, a remodeled barn, a restored saltbox, orchards, fields, upland.

"Here. Stop here."

Steph and Greg tumbled out of the car, scrambled over a tumbledown fieldstone fence. Whooping they dove through apple trees down the slope, into darkening brush. Joe's tract of land, long fallow, lay in a panoplied richness of departing color, tawny tussocks, subdued browns, purple.

He perched with Priscilla on the rocky fence under an overhanging pine. They had talked with Flo before they left. Joe was in fine fettle, charming hell out of everybody. Heart, lungs, blood perfectly normal for a man of his age. Some hypertension. Tomorrow a series of tests.

"Healthy as a potato," Priscilla said. "Maybe a little psychosomatic." She had excluded every other possibility from her mind. "It's so peaceful out here. So peaceful."

Turquoise sky splattered through the plumes of pine above them. She reached up and broke off a plume, whisked it over his cheek. Aromatic. Tickling. Prickling. A stinging titillation.

In stillness, tranquility, clarity. With the sharp tingle of pine needles. The chill roughness of rock.

A ferny green freshness rising up out of the dead stalks scented the evening air.

II

1

The stalled line in front of the brick city hall extended around the corner. Police kept it in order, two abreast, spilling over with babies and tots. Along the lawn, up the short walk and the shallow granite steps, through the grotto of the porch, into the hall half-tiled like a lavatory and floored with cracked terrazzo, and up the narrow stairways that circled the iron-caged elevator shaft. The tenant delegation's four o'clock appointment with the mayor was delayed by a controversy at the head of the third flight of stairs outside the mayoral office. Meanwhile, husbands arriving from the afternoon shift joined the line in the street.

He was nodded and nudged ahead from the foot of the line, the two abreast adroitly shifting position under the stricture of the police to let him through. "It's Lunin. His wife's up there with Kearnsey." At least three hundred, he calculated with practiced eye and a begrudging admiration for Lucas. It was Lucas Ford who was mainly responsible for publicizing, renting buses, pulling the crowd out. But according to the headline stories in the *Tribune* on the continuing dump-truck blockade, the force behind the tenant uprising had been identified by a reliable source as Michael Lunin, past president of EWIU-UV Local 317.

A reporter stalked him. "Say, Mike. Hey." The proof sheet of an advertisement was thrust up at him. "This yours? You running this on Sunday?"

"The Tenants Council is."

"Who's the Tenants Council? Who are the officers?"

"It's listed there. You can read."

"But you're not listed. Is it true you're announcing against Colangelo in a couple of days? Is this part of your campaign to recapture the local?"

He escaped inside, dodging a policeman. "It's Lunin." He was spirited through.

From the thronged stairways, enclosed between scrolled sheet-metal walls and scrolled iron elevator cage, a roar of impatience mounted, punctuated by whistles, catcalls, chants. At the head of the third flight of stairs, a police squad barred further progress, adamant against the surging and bucking below. In the hall beyond the police, Priscilla and Frances Knowlton and the tenant petition collector were holding council. A rosy young chap in clerical garb was chatting on the side with a clutch of city hall lawyers and hangers-on.

"Hey, what's the deal?" he shouted to Priscilla over the restraining arm of a police sergeant.

She flashed a smile at him, all sun and sea-brightness. Removed from him, remote, a stranger in navy blue suit with a frill of white blouse collar, and a hat she must have borrowed perched on the back of her head, with a fluff of veiling flared out over her bangs. Her color was high. Her eyes glinted with the light of battle. Everything was under control.

The tall recessed door of the mayor's office, scaled in height proportionately to the height of the ceilings, opened part way. The three delegates refused to surrender the tenant petitions they were carrying to the mayor's secretary. Priscilla, drowned out by the roar up the stairs, repeated what was evidently a set speech. The door opened wider, revealing an old-fashioned hat tree standing inside in the corner. To this day, it was said, Rod Kearnsey still wore the same hat he had when he was elected twenty years before. He was so far above the usual breed of greedy politician, it was said, he rode to work every day in the downtown bus. He was so concerned with the conservation of funds, not only his own but the taxpayers', that he had had the benches removed from their stanchions in the public parks to preserve them from the incursions of weather, wear and vandalism.

"What's the matter? What's the holdup?" he inquired of the people on the stairs around him.

The mayor had refused to meet with the delegation unless the people were sent away. The delegation had refused to leave unless the mayor met with the people.

"We got him over a barrel."

The line down the stairs was as good-natured as a line outside a ball park, ticket in hand, waiting to be admitted; and as dangerous if denied admission. For the second day the trucks were unable to unload their refuse at the dump. Household trash cans were standing on the curb sides disgorging their overflow into the streets. Waste was accumulating in the factories pre-empting work space, offering a potential hazard to workers. Mayor Kearnsey had to start cracking heads and throwing tenants into the pokey or come to terms.

The tall, paneled, yellow-pine door of the mayor's outer office opened wide. A cheer went up.

The delegation filed inside, Priscilla in the lead clutching the petitions to her bosom. Into the lair of her father's protégé and betrayer. The Independent Labor candidate re-elected time and again by the workers, the small shopkeepers, the foreign-born who vested in him all their lost ideals, out of another time and place, and all their resignation to the nature of life: compromise. The reformist whose promises had achieved no more than a regime of civic penury, whose rectitude had proved as ruinous as corruption.

Sometime, too far back for Rod Kearnsey to remember, he had won a small girl's solemn idolatry. In a hand as hard as nails he had held the hand of a trustful little girl, leading her to the victory platform: the man of the people who would lead the people into a shining tomorrow. When she was sent to bed early, kicking and screaming, he came up to say good night to her with his stories and poems. *My heart's in the highlands, my heart is not here, My heart's in the highlands a-chasing the deer. A-chasing the wild deer and following the roe* . . .

Priscilla emerged from the mayor's office, the mayor courteously holding the door open for her, to announce that despite the lateness and inconvenience of the hour Mr. Kearnsey had consented to hold an open hearing on the dump issue in the city council chamber two floors below.

2

The hearing was a triumph or a tragedy, whichever way one chose to regard it. A triumph in the numbers present. A tragedy in that each one of those present, having gone to the length of bringing himself here, having overcome inner inhibitions and outer obstacles to give rein for once to outrage where outrage was due, encountered as a result precisely what he had expected.

Roderick Kearnsey assumed the presiding chair at the council table, ramrod straight in his seedy dark suit, pinched to the bone. His flying brows and piercing eyes, his starkly jutting nose and his thin mouth, once so intimidating, had retreated behind steel-rimmed glasses and bushy mustache. Kearnsey had rescued Shoreham from bankruptcy. He had ousted from office the Republicans who enriched themselves on three bridges that were never built, and the Democrats who had sold city property to themselves at nominal prices. He had scourged the fat from the municipal rolls, had driven forth the dragon of venality, and now, impregnable in his accomplishment, he wore his probity like a mantle about his meager frame. He handled challengers to his hegemony these days generally by ignoring them. In his last election he had been returned to office with his largest landslide ever.

Presiding at the council table, Kearnsey was flanked by his administrative aides: Alvin Whitehead, his director of public works, on his right; Dr. Cranach, his director of public health on his left;

and, joining them shortly, Lowell Stanton, his director of public housing, considered by many to be the arch villain of the piece. Also, at scattered smaller tables: his city attorney and clerks hastily summoned from drowsy end-of-the-afternoon preoccupations preparatory to leaving for home. From within the well of his preserve, enclosed behind a ponderously carved mahogany balustrade that curved across the width of the chamber, he faced the ranked rows of benches mounting to the rear, filled with tenants and a goodly admixture of interested citizens.

Priscilla flew up and down the stepped aisles in whispered conclaves, then settled modestly to the rear beside her husband.

"Mish! Am I glad you got here!"

"What for? You're doing all right. Did he recognize you?"

"I don't think so. I practically told him you had the whole union out there on the stairs."

He stared at her in consternation. She was too exuberant to be remonstrated with. It was her show. She had pulled it off. Out of some long-laid plan of hers . . . no, not plan, it was never so deliberate as a plan . . . out of some long-buried compulsion, necessity . . . She pushed her bangs back, flipped back her little veil and leaned forward, eyes everywhere, observing, consuming. It was up to Frances Knowlton from here on in. Frances, the tenant chairman, was sitting below in the first row of benches.

"Where's Lucas?" he asked her.

"Lucas?" she said vaguely. "Back at the project, I guess. In charge of the human chain."

She had a man posted by the public telephone outside the council chamber, who was to receive word instantly and report it to her if Kearnsey's police tried any hanky-panky at Tidal Flats while the hearing was in progress.

"Sometimes," he said and put his arm around her, along the back of the bench, "you are so full of baloney."

Rod Kearnsey set the hearing in motion with one of the curt commentaries for which he was celebrated.

The dump? It had been from its inception twenty years ago, he reminded his audience, a reclamation project designed to fill in salt marsh and convert it to use. Many homes and businesses in this city rested on just such areas, similarly reclaimed in the past.

The purpose of the dump? Any city in which the majority of the population derives its living from manufacture must provide a place for the disposal of rubbish, industrial and domestic.

The location of the dump? It is a well-known fact that no matter where a dump is located, it should always be on the other side of town from the adjacent residents.

The future of the dump? The land was nearly filled now, and fill had to settle. After the proper grade was established, roads would be constructed, grass would be planted and recreational facilities would be installed. In that order.

"Change takes time and time takes patience," Rod Kearnsey reminded them, "and patience is always notable by its absence among those very citizens who stand to benefit the most."

Now what was their problem?

A woman strode down the sloping center aisle to the councilmanic rail and held up, outspread, a diaper dusky with soot.

The parade of witnesses beginning with Frances Knowlton was permitted three minutes each. Professionals seconded the tenant spokesmen: an ex-social worker, a retired school principal, an industrial chemist, a lawyer residing out on Bay Point, an official of the Chamber of Commerce. Priscilla had even managed to snare Ellen Hamer of her mother's ban-the-bomb committee, a distinguished conservationist whom Flo had coaxed out of her conservatism. In one fell swoop, extending her three minutes to six, Mrs. Hamer tied up the fallout from this week's H-bomb blast, the sulphuric-acid content of the air over England's industrial midlands, Los Angeles smog, and the dire consequence of filling wetlands upon the food chain, with the fiery cloud over Shoreham Bay.

Courteously the mayor, his mouth sunk into the vise of thumb and forefinger, listened to appeals and demands, resolutions, case histories. Under his scrupulous stewardship the council chamber had not been equipped with such frills as a public address system.

The witnesses confronting the officials could scarcely be heard at times from behind. The words of the officials, directed to the witness, were also at times almost inaudible. Shouting broke out from the crowd. "Louder, louder!" "Dump the dump!" The mayor gaveled it to silence. Hand-lettered signs appeared, excavated on signal from shopping bags. A paper banner was unrolled from lap to lap along a tier of benches and across the center aisle. On a nod from the mayor, the signs were confiscated. The mayor was willing to listen only so long as respect for law and order was maintained. At the first hint of any further disturbance the hearing would be adjourned.

An unruly murmur persisted, compounded by youngsters squirming loose, the bustle of comings and goings. It grew with the testimony of witness after witness, the irresistible logic of their charges. The common mood burgeoned from confidence to certainty. They were too many to be denied. The evidence in their favor was too overwhelming to be evaded.

A state health inspector clumped down the center aisle, brushed through the witnesses at the gate and entered the inner preserve. Announcing himself and citing chapter and verse of a state statute forbidding the maintenance of open dumps, he delivered a legal warning notice to Kearnsey and his associates. The city administration was in clear violation of the law.

Newspaper and radio reporters scuttled forward. Tomorrow's headline: DUMP ORDERED CLOSED.

Applause broke out. Priscilla raced up and down the aisle in an ecstasy of delight and deprecation. "Isn't this great? Isn't it marvelous? Don't move! It won't stick."

The state lacked the enabling legislation to enforce the law upon the city. Still compliance, though not mandatory, was presumed to be obligatory, and non-compliance an act of defiance.

Kearnsey passed the warning notice over the council table to his city attorney. Applause died down lest he make good his promise to walk out. But not the jubilation. They had him on the spot. They had him on the run. They'd make it stick. The right for all the world to see was theirs.

Except for a pointed comment to a witness now and then—"Tell me, sir, where do *you* dump your dump?"—Rod Kearnsey left the burden of response to the directors of his departments.

Mr. Whitehead of Public Works, a scrappy little gentleman with snapping eyes, was not to be exceeded by anyone in his zeal for the public weal. There were tenants at Tidal Flats who stoutly believed that Alvin Whitehead was in league with the scrap-metal dealers who either started or encouraged the fires on the dump. There were some who even insisted that the dump was no longer under the city's control—that Whitehead had leased out long-term franchises on it to a certain scrap dealer and suburban refuse contractors for a price. In his physical presence however, Mr. Whitehead exhibited a devotion to duty impossible to doubt. He drew bulging files on the dump from his red calf brief case and, emitting sparks as he spoke, borrowed refutations from the survey he had been conducting for over two and a half years.

The dump could not be ameliorated, as had been suggested by some, by bulldozing gravel over it every night. Gravel was expensive and gravel laid before the landfill had settled could be a total loss . . . The dump could not be eliminated, as others had suggested, by the addition of an incinerator to the present sewage disposal plant. There were incinerators and incinerators and many of them discharged into the atmosphere as much, if not more, smoke than the present dump did. The cost of an efficient incinerator would run from nine million dollars up, a sum prohibitive for the taxpayers, most of them homeowners; and the cost of incineration about four to five dollars per ton. Even so, there was no guarantee that the incinerator would prove adequate for the job. . . . The dump could not be replaced at this date, as had also been suggested, by a public park. The title to forty lots out there in Tidal Flats had yet to be acquired by the city, and the proprietors, he had discovered after extensive research, could not be traced.

Public Works in the person of Mr. Whitehead was proud of its operation of the dump at its present site and some praise, he thought, was due from a grateful citizenry. The Tidal Flats dump was hardly costing them a cent.

Dr. Cranach, the director of Public Health, took exception to his friend Al Whitehead's statement that the dump posed no hygienic threat to the community. Cranach sprawled in his chair, large and affable, a bulwark of assurance against demands impossible to satisfy. In his budget request to the Board of Appropriations this spring, he was including an item that would, if granted, double the number of exterminators assigned to cope with the problem-potential of rodents. He also needed, if funds were available, an additional public health nurse to service the Bay section. Beyond this, perhaps more emphasis in the schools on teaching good physical habits and more frequent use by the neighborhood of the free chest-X-ray unit . . .

Having yielded thus far to the critics, Dr. Cranach then implied that the hasty dispatch of a state health inspector to this hearing was politically motivated, inspired by opposition parties. Meanwhile, at this very moment, the real menace to the health and safety of the community was expanding so rapidly as to constitute an emergency of alarming proportions. The refuse trucks being blocked at the access routes to the dump must be permitted to proceed with their function at once, even if it required armed police to drive them through.

"All you people here who have lent yourself to this irresponsible action, go back to Tidal Flats right now and see to it that those trucks go through. Otherwise I shall be bound to call upon the mayor to take whatever steps are necessary."

"Are you saying," a man spoke up from the middle row, "that you're going to *shoot?*"

"We have warned you people that unless you keep order . . ."

No one stirred during the flurry of consultation at the council table. Their fate was not to be decided by the olympian accords and discords of department heads. They were the deciders. It was the city that was on trial, not themselves. Neither the somber dark paneling nor the monotonously patterned sheet metal above nor the dull clusters of light nor the faded backsides of downtown stores through the tall windows nor the air itself, dusty and dessicating, could sap their will.

"Howcome Huffsy, the salvage king, has a monopoly on scavenging the dump?" the next witness addressed himself rhetorically to Whitehead. "Is Public Works behind him? Or is he a mustache for the Mafia?"

The last half dozen witnesses parted to let a determined girl propel her daughter through to the forefront.

"Pick up your blouse, honeybunch. Show the doctor your back. Show them."

"Identify yourself. Your name, ma'am?"

"Unless you people keep order . . ."

3

Priscilla slumped back against the bench in relief. "Wow. That does it. He's going to give in. He's got to give in. He can't sit through a thing like this and not give in."

The ruffled collar of her blouse billowed with a misty warmth. Even though she had her word to say that she had been saving for so long, she had resolved when she started counting heads among the witnesses to stay out of the hearing. She had watched it unfold before her like a thing of beauty, a spectacle outside herself.

"If we hold out. If we just don't give in ourselves. Mish, don't you dare . . ."

He had his own plan, concocted with Bostic and the sanitation men yesterday afternoon, that he was to introduce if all else failed. A sensible enough plan, but to Priscilla a token of surrender. Settle for halfway measures? Never. No quarter to the enemy!

"Who says it will settle it?" he said and smoothed the collar of her blouse down over the flat collar of her suit.

"Mish, look at him. We have him in such a bind—he's got to shoot or give in. And you want to supply him with a loophole?"

It remained for Lowell Stanton of Public Housing to turn the tables completely roundabout. Just as Priscilla had her heart fixed on Kearnsey, the tenants had their heart on Stanton. They had been unable during their testimony to refrain from mingling their multiple housing complaints with their dump plea and attacking Stanton as the prime cause of their ills. The sympathizers and expert witnesses had contributed their share to the castigation heaped on him. As the incarnation of bureaucratic arrogance and indifference, Stanton was a much more likely target than Kearnsey who had appointed him.

Several months before, Stanton had imposed a rent increase on the housing projects and, after a week of declining to discuss it with tenants, had summoned the press to his office and dictated his explanation. "The reason for the rent increase is obvious. One-fifth of our apartments are vacant. The increases are essential therefore to compensate for loss of revenue." The reason for the vacancies at a time of housing shortage? "That, too, is obvious. Aside from those on relief who are paying underscale, applicants with income low enough to meet federal requirements cannot be found. Rent based on the income of families in the low-budget bracket therefore has to be raised in order to provide more housing for more people."

He was tagged from then on in Shoreham as What's-That-Again-Stanton.

Throughout the hearing, Stanton had proffered his back to the public. Seated to the left of Cranach and the mayor, he pivoted himself in such a fashion that only his tweedy left shoulder, hunched upward in distaste, and the side of his head were visible. At last, unable to endure any more, he expressed himself with face averted from the chamber.

Suddenly it was clear that Stanton would have preferred never to rent out the housing at all. He had been given a nice lot of buildings to look after, newly constructed, and would have liked to preserve them in their pristine state, the raw brick exteriors, their cool plaster and resinous paint freshness inside, against the depredations of occupancy. He had attempted to be selective, to place the small families and pensioners, the applicants of good

appearance, with the job background and connections to recom-
mend them, in the choicer projects; the sad sacks in the shabby
locations; the non-whites not at all, with few exceptions and those
exceptions all together; the rest on a rotating list as the size apartment for which they were qualified became available. In the last
few years, much against his judgment, he had been compelled by
the state to admit welfare cases, unwed mothers and other un-
desirables, including an influx of migrants from the South and
Puerto Rico. He did his best to prevent these elements from
spreading their damage by assigning them to Tidal Flats on the
dump side where it wouldn't matter as much. He tried to hold
them off when they applied, hoping they would find other quarters. He tried to keep them out. And still they came. And still they
spread, building to building, court to court.

"The dump is none of my business," Stanton began in his low
and penetrating voice, directed toward his fellows at the council
table, "but the tenants are. We are in the business of housing them
and that's all. But . . . I cannot sit here any longer and allow them
to carry on as if they were the epitome of all virtue and the government that shelters them the source of all evil. I cannot sit idly
by and allow this distortion of reality to develop any further. If
there is any dump anywhere let them look to their own premises
and if there is anyone at fault let them look at themselves.

"Tidal Flats! Oh, if only I could write a book! Tidal Flats is less
than ten years old and already it's being reduced to a shambles."

The filthy halls, if one mopped, another didn't. The female
feuds and the fisticuffs. The broken bottles in the courtyards, the
broken windows, the broken lights. "We built a conduit up to the
roof and put a screened light up there and do you think the kids
didn't climb up the conduit and smash the light?" The gambling
and drinking in the open, the petting in the doorways, the roving
juvenile gangs, the instances of rape and incest, the knifings, the
police out there every other Saturday night. The inexperience with
plumbing equipment. More than garbage was dropped out the
windows.

"Personal misconduct! Immorality! Ignorance! If that were all!

Unfortunately wherever there is manure, there are always flies to fatten on it."

Stanton did not mention but somehow conveyed the surreptitious trafficking in numbers, sex, booze, drugs, stolen goods. He mentioned no hustle or hustler by name but he did stress the need for more plainclothes police. And the biggest hustle of all? Stanton granted it a groan. Families moving in from some rathole somewhere left their furnishings behind and as soon as they arrived the door-to-door salesmen descended on them with their time-payment plans . . . the collection agencies . . . the threats of repossession . . . the resort to part-time prostitution, the rackets . . .

"The truth is, these people are incapable of doing anything to help themselves. Land for parks? They'd park their cars all over it. Playground equipment? They'd tear it up by the foundations. What they require first and foremost and I only wish to God we had it in our power to provide it, is: SOMEONE TO TEACH THEM HOW TO LIVE!"

From Stanton's picture of Tidal Flats emerged the portrait of a man desperately trying to contain in one corner of one project a contagion that would, if uncontrolled, filter out into all his projects and the city at large. And more and more it was escaping the boundaries he set. Soon the whole of Tidal Flats would become a condemned village, quarantined by reputation behind the high chain-wire fencing that surrounded it. A dumping ground for the dregs of society, the dump a fount of purity by comparison.

The city attorney left his small table to speak into Stanton's ear. Stanton nodded thoughtfully. For the first time he swung about toward the benches and lifted his eyes over the packed rows upward to the statue of Athena guarding the double doors in the rear.

"Of course," Stanton resumed with an ambient smile, all passion spent, "only about 10 per cent of our tenants ever give us any trouble. The other 90 per cent," he acknowledged, "nobody ever talks about. Many of you here now, I am reliably informed, are not tenants at all and therefore have little acquaintance with the subject. As for those who do claim to be tenants, they are, I can assure you, not at all typical. Obviously they are being misled by a small group, who, I am certain that investigation will reveal, do not belong in public housing."

What's that? What's that again, Stanton?

"To those bona fide tenants who have come in good faith I would offer a piece of advice. Obey the housing rules and most especially see to it that your small children are not sent down the halls with trash bundled in bags or newspapers that become soggy to chutes that are too high for them to reach. The despoliation of Tidal Flats would then, I guarantee you, be substantially abated."

Disorder swept the chamber. Amid a confusion of cries—"Dump Stanton!" "No more Stanton!" "Apologize, apologize!"—Stanton stalked toward the door at the far end of the balustrade. He had driven his assault deep into their ranks: Stop blaming the dump, the dump is merely a scapegoat for your own delinquencies. He had bombarded them with truisms so telling they gave rise at times, over the hisses, to scattered applause: It's not buildings that make slums, it's bad parents who can't or won't control their young. He had planted his boobytrap among them: Do I or don't I belong?

Reporters pelted after Stanton along the balustrade. Was he initiating an investigation into illegal tenancy? Did he have any particular persons in mind? What about the criminal element?

"Shoreham, the asshole of America! And Tidal Flats, asshole of the asshole! We are the refuse swept under the rug of civilization."

It was Lucas—a wraith standing above the topmost bench, up on the white base of the Pallas Athena in the rear—a black stem crowned with a thorny black halo of hair, pale face reduced to anonymity by the twin-muzzled projection of black glasses. He diverted all movement for the moment, denouncing everybody for everything with equal venom: the sweet social worker along with the mayor, the helpful Chamber of Commerce secretary along with Stanton and his stooges. Police swarmed from their posts to pull him down. Tenants swarmed from the benches to rescue him. Lucas plunged from their clutches down the aisle to the balustrade.

"Come on, all you gutless creeps. Come down, jump the gate and take your rightful place. Follow me!"

One minute he saw Lucas and the next minute he didn't. When he broke through to Lucas, nobody was there but Bostic, Willenski, Tidal Flats neighbors. Did the police get him? No. Did anybody see him go? No. He'd gone up in a puff of smoke. He was never there at all.

"Mr. Mayor. Just one moment. If you please."

The imperious voice descending the aisle interrupted the adjournment of the hearing. Veiled hat, navy blue suit with a frill of blouse over the collar approached the rail.

"Are you telling us, Mr. Mayor, that you have no remedy for this situation?"

Rod Kearnsey paused in his preparation for departure to regard the lady. Despite what he was to refer to later as a near-riot in his chamber he allowed her to give her name to the clerk as an additional witness and to take the allotted three minutes.

"Am I right in assuming, Mr. Mayor, that the only thing that stands between us and the removal of that dump is money? That if you had the money you could immediately buy or build as many incinerators as we need, of the kind we need? And in view of this, all the other arguments put forth here this afternoon by these gentlemen are of no account whatsoever?"

Kearnsey permitted himself a twinkle. "Well, Mrs. Lunin. If you can tell me where the money is to be found?"

"I most certainly can."

She had been hoarding it for so long—it swelled out of her, ringing to the rafters.

"You were elected to office by the working people of this city as their representative and for twenty years you have been the front, the mask, for the manufacturers who derive their wealth from us. The money you've saved while you let our schools and our services and our very environment go to pot has been their money."

"Will you come to the point, Mrs. Lunin? If you have a point?"

"The politicians who robbed Shoreham bankrupt don't have a patch on the real thievery that goes on here. The industrial tax exemptions! If I may quote from a speech you delivered your first election night—"

"Your point, Mrs. Lunin?"

"You go to United Vacuum and International Automatics and Royal Steel and all the other major industries and levy a property tax on their inventories and you will have the money . . ."

As she had stood with her guitar on the platform singing that winter day a decade ago before the massed support for the UV strike assembled in Liberty Square, she stood now below, her back to the crowd, challenging the mayor with the secret scandal of his administration. The untaxed inventories. The subtle subsidy borne by the inhabitants, the sacrifice of their own and their children's well-being on the altar of the industries sustained by their labor.

"Levy a property tax on their stock and equipment on a scale commensurate with that paid by anyone who owns a car—"

Sitting up on the bench between Bostic and Willenski, he covered his face and cowered. Any UV worker could have told Priscilla, any worker in any one of Shoreham's major industries: Don't push it, don't say it, don't even think it! A tax like that and UV would be out of Shoreham tomorrow.

People were sidling out, overtired or hungry or simply uneasy. Stanton, so soundly booed a few minutes before, had left his mark. Tidal Flats was going down and the practical-minded were already reviewing their alternatives. And Lucas, the firebrand, had left his mark. Asshole of the asshole—Shoreham was no shantyville! This beautiful city laid between the hills and the sea, with its many tree-lined streets, its blocks of sun-porched three-family houses, its nationality centers and churches; where would you find a better one? And Priscilla was leaving her mark. What taxes? Whose money?

"You located Tidal Flats on the city dump, a population center of over two thousand people, pledging that the fill would be completed inside of five years. Those five years were up five years ago. If a man like you, of your principles and your integrity, refuses to respond to an aroused populace, then democracy is dead! Government without the consent of the governed is tyranny. We beg of you, stop the dumping. Appropriate the money. Start building the Roderick A. Kearnsey Playground and Park. Now!"

She stripped Kearnsey, she flayed him, she blasted him to a cinder with his own long-since meaningless slogans, faithfully reiterated every election year. When she was finished, Kearnsey withdrew his mouth from the forked support of thumb and forefinger and to everyone's surprise blandly inquired, "Anybody else?"

Unmoved by reminders of his beginnings, Kearnsey was lasting it out to the last outburst. A little rebellion every once in a while did no harm. The rebels exercised their right to free assembly, they gave vent to their free speech, they flaunted their demand for redress of grievances and then it was over. The air was cleared. You had your day, you had your say, what more do you want? Go home.

With Bostic and Willenski by his side, he followed Priscilla at the gate. It was Bostic who had insisted that if you're going to ask for anything you have to show them how to give it. But Bostic was distinctly unhappy now. Mae and her job at the civic auditorium, him and his job at UV, the apartment they'd had for years, one of the privileged few colored families. Madder at Lunin than he was at the mayor, he glowered with the hard-headed conviction: If anybody's left holding the bag, it's gonna be me!

It was a minimum request they were making, for just a minor bit of information. The time schedule for the closing of the dump. When.

"According to competent engineers, Mr. Mayor, the dumping has more than filled in the marshland. Fill, you have hills and mountains of fill. The job is now complete.

"All that remains is a grading operation. Using present city equipment you can lay down a six-inch cover of dirt every night, compacting the rubbish as you bulldoze and burying it. With a final topping of about two feet at the end of sixty days, you will have a clear field, leveled off, ready for seeding. You have done it."

Alvin Whitehead popped his head out from the carapace of his back and with snapping blue eyes gobbled up the morsel.

"If we have dirt available for that purpose."

"Sixty days, that's all it requires. Meanwhile no odors, no vermin, no fires."

"I said, Lunin, that we'd take it under advisement. Soil topping costs too much and fills up too fast—"

"Do you have a date, sir, for cessation of this so-called fill operation at Tidal Flats?"

"Certainly."

"When?"

"As soon as possible."

"When is that?" The crowd was breaking up behind them. "Three months? Five months? When?"

Whitehead's eyes skittered humorously over them. Ten years ago, it had been five more years. Five years ago, it had been another five years.

"Five years should do it."

And five years from now?

A vague assurance that from now on the fire department would pay more attention to fire prevention. A glib hint that this summer the neighborhood schoolyard would be kept open for Tidal Flats youngsters to use as a playground, under supervision. That was all they were able to extract by their combined efforts from the combined departments of the city.

With a rigor that ribbed his jaws and a rasp in his throat, Kearnsey reprimanded the trio of men before him, at the same time speeding his dispersing guests on their way.

"All of us want the best for our city, there's no question of that. But it's one thing to advocate and quite another to administer. I spent years meeting with my supporters in little labor halls and when the halls were raided we took to the street corners and when permission to speak on the streets was refused us we rented vacant lots and when the lots were denied us we went to the courts. We contested the parties in power and when we won power from them, they left us an empty shell, a sinking ship, a government so penniless it couldn't pay for the forms to write a purchasing order on. We took what we had to work with and rebuilt as best we could and restored Shoreham to working order.

"If any of you think you can improve on our accomplishment, then get into politics, go out on the streets and convince others of your program. Risk the ridicule and the rocks. And when you've won your struggle and have to put your ideals in practice, let us see how you'll deal with the dilemma of the city dump."

Kearnsey glanced at a paper that had been passed to him and without comment gave it to a clerk to be handed over the gate to the unholy three, Lunin, Bostic and Willenski. It was a telegram sent by Nick Colangelo who had just learned from the radio that EWIU-UV Local 317 was being falsely represented at city hall as a proponent of the Tidal Flats Tenants Council. No such authorization had been voted to Michael Lunin or anyone else purporting . . .

"You see?" Bostic grunted. "Didn't I tell you, you ought to ring Nick in on this? He'd have gone to Judge Rinaldi with it. We'd be in clover."

At the summit of the aisle Priscilla was deep in discussion with a young lawyer from Bay Point. "They'll ask for an injunction against the tenants," the lawyer was counseling her as he joined them, "to stop them from blocking the trucks. Your father's a lawyer, you know you can't buck an injunction."

"But can't *we* ask for our own injunction? Make *them* stop?"

He succeeded in detaching her and hurrying her out. She had the lawyer all lined up, she claimed. A young Republican with political ambitions. If he took legal action on behalf of the tenants, she had persuaded him, he'd have five hundred votes in his pocket, ready-made.

"It went so well. Didn't it go well? You came in just right, Mish. I was so afraid you'd water down— And Lucas just at the height, that was wild. Even Stanton with his insults . . ."

They were halted on the ground floor by a round of applause. The mayor and his contingent issued from the elevator.

"Mrs. Lunin?"

In his faded brown hat and seedy dark suit, a legendary figure, Kearnsey took Priscilla by elbow and hand and drew her aside. "Tell me, how is Joe?"

"Great. Fine. He's up at Sprague for a checkup. Be back in a few days."

The mayor's query startled and disturbed her. "The word sure gets around fast," she groused all the way out to the street. "Why did he ask me that?"

"Lunin—say, Lunin?" Reporters caught up with him. "How long have you lived at Tidal Flats?"

"Since the house we were living in was condemned for the expressway and there was nothing else vacant in our price range. Okay?"

"How about this investigation Stanton is launching?"

"I know as much about it as you do."

"I understand Mr. Colangelo has repudiated—"

"Repudiate!" Priscilla swept grandly on. "Just let him come out and repudiate. A lot of good it'll do him."

"About that UV taxation, Lunin—"

He hurried after his wife. Whether he affirmed or denied it, not a word on the subject of UV taxation would leak out in tomorrow's press. And nothing he could say would change the impression that he was the one to raise the subject here today.

They strode past illuminated store windows of bedspreads on sale, mannequins in furs and Easter lilac; jostled through the flanks of fenders in the parking lot; bundled into the car, slamming doors. Priscilla ripped off her hat. Her hair, released, sprang up like a nest of straw. Stretching out on the seat, with an arch of her hips she began slithering out of her unaccustomed girdle. Oooffff.

"Did we clobber them! I've never been through anything— Not anything— You're not saying anything. Why don't you say something?"

Headlights shot blindingly through the windshield, splintering on the silver sliver of the wiper.

"You were great. Beautiful."

"Go back. There are people we have to ride home. I don't mean that. I mean really. Wasn't it—"

He reached under her skirt and pinched her underthigh, silky cool, and took the girdle she passed him, rolled up with her hose inside, and stuffed it, warmly elastic, into his jacket pocket.

"Now I know who really should be mayor of Shoreham."

"Hey, George, Ginger! Hey, folks—over here! I didn't mean *me*. I meant *it*. I mean three days ago who would have dreamed— You don't mean that. You don't really mean . . ."

"Yes, I do," he said. "Really."

4

Squeezed between him and George in the front seat, Priscilla wriggled out of her jacket. Through her wilted blouse she diffused a feverish and expansive energy. What they had to do next and next. She caught at details as if to let one escape her would invite catastrophe.

"We have to find Lucas. He has the cut for the Sunday ad."

"The *Trib* has the cut," he assured her. "Their reporter showed me the proof when I was going into city hall."

"You saw it? Are you sure? It wasn't just the copy? The last thing they put in is the cut."

"I saw it. They got it. It's there."

"Wait'll you see the ad on Sunday, it's a knockout," Priscilla told their passengers.

"Do you think it'll do any good?"

To Priscilla the question was treason. To admit the possibility of defeat was to surrender to it. To give voice to caution was to sabotage the momentum.

He was stifled by concern for her. What happens when she finds out. . . .

Outside the project, dump trucks, abandoned for the night, lined the streets like slumbering beetles. At the access routes tenant patrols maintained their blockade. The fires that had blazed sky-high behind the buildings were out. The smoke had died down. The blackened fields were pitted with running sores, a blackness that heaved and shuddered, whorls of blackness, shimmering with pools of stagnant water out of which skeletal metal frames reared reaching for the stars. Fumes of burnt rubber, plastics, cotton, a residue of oil hung sodden in the poignant sea air. It would rain before the night was out.

They dropped the passengers off at their doors. "Has anybody around seen Lucas?"

Lucas was here. Lucas was there. Lucas wasn't anywhere.

Stephanie and Gregory were sitting on the Kochis living room floor with the Kochis children, watching TV. Out of the darkness toy pistols shot at ghostly figures massacring each other over overturned saloon tables.

He waited in the open doorway to the hall, holding groceries and bundles of his union mailing, while Priscilla went in to fetch them.

"No trouble at all," Mrs. Kochis said. "Let 'em stay to the end. They're fed. Look what Eddie brought them."

In Hopalong Cassidy outfits, black hats pitched back, they shot from the hip.

"Oh, you shouldn't have," Priscilla said faintly. "I'll pay you back. Come on, kids. Come on now."

A little too sharply, steering a course between gratitude and disapproval, Priscilla tugged at the children. Roused, they resisted her. *Let it be*, he signaled Priscilla from the door. *How can I*, she signaled back at him, *look at them*. Ruination! The Kochis boy sprang up and frantically shoved his fist at Greg whose protests against leaving were drowning out the dialogue. Quick as a cat Mrs. Kochis landed a stinging blow on her son's ear.

"I'll turn the damn thing off!"

With hand over ear, too mesmerized by the scene on the screen to cry out, the boy sank back down to the floor.

"Say, hon, where's my bowling shoes?"

Eddie padded out of the bathroom, all spiffied up in sports shirt and slacks, his hair slicked back from his broad brow in a side-swiped swirl. "Hey." He spotted Priscilla in the living room. "I hear you made a monkey out of Kearnsey."

That set her off. "You should have been there. If he thinks he can buy us out by promising improvements . . ."

"Kearnsey's the best of them," Eddie teased her. "Look at Boston, look at Chicago, look at Jersey City. They spend your dough and what do you get for it? They all sell out. Except the man at the bottom and that's why he's there."

It was useless to argue with Eddie. He changed his premise with every sentence. Priscilla went at him hammer and tongs, and he stood her off laughing. "Stay for coffee," Mrs. Kochis pleaded. "I'll have coffee in a minute."

The telephone was ringing in the Lunin apartment. And Priscilla's brother, Ted, was coming up the stairs.

"You have to remember Kearnsey's a carpenter," Eddie declaimed, edging after Priscilla to the door. "He dropped his plumb line and bob from where he was at and it fell just a fraction short of where he was supposed to start and the more he's built, the farther it's taken him from where he meant to go."

"That's a very intelligent observation," Ted said.

"Teddy!"

The program was over. The kids were led out showing off their loot, the black felt hats whipstitched with white already unraveling, the shiny black paper-leather boots pulled on over their ankles already crumpling. And the guns. Pop pop, poppety-pop.

"Out in Boston Harbor there's an island piled so high with trash—" Eddie pursued them to their door "—it don't pay no more to have the cranes hoist the dump up on top of it. They can't get the bulldozers up there to level it off. Ain't nothing they can do but abandon it. Leave it to the gulls." With a flick of his finger Eddie flipped up under Priscilla's nose. "Leave it to the gulls, doll. Leave it to the gulls."

"That's quite a blockade you have out there," Ted said as soon as they were inside. "How long do you think you can keep it up?"

"As long as we have to," Priscilla said. "Till a special council's convened to allocate the funds for an incinerator." She sailed ahead of them into the kitchen and threw an apron on, tore frozen minute steaks out of their wrappings, began skinning onions into the sink. "They'll have to find someplace else to fill in temporarily. No more here. Not another speck."

"How long, Mish?"

"I'll tell you better next week."

"Don't listen to him, Ted. He's starved. Here." She tossed a bag of potato chips at him. "Break out the beer."

Exchanging glances over her, they settled down at the kitchen table with a couple of beers and a batch of envelopes to be addressed. "Do you honestly think, Mish, that a missive like this," Ted asked hesitantly, "whatever its merits . . ." He was too busy to reply, scrawling away. The mailing had to be out tomorrow for Saturday delivery at the latest.

Ted had stopped off between planes. He was on another consultation trip with Weber, to Dallas overnight and back on Saturday. He had been up at Sprague visiting Joe this afternoon. He had spoken with the chief neurologist. Everything negative so far. Joe was staying the week for further tests and observation. Hot on his brief, dictating to Flo faster than she could take it down.

"Didn't I tell you?" Priscilla waved her red-string onion bag on high.

"But all that talking he did the other night, the accentuation of personality traits. . . ."

"Pfffvvv." She let out a resounding Bronx cheer. "Look who's talking! I'd match you against him anytime." She shot two onions into the garbage pail, scummy, stinking, awful, saving the long-horned sprouts to mince over the steaks. "You should have heard Stanton today. You wouldn't believe . . ."

All Joe's talk that night . . . Joe, at his wits' end, seeing nothing ahead for them but demoralization, trying so hard to rectify . . . none of it had penetrated, none of it made a dent on her.

Ted slung his coat over the back of his chair, unslung his necktie and tackled the envelopes. "Suppose you lose this dump thing," Ted boldly put it to her, "what then?"

"What have we got to lose! We lose, we're where we were. If we win . . . We'll win this one. You can't lose 'em all."

He left Ted with the envelopes to take a quick shower and change for the evening. When he returned to the kitchen they were both at it, in rival session. Priscilla on the mayor, how she had exposed him till now the only way he could save his skin . . . And Ted on his consultation trips. Ted was always quite funny about his trips, holding them off from himself with his air of easy-breezy detachment and embracing them, assuming the importance of one who moves in the world of affairs and becoming the more important by his rejection of it.

Someday he would write a novel, Ted vowed, called *The Tube*. All the suburbanites hopping into their cars in the carport, racing for the expressway, ten minutes later in the office, never having seen any of the towns they passed through en route. Same thing with these trips. Into the car to the airport and out of sight. Down into the same airport they left behind and on to the de luxe motor inn, same one everywhere, and into the motel conference room. Same management reception. The fish eye. What makes you think you can solve what we can't? Cocktail, Dr. Weber. Cocktail, Dr. Barth? Same cocktail. The plant? They never went near it. In two years Weber had been all over the country and hadn't seen one damn thing. Back to the plane.

Ted rocked on his kitchen chair, in shirtsleeves, and entertained them with it. His dark hair, soft as a child's, tumbled over his forehead, a sheen in it that might be the first faint daub of gray. His glasses flickered with self-derisive humor.

"Even the problem," Ted said, "the problem's usually the same. Expansion. Bigness. Five years ago the company started out with a fifty-thousand-dollar investment and now they have a fifty-million-dollar business and suddenly they can't cope, why? They're doing all the same things they did before. It's led to such success. And now? Bring in the outside expert! Help!"

The minute steaks, laced with blood and fringed with browned onions, were shoveled out onto plates. The salad bowl was thumped down on the table, the french fries were shaken about in paper toweling. Priscilla with telephone tucked under her ear, cigarette jigging in the corner of her mouth, sank down at the table with them. "What we did to Kearnsey, that's just the beginning." She left the telephone off the hook and fell to, famished. "Even the welfare cases . . ." Gradually she subsided, yielding the field to Ted, listening to him with puzzled attention.

"Last time Weber and I tubed down to Houston. Texas Micromatics. We were met by the entire corporate board, ten of them. One difference. Ordinarily everyone dresses the same, charcoal suit, white shirt, slim tie, the uniform. Step out of line, sooner or later you're out of a job. But this time half of them arrived in uniform and half of them in Italian shirts, self-conscious, not knowing what to expect.

"What's the problem? Administrative. Five years ago they started out with three hundred employees. Now it's twenty-two thousand. How do you manage that number? In a municipality it's organized along political lines, with democratic participation, at least presumably. But a factory? The sheer weight of it . . .

"We tackled the problem from the top. Executive turnover. All over town the preachers are complaining that these prize parishioners aren't attending church, teachers are complaining the children aren't receiving proper paternal attention, the wives are complaining. . . . All working seventy hours a week, trying to surpass each other at the highest level, make themselves look good. No make-work either. All essential, creative, requiring the best brainpower. Sixty thousand a year and they don't stay. What's wrong?

"We were there three days consulting. Never went near the plant."

Forks and knives wrestled with the gristle. The meat was chewed down anyway, hungrily, with its stringiness, mmm, so good. Salt? More onion, anyone?

On the plane back from Dallas, Ted had run into a physicist, a

Dr. Rennie. Rennie had just been through the same experience, in another plant. But all Rennie could spare was two hours. Cocktail, Dr. Rennie? No cocktail. You'll be here for dinner, Dr. Rennie? No dinner. Rennie had wired ahead for a blackboard to be set up in the motel conference room and right away he took his coat off and started in. What's the problem? A furnace in which they had been making so much compound per so many cubic feet. Up to a few months ago when they enlarged the furnace according to their formulas, quadrupling production. All of a sudden the compound was dissolving on them. Rennie asked them his questions, put their answers up on the blackboard and left. It was all right there on the blackboard. Expansion. Bigness. They had overlooked the primary factor. The effect of maximization.

"All the way back on the plane we kicked it around," Ted said and sucked at a shred of meat trapped in his back teeth. "These feudal oligarchies grown up within the body politic, with only minimal regulation, no government agency over them, no one asking, 'Where's this all going to end up?' The spontaneous tendency of an organism is to keep growing until something intervenes to arrest the process. You know it can't keep growing forever."

Toothpicks were passed around. Their faces were strained with laughter, eyes hardened to aching.

"What are you laughing at, Mish?"

"Growth! I got the same thing from Coffin," he said to Ted and laughed so hard he almost swallowed his toothpick.

"Did you now? On the basis of that thesis, Rennie the physicist and Weber the psychologist went to work on me. Plotted out my future for me. The age of imperialism, wars, revolution, social collapse? Rot! We're at the dawn of the postindustrial epoch. There's so much money being made, according to them, the surplus value if you will is so great, the economic surplus being poured into new investment and new investment into new development. . . . The feedback within the system can cover the cost of anything, wars, wages, the whole bit.

"What's the problem? My problem—their problem—is to spot

the malfunctions, correct the imbalances. Keep it growing. Grow! What could be better? So Rennie took me by the hand . . ."

Rennie had taken Ted, after they landed, to see a friend who headed up an advisory group to industry and government, forecasting production trends in the 1980s.

"Oh, Ted, you wouldn't . . ."

It was an experience. Ted was always interested in new experiences. He found himself on the sixty-first floor of a glass building, a windowed cell floating in midair. Décor in wood tones. Everybody busily working. Somebody from IBM coyly inquiring, "Do you think we're paternalistic?" Outside, gray monoliths, cenotaphs, dragon's teeth.

"And I'm cringing. Shrinking in expectation. The island can only hold so much, it'll maximize until somewhere a self-destruct mechanism is tripped off. Manhattan sinking into the sea? A bolt out of the blue?"

"Ted, you didn't . . ."

"Obviously not. I sent them my published stuff. They were very excited over it. Suggested another group, preparing educational materials to counteract Russian and Chinese propaganda in the underdeveloped nations. Weber gave me his advice. Get out of the university. Get myself placed as a senior analyst. Then come back, if I want to, trailing clouds of glory."

"Ted, what are you trying to tell us?" Turning away from the table, Priscilla studiously scrubbed her bread in the drippings in the grill pan. "The university didn't renew your appointment, is that it? They dropped you?"

No, it wasn't the university. Ted had his reappointment. Another assistantship.

"Upsala then? It fell through? Ted, it was never that definite! You mustn't let it get you down. So long as you know you're on the right path. . . ."

With exuberant examples from her day she urged Ted out of his discouragement.

"Take Frances Knowlton. You know what's giving her all the gumption? That bus boycott down in Montgomery, Alabama.

She's given us so much time, she's not sure she has a job any more with the women she cleans for. And she doesn't care. 'Some things you have to do.' So long as you know you're right. . . ."

"When was Reconstruction, Priscilla? How many years has it taken for them to start moving from the back of the bus to the front?"

The telephone, absent-mindedly restored, was ringing. Lucas's sister worried about Lucas. She'd had an awful fight with him this noon and hadn't seen him since.

Priscilla put the telephone down, perturbed.

"That's funny. I had a fight with him too. Over the photo for the ad. He paid this teen-age camera bug he's been cultivating twenty dollars out of our kitty for the photo. Said he wanted to make him feel professional. Twenty dollars! When all the rest of us are in it for nothing. I blew my stack. Then he got bitter. Started accusing me of being eyewash for the ruling class. Me! Worse than Kearnsey. Worse than Eisenhower! It was getting time to leave for city hall so I left him."

The children, forbidden, had discovered their guns, hidden, and were shooting it out in the bedroom. A hair-raising shriek. Steph had caught her foot in Greg's boot and the binding, unwinding, ripped through the shiny black paper leather.

"Where's the adhesive tape? Why the hell did Eddie have to buy . . ."

Banging each other over the head with their pistols. Attempts to wrench the pistols from them defeated by shrieks to high heaven.

5

The two of them put the children to bed while Priscilla attended to mending the boot. He was to drive Ted to the airport afterward.

"A story! A story!"

Ted wasn't the storyteller, it was Gail.

"Once upon a time," Ted began, lightly, "there was a beautiful princess who could dance and sing and make strudel. One night her prince came home from a journey to a far country and all over the palace tables there was strudel dough. Strudel dough in the kitchen all over the counters, rolled out as thin as gossamer, and in the parlor all over the walls and all over the ceiling and hanging from the lights. And the princess said to the prince, 'Where have you been?' And the prince said, 'Seeking the meaning of life.' 'You're forever seeking for some deep meaning in life,' the princess said to him, 'when there is none. Why can't you just *live?*'

"So they filled the strudel with nuts and raisins and they baked it up and they ate it. And they lived happily ever after."

"Is that all?"

"That's all. You're lucky to get this much."

"Guess what!" Priscilla burst in, shining. "Gray just called, the Republican lawyer out on Bay Point. He's agreed to go before Judge Rinaldi tomorrow with our request for an injunction against the city, at no cost to us."

"But, Priscilla, Gray's just using this," he protested and looked to Ted for confirmation. "As a pawn in whatever game the Republicans . . . Putting Rinaldi on the spot. Rinaldi's a Democrat and he wants to be mayor."

Ted backed him up. "Two birds with one stone. Embarrass Rinaldi. And the administration."

"So what! All the better. You're not leaving, are you? I have a potful of coffee."

They drank their coffee standing in the kitchen, in their coats.

"You see, Ted, if you stick to your path, things can come your way—"

"What path? You wake up one day to the recognition that you're not a theoretician, you're a technician. You hear yourself intruding into every conversation, asserting your views. You resort to such stratagems . . . The child prodigy grown up. The whiz kid that fizzled." The lightness, the detachment was out of it. "They had no right, Pris, no earthly right to impose that on me! It's Joe who should have become so much more than he is. Joe!"

"Ted Ted Ted, don't. The limitation isn't in you! You're not out to cure typhoid one by one. You're clearing the swamp. Those careerist crumbs—"

The man was flying upside down in a tailspin. And Priscilla, exhorting him with her moral example, picked up his flight bag without further ado and took it off to the hall closet. She locked it in and, lacking pockets, wedged the key into her skirt band.

"Dallas-shmallas! You're staying here tonight. Mish, stay out of this."

He went after her, reaching for the key. "Enough now. Cut it out. Give him back his bag."

"I'll handle it, Mish." Ted shushed him down. "This is between the two of us. Sure, sure, I'm right. Only my timing is a little off. Just like Kearnsey. That neighbor of yours—what's his name, Kochis?—wasn't so wrong about old Rod. If he could have started off from scratch. If he could create change in a vacuum. But, no, the past always pervades the present, even the past you think you've eradicated. He was handed just so many options to begin with. He couldn't choose what wasn't there. So he chose the straightest line toward his objective. Maybe just a fraction off. And that fraction off . . ."

"Are you justifying Kearnsey? Are you implying that all this—"

"That fraction off and before you know it you're in the woods so far astray . . . Do you stick to your path? Or do you pull out and cut your losses? Start all over again? Calculating more shrewdly this time the probabilities of one course over another, under this range of circumstance and that? Unless of course you can't withdraw. That first cellular misstep . . ."

"Ted, you've made no misstep! You'll be vindicated."

None of it touched her. It rolled right off her back. Anything Ted could say, Joe could say, he could say. Their wrangle, brother and sister, older and younger, rang piercingly through him. That one choice, deliberately or accidentally made, that begets such a progeny of choices, ramifications, paths leading in all directions and at every fork another choice, each choice precluding all others and once taken, no backing out of it. On the kitchen table he addressed more envelopes, sorted out so many to be dropped off at Ewell's, so many at Amy's, Mabley's. They had counted on the letter house to do the addressing, but at such short notice . . .

"There is something in medicine, Priscilla, called Cannon's Law. The body always tries to maintain equilibrium. It will go to amazing lengths sometimes to compensate for the lack of it. A child is born, for instance, with one leg shorter than the other. Does he limp when he starts to walk? No. He walks equally on both feet. Only when he is examined by a physician, it will be found that he has curvature of the spine."

"Are you implying that you and I— We're all off kilter? Our principles? Our whole existence? Oh."

The shift in Ted's drift was reflected in her face.

"But everything's negative. You said—"

"All I'm saying is it's hard to tell. The presence of an abnormality can be very insidious—the body goes to amazing lengths sometimes. . . . Even when the surgeon gets inside, even when he has the biopsy—"

"There's nothing there! I know there's nothing there!"

"—the growth tissue may be indistinguishable from the substance of the brain itself. Mish, you stay out of this—"

"Nothing! Nothing!"

"There can be 30 to 40 per cent margin of error. Think of the unnecessary excisions that have been made. And the excisions that should have been made while there was still time."

"All this is crazy. Ridiculous. Just an outside possibility they're checking out to eliminate—"

"To determine, Priscilla, to determine! From the disturbance in his field of vision they can just about pinpoint"—Ted groped at the back of her head on the left side, under a rumpled tuft of hair —"where to enter."

Enough, enough! He started up from the table once or twice. Stop, enough! But when he touched her arm, touched Ted in an attempt at restraint, they shook him off. And in some part of himself, in some twitching crinkle of the brain, some twisted crevice of his consciousness, he maliciously, viciously wanted Ted to tell her. Sock her with it. Beat and stomp her with it.

"But his tests, those tests he took?"

"When they tested his vision, he minimized the whole thing. 'Just a little blurred, that's all.' "

"It's *his* eyes. If he says . . . He wouldn't fake a thing like that."

"When they attached the wires for the electroencephalograph"—Ted's hands splayed over his scalp—"they told him to close his eyes, relax. Generally it can localize any acceleration or reduction of electrical activity, any indication of metabolic upset or increase in intracranial pressure. Even deep in the tissues. But you know Joe. He's interested in the apparatus. He has to cross-examine the doctor. He thinks of something he wants to ask about the patient in the next room. He remembers a key phrase he should have given Flo he's afraid he'll forget. His eyes pop open. The alpha rays disappear. If there's any irregularity in his brain waves anywhere, they don't have a good enough chart on it to show it."

"But that's Joe. That's always been Joe. Relax when someone's fiddling around—"

"Now the X rays. He's stalling it. Has to finish some work first. It may be that he dreads the procedure. A needle is sunk in to withdraw cerebral fluid and replace it with air for the picture. Or it may be that his preoccupation with the Kallen case is itself symptomatic. Going over the same material, over and over—"

"Refining it. That's his method. He's a sifter. The more you tell me—"

"We are talking about a tumor of the brain, Priscilla! We can hope you're right, there's nothing there. We can hope that if there is, it's in an operable spot. We can hope it's not advanced enough to affect any vital function. That it can be removed in its entirety without damage to the surrounding area. That it's as harmless as a wart. And that once it's out he'll be back on the job in a couple of weeks. With years of useful life ahead of him."

For once Priscilla stood absolutely still. No flinging of herself about in protest, no gesture sweeping away objections in her path.

Coffee bubbled up black in the glass dome of the pot and he shakily refilled her cup. Forgetting that she liked hers black, he added milk and sugar. For once she didn't reshuffle cups.

"But— They haven't found anything yet. Is that right? Not a thing so far?"

"Right."

"They haven't found a thing and you're already *resigned?* Accepting? Oh, Teddy, don't ever do this to me again. Sink a needle—"

She gulped her coffee. "Ted, darling—"

She kissed him like a drunk on New Year's Eve. "You're flying to Texas an hour from now. You'll be back Saturday night around seven. Right?" She smiled tremulously, wiping her chin off with the back of her hand, tears shimmering, the light in her eyes of faith, the faith that can move mountains. "Until I have reason to believe otherwise, I go on that assumption. Right?"

"You're right." Ted kissed her wet cheeks. "I'm sorry, I shouldn't have— You're right. Of course you're right."

She choked on her coffee and had to be thumped on the back and spluttering, drawing water at the sink, she began to giggle. She bent over the sink in paroxysms of giggles, hanging onto the faucet. Clumsy in their coats they tried to hold her, contain her. She thrust them away.

"It's just . . . It's just . . ."

Joe!

Explosively she spluttered it out, the water in her mouth spritzing over the ruffled front of her blouse. Joe, Joe up there at Sprague with all his courtroom delays and devices, standing off a battery of government attorneys.

"I'm sorry, I'm sorry." Ted tried to soothe her down. "I went overboard. That doctor got to me."

"Watch out for those doctors." She blew her nose in the dish towel, weeping through laughter. "They suck you in from one stage to the next."

Maybe she should go up there, leave everything? No no no, Ted comforted her. To Flo and Joe she was a comfort. At least someone down here doing something constructive.

Pop pop, poppety pop.

"I'll knock their little heads together. I'll murder them. Stop that," she bawled and raced off to the bedroom.

Prrrng prrrrnnng.

She was back at the telephone, answering at first with a subdued quaver.

"Yes, Mr. Gray. Yes." Firming up. "So that's his tactic." Whispering to them over the mouthpiece. "Kearnsey had John Doe restraining orders drawn up to serve on the patrol leaders tomorrow. Before we even went down to the council chamber!"

Frantically she dialed Lucas's sister, line busy. Mrs. Leggett, no answer. Lucas—she had to get hold of Lucas. Lucas had the patrol schedules.

Apologetically she dug Ted's flight bag out of the closet. "I don't know what hit me. Kid stuff. Do you have to go? Do you?"

"I—" Ted took the bag from her. At the door he stood off and surveyed her. "What's that blouse you're wearing, Priscilla?"

The ruffled blouse, too short when bought or shrunken since, drooped out, bedraggled, over the top of her skirt. There was a button out in the middle and a rip underarm.

"Just what miseries of the world do you think you're mitigating by decking yourself out in a rag like that?"

Slowly, incredulously, as if from Ted she expected only compliments for her shortcomings of dress, she tucked her blouse back inside her skirt. There was a red splotch on her lower jaw, the imprint of the telephone.

Man to man they jogged down the stairs. "Was I too rough on her?"

"Better from you," he said to Ted, "than from me."

In masculine complicity they crawled into the car, having chopped her down, having with horror and exaltation demolished the beloved. Priscilla among the natives building the visionary citadel, carrying stone by stone uphill even as the least among them, asking nothing for herself, giving all, here take me! every setback a spur, on with it! every accomplishment a chance for someone else to make it, so what! All her struggles and sacrifices eyewash for the system, all her selflessness an enhancement of it, enabling it to get by?

"Lu-CUSSS," she yelled from the window above. "Has anybody down there seen Lucas?"

III

1

He spent Thursday and Friday evenings and all day Saturday out with his teams visiting members at home. He was received well everywhere and plied with food, he must have gained ten pounds in two days; and with urgencies and emergencies enough for ten Broadway plays. Stewards who were known to be dissatisfied, rank-and-filers who were sources of advice and agitation in their departments, old-time supporters, skeptics from upstairs and downstairs and around the block—they all wished him luck. Membership participation in union affairs was never easily obtained except in time of crisis. But he was struck anew during his visits by the estrangement of the members from their union. "Ah, Mish, it's not what it was." At best, the union functioned as a service geared to meet their everyday problems on the job and provide the framework of principle within which those problems were settled. At worst, it was just another monster on their backs—dues, insurance, taxes, wage deductions! When he spoke of restoring democracy to the local he was regarded with good-natured tolerance. "We'll be rooting for you." "But I'm talking about you!" With their urgencies and emergencies, anticipation whetted, they promised to attend the Sunday meeting. "If you promise it won't be a waste of time."

His only failure was Cranston. He tried sending cautious feelers out to Herb through mutual acquaintances. No response. Marty Rakocszi on his round of bars was tipped off that if he'd be at the Blue Bird Saturday night around ten, he might run into someone interesting. Who it was and what for and why all the mystification, Marty couldn't find out. Ray decided to accompany Marty. Lunin would drop by.

Wound up, nagged by a hundred loose ends, a full night ahead of him, tomorrow upon him, he pulled up outside the airline building Saturday, minutes late, to pick up Ted. Ted was waiting at the curb, happily jiving with a companion.

"Hurtling along all packaged, cellophaned, chlorophylled, sanitized . . ."

Ted swung open the car door and eased in. The companion, burly as an ex-football player in his Burberry coat, ducked his head, the round head of a mischievous freckle-nosed boy, to peer in over the lowered glass and pump Ted's hand.

"Anything I can do for you, just pick up the phone. I'll give you all the help and guidance you need."

They sped over the causeway through rain-swept marsh toward the misty lights of the city. He had some visiting to do out on North Cedarbrook as well as his stop at the Blue Bird later. Ted elected to go along with him. Briefly they exchanged news. No change in Joe except for a siege of headaches. Nothing definite on the X rays, at least nothing definite enough yet for diagnosis. Priscilla was firmly convinced now that Joe's symptoms stemmed from a tooth he'd had trouble with last year. Sometimes a sympathetic nerve . . .

"Who's to gainsay her? Here I am, on schedule," Ted ruefully admitted, "all in one piece. How's the human chain holding up?"

"How do you think?"

The March storm that whipped up Thursday night had diminished their numbers. First thing Friday, the patrol leaders were served with temporary restraining orders, to be heard in superior court sometime next week. Gray was filing the tenants' appeal for a permanent injunction against the city to halt the dumping. Meanwhile they had to lift their blockade or face arrest for contempt of court. Priscilla was all for keeping it up. Gray was dead set against it. If they went to jail, who'd raise the bail? Over the weekend too, go find bondsmen! Lucas Ford had disappeared—in hiding, some thought, or on the lam. Willenski was busy with his folks who had arrived from Detroit to see his infant son, a first grandchild, just two weeks old and different of course from all others ever born. Nevertheless lines had gathered at the access routes in the rain, three deep. Ordered to disperse, they held fast. The police charged. The lines scattered. A couple of guys got their legs whacked. The dump trucks drove through.

On the marshland between airport and city, the road ahead of them was blurred under the headlights in white dervishes of drizzle. He handed Ted the afternoon paper he had brought along and his flashlight from under the seat. Scant of news Saturday, the front page featured a follow-up story on yesterday's rout, with a full account of the tenant leaders including Priscilla Lunin and by extension an allusion to the current status of the Kallen case. And a boxed item, a late flash. Michael (Mish) Lunin, a Tidal Flats resident and three-time loser to Nicholas Colangelo in contests for the presidency of EWIU-UV Local 317, AFL-CIO, was expected to announce his candidacy once again tomorrow afternoon. "Lunin is popularly identified with the faction headed by the late Robert Ucchini, ousted for its alleged pro-Communist leanings. . . ."

"How's Priscilla taking it?"

"With flying colors. It's all out in the open now. Just as well. Feels a lot better about it. Madder than ever at Kearnsey. And full of remorse toward Lucas—she should never have disputed him over paying the teen-ager for that pic, such a smashing picture, terrific talent. She's banking everything now on the impact of it in the ad tomorrow."

"And you? How does this all affect you?"

He held up two fingers, crossed.

Ted was full of his trip, heady with it. Horatio Alger stories. Overnight millionaires. Millionaires many times over. A physicist at MIT who'd gotten out two steps ahead of the un-American

Committee and started his own electronics firm. Now, having made his bundle, he was being summoned to Washington every other week, a science adviser to the President.

And his companion on the plane, Walter Gordon. Ted had formed the academic freedom committee back in the Henry Wallace days to save Walter's job. Walter was a chemist, bats about rocketry. With a friend who had been working for a manufacturer of bug bombs and some backing from his wife's family, he went into hair spray. Pressurized cans.

"The hair spray blasts off. Inside of three years it's being marketed coast to coast under five national brand names and Walter's up to his ears in pressure-packing perfumes, cosmetics, shave cream. The propellant is Du Pont but he owns a couple of valve patents and he has a lab at Columbia—Columbia!—researching measuring devices so he can take on pharmaceuticals too. He enlarges his production facilities to meet demand. And goes public. Gets a reputable investment house to float a stock issue for him, two hundred thousand shares at ten dollars par. Keeps 51 per cent of it for himself.

"The stock buyers, sold on his growth potential, start buying like mad. The investment house rakes in its commission. The value of Walter's stocks shoots up. And he still has his company. Next year he'll declare a split and everyone will make it all over again. So long as the three balls keep coming up on the one-armed bandit, orgasm! Yippee!

"Walter showed me a canceled check out of his wallet made out to him personally for one million dollars. While we sit there flying, he's getting richer by the minute."

The rain-spattered windshield glittered with the lights of a cheap shopping district, the wiper sweeping drops into furrows and waves, the glass fogging up on the inside. Despite his preoccupation with other matters, half-listening to Ted, he was intrigued.

"On his cans or his stocks?" he asked Ted.

"Who the hell can tell? Both. He's running around the country making acquisitions. Offered me a job. Sixteen-five."

Ted was much calmer than he had been two days ago. No shift-ings about in odd postures of humor. No twining of his fingers knotting and unknotting invisible strings.

"You didn't take him up on it?"

"Just a whim on his part. Another feather in his cap. No. Any more than you could take it from Coffin."

It wasn't the same at all. And yet it was. The distaste and the mistrust. The fear of being used to no purpose and cast off or being only too well used, cooperating in the perversion of their abilities. And the pride, as much pride as principle. Too insuffera-bly sure of their own worth to submit themselves to someone else's shenanigans.

"If I stay at the university," Ted said, "what do I have? Students of the status quo. Go on with my research and writing? By the time it's acceptable it'll be out of date. Consulting? This mix of definition and manipulation? Unh unh, I can't sell what I see through."

He didn't pay as much attention to Ted as he should have. His mind was elsewhere. Shaking down beefs. Lemon meringue pie —UV had introduced a template for cutting pie in the cafeteria and simultaneously cut the countermen's pay. The template worked out okay on apple and blueberry but was no good for lemon meringue. During the mealtime rush they had to switch back and forth from template to knife. . . .

"These small plants." Ted lowered the window on his side. "Must be hundreds of them in Shoreham."

They threaded through desultory patches of cinder-block build-ings, a single rod of light piercing murky interiors. Quality Forg-ings. Petersham Plastics. Worm & Gear. Electroplate.

"Just talking to Walter I got an inkling of the initiative and ingenuity that go into them. There are these niches that can be carved out within the monopoly setup. You apply yourself to something simple, genuine, essential. In the real world where to speak is to act. Wheels turn. Things happen. You come to grips with the consequence of your thought."

Ted sounded like Irene when, after years of being in love with a Hungarian musician, she decided to marry Harry, a postal clerk who, lacking in romantic fancy himself, loved her for her romantic fancies. "Harry's a challenge," Irene had said defiantly, displaying the engagement ring Frank had never given her. "Every human being has something if you look hard enough for it." The fires had died down in Irene only too soon. But she did have, nowadays, patience and compassion.

"No razzle-dazzle. No rarefied abstractions," Ted said. "It's a challenge."

Ted didn't sound like Irene. Ted with a fiendish grin, goggled, schussing down the ski slope, squirming in behind the wheel of his stock car, flying blind through the clouds.

"It's hard, dirty, mean," he said to Ted, fully alert to him now. "Soul-destroying. Barth Barrel—you'd be insane."

Hard, dirty, mean, that was just what appealed to Ted. Another Priscilla!

"Joe's not Grover Coffin," Ted said to him. "Nobody's asking you to be Coffin's stooge, will you get that through your head? Joe wasn't trying to buy you."

"I'd be Coffin. I'd be the one—"

"You handle the mechanics of it. I'll deal with the personnel."

"It can't be separated—no, it's out. I can't do it. I'd be going against myself. Everything I've ever stood for."

"Willow Street is just two blocks away, let's cut over . . ."

"No, I haven't got the time now."

"All right, not now. Set a date, we'll take a look. You'll see the possibilities."

"What's the point? It's out. Out—out—out!"

They had never crossed wills before, never had occasion to. The air between them vibrated with such tension, reacting to it he was sick to the stomach, his hands were slippery on the wheel. He speeded up and almost ran down a kid riding a bike in the rainy road. He had to stop the car to catch his breath.

"Ted, you're feeling low, you're grasping at straws— You can always find somebody else."

"No one else would have the interest. When Eckstrom tried taking on a plant superintendent a few years ago, he had three of them in three months. So much has to be done . . ."

Another element had entered his consciousness and he didn't want it there. He didn't want to think about it. With Ted's decision, if it had come to that, the reality outside himself was subtly shifting. He locked it out, preserving against it his familiar space, his perspective.

"Mish, you can't win." Ted rapped the folded newspaper over his knee. "What makes you think that after a story like this, you have the slightest chance? As long as you live you're never going to rid yourself of it. It'll follow you—"

He didn't want to rid himself of it. Bob Ucchini still lived in some part of him.

All through the evening, from the home visits into the Blue Bird and out again, directly and indirectly, verbally and silently, Ted maintained his barrage.

"Even if you were to win, how long do you think you'd last? With John Bennett at the head of the EWIU. Either you play the game or you'll be out on your ear inside of a year."

"And even if you get by with Bennett, how far do you think you'll get with the company? UV has twelve different unions in there now, all at odds with each other. What can you possibly accomplish?"

"Bread-and-butter issues. Pure and simple trade unionism. Round and round the music goes. If we were in a period of militancy when the power of the unions was being used for social good . . ."

"Capitalism their system, pragmatism their philosophy, reformism their politics, the pressure of opposition to the ruling parties sacrificed for the privilege of tailing along. . . ."

"You're out of context, you're bucking the tide of history. Until labor makes the next leap ahead, Mish, it's dead."

His own words ringing in his ears. It's gone, Priscilla, it's over, it's not there! He had said it and said it and now, caught up in the situation, he was going through the process all over again. His hope rekindled and he performed. Is this IT this time? One time it will be.

2

Tonight he was concentrating on Cranston. If Cranston showed up at the meeting tomorrow . . . If there were enough Lunin partisans present to impress Cranston . . . If they could combine forces . . .

If he wasn't barking up the wrong tree.

He had three leads on Cranston out on North Cedarbrook. He drove up and down seeking numbers in the dark. A district of little chicken-coop houses built by Hungarians and Italians when it was still country. And rows of cracker-box houses built by developers in the last few years, which young UV workers began buying up when rents became, with the new expressway, too high and too scarce.

He rang their bells, Ted at his elbow in place of a shopmate. Prepared to listen—that was what took all the time: who married who, who gave who the air, who took off with whose wife to Florida, whose health wasn't so good lately, who had lost a son in Korea and was so heartbroken over it no one could coax him out for anything any more. And prepared with the letter that had been sent out to discuss the issues, with lists of names to check off suggested contacts, with a notebook in which he jotted down details of shop conditions. In turn he had to outline the strategy he intended to follow tomorrow, his limited objectives. At an opportune moment he would mention Cranston, casually.

In the trellised doorway of the first house, a chicken coop, he waited while the second wife, a stranger to him, went in to call Gil Hunyadi, once a Liscomb Street neighbor. Gil, close to retirement now, worked as a millwright with Cranston in Maintenance. They hadn't seen each other in several years. Gil came flying out with open arms.

"Mish, it's you!"

They embraced. All their knowledge of each other, all the years under the bridge rushed together, commingling.

"Gomby"—Gomby was Gil's name in Hungarian—"Gomby *botchy*"—no one, not even a Hungarian, could translate *botchy*, except it was the most respectful term you could use to a Hungarian elder—"how are you?"

The tiny parlor was crammed with overstuffed furniture and the daughter's upright piano, her zither in its case, her pictures on the wall in baby clothes, folk costume, cap and gown, wedding dress.

"Did you hear about Mroz?" Gil mourned. "What the boys did to him? Such a terrible thing, it could never happen before. We were all so close. We cared for each other. We didn't have what to eat in the house, but still when the organizers came in, the women got together and we fed them. Now everybody's making his mint off everybody else. . . ."

About the meeting tomorrow—Gil who had been a charter member of Local 317, who had been through the wars with Boris and Bob, sharpened up out of his nostalgia. Stocky, radiating vigor, playing up to Ted, their audience, he cannily questioned, "And that's all you're after? Mish, don't try to fool me. I'm an old hunky."

Although Gil's was the only friendly reception he expected in his home-visiting tonight, he stepped softly with him.

"You remember that leaflet last Friday? Let's bury Graveyard? I heard somewhere it came out of Maintenance. You guys are the ones that get around."

Gil quieted down, grew guarded. The past was past. The present was his meal ticket. "Friday? Which Friday? Let me see, what day was Friday?"

"Aw come on, Gil. I'm an old hunky too."

"I found mine on the bench. That's all I know about it."

"And Herb Cranston, did you notice his reaction? How did he take it?"

Cranston was Gil's steward. A good steward, Gil insisted, so far as processing grievances was concerned. Herb got after the business agent, he stood in good with Colangelo, he gave service. Very efficient. No complaints there.

"As for anything more—" Meaningfully, as if the walls had ears, Gil flexed his biceps and spread his hands, no soap, and nodded back toward the kitchen—his second wife, she didn't know about such things.

"Didn't Cranston say anything about the leaflet?"

In his knit vest, pulled on for warmth, Gil huddled in his chair. He had been allied with Bob, and all the months of deterioration when he suspected everyone, even his best friend, of being an FBI informant, and his best friends suspected him, brooded about him.

"Well, you know Herb," Gil said. "He's a cool cucumber. Never says a word till he's ready to say it."

His second call, after a maze of roads without name and houses without number: a pink cracker box. They stepped directly into the living room, apologizing for muddy feet. The room was devoid of furniture. The youngster in high school sweat shirt who let them in shouted up the open stairway at the side for his father. The expansion attic was being finished off to accommodate in-laws who would help with the mortgage payments.

Loy Koslow trotted down the stairs with hammer in hand and nails in his teeth. He had been one of Cranston's followers in the Catholic Action Front and the Freedom Caucus and, according to Ewell, still went hunting and fishing with Cranston on occasion.

Loy spit the nails out into the palm of his hand. "Goddamn, one out of every ten you hit it and it bends." Not unfriendly, he dragged chairs away from the kids playing gin rummy in the kitchen. He had five kids on bunk beds in two bedrooms and was planning to fix up the basement for them if he could lick the water problem. A speculator bought the land and filled in the stream on the hillside and the developer built and the realtor sold and none of them figured water has to go somewhere. He knocked at the wall in back of their chairs, look at this dry-wall construction, look at the paint job. Would they excuse the state of the living room? His old lady had a set all picked out last fall, solid maple, none of this veneer stuff, when UV up and transferred Washer-Dryer down South.

"Washing machine—for two years they'll be producing with a green crew. Bad consumer rating, who cares? Beef up the promotion! Add on a hot new feature! Till they have them trained. Meanwhile UV's put through the methods we wouldn't take. Saved, made millions."

Loy didn't have a single UV appliance in his house. Discount or no, when he went out to buy he wanted something that would last.

"I'm in assembly now, I see it every day. Everything's going to hell. The speed-up killed it. There's no pride in your work. Nobody cares. Nobody gives a shit."

Encouraged by Loy's outburst, he egged him on. "You got the letter we sent out? How we need to improve the local? If you come to the meeting tomorrow and bring some of your friends—"

Unfortunately tomorrow was Palm Sunday and though Loy kept the Orthodox calendar, his wife was Spanish and her folks were expecting them over to dinner after church. He'd try to make it there later.

"Just one thing wrong with this country," Loy interjected, suddenly mindful of whom he was talking to. "Money is everything. Anything for a buck. And one thing good about it. If you got the money, you don't need nothing else. All you need is money."

That bit of flag-waving out of the way, Loy toured them through the scantily furnished house—his wife was out for the evening with her ladies of Fatima. He plowed through his rambunctious young, shutting them up—no discipline any more, no respect, even the sisters at school were losing their grip, everything getting out of hand. Drinking beer out of the can, they admired the cornices Loy had put up over the uncurtained windows—scalloped, did that with his coping saw. In the cellar he showed them his workshop. The one best thing about this house, he had a place for his own stuff. An island elevated on a wooden platform over the concrete floor, power equipment firmly implanted, hand tools arrayed on pegboard over his bench, fluorescent light overhead. A series of figurines on a shelf. Animals, saints, ikons Loy had carved out of rare woods he picked up in a wrecker's joint. Was there a market for it, he besought Ted.

The whir in the background, the sump pump he had to install last fall. Eating up electricity whenever it rained. He woke up nights listening to it. "A house is a sponge." What Loy needed out of UV was more overtime. And less women.

"You're always standing up for the women, Lunin. Do you know that in my department they put women assemblers, one twenty-six an hour, into the position of male inspectors who were getting one sixty-five? They got a broad blueprint-reading? Using mechanic's tools . . ."

"Equal pay for equal work." How many times had he said this to the same story in the past few days? "Bring it up at the meeting tomorrow."

"You want the girls to lynch me? If UV had to pay equal, they'd keep the men on."

"What we need . . ." He went into it thoroughly with Loy item by item, Loy nodding agreement. Emboldened, he proceeded further. "Your old clique, do you still get together sometimes?"

"Nowadays? Nothing's together nowadays. Everybody's tending his own turf."

"You have any idea what their thinking is? Is it anything like yours?"

"I only speak for myself. I can't speak for no one but myself."

If the leaflet was Cranston's and if it had been smuggled into the plant by Cranston's old clique, Loy wasn't in on it. Or he was covering up, with more guile than he seemed capable of. He shone with honesty. The beginning wrinkles in his neck stretched with eagerness as he spoke. He was a spontaneous, bubbling spring.

"What about Cranston? You're in touch with him, aren't you?" He decided to lay his cards down with Loy, play it straight. "I'd like to talk with Herb before tomorrow afternoon. At his house, here, my house, anywhere he chooses. Can you arrange it?"

In the bare living room the sump pump whirred up from below. The oil furnace throbbed on, jolting the floor.

"Well, you know Cranston. He's the type you go to him"— Loy threw his head back, granite, frozen-eyed, staring him down —"you won't get nowhere. Cranston wants you, he sends for you."

Up the next street, a new car in front of the house. The living room carpeted wall to wall, picture window draped and curtained, tall lamps—pottery shafts under columnar white shades—on limed oak end tables, furniture in muted tones fairly fresh, a built-in bookcase containing cabineted television, radio, hi-fi. Pretty young wife at her ironing board watching TV as she ironed, baby in high chair, toddler on the floor. Glimpse of kitchen through the doorway, fully equipped. Husband in the bedroom sprawled out on the Hollywood bed, his head propped against the upholstered headboard, bleating away with youthful concentration on his clarinet. Dickey was Cranston's nephew, one year at UV and sore as hell at the seniority system and all the old crocks he couldn't bypass.

"Say, Dickey—" With a touch of his uncle's condescension Dickey removed his clarinet from his mouth to listen to him, wiping off the mouthpiece and his mouth. "—isn't that a new Plymouth out there? I thought you were driving a Chevvy."

"Yah. A salesman come along and he showed me how for the same money by the month I could have a brand new car."

"But it'll take that many more months before you own it."

"Who expects to own it? Another year, another salesman will come along."

Dickey was one of the breed coming in who drove the foremen crazy. He and another welder made a couple of golf club heads one day and used them to bat a ping-pong ball back and forth across the aisle. The boss had to run to the steward for help. "Make them stop!" They didn't give a damn for the steward either. "We just get paid for what we do, don't we? Well, we done it. What's this cat . . . ?"

"You fixed up this place just great," he said to Dickey. "How you paying for it all?"

"Now if you gonna give me a sermon like my folks, how they worked for ten years before they got anything— If we were going to be satisfied with what they had, we'd be back in the horse-and-buggy days."

He settled down on the edge of Dickey's bed. Ted took the vanity bench. Their eyes met. You know, he's right?

"How we paying for it?" The pretty young wife leaned in the doorway with her baby on her hip. "First of the month, first bill collector that shows up he's the one that gets it. The rest of them —'You're too late! Next month.'"

"What if they threaten to repossess?" Ted ventured to suggest.

With her free arm she swept about her wholesale. "'Then take your junk out!' They can have it."

When they married they were both working, making thirty a day between them and it seemed like so much. They bought the house for less than rent and every store in town was shoving credit at them, home decorating magazines and decorators free. And they bought a car to get back and forth to work in. Then the babies started coming and she couldn't just sit here in the house staring at the furniture, no money for sitters, no recreation. So they bought the TV. Now he was working nights and she was working days. On weekends sometimes he played weddings with a small band, had to have the hi-fi to practice along with.

"In other words," he said to Dickey, "you want it all and you want it now."

"Why not?" Dickey lay back on the pillow and blew riffs at the roof. "The country's rich enough."

With Gil Hunyadi he felt that he had gathered a hint or two at least, if he read him right, that he was on the right track. With Loy Koslow he felt that he was making some progress, by way of information at least: that the old groupings had loosened up, that the venom of past antagonisms was dissipating somewhat. But with Dickey he got absolutely nowhere at all.

The union? "Don't give me none of that stuff about how tough it used to be. I got it now."

His uncle, Herb Cranston? "Maybe you can talk to him. Not me. That guy, I swear he's got a poker up his ass."

Outside, he and Ted climbed into the station wagon laughing. "There's your revolution," Ted said to him. "If anybody ever makes it, it'll be Dickey."

A few more visits while he was in the area. Another young fellow, with one son crippled by polio and the second a spastic, demonstrated the gadgets he had devised for his station wagon so he could take his family camping weekends, even sometimes in the winter. He was studying history nights at the university extension, hoping to become a history teacher. The next one a night worker with ten children who was secretly by day a history instructor at St. Francis Xavier College. One sending him to the next and the next and the next.

All united in opinion. Conditions were bad. A leadership vacuum. But the impelling sense of crisis—they were living in perpetual crisis. They covered a hillside denuded of woodland by the bulldozers, on their soggy plots over filled-in streams.

The stories in the evening paper, insofar as he could tell, stirred up more curiosity than controversy.

He drove back toward Cedarbrook through pools that splashed up over his hubcaps and splattered his windows, frustrated, disgusted, sated with the futility of every wild-goose chase he'd ever undertaken. Down slippery black byways, brakes gone, skidding.

Ted tried a bit of horse sense on him, which in his irritation he took to be a thrust. "You ever hear Joe on the horse? The module for the judiciary lines in this state was established by the horse. How far a horse can travel in one day. All the grubby little circuit courts still around, demeaning to the judge, the attorneys, the accused, the witnesses. If only he'd spent his career, Joe said when I saw him, promoting himself into a position to redraw those lines, he'd have accomplished something."

He retorted with a parable that, he thought, more precisely projected his plight. "In my father's village a peasant had a horse stolen. Eight years later gypsies passed through, with a horse the peasant claimed was his. The village council consulted over the theft and advised the peasant to go home and leave his gate open. If the horse returned to his stall, the horse was his. Who did the horse belong to? They left it up to the horse to decide."

He finished lamely, appalled by unintended innuendoes, beyond the reach of explanation. He hadn't even gone into the business with Ted and already who stole what from who! He crossed the high bridge over the railroad track by Shoreham Machine as a train, car after car, passenger windows alight, roared beneath. He laughed aloud, dispelling the unpleasantness.

"What's so funny?"

"My old man. Every time he crosses this bridge and a train passes underneath, every goddam time he says the same thing. 'The crow flies and the dog sits on its tail. But whose tail?' "

Ted digested it awhile. "What does it mean?"

"Beats me. You ask him, he'll groan with the weight of the universe on him. 'But whose tail nobody tells you.' "

United Vacuum soared skyward, its emblem ablaze on the breast of the dark office tower. No Bob Ucchini leading the ranks down Cedarbrook Avenue on a night so cold their heels rang like iron on the pavement, *avanti popolo!* No tangle of howling dogs outside the Blue Bird, frustrated males mounting each other. No little bitch locked up in the backroom, yapping.

Behind roseate windows, the bar cozy on a rainy night. In the semigloom of crimson, blue and puddled purples reflected from the outside sign, in the amber refulgence of the illuminated back-bar mirror, a row of figures pivoted on stools, heads uptilted to the pale flicker of figures in the box mounted under the ceiling. A ghostly leap midcourt. A ball precariously circling the rim of the basket.

Quiet at the bar. Quiet in the booths in back, husbands having a beer with the wife on a Saturday night. The atmosphere skunky as always.

In the last booth in back, Ray and Marty were conversing with a casual acquaintance who had stopped by on his way to the telephone, beer in hand. So it seemed at a glance. Ray and Marty seated together, facing forward. Ray's thin face flushed, eyes chestnut-bright, Reynard the fox, fixed on the acquaintance, the terrain, who was coming in the door, who hadn't come out of the can, appraising, analyzing. Marty with his hat down over his brow, solid, stolid, putting two and two together, adding this up with that, making his survey. A flick of their eyelashes gave him pause. Something about the acquaintance standing over the booth, back to him, caught his attention. The cock of the head, the heavy-set shoulders, the haircut clipped straight across the neck, the thick green plaid jacket, the weighty whole droopy with resigned patience.

Rapidly he backtracked over Ted and dropped into the nearest booth, concealing himself.

"Jesus Christ, am I stupid!"

The fellow who had joined him going into the building after lunch the other day: "I thought Marty was with you." Bucky Stewart signifying in the elaborate protocol of these things that he, as an emissary from Herb Cranston, was willing to conduct talks with Marty, acting as Lunin's representative. Cranston, unwilling as yet to make any direct approach to him, public or private, was feeling out the situation.

The casual encounter had been sought out by Bucky, away from his usual haunts on the other side of town, here at the Blue Bird, Marty's habitual headquarters.

Three more beers back there. They were moseying around each other.

Ray with his tales of his northern Maine childhood, how they used to hang a salt herring over the table and wipe a piece of bread on it.

Bucky with his tales of his young years on the bucket crane.

He knew Bucky. And his famous tales—how the Italian boss would stage the show in the street for the lunchgoers, the crane rising up the structural iron scaffolding of a skyscraper; how the Labrador fishermen with their big hands, good for handling the boom, would feed him their Labrador stew when he caught cold; how the Indian up there waiting to shoot the bolts, never bothered with a safety belt, would throw him a couple of bottles as he swung by, "Say, Bucky, you wanna beer?"

It was never simple for a man of Cranston's temperament to switch position. His commitment to a certain political outlook, his influence over others, his attachment to routines developed over the years—Cranston was torn every which way, inside and out. So he had dispatched Bucky, a reporter who never missed a thing.

"Eckstrom has contracts with various firms, collecting five hundred drums at a time to be reconditioned. Their drums or ours on lease. Our haulage. Walter Gordon can lead us to at least fifty new customers."

He scarcely heard Ted, his ears straining, attuned to the waves emanating from the rear.

"Our first step—to reorganize the production setup. And our second—if we can accumulate sufficient capital in the next few years—to go into manufacture of new drums. We'll have to scrounge around for used equipment, make it work."

Bucky returned with his beer mug to the bar and paid up.

Five minutes after Bucky, he left the tavern with Ted and waited in the wagon, his expectation growing as he waited, for Ray and Marty to come out. They slid into the back seat. He drove around the corner to a side street a few blocks away and parked.

"Okay, shoot."

"Bucky wanted a rundown on what Coffin said to you."

That confirmed the leaflet. Cranston had his sights fixed on Coffin.

"What'd you tell him?"

"That just as Coffin's looking to be elevated from operational vice-president to a soft spot on the top directorate, Shoreham starts blowing up on him. So he tries to defuse it by detaching Lunin—"

"Yeah, yeah," he interrupted impatiently, "what about tomorrow? Did Bucky say anything about tomorrow?"

Bucky had tipped them off that Nick too was looking ahead. There was a move afoot for the next convention to amalgamate the offices of president and business agent, which would enable Nick to quit the plant altogether, spend full time on salary at the local's headquarters. Desk status for life, renewable every two years. He was taking no chances on anyone upsetting the apple-cart now.

"Bucky leaked it to us that he's planning just a short business meeting. A report from his building committee. No general discussion. Nominations to be passed and seconded in the last few secs and go home."

"And Cranston? Didn't Bucky mention what Cranston's aiming for?"

Cranston had no aims. He just wanted to be privy to what they were up to. Without stepping out of line himself, quite content to have them out there fronting for him.

"It was just a fishing expedition."

"Just! Just!" He exploded with it. "All these little leaks? These tips? These probings and proddings?"

"This is an isolated action," Ted warned them. "It has no connection with anything going on anywhere else. No real basis. No destination. Business unionism. The union business."

Through the waves beating in his ears he remotely heard Ted and agreed with him and ignored him.

"Cranston'll be there tomorrow. We'll be there. All that's lacking for godsake is the link-up!"

"They'll co-opt you, they'll swallow you up . . ."

"How does it look, Marty? How many?"

"They'll chop you down, they'll boot you out . . ."

"Touch and go," Marty said. "Touch and go all the way."

3

From where he sat with Ray and Marty in the front row he counted his troops as they drifted in. Ewell behind and to the right of Ray, Cusak behind and to the left of Marty. Quite unconsciously, in self-effacement perhaps, they took seats that fanned back from his on both sides to the middle row and converged again to the back, assuming the diamond formation Cranston had introduced as a means of disrupting the Ucchini meetings.

There was no massive outpouring at the union meeting such as there had been at city hall. The prolonged rain outside cast a pall. In the drafty hall the banks of chairs being shuffled into a dozen meager rows dropped open with the clack of bowling balls. After all the brave talk, the letters sent out and the contacting, Mari giving full time to it, ninety people showed up. Mari herself had telephoned him during the morning that she was down with chills and fever.

Under the drab light his euphoric calculations of last night dwindled. Gil Hunyadi was here and a scattering of the old stalwarts, but not enough of them. Mabley with the Hot Rubber crew, Amy with Rita, and Elsie—edgy, wary of being caught with their individual cause on the wrong public side. The newspaper reports on him, indicating a hot fight in the making, had had an effect. Bucky Stevens arrived and Loy Koslow, but not Cranston. They mingled with the knots of officials before sitting down. He was outnumbered, not so much by Colangelo, who had rallied no more troops than he did, as by the neutrals occupying the core of the diamond. They would tend to vote with the leadership unless and until persuaded that a better course not only existed but could prevail.

In the front row, facing the table at which Colangelo informally presided, he let the reading of the agenda pass without objection or suggestion for amendment. He could not afford any losses at the outset. The success of his strategy depended on avoidance of an attack on Colangelo. If there was to be conflict, it had to issue from the will of the crowd.

Just as Colangelo was about to open the order of business, Herb Cranston walked in, pinkly chilled by the rain. He took a seat by himself in the center of the unoccupied rear row and laid his wet coat—he wore no hat—over the back of the adjoining chair. Settling down to listen, he folded his arms over his chest and raised his head, sleeked hair dripping over his bonily exposed face, in that attitude of detached judgment, the moral arbiter, that had won him converts but no personal popularity. Cranston had scarcely arranged himself when Mari sallied in, ivory pale, her head shrouded in white scarf and muffled in the voluminous raccoon collar of her maroon coat. Mid-aisle she surveyed the empty seats front to rear. Eschewing the women beckoning her to join them, she turned back and sidled into Cranston's row next to him. Ceremoniously she unfastened her coat and removed it, shook the raindrops out of her fur collar, smoothed the fabric, unwound her scarf from over and around her head and threw it back over her shoulders. She sank down beside Cranston, not once glancing at him, with her handbag decorously clasped in her lap.

"In the interest of shortening the meeting, will someone please make a move to dispense with the minutes?"

"I so move."

Colangelo stared suspiciously over the heads twisting toward Mari. Excluded from membership years ago, she attended meetings whenever she pleased, spoke up when it suited her, took part in voice and standing votes. Her mere presence was a provocation. With a shrug Nick resumed. He was avoiding clashes too.

"Do I hear a second?"

Mari seconded, her pleasantly modulated contralto penetrating the drone of responses, the routine that of itself intimidated and stultified, stifled every impulse toward opposition as irrelevant, even unnatural.

Finance report? Reports of the standing committees? The chairman of the building committee delivered his report.

It was Nick Colangelo's dream to remodel the union hall. He had devoted considerable thought to plans for reducing and more efficiently utilizing the space of the one-time church. Those groined vaults above into which heat escaped were to be covered with a flat acoustical tile ceiling, inset with recessed lighting. The offices now crammed behind the dais were to be moved forward into the side aisles and paneled off for executive use, news weekly, records, conferences. Kitchen and membership facilities in the basement would be renovated and the unsightly asbestos-coated piping overhead boxed in. The heating system required a complete overhaul. At a minimum the whole place had to be re-painted, requiring an immediate expenditure of three thousand dollars.

Nick's committee had been poring over estimates for more than a year. There was also the behind-the-scenes jockeying over whose connections would be awarded what contracts. The paint contract with Busoni Bros. had been drawn up during the week and now awaited approval of the membership.

"Brother Chairman?"

"Yes, Brother Cusak?"

"If you're going to make all these other improvements, isn't it a waste to paint now?"

What Cusak really meant was: howcome you gave the contract to another Italian? Were there other bidders? How much? Stirring to life every Italian and non-Italian in the hall.

"Yes, Brother Cusak," Nick agreed, placatingly. "Where to be-gin, that's always the question. With the root or the branches? We have to begin somewhere."

Nick wanted the contract signed today and out of his way. On to the furnace deal, which had to be taken care of this summer.

In his front seat, in an atmosphere that fairly crackled with resistance to the least contrary voice, he waited, watching Nick produce, like rabbits out of a hat, paint color cards to be passed around, architects' projections for the basement kitchen, rings of Formica samples. No mention of the issues that had brought them out on a rainy afternoon. No outlet for the indignation that boiled up day after day, month in month out. Those who had had a heavy holiday dinner after church were struggling against sleep and those who were having a big family dinner later were restless with hunger, anxious to get back to their visiting rela-tives. Minutes were frittered away in a wrangle between chair and floor over home-repair experiences. Most of them would be in

their coats and down the aisle by the time Campbell, reporting for
the nominating committee, announced the slate for next year.

He waited till the rumblings of the crowd wedged into his
back. Mabley and the Hot Rubber crew were openly grousing.
Amy and Rita were complaining rearward to Elsie and Elsie to
Mari. On either side of him, Ray and Marty grimly clutched
their knees, gritting their teeth.

"What about my lemon meringue pie?"

"The suspensions! How about my suspension?"

"Our tool payments—"

"The company's playing tricks with the seniority lists—"

"My service—"

"The pie! The pie!"

With the outcry, he was on his feet.

"Yes, Brother Lunin?" Colangelo, gaveling for order, recognized
him almost too graciously.

If he moved to refer the building report back to committee or
even if, most cooperatively, to accept it as read, his motion would
be followed very likely by a host of exceptions and amendments,
every one of them subject to debate.

"I move that the report of the building committee be tabled."

"Second the motion!" "Second!" "Second!"

"Move the question!"

The entire diamond formation and well over half the core.

"Lunin, you're out of order—"

"Question! Question! Move the question!"

A motion to table was neither debatable nor amendable. It
could not be postponed, committed, divided or reconsidered. It
was overwhelmingly carried.

Promptly Nick took advantage of defeat—he was going to do
what he wanted to anyway with the paint contract—to out-
maneuver him.

"In view of the absence of our business agent and your very
understandable desire to speed things up, I will entertain a
motion to omit items 3 and 4."

Redheaded Fritz of Switch, running up and down like a floor manager at a convention, commandeered the motion through.

Ray was on his feet. "Brother Chairman?"

"We've moved forward to Item 5, Brother Pelletier. Nothing else—"

"I just wanted to say before we go any farther that we ought to give a vote of thanks to Brother Horvath for the fine report he delivered on finances."

"Do you want to put that in the form of a motion?"

"I move . . ."

Unanimous of course.

Ray's motion automatically opened the meeting to reintroduction of any pending old business. In the ensuing dispute a parliamentarian was summoned to the fore.

"All right, Brother Lunin, you have the floor," Nick benevolently conceded. "So long as you keep it short."

He drew his little black book out of his jacket pocket. "I have here a list of one hundred and twenty-two unsettled grievances—"

"Out of order. You know good and well that this is not the place to discuss specific grievances. I can't allow you to make a grandstand play—"

"I'm not discussing them. How can you talk about grievances without going into the company practices that bring them about?"

"Out of order—"

"Let him speak! Let the brother speak!"

"You're out of order, Lunin. Sit down!"

"I am speaking under old business on the membership report. Our membership in some departments, as Brother Horvath's statement on dues indicated, is down 50 per cent. That's why United Vacuum gets away . . ."

He found himself confronted by the sergeant-at-arms, Baldessari the secretary, Fritz and a couple more heavies, moving in on him in a semicircle. Ray and Marty were up beside him.

"It's for your own good, Brother Chairman! It's to strengthen your own hand!" He heard the rustling in the background, the scraping of chairs, the upsurge of his diamond formation. "How can we rebuild this building till we rebuild the membership? I want to make a motion that we expand our membership committee from three to twenty, initiate an all-out drive, every worker a member—"

One second the heavies were closing in on him. He was looking into the turquoise eyes, the squirrel-cheeked grin of a division chairman who, he suddenly recalled, had replaced Arlene Cox. Last October someone came to Arlene and said, "You're no longer chairman here. This guy is." "But I was elected." "That was a mistake." Arlene dropped out of the union and a good part of the division pulled out with her.

The next second the heavies melted away. Nick's gavel was sledge-hammering down on the table. "Get back to your seats, you guys! What's got into you? Lunin, sit down and keep the peace. Quiet back there! Campbell, will you bring in the report of the nominating committee?"

"There's a motion on the floor!" "Second the motion!" "Restate the motion!"

A meeting that might have been resolved with fists and chairs and flying Coke bottles erupted instead into a hassle over conflicting motions, amendments and amendments to amendments, and substitutes for amendments; debates allowed and disallowed, limited and extended; votes polled by voice, show of hands and standing, with groups caucusing in the aisles uncounted and recounted. And unwinding in reverse, the amendments to the amendments approved or disapproved, the amendment to the substitute, the substitute, the motion itself. All nullified upon discovery by a mover that, under the load of appendages turning his intention into its antithesis, he had been misquoted. Amid points of order and calls to order, shouts of yield the floor, yield the chair, read it again! Does a point of personal privilege have precedence over a point of information? At times half of them were poking the other half, "What are we voting on now?" Watching Lunin or Fritz, Mari or Cranston, they rose and subsided. Cranston treading his own straight-and-narrow, judging alternatives according to his own yardstick, was sometimes with one, sometimes with the other, and as often as not abstained.

"To take steps here today to expand the membership committee to twenty, representing all groupings in the plant, whose function it will be to bring in to the next meeting a comprehensive plan for a full membership drive. Said plan to include concrete suggestions for expediting grievances . . . revival of regular departmental meetings . . . submission to the nominating committee of a Labor Unity Slate.

"If we take positive action on this motion, all we have to do now is name our additions to the membership committee."

The diamond formation had a supply of names at its fingertips and Amy had a weekly date for committee meetings on the tip of her tongue.

"What the hell do you think you're doing, Mabley?" Mabley was up front beside the table, addressing the crowd. "Nobody recognized you."

"I'm speaking on the motion."

No one walked out. Women forgot the roasts they had left in the oven. Excitement, drama—in fine fettle the membership overrode motions to close discussion, trampled on Roberts Rules and, recalled to ritual, suspended them and the bylaws as well when they got in the way.

Mari rose to speak on a point of personal privilege. "Recognize her!" "Let her have her say!" There were some present in a mood to lift Colangelo bodily out of his chair if he denied her.

"Brother Colangelo," she began in cadenced and reasoned tones, standing at her seat in back, drawing attention backward toward her, "there are none of us here, including myself, that have any wish to unseat you from office. We want to increase and consolidate our ranks under your leadership. None of us came to break the local up. We want to restore the unity we once had."

Laughter broke out. It was so patently phony. Mari had nothing but contempt for Colangelo.

Pale as the scarf fluffed about her shoulders, she grasped the back of the chair in front of her, supporting herself. But there was nothing weak about her voice. It swelled through the hall, sonorous with certitude.

"We had unity once. We had organization. We had strength. We had the strength that comes of a solidly united organization.

"Remember, remember back in '46 when UV canceled the contract and we struck? You remember, Cranston."

Cranston was sitting back with folded arms, head upcanted and eyes fastened on her hard enough to reach up and drag her back down into her chair.

"Inside of three days we had our people so well organized—ten committees! The strike committee met every day—every dollar budgeted, every discussion recorded, every proposal submitted to the membership, every tactic planned. The picket line—if anybody didn't show up for picket duty he better have a good excuse or he was visited to find out the reason why. The picket signs—remember Ralsky, what an artist he was, everybody chasing after him with slogans. The soup kitchens—they were operating even before the strike began. The funds—over half the foremen were slipping us dough on the side. Public relations—we had reporters following us everywhere, we were on the radio every day and all over the New York *Times, Life, Collier's.* The community—we had the whole community behind us, merchants, churches, lawyers, doctors and dentists, students, all the liberal intellectuals. Education—we were running classes in American history, labor history, economics, foreign relations, nutrition and dressmaking. Entertainment—the talent we rounded up in the shop, Mary what's-her-name, wasn't she a lovely thing? and sing? like an angel. The troupes of dancers who came up from New York to perform for us, the Hollywood stars.

"Every day something new, something different. Oh, the ideas we had, we were so creative with it. And you, Cranston, you—"

All animation now, all gesture, she shook her finger in Cranston's forbidding face.

"You, Cranston, in a Paul Revere outfit up there on a white horse leading us down Bancroft Avenue, swinging your lantern and ringing a bell.

"What happened to it all? Where has it all gone? All of us sitting here in this hall right now, deadheads. Who destroyed it?

"Not you, Cranston, don't give yourself that much credit. And not you, Colangelo, you're not that smart.

"Coffinism! It was destroyed by Coffin. The three-pronged attack. Government regulation through Taft-Hartley, setting us all scrapping among ourselves. Indoctrination of the workers with the Cold War policy. And the get-tough contracts—take it or leave it!

"Let's rebuild our membership, our democratic structure, our unity. . . ."

They were swayed by Mari, by memories long vanished, images of the onetime self flashing out of the darkness. The more recent members usually fidgety under such reminders of things past—the mouthings of veterans of some antique war sunning themselves in their own heroism—sat quiet, no shuffling or shifting about, bemused, scenes they had never known as vivid in their eyes for an instant as if they had lived them.

"Move the question!"

"Call the question!"

If the votes were to be tallied by the number of voices in its favor, the motion would surely carry. For the simple reason that few people saw how an expanded membership committee under Colangelo's leadership could possibly pose a threat to Colangelo.

But Colangelo saw it. As Baldessari reread the motion with its auxiliary stipulations, pausing to argue language now and again with Rakocszi who had also been taking notes, Nick simmered and swelled. The motion gave him no time to pack the membership committee with hand-picked appointees. And it pre-empted his nominating committee, giving his opposition time to inject its candidates into his slate before the next meeting. The little gray man had made a little gray place for himself that was soon at his behest to be painted a nice clean cream. Like the sea creature that after its free-floating larval period sinks to the bottom of the sea and attaches itself to a rock from which it never thenceforth departs, he had his rock here, all set. He carried out instructions

from the union's national office more or less adequately. He con-
formed to the role expected of him by company industrial relations. He was labor adviser to the mayoralty aspirant most likely
to succeed Kearnsey in office. No outside notions required. No
assistance from unpredictable elements needed or wanted.

Thickened, brown and brawny, bristling, Nick rested back
against the table and regarded Lunin, still standing before him in
the front row waiting for his motion to be passed, with glossy
eyes.

"You talk about unity." Nick's basso profundo boomed out.
"There's only one aim of this meeting and that is to produce dis-
unity—"

"You're out of order, Nick," he said to him, practically toe to
toe. "Discussion's closed."

"And there's just one person behind it—"

"Out of order!"

"Chairman, call the question! Question!"

"Baldy, take the chair. Now you all let everybody else talk. Let
me talk, I got a right . . ."

Baldessari assuming the chair behind the table ruled on Nick's
right to talk.

"Let him talk," Cranston from the rear cut through the buzz.

"Is it all right with you, Lunin?" the parliamentarian, fighting a
losing battle, punctiliously inquired.

At that moment he had it within reach: the membership campaign, the electoral coalition, the means by which pressure from
the bottom up might re-energize the organization. But the striving
for fair play in several quarters, strained beyond the ordinary, was
still at work. It wasn't only Colangelo's troops and Cranston's
who were pounding their feet. "Give him leave! Give him leave!"
To refuse Nick was to lose all that he had so far won.

He nodded.

Discussion was reopened as it would have been anyway, he concluded, with or without his nod. He was braced for Nick's assault, all but welcoming it, willing it into being.

"A personal vendetta . . . Secrets I been in on . . ."

Which was it to be? Priscilla? *His wife was always giving me the eye and he couldn't* . . . Miss Bonnie Bluebell? *This blonde in blue* . . . Maria Ucchini? *I wonder who's sharing her pillow now.* . . .

He was ready for it now, allegation for allegation, all his gingerly fears of other years outlived. With the impetuous need of the duelist for satisfaction, a chance to settle old scores, let him do his worst! The trade union leader who sells out over the telephone what he's negotiating over the table. Boss's stooge! Coffin's tool!

He should have known better. Nick was an improviser. Nick seized by inspiration on the materials at hand and put them to use, having sublime faith in the veracity of his own improvisation. There was no Evening in Paris perfume floating around here.

"Unity? When was this unity?" Nick trumpeted, striding up and down before his table. "It's a myth they made up in their sleep, these people that talk about unity. There was always trouble. We were fighting all the time. Not for the benefit of you and me. Not to help Uncle Sam. The somersaults of the Communist Party! The power ploys of the Soviet Union! Stah-leen!

"That'll never happen again. Oh no, we'll never allow that kind of magnetic pole to influence us again. We got rid of that cancer.

"Unity, we never had so much unity as we have now. We're united in the interests of our own nation, our own union, ourselves. And we're going to stay that way.

"With the exception of one small gang. The same old gang. Here."

Nick pulled out of his pants pocket where he had been carrying it around too, transferring it as he changed clothes, the soiled and tattered leaflet. He held it dangling from his fingers like a snotty handkerchief.

"Rabid! Ridiculous! 'Dig your own grave, Graveyard!' The big impersonal corporation run by committee—all of a sudden it's all wrapped up in one person. The kind of a line, out of the dark ages, that solves nothing, that has as its sole objective the sharpening of antagonisms at the bargaining table. We sit down with management to iron out the suspensions and all they want to know is, where did this rag come from?"

Standing directly before him, Nick dropped it into his lap. He drew his legs away overquickly and it fell to the floor.

"Hatchet man!" Nick declared, wagging his head at him more in commiseration than in accusation. "The hatchet man for forces I don't need to name. In the middle of the '46 strike you were put up to get Scottsy, the best field organizer ever sent us, the genius of the Liberty Square rally, and you got him. I know it! And in the middle of contract negotiations when you were president of this local, you were put up to get Frank Gavin, the man who made you, who knew better than any of us what's what in this world, and you stabbed him in the back, you got him. I saw it! And now after being defeated fair and square in three elections, you've been put up once again to get me. Well you won't capture this local from within . . ."

"Coffin's stooge! Company fink! I caught you red-handed—"

Ray and Marty hauled him back down in his chair. If the chair had not been attached to its neighbors by iron brackets in back, he would have had it up over his head. Pinned down, struggling, still a shadow of himself heaved upward, hurling itself. . . .

"As for these suspensions—" Over a scrimmage of hoarse yells, Nick recaptured his audience with a timely reversion to the mundane and the pertinent. "I didn't want to go into it—all right, Mabley, sit down—while we were still working on it, but let me say this much. You want to listen to this? Then listen!"

Nick relaxed back against the table, restored to his customary geniality. As a man whose attitude toward his opponents after he had beaten them down was forgive and forget, he expected the same attitude back in return.

"We have two sets of suspensions here. I have hopes of having the three in Hot Rubber rescinded by tomorrow." He was probably making it up on the spot. "Scratching the warning notices but with the pay loss still in dispute." A good liar always adds the flourish of detail. "Now with the women in Switch I'm not so

sure we can do as well. We're arguing it as a case of contagious hysteria. One woman has been in the hospital recently—
now, Mari, keep your shirt on, it's the only way we can buck it."
That cooked Mari's goose. "And I'd better advise you right now,
Lunin, if you attempt a walkout over this in Switch tomorrow,
it'll just torpedo any chance we have of gaining concessions."

Serenely Nick disposed of all other outstanding grievances by
agreeing yes yes, you're right. Nobody's against you, we're all for
you, something ought to be done about it.

"Only there's talk of recession in the air and that always makes
it that much harder. But with your continued cooperation we'll
keep punching. Now I know you're all in a hurry— What's eating
you, Lunin?"

"Move the question."

"What question?"

"There's a motion on the floor."

It was past five o'clock. Amy and Rita were loudly shuffling
down their row, with a general movement toward exodus in their
wake. Rita who had been muttering her discontent all along let
loose with a broadside.

"Communism! All you have to do is say it and that's the end.
Everybody abdicates."

"Next thing you won't have a union here," Amy prophesied.
"The oldsters quit. The youngsters won't join. We'll be decerti-
fied."

"Brother Chairman! Brother Chairman!"

"Yes, Brother Cranston," Nick recognized him in relief.
"Brother Cranston has the floor. Go ahead, Herb."

With a clack the departers were back in their seats. There had
been nothing quite like this since Cranston's Catholic Action
Front, led on by Tookalook, hounded the Ucchinis out of the
hall.

Aloof, above the turmoil, Cranston allowed the hubbub to subside. The last cough, the last scrapings about died down.

"If the chair will permit me I'd like to address a few words to
Sister Ucchini. Mariuch . . ."

Tall and unbending he stood above her, people clambering up over their chairs for a view of them.

"I did you a great deal of harm once," Cranston said to Mari. "Bob made his mistakes but I made mistakes too. In despoiling him I despoiled myself. If you can find it in your heart to forgive me . . ."

He thrust his hand out to Mari. After a second's hesitation, gazing up at him, unsmiling, she accepted his hand.

"Mish."

Cranston strode down the aisle to the forefront and offered his hand, a firm and kindly grasp, the righteous bastard.

"I thought I was doing good and I did harm."

Stepping back, Cranston fished the discarded leaflet up from the floor. He wiped it off against his pants, smoothed it out and folded it away in his pocket.

"Coffinism! The three-pronged attack. First he got the radicals and the militants. Then he got the union. Now he's got every worker . . ."

"Cranston, get your ass outa here."

"Question! Question! A motion for a membership drive is on the floor." "Vote the motion!"

Ignoring the motion, Colangelo called for the report of his nominating committee. Amid cries of "Dictatorship!" "Bossism!" Campbell delivered the report, rattling off the names. "Any other nominations?" Before anyone could formulate a reply, Colangelo's well-oiled machine, ill-equipped to cope with unforeseen contingencies but otherwise fast on the uptake, was off and away. "Move the nominations be closed." "Second." "Move the question." "All those in favor?" "AYE." "All those opposed?" "NAY! NAY!" "The ayes have it."

The meeting stood adjourned. About thirty members trailed down the aisle after Colangelo. The rest remained in their chairs, stomping their feet against the illegal adjournment.

"Don't leave! This is a continuation of the meeting. Stay where you are!" They couldn't leave now. They were too revved up to leave.

The sergeant-at-arms turned off the lights. Confusion. Shrieks. Someone turned them on again. Off. On. Colangelo reappeared in the doorway, buttoning into his gray-brown raincoat. It was the prerogative of the incumbent officers to have the dissidents evicted from the hall, by the police if necessary.

"You came here calling for unity against the company," Colangelo reproved them. "But if you want to divide the ranks by conducting a rump session—"

"No rump session! It's a continuation . . ."

"Go on and do it. Be my guest."

With a salute of his gloved hand, it's all yours, Nick left them the hall. They weren't that important to him. He didn't have to abide by their decisions.

They went on until six-thirty and even then they could have gone on for hours. A rank-and-file slate of candidates to oppose Colangelo: Lunin for president—no one else would take it; Mabley for vice-president; Cranston for secretary; business agent, wide open; a composite executive board. The job in the weeks ahead mapped out. Two hundred-some dollars chipped in on the table as a starting fund. How to compel Colangelo, taking it to court if they had to, to allow equal watchers and checkers at the polls.

And all through it, Cranston and Mari engaged in a running colloquy, in parallel lines of self-vindication, unconverging:

"But you see, you tied yourselves to a lie. It had to die."

"It was always the problems here that counted, not Russia. Jobs. Peace. Brotherhood . . ."

"The thing that burns me, you always assume that everything good that was ever accomplished around here you did it."

"If the people took power . . ."

"If the state has the monopoly over property, then it has life-and-death power . . ."

When he said good-by to Cranston at his car, Cranston was still absorbed in his own private trauma. Rain dribbled down his bare head into the upturned collar of his coat.

"I thought I was doing right," Cranston reiterated, stricken. "And I did harm. It'll take years to overcome it. Years."

Starting his car, he noticed Mari's car standing alone up against the log under the high wood fence. He took his flashlight and went over to her.

"Something the matter with your car?"

Mari was sitting at the wheel holding her right hand in a peculiar position, up-clenched over her bosom, her left hand clamping the wrist. He seemed to recall her holding her hand like that for some time, her left hand clutched over the wrist like a tourniquet constricting the flow of blood.

"Did you hurt yourself? Are you able to drive home?"

Slowly she gazed about at him, no warmth of busyness, no eagerness in pursuit of political ends; stripped to the self, lost and gone. Releasing her right hand, she gazed down at it in surprise, opened it wide and examined it, the hand that had accepted Cranston's hand.

"I should have cut it off," she said, and with the offending member, a stranger to her, reached for the ignition key.

4

When he arrived home the living room was dark, the apartment was hushed. Priscilla lay stretched out on her back on the bed like a figure carved on a coffin, her hands folded on her chest, her eyes vacant. He was alarmed. Still if it had to do with Joe she wouldn't be lying here like this.

"Where are the kids?"

"Pop took them up to Deering to see Jennie," she answered him after a while tonelessly. "She likes it there. Your dinner's in the oven."

It wasn't Joe then. His younger sister, Jennie, a shy overgrown girl, moved from farm to farm working as a hired hand, taking care of livestock. "Animals are good," Jennie said. "Only people are bad."

He brought his plate into the bedroom. He was emotionally worn out. And exhilarated, racing with snatches of afterthought, a million glittering stars. He hardly knew what he ate.

"How'd it go?"

"Damnedest thing I've ever seen. All the pieces came together. Everything fell into place."

He told her almost with a sense of awe, dumfounded by it. She didn't rise to it.

"How many were there?"

"About ninety in all. We finished up with just under sixty."

"Oh."

It took the wind out of his sails. He sat down on the bed beside her and kissed her. Her mouth was flaccid under his, the little chapped shreds of skin that always prickled so tantalizingly dry on her lips as scaling rust. His hand trailed down over her breast. She was utterly passive. Even her red sweater, the wool always so springy, was limp to his touch. He tugged at her skirt and she smoothed it down over her knees.

"Why bother? You don't even like me."

"Priscilla, you're all knocked out—"

"Not really."

"Get out of your clothes, get into bed, I'll get you an aspirin—"

"I'm perfectly all right."

"A drink then. Would you like a martini without an olive? Or an old fashioned without a cherry?"

"What for? It won't change anything."

"What's hit you, Pris? Why are you acting like this?"

"Isn't this the way you've always thought I should act?"

It took him some time to dig it out of her. He collected the newspapers strewn about the bed, tear sheets of the tenant ad, and stacked them on the bureau. The photo of two boys pyramided on a rubbish heap, so sharp in the glossy and the final proof, was quite blotchy, the black face blotted out. The credit line of the teen-age camera bug Lucas had insisted on paying was overly prominent, in twelve-point bold. Otherwise it was everything she had visualized, three quarters of a page, smashing. THE SHAME OF SHOREHAM. . . .

He undressed himself and undressed her and switched off the bedside lamp and pulled the blankets up over them. Her hands moved slackly through the routine, kneading.

"Lie still. Lie still. Put your arms around me." She put her arms around him. He held her tightly to him, full length, facing her on the pillow, her legs pinioned in his. She was willing enough simply to lift her leg and let him in with the casualness of a hundred half-asleep couplings. But not with a comfortable casualness. Indifference, just do it for godsake and get it over with.

"Now tell me. Start from the beginning."

"You never loved me. You always despised me. Right from that first day on the picket line."

He tried mockery. "Nobody loves you. Everybody hates you. What else?"

"Bostic." It popped out of her in a burst of breath. "Bostic wasn't there at your meeting, was he?"

"Come to think of it, no."

"Gene and Mae are out looking at houses. Most of the people in this building were out this afternoon looking at places to rent or buy with money they haven't got."

"Do you blame them? Do you blame them so much?"

"Why should I blame them? I blame myself. Pushing them into what I think is right when what they want—"

"—is something better than what they have. Believe me, if they didn't push themselves, you couldn't push them. If that's all . . ."

It wasn't all.

"Frances Knowlton was here."

Frances was just about out of her mind. A couple of policemen had invaded her apartment during her absence and discovered that in addition to her own children she had two nieces from South Carolina living with her and attending school here. When her husband arrived home and objected to the cops questioning the kids, he was arrested. Dragged down to headquarters and booked for assaulting an officer of the law, suspicion of defrauding the city, policy slips—though why he would be carrying numbers on him on a Sunday . . . She had to clear out of her apartment by Tuesday or be brought up on charges herself.

"But this is retaliation," Priscilla had told her. "We have to fight it!"

"All this may be all right for you," Frances told her back. "You're just playing at it. With us it's for keeps."

She groaned on her pillow and twisted in his arms, racked with the pain of it, the brutal exclusion.

"And Lucas—Lucas—oh my God, Lucas. I thought I knew Lucas. I thought . . ."

They were all so furious at Lucas these past few days. The outsider who breezes in, whips up a frenzy, then disappears without a trace.

"Mish, you don't know. I was in such despair over you. I threw myself at him. I almost . . ."

She had gone to see Lucas's sister Jean after Frances left hoping that Lucas might have returned, maybe there was something they could do for Frances. Jean was alone—she actually hadn't paid much attention to Jean before. A woman older than Lucas, a madonna with gray-streaked hair. Only she wasn't Lucas's sister. Her husband had died and she was left with two daughters and a son to raise and a living to earn for them. When Lucas came along she was having trouble with her son. Lucas had a habit of attaching himself to families and entering into their troubles, trying to help straighten them out. And he did help, except that his help always culminated in catastrophe.

When Jean first met Lucas he was mixed up with a young colored couple. The husband in and out of reform school from the time he was ten, highly articulate, brilliant. The wife a dear little thing who didn't dare say boo. Both under twenty, with four children, all of them born by Caesarian section, and a fifth one on the way. Lucas persuaded the wife to have herself sterilized after the fifth Caesarian. She went through with it. Whereupon the husband lost his desire for her, it wasn't the same any more. Three months after Lenore had herself tied up she went around boasting of another pregnancy. "Carl and I have done it again." When that fell apart she began going out with another man in order to prove to Carl and herself that she still had her sexual allure. Carl was out nights attending a school Lucas had steered him to. Lenore was dating. The five children were left home alone, locked in. Then Lucas began giving Carl hell for his wife's infidelity, it was Carl's fault, she was a person too with yearnings—which she now voiced only too eloquently—to be fulfilled. Thursday morning in the early hours Lenore had Carl jailed for breach of peace. When Lucas came around to reason with her, she threw him out.

"That was Thursday morning, first thing. Lucas would start helping and he did help. Only in the course of it he'd turn into a regular martinet. A little tyrant."

With Jean it was the same thing. Lucas had moved in with her to help with her son who was in dire need of a father. And Lucas was a father to him until one day he began laying down the law. The boy refused to knuckle under and Lucas began cursing him out, abusing him. Jean had to send the boy away to stay with friends.

"She had a terrible row with Lucas over it lunchtime Thursday. She told him he'd have to pack up and leave."

And in the last few weeks, Mrs. Leggett. Lucas was bent on saving Mrs. Leggett and her daughters from whoredom. Thursday evening after the city hall meeting, late, Lucas returned to the project and knocked on Mrs. Leggett's door. She wouldn't admit him. He kept at it. After about five minutes she opened the door a crack and threw a glass of water in his face. The little girls were up by then and running around in their nighties. It sent Lucas wild. He broke through and grabbed for the man in Mrs. Leggett's bed. The man grabbed for a lamp.

"It all came to a head on Thursday. We all had a brawl with him that day. When he called me up just before city hall, I bawled him out so over the money for that photo. When he called for us to follow him down the aisle and take over the council chamber, nobody followed. Every single one of us, we slaughtered him."

Lucas had crawled out of the woods this morning, forty miles away somewhere, beaten beyond recognition. Fractured skull, concussion, exposure.

"They found an old envelope in his shoe with Jean's address on it and called her to find out if she knew who he might be. She wanted to say no. She should have said no. But she didn't."

"How did Jean find out how . . ."

"Mrs. Leggett's neighbors, upstairs, downstairs, the same floor. They all knew all about it."

"Jesus."

"All this going on—this—" Priscilla thrashed about, writhing on the withered sheet. "And I—zipping around with my little petitions—"

She had always had such resilience. One thing fell by the wayside, she was onto the next thing. Not now.

She knew it all now, everything he had ever held against her. She was everything he had ever wanted for her to be now, wasn't she? Knowing the cost of living, that living costs, that the people she so blithely slapped together, careless of who and what they were, how they felt . . . Knowing it so well and in such measure that she was immobilized by the knowledge.

He tried moralizing. "When a mass action fails, you take it as a personal failure. But that's how nature proceeds, by trial and error. Ted keeps saying that someday there'll come another leap. But what does the next leap come out of? It doesn't come out of nothing. It comes out of this."

"Rah rah rah."

He tried making love to her. Long-boned, shoulder blades sharp as a knife, lean-shanked, chapped shins, abrasive—she was a lump. "Here we are fucking on Lucas's grave." He flung himself back and she leaned up over him and gave him her tit. "Here, suck it. There's nothing there. I don't feel a thing. I haven't felt anything for ages, I've just been pretending to you—me—I wouldn't admit—" She kissed him with all her lack of lust down hard on the mouth and he pulled her down kissing her and all of a sudden out of nowhere it was one of those times when the pleasure given is the pleasure taken, when all the devices of love stimulating response become self-stimulating, when skin meeting skin rises up as if lifted from its moorings by a transcendent suction of the flesh, when out of miscible fluids an osmosis takes place and lingers on and on beyond belief.

"It goes away and comes back . . . Goes away till you think it's gone forever . . . And comes back. . . ."

Dreamily they floated on their barge, murmuring. The telephone rang. It rang again and again. Stopped. Rang again.

"Go answer it," he urged drowsily. "It's for you."

She wouldn't answer it. He got up to take it off the hook, fumbled through the living room to the hall and, dazzled by the light, thinking it might be for him after all, answered. It was for her.

"It's Gray, that lawyer out on Bay Point."

She wouldn't come to the telephone. "What should I tell him?"

"I don't care. Hang up on him."

He spoke to Gray and returned to the bed. "You left a call in for him earlier, he says, about Frances Knowlton. What shall I say to him?"

She didn't know. She didn't care. Dreamily she floated above the wrecks of time. Frances would just have to take care of herself.

"Come on, baby." He dragged her up. "Come, sweetheart." With his arm around her he walked her to the telephone. He placed the telephone in her hand.

"Yes, Mr. Gray. About Mrs. Knowlton. Her husband's in the King Street lockup and she's being evicted—a crass case of . . . Judge Rinaldi's ordering a *study?* Another study? Victory, that's some victory. What kind of victory . . . ?"

She stalked back into the bedroom and began pulling on her clothes, everything that had preceded already forgotten.

"Judge Rinaldi's ordering the city tomorrow to initiate a study of feasible alternatives to the Tidal Flats dump. The judge saves his face. Gray's off the hook. And Kearnsey can just go on sitting on his hands."

She yanked her sweater down over the safety pin that held her skirt band together where the buttons were out.

"We'll kill those bloody bastards!"

Zdyes eta ulitsa, zdyes eta dom, zdyes eta barishnya shto ya lyublyon.

IV

1

Leora was back at her old job in final assembly Monday morning, group leader again, tightening up her crew, cracking down on the weaknesses tolerated by Amy. Nine women perched on their stools around the turntable, trying to catch up with the production figure previously achieved by thirteen of them. A young girl under the tutelage of Tom, the assistant foreman, temporarily replaced Rita at the brusher. Don Pinette drag-rolled down the lanes on roller skates. The electrical activator burst with lights, cascading fireworks. No Pirate Jenny whistled her Threepenny air under the chatter of the presses.

Anchored to their tasks, isolated from one another by the deafening noise, they devoted themselves to the dictates of the machine.

"You know Mahoney in 15-D?" Ewell on the way to the can muttered into his ear.

Yeah, he knew Mahoney. A beer belly. Bigmouth.

"He's talking about dumping you. He gets you alone he's going to dump you out the window."

"Sure. Second floor or third?"

"Don't you go anywhere alone."

His election campaign was on.

He had been at work 2.2 hours when Dirksen tapped him on the shoulder. "You're wanted in Personnel."

"Cheez-zuss Carr-rist!" He threw up his pipe wrench. "You ever gonna let me finish anything?"

This time he thought to wash the grease off his hands, clean up. But Dirksen hustled him down the corridor past the locker room and through the buildings of busy gray production units, allowing him no stops, no detours, no chance to speak to anyone. Puffing and clearing his throat repeatedly, Dirksen delivered him into the tired tan precincts of Employee Relations. At the door of the Labor Conference room upstairs, Dirksen stationed himself outside to wait for him. Tight with apprehension, always apprehensive under such circumstance, but unworried, what can they do me? he sauntered in. What did Graveyard have up his sleeve for him now?

Sewall, the director of personnel, and Kane, director of industrial relations, rose from the side of the conference table and advanced on him with hands extended in greeting. Cordially they shook hands all around. They proffered him a chair across the table. Cozily they all sat down together. With no further preliminaries Sewall began reading from the single mimeographed sheet that lay on the table, a prepared statement. It was in the form of a press release.

" 'The United Vacuum Company, Shoreham, is taking the unusual step of making public the facts surrounding its discharge today of Michael Lunin, a former official of EWIU-UV Local 317, AFL-CIO. According to information brought to the attention of the company by his fellow employees, Mr. Lunin has engaged for several weeks in activities designed to disrupt production and to reflect adversely upon the good name of United Vacuum, its policies and its products.' "

"Just a minute," he interrupted. "I'm not going one step further without union representation."

"The union," Mr. Kane said, "has been notified." He nodded briskly to Sewall, his elder and underling. "Go on, please."

" 'In the past ten days Mr. Lunin has been responsible for at least two work stoppages in violation of the union contract and has interfered on a number of occasions with normal work procedures in the plant. In addition, he has conducted meetings concerned with an internal union situation on company premises and company time. A defamatory leaflet attributed to him—'"

"You're making a hero out of me."

" 'The latest incident occurred last Monday during a visit by distinguished foreign guests. With the aim of discrediting United Vacuum and the United States government—'"

"Now you know damn well that's a complete fabrication!"

"We have sworn testimony. Continue, Sewall."

" '. . . jeopardizing our business and our standing as a defense establishment—'"

"I'm not working in defense. Switch isn't under security clearance."

"We're not at liberty to divulge our future plans for Switch," Sewall accommodatingly departed from his text to explain to him. "With these new weapons systems we don't know what we may be called upon to make."

"That's a historical assumption. Well, I'm fond of historical assumptions too. And I assume that in this atomic age nations are forced to live in peace, if not exactly harmony, together. The future then, if there is to be a future, lies with light buttons, not bomber buttons."

"Sewall, finish up."

" 'Lunin's behavior, it has been attested by a witness, has been directed by an alleged subversive group meeting in secret—'"

Teresa! Teresa hanging over the seat between him and Mari howling out her injuries. . . .

" 'Therefore for the good of our employees, our company and our country we are terminating Mr. Lunin's employment.'"

It stung. It penetrated. It hit him in the solar plexus.

"These charges are false and libelous—"

The accusation that he had hurt the country, this surprisingly was what hurt him the most, most deeply, most unjustly.

"It's perfectly plain I'm planning to run for union office and you're using this pretext—"

It was his country as much as theirs.

"I'll fight in every way open to me—"

"Now, Lunin, you're smart enough to know what this is all about. There's no need to go into it any further. One more detail. Do you want to maintain your insurance?"

He was given the press release as his notice of termination, to take effect immediately. With it out of the way, a nasty job which if anything they resented his foisting upon them, the two became once more their adept selves, dealing with duties more natural to them.

"It's to your advantage to keep the insurance. Save you quite a bit in premiums." Sewall provided him with the forms to have his group insurance converted to an individual policy. "Be sure to notify the paymaster."

"We'll mail out your paycheck, Friday."

They walked him to the door where Dirksen was waiting for him. During a moment's hiatus, while Dirksen telephoned for a guard, they shook hands again with him.

Dirksen and a gray-uniformed guard marched him back to the locker room, cutting him off from return to his department. They stood over him as he stepped out of his coveralls, self-conscious in his sad sack underwear, and pulled on his sports shirt and slacks. He took his towel, soap, comb, extra pair of shoes, emergency plastic raincoat and paper bag with today's lunch in it out of his locker. They accompanied him down the iron-treaded stairs and across the yard, watching to right and left to see that he made no attempt against company property, and all the way out to his car in the parking lot. Followed the car at a half trot into Raymond Street and, joined by a guard from the main gate, watched after him till he reached the corner of Cedarbrook Avenue.

He circled around the office tower, Coffin at the summit inaccessible in his indigo-and-white habitat, and drove along the mall past the blocks of buildings, past the old main entry opposite the barberry-bowered rotunda, past the windows glittering with light, the floors of clattering machinery. All his working life in there. All going on without him. Expelled from the body productive. The brick wall, the implacable brick wall that divided being outside from being inside.

He drove around the twelve blocks of United Vacuum three times. Still in there, his flesh attuned to the rhythm of shuttlings, revolvings, refusing to withdraw itself. His mind geared to it, buzzing with it, searching for the bug in the system, clinging to it in a kind of kinetic afterlife. The familiar faces, the interwoven tissues of association, the momentum of his perspective . . . More than ten years of himself in there, a chunk gouged out of his chest and devoured.

The weather had turned cold after the rain. The air was cold-white. The sun was white. He shivered in the chill of his sweat.

He drove down to the union office to file a discharge grievance. He drove downtown to consult with the attorney who serviced the union. He drove over to the State Employment to register for a job and fill out papers for unemployment compensation. He drove home and sat down with Priscilla to draft a statement for the newspaper in reply to UV's press release. Later he telephoned Nick Colangelo. Nick seemed genuinely concerned. "I'll look into it. Sure. Check."

Next day he learned from the newspaper that the union executive board had rejected his grievance. He was discharged for cause.

The AFL-CIO lawyer regretfully, "I know you're getting a raw deal," bowed out of his case, "You don't stand a chance," and suggested that he move to another city. He had nowhere to move where he'd be any better off. It was his city.

The State Unemployment sent him out on a job and he was accepted by the department foreman. Before he reached home the foreman telephoned Priscilla: there had been a slip-up, there was no job opening in his department.

Within the week he was notified by Unemployment Compensation that the reason for his termination having been tabulated by his employer as Willful Misconduct he was not entitled to Benefits. He prepared an appeal to the Unemployment Commission. Even this had to be fought through.

His wires and registered letters to higher bodies of the union went unanswered. Through Mike Garceau in Springfield, he arranged for a personal meeting with John Bennett, the national president, and Bennett agreed to it. The meeting never materialized.

He submitted his case to Joe Barth's colleagues in the Civil Liberties Union for consideration. His contractual rights had been violated, his property right to his job, his constitutional right to a livelihood. They invited him to the chapter's monthly luncheon at the Red Rooster Inn and there he was advised that his claim to property right in his job and constitutional right to a livelihood held no water and that his contractual rights were outside their purview. No one thought to pay for his lunch. He paid for it himself.

He filed a complaint with the National Labor Relations Board charging collusion between company and union in the denial of rights guaranteed him under the Taft-Hartley Act. A sympathetic young lawyer from the board visited him surreptitiously at home, keeping well out of range of the window and declining the coffee Priscilla brought out. The lawyer had come to urge him confidentially to withdraw his complaint. "Why?" "You're going to lose it. Better for you to withdraw than to lose." He refused to withdraw.

Meanwhile he dug in to help Mabley and Cranston with their election campaign. Cranston offered to come forward as the author of the leaflet. "No, don't expose yourself." Mabley offered to call for a walkout demanding Lunin's restoration to his job. "No, you're not strong enough." Protests broke out against a lack-of-work layoff in the Construct Facilities division—"Due to cancellation or reduction of Government orders, United Vacuum regrets . . ." His apartment was deep in paper: white, buff, yellow, blue.

The plant went on without him. But he went on with the plant.

2

It was a long low structure of corrugated iron, dirty red, with a high-pitched roof from which a series of windows projected at an angle. Chimney stacks in the near front and rear rose as high as the roofs of neighboring three-story houses. Mountains of steel drums piled up in the yard, bung-type and open-head. Battered, rusty, reeking in the sun with the residues of grease and chemicals. The yard crew unloading the trucks wore galoshes.

The first time he viewed the interior of Barth Barrel, from outside on the receiving dock, he whistled.

"Automate it, hell. This ain't even mechanized!"

A clangor of drums filled the interior with a force that, if noise were convertible to energy, would blow the roof off. And heat, the heat of a steam cooker. The floor underfoot was thick with rust shavings, muck. Windows on the ground level were painted green, keeping the outside out and the inside in.

Eyes, ears, nose, flesh assaulted, he followed Eckstrom through an obstacle course of stock and equipment.

At the vats a dozen men, black and Puerto Rican, stripped the bung-type drums, inserting high-pressure jet sprays of boiling alkali solution. In the caustic fumes, tears, round as ball bearings, dripped down their sweaty cheeks. Their shirts hung from their backs in tatters.

The bung-type drums that didn't pass inspection for cleanliness were rolled off, clash-crashing, to the chain gang. At the head of the line a stolid black man, with a cap made of lady's tan nylon stocking over his hair, poured a quart of alkali solution through the bung hole and fed in heavy link chain. While his partner rapidly revolved the drum he chain-whipped the remains of old coating and fill from inner sides, top, bottom. Whang whang whang the chains, with the sound of a thousand rocks iron-split. Round round round the drums in a blur of light, stripped to the raw steel.

Open-head drums traveled upright, lids interspersed, on an ancient belt over gas jets into a burn-off oven spewing blue flame. The oven crew danced attendance, prodding with long rods at the logjams that developed. Blowing their noses, choking. Damn asphalt, always creates this kind of smog. A shock of flames, a conflagration, the whole eighty-foot row of drums catching fire. Batch must have contained some kind of lacquer.

Sandblast chamber rattling with steel shot.

De-denting. A chorus of hammer blows.

Chimes straightened. Takes skill.

Spic and span or the paint won't adhere. Not a fleck of rust or the rust will spread. Smooth as glass. Airtight. Leakproof.

"THEY HAVE SHATTERED ME!"

At the summer bungalow close to Sprague that Flo had rented for Joe's convalescence, Joe came plodding out from his nap last Saturday afternoon onto the sun porch, pushing his feet. Neat in navy blue robe, striped pajamas, meticulously clean. Not aseptic hospital clean, but an extraordinary, striking cleanliness at odds with the neat but normally used furnishings of the porch. His face clean-shaven, smooth as a boy's. Impossible to tell from his appearance that he was sightless in one eye and had not yet fully recovered the sight of the other. He had been visited earlier by an old school friend and the laughter of the visit, reminiscences, some subtle point exchanged, lingered in his eyes. He wore a white stockinette cap on his head. The cap too was meticulously, strikingly clean, covering a drain, presumably, or some other device of postsurgical treatment.

Joe kissed Flo first in greeting though she was staying with him. With a soldierly old world gesture he kissed Gail's shoulder and bowed his head down upon it. He took Priscilla's hands in his and covered them with kisses. He embraced son and son-in-law.

"My children," Joe said. "My dear children."

With a host's concern for their comfort Joe settled them about in glider and wicker chairs. "Flo, where, where is some tea? Do we have, do we have any sherry? Do you know who was here today? Do you know who was here? We sang."

"Isn't he coming along wonderfully?" Flo whispered to them under cover of leaving for the kitchen. "So much better than he was. Trying to get back to his brief."

"We sang."

Roaring with schoolboy laughter, Joe took a position on the inmost oval of the oval braided rug. Mischievously, savoring every word as if it possessed an essential meaning, deliciously funny, he belted out a cockney song.

"*I been waiting at the church, I been waiting at the church—*" He stumbled over a lost phrase, groped frantically for it. "*Till I received this bloody note. 'I can't marry you today, I can't marry you today because—because . . .'*" He wept with laughter, pounding at Ted's arm, don't you get it? don't you get the point? "*'Be- cause—because—'*" He hooted it out with a boy's hilarity. "*'—my wife won't let me.'*"

Annoyed with his stockinette cap, Joe plucked it off. No drain beneath. A cross was painted over his bald head in broad Mercurochrome strokes.

"*'I can't marry you today . . . I can't marry you today . . .'*"

Suddenly as he stood on the oval rug in his music hall attitude, still holding his cap by the peak, his mouth still agape with song, an anguished shriek broke out of him.

"THEY HAVE SHATTERED ME!"

"On to paint, Mish. This way."

Back back-sloping, auburn head forward thrust, Fred Eckstrom swiveled about protuberances, stepped over pitfalls, so accustomed to their presence he wouldn't have known how to walk through the plant without them. This was the established order, his accomplishment. Anyone who bumped or stumbled was a stumblebum. Nobody could move a skid from here to there without Eckstrom's okay. A missing lid, he'd tear the place apart.

Paint was manned by Negroes and Italians under a veteran employee, Italian, who was also president of the union local. Liners applied with a four-head spray with particular attention to bottom rim and junctures. Exteriors enameled in the spray booths in one, two or three colors as specified by the order sheet. Liners first, then exteriors baked in the eighty-foot convection oven. A man crawls into the 400° oven to break up a snag that resists the rod. Atmosphere saturated with alkyds, resins, phenols.

In the shadowless fluorescent glare it was easy as he went along to spot the production problems. The layout had grown up like Topsy, determined by the shape of the building and the site of chimneys and plumbing in the original barrel works.

"Why are the vats there in the middle?" he asked Eckstrom.

"That's where the steam tunnel was for the wooden barrels," Eckstrom said. "Stick around here awhile, young fellow, you'll find out there's a reason for everything."

The paint booths were separated from the bake-on oven, the storage area for the finished drums from the shipping platform, and the considerable footage between crammed tight with umpteen other operations. Drums crisscrossed the floor, backtracking over their routes twice over. Workers darted to and fro in pursuit of their drums; or were shuttled from one job to another as the need arose, from out in the yard to into the ovens; or stood fixed at their tasks, oblivious of what went on before and after, accumulating bottlenecks.

It all had to be broken down into a logical production sequence and as completely as possible conveyorized.

And that was the least of it.

"Glad to have someone back here taking charge," Eckstrom said.

Eckstrom had no intention of relinquishing charge to anyone.

"It's all under control here. You'll catch on. Just don't pay any mind to the gripers. They're jittery, unstable, especially the PRs. Never know what's going on with them."

"This sludge on the floor, isn't it a safety hazard?"

"Shovel it out every night."

"What do you do with it?"

"What does United Vacuum do? Into the trucks. Off to the dump."

Flames shot out of the burn-off chimney stack showering neighboring roofs and clotheslines with fiery cinders.

To Ted, this shanty, this corrugated iron oven, this thrumming drum was the stuff that dreams are made of. Together they would in time transform it into a model enterprise.

To him it was an impossibility of such magnitude in its every aspect that he could hardly bear to contemplate it.

Technically maybe. Humanly, how?